# RED OR DEAD

## DAVID PEACE

*faber and faber*

First published in 2013
by Faber and Faber Limited
Bloomsbury House
74–77 Great Russell Street
London WC1B 3DA

This export paperback edition first published in 2013

Typeset by Ian Bahrami
Printed in the UK by CPI Group (UK) Ltd, Croydon, CR0 4YY

Photo credits: endpapers (front) 1911 Liverpool Transport Strike, courtesy of
Mills Media Group, formerly Carbonara; (back) People's March for Jobs, 1981
© Martin Jenkinson/Alamy; p. 3 © *Daily Mail*/Rex Features;
p. 495 © Keystone/Hulton Archive/Getty Images

The right of David Peace to be identified as author of this work
has been asserted in accordance with Section 77 of the Copyright,
Designs and Patents Act 1988

A CIP record for this book
is available from the British Library

ISBN 978–0–571–28068–1

FSC
www.fsc.org
MIX
Paper from
responsible sources
FSC® C101712

2 4 6 8 10 9 7 5 3 1

In memory of Gordon Burn,
with love and thanks.

Here I am.
I stand at the door and knock.
If anyone hears my voice and opens the door,
I will come in and eat with him,
and he with me.

*Revelation*, Chapter 3, Verse 20

## The Argument III

Repetition. Repetition. Repetition. After the harvest, the failed harvest. Before the harvest, the next harvest. The man knocked on the door.

Come, said a voice from behind the door.

The man opened the door. The man stepped into the room. The man stood in the room. Before the long table, the long shadows.

Sit, said a voice from the shadows.

The man sat down in a chair at the end of the long table.

Yes, asked the voice.

The man blinked. The man tried to keep the tears from his eyes. The man swallowed. The man tried to keep his voice from breaking. And the man said, You are right. The strain has proved much too much. I am tired. And I cannot go on. I have had enough.

Close the door on your way out.

The man tried to stand. The man tried to get back on his feet. But the man could not stand. The man could not get back on his feet.

# RED OR DEAD

William Shankly, in two halves

# THE FIRST HALF

## EVERYDAY IS SATURDAY

*Shankly Among the Scousers*

# 1. TO SEE OURSELS AS OTHERS SEE US

In the winter-time, in the night-time, they remembered him. And then they came to him. In the winter-time, in the night-time. Not cap in hand, not on bended knee. Not this sort. But still they came. Here to Leeds Road, Huddersfield. Here on October 17, 1959. They came –

In the winter-time, in the night-time.

Tom Williams had seen enough. Liverpool Football Club were in the Second Division. They had not won anything since the League title in 1947. And they had never won the FA Cup. Tom Williams telephoned Geoff Twentyman. Geoff Twentyman told Tom Williams the name of the man Liverpool Football Club needed. Tom Williams telephoned Matt Busby. Matt Busby told Tom Williams the name of the man Liverpool Football Club needed. Tom Williams telephoned Walter Winterbottom. Walter Winterbottom told Tom Williams the name of the man Liverpool Football Club needed. Tom Williams had heard enough. Tom Williams telephoned Harry Latham –

In the winter-time, in the night-time.

Tom Williams and Harry Latham drove across the Pennines to Leeds Road, Huddersfield. They did not tell the directors of Huddersfield Town they were coming. They did not ask the directors of Huddersfield Town for complimentary tickets. They did not sit with the directors of Huddersfield Town. At Leeds Road, Huddersfield, Tom Williams and Harry Latham sat as close to the pitch and the home dug-out as they could. Huddersfield Town were playing Cardiff City. But Tom Williams and Harry Latham did not watch Huddersfield Town. They did not watch Cardiff City. They watched the man in the dug-out. The home dug-out. His eyes narrow, his mouth open. Jaw out, neck forward. His arms moving, his fists clenched. Right foot, left foot. Tom Williams and Harry Latham watched this man make every run every player on the pitch made. They watched this man kick every ball every player on the pitch kicked. They watched this man take every free kick. Every corner. And every throw-in. They watched this man make every pass. And every tackle. And Tom Williams and Harry Latham listened to the man in the dug-out. They listened to this man cajoling his players. They listened to this man encouraging his players. And Tom Williams and Harry Latham saw the way the players of

Huddersfield Town listened to the man. The way they listened to this man and the way they obeyed this man. His every command and his every instruction. His every word, the voice of God. And after the whistle, the final whistle, Tom Williams and Harry Latham had seen enough and they had heard enough. They knew this man had fought harder and played harder than any man out there on the pitch. And Tom Williams and Harry Latham knew this was the man they needed for Liverpool Football Club. This was the man they wanted for Liverpool Football Club. The only man for Liverpool Football Club –

In the winter-time, in the night-time. The only man.

In the shadows of the hills, in the shadows of the mills. Under the stands and on the slope. Tom Williams and Harry Latham saw the man they needed, the man they wanted. Under the stands, on the slope. Tom Williams and Harry Latham walked towards the man. And Tom Williams said, Good evening, sir. I don't know if you remember me, but my name is Tom Williams and I am the chairman of Liverpool Football Club and this is Harry Latham, one of our directors. I wonder if we might have a word with you, Mr Shankly?

I remember you, said Bill Shankly. And they are not for sale.

Tom Williams smiled. Tom Williams shook his head. And Tom Williams said, We're not here for Law or Wilson. We are here to talk to you, Mr Shankly. We are here to ask you a question.

Then ask it, said Bill Shankly.

Tom Williams said, How would you like to manage the best football club in the country, Mr Shankly?

Why, asked Bill Shankly. Matt Busby packing it in, is he?

Tom Williams smiled again. And Tom Williams said, Very funny, Mr Shankly. But you know what I'm talking about. I'm talking about Liverpool Football Club. How would you like to manage Liverpool Football Club, Mr Shankly?

I thought you didn't want me for your football club, said Bill Shankly. I thought you didn't think I was good enough for Liverpool?

Tom Williams shook his head again. And Tom Williams said, I never said that, Mr Shankly. I never said that.

You didn't need to.

I wasn't the chairman then, Mr Shankly. But I am the chairman now. And so now I'm asking you if you would like to manage Liverpool Football Club, Mr Shankly?

I thought you already had a manager? Mr Taylor? Phil Taylor?

It has not been made public yet. Nothing has been announced yet. But Mr Taylor is not a well man. He has asked me to relieve him of his duties. As I say, nothing has been announced yet, nothing made public yet. But we'd like to sort out something before it is.

Under the stands, on the slope. There was the sound of joking, laughter from the Huddersfield Town dressing room.

We might've lost today, said Bill Shankly. But we're not doing too badly here, you know, Mr Williams?

Tom Williams said, We know that. We can see that. And that's why we want you, Mr Shankly.

Well, said Bill Shankly. I'll not be rushed. But I will consider it.

In the winter-time, in the night-time. Tom Williams held out his hand. And Tom Williams said, Thank you, Mr Shankly. That is all I ask. Goodnight, Mr Shankly. Goodnight.


## 2. IN NIGHTS OF POSSIBILITY, IN DAYS OF OPPORTUNITY

In their house in Huddersfield. In their kitchen at the table. Bill ate and Bill talked. Firing out his words, wolfing down his tea. Bill ate and Bill talked. But Ness said nothing, Ness ate nothing. Ness put down her knife and her fork on her plate. And Ness got up from the table.

Bill frowned. And Bill said, You've not finished your tea, love.

Ness picked up the plate and walked over to the bin. Ness pushed the meat and the vegetables off the plate and into the bin.

Bill shook his head. And Bill said, What a waste.

Ness walked over to the sink. Ness put the plug in the sink. Ness turned on the taps. Ness put her plate, her knife and her fork on top of the pans in the sink. Ness squeezed washing-up liquid into the sink. Ness turned off the taps. Ness picked up the scrubbing brush. Ness began to wash the plate and the pans. The knife and the fork.

Where is Liverpool, Daddy, asked one of their daughters.

Bill smiled. And Bill said, It's by the seaside, love.

Ness stopped washing the plate and the pans. The knife and the fork. Ness looked up from the sink. Ness stared out into the dark garden. And Ness said, We're settled here. We've got a nice house. We've got good friends. The girls like their schools. They're happy here. I'm happy here. I don't want to leave, love.

Bill said, I know, love. I know.

. . .

In his car, at the wheel. Driving down this road, driving up that road. Bill saw a telephone box on a corner up ahead. And Bill braked. Suddenly. Bill pulled over. Bill got out of his car. And Bill went into the phone box. Bill took out a piece of paper from the pocket of his coat. Bill dialled the telephone number on the piece of paper. Bill listened to the phone ring. Bill heard a voice answer. Bill dropped two coins into the phone. And Bill said, Mr Williams? This is Bill Shankly.

Good evening, Mr Shankly. What can I do for you?

Bill said, I've been thinking about your offer.

I'm very glad to hear that, said Tom Williams. So what have you been thinking, Mr Shankly?

Bill said, I'm interested. But I have a number of conditions.

Go on, Mr Shankly.

Well, I have to have total control of the playing and the coaching staff. I have to decide on the training methods and the playing style. I have to select the team without any interference from you or the directors. And if I feel we need new players, then you and the directors must make the money available for me to buy the players I want. And I also want a salary of £2,500. And so if you cannot accommodate all these conditions, then I'm afraid I'm not interested.

May I ask what Huddersfield are paying you, Mr Shankly?

Bill said, £2,000 a year.

Then I think we can accommodate all your conditions, said Tom Williams. I am sure we can, Mr Shankly.

Bill said, Then I accept your offer.

Thank you, said Tom Williams. Then we'll be in touch again. Goodnight, Mr Shankly. Goodnight.

. . .

In their house in Huddersfield, their home in Huddersfield. In the night and in the silence. In his chair. Bill put down the newspaper. And in the night and in the silence. Bill closed his eyes. Liverpool Football Club had come to Leeds Road, Huddersfield. In the twentieth minute, Les Massie had scored. And Huddersfield Town had won. Liverpool Football Club had lost. Huddersfield Town were sixth in the Second Division. Liverpool Football Club were tenth in the Second Division. But no one was happy. Ten days before, Phil Taylor had announced his resignation as manager of Liverpool Football Club. Bill remembered his words. The words Bill had read in the newspaper. Bill could not forget his words. Phil Taylor had said, In my opinion, the club has enjoyed reasonable success. My three years have resulted in a third and two fourth-place positions. However, the strain of it all has proved too much for me. And so, great as my love is for Liverpool Football Club, I have decided to resign. I made promotion my goal. I set my heart on it. I strove for it with all my energy. But such striving was not enough. Now the time has come to hand over to someone else.

In the night and in the silence. In his chair. Bill opened his eyes again. The grapevine was alive with rumours. Rumours that Liverpool Football Club wanted Bill Shankly to be their new manager. Rumours Liverpool Football Club had denied. In his chair. Bill picked up the newspaper again. Mr Lawson Martindale, one of the senior directors of Liverpool Football Club, had said, Any names mentioned in connection with the vacancy are only conjecture. There is no certainty about the matter. Nor can there be until we have examined all the applications. We particularly desire secrecy. And we are hopeful that we shall have many first-class men seeking the job. But we do not wish to cause them, or their clubs, any embarrassment.

. . .

In the ground at Leeds Road, before the door to the Huddersfield Town boardroom. Bill touched his tie, Bill straightened his tie. And then Bill knocked on the door to the boardroom.

Come, said a voice from behind the door.

Bill opened the door. Slowly. Bill stepped into the boardroom.

Sit, said Stephen Lister, the chairman of Huddersfield Town.

Bill walked to a chair at the end of a long table. Bill sat down in the chair. Bill looked up the long table at Stephen Lister and the directors of Huddersfield Town Football Club. Bill coughed. And then Bill said, This will be my last weekly report. I have received an offer from Liverpool Football Club. And I have decided to accept their offer.

9

Stephen Lister and the other directors did not speak.

Bill coughed again. And then Bill said, I realise that this may come as something of a shock to you all. But I have decided to go because I would like to take up the challenge of managing a big club in a big city. And Liverpool Football Club is a big club in a big city.

The chairman and the directors still said nothing.

Bill coughed. And then Bill said, But I want you to know I have taken this decision very reluctantly. I have enjoyed my time in Huddersfield. And the club has always been very good to me.

Stephen Lister and the directors looked at each other. They patted their bellies, they stroked their chins. They began to mutter, they began to whisper. This name and that name.

I wonder if Harry Catterick would be interested in coming here, said Hayden Battye. A decent chap, I hear . . .

Bill laughed. Bill shook his head. And Bill said, Harry Catterick? But Wednesday are a much bigger club than this.

I think the very least you could do, said Stephen Lister, is to give us one month's notice, Shankly. You will continue in your duties until the end of the month, until the end of December.

Bill said, Fine. If that is what you want.

Close the door on your way out.

. . .

In the corridor, outside his office at Leeds Road. Bill saw Eddie Brennan, the assistant club secretary of Huddersfield Town. And Bill said, I've got something to tell you, Eddie. Something to tell you. I'm leaving, Eddie. I've been offered the Liverpool job and I've accepted it. So I'm leaving, Eddie. I'm off, I'm off. And I can't wait, Eddie. I can't wait. A big club, Eddie. A massive club. So much potential, Eddie. So much potential. You've been there, Eddie. You know. That crowd, Eddie. That city. What a crowd, Eddie! What a city! And they're going to back me, Eddie. The board. They're going to back me all the way, Eddie. Give me all the money I need. Not like here, Eddie. Not like this place. Never be anything, Eddie. This place. No potential, Eddie. No ambition. No money, Eddie. Nothing. Same with Carlisle, same with Grimsby. Same with Workington, same as here. Not like Liverpool, Eddie. What a club! What a city, Eddie! All that potential, all that ambition. I tell you, Eddie. I've been waiting my whole life for this. My whole life, Eddie. For a chance like this. It's the chance of a lifetime, Eddie. The bloody chance of a lifetime. And I can't wait, Eddie. I just can't wait. So what do you think, Eddie?

We'll miss you, said Eddie Brennan. I know that, Bill.

Bill said, And I'll miss you, Eddie. I will. But you've got to go where the work is, Eddie. Where you are wanted. Where you will be appreciated, Eddie. Appreciated and supported.

I supported you, said Eddie Brennan. And I appreciated you.

Bill nodded. And Bill said, I know that, Eddie. I know that. And I appreciated you, Eddie. I did. And I do, Eddie. I really do.

And I believed you, too, said Eddie Brennan.

. . .

In the boardroom at Leeds Road, at the long table. Bill and Stephen Lister sat down before the local press –

Isn't it true you've simply had a bellyful, asked the reporter from the *Huddersfield Examiner*. A bellyful of walking a financial tightrope, Bill? Of trying for promotion while balancing the books? Isn't that the reason you're off to Liverpool, Bill? Because you've had a bellyful of Huddersfield Town?

Bill shook his head. And Bill said, No. It's going to be a wrench to say goodbye. My wife and family have made more friends in Huddersfield than in any other town we've ever lived in before.

It was certainly a bolt from the blue, said Stephen Lister. It was the very last thing we were expecting. But Mr Shankly put his position before the board and, after expressing our regret at the prospect of losing his services, we have agreed that Mr Shankly shall join Liverpool Football Club. Mr Shankly has no contract with Huddersfield Town, but he considers it only fair to the club that he should stay at Leeds Road for a month in order to give us the opportunity of making a new appointment before he leaves us. Liverpool are getting a good man. Thank you.

. . .

In the boardroom at Leeds Road, before the chairman. Bill touched his tie. And Bill said, You wanted to see me, Mr Lister?

There is no point you hanging around here like a spare part, said Stephen Lister. Not now everyone knows you're going. If you wish to go to Liverpool now, then you can go. We'll not stand in your way, Shankly. We'll not hold you to your month's notice.

Bill held out his hand. And Bill said, Thank you, Mr Lister.

Close the door on your way out, Shankly.

. . .

In another boardroom, at another long table. Bill and Tom Williams sat down before the local press. And Horace Yates, from the *Liverpool Daily Post*, and Leslie Edwards, from the *Liverpool Echo*, opened their notebooks, took out their pens and waited –

Gentlemen, said Tom Williams. The board of Liverpool Football Club would like to announce that all applications for the position of manager have been considered. Of the small number who came up to the requirements, the board decided to ascertain the services of Mr William Shankly, of Huddersfield Town FC, and have offered the management to him.

Bill nodded. Bill smiled. And then Bill said, I am very pleased and proud to have been chosen as manager of Liverpool Football Club. Liverpool is a club of great potential. I have known Mr Williams a long time and I have always considered him to be one of football's gentlemen. He has been at Liverpool Football Club since the club began. He is devoted to Liverpool Football Club. And I am confident that we will be able to work well together. It is my opinion that Liverpool have a crowd of followers which ranks with the greatest in the game. They deserve success and I hope in my small way to be able to do something towards helping them achieve it. But I make no promises except that, from the moment I take over, I shall put everything I have into the job I so willingly undertake. This appointment is a challenge for me. I rank it similar to that confronting Joe Mercer when he left Sheffield United for Aston Villa. Or when Alan Brown left Burnley to go to Sunderland. These clubs, like Liverpool, are amongst the top-grade teams in the football land. So when the challenge was made to me, I simply could not refuse to accept it. There is a job to be done. Perhaps a big job. But with the cooperation of Mr Williams, the directors and staff, I feel certain we shall see the task through together. I am not a lazy man. I like to get down to it and set the example which I want following from the top of the club to the bottom. I make few promises. But one of them is that, in everything I do, I hope there will be patent common sense attached to it. Common sense and hard work. Together, hard work and common sense bring success. That is what I believe. In football and in life.

How would Mr Shankly reflect on his time as manager of Huddersfield Town, asked Horace Yates, from the *Liverpool Daily Post*. Would he say he had been a success at Huddersfield?

Bill nodded again. And Bill said, Yes, I would. When I took over at Huddersfield three years ago, I had only a team of boys to go to work on. Indeed, they are still boys, most of them. I would not be human if I were not pleased with the way in which players like Law, McHale, Massie and Wilson have advanced under my direction. I guided them from their junior beginnings to League football. My signings have been Ray Wood of Manchester United, who I consider to be the best goalkeeper in the Second Division, and Derek Hawksworth. I don't think either of them have let me down. I believe I am leaving Huddersfield Town in a better, stronger position than when I took over three years ago and so I consider that to be a success. That I have been a success at Huddersfield. And I hope they would agree.

But the burning ambition of every Liverpool supporter, said Leslie Edwards, from the *Liverpool Echo*, is to see this football club restored to the First Division. How do you feel about that?

Bill nodded. And Bill said, Nobody realises more than I do what a tough job that is likely to be. But I have gained a lot of experience of Second Division football and so I know the difficulties. But I think we can do it. In fact, I know we can do it.

. . .

In their house in Huddersfield, in the bedroom. Bill waited for the dawn, Bill waited for the light. And Bill got out of bed. Bill shaved, Bill washed. Bill put on his suit, Bill put on his tie. And Bill went downstairs. Bill ate breakfast with Ness and their daughters. Bill kissed them goodbye. Bill went out of the house, Bill got into his car. And Bill drove across the Pennines. Past Manchester –

Into Liverpool. To Anfield.

In the ground, in the office. Bill shook hands with Jimmy McInnes, the club secretary. Bill knew Jimmy McInnes. Bill knew Jimmy came from Ayr. Bill knew Jimmy had played for Third Lanark and for Liverpool Football Club. Jimmy introduced Bill to the receptionist, the ticket administrators, the cleaners and the groundsman,

Arthur Riley. Bill knew Arthur Riley. Bill knew Arthur had worked for Liverpool Football Club for over thirty years. Arthur took Bill to meet the coaching staff. Under the stands, down a corridor. Among the boots, the dirty boots –

This is Bob Paisley, said Arthur Riley. Bob is the first-team trainer. This is Joe Fagan. Joe is in charge of the reserves. This is Reuben Bennett. Reuben takes most of the training. And this is Albert Shelley. Albert used to be the first-team trainer. He's supposed to be retired. But Albert still comes in every day. Albert does whatever needs doing. Albert does everything and anything.

Bill nodded. And Bill said, I know Bob. Me and Bob played against each other on many occasions. We had many a good scrap. And I know Joe. I tried to sign Joe when I was at Grimsby and he was at Manchester City. I know Reuben. Reuben used to work with my brother Bob at Dundee. And I know Albert. I know he lives and breathes Liverpool Football Club. I know you all do. And so I know you men are all good men. True football men. But I also know you fellows have all been here a long time. And so I know you'll all be worried about me coming in. A new feller with new ways. Different ways. Maybe wanting to bring in new trainers with him. His mates. Well, I'm not going to do that. But I do have my ways. My methods and my systems. And they will be different ways. But I am here to work with you. Not against you. I am here to work in cooperation with you. As a team. And so gradually I will lay down my plans and then gradually we will be on the same wavelength. And, in return, I ask for only one thing. Loyalty. I want loyalty. So I don't want anybody to carry stories about anyone else. The man who brings the story to me will be the man who gets the sack. I don't care if he's been here fifty years. He'll be the one who goes. Because I want everyone to be loyal to each other. To the team. And to the club. So everything we do will be for Liverpool Football Club. Not for ourselves. Not as individuals. But for the team. For Liverpool Football Club. Total loyalty. That is all I ask. Because that loyalty makes strength. And that strength will bring success. I promise you.

. . .

In their house in Huddersfield, in their kitchen. Bill and Ness cleared the table. Bill and Ness washed the pots. And then Ness made a cup of tea for her and Bill. Bill and Ness took their cups of tea into the other room. Bill and Ness sat down with their cups of tea. In front of the television. And Bill said, So how was your day then, love?

Mine was fine, said Ness. But how was yours?

Bill nodded. And Bill said, It went well, love. It went well. Thank you, love. They are all good men.

That's good then, said Ness.

Bill said, Aye.

But it's a long drive, said Ness. You must be tired, love.

Bill nodded again. And Bill said, It is, love. And I am a bit tired. But it's a good city, love. More like a Scottish city. Good people, love. Like Scottish people. I can tell, love. Like Glasgow. So I think you'd like it, love. And the girls would, too.

Yes then, said Ness. I'd like to go over, love. To have a look then. And maybe even look at some houses, love. If you have time?

Bill smiled. And Bill said, Aye. On Sunday then.

. . .

In Liverpool, at Anfield. Bill walked around the ground with Arthur Riley. Bill looked at the turnstiles and Bill looked at the stands. Bill looked at the seats and Bill looked at the toilets. Bill looked at the dressing rooms and Bill looked at the tunnel. And then Bill walked out onto the pitch. The Anfield pitch. Bill stood on the pitch, Bill stamped on the pitch. Once, twice. Bill shook his head. Once, twice. And Bill said, How do you water this pitch, Arthur? Where do you keep your watering equipment?

There isn't any, said Arthur Riley. There's no water.

Bill said, No water? So what do you do?

There's a tap in the visitors' dressing room, said Arthur Riley. We run a pipe from there out here.

Bill looked down at the pitch. The Anfield pitch, the Anfield grass. Frozen and bare, hard and barren. Bill shook his head again. And Bill said, You run a pipe? That's no bloody good, is it?

I know, said Arthur Riley. But what can we do?

Bill said, We can fix it. We can buy some bloody equipment. That's what we can do, Arthur.

I've been saying that for years, said Arthur Riley. But there's no money. No money here.

Bill smiled. And Bill said, Leave that to me. I'll get you the money, Arthur. Trust me.

I do, said Arthur Riley. You're the Boss.

Bill smiled again. And Bill said, I am. Now let's you and me go and have a look at the training ground. Let's go out to Melwood.

You're not going to like it, said Arthur Riley. You're not going to be happy, Boss. I can tell you that for nothing.

Bill shrugged. And Bill said, How bad can it be, Arthur? It can't be any worse than this place, can it?

. . .

In Liverpool, in the car. Bill and Ness drove from house to house. This house for sale and that house for sale. This house too big, that house too small. Outside the last house, back in the car. Bill shook his head. And Bill said, I'm sorry. love. That was a waste of time.

No it wasn't, said Ness. There's no rush, love. Better to find the right house than any old house. Better to take our time, better to wait, love. And at least we can have Christmas in Huddersfield.

Bill nodded. And Bill said, Yes. With our friends.

On their way back home, home to Huddersfield. Bill stopped the car at Melwood in West Derby. Bill and Ness got out of the car. It was cold and it was dark. There were trees and there were bushes. There were hills and there were hollows. There was an air-raid shelter and there was a cricket pitch. There was an old wooden pavilion. In the cold and in the dark. Bill and Ness stood in the middle of the training pitch. They felt the long grass and the uneven ground beneath their feet. Bill shook his head again. And Bill said, What do you think, love? Have I made a mistake in coming here? A big mistake, love?

No, you haven't, said Ness. You want to get into the First Division. You want to win the League. You want to win the Cup. So this is your chance. The chance you have been waiting for. The chance you have been working for. Your whole life. You are not a coward. And you are not a shirker. So you will do it, love. I know you will.


## 3. WHAT IS TO BE DONE

In the winter, in the morning. The players of Liverpool Football Club were packed into the old wooden pavilion at the Melwood training ground in West Derby. All forty of them. They were here to meet their new manager. And they were nervous. They were worried. All forty of them. They had all heard the stories about Bill Shankly. One of them whispered, The man's a fanatic. A bloody mad man. He'll come in here like a fucking hurricane. We'll all be for the chop, lads, I tell you.

Some of them nodded. And another one said, Yeah. I heard that story about him at Carlisle, when he was manager at Carlisle. And they were two down at half-time. And they come into the dressing room. And the first thing Shankly does is he grabs their captain. He grabs him by the throat and he says, Why did you kick off the way you did? And the captain says, Because I lost the toss, Boss. So Shankly says, Well, what did you call? And the captain says, Tails. And then Shankly calls him every name under the sun. Every bloody name there is. In front of the whole fucking changing room. And then Shankly says, You never call tails. Everyone knows that. You never call tails.

In the pavilion, in the corner. Bob Paisley looked up from his *Sporting Life*. Bob Paisley laughed. And Bob Paisley said, But the feller was right, wasn't he? The Boss was right.

Now the players of Liverpool Football Club heard footsteps on the wooden stairs outside. Fast steps, heavy steps. And now Bill Shankly walked into the pavilion. Bill Shankly looked around the room. From player to player. All forty of them –

We're going to start from the beginning again, said Bill Shankly. We're going to start from scratch. And so every man here will have the chance to prove himself. Prove himself good enough to play for Liverpool Football Club. Good enough to help Liverpool Football Club get back into the First Division. Back where we belong. Because that's all I'm interested in –

Promotion, lads!

. . .

On Saturday 19 December, 1959, Cardiff City came to Anfield, Liverpool. That afternoon, twenty-seven thousand, two hundred and ninety-one folk came, too. In the twelfth minute, Tapscott scored. In the thirty-fourth minute, Watkins scored. In the fifty-seventh minute, Tapscott scored again. And in the sixty-seventh minute, Bonson scored. And Liverpool Football Club lost four–nil to Cardiff City. At home, at

Anfield. It was Bill Shankly's first game as the manager of Liverpool Football Club. But Bill Shankly had not picked the team that day. Bill Shankly had refused. Bill Shankly had said, I have not seen enough. I do not know the players well enough. So I cannot pick the team.

And so the directors and the coaching staff of Liverpool Football Club had picked the team for that match.

After the whistle, the final whistle. Among the shouting and among the bawling. Before the stands, before the Kop. The shouting in the stands and the bawling on the Kop. Bill Shankly stood up. In front of the stands, in front of the Kop. Among the insults and among the jokes. Bill Shankly walked along the touchline. The Anfield touchline. Bill Shankly walked down the tunnel. The Anfield tunnel. Bill Shankly walked up the stairs. The Anfield stairs. Bill Shankly opened the dressing-room door. The home dressing-room door. Bill Shankly stood in the centre of the dressing room. The Liverpool dressing room. Before the players, the Liverpool players. Bill Shankly looked from player to player. Liverpool player to Liverpool player. From Slater to Jones, Jones to Moran, Moran to Wheeler, Wheeler to White, White to Campbell, Campbell to Morris, Morris to Hunt, Hunt to Hickson, Hickson to Melia and Melia to A'Court. And Bill Shankly smiled –

There will always be times when we get beaten, said Bill Shankly. There will always be times when we lose. But the important thing is what we take away from that beating, what we learn when we lose. Because we'll always learn more from a loss than a win. So remember that and learn that, lads. And I'll see you all on Monday.

. . .

On the Monday, in the morning. The players of Liverpool Football Club were running laps around the training pitch at Melwood. All forty of them. And the players of Liverpool Football Club were watching Bill Shankly, Bob Paisley, Joe Fagan, Reuben Bennett, Albert Shelley, Arthur Riley, Tom Bush and Eli Wass –

Bill Shankly, Bob Paisley, Joe Fagan, Reuben Bennett, Albert Shelley, Arthur Riley, Tom Bush and Eli Wass standing in a line across one end of the training pitch at Melwood. Each with a sack in one hand, each with a trowel in the other. And Bill Shankly smiled –

Right then, said Bill Shankly. Let's make a start.

And Bill Shankly, Bob Paisley, Joe Fagan, Reuben Bennett,

Albert Shelley, Arthur Riley, Tom Bush and Eli Wass began to walk across the training pitch. Slowly. Their heads bent forward, their eyes staring down. Down at the ground, down at the pitch. Slowly. Bill Shankly, Bob Paisley, Joe Fagan, Reuben Bennett, Albert Shelley, Arthur Riley, Tom Bush and Eli Wass picked up every stone they saw. Every bit of brick, every piece of broken glass. Every rock and every pebble. They pulled up every weed they found. Every dandelion and every thistle. They put the stones into their sacks, they put the weeds into their sacks. They used the heels of their boots to tread down the ground. To fill in every divot, to fill in every hole. From one end of the training pitch to the other end. And when they reached the other end, they turned and walked back. Slowly. Picking up the stones they had missed. The bits of brick, the pieces of broken glass. Pulling up the weeds they had missed. The dandelions and the thistles. Treading down the ground. Every divot and every hole. And when they came to the place where they had started, then they turned again. And they began to walk back towards the other end again. Slowly. Picking up the stones, pulling up the weeds.

And the players of Liverpool Football Club kept running their laps of the training pitch. All forty of them. The players of Liverpool Football Club watching the eight men. The eight men picking up the stones, the eight men pulling up the weeds. With their sacks and with their trowels. And the players of Liverpool Football Club glanced at each other. They shook their heads, they rolled their eyes. And the players of Liverpool Football Club slowed their pace.

Reuben Bennett looked up from the ground. From the stones and from the weeds. And Reuben Bennett shouted, Pick up them feet, lads. No slacking now! No bloody slacking, lads!

Bill Shankly, Bob Paisley, Joe Fagan, Reuben Bennett, Albert Shelley, Arthur Riley, Tom Bush and Eli Wass reached the other end of the training pitch for the twelfth time. They had eight sacks of stones and weeds. Eight full sacks of stones and weeds –

Right, said Bill Shankly. It's no bowling green. Not yet. But it'll do for today. It's a start. For now.

Reuben Bennett blew his whistle. Reuben Bennett shouted, Last lap, lads. And it's a race! Go!

And the players of Liverpool Football Club sprinted around the training pitch. All forty of them. And Bob Paisley gathered the fastest twenty on one half of the pitch. And Joe Fagan gathered the slower twenty on the other half. Bill Shankly went into the pavilion. Bill Shankly came back out carrying a big bag of balls. Bill Shankly stood in the centre of the training pitch. And Bill Shankly smiled –

Right then, said Bill Shankly. Enough running around the houses. We're going to play some football, lads . . .

The players of Liverpool Football Club rubbed their hands together. The players of Liverpool Football Club smiled.

And Bill Shankly smiled again –

We're going to play some five-a-sides, said Bill Shankly. Have ourselves a wee little FA Cup, boys . . .

The players of Liverpool Football Club hopped from foot to foot. The players of Liverpool Football Club grinned.

Bill Shankly grinned, too. Bill Shankly looked at the players gathered around Joe Fagan. The players who had been the slowest twenty around the training pitch. Bill Shankly took off his sweater. Bill Shankly took off his shirt. Bill Shankly took off his vest. And Bill Shankly laughed. And Bill Shankly said, Merry Christmas, lads. It's shirts versus skins. Merry Christmas, boys!

. . .

In the afternoon, after their lunch. The directors of Liverpool Football Club were sitting in the boardroom at Anfield. The directors of Liverpool Football Club were waiting for Bill Shankly. The directors of Liverpool Football Club heard the footsteps in the corridor outside. The fast steps, the heavy steps. And then the knock upon the boardroom door. Fast and heavy. And Tom Williams said, Come.

Bill Shankly opened the door. Bill Shankly stepped into the boardroom. Bill Shankly looked around the boardroom. From director to director. And Bill Shankly waited.

Tom Williams said, Sit down.

Bill Shankly sat down at the long table. Bill Shankly looked up the long table at the directors of Liverpool Football Club.

Tom Williams smiled at Bill Shankly. And Tom Williams said, Well then, Mr Shankly. How is it going? How are you getting on?

I have been here a week now, said Bill Shankly. And for that week, I have held my tongue but I have kept my eyes open. And frankly, gentlemen, I do not like what I have seen. There are many things that need changing, many things that need doing. First and foremost, this ground is an embarrassment and an eyesore. It needs cleaning up and it needs renovating. For a start, the pitch needs proper watering equipment. And then there are the toilets. The toilets are a disgrace. Most of them don't even flush. And so they stink!

The directors of Liverpool Football Club looked at each other. And one director asked, Which toilets are you talking about?

All of them, said Bill Shankly. All of the ones in the stands.

The ones the spectators use?

Yes, said Bill Shankly. The ones in the stands. The ones the people who pay to watch Liverpool Football Club have to use. Those people who pay my wages. Those people, their toilets.

Tom Williams said, Well, we will certainly take your suggestions under consideration. Was there anything else, Mr Shankly?

Aye, said Bill Shankly. There certainly is. There is Melwood. That place is worse than here. It's not fit for a Sunday kick-about, let alone training sessions for professional footballers. The pitch is a deathtrap. It's a wonder no one has broken their leg on it. And that pavilion is no better. One big gust of wind and that thing will fall down. And the kits the players wear for training. They are in tatters. They are nothing but rags. A tramp would turn up his nose at them. It's not good enough for Liverpool Football Club.

Again the directors of Liverpool Football Club looked at each other. And another director asked, So what do you suggest, Shankly?

I suggest you get the players some new training kits, said Bill Shankly. And I suggest you get me some tins of paint. I'm not asking you to bring in the painters and the decorators. Just get the players their kits and get me some paint. And then I'll do the rest.

Tom Williams said, Well, I think we'd all agree you certainly make a very powerful case, Mr Shankly. And, as I say, we will certainly consider your suggestions. Thank you, Mr Shankly.

Good, said Bill Shankly. Because I am here to do a job of work. And I will do it. And so I expect you all to do yours, too.

. . .

On Boxing Day, 1959, Liverpool Football Club travelled to the Valley, London. In the thirty-fourth minute, Fryatt scored. In the seventy-fourth minute, Fryatt scored again. And in the ninetieth minute, Lawrie scored. And Liverpool Football Club lost three–nil to Charlton Athletic. Away from home, away from Anfield –

After the whistle, the final whistle. In the dressing room, the away dressing room. The players of Liverpool Football Club looked at Bill Shankly. And Bill Shankly looked at the players. From player to player, Liverpool player to Liverpool player. From Slater to Molyneux, Molyneux to Moran, Moran to Wheeler, Wheeler to White, White to Campbell, Campbell to Melia, Melia to Hunt, Hunt to Hickson, Hickson to Harrower, Harrower to Melia and Melia to A'Court. From dejected player to dejected player. And Bill Shankly smiled –

We only conceded three this time, said Bill Shankly. So that's better than the last time. But it's still a defeat. So we still have a lot to learn. And so I'll see you all tomorrow morning. Bright and early!

. . .

In the morning, the dark and early morning. Again. The players of Liverpool Football Club were running laps around the training pitch at Melwood. All forty of them. And again. Bill Shankly, Bob Paisley, Joe Fagan, Reuben Bennett, Albert Shelley, Arthur Riley, Tom Bush and Eli Wass were standing in a line across one end of the training pitch at Melwood. Again. Each man with a sack in one hand, each man with a trowel in the other. And again. Bill Shankly smiled –

Right then, said Bill Shankly. Let's start again.

And again. Bill Shankly, Bob Paisley, Joe Fagan, Reuben Bennett, Albert Shelley, Arthur Riley, Tom Bush and Eli Wass began to walk across the training pitch. Again. Their heads bent forward, their eyes staring down. Down at the ground, down at the pitch. Again.

Picking up every stone they saw. Every bit of brick and every piece of broken glass. Again. Pulling up every weed they found. Every dandelion and every thistle. Again. Putting the stones into their sacks, putting the weeds into their sacks. Again. Using the heels of their boots to tread down the ground. Every divot, every hole. Again. From one end of the training pitch to the other end. Again. Reaching the other end, then turning and walking back. Again. They picked up the stones they had missed. The bits of brick, the pieces of broken glass. Again. They pulled up the weeds they had missed. The dandelions and the thistles. Again. They trod down the ground. Every divot and every hole. And again. When they came to the place where they had started, then they turned again and they began to walk back towards the other end. Again. Picking up the stones, pulling up the weeds.

And again. The players of Liverpool Football Club kept running their laps of the training pitch. All forty of them. But today the players of Liverpool Football Club did not watch the eight men working. The eight men picking up the stones, the eight men pulling up the weeds. With their sacks and with their trowels. Today the players of Liverpool Football Club did not slow their pace. All forty of them. Today the players of Liverpool Football Club did not slack.

And again. Bill Shankly, Bob Paisley, Joe Fagan, Reuben Bennett, Albert Shelley, Arthur Riley, Tom Bush and Eli Wass reached the other end of the training pitch for the twelfth time. Again. They had eight sacks of stones and weeds. But today the eight sacks of stones and weeds were not quite as full. Again. Bill Shankly smiled –

It's still no bowling green, said Bill Shankly. Not yet. But it's getting better. So we're getting there, gentlemen.

And again. Reuben Bennett blew his whistle. Again. Reuben Bennett shouted, Last lap, lads!

And today the players of Liverpool Football Club knew it was a race. For dear life. The players of Liverpool Football Club tore around the training pitch. All forty of them. And again. Bill Shankly went into the pavilion. Again. Bill Shankly came back out carrying a big bag of balls. Again. Bill Shankly stood in the centre of the training pitch. Again. Bill Shankly took off his sweater. Bill Shankly took off his shirt. Bill Shankly took off his vest. Again. Bill Shankly smiled –

Right then, lads. Let's play some five-a-sides again!

Bob Paisley, Joe Fagan and Reuben Bennett put the players of Liverpool Football Club into eight teams of five. And Bob Paisley, Joe Fagan and Reuben Bennett divided up the training pitch into four smaller pitches. Bob Paisley, Joe Fagan and Reuben Bennett would be the referees. And Albert Shelley would be the fourth referee. Bill Shankly would not be a referee. Bill Shankly would not stand on the touchline watching. If there was a game of football to be played, then Bill Shankly played. Bill Shankly played –

He played and he ran. Over every inch of grass. Over every blade. Bill Shankly ran. He ran and he shouted. Calling. Constantly calling for the ball. Every ball. Demanding the ball. Every ball. Getting the ball. Every ball. Receiving and then passing the ball. And running again. Over every inch of grass. Every blade. Running and shouting. Calling. Demanding. Receiving and passing. On and on. Over and over. Game after game. Running and shouting. Calling and demanding. Receiving and passing. Until his team had beaten each of the other seven teams, beaten every one of them into the ground. And Bill Shankly stood, Bill Shankly tall. Stripped to his waist, sweat down his chest. His chest heaving, his back steaming. In the winter, in the morning. Bill Shankly standing, Bill Shankly tall –

His boot upon the ball. His arms raised,

his fists clenched. Victorious.

. . .

On Monday 28 December, 1959, Charlton Athletic came to Anfield, Liverpool. That day, twenty-five thousand, six hundred and fifty-eight folk came, too. Two months ago, when Dave Hickson had made his debut against Aston Villa, when Dave Hickson had scored twice against Aston Villa, when Liverpool Football Club had beaten Aston Villa two–one, almost fifty thousand folk had been at Anfield, Liverpool. But not today. Today there were empty seats in the stands, today there were empty spaces on the Kop. And there was silence, too. But in the fifty-eighth minute, Jimmy Harrower slipped the ball to Tommy Leishman, who chipped it up for Alan A'Court to head into the Charlton net. Five minutes later, Jimmy Harrower put Roger Hunt through to shoot and score a second. And Liverpool Football Club beat Charlton Athletic two–nil. At home, at Anfield. There was still silence. No insults, no bawling. Just

silence –

But not after the whistle, the final whistle. Not in the dressing room. In the home dressing room. Bill Shankly was tap-dancing from player to player. From Slater to Molyneux, Molyneux to Moran, Moran to Wheeler, Wheeler to White, White to Leishman, Leishman to Melia, Melia to Hunt, Hunt to Hickson, Hickson to Harrower and Harrower to A'Court. Bill Shankly patting their backs, Bill Shankly shaking their hands. All of their backs and all of their hands. Tap-dancing and singing, singing their praises, all of their praises –

Well done, boys. Well done. You were great, lads. You were

great. Each and every one of you, boys. I could not have asked for more. And this is only the start, lads. Only the beginning. And so I'll see you all first thing tomorrow, boys.

. . .

On Saturday 2 January, 1960, Liverpool Football Club travelled to Boothferry Park, Hull. In the thirty-first minute, Jimmy Melia scored. And Liverpool Football Club beat Hull City one–nil. Away from home, away from Anfield.

One week later, Leyton Orient came to Anfield, Liverpool. That afternoon, forty thousand, three hundred and forty-three folk came, too. In the first minute, Roger Hunt scored. In the sixty-second minute, Foster scored for Leyton Orient. But in the last minute, Roger Hunt scored again. And Liverpool Football Club beat Leyton Orient two–one in the Third Round of the FA Cup. At home, at Anfield –

After the whistle, the final whistle. In the tiny office, before the small desk. Horace Yates, of the *Liverpool Daily Post*, watched Bill Shankly jump up from behind the desk in the office. Horace Yates watched Bill Shankly pace the room. He watched him pace and he listened to him talk. Ten to the dozen, one hundred miles an hour –

Talking and pacing, pacing and talking,

talking about the future,

the future now –

The gates of Anfield, the gates of Melwood are wide open. Wide open, Horace. To every schoolboy and every youth on Merseyside. The gates are open, Horace. They need feel no embarrassment. No shyness, Horace. They must come and report for coaching and training. Every one of them. Every lad who has ever kicked a ball within one hundred miles. They are all welcome. All welcome, Horace. And we will watch them all. So any boy, any lad, who has any potential, we will develop that potential. That is my promise. To give every boy, every lad who comes through these gates the opportunity. The opportunity, Horace. Because that is what I believe in. Giving people, whoever they may be, wherever they may come from, giving them that opportunity. That opportunity, Horace. Because without opportunity, there is no chance for talent. And so if any boy, if any lad, has any talent in them at all, we will do our very best to bring it out of them. Our very best, Horace. Because that is what I believe in. Finding that talent. Then giving that talent the opportunity. Bringing out that talent. Then developing that talent. So they are all welcome. They are all welcome, Horace –

The more the better. The more the merrier . . .

Bill Shankly sat back down behind the desk. Bill Shankly looked across the desk at Horace Yates –

You know, it's not such a giant step from school to League football these days. Not such a long stride, Horace. Not these days. And when you think how difficult it is to find experienced players. And then how costly it is to procure them. It makes more sense to look much closer to home, does it not? And I just cannot believe, I simply refuse to believe, in a city as soccer-conscious, as soccer mad as Liverpool, that we cannot find the talent we need. The boys we need. And if we get enough of them . . .

Bill Shankly jumped back up onto his feet, Horace Yates jumping out of his skin in his chair. Bill Shankly pacing the room again, Horace Yates turning his neck again. Horace Yates writing as fast as he could, Bill Shankly talking as fast as he could –

If enough of them come, then we are sure to get a percentage of winners. I am certain of that, Horace. I know that. I know that within three years of them leaving school, these boys could be in the first team. I know that. So I know it is not even that long term. Not as long term as the cynics might say. Not so long term, Horace. Not when you can't get the ready-made material. Not when it is so difficult. So heartbreaking. Look at Roger Hunt. How many more Roger Hunts are out there now, playing for their school, playing in their street? Look how many we found at Leeds Road. At Huddersfield, Horace. In a town that size. A town that small, Horace. It should be much easier here, in this city, with its size, with all its people, with all its history, all its passion. Its passion for football, Horace. I refuse to believe there aren't the boys, aren't the lads, out there who think, who eat, who sleep football. Just hankering after a career in soccer, just waiting for the chance. For the opportunity. The opportunity, Horace. And so all I ask is for those boys, those lads, to give me the opportunity, to give me the chance to help them achieve their goal, to achieve their dream. If they give me the chance, Horace, I will give them the chance . . .

Talking and pacing, pacing and talking,

jabbing his finger into the chest of Horace Yates, looking into the eyes of Horace Yates, saying –

Football is my life. My life, Horace. And so I do not mind how long it takes, how much time I spend among these boys, these lads. Because I have great hopes. Great hopes, Horace. And I know the boys, the lads of Liverpool, I know they will not let me down. They will not let me down. And so to me the sky is the limit. The sky is the limit, Horace. And so the gates are open. The gates are open, Horace. And they will stay open. For as long as I am at Liverpool Football Club, the gates will always be open. Always open, Horace. Always.

. . .

On Saturday 16 January, 1960, Sheffield United came to Anfield, Liverpool. That afternoon, thirty-three thousand, two hundred and ninety-seven folk came, too. In the ninth minute, Jimmy Melia scored. In the fifteenth minute, Roger Hunt scored. And in the sixty-eighth minute, Roger Hunt scored again. Fifteen minutes later, Dave Hickson was sent off. But Liverpool Football Club still beat Sheffield United three–nil. At home, at Anfield –

Every morning, every morning of the week. In the ground, in the dressing room. The players and the coaching staff of Liverpool Football Club took off their suits and ties. And their shoes. Every morning. The players and the coaching staff of Liverpool Football Club put on their tracksuit bottoms and their sweaters. And their boots. Every morning. The players and the coaching staff of Liverpool Football Club walked out of the dressing room and down the corridor. The players and the coaching staff of Liverpool Football Club walked out of the ground and into the car park at Anfield. Every morning. The players and the coaching staff of Liverpool Football Club climbed on board the bus to Melwood. Every morning. The players and the coaching staff of Liverpool Football Club travelled on the bus to Melwood to train. And every morning, after training and a nice cup of tea. The players and the coaching staff of Liverpool Football Club climbed back on board the bus. And every morning. The players and the coaching staff of Liverpool Football Club travelled back to Anfield. Every morning. The players and the coaching staff got off the bus in the car park at Anfield and walked back into the ground. Every morning. The players and the coaching staff of Liverpool Football

Club walked back down the corridors and back into the dressing room. Every morning. The players and the coaching staff took off their boots. Their sweaters and their tracksuit bottoms. And every morning. The players and the coaching staff of Liverpool Football Club went into the showers and into the baths. Every morning. The players and the coaching staff of Liverpool Football Club washed and then changed back into their suits and ties. And their shoes. And then every morning. The players and the coaching staff of Liverpool Football Club said, Goodbye. See you tomorrow. Take care now. See you. This was the Liverpool way. Every morning –

The Anfield way –

And every morning. A young lad with a broom in his hand stood by the bus in the car park at Anfield. Every morning. The young lad with the broom in his hand watched the players and the coaching staff of Liverpool Football Club climb aboard the bus to Melwood. And every morning. The young lad dreamt of the day he would no longer have a broom in his hands. The day he would have boots on his feet. The day he would climb aboard the bus to Melwood –

What's your name, son, asked Bill Shankly.

The young lad jumped. Out of his dreams, into the car park. And the young lad said, Christopher Lawler, sir.

What are you doing just standing here, son, asked Bill Shankly. Why aren't you changed? Why aren't you on the bus, lad? Hurry up.

The young lad said, But I have my work to do, sir. My work.

And what work is that, son, asked Bill Shankly.

The young lad said, During the day, I have to clean the place up, sir. That's my job. That is my work, sir.

So when do you do your training, son, asked Bill Shankly. When do you play your football, lad?

We do our training at night, sir.

You train at bloody night?

Yes, sir. At night. All the boys do.

Not any more you don't, son, said Bill Shankly. So you go now and you get all the boys together, all the ground-staff lads. And you tell them to get changed and get on board this bus. Because you are here to play football first and to clean up second. So you'll play your football during the day and you'll do your cleaning at night. Is that clear, son? Is that understood?

Yes, sir.

Well, don't just stand there then, son. Get to it. Hurry up, lad! We haven't got all bloody day. We've got football to play!

. . .

After their lunch, in the afternoon. The directors of Liverpool Football Club were sitting in the boardroom at Anfield. The directors of Liverpool Football Club were waiting for Bill Shankly. Again. The directors of Liverpool Football Club heard the footsteps in the corridor. Again. The fast steps, the heavy steps. And the knock upon the door.

Tom Williams said, Come.

Bill Shankly opened the door. Bill Shankly stepped into the boardroom. Again. Bill Shankly looked around the boardroom –

You wanted to see me, asked Bill Shankly.

Tom Williams said, Yes. Sit down, please, Mr Shankly.

Bill Shankly sat down at the long table. Bill Shankly looked up the long table at the directors of Liverpool Football Club.

Tom Williams said, I am afraid you have upset the routine of the club, Mr Shankly. The young boys are needed to help the staff clean up the stadium. That is their job, Mr Shankly.

I know that, said Bill Shankly. I know that is *part* of their job. But first and foremost they are here to play football. They can still do their cleaning, they can still help the ground staff, but they can do it at night. During the day they should be playing football. They should be training. Developing. Not cleaning toilets.

Tom Williams smiled. And Tom Williams said, We all know how passionately you feel about bringing on the younger players, Mr Shankly. That is one of the reasons we wanted you to be the manager of Liverpool Football Club. Because of your success with the younger players at Huddersfield Town. But we have our routines. We have our ways. And if you don't agree with those routines, those ways, then you should come to us first, Mr Shankly.

Well, if you don't want me to develop these boys, these lads . . .

We never said that, Mr Shankly. We are not saying that.

Then you need to let me buy some players. Some decent players. Because frankly speaking, the players you have got here are not good enough for Liverpool Football Club.

Tom Williams sat back in his chair. And Tom Williams said, And so who do you have in mind, Mr Shankly? Which players should we buy? Go on then, Mr Shankly. Please give us their names.

Well, said Bill Shankly. I can tell you two names.

Tom Williams said again, Go on . . .

Denis Law of Huddersfield Town, said Bill Shankly. And Jack Charlton of Leeds United. For starters, that is. Just for starters.

The directors of Liverpool Football Club smiled. The directors of Liverpool Football Club laughed. And one of them said, Denis Law? Mr Shankly, you must know better than any man how much Law would cost. Huddersfield are already asking over fifty grand for the lad. He's a player for the likes of Arsenal or Spurs. For Manchester United or City. Not for Liverpool Football Club.

And there's your problem, said Bill Shankly. Right there. Right bloody there. Your thinking is the problem. You should be thinking Denis Law *is* a player for Liverpool Football Club. That *only* players as good as Denis Law can play for Liverpool Football Club . . .

But we don't have the money, Mr Shankly.

You don't have the ambition!

Tom Williams sat forward in his chair. Tom Williams put his hands out before him. And Tom Williams said, Mr Shankly, Mr Shankly, please. We all want the best for Liverpool Football Club. The very best. But we simply don't have the money for Denis Law. I wish we did. I really do. But we don't. But now what about Jack Charlton? Do you honestly think Leeds United would sell him? They are fighting for their lives in the First Division. They are hardly likely to sell one of their best players now, are they, Mr Shankly? Their centre-half?

I think they might. I think it's at least worth asking.

Well then, ask them, Mr Shankly. Ask them.

. . .

After their late lunch, in the late afternoon. The directors of Leeds United Association Football Club were sitting in the boardroom at Elland Road, Leeds. The directors of Leeds United Association Football Club heard the footsteps in the corridor outside. The fast steps, the heavy steps. The knocks upon the door. Fast and heavy.

The chairman of Leeds United said, Come!

Bill Shankly opened the door. Bill Shankly stepped into the

boardroom at Elland Road. Bill Shankly looked around the board room. From director to director. And Bill Shankly smiled –

My name is Bill Shankly. I am the manager of Liverpool Football Club. And I'm here to buy Jack Charlton.

The directors of Leeds United Association Football Club stared down the long table at Bill Shankly. And then their chairman asked, And how much would you be willing to pay for Charlton?

Fifteen thousand pounds, said Bill Shankly.

The directors of Leeds United Association Football Club shook their heads. And their chairman said, Charlton will cost you twenty thousand, Shankly. Twenty thousand pounds. And not a penny less.

How about eighteen thousand pounds, said Bill Shankly.

Twenty thousand pounds, Shankly.

Fine, said Bill Shankly. Twenty thousand pounds it is then. But I'll need to make a telephone call.

The directors of Leeds United Association Football Club smiled. And their chairman said, Then make your call, Shankly.

After his early dinner, in the early evening. Tom Williams picked up the telephone in his hallway. And Tom Williams said, Yes?

Mr Williams? This is Bill Shankly.

Tom Williams said, Good evening, Mr Shankly. What can I –

I'm at Elland Road. At Leeds. And I have fantastic news. Unbelievable news! Leeds United will sell Jack Charlton to us. They will sell him. It's unbelievable. It's fantastic news!

Tom Williams said, I'm very glad to hear that, Mr Shankly. And so how much are they asking for Charlton?

Twenty thousand pounds. Just twenty thousand pounds, sir.

Tom Williams sighed. And Tom Williams said, But we sanctioned eighteen thousand pounds, Mr Shankly.

I know that. I know that, sir. But for two thousand pounds more, just two thousand pounds more, they will sell him. And then Jack Charlton will be a Liverpool player.

Tom Williams sighed again. And Tom Williams said, Mr Shankly, as you know, I have spoken with the other directors and I am afraid we can go no higher than eighteen thousand pounds. That is our final offer. Eighteen thousand pounds.

But I know they will not sell him for eighteen thousand pounds,

Mr Williams. They are asking for twenty thousand pounds. Just another two thousand, Mr Williams . . .

Tom Williams said, But our offer is eighteen thousand pounds.

Mr Williams, I have watched Jack Charlton since he was in his teens. I have watched him many times. He plays with authority. He plays with courage. He will be the very backbone of Liverpool Football Club. The very backbone, Mr Williams. And all they want is another two grand. Another two grand and he'll be ours. Ours . . .

Tom Williams said, I am sorry, Mr Shankly. It's eighteen thousand pounds. That is our final offer. Goodbye, Mr Shankly.

After their brandies, with their cigars. The directors of Leeds United Association Football Club were sitting in the dining room at Elland Road. The directors of Leeds United Association Football Club heard the knock upon the door. Not so fast and not so heavy.

The chairman of Leeds United said, Come!

Bill Shankly opened the door. Bill Shankly stepped into the dining room. Bill Shankly looked around the table. From director to director. And Bill Shankly waited.

The chairman of Leeds United said, Well then, Shankly? What do you have to say for yourself?

Our offer is eighteen thousand pounds, said Bill Shankly.

Close the door on your way out, Shankly.

. . .

On Saturday 30 January, 1960, Manchester United came to Anfield, Liverpool. That afternoon, fifty-six thousand, seven hundred and thirty-six folk came, too. In the rain and in the wind. Fifty-six thousand, seven hundred and thirty-six folk to watch Liverpool Football Club play Manchester United in the Fourth Round of the FA Cup. At home, at Anfield. In the dressing room, the home dressing room. The players of Liverpool Football Club looked up from the benches. The players of Liverpool Football Club looked at Bill Shankly. Bill Shankly in his best coat, Bill Shankly in his best hat. Bill Shankly looked around the dressing room. From player to player. From Slater to Molyneux, Molyneux to Moran, Moran to Wheeler, Wheeler to White, White to Leishman, Leishman to Melia, Melia to Hunt, Hunt to Hickson, Hickson to Harrower and Harrower to A'Court. Bill Shankly rubbed his hands together. And Bill Shankly smiled –

What a day this is, boys. What a great day! The crowd that are here, the people that are here. There must be sixty thousand. Sixty bloody thousand. And the team that is here, the manager who is here. Just across that corridor, in that dressing room. I mean, I know Matt well. Very well. He was a player I admired and he is a manager I admire. A man I admire. The things Matt has done at United. The teams he has built, the club he has built. The way United play, the way United work. It is an inspiration, boys. An inspiration to us all. I mean, I don't need to tell any of you what he has been through, what that team have been through. I mean, I'll never forget that day. I was in my office at Leeds Road when the telephone rang with the news. The news from Munich. And I drove straight back home. I put on the television and I waited for news. I waited and I prayed. But then I heard Harold Hardman, the chairman of Manchester United. I heard him say that Matt had died. That Matt was dead. And I could not believe it, boys. I refused to believe it. And I don't mind telling you, I got down on my knees and I prayed. I prayed like I had never prayed for anything before. And my prayers were answered. Thank God. Matt survived. But Tommy Curry was one of the dead. One of those twenty-three dead. And I knew Tommy well, from my time at Carlisle. And Tommy was dead. And eight of those players. Men we knew. Men who died. But Matt survived. Against all the odds. He refused to give in, he refused to surrender. And he went back to work, he went back to United. He began again. He built them back up again. He resurrected them. And here they are. A new team, a new United. And so Matt is an inspiration to me, boys. An inspiration. And so let his team be an inspiration to you, boys. An inspiration. But don't you forget to beat them, boys. And if you cannot beat them, then make sure you learn from them. And you enjoy every bloody minute of the lesson . . .

In the thirteenth minute, Charlton scored. In the thirty-sixth minute, Wheeler equalised. In the forty-fourth minute, Charlton scored again. In the sixty-ninth minute, Bradley scored. And Liverpool Football Club lost three–one to Manchester United in the Fourth Round of the FA Cup. At home, at Anfield –

After the match, after the final whistle. In the rain and in the wind. Matt Busby walked down the touchline. The Anfield touchline. Matt Busby smiled at Bill Shankly. Matt Busby put a hand on Bill

Shankly's shoulder. Matt Busby shook Bill Shankly's hand. And Matt Busby said, You showed plenty of fight today, Bill. And plenty of spirit, too. So you'll be all right, Bill. You'll be all right.


## 4. AFTER THE SEASON, BEFORE THE SEASON

In the empty, semi-detached house on Bellefield Avenue, West Derby, Liverpool. Bill and Ness went through the rooms. Bill and Ness went up the stairs. Bill and Ness went into one of the bedrooms. Bill and Ness stood in the window. Through the glass, through the trees. Bill and Ness could see men kicking footballs on a pitch.

What team is that, asked Ness.

Bill said, Everton.

Is that where Everton train then, asked Ness.

Bill nodded. And Bill said, Yes. That's Bellefield, love.

That's handy then, said Ness. You'll be able to keep your eye on them then, love, won't you?

Bill smiled. And Bill said, Aye, I will. I certainly will, love.

So you like this house then, asked Ness.

Bill said, If you do.

I do, love.

. . .

In the office, at the desk. Bill opened up the newspaper. Again. Bill looked down at the final League table for the 1959–60 season. Aston Villa were Second Division Champions with fifty-nine points. Cardiff City were runners-up with fifty-eight points. Cardiff City had been promoted to the First Division with Aston Villa. Liverpool Football Club were third with fifty points. Liverpool Football Club had not been promoted. Huddersfield Town had not been promoted either. Huddersfield Town had finished sixth with forty-seven points. Since Bill had left Leeds Road, since Bill had come to Anfield, Liverpool Football Club had won eleven games, drawn five and lost five. In the office, at the desk. Bill opened a drawer. Bill took out a pair of scissors and a pot of glue. Bill cut out the final League table for the 1959–60 season from the newspaper. Bill opened his book. His book of names, his book of notes. Bill stuck the final League table in his book. His book of names, his book of notes. In the office, at the desk. Bill turned the pages of his book. The pages of names, the pages of notes. The names of players, the notes on players. Bill had moved on Doug Rudham, Fred Morris, Reg Blore and Barry Wilkinson. Bill had brought in Kevin Lewis from Sheffield United. Bill had brought in Alf Arrowsmith from Ashton United. Alf Arrowsmith was seventeen years old. Bill had wanted to bring in more players. More experienced players. Better players. Bill still wanted to bring in more players. In the office, at the desk. Bill closed his book. His book of names, his book of notes. Again.

. . .

In the car park at Anfield. In his tracksuit bottoms, in his sweater, Bill was standing in the car park at Anfield. Bill was looking for the bus to Melwood. The bus was not here. The players of Liverpool Football Club came out of the stadium. In their tracksuits, in their sweaters. Bill greeted every one of the players of Liverpool Football Club. Bill shook their hands, Bill patted their backs. Bill asked after their families, Bill asked after their holidays. Bob, Joe, Reuben, Arthur and Albert came out of the stadium. And Bill looked at his watch. Bill looked at Bob, Joe, Reuben, Arthur and Albert. And Bill said, Where's the bloody bus? It's the first day of pre-season training. And the bus is not here, the bus is late. What's going on?

We don't use the bus in the summer, said Albert. We never have, Boss. Not in the first week. The first week we always run out to Melwood, Boss. And then we run back here . . .

Bill said, You run to Melwood?

Yes, said Albert. We run to Melwood. It's road-work. To build up their fitness, their strength . . .

Bill shook his head. Bill took Bob, Joe, Reuben, Arthur and Albert to one side. And Bill said, I don't believe in road-work. I never have. The players do their playing on grass. So they should do their running on grass. Not on roads. Not on concrete. There's no surer way for a player to pull a muscle or to injure himself than on a road. On the grass. That's the way to build up their fitness, to build up their strength. That's my way. On the grass. And with a ball. A bloody football!

Bob, Joe, Reuben, Arthur and Albert looked at each other. Bob, Joe, Reuben, Arthur and Albert nodded. And then Bob said, I'll go and ring the driver then, Boss. I'll go and give him a call . . .

Bill looked at his watch again. And Bill said, Thank you, Bob. But we're wasting time. There's no bloody time. So we'll walk out to Melwood today. Slowly. But then we'll get the bus tomorrow.

. . .

In their new house in Liverpool, in their new bedroom in the old bed. Bill waited for the dawn, Bill waited for the light. The new dawn and the new light. And then Bill jumped out of bed. Bill shaved and Bill washed. Quickly. Bill put on his suit and Bill put on his tie. Quickly. Bill went down the stairs and Bill ate breakfast with Ness and their daughters. Quickly. Bill kissed them goodbye and Bill went out of the house. Quickly. Bill got into his car and Bill drove to Anfield.

In the ground, in the office. Bill looked at his watch. And Bill paced and Bill paced. And Bill heard the people coming, coming to Anfield. Through the turnstiles, into the stands. And then Bill stopped pacing. Bill looked at his watch again. And now Bill smiled.

In the dressing room, the home dressing room. Bill looked from player to player. From Slater to Byrne. From Byrne to Moran. From Moran to Wheeler. From Wheeler to White. From White to Leishman. From Leishman to Lewis. From Lewis to Hunt. From Hunt to Hickson. From Hickson to Melia. From Melia to A'Court. And Bill clapped his hands. Bill smiled. And Bill said, This is it, boys. The start. The real start, lads. The start of it all. The first game of the new season, boys. At home to Leeds United. A great chance to lay down our marker, lads. A great opportunity to show the world what we are about.

And there will be over forty thousand people here to see us, boys. To see what we are about. And so this is our chance, lads. Our chance to show the people that we mean business. The business of promotion. Because that is the only business that matters, boys. The only thing that matters. And so you go out there today, lads. And you show these people who have come here today, who have paid their money today. You show these people that they were right to come, right to pay to see us play today, boys. Because this season we mean business. This season we will win the League, lads. And we'll get promoted.

In the dug-out, on the bench. The Anfield bench. Bill stared out at the players of Liverpool Football Club on the pitch. The Anfield pitch. In the sun, the players of Liverpool Football Club shining. In the sun, in their kits. Their red shirts, their white shorts. And their white socks. And in the dug-out, on the bench. The Anfield bench. Bill heard the whistle blow, Bill heard the crowd roar. The Anfield crowd. And in the dug-out, on the bench. Bill sat forward on the edge of his seat. On the very edge of his seat. His eyes darting, his hands moving. And his legs twitching. With every ball, with every kick. And with every pass. With every tackle and with every shot. His eyes darting, his hands moving. His legs twitching. With every ball. Every kick and every pass, every tackle and every shot. And in the twenty-eighth minute, Kevin Lewis scored his first goal for Liverpool Football Club. Seven minutes later, Dave Hickson scored a second. And in the dug-out, on the bench. Bill heard the final whistle blow. And Bill heard the crowd cheer. The Anfield crowd. And in the dug-out, on the bench. The Anfield bench. Bill smiled. Bill got to his feet. And Bill walked down the touchline. The Anfield touchline.

In the dressing room, the home dressing room. Bill danced from player to player. From Bert to Gerry. From Gerry to Ronnie. From Ronnie to Johnny. From Johnny to Dick. From Dick to Tommy. From Tommy to Kevin. From Kevin to Roger. From Roger to Dave. From Dave to Jimmy. And from Jimmy to Alan. Bill danced and Bill sang. Bill sang the praises of every player, of every man. Patting their backs and shaking their hands. Patting Bob and Reuben on their backs, shaking Bob and Reuben by their hands. And Bill said, Well done, boys. Well done. You were magnificent, lads. Magnificent. Each and every one of you, boys. I could not have asked for more. But this is only the start, lads. Only the start. You know that, boys. We all know that. But if you play like that, lads. If you play like that every game. Every match, boys. Then this will be our season. Our season, lads.

. . .

In the dressing room, the home dressing room. On the bench, in the silence. Bill shook his head and Bill sighed. Bill shook his head again and Bill closed his eyes. Four days after Liverpool Football Club had beaten Leeds United, Liverpool Football Club had lost four–one at Southampton. Three days after that, Liverpool Football Club had drawn one-all at Middlesbrough. And then today, Liverpool Football Club had lost one–nil to Southampton. At home, at Anfield. Today, Liverpool Football Club had just three points from their first four games. And in the dressing room, the home dressing room. On the bench, in the silence. Bill opened his eyes again, Bill shook his head again. Bill cursed. And Bill said, It's not good enough. Not good enough for me and not good enough for Liverpool Football Club. For the supporters of Liverpool Football Club. Not bloody good enough!

. . .

In the boardroom, the Anfield boardroom. In the chair at the end of the long table. Bill said, Well, what?

Well, what do you have to say about the start we have made to the new season, asked the directors of Liverpool Football Club.

It's not good enough, I know that.

And so what are you planning to do about it, Mr Shankly?

Bill smiled. And Bill said, I was going to ask you the same question. The very same question.

What do you mean by that, Mr Shankly? You are the manager. We are asking *you* what *you* are going to do about the results. We are asking *you*, Mr Shankly.

Bill smiled again. And Bill said, But I asked you for Brian Clough. And you would not give me Brian Clough. I asked you for Dave Mackay. But you would not give me Dave Mackay. I asked you for Jack Charlton but you would not give me Jack Charlton.

But you also asked us for Kevin Lewis, said the directors of Liverpool Football Club. And we gave you the money for Kevin Lewis. We gave you thirteen thousand pounds for Kevin Lewis. A club record. And just last week, you asked us for Gordon Milne. And we gave you the money for Gordon Milne. We gave you sixteen thousand pounds for Gordon Milne. Again, a club record. And you asked us for this lad Arrowsmith. And we gave you the money. And let's not forget we also gave you the money for Sammy Reid. Eight thousand pounds for a man who never played for the first team. Eight thousand pounds for a man we have now sold to Falkirk. So we have given you the money, Mr Shankly. We have given you the best part of forty thousand pounds. So we have given you the money, Mr Shankly.

Bill shook his head. And Bill said, But I was promised sixty thousand pounds. When I accepted the position as manager of Liverpool Football Club, I was promised sixty thousand pounds to spend on new players. Sixty thousand pounds to rebuild the team.

That is not quite true, said Tom Williams. We told you money was available if the right players became available. And we have given you that money. We have given you forty thousand pounds, Mr Shankly. But it is not a bottomless pit. We do have our limits.

Bill looked up the long table at the chairman of Liverpool Football Club. And Bill said, So you are saying there is no more money? Is that what you are saying, Mr Williams?

No, said Tom Williams. That is not what we are saying. What we are saying is you have had money. But there are limits to that money, Mr Shankly. There have to be limits.

Bill shook his head again. And Bill said, So what would you have me do? You'd have me make do, would you? Make do with the players we have? When I have already told you some of these players are not good enough. Not good enough to win us promotion.

But can you be so sure of that, Mr Shankly, asked one of the directors of Liverpool Football Club. What makes you so certain? Players don't become bad players overnight.

Bill laughed. And Bill said, Who exactly are you talking about? Which players would these be?

Liddell.

Bill laughed again. And Bill said, Billy Liddell is thirty-eight years old. Thirty-eight years old!

But he has been a fantastic servant to this club, said another of the directors of Liverpool Football Club. A great player.

Bill said, I know Billy Liddell *was* a great player. He had a powerful shot with either foot. He could head the ball like the blast from a gun. He was as hard as granite. And he was fast. But not any more. Not now. Not these days. Not today!

Maybe he just needs more games, said another director.

Bill shook his head. And Bill said, More games? Billy Liddell has played over five hundred games for Liverpool Football Club. The man needs a testimonial. Not more bloody League games.

Mr Shankly, said Tom Williams. Mr Shankly, please. All we are saying is perhaps we already have the players we need. Perhaps you should look again at the players we have.

At Billy Liddell? Thirty-eight-year-old bloody Billy Liddell?

Perhaps not Billy Liddell, said Tom Williams. But what about

Harrower or Morrissey? They have not played this season . . .

Bill looked up the long table at the chairman and the directors of Liverpool Football Club. And Bill said, So now you're telling me who to select? Who to pick? Is that it?

No, said Tom Williams. We are not telling you who to pick, who to select. We are simply asking you to look again at the players we have, to think again . . .

Bill got up from the chair at the end of the long table. Bill looked from director to director. And Bill said, Fine then. I'll think again, I will think again. I promise you that, gentlemen.

. . .

In his car. Bill cursed. It had been the same at Carlisle. On the road to Manchester. Bill cursed again. The same at Grimsby, the same at Workington. In the car park at Old Trafford. Bill cursed again. The same at Huddersfield. And in the office at Old Trafford. Bill cursed and Bill said, It's always the same. Fight and argue. That is all I ever do. It's always the same. And I've had enough, Matt. I'm going to quit, I'm going to resign. I swear to you, Matt.

Matt Busby stopped stirring his tea. He put the teaspoon down in the saucer. He looked up from his cup. And Matt Busby smiled –

You're not a quitter, Bill. You're not going to resign . . .

I am, Matt. I am. I've had enough, Matt. Enough.

Matt Busby picked up his cup. He took a sip of tea. He put the cup back down in the saucer. And Matt Busby looked at Bill –

So you've another job to go to then, Bill? Something else lined up, have you? Lined up just waiting for you, Bill?

No, Matt. No. But I don't care, Matt. I don't care any more.

Matt Busby took another sip of tea. He put the cup down again. He looked at Bill again. And Matt Busby sighed –

But then what about Nessie and the girls, Bill? You can't just quit, you can't just walk away. Think of your family, Bill . . .

But I don't care, Matt. I really don't care.

Matt Busby shook his head –

If you had another job to go to, if you had a better opportunity, then that would be one thing, and then things would be different. But you haven't, Bill. You haven't. You've nothing, Bill. Nothing. And I honestly don't think you'll find anything better than this, a better opportunity than this one you have now, Bill. I really don't think so. I really don't, Bill. And I also don't think you want to be sat at home all day now, do you? Under Nessie's feet all day, Bill. Now that wouldn't be for you, would it? That wouldn't be for you at all, Bill.

I don't care, Matt. I really don't care.

But you do care, Bill. I know you care. I know you do, Bill.

Bill shook his head. And Bill said, But you don't know what it's like, Matt. You don't know what it's like. It's hard enough trying to win the battles on the pitch, Matt. You know that. But then I've got all these constant bloody battles off the pitch, Matt. Just trying to make them realise what it is we're working for . . .

But I do know, Bill. I do know. And you know I know. And you also know it's always hard work. You knew that when you took the job, Bill. That it would be a hard job. That it's always a hard job. Always. It was the same for me. And it's *still* the same for me. It's still hard work, Bill. Always hard work.

I know that, Matt. I do know that. But at Grimsby, at Huddersfield, I knew the limitations. And so I knew I had taken them as far as I could. I knew I'd reached the limits of their ambitions. And so I knew that it was pointless to stay on. But I thought it would be different at Liverpool. I thought there would be more ambition. More ambition and more potential. Ambition and potential to succeed.

And there is, Bill. There is. You were right.

Bill shook his head again. And Bill said, But I tell them we need a goalkeeper. And they say the one we have got is good enough. But what they really mean is, he's good enough to keep them in the top half of the Second Division. In the top half of the Second Division, with gates of just over twenty thousand. That's all they want. Top half of the Second Division. With gates over twenty thousand. That's good enough for them, Matt. That's all they want.

But it's not good enough for you, said Matt Busby. It's not what you want, Bill. I know that, I know that. And that's also why I know you should not quit, Bill. Why I know you should not walk away now. Because Liverpool do have the potential. And no other club has that same potential. But only you have the ambition. No other manager has that same ambition. And so if you stick with it, things are bound to break for you, Bill. They are bound to break. I promise you, Bill. But not if you quit. Not if you walk away now, Bill. Before you have hardly begun, before you have hardly started.

## 5. THE HAMMER AND THE NAILS

On Saturday 3 September, 1960, Liverpool Football Club beat Brighton and Hove Albion with two goals from Jimmy Harrower. Four days later, Liverpool Football Club drew two-all with Luton Town. Then Liverpool Football Club lost one–nil at Ipswich Town and two–one at Luton Town. Liverpool Football Club had played eight games this season. But Liverpool Football Club had won just twice this season. Liverpool Football Club had only six points from a possible sixteen. Liverpool Football Club were seventeenth in the Second Division. Liverpool Football Club were going backwards, Liverpool Football Club were falling. And their gates were falling, too. Forty-three thousand and forty-one folk had come to Anfield for the first game of the season. Thirty-seven thousand, six hundred and four folk for the next home match. The match Liverpool Football Club had lost one–nil to Southampton Football Club. Only twenty-seven thousand, three hundred and thirty-nine folk had come to Anfield for the game against Luton Town. In the pubs and in the clubs of Liverpool, folk began to question Bill Shankly. Folk began to ask if Bill Shankly was the right man to manage Liverpool Football Club. Folk began to ask what exactly were Bill Shankly's qualifications for the job. What had Bill Shankly ever done? What had Bill Shankly ever won?

. . .

After the game at Kenilworth Road, the defeat to Luton Town. After Liverpool Football Club had come back home, home to Anfield. Bob Paisley had gone into the ground, Bob Paisley had gone under the stands. Among the piles of dirty boots, on an upturned beer crate. Bob Paisley took out his copy of the *Sporting Life*, Bob Paisley looked down at his copy of the *Sporting Life*. And then Bob Paisley heard footsteps in the corridor. Fast steps, heavy steps. Bob Paisley looked up from his copy of the *Sporting Life*. Bob Paisley saw Bill Shankly. In the doorway to the boot room. And Bob Paisley said, Hello, Boss.

Hello, Bob. Hello, said Bill Shankly. Are you busy, Bob? Or

42

do you have the time? The time for a chat, Bob?

Bob Paisley smiled. And Bob Paisley said, I've always the time, Boss. Come in. Have a seat, Boss.

Thank you, Bob, said Bill Shankly. And Bill Shankly walked into the boot room. Bill Shankly sat down on an upturned beer crate.

Bob Paisley smiled again. And Bob Paisley said, Now what's on your mind, Boss? What's on your mind?

No doubt the same as what's on yours, said Bill Shankly.

Bob Paisley nodded. And Bob Paisley said, Aye, Boss. Aye. It's been a bad start, Boss. A very bad start.

I keep going over things in my mind, said Bill Shankly. Over the things I've done, Bob. All the things I've done. Over and over, round and round, Bob. In my mind. Over and over, round and round, Bob. Wondering where I've gone wrong. Where I'm going wrong, Bob. And how to put it right. How to bloody fix it, Bob.

Bob Paisley nodded again. And Bob Paisley said, Aye, Boss. I'm the same. It's the same with me, Boss.

But I know it's me, Bob. It must be me. It's my fault, Bob.

Bob Paisley shook his head. And Bob Paisley said, No, Boss. No. It's not you, Boss. It's not you. It's never one man, Boss. It's all of us. It's every one of us, Boss.

Thank you, said Bill Shankly. Thank you, Bob. But Albert was right. You were all right, Bob. The players were not fit enough. The players *are* not fit enough. They were used to the road-work. They were used to the running. I should have listened to you, listened to you all.

Bob Paisley shook his head again. And Bob Paisley said, No, Boss. No. You were right, Boss. You were right. The players do their playing on the grass. So they should do their running on the grass. You were right, Boss. And you are still right. Still right, Boss.

But the players are just not fit enough, said Bill Shankly. I know that and you know that, Bob. We can see that.

Bob Paisley nodded. And Bob Paisley said, You remember you told us how you used to spend your summers? When you were a player yourself, Boss? How you used to go back to Glenbuck. Every summer. How you used to spend your days running across the fields and up the hills. Every day. Then how you spent your nights playing football with the men from the village. Every night.

Aye, said Bill Shankly. It was no holiday. No summer holiday. But my mother never believed in holidays. She used to say, Every day you wake up and you can get up and you can do your work, then that is a holiday. That is what she believed. That is how she raised us.

Bob Paisley smiled. And Bob Paisley said, Not many that believe that now, Boss. Not many that were raised that way. Not these days, Boss. Not in our team. Not this lot, Boss. They'll have been sat in their deckchairs. On the front. Or sat on their sofas. In front of their televisions. Eating chips, drinking beer. Getting fat, getting lazy. That's how this lot'll have spent their sodding summers.

Aye, said Bill Shankly again. Aye. You're right there, Bob.

Bob Paisley nodded. And Bob Paisley said, But you were right, too, Boss. Right to ease them back in. No good giving them bloody heart attacks on their first day back. No good at all.

Aye, said Bill Shankly. But we need to pick up the pace now.

Bob Paisley nodded again. And Bob Paisley said, Yes, Boss. We need to pick up the pace. We need to make them sweat.

Bill Shankly sprang forward on the upturned beer crate. Bill Shankly took out a book from his jacket pocket. A notebook. Bill Shankly flicked through the pages. The pages of notes. And then Bill Shankly stopped. Bill Shankly thrust the open book at Bob Paisley –

Look at that, said Bill Shankly. Look at that, Bob! It might just be the answer. It might just be what we need, Bob.

Bob Paisley took the book from Bill Shankly. Bob Paisley stared down at the lines on the page. The lines of a sketch, the lines of a diagram. And Bob Paisley said, What is it, Boss? What is it?

It's a box, said Bill Shankly. It's a box, Bob!

What kind of box, Boss?

A box to make them sweat, Bob. A box to make them sweat.

Bob Paisley looked back down at the lines on the page. The lines of a sketch, the lines of a diagram. The lines of a box. Bob Paisley nodded. And Bob Paisley said, Then what are we waiting for?

We'll need some wood, said Bill Shankly. Plenty of wood, Bob.

Bob Paisley said, I can get us the wood, Boss. Plenty of wood.

And we'll need some hammers, Bob. And some nails.

I've got the hammers, Boss. And I've got the nails.

And in the night, back out at Melwood. Bill Shankly and Bob

Paisley built the box. Out of wood, with hammers. And with nails. Four large boards, eight feet high. Ten yards apart. That was the box, the box for the players. The box to make the players sweat, the box to make the players work. Two players in the box. And a ball over the top into the box. The first player shoots against one board. First time. The other player hits the same ball on the rebound. First time. Ball after ball. Every second, another ball. Into the box. Every second for one minute. Ball after ball. Into the box. Then for two minutes. Ball after ball. Into the box. Then for three minutes. Ball after ball. Into the box. Again and again. Ball after ball. Into the box. Every second. Shot after shot. Every second. Inside the box. Every player. Player after player. Into the box, inside the box. The players working in the box, the box working on the players. Because the box worked –

The box bloody worked.

. . .

In September, 1960, Liverpool Football Club beat Scunthorpe United and they beat Leyton Orient. In October, 1960, Liverpool Football Club beat Derby County and they beat Lincoln City. And they drew with Portsmouth Football Club. They beat Huddersfield Town and they drew with Sunderland Football Club. But in November, 1960, Liverpool Football Club beat Plymouth Argyle. They beat Norwich City and they beat Charlton Athletic.

On Saturday 26 November, 1960, Sheffield United came to Anfield, Liverpool. That afternoon, thirty-nine thousand, nine hundred and ninety-nine folk came, too. Sheffield United were top of the Second Division. In the thirtieth minute, Jimmy Harrower scored. In the fifty-fifth minute, Dave Hickson scored. In the sixty-third minute, Harrower scored again. And in the seventy-seventh minute, Harrower scored his third. And Liverpool Football Club beat Sheffield United four–two. That evening, Liverpool Football Club had twenty-six points. And Liverpool Football Club were second in the Second Division.

In December, 1960, Liverpool Football Club beat Swansea Town and they drew at Leeds United. On Boxing Day, 1960, Liverpool Football Club beat Rotherham United. That evening, Liverpool Football Club were unbeaten in fourteen games. And Liverpool Football Club were still second in the Second Division.

On Tuesday 27 December, 1960, the day after Boxing Day,

Liverpool Football Club travelled to Millmoor to play Rotherham United again. And Liverpool Football Club lost one–nil. Four days later, on New Year's Eve 1960, Middlesbrough Football Club came to Anfield, Liverpool. That New Year's Eve, thirty-four thousand, six hundred and fifty-four folk came, too. In the twenty-first minute, Alan A'Court scored. In the thirty-fifth minute, Kevin Lewis scored. In the fifty-sixth minute, Lewis scored again. But Liverpool Football Club lost four–three to Middlesbrough Football Club. At home, at Anfield –

After the whistle, the final whistle. In the dressing room, the home dressing room. The players of Liverpool Football Club looked at Bill Shankly. Bill Shankly standing in the dressing room, Bill Shankly staring at the players. From player to player. From Slater to Molyneux. From Molyneux to Byrne. From Byrne to Campbell. From Campbell to White. From White to Leishman. From Leishman to Lewis. From Lewis to Hunt. From Hunt to Hickson. From Hickson to Harrower. From Harrower to A'Court. And Bill Shankly said, You tried your best, boys. You tried your very best. Each and every one of you, lads. Every single one of you. And so I could not have asked for more, boys. Nothing more. But I know we have lost twice in a row now, lads. And no one likes it. None of us, boys. Not one single one of us. But we went fourteen games without losing, lads. And so I know we can go another fourteen games without losing. Another forty, boys! I know we can, I know we can. So this is not the end, lads. Not the end. This can still be our season, boys. I know it can be. Our season for promotion, lads!

. . .

On Saturday 7 January, 1961, Coventry City came to Anfield, Liverpool. That afternoon, fifty thousand, nine hundred and nine folk came, too. Fifty thousand, nine hundred and nine folk to watch Liverpool Football Club play Coventry City in the Third Round of the FA Cup. In the thirty-seventh minute, Roger Hunt scored. In the fortieth minute, Kevin Lewis scored. In the sixty-first minute, Jimmy Harrower scored. And Liverpool Football Club beat Coventry City three–two in the Third Round of the FA Cup. At home, at Anfield. One week later, Liverpool Football Club lost to Brighton and Hove Albion in the League. One week after that, Sunderland Football Club came to Anfield, Liverpool. That afternoon, forty-six thousand, one hundred and eighty-five folk came, too. Forty-six thousand, one hundred and eighty-five folk to watch Liverpool Football Club play Sunderland Football Club in the Fourth Round of the FA Cup. In the third minute, Hooper scored. In the fourteenth minute, Lawther scored. And Liverpool Football Club lost two–nil to Sunderland Football Club in the Fourth Round of the FA Cup. At home, at Anfield. Liverpool Football Club were out of the FA Cup. Again.

. . .

In February, 1961, Liverpool Football Club beat Scunthorpe United. They beat Leyton Orient. They beat Derby County. And they beat Lincoln City. In March, 1961, Liverpool Football Club drew with Portsmouth Football Club. They beat Huddersfield Town. They lost to Swansea Town and they drew with Plymouth Argyle. On the last day of March, 1961, Liverpool Football Club beat Bristol Rovers three–nil. At home, at Anfield. That evening, Liverpool Football Club were third in the Second Division. Sheffield United were second and Ipswich Town were first. But just one point separated Liverpool Football Club and Sheffield United. Just one point, one single point –

On Tuesday 4 April, 1961, Liverpool Football Club travelled to Bramall Lane, Sheffield. In the seventy-second minute, Johnny Morrissey scored for Liverpool Football Club. But Liverpool Football Club could only draw one-all with Sheffield United. That night, Liverpool Football Club had forty-seven points. Sheffield United had forty-eight points and Ipswich Town had fifty-two points. Three days later, Liverpool Football Club travelled to the Eastville Stadium, Bristol. Bristol Rovers were fighting for their lives, Liverpool Football Club were fighting for promotion. And Bristol Rovers beat Liverpool Football Club four–three. That day, Sheffield United won. Four days after that, Liverpool Football Club beat Charlton Athletic two–one. That same day, Sheffield United won again. On Saturday 15 April, 1961, Liverpool Football Club travelled to Carrow Road, Norwich. And Norwich City beat Liverpool Football Club two–one. That day, Sheffield United won again. That night, Liverpool Football Club had forty-nine points. Sheffield United had fifty-four points and Ipswich Town had fifty-five points. Four days later, Sheffield United beat Derby County. Sheffield United now had fifty-six points. That night, Sheffield United were promoted in second place and Ipswich Town were promoted as Champions. Liverpool Football Club were not promoted. Liverpool Football Club finished third in the Second Division. Third again.


## 6. P.S. FIND PEOPLE WHO ARE TOUGHER

In the boardroom, in the chair at the end of the long table. Bill looked at the directors of Liverpool Football Club. And Bill waited.

It's been a good season, said Tom Williams. Quite a good season, Mr Shankly. Yes, we have finished third again. Yes, we have missed out on promotion again. But we have two more points than we did at the end of last season. And so that is an improvement, Mr Shankly. A visible improvement. Unfortunately, our home gates are a little down on last season. But not by much, not so very much. And we all know Rome was not built in a day, we all know that. So keep up the good work, Mr Shankly. And better luck next season.

. . .

In the office, at the desk. Bill opened up the newspaper. Again. Bill looked down at the final League table for the 1960–61 season. Liverpool Football Club had played forty-two games in the Second Division in the 1960–61 season. They had won fourteen games at home, at Anfield. Lost five and drawn two. They had won seven games away, away from Anfield. Drawn five and lost nine. Liverpool Football Club had scored forty-nine goals at home and thirty-eight goals away. They had conceded twenty-one goals at home and thirty-seven away. In the office, at the desk. Bill opened a drawer. Bill took out a pair of scissors and a pot of glue. And Bill began to cut out the final League table for the 1960–61 season from the newspaper. Bill did not believe in luck. Bad luck or good. Bill knew it was never a matter of luck, never a question of luck. Bill knew luck was just another excuse for failure. Bill knew luck was what men like the directors of Liverpool Football Club told men like him when things did not work out, when things did not go the way men like him wanted them to go. Bill thought the word luck should be cut out of the dictionary, struck from the English language. Banished and forgotten. In the office, at the desk. Bill heard footsteps in the corridor. Slow and careful steps. And a knock upon the door. A slow and careful knock. Bill put down the scissors. Bill looked up from the desk. And Bill said, Yes?

The door opened. Slowly and carefully. A round-faced man in an ill-fitting suit stood in the doorway.

Bill said, Can I help you?

Mr Shankly, said the man. I don't think we've been properly introduced, but my name is Eric Sawyer. I've just been appointed to the board of directors. I wondered if you had a moment?

In the office, behind the desk. Bill smiled. Bill stood up. And Bill said, I've always a moment. Please come in, please have a seat. And would you like a cup of tea, Mr Sawyer?

That would be very nice, Mr Shankly, said Eric Sawyer. If you have the time. Thank you very much, Mr Shankly.

Bill went out of the office. Bill went down the corridor. And Bill asked one of the secretaries to bring in a pot of tea. Then Bill came back up the corridor. Bill came back into the office. Bill sat back down behind the desk. Bill smiled at Eric Sawyer. And Bill said, The tea will be just a minute. Now what can I do for you, Mr Sawyer?

Well, said Eric Sawyer. Like most directors, I'm afraid I don't know very much about football, Mr Shankly. Not very much at all.

Bill laughed. And Bill said, That's a very honest thing for you to say, Mr Sawyer. In fact, that's the most honest thing I've ever heard a director say in my life. Maybe the only honest thing!

But I know you know about football, said Eric Sawyer. I know you know a lot, Mr Shankly. Perhaps all there is to know about football. And so I also know you must be bitterly disappointed that we have not been promoted this season.

I am, Mr Sawyer. I am.

Well, I want you to know, Mr Shankly, that I am here to help you. I am here to help you gain promotion. To help you get Liverpool Football Club back into the First Division. That is why I have been appointed to the board of Liverpool Football Club.

There were footsteps in the corridor again, a tap upon the door now. And one of the secretaries brought in a pot of tea. Two cups and two saucers. The secretary put down the tray on the desk.

Bill said, Thank you. Thank you very much.

As you know, said Eric Sawyer, Mr Moores is the chairman of Everton Football Club. But he also has a lot of shares in this club. In

Liverpool Football Club. And so Mr Moores would like to see Liverpool Football Club succeed, too. Not just Everton, but Liverpool Football Club, too. Mr Moores believes this city deserves two successful football clubs. Not just one.

Bill poured the tea into the two cups. Bill handed one cup to Eric Sawyer. And Bill said, I am listening, Mr Sawyer. Please go on.

Eric Sawyer took the cup of tea from Bill. And Eric Sawyer said, Thank you, Mr Shankly. Now Mr Moores cannot sit on both boards of directors. Not as the chairman of Everton Football Club. So Mr Moores nominated me in his place. To sit on the board of Liverpool Football Club. I am an accountant by trade. And I have worked for Mr Moores for many years at Littlewoods. I am the executive in charge of finance at Littlewoods. That is my job.

Bill smiled. And Bill said, So you know about money then, Mr Sawyer? You are one of the money men then?

Yes, said Eric Sawyer. I am a money man, if you like. And so yes, I know about money. So I know the finances of Liverpool Football Club are a mess. I know they need sorting out. And fast.

Bill sighed. Bill put down his cup. And Bill said, So I suppose you are here to tell me there is no more money, Mr Sawyer? No more money for new players? Is that why you are here, sir?

Quite the opposite, Mr Shankly. Quite the reverse. As I told you, I do not know much about football. But I do know the players we have at Liverpool Football Club are not good enough to get us promoted to the First Division. So I know we need to buy new players. And that if we buy new players. The right players. Then Liverpool Football Club will be promoted to the First Division. And if Liverpool Football Club are promoted to the First Division, then the gates will increase. There will be no more average gates of twenty-odd thousand. Not if Liverpool Football Club are in the First Division. If Liverpool Football Club are in the First Division, then the potential is here for gates of fifty thousand or more. I know that and Mr Moores knows that. But first we have to get promoted. And to get promoted we will need to spend money on new players. So I am here to tell you that if you can find the players, the right players, then I will get you the money, Mr Shankly. I will get you the money.

. . .

50

In the house, in their kitchen. Bill and Ness cleared the table. Bill and Ness washed the Sunday pots. And then Ness made a cup of tea for her and Bill. Bill and Ness took their cups of tea into the other room. In the other room, in their chairs. Bill and Ness sat down with their cups of tea and the Sunday papers. Bill with the back pages and Ness with the crossword. Bill and Ness could hear the girls upstairs, listening to their records. Dancing and singing. And carrying on . . .

Bill jumped up from his chair. And Bill shouted, Jesus Christ!

Ness jumped, too. Ness looked up from her crossword. And Ness saw Bill. Bill dancing around the room, Bill waving the *Sunday Post* about, sheets of the newspaper falling onto the carpet, Bill clutching this one page and Bill saying, Where's the telephone, love? Where is it? Where's the phone, love?

The phone's in the hall, said Ness. Where it always is, love.

Bill nodded. Bill grabbed his address book from the arm of his chair. Bill dashed out of the room, Bill sprinted into the hall. Bill flicked through the pages of his address book. Bill picked up the telephone. Bill read the number in his address book again. Bill dialled the number. And Bill waited. And Bill waited. And then Bill said, Mr Sawyer? Mr Sawyer. It's Bill Shankly. You'll never believe what I've just read in the paper. In the *Sunday Post*. The boy wants to go, the boy wants to leave. There's not a moment to lose . . .

Back in the other room, back in her chair. Ness put down her crossword. Ness stood up. Ness came out into the hall. Ness opened the cupboard door. Ness took out Bill's coat, Ness took out Bill's hat. Ness opened the front door. And Bill said, Thank you, love. Thank you.

Outside their house on Bellefield Avenue, at their gate. Bill looked at his watch again, Bill looked up the street again. Bill looked at his watch again and Bill looked up the street again. Bill saw a Rolls-Royce turn into the street. And Bill ran halfway down the street to meet the Rolls, Bill waving his hat in his hand. The Rolls pulled up. Bill opened the door. And Bill said, Hello, Mr Williams. Hello, Mr Reakes. Now how fast will this thing go?

What time do we have to be there, asked Tom Williams.

Bill said, We're already late. We're already late.

Bill had already tried to sign Ian St John once before. At Huddersfield. Bill and Eddie Boot had driven all the way from

Huddersfield up to Falkirk. The Scotland national team were playing a Scottish Second Division select. Bill and Eddie Boot had come to watch a player called Ron Yeats. Ron Yeats played for Dundee United in the Scottish Second Division. Ron Yeats was worth the trip. Ron was a huge man, but Ron was a quick man. But that night, Bill and Eddie Boot also saw Ian St John play. Ian St John played for Motherwell in the Scottish First Division. That night, Ian St John was playing for the Scotland national team. He was punchy and he was strong. He was a box of tricks. And he gave Ron Yeats a game. What a battle they had, St John and Yeats. Bill had seen enough, Bill had seen plenty. Bill and Eddie Boot had driven back down to Huddersfield. And Bill had asked the directors of Huddersfield Town Association Football Club for the money to sign Ron Yeats and Ian St John. But the directors of Huddersfield Town Association Football Club had said, No. We cannot afford to buy Yeats and St John, Shankly . . .

And Bill had said, Christ! You can't afford *not* to buy them.

On the road to Scotland, in the Rolls-Royce. Again Bill said, We can't afford *not* to buy St John, Mr Williams. We can't afford not to. We didn't get Clough. Sunderland got Clough. We can't let that happen again, Mr Williams. We have to get St John. And we can. We can. I know we can. Because he wants to leave. He wants to go. And he wants to come to England. The boy wants to play his football in England. But Motherwell are no fools. They know what they have. They know what he's worth. So they'll have told other clubs. Other directors. And so they'll be in their cars. They'll be on their way. So we have to hurry. We have to be quick. Because we have to get Ian St John. We have to buy the boy. We cannot afford *not* to buy him!

Mr Williams nodded. And Mr Reakes stepped on it.

On the road back to England, in the Rolls-Royce. Bill sat between Ian St John and his wife. On the back seat. Bill was smiling and Bill was talking. Ten to the dozen. One hundred miles an hour. Bill said, Just think of all the goals you'll score, son. We'll be promoted in no time. In no time at all, son. With the goals you will score. We'll be Second Division Champions, son. First Division Champions. We'll win the FA Cup, son. We'll play in Europe. We'll win the European Cup, son. We will win the bloody lot. With the goals you will score, son. We will be the greatest team in England. The greatest team in Europe, son. With the goals you will score. I promise you we will, son. Because I know we bloody will!

. . .

In the house, in their front room. In the night and in the silence. In his chair. Bill closed his book. His book of names, his book of notes. And Bill closed his eyes. Liverpool Football Club had paid thirty-seven thousand, five hundred pounds for Ian St John. A club record. Plus one thousand pounds, in cash, under the table to Ian St John. A week later, Liverpool Football Club had gone to Goodison Park to play Everton Football Club in the Liverpool Senior Cup. Liverpool Football Club had lost four–three. But Ian St John had scored all three Liverpool goals. On his debut, a hat-trick. In the night and in the silence. In his chair. Bill opened his eyes again, Bill opened his book again. His book of names, his book of notes. Bill turned the pages. The pages of names, the pages of notes. Ticks and crosses. Bill had got Ian St John. And Bill had moved on Bobby Campbell, Alan Arnell and James Harrower. Then Bill had moved on Alan Banks, John Nicholson and Dave Hickson. And Billy Liddell had had his testimonial. In the night and in the silence. In his chair. Bill stared down at the pages. The pages of names, the pages of notes. All the ticks and all the crosses. But in the night and in the silence. In his chair. Bill was not satisfied. Too many crosses and not enough ticks. And no sense of satisfaction. There never was, never could be. Bill did not believe in satisfaction. That was another word Bill thought should be cut out of the dictionary. Satisfaction. Another word that should be struck from the English language. Banished and forgotten. In the night and in the silence. In his chair. Bill could not forget Yeats. Ron Yeats and Ian St John. Their names were forged together in Bill's mind. Forged together since that night Bill and Eddie Boot had watched the Scotland national team play that Scottish Second Division select. In the night and in the silence. In his chair. Bill might have got Ian St John. But still Bill wanted Ron Yeats. What a player he was. What a man he was. Six foot three. A giant. A colossus. Not a man you forgot. In the night and in the silence. In his chair. Bill closed his book. His book of names, his book of notes. Bill picked up his address book from the arm of the chair. And Bill got up from his chair. Bill went out into the hall. Bill picked up the telephone. Bill dialled a number. And Bill said, Hello,

Jerry? It's Bill Shankly. How are you, Jerry? How's Dundee United?

I'm fine, said Jerry Kerr. Well, I *was* fine. How are you, Bill?

Bill said, I'm fine, too, Jerry. Very fine. Thank you very much.

Good, said Jerry Kerr. That's fantastic news, that's great news. We're both fine. Thanks for calling, Bill. Goodnight now . . .

Bill laughed. And Bill said, Not so fast, Jerry. Not so fast.

But he's not for sale, Bill. Like I tell you every time. The man is not for sale. He helped us gain promotion. He's helped keep us in the First Division. And we couldn't have done it without him. We know that and he knows that. And so he's happy here. We're all happy.

Bill laughed again. And Bill said, Congratulations, Jerry. Congratulations. I am very pleased for you, Jerry. Very pleased. I could not be more pleased for you, Jerry. But I also know what a struggle it is to stay in that division. What a struggle it is, Jerry. So I know you must have your eye on a few new players. A few new players, Jerry. To freshen things up a bit, liven things up, you know?

Well, said Jerry Kerr. A few new players would be nice. Aye. I won't deny you that, Bill. I can't deny you that. But there's the ones you want and then there's the ones you can afford. You know that, Bill. You know how it is. It's always a question of money, Bill . . .

Bill said, Aye, Jerry. Aye. You don't have to tell me that, Jerry.

I know, said Jerry Kerr. I know I don't, Bill.

Bill said, Aye. It's always a question of money, Jerry.

Aye, it's always the money, said Jerry Kerr. Well, thank you, Bill. Thank you for calling. Now you take care, Bill. And you give my regards to your lovely wife. To Nessie and the girls, Bill . . .

In the house, in their hallway. Bill put down the telephone. In the night, in the silence. Bill smiled. And Bill picked up the phone again. And Bill dialled another number.

. . .

At the station, on the platform at Dundee. Bill shook hands with Duncan Hutchinson, one of the directors of Dundee United Football Club. And Bill said, Well, thank you for the lift back here, sir. It's a great shame the way things have turned out. I mean, things have not gone the way I hoped, the way I wanted. But it was very good of you to still give us a lift back here, sir. And save us a cab fare.

Yes, said Duncan Hutchinson. It's a great shame, Mr Shankly.

Bill nodded. And Bill said, Aye. It is that. But if a club says a player is not for sale, then there is not much more to say . . .

At the station, on the platform. Duncan Hutchinson leaned forward. And Duncan Hutchinson whispered in Bill's ear, No, it's a great shame because I bet for thirty thousand, Yeats would be yours.

Bill looked at Duncan Hutchinson. And Bill said, Really?

Duncan Hutchinson nodded, Duncan Hutchinson winked.

On the train, in their carriage. At their table, in his seat. Bill looked out of the window as the train pulled out of Dundee station. And Bill smiled. Bill turned to look across at Sidney Reakes and Eric Sawyer. In their seats, at their table. And Bill said, You remember you told me, if I can find the players, you can get me the money?

Yes, said Eric Sawyer. Of course, I remember.

Bill laughed. And Bill said, Good. I'm glad you do. Because we're getting off at Waverley. At Edinburgh.

Edinburgh, asked Sidney Reakes. Why are we getting off in Edinburgh, Mr Shankly?

Bill laughed again. And Bill said, So you can make some phone calls. So he can get me the money. The money I need.

. . .

In the lounge of the North British Hotel in Edinburgh. At a table, in a chair. Bill looked up and Bill saw Ron Yeats. Ron Yeats striding into the lounge, Ron Yeats looking around the room. And Bill sprang up from his chair. Bill ran across the room. Bill grabbed Ron Yeats by the hand. And Bill said, Christ! What a player you are, Ron. What a man you are! You are the biggest defender I have ever seen, Ron. You must be seven feet tall, I swear. Seven foot tall, Ron!

Actually, I'm six foot three, said Ron Yeats.

Bill smiled. And Bill said, But you look seven foot, Ron. You look seven foot. But you're also quick, Ron. You're the quickest defender I've ever seen. The very quickest, Ron.

Thank you very much, said Ron Yeats. By the way, where exactly is Liverpool, Mr Shankly?

Bill said, In the First Division, Ron. The First Division.

I meant whereabouts in England, Mr Shankly. Whereabouts is Liverpool in England. But that's not true, Mr Shankly. The club are in the Second Division. I know that much, Mr Shankly.

Bill laughed. And Bill said, Not with you in the team, Ron. Not with you in the team. With you in the team, we'll be in the First Division, Ron. The Big League.


## 7. TO BEGIN AGAIN, AT THE BEGINNING AGAIN

In the last week of June, 1961. Bob Paisley, Joe Fagan, Reuben Bennett, Arthur Riley and Albert Shelley walked up the stairs to the boardroom of Liverpool Football Club. The directors of Liverpool Football Club were still on their holidays. But Bill Shankly was not on his holidays. Bill Shankly was sitting in a chair in the boardroom of Liverpool Football Club with the door open. Bill Shankly was waiting for Bob, Joe, Reuben, Arthur and Albert. Bill Shankly smiling –

Come in, said Bill Shankly. And sit down, sit down . . .

Bob, Joe, Reuben, Arthur and Albert sat down around the long table in the boardroom. They looked at the books spread out on the long table. The books of names, the books of notes. They looked at the sheets of paper piled up on the table. And they looked at Bill Shankly.

Bill Shankly picked up one of the piles of papers. Bill Shankly handed Bob, Joe, Reuben, Arthur and Albert each a sheet of paper. A sheet of names, a sheet of dates. And Bill Shankly smiled again –

Gentlemen, said Bill Shankly. These are all our fixtures for the season. The coming season, the new season . . .

Bob, Joe, Reuben, Arthur and Albert each looked down at the typed sheet of paper. The sheet of names, the sheet of dates. The names of clubs, the dates of fixtures. And then Bob, Joe, Reuben, Arthur and Albert all looked back up at Bill Shankly. Smiling –

Gentlemen, said Bill Shankly again. This season we're going to take no chances. We're going to leave nothing to chance. We're going to leave no stone unturned. We're going to look under every stone. And find out all there is to know. Everything there is to know. Everything there is to know about every one of these teams on this sheet of paper. Every single thing there is to know about every single one of these teams. Every single thing, every last thing . . .

Bob, Joe, Reuben, Arthur and Albert each looked down at the typed sheet of paper again. The sheet of names, the sheet of dates. The names of clubs, the dates of fixtures. And Bob, Joe, Reuben, Arthur and Albert all nodded.

Bill Shankly picked up a second pile of papers. A massive pile of papers. The papers bound in five separate sheaves. Bill Shankly handed Bob, Joe, Reuben, Arthur and Albert each a sheaf of paper –

And this is a list of fixtures for every team in our division. Every game every team in our division will play this season. Every single game for every single team. They are all listed here . . .

Bob, Joe, Reuben, Arthur and Albert each looked down at the sheaf of paper in their hands. And Bob, Joe, Reuben, Arthur and Albert flicked through the pages. The pages of names, the pages of dates. The names of every single club in the division, the dates of every single one of their fixtures. Forty-one names, one thousand, seven hundred and twenty-two dates –

Gentlemen, said Bill Shankly. This season we are going to watch every team in our division. Every single team. Before they come to us, before we go to them. Because we need to know every thing there is to know about every team. Every single thing about every single team. Their strengths and their weaknesses. And so we need to watch them all. Before they come to us, before we go to them. And then we are going to come back here and we are going to talk about them. Discuss them and analyse them. Their strengths and their weaknesses. And so then we will know every single thing there is to know about every single team. And then we will be prepared. Before they come to us, before we go to them. We will be prepared.

Bob, Joe, Reuben, Arthur and Albert all looked up from the sheaves of papers in their hands. And Bob, Joe, Reuben, Arthur and Albert all nodded again.

So we need to study these fixtures, said Bill Shankly. And then we need to decide which one of us will go to which one of these games. If we have no game, I am happy to go. More than happy to go. And any one of you is welcome to join me. Particularly if you don't mind driving. But if we have a game, then one of you will have to go . . .

Bob, Joe, Reuben, Arthur and Albert all nodded again.

Bill Shankly picked up the last pile of papers. Another list of names, another list of dates. And Bill Shankly handed Bob, Joe, Reuben, Arthur and Albert these last papers –

But enough about them, said Bill Shankly. Enough about the opposition. These are the names of every player we have on the books at Liverpool Football Club. And these are the dates of every training session we have scheduled at Liverpool Football Club. And so what I want us to do now, what I want us to do today, is to go through every player and every date and plan every training session for every player at Liverpool Football Club. Every single session for every single player. Because this season we're going to take no chances. We're going to leave nothing to chance. Because this season Liverpool Football Club will be promoted. This season Liverpool Football Club will be Champions. Together, gentlemen. We will be Champions!

Bob, Joe, Reuben, Arthur and Albert all looked up from the papers in their hands. Bob, Joe, Reuben, Arthur and Albert all nodded again. And Bob, Joe, Reuben, Arthur and Albert all smiled.

. . .

In the first week of July, 1961. On the first day of their pre-season training. The players of Liverpool Football Club gathered in the car park at Anfield. In their new kits, their brand-new training kits. In the sun, the July sun. Bill Shankly came out of the stadium. He greeted every player. He shook their hands, he patted their backs. He asked after their families, he asked after their holidays. And then Bob, Joe, Reuben, Arthur and Albert joined Bill Shankly and the players of Liverpool Football Club in the car park at Anfield. And in the sun, the July sun. They all walked out to Melwood. And the players jogged once around the training pitch. Then the players passed the ball back and forth, in pairs, back and forth to each other for twenty minutes. Then the players jogged once more around the training pitch. And then in the sun, the July sun. The players and the coaching staff of Liverpool Football Club all walked back to Anfield.

On the second day of their pre-season training. The players and the coaching staff of Liverpool Football Club all gathered in the car park at Anfield. Then the players and the coaching staff of Liverpool Football Club all jogged out to Melwood. And the players ran once around the training pitch. Then the players passed the ball back and forth, in threes, back and forth to each other for thirty minutes. Then the players ran once more around the training pitch. Then the players and the coaching staff of Liverpool Football Club all jogged back to

Anfield. And on the third day of their pre-season training. The players and the coaching staff of Liverpool Football Club all gathered in the car park at Anfield. Then the players and the coaching staff of Liverpool Football Club all ran out to Melwood. And the players ran twice around the training pitch. Then the players passed the ball back and forth, in fours, back and forth to each other for forty minutes. Then Reuben blew his whistle. And Bill Shankly gathered the players in the middle of the training pitch. Bill, Bob, Joe, Reuben, Arthur and Albert divided the thirty players into six groups of five.

And Bill Shankly smiled –

Right then, lads, said Bill Shankly. Enough bloody running. We're going to play some football! Some five-a-sides, lads . . .

In the second week of their pre-season training. The players of Liverpool Football Club gathered in the car park at Anfield. Bill Shankly came out of the stadium. He greeted every player. He shook their hands, he patted their backs. He asked after their families, he asked after their weekends. And then Bob, Joe, Reuben, Arthur and Albert joined Bill Shankly and the players of Liverpool Football Club in the car park at Anfield. And they all climbed on the bus to Melwood. And when the players of Liverpool Football Club arrived at Melwood, when the players of Liverpool Football Club got off the bus at Melwood, the players of Liverpool Football Club saw the box on the training pitch at Melwood. The box ready for them, the box waiting for them. And the players groaned. And the players laughed. And the players of Liverpool Football Club ran twice around the training pitch. Then the players passed the ball back and forth, in pairs, back and forth for twenty minutes. And then the players went into the box. In pairs. And a ball came over the top into the box. And the first player shot against one board. First time. Then the other player hit the same ball on the rebound. First time. Ball after ball. Every second, another ball. Into the box. Every second for one minute. Ball after ball. Into the box. Then for two minutes. Ball after ball, into the box. Then for three minutes. Ball after ball, into the box. Again and again. Ball after ball, into the box. Every second. Shot after shot. Every second. Inside the box. Every player. Inside the box. Player after player. Pair after pair. Into the box. The players working in the box, the box working on the players. Then Reuben blew his whistle. And Bill Shankly gathered the players in the middle of the training pitch. And Bill Shankly smiled –

Right then, lads. Enough bloody exercises. Now we're going to play some football! Some five-a-sides, lads . . .

And that was the second week of their pre-season training. And the third week. And the fourth. And the fifth. The players of Liverpool Football Club did not practise set pieces. They did not practise corners and they did not practise free kicks. The players of Liverpool Football Club practised passing. Always forward, always faster. Faster and faster, always forward. Always forward –

And always to a red shirt,

always to a red shirt,

a red shirt.

. . .

On Saturday 19 August, 1961, on the first Saturday of the new season, Liverpool Football Club travelled to the Eastville Stadium, Bristol. And before the whistle, the first whistle of the new season. In the dressing room, the away dressing room. The players of Liverpool Football Club looked up at Bill Shankly. Bill Shankly in the centre of the dressing room, the away dressing room. Bill Shankly looking around the dressing room, the away dressing room. From player to player, Liverpool player to Liverpool player. From Slater to White, White to Byrne, Byrne to Milne, Milne to Yeats, Yeats to Leishman, Leishman to Lewis, Lewis to Hunt, Hunt to St John, St John to Melia, Melia to A'Court. And Bill Shankly rubbed his hands together –

This is it, said Bill Shankly. This is it, boys! Everything we've been doing. Everything we've been working for, boys. It was all for this moment, all for this game. This first game of the season, boys. This season that will be our season. Our season, boys . . .

In the seventh minute of this first game of this new season, Kevin Lewis scored. And in the fifty-fifth minute, Hills scored an own goal. And Liverpool Football Club beat Bristol Rovers two–nil. Away from home, away from Anfield. In the first game of the new season.

On Wednesday 23 August, 1961, Sunderland Football Club came to Anfield, Liverpool. That night, forty-eight thousand, nine hundred folk came, too. On a Wednesday night, for the first home game of the season. In the forty-eighth minute of the first home game of the season, Roger Hunt scored. In the seventy-eighth minute, Kevin

Lewis scored. And in the eighty-third minute, Hunt scored again. And Liverpool Football Club beat Sunderland Football Club three–nil. At home, at Anfield. In the first home game of the season.

After the whistle, the final whistle. In the dressing room, the home dressing room. Bill Shankly sat down beside Ron Yeats. And Bill Shankly smiled. Bill Shankly laughed –

That lad Clough is some player, said Bill Shankly. And I tried to sign him. But tonight he never had a sniff, son. He never had a touch. Because you marked him out of the game, son. You made him look ordinary. And that is why I signed you, son. And that is why I made you the captain of Liverpool Football Club. Well done, son.

Three days later, Leeds United came to Anfield, Liverpool. That afternoon, forty-two thousand, nine hundred and fifty folk came, too. In the sixth minute, Roger Hunt scored. In the forty-eighth minute, Hunt scored again. In the fifty-third minute, Kevin Lewis scored a penalty. In the sixty-eighth minute, Jimmy Melia scored. And in the seventy-fourth minute, Hunt scored his third. And Liverpool Football Club beat Leeds United five–nil. At home, at Anfield.

And after the whistle, the final whistle. In the dressing room, the home dressing room. Bill Shankly sat down beside Roger Hunt. And Bill Shankly smiled. Bill Shankly laughed –

That lad Charlton is some player, said Bill Shankly. And I tried to sign him. But today he could not get near you, son. Today you made him look very ordinary. Well played, son.

On Wednesday 30 August, 1961, Liverpool Football Club travelled to Roker Park, Sunderland. In the twenty-sixth minute, Roger Hunt scored. In the thirty-ninth minute, Ian St John scored. In the sixty-ninth minute, Hunt scored again. And in the ninetieth minute, the very last minute, St John scored again. And Liverpool Football Club beat Sunderland Football Club four–one. Away from home, away from Anfield. That night, that season, Liverpool Football Club had played four games and they had won four games. They had scored fourteen goals and they had conceded only one. It was a good start. A very good start. But it was only a start,

only the start.

. . .

In September, 1961, Liverpool Football Club beat Norwich City

61

and they beat Scunthorpe United. And they drew with Brighton and Hove Albion. But then Liverpool Football Club beat Newcastle United. They beat Bury Football Club. And they beat Charlton Athletic.

On Wednesday 4 October, 1961, Newcastle United came to Anfield, Liverpool. Last season, the average gate at Anfield had been just twenty-nine thousand, six hundred and three. This season, the average gate was over forty-six thousand. Tonight, fifty-two thousand, four hundred and nineteen folk had come to Anfield. On a Wednesday night. In the thirty-eighth minute, Kevin Lewis scored. And in the seventy-fifth minute, Roger Hunt scored. And Liverpool Football Club beat Newcastle United two–nil. At home, at Anfield. That night, that season, Liverpool Football Club had played eleven games. They had scored thirty-one goals and they had conceded only four. They had won ten of those games and they had drawn only one. Liverpool Football Club were unbeaten. Liverpool Football Club had twenty-one points. Liverpool Football Club were top of the Second Division.

After the whistle, the final whistle. In the dressing room, the home dressing room. The players of Liverpool Football Club looked up at Bill Shankly. Bill Shankly dancing from player to player. From Bert Slater to Dick White, from Dick to Gerry Byrne, from Gerry to Gordon Milne, from Gordon to Ron Yeats, from Ron to Tommy Leishman, from Tommy to Kevin Lewis, from Kevin to Roger Hunt, from Roger to Ian St John, from Ian to Jimmy Melia and from Jimmy to Alan A'Court. Bill Shankly patting their backs, Bill Shankly shaking their hands. Singing their praises, all of their praises. And then Bill Shankly stood in the centre of the dressing room. In the home dressing room. Bill Shankly put his finger to his ear –

Could you hear that, boys, asked Bill Shankly. Did you hear that sound, lads? That was the sound of over sixty thousand folk. The sixty thousand folk who came here tonight to see you, boys. To see you play, lads. After working all day, after working all week. They came here to see you play, boys. And they saw you play, lads. And they liked what they saw, they loved what they saw. And so they were not only applauding you, boys. They were not only cheering you, lads. Those sixty thousand folk, they were singing, boys. They were singing, lads. Singing your names, all of your names. And singing our name, the name of Liverpool Football Club. Liverpool Football Club . . .

And can you hear that, boys? Do you still hear that, lads? Because they are still singing, still singing the name of Liverpool Football Club. Because of you, boys. Because of you. They don't want to go home, lads. They never want to leave . . .

Because of you, because of you . . .

The Kop are still singing . . .

## 8. THE SONG OF THE COUNTER-PLAN

Upstairs in the house, in their bedroom. Bill was standing in the window. Bill was staring out through the glass at the trees. Downstairs in the house, in their kitchen. Ness and the girls were clearing away the tea things. Washing up the pots, putting away the plates. They were chatting and they were laughing. But upstairs in their bedroom, at the window. Bill could only hear the Kop. In his ears, in his mind. Bill still heard the Kop applauding, Bill still heard the Kop cheering. And singing, still singing. In his ears, in his mind. The Kop was still singing. But now standing in the window, staring through the glass. Now Bill saw the branches of the trees. The branches of the trees moving, the leaves on the branches falling. The first spits of rain on the window pane. And in their bedroom, at the window. Bill looked up through the trees to the sky. And Bill saw the clouds in the sky. The dark clouds moving in the dark sky. Night drawing in. Bill reached up. Bill closed the little window. And Bill drew the curtains.

In the house, in their front room. Bill got up from his chair. Bill kissed Ness on her cheek. And Bill said, Goodnight, love. Goodnight. I won't be long, love. I won't be long . . .

In the house, in their front room. In the night and in the silence. In his chair. Bill stared down at his book. His book of names, his book of notes. The pages of names, the pages of notes. And Bill cursed. Ian St John had not played today and Ron Yeats had not played today. Ian St John and Ron Yeats had been selected to play for the Scottish national team against Northern Ireland. Ian St John and Ron Yeats had travelled to Belfast. Ron Yeats had not even played for Scotland. Ron Yeats had sat in the bloody stands in Belfast. And Liverpool Football Club had lost two–nil to Middlesbrough Football Club. For the first time this season, Liverpool Football Club had bloody lost. For the first time this season, Liverpool Football Club had gone backwards. Backwards in time. In the night and in the silence. In his chair. Bill sighed. And Bill closed his book. His book of names, his book notes. And Bill closed his eyes. In the night and in the silence. In his chair. Bill heard the rain falling on their house. Bill heard the wind blowing around their house. And Bill knew the dangerous months were here. These dangerous months, these winter months. These months of short days, these months of long nights. Nights of rain and days of mud, days of injury and nights of hurt. In these winter months, these dangerous months. Bill knew you had to be prepared. Prepared for the injuries, prepared for the hurt. For the hurt and for the pain. You always had to be prepared. For pain and for hurt.

In the house, in their front room. In the night and in the silence. In his chair. Bill opened his eyes again. Bill looked at his watch. Bill put his book to one side. His book of names, his book of notes. And Bill got up from his chair. Bill walked out of the front room. Bill walked into the kitchen. And Bill switched on the light. Liverpool Football Club had beaten Walsall Football Club six–one. At home, at Anfield. Lewis had scored. Melia had scored. Hunt had scored. Then Hunt had scored again. St John had scored. And then Hunt had scored again, his third. His second hat-trick of the season. Roger Hunt had now scored sixteen goals this season. In the night, in the kitchen. Bill walked over to the cupboards. And Bill opened one of the drawers. Liverpool Football Club had lost two–nil to Derby County. Away from home, away from Anfield. Liverpool Football Club were still first in the Second Division. But Liverpool Football Club had now lost twice in their last three games. In the night, in the kitchen. Bill took out the tablecloth. And Bill closed the drawer. Liverpool Football Club had drawn three–three with Leyton Orient. At home, at Anfield. Bill had kept faith with the same team who had lost to Derby County. Bill had picked the same eleven players to play against Leyton Orient. And at home, at Anfield. Liverpool Football Club had drawn. The first point Liverpool Football Club had dropped. At home, at Anfield. In the night, in the kitchen. Bill walked over to the table. And Bill spread the tablecloth over the table. Liverpool Football Club had beaten Preston North End. Bill had dropped Kevin Lewis and Bill had brought in Ian

Callaghan from the reserves. And Ian Callaghan had scored. It was Ian Callaghan's first goal for Liverpool Football Club. In the night, in the kitchen. Bill walked back over to the cupboards. And Bill opened another of the drawers. Liverpool Football Club had drawn one-all with Luton Town. Bill had kept faith with Ian Callaghan. But Roger Hunt was not fit, Roger Hunt was injured. So Bill had brought back Kevin Lewis. And Kevin Lewis had scored. Kevin Lewis had made his point. But that was all Liverpool Football Club had got. A point. In the night, in the kitchen. Bill took out the cutlery. And Bill closed the drawer. Liverpool Football Club had beaten Huddersfield Town. Roger Hunt was fit again, Roger Hunt could play again. But Bill had kept faith with Ian Callaghan. Bill had dropped Kevin Lewis again. In the night, in the kitchen. Bill walked back over to the table. And Bill laid four places at the table. Liverpool Football Club had beaten Swansea Town five–nil. Bill had kept faith with the same team. And Liverpool Football Club now had thirty-one points. Liverpool Football Club still first in the Second Division. Leyton Orient second, Leyton Orient with twenty-three points. Liverpool Football Club eight points clear of Leyton Orient. In the night, in the kitchen. Bill walked back over to the cupboards. And Bill opened one of the cupboards. Folk were beginning to say that promotion was assured, folk were beginning to think promotion was a foregone conclusion. In the night, in the kitchen. Bill took out the crockery. And Bill closed the cupboard. Bill knew folk often talked rubbish, Bill knew folk often got things wrong. In the night, in the kitchen. Bill walked back over to the table. And Bill put a bowl and a plate in each of the four places at the table. Bill knew nothing was ever assured, Bill knew there were no foregone conclusions. In the night, in the kitchen. Bill walked over to the pantry. And Bill opened the pantry door. Not in life. And not in football. In the night, in the kitchen. Bill took out the salt and pepper pots. The jar of honey and the jar of marmalade. And Bill closed the pantry door. Liverpool Football Club had lost two–nil to Southampton Football Club. Away from home, away from Anfield. In the night, in the kitchen. Bill walked back over to the table. Bill put the salt and pepper pots on the table. And Bill put the jar of honey and the jar of marmalade on the table. Backwards and forwards. One step forwards, two steps backwards. Backwards and forwards. In the night, in the kitchen. Bill looked down at the cutlery and the crockery. The salt and pepper pots. The jar of honey and the jar of marmalade. Backwards and forwards. Bill turning things over, Bill thinking things over. Over and over. In the night, in the kitchen. Bill sat down at the table. And Bill stared across the table at the cutlery and the crockery. The salt and pepper pots. The jar of honey and the jar of marmalade.

In the house, in their kitchen. In the night and in the silence. At the table, in the chair, Bill stood up. Bill walked back out of the kitchen. Bill walked back into the other room. Bill walked back over to the other chair. Bill picked up his book from the arm of the chair. His book of names, his book of notes. Bill went back out of the room. Bill went back into the kitchen. Bill sat back down. In the night, in the kitchen. At the table, in the chair. Bill opened his book again. His book of names, his book of notes. And Bill stared down at the pages of his book again. The pages of names, the pages of notes. And Bill turned the pages again. Again and again. These pages of names, these pages of notes. Backwards and forwards, again and again. Through all these names, through all these notes. All the players and all the games. The games still to come and the games that had been. Again and again, forwards and backwards. In the night, in the kitchen. Bill stopped turning the pages. The pages of names, the pages of notes. Bill closed the book. The book of names, the book of notes. And at the table, in the chair. Bill closed his eyes again –

It was half-time, half-time in the game against Plymouth Argyle, half-time in the twenty-first game of the season, half-time in the 1961–62 season. Half-time and Liverpool Football Club were drawing one-all with Plymouth Argyle. At home, at Anfield. Bill walked into the dressing room, the home dressing room. And Bill sat down on the bench beside Johnny Wheeler. Johnny Wheeler had come in for Tommy Leishman. Tommy Leishman was injured, Tommy Leishman could not play. So Bill had brought in Johnny Wheeler. Bill had had no choice. In the dressing room, on the bench. Bill put his hand on the top of Johnny Wheeler's thigh. Bill gripped it hard. And Bill said, Christ, you are playing well today, John. You are playing well. As well as I've ever seen you play, John. And Christ, I've seen you play some games. Some great games, John. But today you are turning back the tide. Rolling back the years, John. But I know you must be feeling those years by now. Feeling every one of those years, John. But forty-five more minutes. Forty-five more minutes, John. That is all I ask. That's all I ask of you, John. Just give forty-five more minutes like the last forty-five minutes. Can you do that for me, John?

Johnny Wheeler nodded.

Bill patted Johnny Wheeler's thigh. Bill patted it gently. And Bill said, Thank you, John. Thank you.

Back in the dug-out, the home dug-out. Bill watched and Bill waited. Bill waited and Bill watched. And in the eightieth minute, Ian St John scored. And Liverpool Football Club beat Plymouth Argyle two–one. At home, at Anfield. And after the whistle, the final whistle. In the dug-out, the home dug-out. Bill stood up again. Bill walked down the touchline, the Anfield touchline again. Liverpool Football Club had now played twenty-one games. Liverpool Football Club now had thirty-three points. Liverpool Football Club were still first in the Second Division. But it was still half-time, still only half-time. Liverpool Football Club still had half the season to come. Liverpool Football Club still had twenty-one games to play. But Johnny Wheeler would never play another game for Liverpool Football Club.

In the house, in their kitchen. In the night and in the silence. At the table, in the chair. Bill opened his eyes again. And Bill got up from the chair again, up from the table again. Bill walked over to the wall. Bill switched off the light. Bill walked up the stairs. Liverpool Football Club had beaten Bristol Rovers two–nil. At home, at Anfield. Liverpool Football Club had thirty-five points. Liverpool Football Club still first in the Second Division. Leyton Orient still second, Leyton Orient with twenty-seven points. Bill went into the bathroom. Bill switched on the light. Bill washed his face, Bill cleaned his teeth. And then Bill looked up into the mirror. Liverpool Football Club had lost to Leeds United. Away from home, away from Anfield. In the bathroom, in the mirror. Bill could hear the wind blowing around the house. In a gale, a winter gale. Liverpool Football Club had lost to Rotherham United. Away from home, away from Anfield. Again. Liverpool Football Club still had thirty-five points. Liverpool Football Club still first in the Second Division. Leyton Orient still second, Leyton Orient now with thirty-one points. And now with a game in hand. In the bathroom, in the mirror. Bill turned away. Bill switched off the light. And Bill walked into the bedroom. In the bedroom, in the dark. Bill got undressed. In the dark and in the cold. Rotherham United should have come to Anfield, Liverpool. And Liverpool Football Club should have had the chance to put things right. To make amends, to take revenge. But in the dark and in the cold. The weather was against Liverpool Football Club. And the game was postponed. Leyton Orient's game was not postponed. Leyton Orient played Swansea Town. And Leyton Orient beat Swansea Town three–one. Leyton Orient now had thirty-three points. In the dark and in the cold. Bill put on his pyjamas. Liverpool Football Club still had thirty-five points. Liverpool Football Club still first in the Second Division. Just. In the dark and in the cold. Bill got into bed. But Bill did not close his eyes. Bill did not go to sleep. In the dark, in their bed. Bill stared up at the ceiling. In the dark, in their bed. Bill was still thinking things over, Bill was still turning things over. Over and over. In the dark, in his mind. The games that had been and the games-to-come, the players he had picked and the players he might. Thinking who should step down and who should step up, thinking who was ready and who was not. Ready to step up, ready or not. In the dark, in his mind. Wondering who was deserving of faith and who was not. Wondering, always wondering. Bill was always wondering. In the dark, in their bed. Bill could not close his eyes. Bill could not sleep, Bill just could not sleep.

Upstairs in their bedroom, at the window. Bill drew back the curtains. Bill looked out through the glass at the trees, up through the trees to the sky. The sky and the dawn. And Bill smiled. Downstairs in the house, in their kitchen. Ness and the girls were clearing away the breakfast things. Washing up the pots, putting away the plates. They were chatting and they were laughing. Upstairs in their bedroom, at the window. Bill smiled again. And Bill turned away from the window. Bill walked over to the bed. Bill picked up his shirt and Bill put on his shirt. His brand-new red shirt. Bill went to the dressing table. Bill opened the top drawer. Bill took out his cufflinks. His gold cufflinks. Bill closed the drawer. Bill did up the cuffs of his shirt. His brand-new red shirt. Bill went to the wardrobe. Bill opened the doors. Bill took out his suit. His freshly cleaned grey suit with the white pinstripe. Bill left the wardrobe doors open. Bill walked over to the bed. Bill laid out the suit on top of the bed covers. Bill took the trousers from the coat hanger. Bill put on the trousers of his suit. His freshly cleaned grey suit with the white pinstripe. Bill went back to the dressing table. Bill opened the second drawer of the dressing table. Bill took out a red tie. The red tie his daughters had given him for Christmas. The red tie Bill had never worn before. Bill closed the drawer. Bill walked back to the wardrobe. The doors still open. Bill stood before the mirror on the back of one of the doors. Bill put on his tie. His red tie. Bill went back over to the bed. Bill picked up the jacket from the bed. Bill took the jacket from the coat hanger. Bill put on the jacket of his suit. His freshly cleaned grey suit with the white pinstripe. Bill walked back over to the dressing table. Bill opened the top drawer of the dressing table again. Bill took out one white handkerchief and one red pocket square. Bill closed the drawer. Bill put the white handkerchief in his left trouser pocket. Bill laid the red pocket square on the top of the dressing table. It looked like a red diamond. Bill brought the bottom point of the red pocket square up to the top point. It looked like a red triangle. Bill brought the left corner of the triangle to the right corner and then the right corner to the left corner. It looked like a long red rectangle with a point at the top. Bill folded the bottom almost towards the top. Bill walked back over to the mirror on the back of the wardrobe door. Bill stood before the mirror. Bill placed the red pocket square in the breast pocket of his grey jacket. Bill looked in the mirror. Bill adjusted the pocket square until just enough of the point was coming out of the pocket. The red point out of the grey pocket. Bill stepped back a little from the mirror. In the house, their semi-detached house on Bellefield Avenue, West Derby. In the bedroom, in the mirror. Bill looked at himself, Bill saw himself. And Bill smiled. Today, Chelsea Football Club were coming to Anfield, Liverpool. Today, the world would be coming to Anfield, too. Today, Bill knew the world would be watching Liverpool Football Club. And Bill could not wait, Bill just could not wait.


9. THE MARCH TO APRIL

On Saturday 6 January, 1962, the world and forty-eight thousand, four hundred and fifty-five folk came to Anfield, Liverpool. *Oh, when the saints.* The world and forty-eight thousand, four hundred and fifty-five folk to watch Liverpool Football Club play Chelsea Football Club in the Third Round of the FA Cup. *Go marching in.* The world and the Kop. *Oh, when the saints go marching in.* The Kop clapping, the Kop cheering. *Lord, how I want to be in that number.* The Kop shouting and the Kop singing. *When the saints go marching in.* A wall of sound, a sea of noise. *We are travelling in the footsteps.* A sound so great the Chelsea players trembled on the pitch. *Of those who've gone before.* A noise so loud the Chelsea players could not hear the referee blow his whistle. *And we'll all be reunited.* In a din, a din. *On a new and sunlit shore.* A din so deafening, a din so intimidating. *Oh, when the saints, go marching in.* That never let up and never subsided, that had the Chelsea players kicking the ball anywhere. *Oh, when the saints go marching in.* Anywhere for a moment's peace, for a moment's respite. *Lord, how I want to be in that number.* But there was no peace, there was no respite. *When the saints go marching in.* Not from the din and not from the team. *And when the sun, refuse to shine.* The team in red shirts, white shorts and white socks. *Oh, when the sun refuse to shine.* The team that came again and again at the Chelsea players. *Lord, how I want to be in that number.* Again and again, wave after wave, attack after attack. *When the sun refuse to shine.* The sound behind the team in red shirts, white shorts and white socks. *And when the moon, turns red with blood.* The noise of forty-eight thousand, four hundred and fifty-five folk clapping and cheering, shouting and singing. *Oh, when the moon turns red with blood.* The din and then the roar. *Lord, how I want to be in that number.* The roar in the sixteenth minute as Ian St John scored. *When the moon turns red with blood.* The roar of a goal. *Oh, when the trumpet, sounds its call.* A Liverpool goal. *Oh, when the trumpet sounds its call.* The roar and then, then a sudden silence. A sudden silence as Tambling equalised for Chelsea. One-all. One-all and Bill Shankly was on his feet. On his feet, his arms outstretched. Cajoling his team, rallying his team. Orchestrating and conducting. Not only the team. Orchestrating and conducting the crowd. *Lord, how I want to be in that number.* The forty-eight thousand, four hundred and fifty-five crowd inside Anfield, Liverpool. *When the trumpet sounds its call.* The crowd and the Kop. *Some say this world of trouble.* The Kop clapping again, the Kop cheering again. *Is the only one we need.* Shouting again and singing again. *But I'm waiting for that morning.* Roaring. *When the new world is revealed.* Roaring again in the twenty-eighth minute as Roger Hunt scored. *Oh, when the new world is revealed.* Two–one. *Oh, when the new world is revealed.* Roaring again in the forty-first minute as St John scored his second. *Lord, how I want to be in that number.* Three–one. *When the new world is revealed.* Roaring again as Jimmy Melia hit one post. *Oh, when the saints.* Roaring again as Ian Callaghan hit the other. *Go marching in.* Roaring again and again as Bonetti made save after save. *Oh, when the saints go marching in.* Then roaring again, louder than ever, roaring again in the forty-fourth minute as Alan A'Court scored. *Lord, how I want to be in that number.* Four–one –

*When the saints go marching in . . .*

At half-time, in the dressing room, the home dressing room. With a cup of tea or with a slice of orange. The players of Liverpool Football Club sat on the benches and the players of Liverpool Football caught their breath. And Bill Shankly, Bob Paisley and Reuben Bennett went from player to player. From Slater to Molyneux, Molyneux to Byrne, Byrne to Milne, Milne to Yeats, Yeats to Leishman, Leishman to Callaghan, Callaghan to Hunt, Hunt to St John, St John to Melia and Melia to A'Court. Praising them and cautioning them. Praising them for the job they had done, cautioning them for the job to come. The job still half done,

a half still to come –

The referee blew his whistle again and the forty-eight thousand, four hundred and fifty-five folk began to clap again, began to cheer again. But they did not clap as often, they did not cheer as much. They still shouted and they still sang. But they did not shout as loud, they did not sing as long. The forty-eight thousand, four hundred and fifty-five folk inside Anfield, Liverpool, began to think the job was done, began to think the game was over. But in the sixty-seventh minute, Tambling scored again. Four–two. Nine minutes later, Bridges scored. Four–three. And now the forty-eight thousand, four hundred and fifty-five folk did not clap at all, they did not cheer at all. They did not shout and they did not sing. The forty-eight thousand, four hundred and fifty-five folk inside Anfield, Liverpool, held their breath. In silence. For minute after minute. They held their breath. In silence. For long minute after longer minute. They held their breath. In silence. For eternal minute after eternal minute. They held their breath –

In silence. Silence

until, until,

until –

The referee raised his hand. Slowly. The referee put the whistle to his lips. Slowly. The referee spread his arms wide. And then, for the final time, for the last time, the referee blew his whistle, his whistle that became the roar, the roar of forty-eight thousand, four hundred and fifty-five Liverpool folk clapping and cheering, shouting and singing, the roar that became a cry, one huge and joyous cry of victory, of victory and of celebration, of communal victory,

of communal celebration –

*Oh, when the reds.* Liverpool Football Club had beaten Chelsea Football Club four–three. *Go marching in.* Liverpool Football Club had won. *Oh, when the reds go marching in.* And the world had watched. *Lord, how I want to be in that number.* The world had watched Liverpool Football Club. *When the reds go marching in . . .*

And the world had heard –

*Go marching in! In! In . . .*

Had heard the Kop –

*The Reds! Reds! Reds . . .*

The Spion Kop –

*Go marching in, go marching on . . .*

 . . .

One week after Liverpool Football Club had beaten Chelsea Football Club in the Cup, Norwich City came to Anfield, Liverpool. And Liverpool Football Club beat Norwich City in the League. Just. Liverpool Football Club were still first in the Second Division. Just. Liverpool Football Club now had thirty-seven points. But Leyton Orient now had thirty-five points. They had won eight games in a row and they were unbeaten in twelve. One week later, Leyton Orient won again. Leyton Orient now had thirty-seven points. But Liverpool Football Club had only thirty-eight points. Liverpool Football Club had drawn one-all with Scunthorpe United. Away from home, away from Anfield. On Saturday 27 January, 1962, Liverpool Football Club went to Boundary Park, Oldham. And Liverpool Football Club beat

Oldham Athletic two–one in the Fourth Round of the FA Cup. One week after that, Brighton and Hove Albion came to Anfield, Liverpool. And Liverpool Football Club beat Brighton and Hove Albion three–one. One week later, Liverpool Football Club beat Bury Football Club three–nil. Roger Hunt had scored all three goals. His fourth hat-trick of the season. Roger Hunt had now scored twenty-nine goals in twenty-eight games. And Liverpool Football Club now had forty-two points. Liverpool Football Club still first in the Second Division.

On Saturday 17 February, 1962, Preston North End came to Anfield, Liverpool. That afternoon, fifty-four thousand, nine hundred and sixty-seven folk came, too. Fifty-four thousand, nine hundred and sixty-seven folk to watch Liverpool Football Club play Preston North End in the Fifth Round of the FA Cup. Fifty-four thousand, nine hundred and sixty-seven folk to watch Liverpool Football Club draw nil–nil with Preston North End. Three days after that, Liverpool Football Club travelled to Deepdale, Preston. And Liverpool Football Club were twenty-five minutes late. Because of the traffic around the ground. Because of the crowd around the ground. The gates of the ground had to be closed half an hour before kick-off. And inside the ground, Liverpool Football Club drew nil–nil with Preston North End again. Nil–nil again, after extra time. There was nothing to choose between the sides. Four days later, Middlesbrough Football Club came to Anfield. Ian St John scored two goals. And Roger Hunt scored three. His fifth hat-trick of the season. And Liverpool Football Club beat Middlesbrough Football Club five–one. Two days after, just two days later, on Monday 26 February, 1962, Liverpool Football Club travelled to Old Trafford, Manchester. Forty-three thousand, nine hundred and forty-four folk came, too. Forty-three thousand, nine hundred and forty-four folk to watch Liverpool Football Club play Preston North End in the second replay of the Fifth Round of the FA Cup. On a snow-covered, frozen pitch. Where players slipped, where players fell. In the snow, on the pitch. They slipped and they fell. All except Peter Thompson. And in the two hundred and sixty-sixth minute of the tie, the tie that over one hundred and thirty-six thousand folk had paid to watch, Peter Thompson kept his feet. He did not slip, he did not fall, And Peter Thompson scored –

The only goal.

After the whistle, the final whistle. In the dressing room, their dressing room at Old Trafford. The players and the coaching staff of Preston North End were celebrating. And then the players and the coaching staff of Preston North End heard a knock upon the dressing-room door. And the players and the coaching staff of Preston North End saw Bill Shankly step into their dressing room, the Preston dressing room. And Bill Shankly went from player to player. Patting their backs, shaking their hands. Bill Shankly congratulated them all. And then Bill Shankly sat down on the bench next to Peter Thompson. Bill Shankly patted his back, Bill Shankly shook his hand –

Christ, you played well, said Bill Shankly. Over all three games, son. You were the best player on the pitch. The best player by far, son. And so I won't forget you. I won't forget you, son. So don't you forget me. Don't you forget me, son . . .

. . .

The morning after the night before, the cold morning after the Cup night before. The directors of Liverpool Football Club were sitting in the boardroom at Anfield. Again. The directors of Liverpool Football Club were waiting for Bill Shankly. And again. The directors of Liverpool Football Club heard the footsteps in the corridor outside. Again. The fast steps, the heavy steps. Again. The knock upon the boardroom door. Again. Fast and heavy, very fast and very heavy.

And Tom Williams said, Come in, please.

Bill Shankly opened the door. Again. Bill Shankly stepped into the room. Again. Bill Shankly looked around the boardroom. Again. From director to director. And again. Bill Shankly waited.

Tom Williams said, Sit down, please.

Bill Shankly walked to the end of the long table. Again. Bill Shankly sat down in the empty chair at the end of the table. And again. Bill Shankly looked up the long table.

The directors of Liverpool Football Club looked back down the long table at Bill Shankly. The directors of Liverpool Football Club smiled down the long table at Bill Shankly. And Tom Williams said, Bad luck in the Cup, Mr Shankly. Hard luck. But it is still a good season, Mr Shankly. A very good season. And we are all still behind you, Mr Shankly. We are all still sure we can get promotion. And we are all still sure you are the man who can get us promotion.

I'm very pleased to hear that, said Bill Shankly. But if we are to get promoted, if we are to be Champions. If we are sure to be promoted, if we are sure to be Champions. Then we need a new goalkeeper. We need to buy a new goalkeeper.

The directors of Liverpool Football Club looked at each other. The directors of Liverpool Football Club shook their heads. And Tom Williams said, But we have a good goalkeeper, Mr Shankly. A very good goalkeeper who has helped take us to the top of the table. We are still first in the Second Division. We are still at the top of the table, Mr Shankly. The very top of the table . . .

I know very well where we are, said Bill Shankly. Very well where we are now. But it is still only February. If we want to be top of the table at the end of the season, if we want to be top when it matters. Then we need a new goalkeeper. We need a new bloody keeper.

The directors of Liverpool Football Club looked at each other. Again. The directors of Liverpool Football Club shook their heads. And Tom Williams said, But what is wrong with the keeper we have, Mr Shankly? What is the problem with the keeper we have?

He is too short, said Bill Shankly. And he has let in twenty-seven goals in the League. And five in the Cup. Because he is too short.

Tom Williams said, He was just unfortunate in the Cup, Mr Shankly. He was just very unlucky against Preston . . .

He wasn't unfortunate, said Bill Shankly. He wasn't unlucky. He was too short. And that is one of the reasons we lost. Because he was too short. Because he *is* too short. It has nothing to do with fortune. Nothing to do with luck. It has everything to do with size. Everything to do with size. The man is simply too short.

Eric Sawyer asked, So who do you want, Mr Shankly? Who do you have in mind to replace him?

Jim Furnell, said Bill Shankly. From Burnley.

Eric Sawyer asked, But would Burnley really sell him?

Yes, said Bill Shankly. Burnley will sell him.

And how much would they want for him?

Eighteen thousand pounds.

The directors of Liverpool Football Club looked at each other. Again. The directors of Liverpool Football Club looked down the long table at Bill Shankly. And Tom Williams said, But how can you be so certain, Mr Shankly? How can you be so sure Burnley will sell us this man Furnell for eighteen thousand pounds?

Because I have already asked them, said Bill Shankly. I've already asked and they've already agreed. That's why I am so certain.

. . .

On Saturday 3 March, 1962, Liverpool Football Club travelled to Fellows Park, Walsall. But Bert Slater did not travel to Fellows Park, Walsall. Bill Shankly had dropped Bert Slater. Bert Slater had played ninety-six consecutive games for Liverpool Football Club. But Bert Slater would never play another game for Liverpool Football Club. On Saturday 3 March, 1962, Jim Furnell travelled to Fellows Park, Walsall. It was Jim Furnell's first match for Liverpool Football Club. Jim Furnell conceded one goal on his debut. And Liverpool Football Club drew one-all with Walsall Football Club. One week after that, Derby County came to Anfield, Liverpool. And Liverpool Football Club beat Derby County four–one. Liverpool Football Club were still first in the Second Division. And Leyton Orient were still second.

On Saturday 17 March, 1962, Liverpool Football Club travelled to Brisbane Road, London. Ten minutes before kick-off, Bill Shankly burst into the away dressing room at Leyton Orient. Bill Shankly took a photograph from his pocket. Bill Shankly showed the photograph to every player, to Furnell, Byrne, Moran, Milne, Yeats, Leishman, Callaghan, Hunt, St John, Melia and A'Court –

Do you know who this man is, lads? Do you know this man? This man is Dave Dunmore. He used to play for Tottenham Hotspur, he used to play for West Ham United. But now he plays for Leyton Orient. He is the best player they have. The only good player they have. Whenever he plays, they win. But I've just seen their team sheet, lads. And guess what I've just seen? Today there is no Dave Dunmore for Leyton Orient. Today Dave Dunmore is injured. And this team cannot win without Dave Dunmore. And they have not won at home since the thirteenth of January this year. And so I know they cannot win at home today either. Not at home. Not today. Not without Dave Dunmore. They cannot win. I know they cannot win . . .

First Leyton Orient scored. In the mud and in the wind. Then in the eightieth minute, Alan A'Court equalised. In the mud and in the wind. Then Leyton Orient scored again. But in the mud and in the wind. In the eighty-ninth minute, A'Court scored again. And in the London mud, in the southern wind. Liverpool Football Club now had forty-eight points and Leyton Orient now had forty-three points. But Liverpool Football Club had two games in hand over Leyton Orient. And Liverpool Football Club were still first in the Second Division. Still at the very top of the table.

. . .

On Saturday 24 March, 1962, Preston North End came to Anfield. That afternoon, thirty-nine thousand, seven hundred and one folk came, too. Jimmy Melia scored one. Ian St John scored one. And Roger Hunt scored two. And Liverpool Football Club beat Preston North End four–one. Four days after that, Rotherham United came to Anfield. That night, thirty-two thousand, eight hundred and twenty-seven folk came, too. Roger Hunt scored one and Ian St John scored a hat-trick. And Liverpool Football Club beat Rotherham United four–one. Three days later, Liverpool Football Club travelled to Kenilworth Road, Luton. And Liverpool Football Club lost one–nil. One week after that, Huddersfield Town came to Anfield. That afternoon, thirty-eight thousand and twenty-two folk came, too. And Liverpool Football Club drew one-all. At home, at Anfield. That night, Liverpool Football Club had fifty-three points. Liverpool Football Club still first in the Second Division. But that day, Leyton Orient had won. Leyton Orient now had forty-eight points. And there were still six more games to go, still six more games to play. More games to win,

more games to lose –

On Saturday 14 April, 1962, Liverpool Football Club should have travelled to Vetch Field, Swansea. And Liverpool Football Club should have played Swansea Town. But there had been an outbreak of smallpox in South Wales. And Liverpool Football Club's game against Swansea Town was postponed. Leyton Orient's game was not postponed. But Leyton Orient lost. If Liverpool Football Club won their next match, then Liverpool Football Club would be promoted. Promoted to the First Division. If Liverpool Football Club won their next match. Their next match at home to Southampton Football Club. If Liverpool Football Club beat Southampton Football Club, then Liverpool Football Club would be promoted. If Liverpool Football Club won. If they won, if they won. If, if –

Always if, if –
Always –
If, if –

This was the day, this was the hour. In the rain and in the wind. Arthur Riley and Jimmy McInnes stood on the Anfield pitch with Bill Shankly. In the rain and in the wind. They watched Mr Holland walk out of the Anfield tunnel and onto the Anfield pitch. Mr Holland was the referee. In the rain and in the wind. Mr Holland looked down at the Anfield pitch. Mr Holland pressed his shoe down into the Anfield pitch. Mud and water came up from out of the Anfield pitch. Mud and water came up over the top of his shoe. Mud and water onto his sock, mud and water into his shoe. In the rain and in the wind. Mr Holland looked up at the sky. The sky and the clouds, the dark clouds in the dark sky. Mr Holland looked back down at Arthur Riley, Jimmy McInnes and Bill Shankly. And Mr Holland shook his head.

Come on now, said Bill Shankly. A wee bit of rain never hurt anyone, Mr Holland. Never hurt anyone . . .

In the rain and in the wind. Mr Holland looked back down at his shoe. In the mud and in the water. Mr Holland looked back up at the sky. The dark sky and the dark clouds. And Mr Holland looked back down at his watch. His watch ticking. Ticking. Ticking.

And the forecast is for blue skies, said Bill Shankly. Blue skies, Mr Holland. Blue skies and sunshine. Beautiful April sunshine!

Mr Holland looked at Bill Shankly. Mr Holland shook his head again. And Mr Holland said, What forecast is that, Mr Shankly?

Mine, said Bill Shankly. But I'm rarely wrong.

Arthur Riley and Jimmy McInnes both nodded. And they both said, Mr Shankly's right, Mr Holland. He's rarely wrong. You'll find he's usually right about most things.

In the rain and in the wind. Mr Holland smiled. And Mr Holland said, Well, let's hope so then. Let's hope he's right today.

On Saturday 21 April, 1962, forty thousand, four hundred and ten folk came to Anfield, Liverpool. In the rain and in the wind. Forty thousand, four hundred and ten folk hoping to see Liverpool Football Club promoted to the First Division. In the rain and in the wind. Forty thousand, four hundred and ten folk praying to see Liverpool Football Club promoted to the First Division. In the rain and in the wind. If

78

Liverpool Football Club won. In the rain and in the wind. If, if.

Before the match, in the dressing room. The home dressing room. Kevin Lewis sat on the bench. On the dressing-room bench. Kevin Lewis stared down at his boots. And then Kevin Lewis felt an arm around his shoulder. And Kevin Lewis looked up –

Today's your day, said Bill Shankly. Today is your day, son. Your day to prove me wrong. To prove what a fool I've been. Not to let you play more games, not to let you have more chances. But today you have your chance. Today's your chance, today's your day. So are you ready, son? Are you ready? To prove me wrong, to take your chance. And to make your point today, son?

Kevin Lewis nodded.

Good lad, said Bill Shankly. And Bill Shankly stood up. Bill Shankly walked into the centre of the dressing room. The home dressing room. And Bill Shankly looked around the dressing room. The Liverpool dressing room. From player to player. From Furnell to Byrne, Byrne to Moran, Moran to Milne, Milne to Yeats, Yeats to Leishman, Leishman to Callaghan, Callaghan to Hunt, Hunt to Lewis, Lewis to Melia, Melia to A'Court. And Bill Shankly smiled. In the centre of the dressing room. Bill Shankly rubbed his hands together –

I know after today there are still five more games to go, lads. Five more games to play. But I don't know about you, lads. I don't know about you. But I don't like waiting, lads. I hate waiting. I don't want to wait, lads. We've all waited long enough. And Liverpool Football Club have waited long enough. Too long, lads. We've all waited too long. So I want to win today. Today! Because I want us to be promoted today. Today! Not tomorrow, not next week. Today! Because this is the day. This is the hour. We can win today and we can be promoted today. No more tomorrows. No more ifs. No more maybes. We can win today and we can be promoted today. Because this is the day, lads. This is the hour. We will win and we will be promoted. Today! Liverpool Football Club will be promoted. Today!

In the nineteenth minute, Kevin Lewis made his point. Ten minutes later, Kevin Lewis made his point again. And Liverpool Football Club beat Southampton Football Club two–nil. They had won. Liverpool Football Club had won the match and Liverpool Football Club had won promotion to the First Division –

After the whistle, the final whistle, the players of Southampton Football Club formed a guard of honour. In the rain and in the wind. The players of Southampton Football Club applauded the players of Liverpool Football Club off the pitch. But in the rain and in the wind, no one could hear their applause. No one could hear the rain or the wind. The forty thousand, four hundred and ten folk inside Anfield, Liverpool, would not go home. In the rain and in the wind. The forty thousand, four hundred and ten folk inside Anfield, Liverpool, refused to leave. They clapped and they cheered. They shouted and they sang. And they called and they chanted. In the rain and in the wind. They called for the players of Liverpool Football Club, they chanted for the players of Liverpool Football Club. WE WANT THE REDS! WE WANT THE REDS! WE WANT THE REDS! Over and over, again and again. In the rain and in the wind. They called and they chanted. WE WANT THE REDS! WE WANT THE REDS! WE WANT THE REDS! Again and again, over and over. In the rain and in the wind. WE WANT THE REDS! WE WANT THE REDS –

WE WANT THE REDS!

Long after the whistle, the final whistle. Still in the rain, still in the wind. No one would go, no one would leave. And up in the directors' box, Tom Williams tried to address the crowd. To thank the crowd and to thank the players. But no one could hear, no one was listening. No one going, no one leaving. And so up in the directors' box, Tom Williams invited Bill Shankly to address the crowd –

One of the hardest things in football, said Bill Shankly. Is to win the Second Division. And to be promoted. And so this is the happiest day of my football life. My football life so far . . .

But in the rain and in the wind. The public address system was not loud enough. Not loud enough to silence the crowd. The crowd and the Kop. In the rain and in the wind. Their cheering and their chanting. In the rain and in the wind. The Kop cheering and the Kop chanting, WE WANT THE REDS! WE WANT THE REDS!

OH, WE WANT THE REDS!

THE REDS! THE REDS!

THE REDS!

No one going, no one leaving. In the rain and in the wind. Tom Williams told Bill Shankly he had better go back down to the dressing room. And fast. Bill Shankly ran back down to the dressing room. Fast. Bill Shankly burst into the dressing room, the home dressing room –

You'll have to go back out there, said Bill Shankly. You'll all have to go back out there, boys. The crowd want you. The crowd still want you, lads. So give the crowd a lap of honour. Give them what they want, boys. What they deserve. And you deserve . . .

And in their shorts and in their socks, the players of Liverpool Football Club ran back up the tunnel. The Anfield tunnel. And the players of Liverpool Football Club ran back out onto the pitch. The Anfield pitch. And the supporters of Liverpool Football Club roared, the supporters of Liverpool Football Club cried, REDS! REDS! REDS!

But the players of Liverpool Football Club could not give the crowd their lap of honour. The players of Liverpool Football Club could not get but twenty yards. On the pitch, the Anfield pitch. The crowd swallowed up the players, the crowd took up the players. Into their arms and into their hearts. And on the pitch, the Anfield pitch. The police had to rescue the players. The police had to help the players. Back down the tunnel, back to the dressing room. Back to their mugs of champagne, back to their celebration. In the dressing room, the home dressing room. Bill Shankly clapped his hands together –

Now you know what it means, laughed Bill Shankly. What it means to play for this club, boys. To play for Liverpool Football Club!

. . .

After the champagne, after the celebrations. The directors of Liverpool Football Club looked down the long table at Bill Shankly. The directors of Liverpool Football Club smiled at Bill Shankly. And the directors of Liverpool Football Club said, Well done, Mr Shankly. Well done indeed! What a season it has been, Mr Shankly. What a great season! The best season in years, Mr Shankly. The very best in years! And as a token of our gratitude, Mr Shankly. As a token of our thanks, we would like to present you with this cigarette box. This engraved silver cigarette box. There is one box for you, Mr Shankly. And there is one for all your staff. And one for every player. As a token of our gratitude. As a token of our thanks, Mr Shankly.

Thank you, said Bill Shankly. Thank you very much, gentlemen. But I just hope no one here in this room, no one here at this table, thinks that this is satisfactory. That this is enough?

The directors of Liverpool Football Club stopped smiling. The directors of Liverpool Football Club looked back down the long table at Bill Shankly. And the directors of Liverpool Football Club said, What do you mean, Mr Shankly? What do you mean? Were you hoping for something more, Mr Shankly? Is this box not enough?

I do not mean the box, said Bill Shankly. I mean promotion. I mean, I hope no one in this room, no one at this table, thinks promotion is enough. That promotion is satisfactory. Yes, Liverpool Football Club are back in the First Division. Back in the Big League. But that is only where Liverpool Football Club belong. Only where they should have been all along. In the First Division, in the Big League. So the next time you come bearing gifts, bringing presents, it will be because we've won the Big League. Because Liverpool Football Club have won the First Division. And the FA Cup. And the European Cup. And every cup there is to win. Because only that will be satisfactory, gentlemen. When Liverpool Football Club have won everything there is to win, when Liverpool Football Club have conquered the world. Only that will be enough.

## 10. THOSE WHO DEPRIVE THE TABLE OF MEAT

In Blackpool, on the North Shore. In his deckchair, in the sun. Bill looked out across the beach, out across the sands, towards the water, towards the sea. In the sun. Ness was sat in the deckchair next to Bill. Ness had a newspaper on her lap. Her crossword done, her eyes closed now. In the sun. The girls had gone for a walk on the promenade. To the arcades and the amusements. In the sun. Bill closed his eyes now. Bill listened to the waves, Bill listened to the gulls. And Bill heard the voices of children. Children laughing, children playing. In the sun. Bill opened his eyes. Bill looked out across the beach again, out across the sands again. And Bill saw the buckets and the spades. The balls and the games. In the sun. The balls on the beach, the games on the sands. In the sun. Bill got up from his deckchair. Bill took off his shirt and Bill took off his vest. Bill walked down onto the beach, down onto the sands. There was always a game, always another game.

. . .

In the boardroom, the Anfield boardroom. There were no directors. The directors of Liverpool Football Club were still on their holidays. But Bill was not on his holidays. Not any more. And Bob, Joe, Reuben, Arthur and Albert were not on their holidays. Not any more. In the boardroom, the Anfield boardroom. Bill, Bob, Joe, Reuben, Arthur and Albert were back at work. Their books spread out on the long table. Their books of names, their books of notes. Their sheets of paper piled up on the table. Their sheets of names, their sheets of dates.

And Bill said, We all know we won the Championship in the first month of the season. We all know in that first month we were fitter, we were stronger and we were more competitive than any other team in the League, than any other team in the Second Division. We all know that is how we won promotion, why we were the Champions. But we all know that was in the Second Division. In a different league. Now we are in the First Division. Now we are in the Big League. Now we will need to be even fitter, even stronger and even more competitive. And we also know, in itself, that will not be enough. Not enough in the First Division. In the Big League. We will need to have more artistry, we will need to have more vision. In short, we will need to have more skill. We will need to have *much* more skill . . .

Joe, Reuben, Arthur and Albert nodded. And Bob said, And we will need to have more guile, Boss. And we will need to have more confidence. More guile and more confidence, Boss.

Bill nodded. And Bill said, You are right, Bob. You are exactly right. We will need to give the players more guile and we will need to give the players more confidence. Exactly, Bob . . .

Everybody nodded, everybody agreed.

Bill picked up the piles of papers. The piles of names, the piles of dates. Bill handed out the piles of paper. The names of clubs, the names of players. The dates of fixtures, the dates of training. Bob, Joe, Reuben, Arthur and Albert flicked through the pages. The pages of names, the pages of dates. And Bill, Bob, Joe, Reuben, Arthur and Albert studied every page. Every page of names, every page of notes. And Bill, Bob, Joe, Reuben, Arthur and Albert discussed every page. Every club and every player. They planned every detail for every date. The details and the dates of every fixture, the details and the dates of every training session. Who, when and where. Who would do what, when they would it, and where they would do it. Page after page, hour after hour, day after day. They studied and they discussed. They discussed and they planned. Every date and every detail. Every single date, every last detail. Hour after hour, day after day –

Again. There would be the walks out to Melwood. The walks and then the jogs. Again. There would be the first jogs around the training pitch. The jogs and then the runs. Once and then twice. Again. There would be six groups. Again. At the start of the season, the players would be put into one of the groups: A, B, C, D, E or F. Again. The names of the players, the group they were in, would be listed on the noticeboard. Again. Each group would be given a different exercise, a physical exercise. A would be weight-training. B would be skipping. C would be jumping. D would be squats. E would be abdominal exercises. And F would be sprints. Again. Reuben would then blow his whistle. Again. The groups would then move onto the next exercise. Again and again, whistle after whistle. Until each group had completed each exercise. Then the whistle. Again. Each group would be given a different exercise, a football exercise. A would be passing. B would be dribbling. C would be heading. D would be chipping. E would be controlling. F would be tackling. Again. Reuben would then blow his whistle. Again. The groups would then move onto the next exercise. Again and again, whistle after whistle. Until each group had completed each exercise. Then the whistle. Again. The training boards would come out. Fifteen yards apart. To keep the ball in play, to keep the players moving. The players moving, the ball moving. To play the ball against one board, to take the ball and control the ball, to turn with the ball and dribble with the ball. Up to the other board, with just ten touches. To play the ball against the other board, to pull the ball down and turn. Again. To turn again and dribble again. Back down to the first board, with just ten touches. Then the whistle. Again. The sweat box would come out. Again. Ball after ball, into the box. Every second, another ball. For one minute, then for two minutes, then for three minutes. Again and again, whistle after whistle. Until each player in each group had been on the boards, until each player in each group had been in the box. Then the whistle. Again. There would be three-a-sides. Three-a-sides and then five-a-sides. Five-a-sides then seven-a-sides. Seven-a-sides then eleven-a-sides. Again and again.

Hour after hour. Day after day. Week after week. Until the players were prepared, until the players were ready. Prepared for the new season, ready for the new season. Prepared for the First Division, ready for the Big League. Everything planned. Down to the last detail. Everything prepared. Down to the last detail. Until Liverpool Football Club were prepared, until Liverpool Football Club were ready. So there would be no shocks, so there would be no surprises. Only plans, only preparations. No shocks and no surprises.

. . .

In his office, at his desk. Bill jumped to his feet. The telephone still in his hand, Horace Yates still on the line. The room spinning, the world turning. And Bill said again, They did *what*?

They've sold Johnny Morrissey to Everton, repeated Horace.

Bill said, I just don't believe it, Horace. I refuse to believe it.

But it's true, said Horace. I thought you knew, Bill.

Bill said, The bastards. The bastards.

I'm sorry, Bill. I'm sorry you had to hear it from me . . .

But Bill had dropped the phone and Bill was gone. Out the door, down the corridor. Into the office of the club secretary. On his feet, his arms wide. Jimmy McInnes was shaking his head –

I swear I didn't know, Boss. I only just found out myself . . .

Bill said, I'm not having it, Jimmy. I'm not standing for it. Not behind my back, behind my back. I'm going up there now, Jimmy, I'm going in there now. I'm going to have it out with them now . . .

But there's no one there, said Jimmy McInnes. There's no one there, Boss. They've already left. They've all gone home . . .

Well, you get them on the phone. You tell them to get back here. You tell them, Jimmy. You tell them Bill Shankly wants to see them. And see them now, Jimmy And if he doesn't see them, then they'll never see Bill Shankly again. Never again!

Jimmy McInnes nodded. He picked up the phone. Then he looked up. But Bill was gone again –

Back down the corridor, back into the office. Back behind the desk, back in the chair. Bill took out a piece of paper. Bill put the piece of paper into his typewriter. And Bill began to type. To bang the keys, to pound the keys. The noise of the keys, the sound of the keys. Echoing down the corridor, ringing round the stadium. And then Bill stopped typing. And Bill ripped the paper out of the machine. Bill slammed the paper down onto his desk. Bill took out his pen. Bill unscrewed the cap. And Bill scrawled his name, Bill scrawled his signature. Across the bottom of the paper, across the bottom of the letter. And then Bill put down the pen. And Bill folded up the letter. Bill stuffed the letter into an envelope. Bill thrust the envelope into his jacket pocket. Bill snatched his car keys off the top of the desk. And Bill stood up. Bill grabbed his hat from the hook on the back of the door. And Bill stormed out of his office. Bill slammed the door. Bill went down the corridor. Bill went out of the stadium. Bill went across the car park. Bill got into his car. Bill turned the key. And Bill drove. And Bill cursed. The bastards. The fucking bastards –

The treacherous fucking bastards.

In his office, at his desk. Matt Busby put his teaspoon down in the saucer. And Matt looked up from his cup –

When I'd just become the manager here, Bill. When I was still very raw in the job. I was sat in the directors' box. And this one director he was sat behind me. And during the game, he leaned forward, this man, and he said, said in a voice so that everyone could hear, why didn't you do so-and-so, Busby, why didn't you do this and why didn't you do that? And I sat there and I thought, Shall I turn round now and give him a blast? Because I wanted to, Bill. I wanted to. But I thought about it and I bit my tongue and I waited. And then, at the right moment, the moment that was convenient to me, which just happened to be in the gents, very convenient. I went up to this man, this director, and I said, Never dare say anything like that to me when other people can hear you. And this director, this man, he went pale and he never did say anything again. He never did. But at the next meeting, the next board meeting. I put it on the agenda. The very top of the agenda. *No interference by directors.* That's what I wrote . . .

But Matt, they've sold Morrissey! Bloody Morrissey.

Let me finish, Bill, said Matt Busby. Let me finish. Because that was not the end of it. That's just the legend. The story I always tell. But there was more. More battles than you know. And this one will make you smile, Bill. Even today. Feeling like you do. It'll make you smile. Because back in the 1947–48 season, we were having a bit of an indifferent spell. As everyone does, as every team does. And Jimmy

Gibson was still the chairman then. And you know what Jimmy was like. He was always anxious, he was always worried. And he thought the answer to our troubles was to sign somebody. Anybody. And he was right, we did need somebody. We did. But not just anybody. But every time he saw something in the paper, about some player being on offer, he would come and ask me if I was going to buy this player. And each time, I'd tell him no. Because it was not the player we needed, not the man I required. But finally, one day, he comes to me about this Newcastle player. I can't remember who, but the man was transfer-listed. The man was available. And so Jimmy comes to me and asks me if I'm going to sign him. And I said, No. He's no good for us. And Jimmy snaps. He says, Well, I'm not asking you to sign him. I'm *telling* you to sign him. To sign him and to play him. But I said, No, Mr Gibson. I will not sign him. And I will remind you of two things. I am here to manage the club and part of management is giving you advice. And the second is that I lived long before I ever saw you. So my answer is no and let that be the end of it. Well, Bill, I tell you. I thought the man was going to have a fit. He started to brandish that stick of his about. You remember that stick he had? I thought he was going to hit me with it. But he stamped off out of the room. And I'll be honest with you, Bill. I thought maybe I had overdone it. I thought maybe this time I had gone too far. But, anyway, fifteen minutes later, there's a knock on my door. And in he comes. And he says, Mr Busby, you are a very strong-minded person. You know what you want. And I like that. And I respect that. And so I have come back to say I am sorry this has happened. But it will not happen again. We will carry on as we were. And from that day, he neither interfered with my decisions nor brooked any interference from anyone else. And even when he was sick, even when he was dying, Jimmy Gibson would send for me and he would ask me, Is there anybody interfering with you, Mr Busby? If there is, then the man will have to go. That man will have to go . . .

Bill smiled. Bill nodded. And Bill picked up his cup.

But it didn't happen overnight, said Matt Busby. Not overnight, Bill. There were still many more battles. And there are still many battles. There are always battles. Always battles. But I never resigned, Bill. I have never resigned. Because I would never let them force my hand. I would never let them dictate the terms to me. So I never resigned, Bill. I've never resigned. Because I would never give them the satisfaction, Bill. I would never give them that satisfaction. And so that is my advice to you, Bill. Never give them the satisfaction.

. . .

In the boardroom, the Anfield boardroom. In the chair, the chair at the end of the long table. Bill stared down the long table at the directors of Liverpool Football Club. And Bill waited.

But Morrissey did not play a single game last season, said the directors of Liverpool Football Club. Not one in the season in which we were promoted, in which we were Champions. A'Court played in his position. In every game. So we thought Morrissey was not needed. We thought he was surplus to our requirements. We thought you would not mind, Mr Shankly. We thought you would not object.

Bill said, Well, you were wrong. You were all bloody wrong. Because I do mind. And I do object. Because he was far from surplus to our requirements. He was needed. He is only twenty-two years old. He is a fine prospect. And Harry Catterick obviously agrees. Obviously agrees with me. That is why Everton Football Club have bought him. That is why they have paid ten thousand pounds for him. And that should tell you everything. That should tell you what a mistake you have made. Against my wishes. And behind my back.

We did not realise you would feel so strongly about this, said the directors of Liverpool Football Club. But now the deal is done.

Bill nodded. And Bill said, Aye. The deal is done. But I still feel very, very strongly about it. Very, very strongly that you have made a mistake. A very, very grave mistake. And let me tell you another thing I feel very, very strongly about. Let me tell you this: if you ever go against my wishes again, if you ever go behind my back again. Then it will be the last time. The very last time. Because I am the manager of Liverpool Football Club. And so I decide who stays and who goes. Who plays and who doesn't. And if anyone in this room, if anyone around this table, does not accept that I am the manager of Liverpool Football Club, does not agree that I am the man who decides who stays and who goes, who plays and who doesn't, then they should say so now, they should speak up now. And then I'll be gone. I'll be on my way. So speak up now. Speak up now . . .

In the boardroom, the Anfield boardroom. There was silence.

And in the boardroom, the Anfield boardroom. At the end of the table, the long table. Bill got to his feet. And Bill walked out of the boardroom, the Anfield boardroom. Bill went back down the stairs. Bill went back into his office. Bill closed the door. And Bill sat back down. At his desk, in his chair. Bill took out the envelope from his jacket pocket. Bill opened the bottom drawer of his desk. And Bill put the envelope in the drawer. And Bill shut the drawer. For now.


## 11. IN THE BIG TIME

On Saturday 18 August, 1962, on the first day of the 1962–63 season, Blackpool Football Club came to Anfield, Liverpool. That afternoon, fifty-one thousand, two hundred and seven folk came, too. Fifty-one thousand, two hundred and seven folk to watch Liverpool Football Club's first game in the First Division for eight seasons –

Before the whistle, the first whistle of Liverpool Football Club's first game in the First Division. In the dressing room, the home dressing room. Jim Furnell, Gerry Byrne, Ronnie Moran, Gordon Milne, Ron Yeats, Tommy Leishman, Kevin Lewis, Roger Hunt, Ian St John, Jimmy Melia and Alan A'Court sat on the benches. In their kits and in their boots. Jim Furnell, Gerry Byrne, Ronnie Moran, Gordon Milne, Ron Yeats, Tommy Leishman, Kevin Lewis, Roger Hunt, Ian St John, Jimmy Melia and Alan A'Court waited for Bill Shankly. In their kits and in their boots. Jim Furnell, Gerry Byrne, Ronnie Moran, Gordon Milne, Ron Yeats, Tommy Leishman, Kevin Lewis, Roger Hunt, Ian St John, Jimmy Melia and Alan A'Court heard the footsteps in the corridor outside the dressing room. The fast steps, the heavy steps. And Jim Furnell, Gerry Byrne, Ronnie Moran, Gordon Milne, Ron Yeats, Tommy Leishman, Kevin Lewis, Roger Hunt, Ian St John, Jimmy Melia and Alan A'Court looked up from the benches. And now Jim Furnell, Gerry Byrne, Ronnie Moran, Gordon Milne, Ron Yeats, Tommy Leishman, Kevin Lewis, Roger Hunt, Ian St John, Jimmy Melia and Alan A'Court saw Bill Shankly. Bill Shankly in his hat and coat, Bill Shankly on pins and needles –

What a day, said Bill Shankly. What a day this is, boys! Can you hear that crowd? Can you hear them, lads? They cannot wait and I cannot wait. Because this is what we have been waiting for, boys. This is what we have been working for. The Big League, lads! This is what we have been dreaming about and what the supporters have been dreaming about. Playing in the Big League, boys. This is what it's all about. And so this is where it all starts, lads! Today . . .

In the eightieth minute, Kevin Lewis scored. But Liverpool Football Club lost two–one to Blackpool Football Club. In their first game in the First Division and for the first time since New Year's Eve of 1960. At home, at Anfield. Liverpool Football Club had lost.

On Wednesday 22 August, 1962, Liverpool Football Club travelled to Maine Road, Manchester. And Liverpool Football Club drew two-all with Manchester City. On Saturday 25 August, 1962, Liverpool Football Club travelled to Ewood Park, Blackburn. And Liverpool Football Club lost one–nil to Blackburn Rovers. That evening, Liverpool Football Club had one point from three games. That evening, in the first published League table of the new season, Everton Football Club were joint top of the First Division with Wolverhampton Wanderers. And that evening, Liverpool Football Club were joint bottom of the First Division with Leyton Orient.

On Wednesday 29 August, 1962, Manchester City came to Anfield, Liverpool. That evening, forty-six thousand and seventy-three folk came, too. In the third minute, Ian St John scored. In the fifty-fifth minute, Roger Hunt scored. In the sixty-fifth minute, Alan A'Court scored. And four minutes later, Hunt scored again. And Liverpool Football Club beat Manchester City four–one. At home, at Anfield. Liverpool Football Club had won their first game in the First Division. In the Big League –

In September, 1962, Liverpool Football Club beat Sheffield United. Then they lost at West Ham United, then they lost at Nottingham Forest. Then they beat West Ham United at home, then they drew with Ipswich Town at home. Liverpool Football Club were now eleventh in the First Division. Everton Football Club still second in the First Division.

. . .

In the night, they came. With cans of paint, through the park. Between the houses and over the walls. In the night, they came. Into Goodison Park, with cans of paint. To paint the goals and to paint them red. The Everton goals, they painted them red –

The Everton goals, at Goodison Park –

On Saturday 22 September, 1962, seventy-two thousand, four hundred and eighty-eight folk came to Goodison Park, Liverpool. Seventy-two thousand, four hundred and eighty-eight folk to watch the first League meeting of Everton Football Club and Liverpool Football Club for eleven years. Not since 1951 had these two football clubs played each other in a League fixture. Not until today. Today the shops of Liverpool were empty, today the streets of Liverpool were deserted. But there was no peace, there was no quiet. The ground shook, the air roared. Back across the city, out across the river. The ground shook and the air roared. It shook and it roared with the voices of the seventy-two thousand, four hundred and eighty-eight folk packed inside Goodison Park, Liverpool –

Before the whistle, the first whistle. In the dressing room, the away dressing room. In their kits and in their boots. Jim Furnell, Gerry Byrne, Ronnie Moran, Gordon Milne, Ron Yeats, Tommy Leishman, Ian Callaghan, Roger Hunt, Kevin Lewis, Jimmy Melia and Alan A'Court were shaking, too. Not with nerves, but with laughter –

And it's taken them all bloody morning to repaint those goals, said Bill Shankly. So it's no bloody wonder Harry Catterick's looking glummer than usual, lads. By, he's a miserable man is Harry. And I've just seen him, lads. In the corridor. And he's looking even glummer today, lads. Even more miserable than usual. And I know why, lads. I know why. Because I said to him, I said to Harry, All that money you have and the only player you can find to buy is one we don't want. A player we don't need. That lad Morrissey. I said to Harry, You know why we don't want him, why we let you have him? Because he's only got the one leg has Morrissey. His right leg. And he needs that one to stand on. So he was no use to us. That one-legged lad. And so you did us a favour, Harry. Taking Johnny Morrissey, poor Johnny Morrissey. So thank you, Harry, I said, Thank you very much, Harry. It was very good of you, Harry. It was very kind of you . . .

But in their kits and in their boots. Jim Furnell, Gerry Byrne, Ronnie Moran, Gordon Milne, Ron Yeats, Tommy Leishman, Ian Callaghan, Roger Hunt, Kevin Lewis, Jimmy Melia and Alan A'Court were no longer listening to Bill Shankly. Now in their kits and in their boots. Jim Furnell, Gerry Byrne, Ronnie Moran, Gordon Milne, Ron

Yeats, Tommy Leishman, Ian Callaghan, Roger Hunt, Kevin Lewis, Jimmy Melia and Alan A'Court were listening to the voices of the seventy-two thousand, four hundred and eighty-eight folk inside Goodison Park. In their kits and in their boots. They were listening and they were trembling. Not with laughter, now with fear. Their faces pale and their legs shaking. They could hardly stand, they could hardly walk. Out of the away dressing room, down the Goodison corridor. Onto the pitch and into the arena. Into the arena. The arena waiting,

waiting and baying, baying for blood,

their red, red blood –

In the first minute, the very first minute, Jim Furnell collected the ball, his back to the Park end, the noise from the Park end deafening, Furnell still trembling as he bounced the ball once, trying to steady himself, steady himself to kick the ball back up the field, the referee already running back up the field, his back to Furnell, Furnell bouncing the ball, Furnell dropping the ball, the ball running loose, Roy Vernon nipping in, Vernon saying, Thank you very much, Jim. Thank you very much as he rolled the ball into the net, into the net as the crowd roared with laughter, roared in celebration as Furnell held his head in his hands, his head in his hands and the ball in the goal –

Now the referee turned. Now the referee blew his whistle. And the referee shook his head. The referee disallowed the goal. The referee awarded a free kick to Liverpool Football Club. A free kick for an infringement by Vernon on Furnell. And now the crowd roared, roared with indignation, roared with injustice, shouting of cheat and deceit, of robbery and theft, baying for righteousness, righteousness and the blood of the referee, his red, red blood –

And the players of Liverpool Football Club stared down at the ground, the pitch and the grass. The players of Liverpool Club would not look up. From the ground, the pitch and the grass. The players of Liverpool Football Club could not look up. And seven minutes later, the ball was in the back of their net again. But again the referee blew his whistle. Again the referee shook his head. Again the referee disallowed the goal. Again the referee awarded a free kick to Liverpool Football Club. A free kick for an offside against Stevens. And again the crowd roared with indignation, roared with injustice, shouting of cheat and deceit, of robbery and theft, baying for righteousness, righteousness and the blood of the referee, his red, red blood. And still the players of Liverpool Football Club stared down at the ground, the pitch and the grass. Still the players of Liverpool Football Club would not look up. From the ground, the pitch and the grass. Still the players of Liverpool Football Club could not look up. And now Everton came at them again. Again and again. Ball after ball. Into the Liverpool penalty area. Again and again. Ball after ball until one ball, one ball bounced up against the hand of Gerry Byrne, the hand of Gerry Byrne in the Liverpool penalty area. And again the referee blew his whistle. But now the referee nodded. And now the referee pointed to the penalty spot. And now Vernon placed the ball upon the penalty spot. And Vernon placed the ball in the back of the Liverpool goal. And now the crowd roared with laughter, roared in celebration, in celebration of justice, of justice done –

But now, in amongst that laughter, in amongst that celebration, now other voices began to rise, began to echo, quietly and slowly, then louder and faster. *LI-VER-POOL, LI-VER-POOL, LI-VER-POOL . . .*

And now the players of Liverpool Football Club looked up from the ground, from the pitch and from the grass. Now the players of Liverpool Football Club looked for each other. And on the pitch and on the grass. They found each other. And now the players of Liverpool Football Club looked for the ball. And they found the ball. And now they moved forward with the ball, forward with each other, into the Everton half, towards the Everton goal, Callaghan hooking the ball into the Everton penalty area, Lewis hitting that ball, hitting that ball on the volley, on the volley and into the back of the Everton net, the ball in the back of the Everton goal. And now it was one-all –

At half-time in the dressing room. In the away dressing room at Goodison Park. Bill Shankly, Bob Paisley, Joe Fagan and Reuben Bennett went from player to player. Praising each player, encouraging each player. Bill Shankly, Bob Paisley, Joe Fagan and Reuben Bennett filling each player with confidence, filling each player with belief. Confidence in themselves, belief in themselves. Confidence in each other, belief in each other. In themselves and in each other. And now the players were listening to Bill Shankly, Bob Paisley, Joe Fagan and Reuben Bennett. Now the players were not listening to the voices of the seventy-two thousand, four hundred and eighty-eight folk inside

Goodison Park. Now they stood back up, now they walked back out. Back out of the dressing room, back down the corridor. Back onto the pitch, back into the arena. Still hearing those words of Bill Shankly, Bob Paisley, Joe Fagan and Reuben Bennett, still hearing that chant of *LI-VER-POOL, LI-VER-POOL, LI-VER-POOL . . .*

In the second half, the players of Liverpool Football Club played with enthusiasm, they played with thrust. But the players of Everton Football Club had the guile, they had the skill. In the sixty-third minute, a shot from Vernon was blocked, blocked only to fall to Johnny Morrissey. Morrissey shot but Ronnie Moran got to the ball. The ball on the line. And Moran cleared the ball off the line. But the referee blew his whistle. The referee nodded. And the referee said the ball had crossed the line. Into the goal. And the referee awarded a goal. A goal to Everton. A goal to Johnny Morrissey. His first for Everton Football Club. And the players of Liverpool Football Club looked to the bench, the Liverpool bench. And the players of Liverpool Football Club saw Bill Shankly. Up on his feet, his finger in the air. Pointing into the air, pointing to the voices. In the air, the Liverpool voices. *LI-VER-POOL, LI-VER-POOL, LI-VER-POOL.* Bill Shankly with his arms outstretched now, Bill Shankly with his palms open now. Urging his boys to keep their eyes from the ground, urging his lads to keep their heads up. To keep looking for each other, to keep looking for the ball. To keep going forward, forward to the goal. Bill Shankly never looking at the clock, Bill Shankly never looking at his watch. Bill Shankly knowing the time, the time would come. On the wing, down the wing. In the eighty-ninth minute, Alan A'Court looped the ball into the centre of the Everton penalty area. Kevin Lewis headed the ball down. Down to the feet of Roger Hunt. And Roger Hunt rolled the ball across the line. Across the line, into the net. The net of the goal that had been painted red overnight, that had taken the groundsmen all morning to clean and repaint, that Everton goal that was now red again, red again in the eighty-ninth minute –

Red again.

. . .

One week after Liverpool Football Club had drawn two-all with Everton Football Club, Liverpool Football Club travelled to Molineux, Wolverhampton. And Liverpool Football Club lost three–

two to Wolverhampton Wanderers. One week later, Bolton Wanderers came to Anfield, Liverpool. That afternoon, forty-one thousand, one hundred and fifty-five folk came, too. And in the thirty-seventh minute, Roger Hunt scored. And Liverpool Football Club beat Bolton Wanderers one–nil. One week after that, Liverpool Football Club lost three–nil to Leicester City. That evening, Liverpool Football Club were thirteenth in the First Division. After thirteen games, they were thirteenth. In the Big League. Everton Football Club were first. In the First Division. Everton Football Club top –

In the Big League –

After the game at Filbert Street, after Liverpool Football Club had travelled back to Anfield. Bob Paisley walked down the corridor. Bob Paisley knocked on the door to the office of Bill Shankly. Bob Paisley opened the door. And Bob Paisley saw Bill Shankly sat behind his desk. Bill Shankly turning the pages of a book, Bill Shankly staring at the pages of the book. And Bob Paisley said, I'm afraid I've got some bad news, Boss. Some very bad news . . .

Is there any other kind of news these days, asked Bill Shankly. So go on then, Bob, what is it now?

Bob said, Well, it turns out Jim Furnell has broken a finger.

He's broken a finger, said Bill Shankly. Only the one?

Bob nodded. And Bob said, Yes. Only the one, Boss. But it's broken all right. And so he cannot play, Boss. Not for a while . . .

Go on, said Bill Shankly. So what's the bad news, Bob?

Bob said, Well, that *is* the bad news, Boss.

Bad news, laughed Bill Shankly. That's not bad news, Bob. That's great news! The best news we've had all season, Bob.

How is that great news, Boss? Our keeper is out.

Because it saves me breaking all his other fingers. It saves me telling him he's dropped. It saves me telling him Tommy Lawrence has got his shirt. That Tommy's got his shirt and he'll never give it back. It saves me telling Jim Furnell he'll never play for Liverpool Football Club again. That's why it's great news, Bob. Great news!

And on Saturday 27 October, 1962, Liverpool Football Club travelled to the Hawthorns, Birmingham. But Liverpool Football Club lost one–nil to West Bromwich Albion. It was Tommy Lawrence's first game in goal for Liverpool Football Club.

. . .

In the night, the long night. Sidney Reakes, Eric Sawyer and Bill Shankly drove up to Glasgow. They parked outside the Central Hotel on Gordon Street. They walked into the bar of the Central Hotel. And they saw Willie Stevenson sat at the bar. Willie was smoking a Padron Serie 1926 cigar, Willie sipping a Courvoisier cognac.

Good evening, said Bill Shankly. That's a very fine suit you are wearing, Billy. Did you buy that in Australia?

Willie Stevenson looked up from his brandy. Willie smiled. And Willie said, No. I bought it on Savile Row, Mr Shankly.

Aye, said Bill Shankly. That makes more sense. I didn't think they made suits as fine as that Down Under. Must be hard to find cigars like that one, too. And a decent brandy. They are not known for their cigars or for their brandy, are they? The Australians?

Willie Stevenson smiled again. And Willie said, No, they are not. You are right, Mr Shankly. But I did not go there for their brandy or for their cigars. I went to Australia for their weather. And I went there to play some football. To play some football . . .

Ah yes, said Bill Shankly. The football. But do they play any football down there? Football like we do, like we play? I heard they had different rules in Australia, Billy?

Willie Stevenson shook his head. And Willie said, They have their Australian Rules football. But they also play football like we do. Soccer. With the same rules.

Well, I'm glad to hear that, said Bill Shankly. I'm very glad. So then what brought you back, Billy? Back here to Glasgow, back to Rangers. Why didn't you stay down there, Billy? In the sunshine?

Willie Stevenson took a sip of his cognac. Willie sighed, Willie shook his head. And Willie said, Well, I couldn't get the permission I needed, Mr Shankly. The clearance to play.

Oh, I'm very sorry to hear that, said Bill Shankly. I'm very sorry indeed. And so that's why you've had to come back then, Billy? Back here to Glasgow, back to Rangers. And back to their reserves?

Willie Stevenson nodded. And Willie said, Yes. But obviously I'm hoping not to be playing in the reserves. I'm hoping for some first-team football. To be playing some proper football . . .

Is that right, asked Bill Shankly. Well then, I hope that happens for you, Billy. I really do. But I must say, I would be worried . . .

Willie Stevenson took another sip of his brandy. And then Willie said, And why would you be worried, Mr Shankly?

Well, I'm not a man who normally believes much in luck, said Bill Shankly. Good luck or bad, Billy. I believe a man makes his own luck. Through his determination and through his skill. His determination to use what skill he has, his determination to make that skill work for him. Through hard work, not through luck. But I have to say, Billy. I think you are a very unlucky man . . .

Willie Stevenson stared down at the end of his cigar. And Willie said, Oh, really? Do you now? So why is that, Mr Shankly? Why do you think I am an unlucky man?

Well, I can tell you why, said Bill Shankly. I can tell you why in two simple words: Jim Baxter. Jim Baxter is a great player. A great player for Rangers Football Club. But you are a great player, too. A player of great ability, a player of great vision. And for you to find yourself in the same squad as a player like Jim Baxter, a player in the very same position as yourself. Now that is unlucky. That is why you are an unlucky man, Billy. But it happens. It happens in football.

Willie Stevenson took another sip of his brandy. And then Willie nodded. And Willie said, And it's happened to me . . .

Yes, said Bill Shankly. It's happened to you. But you're not the first and you won't be the last. I've seen it before, many times before. And it's never nice, Billy. Never pleasant. Because it reduces a man. It reduces a man to hoping for the worst for another man, for his teammate. Reduces him to sitting in bars, drinking and brooding, hoping that the other man gets injured, or loses his form. And that's no way for a man to live, Billy. For any man to live. Hoping for the worst for another man, his fellow man, his teammate. Drinking and brooding, hoping for the worst, for a broken leg for another man. For a bloody piano to fall from the sky onto the head of another man. That's no way to live, is it, Billy? Not for a man of your ability, a man of your talent.

Willie Stevenson nodded. And Willie said, So then what do you suggest I do about it, Mr Shankly?

Well, I suggest you change your luck, said Bill Shankly. And I suggest you change your life, Billy. It might not have worked out for you in Australia. But it can work out for you in Liverpool. So I suggest you join us, Billy. I suggest you join Liverpool Football Club. Where you can play some football. Some first-team football. In the First Division, in the Big League. Where you belong, Billy. A player of your ability, a player of your vision. At Liverpool Football Club, Billy. In the First Division, in the Big League. Where you bloody belong.

Willie Stevenson said, I'll need to have a think about it.

Well, I'll tell you what, said Bill Shankly. Why don't we take you for a little drive, Billy? Take you for a wee drive so you can have your little think? How about we all do that, Billy?

Willie Stevenson nodded. Willie put out his cigar, Willie finished his cognac. And then Willie followed Bill Shankly, Eric Sawyer and Sidney Reakes out of the bar and into the street to the car.

Willie Stevenson looked at the Rolls-Royce. Willie whistled. Willie looked at Bill Shankly. And Willie said, This is a very nice car, Mr Shankly. I've never been in a Rolls-Royce before . . .

Really, said Bill Shankly. This is the first time you've ever been in a Rolls-Royce? Well, I am surprised, Billy. I must say, I am very surprised. A man of your style, a man of your taste. But I suppose we do get a wee bit blasé down in Liverpool. I mean, riding around in our Rolls-Royces all day. Perhaps we do get a wee bit blasé, Billy.

You mean you've got more? More than one?

Oh aye, said Bill Shankly. I've got ten Rolls-Royces down in Liverpool, Billy. And I've a mind to buy another. I'm always on the look out for another Rolls-Royce, Billy.

. . .

On Saturday 3 November, 1962, Burnley Football Club came to Anfield, Liverpool. That afternoon, forty-three thousand, eight hundred and seventy folk came, too. And in the fiftieth minute, Ian St John scored. But Liverpool Football Club lost two–one to Burnley Football Club. It was Willie Stevenson's first game for Liverpool Football Club. At home, at Anfield. That night, Liverpool Football Club were nineteenth in the First Division. This season, Liverpool Football Club had played fifteen games in the First Division. They had lost eight games and they had drawn three games. In the First Division, in the Big League. Liverpool Football Club had won only four games. In the pubs and in the clubs of Liverpool, folk began to talk of the gulf in class. The gulf between the Second Division and the First Division, the gulf between the little leagues and the Big League. Between the little boys and the Big Men. Between your Liverpools and Leyton Orients and your Evertons and Manchester Uniteds –

On Saturday 10 November, 1962, Liverpool Football Club travelled to Old Trafford, Manchester. That afternoon, forty-three thousand, eight hundred and ten folk came, too. Forty-three thousand, eight hundred and ten folk to watch the Big Men play the little boys –

Before the whistle, the first whistle. In the dressing room, the away dressing room. Tommy Lawrence, Gerry Byrne, Ronnie Moran, Gordon Milne, Ron Yeats, Willie Stevenson, Ian Callaghan, Roger Hunt, Ian St John, Jimmy Melia and Alan A'Court watched Bill Shankly. In the dressing room, the away dressing room. Bill Shankly in his coat, Bill Shankly in his hat. In the mirror, the dressing-room mirror. Adjusting the lapels of his coat, adjusting the brim of his hat. In the mirror, the dressing-room mirror. Bill Shankly smiled –

You all know what I think of Matt, lads. The respect I have for Matt. For all that he has done, for all that he has achieved. And we all know we have not had the best of starts ourselves, we all know the position we are in. But it breaks my heart to see the season Matt is having, the results United have had. And today, to see the team Matt is forced to field. It breaks my heart, it really does. They are a shadow of their former selves, they really are. It's no wonder Matt is always on the phone to me, asking me if any of you are on offer, available for transfer. I know for a fact he'd take any one of you, any one of you, boys. Because they are a makeshift side, this side today. A makeshift United. And so it breaks my heart, lads, it really does. Because today we're going to turn the corner, we're going to turn our season around. So it breaks my heart because we're going to do it here, here today. But then again, they've had the glory long enough, lads. They've had it long enough. And so now it's our turn, boys . . .

In the first half, Herd scored for United. In the second half, Ian St John equalised. Halfway through the second half, Quixall scored a penalty. Then with five minutes to go, Jimmy Melia equalised. And then with one minute to go, Liverpool Football Club were awarded a free kick twenty-five yards from the United goal. Ronnie Moran stepped up. Moran shot. From twenty-five yards out. Moran scored. But then in the very last second of the game, with the very last kick of the match, Giles equalised. And Liverpool Football Club drew three-all with Manchester United –

After the whistle, the final whistle. Matt Busby walked down the touchline at Old Trafford. Matt Busby shook Bill Shankly's hand. Matt Busby smiled. And Matt Busby said, I should've kept my mouth shut, Bill. I should have let you resign that day!

I'll take that as a compliment, Matt.

Matt Busby smiled again. And Matt Busby said, And so you should, Bill. So you should. That's a good side you've got there, Bill. A very good side, the best side we've played so far.

Thank you, said Bill Shankly. Thank you very much, Matt. But I know we have only just begun. Today was only the start.

. . .

Every morning, Liverpool Football Club trained in the wind. Liverpool Football Club played in the wind. And Liverpool Football Club beat Arsenal Football Club in the wind. Every morning, Liverpool Football Club trained in the rain. Liverpool Football Club played in the rain. And Liverpool Football Club beat Leyton Orient in the rain. Every morning, Liverpool Football Club trained in the mud. Liverpool Football Club played in the mud. And Liverpool Football Club beat Birmingham City in the mud. Every morning, Liverpool Football Club trained in the fog. Liverpool Football Club played in the fog. And Liverpool Football Club beat Fulham Football Club in the fog. Every morning, Liverpool Football Club trained in the sleet. Liverpool Football Club played in the sleet. And Liverpool Football Club beat Sheffield Wednesday in the sleet. Every morning, Liverpool Football Club trained in the gales. Liverpool Football Club played in the gales. And Liverpool Football Club beat Blackpool Football Club in the gales. Every morning, Liverpool Football Club trained in the wind and in the rain, in the mud and in the fog, in the sleet and in the gales. Liverpool Football Club played in the wind and in the rain, in the mud and in the fog, in the sleet and in the gales. And Liverpool Football Club beat Blackburn Rovers in the wind and in the rain, in the mud and in the fog, in the sleet and in the gales. And in the wind and in the rain, in the mud and in the fog, in the sleet and in the gales, Liverpool Football Club won seven games in a row. And now Liverpool Football Club were fifth in the First Division. But then the snow came. And then the ice came. So the snow stayed,

and the ice stayed –

The Big Freeze –

Everything frozen, everything stopped. Fixtures postponed, matches abandoned. The country battered by blizzards, the land blanketed in snow. Drifts reached twenty feet, gales reached one hundred and nineteen miles an hour. Mile-long sheets of ice stretched out across the sea. It was the coldest winter since 1740. And between 22 December, 1962, and 12 February, 1963, Liverpool Football Club could not play a single League game. But on Wednesday 9 January, 1963, after two postponements, Liverpool Football Club travelled to the Racecourse Ground, Wrexham. And in the nineteenth minute, Roger Hunt scored. In the seventy-second minute, Kevin Lewis scored. And in the eighty-ninth minute, Jimmy Melia scored. And Liverpool Football Club beat Wrexham Football Club three–nil in the Third Round of the FA Cup.

On Saturday 26 January, 1963, Liverpool Football Club travelled to Turf Moor, Burnley, for a game that had been only fifty–fifty, had been only touch and go. And in the twenty-fifth minute, Kevin Lewis scored. But Liverpool Football Club drew one-all with Burnley Football Club in the Fourth Round of the FA Cup. The replay was scheduled for the following Wednesday. But the following Monday, the draw for the next round of the FA Cup was postponed. That Monday, the Football League season was extended until the nineteenth of May. And the following Wednesday, the replay between Liverpool Football Club and Burnley was postponed –

Indefinitely.

But Liverpool Football Club borrowed halls. Halls from schools. And Liverpool Football Club trained in the halls. The halls of schools. Liverpool Football Club organised friendly games. Friendly games overseas. Liverpool Football Club braved the seas. The Irish seas. And Liverpool Football Club travelled to Ireland. Liverpool Football Club trained in Dublin. Liverpool Football Club played in Dublin. And Liverpool Football Club beat Drumcondra Football Club five–one at Tolka Park, Dublin. And then Liverpool Football Club travelled back. Back to Merseyside, back to school. Again. In borrowed halls. Liverpool Football Club trained and Liverpool Football Club prepared. Prepared to play, ready to play –

Prepared and ready.

And every day, Arthur Riley and his staff cleared the snow from the ground, the snow from the pitch. Every day, bit by bit, patch by patch. Arthur Riley and his staff placed braziers on the ground, on the pitch. They lit the braziers to warm the ground, to thaw the pitch. They moved the braziers across the ground, across the pitch. Every day, bit by bit, patch by patch. Arthur Riley and his staff put sand upon the ground, sand upon the pitch. To protect the ground, to protect the pitch. Until the ground was prepared,

until the pitch was ready –

Prepared and ready.

On Wednesday 13 February, 1963, Aston Villa came to Anfield, Liverpool. In the snow and in the ice. That evening, forty-six thousand, three hundred and seventy-four folk came to Anfield, too. In the snow and in the ice. In the eighteenth minute, Roger Hunt scored. In the twenty-fifth minute, Ian St John scored. In the twenty-ninth minute, St John scored again. And in the sixty-sixth minute, Hunt scored again. And Liverpool Football Club beat Aston Villa four–nil. At home, at Anfield. In the snow and in the ice. Three days after that, Wolverhampton Wanderers came to Anfield, Liverpool. Again in the snow, again in the ice. That afternoon, fifty-three thousand, five hundred and seventeen folk came to Anfield, too. In the snow and in the ice. In the seventh minute, Kevin Lewis scored. In the forty-seventh minute, Ian St John scored. In the fifty-second minute, Lewis scored again. And in the eighty-seventh minute, St John scored again. And Liverpool Football Club beat Wolverhampton Wanderers four–one. At home, at Anfield. In the snow and in the ice. That evening, Liverpool Football Club had not lost in their last twelve games. Liverpool Football Club had won their last nine League games. Liverpool Football Club still fifth in the First Division. Liverpool Football Club still prepared. Liverpool Football Club still ready. Prepared for Burnley, ready for their replay –

On Wednesday 20 February, 1963, Burnley Football Club came to Anfield, Liverpool. That evening, fifty-seven thousand, nine hundred and six folk came to Anfield, too. Fifty-seven thousand, nine hundred and six folk to watch Liverpool Football Club play Burnley

Football Club in the Fourth Round replay of the FA Cup. In the forty-fifth minute, Ian St John scored. But at half-time, the score was one-all. And at full time, the score was still one-all. And after twenty-nine minutes of extra time, the score was still one-all. But then in the Burnley goal, Blacklaw went to kick the ball upfield, upfield for the very last kick of the match. But when Blacklaw went to kick, Blacklaw delayed his kick. And when Blacklaw kicked the ball, the ball hit Ian St John. St John pounced on the ball, St John darted past Blacklaw. Blacklaw grabbed St John, Blacklaw stopped St John. And the referee blew his whistle. The referee pointed to the penalty spot. Moran placed the ball on the penalty spot. And Moran slammed the ball into the Burnley net. With the very last kick, in the very last second. Anfield erupted. In the very last second, with the very last kick, Liverpool Football Club were in the Fifth Round of the FA Cup –

Liverpool Football Club had been prepared. Liverpool Football Club had been ready. Prepared to play, ready to win –

Always prepared, always ready.

But then the snow came again. And then the ice came again. And so the snow stayed again, and the ice stayed

again. Again the Big Freeze,

still the Big Freeze –

On Saturday 23 February, 1963, Liverpool Football Club should have travelled to Burnden Park, Bolton. Liverpool Football Club should have played Bolton Wanderers. But the game was postponed. Two weeks later, there were still braziers on the Anfield ground, still sand upon the Anfield pitch. But Leicester City still came to Anfield, Liverpool. And that afternoon, fifty-four thousand, eight hundred and forty-two folk still came, too. Fifty-four thousand, eight hundred and forty-two folk surging, fifty-four thousand, eight hundred and forty-two folk singing *LI-VER-POOL, LI-VER-POOL, LI-VER-POOL. LI-VER-POOL, LI-VER-POOL, LI-VER-POOL. LI-VER-POOL, LI-VER-POOL, LI-VER-POOL . . .*

Liverpool Football Club were fifth in the First Division. Leicester City were second in the First Division. Leicester City had won their last eight League games. Liverpool Football Club had won their last nine League games. But Leicester City beat Liverpool Football Club two–nil. At home, at Anfield. Leicester City silenced the

fifty-four thousand, eight hundred and forty-two folk inside Anfield.
No more surging, no more singing –
 Now only silence,
 only silence.


## 12. A DRESS REHEARSAL

In the house, in their kitchen. In the night and in the silence. At the
table, in the chair. In the night and in the silence. Bill stared at the
bowls and the plates, the salt and pepper pots, the jars of honey and
marmalade. Bill picked up the bowls and the plates, the salt and pepper
pots, the jars of honey and marmalade. Bill moved the bowls and the
plates, the salt and pepper pots, the jars of honey and marmalade to the
edges of the cloth, to the sides of the table. Bill picked up the four
forks and the four knives and the four spoons. Bill held the four knives
and the four forks and the four spoons in his hand. Bill stared down at
the tablecloth. Bill placed one spoon on the cloth. *Banks.* Bill placed
two other spoons in front of the first spoon. *Sjöberg, Norman.* Bill
placed three forks in front of the spoons. *McLintock, King, Appleton.*
Bill placed the four knives in front of the three forks. *Riley, Cross,
Gibson, Stringfellow.* Bill placed the last fork in front of the four
knives. *Keyworth.* At the table, in the chair. In the night and in the
silence. Bill stared down at the three spoons, the four forks and the
four knives. And the three spoons, the four forks and the four knives
began to move. They began to turn. And the three spoons, the four
forks and the four knives would not stop moving. They would not stop
turning. The three spoons, the four forks and the four knives spinning
and swirling before his eyes. Like cogs. Moving and turning, spinning
and swirling before Bill's eyes. Like gears. Moving and turning,
spinning and swirling. Never pausing, never stopping. Only moving,
only turning. Like cogs. Always spinning, always swirling. Like gears.
At the table, in the chair. In the night and in the silence. Bill felt
nauseous, Bill felt sick. Bill dropped the last spoon onto the kitchen
floor. Bill rubbed his eyes. At the table, in the chair. In the night and in
the silence. Bill stood up. Bill walked back out of the kitchen. Bill
walked back into the other room. Bill walked back over to the other

chair. Bill picked up his book from the arm of the chair. His book of names, his book of notes. Bill walked back out of the room. Bill walked back into the kitchen. Bill sat back down. At the table, in the chair. In the night and in the silence. Bill stared back down at the three spoons, the four forks and the four knives. Bill took out his pen. His red pen. Bill opened his book. His book of names, his book of notes. And at the table, sat in the chair. In the night and in the silence. Bill began to write. To write down names, to write down notes. To draw squares, to draw arrows. To make diagrams, to make plans. At the table, in the chair. In the night and in the silence. Before the spoons, before the forks. And before the knives –

It was already light again,

already morning

again.

. . .

In the dressing room, the away dressing room at Highbury. Bill took his hat off the back of the dressing-room door. And Bill put on his hat. Bill pulled the brim of his hat down low. Bill opened the dressing-room door. Bill stepped out into the corridor at Highbury. And Bill saw the gentlemen of the London sporting press. Bill stuck out his jaw, Bill held up his finger. And Bill said, What an encounter that was. An encounter of epic proportions! Furiously fast and instinctively skilful. It was a battle to delight even the most demanding of *you*. And more-than-ample reward for those who endured the foulest of weathers to watch it. More-than-ample reward! To witness such collective enthusiasm. Such rare courage! Such insistence upon attack. And it was a battle, was it not, of two equally powerful but too equally skilful wing-halves? Their boy Eastham and our man Melia. What a battle, what an encounter! One or the other, forever springing forward, forever galloping into enemy territory. Even in such rank conditions, even in such treacherous mud. Neither player could be impeded, neither man could be restrained. You saw the way Melia pounced on every ball. The way he shrugged off every tackle. The sudden changes of direction, the quick feints this way and then that. And then the balls, then the passes he sent. What balls, what passes. The way he sent St John through, the way he put Hunt through. Time and time again. Despite the conditions, despite the mud. And then there was Yeats.

What a player he is, what a man he is. He stood astride the middle like a colossus. A colossus of flesh and a colossus of blood. Time and time again, calmly swatting away the pin-pricks of their passes, swatting them away like an irritating fly. The player was immoveable, the man was imperious. A colossus of flesh, a colossus of blood! As the battle raged about him. But what a battle, what an encounter! You gentlemen must surely count yourselves amongst the luckiest men on earth to have seen such a game, to have witnessed such a match. And to be paid for that pleasure, to be paid for that privilege, into the bargain. To be bloody paid to watch it, to be bloody paid to write about it. I tell you, I envy you, gentlemen. I truly do. I envy you men, I truly do!

But what about next week, asked the gentlemen of the London sporting press. Who will win next week, Bill? In the Cup?

Bill smiled, Bill laughed. And Bill said, Have you not been listening? Have you not heard a word I've said? Next week there can be only one victor. Next week there will be only one winner. Liverpool Football Club. You mark my words. And so you come back and see. Because I'm never wrong. I'm never wrong.

. . .

On the train, the train back to Liverpool. In the carriage, in his seat. Bill closed his book. His book of names, his book of notes. And in the carriage, in his seat. Bill closed his eyes. And Bill felt the wheels of the train beneath him now. Turning, turning. Their movement and their rhythm. Round and round. Movement and rhythm. Forward, always forward. *LI-VER-POOL.* Sweeping Arsenal off the ball, their passes astray and their shooting awry. *LI-VER-POOL.* Again and again, as Liverpool came. *LI-VER-POOL.* Forward, always forward. *LI-VER-POOL.* Always five forward. *LI-VER-POOL.* Callaghan, Hunt, St John, Melia and Lewis. *LI-VER-POOL.* Always backed, always reinforced by Milne and by Stevenson. *LI-VER-POOL.* Forward, always forward. *LI-VER-POOL.* But built on stone, built on rock. *LI-VER-POOL.* Yeats again immoveable, Yeats again imperious. *LI-VER-POOL.* At the back between Byrne and Moran. *LI-VER-POOL.* Yeats, Byrne and Moran protecting Lawrence, shielding Lawrence. *LI-VER-POOL.* Building from the back, but building always forward. *LI-VER-POOL.* At every chance, at every opportunity. *LI-VER-POOL.* A throw-in on the left. *LI-VER-POOL.* A deception by Hunt. *LI-VER-*

POOL. Hunt slipping the ball through to Melia. *LI-VER-POOL.* Melia shooting. *LI-VER-POOL.* Melia scoring. *LI-VER-POOL.* One–nil. *LI-VER-POOL. LI-VER-POOL. LI-VER-POOL.* And then on a corner. *LI-VER-POOL.* Another corner. *LI-VER-POOL.* A corner from Lewis. *LI-VER-POOL.* The ball swirling. *LI-VER-POOL.* And their man Barnwell, under no pressure at that moment, but having been harried for an hour, their man Barnwell handling the ball, handling out of the pressure, the imagined pressure, handling out of fear, the very real fear. *LI-VER-POOL.* And then the penalty. *LI-VER-POOL.* And then the goal. *LI-VER-POOL.* From the spot. *LI-VER-POOL.* By Moran. *LI-VER-POOL.* Two–nil. *WE WANT THREE!* The noise from the Liverpool supporters. *WE WANT THREE!* The Liverpool supporters packed into the North Stand. *WE WANT THREE!* Urging Liverpool Football Club forward. *LI-VER-POOL.* Rhythmically. *LI-VER-POOL.* Over and over. *LI-VER-POOL.* Forward, always forward. *LI-VER-POOL.* Movement and rhythm. *LI-VER-POOL.* Round and round. *LI-VER-POOL.* Their movement and their rhythm. *LI-VER-POOL.* Turning, turning. *LI-VER-POOL.* Like the wheels of a train. And in the carriage, in his seat. Bill opened his eyes again. And Bill looked down the carriage. Bob, Joe and Reuben were sat further down the carriage with the players. Tonight the players were not playing cards or reading books. Tonight the players were laughing and singing. *WE'RE GOING TO WIN THE CUP.* Tonight the players were drinking. *WE'RE GOING TO WIN THE CUP.* Tonight the players were celebrating. *EE-AYE-ADDIO, WE'RE GOING TO WIN THE CUP.* Today Liverpool Football Club had beaten Arsenal Football Club two–one in the Fifth Round of the FA Cup. And in the carriage, in his seat. Bill smiled. He had not been wrong, he had not been wrong.

. . .

In the dug-out, on the bench. The Anfield bench. Bill was nervous. And on the pitch, the Anfield pitch. The players of Liverpool Football Club were nervous. And in the stands, the Anfield stands. The forty-nine thousand and thirty-six supporters of Liverpool Football Club were nervous, too. Twice now, Byrne had had to clear off the Liverpool goal line. Time and again, Byrne's tackles, Byrne's interceptions, had kept Liverpool Football Club in the FA Cup. And now with nine minutes to go, with a hush across the ground, the

Anfield ground, it was Byrne again, Gerry Byrne again who intercepted another West Ham ball, Byrne again who passed to Gordon Milne, so Milne could send Willie Stevenson away, away over the halfway line, over the halfway line and on to Jimmy Melia, Melia who then passed to Roger Hunt, Hunt still well to the left of the West Ham goal. But this time, and only this time, there was no challenge, no West Ham challenge. And as their keeper came, as Standen came, Hunt screwed the ball, the ball round Standen from an incredible angle, an incredible angle and into the back of the net. *We're going to win the Cup.* At last, at last. The ball in the back of the West Ham net and Liverpool Football Club in the hat. *We're going to win the Cup.* At last, at last. In the hat for the draw for the semi-finals of the FA Cup –

*Ee-aye-addio, we're going to win the Cup!*

. . .

In the dug-out, on the bench. The Anfield bench. Bill was furious. The players of Liverpool Football Club had been outplayed, the players of Liverpool Football Club had been outclassed. And the fifty-four thousand four hundred and sixty-three supporters of Liverpool Football Club had been silenced. Liverpool Football Club were losing two–nil to Tottenham Hotspur. At home, at Anfield. In the dug-out, on the bench. Bill stood up. Bill walked down the touchline. Bill walked down the tunnel. Bill walked into the dressing room. Bill left the dressing-room door open. Bill looked around the dressing room. Bill pointed out of the dressing-room door. Bill pointed out into the corridor. And Bill said, Do you hear that sound? That is the sound of laughter. Laughter from the Tottenham dressing room. Because they are laughing at you, they are laughing at Liverpool Football Club. They are thinking the job is done, they are thinking they have beaten Liverpool Football Club. That you have given up, that Liverpool Football Club have submitted. Given up and bloody submitted –

Bill turned back to the dressing-room door. Bill slammed the dressing-room door shut. Bill looked back around the dressing room again. Bill pointed at each player of Liverpool Football Club. And Bill said, Well, let me tell you. Each and every one of you. I despise the word submission, I loathe the word submission. It should be cut out of the dictionary. It should be struck from the language. It should be banished. It should be forgotten. Because I won't have it. I refuse to have it! Not here at Anfield. Not at Liverpool Football Club!

In the dug-out, on the bench. Bill did not look at his watch. Bill just waited for the moment to come. The moment Bill knew would come. The moment when Stevenson scored, the moment when Melia equalised, the moment when St John scored, the moment when Lewis scored and the moment when Melia scored again. His second goal, their fifth goal. And Liverpool Football Club had come from two goals down at half-time to beat Tottenham Hotspur five–two at full time.

. . .

In the dug-out, on the bench at White Hart Lane. Three days later, just three days later. Again. Bill did not look at his watch. Again. Bill waited for the moment to come. But this time the moment did not come. Again. Tottenham Hotspur scored first. Again. Liverpool Football Club equalised. But then Tottenham scored. Again. Tottenham scored. Again. Tottenham scored. And then Liverpool scored. But again. Tottenham scored. And again. And again. And Tottenham Hotspur beat Liverpool Football Club seven–two.

. . .

In the house, in their front room. In the night and in the silence. In his chair. Bill stared down at his book. His book of names, his book of notes. Bill turned the pages of the book. The pages of names, the pages of notes. Tottenham Hotspur had taught Liverpool Football Club a lesson. In the night and in the silence. In his chair. Bill kept turning the pages. The pages of names, the pages of notes. Three days later, Nottingham Forest had taught them another lesson. Nottingham Forest had beaten them two–nil. At home, at Anfield. Byrne had been injured, Byrne had not played. Moran had been injured, Moran had not played. Backwards and forwards, forwards and backwards. Two days after that lesson, Liverpool Football Club had drawn nil–nil with Fulham Football Club. Away from home, away from Anfield. Byrne had been injured, Byrne had not played. Moran had been injured, Moran had not played. Yeats had been injured, Yeats had not played. Callaghan had been injured, Callaghan had not played. In the night and in the silence. In his chair. Bill stopped turning the pages. The pages of names, the pages of notes. Bill rubbed his eyes. And Bill closed his book. His book of names, his book of notes. In the night and in the silence. In his chair. Bill stood up. Bill walked back into the kitchen. In the night and in the silence. Bill sat back down at the table, in the chair. The bowls and the plates, the salt and pepper pots, the jars of honey and marmalade around the edges of the cloth, at the sides of the table. In the night and in the silence. At the table, in the chair. Bill stared back down at the three spoons on the cloth. *Banks, Norman, Sjöberg.* Bill stared at the three forks. *McLintock, King, Appleton.* Bill stared at the four knives. *Riley, Cross, Gibson, Stringfellow.* And Bill stared at the last fork. *Keyworth.* And again the three spoons, the four forks and the four knives began to move. They began to turn. Again the three spoons, the four forks and the four knives would not stop moving. They would not stop turning. Moving and turning, spinning and swirling. Spinning and swirling, swirling and swirling. Never pausing, never stopping. Swirling and swirling. In the night and in the silence. At the table, in the chair. Bill rubbed his eyes. Swirling and swirling. In the night and in the silence. At the table, in the chair. Bill closed his eyes. Swirling and swirling. And in the night and in the silence. At the table, in the chair. Bill said his prayers. Five prayers for five players. One for Gerry Byrne. One for Ronnie Moran. One for Ron Yeats. One for Ian Callaghan and one for Jimmy Melia. And then in the night and in the silence. At the table, in the chair. Bill said one last prayer –

A prayer against a curse.

Four times before, Liverpool Football Club had reached the semi-finals of the FA Cup. Twice Liverpool Football Club had won their semi-final matches. Twice Liverpool Football Club had reached the final of the FA Cup. Twice Liverpool Football Club had reached Wembley. But Liverpool Football Club had never won the FA Cup. Folk said the Liver Birds would have to fly off the Liver Building, off the Liver Building and out over the Mersey before Liverpool Football Club ever won the FA Cup. Folk said Liverpool Football Club were cursed in the Cup. Folk said Liverpool Football Club would never win the FA Cup. Never win the Cup. The Cup was cursed for Liverpool Football Club. But Bill did not believe in curses –

Bill believed in prayers.

. . .

On the Liver Building, on their towers. In the rain and in the wind. On Saturday 27 April, 1963, one Liver Bird was still looking out to sea, one Liver Bird still looking back across the city. Their wings were spread, but their wings still fixed. In the rain and in the wind. The Liver Birds had not flown away. But on Saturday 27 April, 1963, Liverpool Football Club had travelled away. Away to Sheffield, away to Hillsborough. In the rain and in the wind. Sixty-five thousand folk would travel to Hillsborough, too. Folk from Liverpool and folk from Leicester. In the rain and in the wind. Sixty-five thousand folk would travel to watch Liverpool Football Club play Leicester City in the semi-final of the FA Cup. But on the bus, the Liverpool bus. There was no Jimmy Melia. Jimmy Melia was injured, Jimmy Melia would not play. On the bus, the Liverpool bus. There was Chris Lawler. Chris was still only nineteen years old. And Chris was a right-back. But Chris liked to push forward, Chris liked to attack. And Bill knew Liverpool Football Club had to push forward, Liverpool Football Club had to attack. And so Bill had told Chris Lawler to get on the bus, the Liverpool bus. Because Chris was going to play in the semi-final of the FA Cup. But not at right-back, at right-half. So Chris could push forward, so Chris could attack. But on the bus, the Liverpool bus. Bill knew it was a gamble. In the rain and in the wind –

A gamble and a prayer.

On the pitch, the Hillsborough pitch. In the rain and in the wind. From the first minute to the last, Liverpool Football Club attacked. Attacked and attacked, again and again. They attacked and they attacked. Again and again. They came and they came. Forcing corner after corner. Save after save from Gordon Banks. Again and again, Banks dived. Again and again, Banks punched. Again and again, Banks caught. Again and again, Banks saved. Saved and saved again. From attack after attack. Chance after chance. Shot after shot. Thirty times Liverpool Football Club shot and thirty times Banks saved. Three times Leicester City attacked. *The three spoons, the four forks and the four knives.* Three times. *Moving and turning.* Only three times in the whole of the match. And all three times in the first eighteen minutes of the match. *Spinning and swirling.* In the sixteenth minute, Dave Gibson passed out to Howard Riley. *A knife to a knife.* Ronnie Moran came to intercept. Moran handled. And the referee blew his whistle. The referee awarded a free kick to Leicester City. *The three spoons, the four forks and the four knives.* From thirty-five yards out, Riley dropped the ball at the far post of the Liverpool goal and up went Ken Keyworth. *A knife to a fork*. But Liverpool Football Club were deceived by Keyworth. *Deceived by a fork*. And in drifted Stringfellow, the gaunt and bony body of Mike Stringfellow, drifting in from the wing to rise clear, to rise clear of Liverpool Football Club, to rise clear and head the ball down, down into the net. *A knife to a knife*. One–nil. *One knife in all their hearts . . .*

Their bloody, beaten hearts.

In the dressing room, the dressing room at Hillsborough. Bill looked from Tommy to Gerry, Gerry to Ronnie, Ronnie to Gordon, Gordon to Big Ron, Big Ron to Willie, Willie to Cally, Cally to Roger, Roger to the Saint, the Saint to Chris and from Chris to Kevin. And Bill said, Come on now, boys. Dry those tears and lift up those chins. Because this will not be the only time, boys. Not our only chance. I promise you that, boys. We will have other chances and we will have other opportunities. Many other chances and many other opportunities, boys. So dry those tears and lift up those chins. Because we are a team on the rise, boys. Because we are on the rise. We are on the rise!

And in the dressing room, the dressing room at Hillsborough. The players of Liverpool Football Club nodded.

But in the dressing room, the dressing room at Hillsborough. Bill knew the players of Liverpool Football Club were only half listening. And in the dressing room, the dressing room at Hillsborough. Bill watched the players take off their boots and their kits. In silence. Bill watched the players go into the bath. In silence. Bill watched the players put on their suits and ties. In silence. Bill watched the players go back out to the bus, the Liverpool bus.

And on a bench in the dressing room, the empty dressing room at Hillsborough. Bill sat down. And on the bench, in the empty dressing room at Hillsborough. Bill heard voices. *We're going to win the Cup*. Voices and laughter. *We're going to win the Cup*. Laughter and song. *Ee-aye-addio*. Song and celebration. *We're going to win the Cup!* From the other dressing room, the winners' dressing room. And on the bench, in the losers' dressing room. At Hillsborough, in Sheffield. Now Bill tried to stand, now Bill tried to get back on his feet. To leave this room, to leave this ground. To go back home, to go back home. But on the bench, in the losers' dressing room. Bill could not stand. Bill could not get back on his feet. His jacket stuck to his shirt.

His shirt stuck to his vest. His vest stuck to his skin. His skin stretched, his muscles ached. They ached and they screamed. Beneath his skin, within his flesh. Through his bones and through his blood. His red, red blood. And on the bench, in the losers' dressing room. Bill closed his eyes, Bill closed his eyes. But on the bench, in the losers' dressing room. Now Bill could hear other voices. Quietly, slowly. Beginning to rise, beginning to echo. *When you walk through the storm.* Other voices. *Hold your head up high.* Beginning to rise. *And don't be afraid of the dark.* Beginning to echo. *At the end of the storm.* Quietly and slowly. *Is a golden sky.* Other voices, another song. *And the sweet silver song of the lark.* Rising. *Walk on, through the wind.* Echoing. *Walk on, through the rain.* Quietly and slowly. *Though your dreams be tossed and blown.* Around the ground. *Walk on, walk on, with hope in your heart.* Down the tunnel. *And you'll never walk alone.* Into the dressing room. *You'll never walk alone.* The losers' dressing room. *Walk on, walk on, with hope in your heart.* At Hillsborough, in Sheffield. *And you'll never walk alone.* The Liverpool voices, a Liverpool song. *You'll never walk alone.* And on the bench, in the losers' dressing room. Now Bill heard these voices, Bill listened to this song. These Liverpool voices, this Liverpool song. Their voices and their song. And Bill opened his eyes again. Bill tried to stand again, Bill tried to get back on his feet again. And now Bill stood up again. Now Bill got back on his feet again.


## 13. A MAN OF THE MASSES


After the season, before their summer holidays. In the boardroom, the Anfield boardroom. The directors of Liverpool Football Club looked down the long table at Bill Shankly. The directors of Liverpool Football Club smiled at Bill Shankly. And the directors of Liverpool Football Club said, It has been a good season, Mr Shankly. A very good season. We reached the semi-final of the FA Cup and we finished eighth in the League. And with an average home attendance of almost forty-three thousand. So it was a good season, Mr Shankly. A very good season. So well done, Mr Shankly. Well done, indeed.

After the season, before the next season. In the boardroom, the

Anfield boardroom. Bill Shankly stared up the long table at the directors of Liverpool Football Club. Bill Shankly listened to the clock ticking. And Bill Shankly said nothing.

Tom Williams placed a document on the long table. And Tom Williams said, Now what about this contract, Mr Shankly?

I have never had a contract before, said Bill Shankly. And I have never asked you for one, Mr Williams. I have never wanted one.

Tom Williams nodded. And Tom Williams said, I know that, Mr Shankly. I know that. But we would like to offer you a contract. We would like you to have a contract. And this contract is for three years. And we believe the terms of this contract are very satisfactory. For us and for you, Mr Shankly. For us and for you . . .

If the directors of Liverpool Football Club do not like me, said Bill Shankly, then they can sack me. And if I do not like the directors of Liverpool Football Club, then I can go. Those are the sort of terms that are satisfactory to me, Mr Williams. For me and for you . . .

After their summer holidays, before their next holidays. In the boardroom, the Anfield boardroom. The directors of Liverpool Football Club looked down the long table at Bill Shankly. Again. The directors of Liverpool Football Club smiled at Bill Shankly.

Tom Williams placed a document on the long table. Again. And Tom Williams said, We know other football clubs are interested in your services, Mr Shankly. We have listened to the grapevine, we have heard the rumours. And so we know other clubs have made overtures for your services, Mr Shankly. But we want you to know how much we appreciate your services at Liverpool Football Club. The things you have done, the things you have achieved. How much we value those achievements. How much we value you, Mr Shankly. And so we do not want to lose you, Mr Shankly . . .

Thank you, said Bill Shankly.

Tom Williams looked down at the document on the table again. And Tom Williams said, But to speak frankly, Mr Shankly. We are worried about these rumours, very worried about these overtures from other clubs. We are very worried we will lose you, Mr Shankly. Because we want to keep you here at Liverpool Football Club. We want you to stay here at Liverpool Football Club, Mr Shankly. Because we want you to stay and build upon the things you have already done. The things you have already achieved, Mr Shankly. Because we know you want to keep building. We know you want to achieve much more, Mr Shankly. And we want you to know, we share your desire. We share your hunger, Mr Shankly. Your desire to keep building, your hunger to achieve more. As you know, the old Kemlyn Road Stand is being demolished. A new stand, a cantilevered stand is being built. We are spending three-hundred and fifty thousand pounds to build that stand. Three hundred and fifty thousand pounds because we believe in your desire, Mr Shankly. We share your hunger. Your belief in Liverpool Football Club, Mr Shankly. Your vision for Liverpool Football Club. So, of course, we do not want to lose you, Mr Shankly. To lose your desire, to lose your hunger. To lose your belief, to lose your vision. And so we want you to have a contract. A contract that demonstrates our faith in your belief. A contract that shows our commitment to your vision. So we want you to sign a contract, Mr Shankly. To sign this contract, this contract for five more years . . .

Thank you, said Bill Shankly again. Thank you very much, Mr Williams. I appreciate your candour, I appreciate your concern. And I also appreciate your commitment, Mr Williams. And so I will take this contract home with me today. And I will certainly consider it. I'll consider it carefully, Mr Williams. And then I will call you.

Tom Williams smiled. And Tom Williams said, Thank you, Mr Shankly. I look forward to your call. Now was there anything else? Anything else we can do for you today, Mr Shankly?

Yes, said Bill Shankly. Yes, there is. I want to sign Peter Thompson from Preston North End. And so I want thirty-seven thousand pounds, please, Mr Williams.

Tom Williams looked down the long table at Bill Shankly. Tom Williams picked up the document from the table. Tom Williams passed the document down the long table to Bill Shankly. And Tom Williams said, Well, we will certainly consider it, Mr Shankly. We will consider it very carefully. And I will have an answer for you, Mr Shankly. When you have an answer for me, Mr Shankly, I will have an answer for you.

. . .

Before his deadline, his deadline looming. In the office of Bill Shankly, before the desk of Bill Shankly. Horace Yates was writing,

writing as fast as he could. As fast as Bill Shankly was saying –

Well, I suppose it is the modern trend to have agreements such as this, Horace. So I suppose I have simply fallen into line. With the modern trend, Horace. With the modern times. Because you can't ignore the trends, Horace. You can't ignore the times . . .

Horace Yates stopped writing. Horace Yates looked up from his notes at Bill Shankly. Bill Shankly was on his feet again, Bill Shankly was in full flight again –

And anyway, Horace. I don't mind anybody knowing I intend to stay at Liverpool Football Club. Because Liverpool Football Club has become my second home. My second home, Horace. And I don't mind anybody knowing that. In fact, I want everybody to know that. So write that down. Write that down, Horace! Because deep down in my heart. Deep down in my heart, Horace. I never wanted to leave Liverpool Football Club. Because I have been completely captivated by Liverpool Football Club. My heart completely captivated by the atmosphere here at Anfield. Because it is without an equal, Horace. Without an equal anywhere in the country. Because we have the finest supporters in the country. The very finest supporters, Horace. And deep down in my heart. Deep down in my heart, Horace. I regard myself as just one of them. Just another one of them, Horace. Because I share their feelings. I share their feelings and their hopes, Horace. Their hopes and their dreams. I share their dreams, Horace . . .

Horace Yates stopped writing again. Horace Yates looked up from his notes again. Bill Shankly was back behind his desk again, Bill Shankly back in his chair. Again. Bill Shankly saying –

And the atmosphere could not have been more cordial, Horace. The atmosphere could not have been happier. When Mr Williams and I shook hands on the deal, Horace. When we shook hands on the deal.

Horace Yates said, Yes. But things have not always been so cordial. Things have not always been so happy, Bill. You have told me so yourself. Told me many times before, Bill . . .

You are correct, said Bill Shankly. You are right, Horace. And it would be idle to pretend there have not been some uneasy moments. It would be wrong to pretend otherwise . . .

Horace Yates stopped writing. Horace Yates looked up from his notes. And Horace Yates waited. Waited for Bill Shankly to spring back up again, waited for Bill Shankly to start back up –

But all those moments are a thing of the past now. A thing of the past, Horace. Now we can go forward. Forward into a new era, Horace. Together. Together, Horace. Because Liverpool Football Club are making giant strides in the right direction. Giant strides, Horace. And a lot of the spadework has already been done. A lot of the spadework, Horace. And so we have built a very substantial foundation on which to build. A very substantial foundation, Horace. Yes, much more work remains to be done. Hard work, Horace. But I believe we will be one of the truly great clubs of our time. I am convinced Liverpool Football Club will be one of the truly great clubs of our time and of all our time. And so I will never be truly content until we are the undisputed Champions of the land. I will never truly rest until Liverpool Football Club are the undisputed Champions of the land. And so I will strive to make us the Champions of the land, Horace. With every muscle in my body. With every single muscle, Horace. I will work until the day Liverpool Football Club are Champions. Undisputed Champions, Horace! And I'll tell you this. I'll tell you this, Horace. That day is not so very far away.

. . .

In the summer, before the new season. Peter Thompson turned into the car park at Anfield Road, Liverpool. And Peter Thompson saw hundreds of people gathered around the main door to Anfield, Liverpool. Peter Thompson parked his car in the car park. And Peter Thompson saw television cameras, radio and newspaper reporters gathered at the door to Anfield. Peter Thompson walked across the car park and through the crowd to the door. And Peter Thompson saw Bill Shankly waiting at the door. And Peter Thompson said, Hello, Mr Shankly. Are you expecting someone famous?

Yes, said Bill Shankly.

Peter Thompson looked around him. At the television cameras. At the radio and newspaper reporters. And Peter Thompson said, Who? Who are you expecting, Mr Shankly?

You, said Bill Shankly.

Peter Thompson said, Me? I'm not famous, Mr Shankly.

You soon will be, said Bill Shankly. Because when you sign for Liverpool Football Club, I'm going to make you the greatest player of all time, son. Greater than Stanley Matthews. Greater even than Tom Finney. Because you are already faster than either of them. And I'm going to make you even faster, son. I'm going to make you so fast you can catch pigeons. You'll be the fastest player in England, son.

Peter Thompson said, No, Mr Shankly. Not me . . .

Yes you, son, said Bill Shankly. You, son.

. . .

After the training, before the training. Under the stands, among the boots. Bill Shankly, Bob Paisley, Joe Fagan, Reuben Bennett and Albert Shelley talked about the players. About this player and about that player. This first-team player and that reserve-team player, this older player and that younger player. Who should step down and who could step up. Who was ready and who was not. About Alf Arrowsmith, Phil Ferns, Alan Jones, Chris Lawler, Tommy Smith, Bobby Thomson and Gordon Wallace. About who should stay and about who should go. Liverpool Football Club had sold Tommy Leishman to Hibernian Football Club for ten thousand pounds. Liverpool Football Club had sold Kevin Lewis to Huddersfield Town for eighteen thousand pounds. Under the stands, among the boots. Bill Shankly, Bob Paisley, Joe Fagan, Reuben Bennett and Albert Shelley talked about every player. Every first-team player and every reserve-team player. About who should play and who should not. In the first game of the season, the first game of the new season –

On Saturday 24 August, 1963, Liverpool Football Club travelled to Ewood Park, Blackburn. That afternoon, Lawrence, Byrne, Moran, Milne, Yeats, Stevenson, Callaghan, Hunt, St John, Melia and Thompson played for Liverpool Football Club. And in the sixty-fifth minute of the first game of the new season, Ronnie Moran scored. And ten minutes later, Ian Callaghan scored. And Liverpool Football Club beat Blackburn Rovers two–one in the first game of the new season. Four days after that, Nottingham Forest came to Anfield, Liverpool. That evening, forty-nine thousand, eight hundred and twenty-nine folk came, too. And in the fifty-fourth minute, McKinlay scored an own goal. But that evening, Liverpool Football Club still lost two–one to Nottingham Forest. At home, at Anfield.

On Saturday 31 August, 1963, Blackpool Football Club came to Anfield, Liverpool. That afternoon, forty-two thousand, seven hundred and sixty-seven folk came, too. In the sixty-third minute, Liverpool Football Club were awarded a penalty. Ronnie Moran took the penalty. But Tony Waiters saved the penalty. In the eighty-third minute, Jimmy Melia scored. But that afternoon, Liverpool Football Club still lost two–one to Blackpool Football Club. Again at home, again at Anfield. And that evening, in the first published League table of the 1963–64 season, Liverpool Football Club were fifteenth in the First Division. And Leicester City were first in the First Division.

The day after Bill Shankly turned fifty, Liverpool Football Club travelled to the City Ground, Nottingham. And Liverpool Football Club drew nil–nil with Nottingham Forest. Four days after that, Liverpool Football Club travelled to Stamford Bridge, London. In the ninth minute, Ian St John scored. In the seventy-second minute, Roger Hunt scored. And in the last minute, the very last minute, St John scored again. And Liverpool Football Club beat Chelsea Football Club three–one. Two days later, Liverpool Football Club travelled to Molineux, Wolverhampton. In the first minute, the very first minute, Roger Hunt scored. In the fifty-fifth minute, Jimmy Melia scored. And in the sixty-ninth minute, Hunt scored again. And Liverpool Football Club beat Wolverhampton Wanderers three–one. Five days later, West Ham United came to Anfield. That afternoon, forty-five thousand, four hundred and ninety-seven folk came, too. And in the sixty-fifth minute, Roger Hunt scored. But that afternoon, Liverpool Football Club still lost two–one to West Ham United. At home, at Anfield. Liverpool Football Club had played three games. And Liverpool Football Club had lost all three games. At home,

at Anfield. Two days later. In the dressing room, the home dressing room. There was no Tommy Lawrence. Tommy Lawrence was injured. There was no Ian St John. Ian St John was injured. In the dressing room, the home dressing room. Bill Shankly closed the door. And Bill Shankly went from player to player. From Furnell to Byrne, Byrne to Moran, Moran to Milne, Milne to Yeats, Yeats to Ferns, Ferns to Stevenson, Stevenson to Callaghan, Callaghan to Hunt, Hunt to Arrowsmith, Arrowsmith to Melia and from Melia to Thompson. And Bill Shankly sat down beside each player, Bill Shankly put an arm around each player. And Bill Shankly spoke to each player –

I know you want to do well, said Bill Shankly. I know you want to play well, son. For Liverpool Football Club, for this crowd tonight. But I also know the pressure that brings. That desire to do well. That desire to play well. The pressure of that desire. The desire to please this crowd. The desire to please these people. And I know the weight that brings. The weight of that expectation. It is heavy. I know. That pressure. I know. That weight. But remember this. If I did not feel you could play well. If I did not feel you could carry that weight. Then I would not have bought you, son. And I would not have picked you. I bought you, son. And I picked you. Because I know you can carry that weight, son. Because I know you are the best . . .

In the first minute, the very first minute, Alf Arrowsmith scored his first goal, his very first goal for Liverpool Football Club. In the thirty-third minute, Peter Thompson scored his first goal, his very first goal for Liverpool Football Club. In the fifty-seventh minute, Ian Callaghan scored. In the sixty-seventh minute, Roger Hunt scored. In the seventy-ninth minute, Gordon Milne scored. And in the eighty-seventh minute, Hunt scored again. And Liverpool Football Club beat Wolverhampton Wanderers six–nil. Six–nil. At home, at Anfield.

Five days later, Liverpool Football Club travelled to Bramall Lane, Sheffield. And no one scored for Liverpool Football Club. And Liverpool Football Club lost three–nil to Sheffield United.

On Saturday 28 September, 1963, Everton Football Club came to Anfield, Liverpool. That afternoon, fifty-one thousand, nine hundred and seventy-three folk came, too. The game had been sold out for weeks, the gates had been locked for hours. Before the kick-off. Bill Shankly walked down the corridor. Bill Shankly opened the dressing-room door. Bill Shankly stepped inside the dressing room. The home dressing room. Bill Shankly closed the dressing-room door. Bill Shankly took off his hat. Bill Shankly hung his hat on the back of the door. And Bill Shankly looked around the dressing room. From player to player. From Lawrence to Byrne, Byrne to Ferns, Ferns to Milne, Milne to Yeats, Yeats to Stevenson, Stevenson to Callaghan, Callaghan to Hunt, Hunt to St John, St John to Melia and from Melia to Thompson. And Bill Shankly smiled. Bill Shankly took a piece of paper from his jacket pocket. Bill Shankly pinned the piece of paper to the wall of the dressing room. The home dressing-room wall –

I've just seen Harry, said Bill Shankly. Old Harry Catterick, lads. In the corridor. By, he's a miserable man is Harry. He's always miserable is Harry. But he's not only miserable today. Today he's tired, too. Exhausted. Knackered. And shattered. And he's not the only one. They are all tired. All exhausted, all knackered. The whole team shattered. And do you know why, lads? Do you know why they are all so tired? So exhausted, knackered and shattered?

In the dressing room, on the benches. In their kits and in their boots. The players of Liverpool Football Club looked at Bill Shankly. And the players of Liverpool Football Club shook their heads.

Bill Shankly smiled again. And Bill Shankly tapped the piece of paper he had pinned to the wall of the dressing room –

Because of this, said Bill Shankly. This, lads . . .

In the dressing room, on the benches. In their kits and in their boots. The players of Liverpool Football Club stared up at the piece of paper pinned to the dressing-room wall. The piece of paper, a map of Europe. A map of Europe with one big thick red line drawn across it. One big thick red line drawn from Liverpool to Milan.

Bill Shankly put his finger on the piece of paper. On the map of Europe. Bill Shankly moved his finger along the red line from Liverpool to Milan. And then Bill Shankly moved his finger back along the red line from Milan back to Liverpool –

Do you know how far it is, asked Bill Shankly. How far it is from Liverpool to Milan, lads?

In the dressing room, on the benches. In their kits and in their boots. The players of Liverpool Football Club stared at the piece of paper pinned to the dressing-room wall. Again. The players of Liverpool Football Club shook their heads.

Well, I'll tell you, said Bill Shankly. I'll tell you, lads. It's eight hundred miles. As the crow flies. From Liverpool to Milan. And it's eight hundred miles back again. As the crow flies. That's one thousand, six hundred miles, lads. So that's how far Everton Football Club have travelled this past week. One thousand, six hundred miles! And I'll tell you this, lads. I'll tell you this. When you've been beaten. When you've been knocked out of the European Cup. That will feel more than one thousand, six hundred miles, lads. That will feel more like ten thousand miles, lads. One million miles! And you know what, lads? You know what old Harry had them doing? The minute they got back from Milan. After they had been beaten. After they had been knocked out the European Cup. After they had travelled one thousand, six hundred miles. You know what old Harry had them all doing? The very next day? The day after they got back from Milan in Italy?

In the dressing room, on the benches. In their kits and in their boots. The players of Liverpool Football Club stared up at Bill Shankly. And the players of Liverpool Football Club shook their heads.

Well, I'll tell you, said Bill Shankly again. I'll tell you, lads. Because I know. Because I could see them. From my house, from my window. I could see what Harry had them doing. And you won't believe it, boys. You just won't believe it. The day after they got back. The day after they were beaten by Internazionale of Milan. The day after they were knocked out of the European Cup. The day after they had travelled one thousand, six hundred miles. Harry had them doing a commando course. A commando course, boys! Up at Bellefield. Running the legs off them. But I know why, lads. I know why Harry did it. Because he knows how fit *you* all are. How hard *you* all train. And so he was worried was Harry. And so he's trying to keep up with our training. But he can't, boys. They can't. And Harry's delusional if he thinks they can. The man is simply delusional. Even on a good day. And this was not a good day. This was the day after they got back from Milan. The day after they had been beaten by Internazionale of Milan. They day after they had been knocked out of the European Cup. The day after they had travelled one thousand, six hundred miles. A very bad day. But I could see them, boys. From my house, from my window. I could see them. And I tell you, boys. I tell you. They were exhausted. They were knackered. And they were shattered. They couldn't keep up. They were dropping like flies. Left, right and centre. Dropping like flies they were, boys. The lot of them. So they are already finished, boys. They are already beaten. Before the whistle's even been blown, before they've even kicked a ball. So all you have to do today, boys. All you have to do today is finish the job. Finish the job, boys. And put them out of their misery. For Chrissakes, lads. You'll be doing them a favour. So for the love of God, boys. Please put them out of their misery, lads. Out of their bloody misery . . .

Two minutes before half-time, Ian Callaghan scored. Three

minutes after half-time, Callaghan scored again. Roy Vernon scored for Everton Football Club. But it didn't count, it didn't matter. Liverpool Football Club had beaten Everton Football Club two–one. At home, at Anfield. Bill Shankly burst into the dressing room. The home dressing room. And Bill Shankly danced from player to player. Bill Shankly patted their backs, Bill Shankly shook their hands. All of their backs, all of their hands. And then Bill Shankly stood in the centre of the dressing room. And Bill Shankly grinned –

Do you know what you have achieved today, boys? What you have done today? You have not only beaten Everton Football Club. You have beaten the Champions. You have beaten the Champions of England, boys. And so now you can have nothing to fear. Nothing to fear for the rest of the season, boys. Because you have beaten the Champions of England. The best team in this land. And so if you can beat them, boys. If you can beat the Champions of England. Then you can beat any team. Any team in the land, boys. And every team! You can beat every team in the land. I know you can. Because today you have shown me you can. And so today I know you can be the Champions. I know we can be the Champions of England, boys!


## 14. AFTER THE PASSION, BEFORE THE PASSION

In the office, at the desk. On the last Monday in October, 1963. Bill opened up the newspaper again. And Bill looked down at the League table again. The League table as it stood on Monday 28 October, 1963. This month, Liverpool Football Club had played three matches at home, at Anfield. And Liverpool Football Club had beaten Aston Villa, Sheffield Wednesday and West Bromwich Albion. Liverpool Football Club had played one match away, away from Anfield. And Liverpool Football Club had beaten Ipswich Town. This season, Liverpool Football Club had played fourteen matches. That Monday, Liverpool Football Club had nineteen points. That Monday, Liverpool Football Club were third in the First Division. On goal average, with nineteen points. Arsenal, Everton, Tottenham Hotspur and Manchester United all had nineteen points, too. Sheffield United had twenty-one points. Sheffield United were top of the First Division. Sheffield United were the sixth team to be top of the First Division this season. In the office, at the desk. Bill opened one of the drawers. Bill took out the pair of scissors and the pot of glue. Bill cut out the League table from the newspaper. Bill stuck the League table for Monday 28 October, 1963, into his book. His book of names, his book of notes. And in the office, at the desk. Now Bill took out his diary. His diary of dates, his diary of fixtures. Bill turned the pages of his diary. The pages of dates to come, the pages of fixtures to come. The twenty-eight fixtures to come, the twenty-eight opportunities to come. The twenty-eight opportunities to win, the twenty-eight opportunities to be the Champions –

The Champions of England.

And in the office, at the desk. Now Bill turned back through the pages of his diary. The pages of dates, the pages of fixtures. To the next fixture, to the next Saturday. And Bill stared down at that next fixture, that next Saturday. That next Saturday, Leicester City Football Club would come to Anfield, Liverpool. In the office, at the desk. Bill closed his diary. His diary of dates, his diary of fixtures. And in the office, at the desk. Bill stared down at the pair of scissors. The blades.

. . .

Upstairs, in their house. In the night and in the silence. Ness and the girls were asleep. Downstairs, in their house. In the night and in the silence. At the kitchen table, in a chair. Bill stared down at the three spoons, the four forks and the four knives. Again. The three spoons, the four forks and the four knives moving. Again. The three spoons, the four forks and the four knives turning. Moving and turning. Again and again and again and again. Spinning and swirling. Again and again and again and again. In the night and in the silence. At the table, in the chair. Bill closed his eyes. The three spoons, the four forks and the four knives always spinning. Again and again and again and again. The three spoons, the four forks and the four knives always swirling. Again and again and again and again. In the night and in the silence. At the table, in the chair. Bill opened his eyes. Bill picked up the three spoons, the four forks and the four knives. And Bill threw the three spoons, the four forks and the four knives across the kitchen. The three spoons, the four forks and the four knives clattered on the kitchen floor. In the night and in the silence. At the table, in the chair. Bill stood up. Bill walked out of the kitchen. Bill walked into the other room. In the night and in the silence. Bill picked up his diary from the arm of the chair. His diary of dates, his diary of fixtures. Bill turned through the pages of his diary. The pages of dates to come, the pages of fixtures to come. Looking for one date, looking for one fixture. Until Bill found the date, until Bill found that fixture. And in the night and in the silence. Now Bill stared down at the date. Saturday 28 March, 1964. Easter Saturday. Bill stared down at the fixture. Leicester City. Away, at Filbert Street. And in their house. In the night and in the silence. Bill closed his eyes. And Bill made a promise. Bill made a vow. His promise, his vow. Never again would Leicester City beat Liverpool Football Club. Never,

ever again.

. . .

In the pavilion at Melwood, the repainted and refurbished pavilion at Melwood. In front of the players of Liverpool Football Club, the entire squad of Liverpool Football Club. Bill held up the newspaper. Bill held up the back page of the newspaper. The League table on the back page of the newspaper. The last League table for November, 1963. And Bill said, We won at Bolton. We beat Fulham. We won at United. And we beat Burnley. And look where we are now, boys. Look where we are. We are top, lads. Top of the First Division. For the first time since 1947, boys. Liverpool Football Club are top of the First Division. So well done, lads. Well done! But I have to tell you something, boys. Something you're not going to want to hear. It doesn't count, lads. It doesn't matter who is top of the First Division in November. Nobody cares, boys. The only thing that counts is who is top of the First Division in April. On the last day of the season, lads. That is all that matters. All anybody cares about, boys. And so we might be top now in November. But now we have to stay there, lads. Through December and into January. January into February, February into March. All the way to April, boys. We have to stay there. We have to stay on the top, lads. And so I have to tell you something else. Something else you're not going to want to hear, boys. It's going to be tough and it is going to be hard. Hard work, lads. But let me tell you one last thing. After all that hard work, boys. It'll be worth it. Well worth it, lads. Because we will be Champions. The Champions of England, boys! If we work hard. If we all work hard together, lads . . .

Out on the training ground, out in the rain. The players ran round the training pitch at Melwood. And Bill ran round the training pitch at Melwood. Bill laughing, Bill joking. In the rain, the players heard the whistle. And in the rain, the players split into their groups. And the players lifted weights. The players skipped. The players jumped. The players did squats. The players did abdominal exercises. The players sprinted. And in the rain, Bill lifted weights. Bill skipped. Bill jumped. Bill did squats. Bill did abdominal exercises. Bill sprinted. Bill laughing, Bill joking. Then in the rain, the players heard the whistle again. And in the rain, the players passed the ball. The players dribbled with the ball. The players headed the ball. The players chipped the ball. The players controlled the ball. The players tackled. And in the rain, Bill passed the ball. Bill dribbled with the ball. Bill headed the ball. Bill chipped the ball. Bill controlled the ball. Bill tackled. Bill laughing, Bill joking. In the rain, the players heard the whistle again. In the rain, the players went between the training boards. The players moving, the ball moving. Playing the ball against one board. Then taking the ball, controlling the ball. Turning with the ball, dribbling with the ball. Up to the other board. In just ten touches. Playing the ball against the other board. Then pulling the ball down, turning again and dribbling again. Back down to the first board. In just ten touches. And in the rain, Bill went between the training boards. Bill moving, the ball moving. Bill playing the ball against one board. Then taking the ball, controlling the ball. Bill turning with the ball, dribbling with the ball. Up to the other board. In just ten touches. Bill playing the ball against the other board. Then pulling the ball down, turning again and dribbling again. Back down to the first board. In just ten touches. Bill laughing, Bill joking. And in the rain, the players heard the whistle yet again. And in the rain, the players went inside the sweat box. Ball after ball, into the box. Every second, another ball. For one minute, then for two minutes, then for three minutes. Ball after ball, into the box. And in the rain, Bill went into the sweat box. Ball after ball, into the box. Every second, another ball. For one minute, then for two minutes, then for three minutes. Bill laughing, Bill joking. In the rain, the players heard the whistle. In the rain, they played three-a-sides. Three-a-sides then five-a-sides. Five-a-sides then seven-a-sides. Seven-a-sides then eleven-a-sides. And in the rain, Bill played in the three-a-sides. Three-a-sides then five-a-sides. Five-a-sides then seven-a-sides. Seven-a-sides then eleven-a-sides. Bill laughing, Bill joking. And then in the rain, the players ran one last time around the training pitch. And in the rain, Bill ran one last time around the training pitch. Bill laughing, Bill joking. And in the rain, the players got back on the bus. In the rain, Bob, Joe, Reuben and Albert got back on the bus. And in the rain, Bill got back on the bus. Bill laughing, Bill joking. In the rain, they all travelled back to Anfield. Everybody laughing, everybody joking. In the rain, they all got off the bus. Laughing and joking. In the rain, the players went into Anfield. In the rain, Bill went into Anfield. Bill laughing, Bill joking. In the dressing rooms, the players took off their boots, the players took off their tracksuits. In the dressing rooms, Bill took off his boots, Bill took off his sweater and his tracksuit bottoms. Bill laughing, Bill joking. The players went into the baths. And Bill went into the baths. Bill laughing, Bill joking. The players washed and changed. And Bill washed and changed. Bill laughing, Bill joking. The players said goodbye. And Bill said goodbye. Bill still laughing, Bill still joking. And the players went out to their cars. The players went back to their houses. Laughing and joking. But Bill did not go out to his car. Bill did not go back to his house. Bill not laughing now, Bill not joking now. Bill still looking, Bill still listening. Always looking, always listening. And learning, Bill was always learning. Learning and working –

Bill was always working.

. . .

In the kitchen, at their table. Bill tried to swallow his Sunday dinner, Bill tried to join in the family conversation. But Bill could not swallow his dinner, Bill could not join in the conversation. In the kitchen, at the table. The girls finished their dinner. And Ness finished her dinner. The girls stood up. And Ness stood up. The girls began to clear away the plates. Ness began to run the water in the sink. In the kitchen, at the table. Bill stood up. Bill walked over to the sink. Bill put his hand on Ness's arm. And Bill said, Leave it, love. I'll do it . . .

Ness dried her hands. The girls put down the plates. Ness smiled. The girls smiled, too. Ness went into the front room and her crossword. And the girls went up to their room and their records.

Bill walked back over to the table. Bill picked up the plates.

Bill walked back to the sink. Bill put the plates in the sink. Bill walked back over to the kitchen table. Bill picked up the salt and pepper pots. Bill put them in the cupboard. Bill walked back over to the table. Bill took the cloth off the table. Bill walked over to the back door. Bill opened the back door. Bill stepped outside. Bill stood on the step. Bill shook the cloth. Bill stepped back into the kitchen. Bill closed the door. Bill folded up the tablecloth. Bill put the cloth in the drawer. Bill walked back over to the sink. Bill turned on the taps. Bill squeezed washing-up liquid into the sink. Bill turned off the taps. Bill picked up the scrubbing brush. Bill washed up the plates. Bill washed up the pans. Bill washed up the knives and forks. Bill put them on the draining board. Bill pulled out the plug. Bill dried his hands. Bill picked up the tea towel. Bill dried up the pans. Bill dried up the plates. Bill dried up the knives and forks. Bill put the pans in one cupboard. Bill put the plates in another. Bill put the knives and forks in the drawer. Bill walked back over to the sink. Bill picked up the dishcloth. Bill wiped down the draining board. Bill turned on the taps again. Bill rinsed the dishcloth under the taps. Bill turned off the taps. Bill squeezed the water out of the dishcloth. Bill put the dishcloth down next to the bottle of washing-up liquid. Bill turned around. Bill looked round the kitchen. Bill turned back to the sink. Bill bent down. Bill opened the cupboard under the sink. Bill took out a bucket from under the sink. Bill bent back down. Bill opened a box under the sink. Bill took out a Brillo pad from the box. Bill closed the cupboard door. Bill picked up the bucket. Bill put the bucket in the sink. Bill turned on the taps again. Bill filled the bucket half full. Bill turned off the taps. Bill took the bucket and the Brillo pad over to the cooker. Bill put down the bucket in front of the cooker. Bill opened the oven door. Bill looked inside the oven. Bill could see the dirt. Bill could smell the fat. Bill knelt down on the kitchen floor. Bill unbuttoned the cuffs of his shirt. Bill rolled up the sleeves of his shirt. Bill picked up the Brillo pad. Bill sank the Brillo pad into the bucket of water. Bill pulled the Brillo pad back up, out of the water. Bill squeezed the water from the Brillo pad. The wet, steel wool. Bill squeezed it tighter. Bill put his hand inside the oven. Into the dirt, amongst the fat. In the kitchen, on the floor. On his knees, Bill began to scrub. Liverpool Football Club had lost to Blackburn Rovers. On his knees, Bill began to scour. Liverpool Football Club had lost to West Ham United. On his knees, Bill began to clean. Liverpool Football Club had lost to Everton. On his knees, to clean and clean again. Liverpool Football Club were no longer top of the First Division. Liverpool Football Club were now fourth in the First Division. On his knees, until there was no more dirt, there was no more fat. And Liverpool Football Club were top again, and still top again, and in the Cup again, in the Sixth Round of the FA Cup again.

. . .

Under the stands, in the office. Not at his desk, not in his chair. Bill was pacing and Bill was pacing. Back and forth, across the room. Three strides back and three strides forth. Swansea Town were in the Second Division. In the doldrums of the Second Division. Liverpool Football Club were in the First Division. Near the very summit of the First Division. Folk were saying Liverpool Football Club were certain to knock Swansea Town out of the FA Cup. Folk were saying Liverpool Football Club were certain to reach the semi-finals of the FA Cup. Again. Folk were saying Liverpool Football Club could reach the final of the FA Cup. Folk were saying Liverpool Football Club could win the FA Cup. Folk were saying Liverpool Football Club could win the League, too. Folk were saying Liverpool Football Club could win the League and the Cup. Folk were saying Liverpool Football Club could do the Double. The Double! Under the stands, in the office. Not at his desk, not in his chair. Still pacing and still pacing. Back and forth across the room. Bill had his fingers in his ears –

In the dressing room, the home dressing room. Bill looked from player to player. And then Bill raised his finger in the air. His finger to his ear. And Bill said, Do you hear that noise, boys? Do you hear that sound? What a noise it is. What a sound it is. That is the noise of Anfield. That is the sound of Liverpool Football Club. And you are used to that noise. You are used to that sound. Because that is our noise. That is our sound. But across that corridor. In that dressing room. The players of Swansea Town have never heard a noise like that before. They have never heard a sound like that before. And they will be frightened, boys. And they will be intimidated. They will be pale and they will be shaking. And when you walk out into that corridor. When you walk out onto that pitch. You will see how frightened they are. How intimidated they are. But you can have no compassion for them, boys. No sympathy for them. Because not a ball has been kicked yet. The match is not won yet. And so nothing is certain, boys. Nothing is certain. Not until you have won the match. Not until you have beaten Swansea Town. Only then can you have any compassion for them. Any sympathy for them. When you have won the match. When you have beaten Swansea Town . . .

. . .

In the drive, in the car. Bill turned off the engine. In the night. Bill stared out through the car window at the house, at their home. In their home, in the night. Ness and the girls would be asleep. Their house warm, their house silent. In the drive, in the car. Bill gripped the steering wheel. Tight. And Bill glanced up into the rear-view mirror. Liverpool Football Club's assault had never ceased, Liverpool Football Club's barrage had never lifted. Bill knew what pressure was. Swansea Town had reeled, Swansea Town had tottered. Pressure was trying to find a job. But Swansea Town had refused to collapse, Swansea Town had refused to crumple. Pressure was trying to keep a job. And in the thirty-seventh minute, Swansea Town had scored. And two minutes later, Swansea Town had scored again. Pressure was trying to live on fifty shillings a week. Liverpool Football Club's assault had only became more ferocious. Their barrage only more intense. Pressure was trying to feed your family on fifty shillings a week. Time and time again, Liverpool Football Club had attacked and attacked. But time and time again, Dwyer had saved and saved. Pressure was not trying to win the League. But just after the hour, Peter Thompson had scored. Now the assault unceasing, now the barrage unending. Pressure was not trying to win the Cup. In the eightieth minute, the referee had blown his whistle. The referee had pointed to the penalty spot. Ronnie Moran had placed the ball on the penalty spot. That was not pressure. Moran had stepped back. Moran had run up. And Moran had shot. The ball high, the ball wide. Moran had missed. That was work. Your work. But still Liverpool Football Club had attacked and attacked. They never flagged, they never tired. That was your reward. In the final five minutes, the last five minutes, Dwyer had saved and saved and saved and saved again. Your work *was* your reward. Until there were no more minutes, until there was no more time. Until Swansea Town had beaten Liverpool Football Club. Until Swansea Town had knocked Liverpool Football Club out of the FA Cup. Until there could be no more talk of the semi-final. No more talk of the final, no more talk of the Double. Until there was no more talk. No more talk. In the drive, in the car. Until there was only silence. Only silence. In the drive, in the car. In the night and in the silence. Bill put his hand inside his coat. Bill put his hand inside his jacket. And Bill took out his diary. His diary of dates, his diary of fixtures. The dates to come, the fixtures to come. In the drive, in his car. Bill turned the pages of the diary. The pages of dates, the pages of fixtures. Backwards and forwards. Counting the dates, counting the fixtures. The dates to come, the fixtures to come. There were two more months to the season, thirteen more matches to come. In the drive, in the car. Bill stopped turning the pages. The pages of dates, the pages of fixtures. Bill stared down at one page. One page of dates, one page of fixtures. The Easter dates, the Easter fixtures. In the drive, in the car. In the night and in the silence. Bill gripped the steering wheel. Tighter. Bill closed his eyes. Again. Bill prayed for resurrection. Again.


## 15. ALL POWER TO THE KOP!

On Wednesday 4 March, 1964, Liverpool Football Club travelled to Hillsborough, Sheffield. At half-time, Sheffield Wednesday were beating Liverpool Football Club two–nil. With twenty-two minutes to go, Sheffield Wednesday were still beating Liverpool Football Club two–nil. If Sheffield Wednesday beat Liverpool Football Club, Sheffield Wednesday would be second in the First Division. If Liverpool Football Club lost to Sheffield Wednesday, Liverpool Football Club would be sixth in the First Division –

Sixth in the First Division,

and out of the cup. But in the seventieth minute, Ian St John scored. And a cry went up, a roar. *LI-VER-POOL, LI-VER-POOL, LI-VER-POOL.* And then from out of that cry, from out of that roar, a different sound. *Walk on, walk on, with hope in your heart.* The sound, a song. *And you'll never walk alone.* A song from the supporters of Liverpool Football Club. *You'll never walk alone.* Echoing, rising. *Walk on, walk on, with hope in your heart.* Around the ground. *And you'll never walk alone.* And onto the pitch. *You'll never walk alone.* And in the last minute, in the very last minute, with Liverpool Football Club still losing two–one, with Liverpool Football Club still sixth in the First Division, still sixth in the First Division and out of the Cup, Willie Stevenson rose from out of a crowd of players. To meet the ball, to head the ball. Into the goal, from out of a crowd. *LI-VER-POOL, LI-VER-POOL, LI-VER-POOL.* And that night, Liverpool Football Club were no longer sixth in the First Division. That night, Liverpool Football Club were second in the First Division. Liverpool Football Club with forty points. But that night, Tottenham Hotspur were still first in the First Division. Tottenham Hotspur with forty-four points. But Tottenham Hotspur had played two games more than Liverpool Football Club. And Tottenham Hotspur still had to play Liverpool Football Club. Twice. Home and then away.

On Saturday 7 March, 1964, Ipswich Town Football Club came to Anfield, Liverpool. That afternoon, thirty-five thousand, five hundred and seventy-five folk came, too. In the forty-first minute, Ian St John scored. In the forty-eighth minute, Roger Hunt scored. In the fifty-fifth minute, Alf Arrowsmith scored. In the seventieth minute, Peter Thompson scored. Two minutes later, Hunt scored again. And in the eighty-third minute, Arrowsmith scored again. And Liverpool Football Club beat Ipswich Town six–nil. At home, at Anfield. It was the fourth time this season that Liverpool Football Club had scored six goals. At home, at Anfield. That afternoon, Tottenham Hotspur lost four–two to Everton Football Club. That evening, Tottenham Hotspur were still first in the First Division. Tottenham Hotspur still had forty-four points. But Liverpool Football Club now had forty-two points. Blackburn Rovers also had forty-two points. And Everton Football Club now had forty-two points, too. But Liverpool Football Club had still played fewer games than Tottenham Hotspur, Blackburn Rovers and Everton Football Club. Liverpool Football Club still had games in hand. More games to come –

On Saturday 14 March, 1964, Liverpool Football Club travelled to Craven Cottage, London. And in the rain and in the mud, Liverpool Football Club lost one–nil to Fulham Football Club. In the rain and in the mud. It was a blow, a serious blow. That afternoon, Everton Football Club beat Nottingham Forest six–one. That evening,

Everton Football Club and Tottenham Hotspur both had forty-four points. That evening, Tottenham Hotspur and Everton were first and second in the First Division. That evening, Liverpool Football Club were fourth in the First Division. In the rain and in the mud. It was a blow, a very serious

blow.

Six days later, on the evening before Grand National Day, Bolton Wanderers came to Anfield, Liverpool. That evening, thirty-eight thousand, five hundred and eighty-three folk came, too. In the twenty-eighth minute, Alf Arrowsmith scored. And in the forty-third minute, Ian St John scored. And Liverpool Football Club beat Bolton Wanderers two–nil. At home, at Anfield. That evening, Liverpool Football Club had forty-four points. That evening, Liverpool Football Club were first in the First Division. Again. On goal average. First again, for now. The next day, Everton Football Club beat Blackburn Rovers two–one. That evening, Everton Football Club had forty-six points. And Everton Football Club were first in the First Division.

On Good Friday, 1964, Liverpool Football Club travelled to White Hart Lane, London. That Good Friday, the gates at White Hart Lane were closed an hour before kick-off. That Friday, fifty-six thousand, nine hundred and fifty-two folk came to White Hart Lane, London. And on Good Friday, 1964, just before the half-hour, Liverpool Football Club broke out of defence. Quickly. The long pass to Arrowsmith. Quickly. The square flick to Hunt and an error by Henry. And quickly, Hunt scored. That Good Friday, just after the hour, Byrne passed to Arrowsmith. Quickly. Arrowsmith passed to Thompson. Quickly. The flick to St John, the chip over the defence. And again, there was Hunt. And again quickly, Hunt scored. That Friday, three minutes later, the deep centre into the box from Callaghan. Quickly. And again, there was Hunt. And again quickly, Hunt scored. His third, his hat-trick. And on Good Friday, 1964, Liverpool Football Club beat Tottenham Hotspur three–one. Away from home, away from Anfield.

. . .

That evening, that Good Friday evening. At their hotel, in the dining room. Bill Shankly, Bob Paisley, Joe Fagan and Reuben Bennett were still sitting around their table. The players of Liverpool

Football Club had already gone up to their rooms. Up to their beds. Tomorrow, Liverpool Football Club would travel to Filbert Street, Leicester. Tomorrow, Liverpool Football Club would play Leicester City. Away from home, away from Anfield. Now the dining room was deserted, now the dining room silent. The waiters began to clear the tables, to take away the plates. The spoons, the knives and the forks –

Stop, shouted Bill Shankly. Please wait! Please leave the knives and the forks. And the spoons . . .

And the waiters left the knives, the forks and the spoons on the white tablecloth. In piles.

In the dining room, at their table. Bill Shankly stood up. Bill Shankly reached across the table. And Bill Shankly picked up three dirty spoons, four dirty forks and four dirty knives. Bill Shankly arranged the three dirty spoons, the four dirty forks and the four dirty knives on the white tablecloth. And Bill Shankly stared down at the three spoons, the four forks and the four knives on the tablecloth –

This will be them, said Bill Shankly. This will be Leicester City. They are not the team they once were. They have had injuries, they still have injuries. But the system will be the same. Banks, Norman, Appleton dropping back, McLintock, King, Cross, Hodgson, Sweenie, Roberts, Gibson and Stringfellow. That will be Leicester City tomorrow. That's what we all think? Yes?

Bob Paisley, Joe Fagan and Reuben Bennett stared down at the three spoons, the four forks and the four knives. And Bob Paisley, Joe Fagan and Reuben Bennett nodded.

Right, said Bill Shankly. And Bill Shankly walked over to another table. A table already set for breakfast. Bill Shankly picked up three clean spoons, three clean forks and five clean knives. Bill Shankly walked back over to their table. Bill Shankly arranged the three clean spoons, the three clean forks and the five clean knives on the white tablecloth –

And then this will be us, said Bill Shankly. This will be Liverpool Football Club. We have had our injuries, too. We still have our injuries. Still no Big Ron. But this will be our system tomorrow, our team for tomorrow. Tommy Lawrence. Gerry. Ronnie Moran. Milne. Young Lawler. Billy Stevenson. Callaghan. Hunt. St John. Arrowsmith. And Peter Thompson. That will be us, our team? Yes?

Bob Paisley, Joe Fagan and Reuben Bennett stared down at the three clean spoons, the three clean forks and the five clean knives. And Bob Paisley, Joe Fagan and Reuben Bennett nodded again.

Bill Shankly pointed to the five clean knives –

Callaghan, Hunt, St John, Arrowsmith and Thompson. Those are our knives. Five knives . . .

Now Bill Shankly picked up one of the five clean knives. And Bill Shankly waved the knife at Bob Paisley, Joe Fagan and Reuben Bennett. And pointed it –

This looks like a knife, said Bill Shankly. But it's not a knife! It's a fork. A fork called Ian St John. St John will wear the number-nine shirt. He will be listed as a forward. As a knife. But St John will be a fork. A secret fork. Because he will drop back. And so then St John will be a fork and a key. He will be the key for us! Ian St John will be the key that unlocks Leicester City Football Club!

Bob Paisley, Joe Fagan and Reuben Bennett stared at the knife in Bill Shankly's hand. The knife pointing at them. And Bob Paisley, Joe Fagan and Reuben Bennett nodded. They nodded and they smiled, they smiled and they laughed.

. . .

On Easter Saturday, 1964, Liverpool Football Club travelled to Filbert Street, Leicester. In the rain and in the mud. On Easter Saturday, 1964, St John had the speed, St John had the stamina. In the mud and in the rain. St John had the strength and St John had the skill. In the rain and in the mud. St John juggled the ball from chest to thigh, St John juggled the ball from thigh to instep. In the mud and in the rain. Like it was cotton wool, the ball was cotton wool. In the rain and in the mud. One minute St John was Doctor Jekyll, the next St John was Mister Hyde. In the mud and in the rain. St John linked defence to attack. From the middle of the pitch, from the heart of the game. St John turned defence into attack. In the rain and in the mud. In the seventeenth minute, St John passed the ball out to Thompson. Down the left, past four men. Thompson crossed the ball to Hunt. On the edge of the penalty area, from the edge of the penalty area. Hunt shot. A shot that nicked Norman, that grazed the outstretched fingers of Banks, that squeezed inside the post and into the goal. In the mud and in the rain. In the eighty-fifth minute, St John passed to Arrowsmith.

A perfect pass, through a pinhead. And Arrowsmith scored. In the rain and in the mud. Ian St John had unlocked Leicester City. In the mud and in the rain. Liverpool Football Club had beaten Leicester City two–nil. In the rain and in the mud –

At last, at last.

. . .

On Easter Sunday, 1964, in his office. The camp bed sitting in the corner. The bags of mail standing on the floor. The bags and bags of mail. The stacks of letters on his desk. The stacks and stacks of letters. In his office, at his desk. Jimmy McInnes heard the footsteps in the corridor outside. The fast steps, the heavy steps. And Jimmy McInnes looked up from the stacks of letters on his desk. The stacks and stacks letters. And Jimmy McInnes saw Bill Shankly standing in the doorway. Bill Shankly smiling, Bill Shankly grinning –

Happy Easter, said Bill Shankly. Happy Easter to you, Jimmy!

Jimmy McInnes blinked, Jimmy McInnes smiled. And Jimmy McInnes said, Thank you, Bill. Thank you. And two great results, Bill. Well done. Congratulations, Bill . . .

Oh, I wish you could have been there, said Bill Shankly. I really wish you could have been there, Jimmy. At Tottenham and at Leicester. The boys were magnificent, Jimmy. Every single one of them. I could not have asked for more, Jimmy. Not from any one of them. They were all superb, Jimmy. Absolutely superb!

Jimmy McInnes smiled again. And Jimmy McInnes said, That's what I heard, Bill. That's what people tell me. And it bodes well for tomorrow, Bill. Very well for tomorrow . . .

Aye, said Bill Shankly. Tomorrow will be another good day. I can feel it, Jimmy. I can feel it. I am not worried, Jimmy. Not worried at all. I am excited, Jimmy. I'm excited for tomorrow. There'll be a full house, Jimmy. And on Saturday for United. Two full houses . . .

Jimmy McInnes looked down at the letters on his desk. The stacks and stacks of letters. The bags of mail standing on the floor. The bags and bags of mail. And Jimmy McInnes said, You're right there, Bill. You're right. We'll have to turn away thousands, I reckon. I've already been onto the police. Asking for more police. For tomorrow and for Saturday. The demand is simply enormous, Bill. The demand for tickets. It's unbelievable, Bill. To be honest with you, it's hard for me to keep up. To keep up with the demand for tickets, Bill . . .

But that's the way it should be, said Bill Shankly. That's the way I've always wanted it to be, Jimmy. The way I've always dreamt it would be. The way it deserves to be, Jimmy. For this club, for Liverpool Football Club. The way it has to be, Jimmy. So this is the way it should be. And the way it should always be, Jimmy. Always . . .

Jimmy McInnes pointed to one of the bags of mail. One of the bags of mail standing by the door. And Jimmy McInnes said, Well, that bag over there is for you, Bill. That bag is all fan mail for you . . .

That's unbelievable, said Bill Shankly. That's fantastic, Jimmy. And I'll answer them all. I promise you that, Jimmy. I promise you that. I'll answer them all, Jimmy. Every single one of them . . .

Jimmy McInnes nodded. Jimmy McInnes smiled. And Jimmy McInnes said, I know you will, Bill. I know you will.

But what about all the other bags, asked Bill Shankly. Who are all the other bags for, Jimmy? Are they for the players then?

Jimmy McInnes said, No. They are all for me, Bill. All for me.

You see, laughed Bill Shankly. You're still the most popular man at Anfield, Jimmy. You are still the most popular man at Liverpool Football Club. Without a doubt, Jimmy. Without a doubt!

Jimmy McInnes shook his head. And Jimmy McInnes said, No, Bill. I'm not. I wish I was, Bill. I really do. But I'm not, Bill. I'm the most unpopular man at Liverpool Football Club . . .

Nonsense, said Bill Shankly. Nonsense, Jimmy. I know you try to make as many people happy as you can. I know you do, Jimmy.

Jimmy McInnes nodded again. Jimmy McInnes smiled again. And Jimmy McInnes said, Well, I try, Bill. I really do try.

And that's all I ask, said Bill Shankly. All I ever ask from anyone, Jimmy. That we try, try to make the people happy . . .

Jimmy McInnes nodded, Jimmy McInnes smiled. And Jimmy McInnes looked back down at the letters on his desk. The stacks and stacks of letters on his desk. And in his office, at his desk. Jimmy McInnes heard the footsteps in the corridor outside again. The fast steps and the heavy steps, walking away.

. . .

After his lunch, his Easter lunch. In his house, in his lounge. Ron Yeats heard the telephone ringing. Ringing and ringing. Ron

Yeats stood up. Ron Yeats walked over to the telephone. Ron Yeats picked up the phone. And Ron Yeats said, Hello? Hello . . .

It's me, Ron. It's me. The Easter Bunny, son. Now how are you? How are you feeling today, Ron? Are you feeling better now?

Yes, Boss. Thank you. I'm feeling fine –

That's great news, Ron. The very best news! But I hope you're not stuffing yourself full of Easter eggs now, son?

No, Boss. No. I would never –

That's great news, Ron. Great news! So you're fit enough to play tomorrow then, son? You're ready to play tomorrow, are you?

Yes, Boss. Of course I am. I'm desperate to play . . .

Oh, that's music to my ears, Ron. To hear you say that. Because I was worried, son. I was worried that if you weren't fit enough to play tomorrow, then you might never get back in the side, Ron. The way they are playing. I was very worried you might not get back in the team, son. If you were still not fit enough . . .

But I am fit enough, Boss! I know I am. I'm ready, Boss. And I'm desperate, Boss. I'm desperate to play . . .

Well, you know me, Ron. You know me. I make no promises, son. No promises I cannot keep. But if you get yourself down here tomorrow, Ron. Bright and early. Then we'll have a see, shall we, son? We'll have a see if you're fit enough to play. If you can play . . .

Thank you, Boss. Thank you very much.

But mind you stay off that chocolate now, Ron. Mind you stay away from those Easter eggs. Because they are a poison, son. To a man like you. Nothing but a poison to a man like you, Ron.

. . .

On Easter Monday, 1964, Tottenham Hotspur came to Anfield, Liverpool, LI-VER-POOL, LI-VER-POOL. That afternoon, fifty-two thousand, nine hundred and four folk came, too. Fifty-two thousand, nine hundred and four folk locked inside Anfield, Liverpool, LI-VER-POOL, LI-VER-POOL. Ten thousand folk more locked outside Anfield, Liverpool, LI-VER-POOL, LI-VER-POOL. Surging and shoving, shoving and surging. Outside Anfield, inside Anfield, LI-VER-POOL, LI-VER-POOL, LI-VER-POOL. In the thirty-sixth minute, Ian St John took a pass from Ronnie Moran. And St John scored for LI-VER-POOL, LI-VER-POOL, LI-VER-POOL. Two minutes later, Gerry Byrne passed to Alf Arrowsmith. Arrowsmith flicked on to St John, St John coming from deep. And St John shot low and St John scored again for LI-VER-POOL, LI-VER-POOL, LI-VER-POOL. But then Brown lobbed in a ball. Yeats headed out the ball. But Mullery volleyed the ball back. And Mullery scored. But in the fifty-third minute, Ian Callaghan left Henry spinning. Callaghan found Peter Thompson in the centre. Thompson shot. Arrowsmith stuck out a foot, Arrowsmith diverted the shot. Into the goal for LI-VER-POOL, LI-VER-POOL, LI-VER-POOL. And LI-VER-POOL, LI-VER-POOL, Liverpool Football Club had beaten Tottenham Hotspur three–one. At home, at Anfield, Liverpool, LI-VER-POOL, LI-VER-POOL. And that evening, LI-VER-POOL, LI-VER-POOL, Liverpool Football Club had fifty points. Everton Football Club had forty-nine points. And Manchester United had forty-seven points. That evening, LI-VER-POOL, LI-VER-POOL, Liverpool Football Club were first in the First Division. For now. There were still six more games to go, still six more games to play –

On Saturday 4 April, 1964, Manchester United came to Anfield, Liverpool, LI-VER-POOL, LI-VER-POOL. Fifty-two thousand, five hundred and fifty-nine folk came, too. Fifty-two thousand, five hundred and fifty-nine folk locked inside Anfield, Liverpool, LI-VER-POOL, LI-VER-POOL. In the sunshine. In the bright and brilliant sunshine. Again, ten thousand folk more were locked outside Anfield, Liverpool, LI-VER-POOL, LI-VER-POOL. Surging and shoving, shoving and surging. Again. Outside Anfield, inside Anfield, LI-VER-POOL, LI-VER-POOL, LI-VER-POOL. And in the sunshine. In the bright and brilliant sunshine. From the first whistle of the game, from the first second of the match, LI-VER-POOL, LI-VER-POOL, LI-VER-POOL attacked. LI-VER-POOL, LI-VER-POOL, LI-VER-POOL sought an early paralysing blow. In the sunshine. In the bright and brilliant sunshine. In the fifth minute, LI-VER-POOL, LI-VER-POOL, LI-VER-POOL won a corner. Peter Thompson took it. Ron Yeats rose for it. Gregg let the ball slip. Roger Hunt back-heeled it. And Ian Callaghan cracked it into the back of the net for LI-VER-POOL, LI-VER-POOL, LI-VER-POOL. And again in the sunshine. In the bright and brilliant sunshine, LI-VER-POOL, LI-VER-POOL, LI-VER-POOL attacked. Again LI-VER-POOL, LI-VER-POOL,

LI-VER-POOL came. And Gregg saved. From Ian St John. From Hunt. From Alf Arrowsmith. Again and again and again LI-VER-POOL, LI-VER-POOL, LI-VER-POOL never let up, LI-VER-POOL, LI-VER-POOL, LI-VER-POOL never relented. In the sunshine. In the bright and brilliant sunshine. In the thirty-ninth minute, LI-VER-POOL, LI-VER-POOL, LI-VER-POOL made United bow down again. With Gregg stranded, Callaghan shot. Law blocked the shot on his own goal line. The ball flew back to Callaghan. But Callaghan did not shoot, Callaghan crossed to Arrowsmith. And Arrowsmith headed the ball into the goal for LI-VER-POOL, LI-VER-POOL, LI-VER-POOL. But in the sunshine. In the bright and brilliant sunshine. Still LI-VER-POOL, LI-VER-POOL, LI-VER-POOL attacked and attacked and attacked. In the sunshine. In the bright and brilliant sunshine. In the second half, St John hit the post for LI-VER-POOL, LI-VER-POOL, LI-VER-POOL. Gregg saved point-blank from Hunt of LI-VER-POOL, LI-VER-POOL, LI-VER-POOL. And then in the sunshine. In the bright and brilliant sunshine. In the fifty-second minute, Gordon Milne passed to St John. LI-VER-POOL, LI-VER-POOL, LI-VER-POOL. St John passed to Hunt. LI-VER-POOL, LI-VER-POOL, LI-VER-POOL. Hunt to Arrowsmith. LI-VER-POOL, LI-VER-POOL, LI-VER-POOL. And Arrowsmith put the ball in the net again. In the net again, in the sunshine. In the bright and brilliant sunshine, LI-VER-POOL, LI-VER-POOL, LI-VER-POOL beat Manchester United three–nil. At home, at Anfield, LI-VER-POOL,

LI-VER-POOL, LI-VER-POOL –

After the whistle, the final whistle. Matt Busby walked down the touchline. The Anfield touchline. And Matt Busby shook Bill Shankly's hand. Matt Busby squeezed Bill Shankly's hand. And Matt Busby looked up at the Kop. The Spion Kop. Still swaying and still surging, still surging and still singing LI-VER-POOL, LI-VER-POOL, LI-VER-POOL. And Matt Busby said, You are worse than that lot, Bill. With all your enthusiasm and with all your excitement, Bill . . .

Don't say that, said Bill Shankly. Please don't say that, Matt. I'm not worse than them. I'm the same as them, Matt. The same . . .

Matt Busby smiled, Matt Busby touched his ear. And Matt Busby said, You're right, Bill, You are right. But do you hear that, Bill? Do you hear that? They have recognised a kindred spirit, Bill. They have recognised you as one of their own. You as one of them, Bill . . .

*Shankly! Shankly! Shankly! Shankly! Shankly! Shankly . . .*

Bill Shankly smiled at Matt Busby. And then Bill Shankly turned to face the Kop. The Spion Kop. Bill Shankly raised his hands above his head. And Bill Shankly saluted the Kop. The Spion Kop –

*Shankly! Shankly! Shankly! Shankly! Shankly . . .*

Matt Busby smiled again. And Matt Busby said, They have taken you to their hearts, Bill. To their very hearts.

*Shankly! Shankly! Shankly! Shankly . . .*

Aye, said Bill Shankly. They have, Matt. And I have taken them to mine. To my own heart, too . . .

*Shankly! Shankly! Shankly . . .*

But now they'll never let you go, Bill. You know that? Now they'll never let you leave, Bill. I hope you know that?

*Shankly! Shankly . . .*

Aye, Matt. I do know that. But I would never leave them, Matt. I would never go. Not now, Matt. Not now. Because I could never leave *them*, Matt. I could never let *them* go . . .

*SHANK-LEE!*

. . .

On Tuesday 14 April, 1964, Liverpool Football Club travelled to Turf Moor, Burnley. And that evening, the Spion Kop travelled to Turf Moor, too. Thousands and thousands of them, twenty thousand of them. A Red Convoy. On buses, on trains. A Red Line. In cars, on foot. A Red Army. On the march, the march to victory. In the twentieth minute, Alf Arrowsmith scored. In the fifty-second minute, Ian St John scored. And in the fifty-ninth minute, Arrowsmith scored again. And Liverpool Football Club beat Burnley Football Club three–nil. Away from home, away from Anfield. That night, Liverpool Football Club were still first in the First Division. Liverpool Football Club now had fifty-four points. Liverpool Football Club now needed only one more point. Only one more point from their last four games. Only one more point to be Champions. The Champions of England –

On Saturday 18 April, 1964, Arsenal Football Club came to Anfield, Liverpool. Again in the sunshine. The lovely, spring sunshine. Forty-eight thousand, six hundred and twenty-three folk came, too. In the sunshine. The lovely, spring sunshine. Forty-eight thousand, six hundred and twenty-three folk locked inside Anfield, Liverpool. In the sunshine. The lovely, spring sunshine. Ten thousand, twenty thousand, locked out of Anfield, Liverpool. In the sunshine. The lovely, spring sunshine. Red balloons floated in the sky. Over Anfield, across Liverpool. In the sunshine. The lovely, spring sunshine. Red balloons bounced on the ground. Outside Anfield, inside Anfield. In the sunshine. The lovely, spring sunshine. The Anfield crowd sang, the Spion Kop sang. In the sunshine. The lovely, spring sunshine. With flair and with wit. In the sunshine. The lovely, spring sunshine. The crowd sang, the Kop sang. In the sunshine. The lovely, spring sunshine. The crowd swayed, the Kop swayed. In the sunshine. The lovely, spring sunshine. They sang in rhythm, they swayed in rhythm. In the sunshine. The lovely, spring sunshine. They sang and they swayed. In the sunshine. The lovely, spring sunshine. They sang as one, they swayed as one. In the sunshine. The lovely, spring sunshine. They sang and they swayed, they swayed and they waited. In the sunshine. The lovely, spring sunshine. They waited and they prayed. In the sunshine. The lovely, spring sunshine. For LI-VER-POOL, LI-VER-POOL, LI-VER-POOL. In the sunshine. The lovely, spring sunshine. For LI-VER-POOL, LI-VER-POOL, Liverpool Football Club. In the sunshine. The lovely, spring sunshine. At home, at Anfield, Liverpool, LI-VER-POOL,

LI-VER-POOL –

Before the whistle, the first whistle. In the dressing room, the home dressing room. On the benches. In their kits and in their boots. Tommy Lawrence, Gerry Byrne, Ronnie Moran, Gordon Milne, Ron Yeats, Willie Stevenson, Ian Callaghan, Roger Hunt, Ian St John, Alf Arrowsmith and Peter Thompson looked up at Bill Shankly. Bill Shankly standing in the middle of the dressing room, Bill Shankly pointing his finger into the air –

The top of the mountain is in sight, said Bill Shankly. The very summit of the mountain, boys. And today you *will* reach that summit. You *will* stand on the very top of the mountain, boys. But you will not be standing there alone, no. You will be standing there with the tens of thousands here today. Inside Anfield. And the tens of thousands outside here. Outside Anfield today. You will stand there with them, boys. And you will stand there as one. So go out there now, boys. Go out there now and reach that summit. Go out there now and stand on the very top of the mountain, boys. And give these people what they deserve, give these people what they want. Go out there now and make these people happy, boys . . .

In the sunshine. The lovely, spring sunshine. After just seven minutes, Ian St John scored for LI-VER-POOL, LI-VER-POOL, LI-VER-POOL. But Arsenal Football Club did not capitulate, Arsenal Football Club did not surrender. And in the sunshine. The lovely, spring sunshine. The players of Liverpool Football Club began to feel anxious. And the players of Arsenal Football Club sensed that anxiety. The players of Liverpool Football Club began to make errors. And the players of Arsenal Football Club exploited those errors. Baxter missed by inches. Again. Baxter missed by inches. Gerry Byrne cleared off the Liverpool goal line. And Arsenal won a penalty. Eastham stepped up. Eastham struck the ball. Lawrence dived. Lawrence reached the ball. Lawrence pushed the ball around the upright. Tommy Lawrence had saved the penalty for LI-VER-POOL, LI-VER-POOL, LI-VER-POOL. Now there would be no more anxiety, now there would be no more errors. In the sunshine. The lovely, spring sunshine. Lawrence, Byrne, Moran, Milne, Yeats, Stevenson, Callaghan, Hunt, St John, Arrowsmith and Thompson shone. In the sunshine. The lovely, spring sunshine. They shone like diamonds. And they cut like diamonds. In the sunshine. The lovely, spring sunshine. LI-VER-POOL, LI-VER-POOL, LI-VER-POOL cut Arsenal Football Club to pieces. And in the sunshine. The lovely, spring sunshine. In the thirty-eighth minute, Peter Thompson turned Arsenal inside and out, this way and that. And Thompson sent a perfect centre to the post. St John rose to head square for Arrowsmith. For Alf Arrowsmith to nod home. Into the Arsenal goal. *London Bridge is falling down.* In the sunshine. The lovely, spring sunshine. In the fifty-second minute, Thompson beat Magill. Inside and out. Both ways. In a single, surging movement. Thompson unleashed a shot. From the edge of the penalty area. Into the Arsenal goal. *Falling down.* In the sunshine. The lovely, spring sunshine. Five minutes later, Thompson repeated the dose. From an inside-right position. *London Bridge is falling down.* In the sunshine. The lovely, spring sunshine. In the sixtieth minute, Gordon Milne passed to Thompson. Thompson flicked on to Hunt. Roger Hunt shot.

A thundering shot. Into the back of the net. *POOR, OLD LONDON!* In the sunshine. The lovely, spring sunshine. LI-VER-POOL, LI-VER-POOL, Liverpool Football Club beat Arsenal Football Club five–nil. In the sunshine. The lovely, spring sunshine. LI-VER-POOL, LI-VER-POOL, Liverpool Football Club were the Champions. In the sunshine. The lovely, spring sunshine. LI-VER-POOL, LI-VER-POOL Liverpool Football Club were the Champions of England –

LI-VER-POOL, LI-VER-POOL, LI-VER-POOL . . .

*WE LOVE YOU, YEAH, YEAH, YEAH . . .*

LI-VER-POOL, LI-VER-POOL, LI-VER-POOL . . .

*WE LOVE YOU, YEAH, YEAH, YEAH . . .*

And in the sunshine. The lovely, spring sunshine. The new Champions of England ran around the pitch. The Anfield pitch. In the sunshine. The lovely, spring sunshine. The new Champions of England ran a lap of honour around the ground. The Anfield ground. In the sunshine. The lovely, spring sunshine. Ron Yeats carried the trophy around the stadium. The Anfield stadium. In the sunshine. The lovely, spring sunshine. Not the real Football League Championship trophy. Not the Lady. The Football League had refused to let Everton Football Club courier the trophy across the park. But in the sunshine. The lovely, spring sunshine. No one cared. In the sunshine. The lovely, spring sunshine. Ron Yeats carried a papier-mâché trophy around the pitch. The Anfield pitch. A red papier-mâché trophy around the ground. The Anfield ground. And in the sunshine. The lovely, spring sunshine. The Kop sang, the Spion Kop sang. And everybody sang, everyone sang, *WE'VE WON THE LEAGUE! WE'VE WON THE LEAGUE . . .*

*EE-AYE-ADDIO, WE'VE WON THE LEAGUE!*


16. TOP OF THE WORLD

In the house, in their kitchen. At the window. Bill stared out at the sheets on the line. In the sun. The white sheets, drying on the line. And in his eyes, in his mind. Bill saw another sheet, another white sheet. In his eyes, in his mind. A white sheet held aloft, aloft on the Spion Kop. In his eyes, in his mind. The white sheet painted with two words, two words in bold capitals. In his eyes, in his mind. In capitals, in red. In his eyes, in his mind. **SHANKLY'S CHAMPIONS**. In the kitchen, at the window. Bill smiled. And Bill turned away from the window. Bill walked back over to the kitchen table. Bill sat back down in the chair. And Bill stared back down at the table. At the piles of letters, at the piles of telegrams. The letters of thanks, the telegrams of congratulation. The thanks from their supporters, the congratulations from his colleagues. Men he had played with, men he had played against. Managers he had pitted his wits against, managers he had beaten. At the table, in the chair. Bill went through the letters, Bill went through the telegrams. The letters of thanks, the telegrams of congratulation. Backwards and forwards. The many letters of thanks, the many telegrams of congratulation. Forwards and back. At the table, in the chair. Bill kept coming back to one telegram, one telegram of congratulation. A telegram of congratulation from Jackie Milburn. Jackie Milburn was the manager of Ipswich Town Football Club. Liverpool Football Club had played Ipswich Town twice this season. And Liverpool Football Club had beaten Ipswich Town twice this season. Ipswich Town had finished twenty-second in the First Division this season. And Ipswich Town had been relegated from the First Division. Two years ago, Ipswich Town had been first in the First Division. Ipswich Town had been the Champions. The Champions of England. At the table, in the chair. Bill put down the telegram of congratulations from Jackie Milburn. And Bill turned back to the window. The light had changed, the sun had gone. There were spits of rain on the window pane. At the table, in the chair. Bill stood up again. Bill walked back across the kitchen. Bill opened the back door. Bill went out into the back garden. The spits were now a shower. And Bill began to take the sheets down off the line. The shower now a downpour. Bill brought the sheets back in. Out of the rain, into the house. Bill shut the door behind him. In the house, in their kitchen. The sheets in his arms. At the window. Bill stared out at the line. In the garden, in the rain. The pouring rain. The empty, hanging line. Redundant in the rain. No use to anyone. In the house, in their kitchen. The damp sheets in his arms. At the window. Bill knew the time of the greatest victory was also the time of the greatest danger. These hours when the seeds were sown, these days when the seeds were planted. The seeds of complacency, the seeds of idleness. Watered with song, drowned with wine. The seeds of defeat. In showers of praise. That hypnotised men, that intoxicated men. And blinded men. Holes for their eyes, stitches for their lids. Finished men, forgotten men. In their houses, in their kitchens. At their windows. Redundant in the rain.

. . .

In the hotel, in the dining room. After the laps of honour. The many laps of honour. At the celebration dinner. The many celebration dinners. Tom Williams and Sidney Reakes stood up. Tom Williams was now the president of Liverpool Football Club. Sidney Reakes was now the new chairman of Liverpool Football Club. Tom Williams and Sidney Reakes raised their glasses. They proposed a toast –

To Bill Shankly, said Tom Williams. This success is all down to one man. And to one man alone. To Bill Shankly! Bill Shankly is the greatest manager in the world!

In the dining room, at the table. Bill sprung up. Bill shook his head. And Bill said, No, no, no! The success of Liverpool Football Club is no one-man affair. We are a team. We are a working-class team! We have no room for individuals. No room for stars. For fancy footballers or for celebrities. We are workers. A team of workers. A team of workers on the pitch and a team of workers off the pitch. On the pitch and off the pitch. Every man in our organisation, every man in our team. He knows the importance of looking after the small things, he knows how the small things add up to the important things. From the chairman to the groundsman, every man is a cog in the machine. A cog in the team. And every cog has functioned perfectly. In the team. Every man has given one hundred per cent. For the team. And so the team has won. The team are champions, a team of champions. We are all a team of champions! We are all a team. A team, a team . . .

But amid the popping of corks, amid the clinking of glasses. The slapping of backs and the singing of songs. Amid the celebrations, amid the congratulations. The accolades and the praise. No one could hear Bill. No one was listening to Bill.

. . .

His jacket stuck to his shirt. His shirt stuck to his vest. His vest stuck to his skin. His skin stretched, his muscles taut. Bill opened his eyes. And Bill tried to shift in his seat. His skin burning, his muscles straining. Bill could not shift in his seat. Burning, straining. Bill tried to move his hands. His hands locked tight around the armrest of his seat. His knuckles white. Bill forced open the fingers of his right hand. Bill raised his right arm. Bill brought his right hand over to the left sleeve of his jacket. Bill pulled up the left sleeve of his jacket. Bill stared down at his watch. His watch on his left wrist. The aeroplane shuddered. Again. Bill gripped the armrests of his seat. The aeroplane dipped. Again. Bill closed his eyes. Again. Bill tried to think of films. The films he had seen in Muirkirk. American films. Bill tried to think of boxers. The fights he had heard on the radio. American fights. Bill tried to think of gangsters. The books he had borrowed from the library. American books. And Bill tried to remember the reasons why he was flying to America. Flying to America to join Liverpool Football Club on their tour of the United States. The reasons Liverpool Football Club had agreed to this tour of the United States. This tour he had been against. This tour he knew would exhaust them. This tour he knew would weaken them. Bill tried to remember the reasons Liverpool Football Club were not at home. The reasons he wasn't at home. In Liverpool. Or in Blackpool. Or Glasgow. Anywhere but here, on this aeroplane, with his jacket stuck to his shirt, his shirt stuck to his vest, his vest stuck to his skin, at thirty thousand feet, above the sea, flying to America.

. . .

In the hotel in New York City, in a chair in the lounge. In his blazer, his Liverpool Football Club blazer. Bill saw Bob. Bob walk into the lounge, Bob look around the room. Bob looking for Bill –

There you are, said Bob. There you are, Boss. I've been looking everywhere for you! You'll never guess what I've found, Boss? I've found Jack Dempsey's bar! It's just around the corner, Boss. On the very next block! Come on, Boss. The man might even be there . . .

Bill looked at his watch. Bill shook his head. And Bill said, Are you mad, Bob? It's half past eleven. I'm away to my bed, Bob.

Bob looked at his own watch. And Bob shook his head –

It's not half eleven, said Bob. It's only half six, Boss. It's still early. It's only half past six in the evening, Boss . . .

Bill looked at his watch again. Bill shook his head again. And Bill said, It's half past eleven, Bob. Your watch must be wrong.

No, said Bob. You've got the wrong time, Boss. It's half past eleven in England. But it's only half past six here.

Bill shook his head. And Bill said, You're wrong, Bob. You're mistaken. No American is going to tell me what time it is. I know what time it is, Bob. It's half past eleven. And so it's time for bed, Bob. So you sleep well now, too. And I'll see you in the morning, Bob . . .

. . .

In the hotel, in the corridor. In his blazer, his Liverpool Football Club blazer. With a sheet of paper in one hand. A sheet of names, a sheet of numbers. Bill knocked on Bob's door. And Bill waited. And Bill waited. And then Bill knocked again. And Bill waited. And then the door opened. And Bill saw Bob. Bob still rubbing his eyes, Bob still wearing his pyjamas. And Bill said, What's wrong with you, Bob? Are you ill? Are you sick, man? Are you not well?

No, said Bob. I'm fine, Boss. I was asleep.

Asleep? Jesus Christ, Bob. It's eight o'clock in the morning. It's breakfast time, Bob. It's time to go through the team. The team for the game, Bob. The game today . . .

Just a minute then, smiled Bob. Just a minute, Boss.

. . .

On the pitch at Soldier Field, Chicago. Bill was not watching the players of Liverpool Football Club practise for their friendly. Bill was looking up at the stadium. At the Roman columns. Now Bill turned to the groundsman. And Bill said, This is a famous place. A very famous place. I've heard of this place. This is the very place where Jack Dempsey fought Gene Tunney in 1927, is it not?

Yes, said the groundsman. This is the place. There were over one hundred thousand people here that night. Gloria Swanson was here, Al Capone was here. There were the Astors and the Vanderbilts. There were politicians and there was even royalty . . .

Bill nodded. And Bill said, I know, I know that. I listened to it on the radio. And I remember every round. Every jab and every feint. Every punch and every blow. But where exactly was the ring then?

It must have been over there, said the groundsman, pointing to the centre of the pitch where the players of Liverpool Football Club were practising. That's where the ring would have been that night.

Bill said, Are you certain? I don't want any guesses now.

Yes, said the groundsman. I am certain. In that centre circle.

Bill nodded. Bill turned around. Bill looked for Bob. Bill saw Bob. And Bill shouted, Bob! Bob! Come over here with me. Follow me, over here. And bring a ball, Bob. Bring a ball over here . . .

Bill took off his coat. Bill took off his jacket. Bill made a goal with his coat and with his jacket. And Bill said, Come on, Bob. Come on! To me, to me. Pass the ball to me, Bob . . .

Bob passed the ball to Bill. Bill took the ball. Bill passed it back to Bob. Bob took the ball. Bob passed it back to Bill. Bill turned. And Bill shot. And Bill scored. Between his coat, between his jacket. Bill scored a goal. On Soldier Field, Chicago. In the place where Jack Dempsey fought Gene Tunney. On the site of the Long Count –

Bill looked at his watch. His watch on his left wrist. His Liverpool watch, with Liverpool time. And Bill picked up his jacket, Bill picked up his coat. Bill put on his jacket, Bill put on his coat. And Bill went back to Liverpool. Bill went back home.

. . .

In the house, in their front room. In the night and in the silence. In his chair. Bill picked up the paper again. The evening paper. Bill turned to the back pages again. The sports pages. Stan Cullis had been sacked as the manager of Wolverhampton Wanderers. In 1949, as manager of Wolverhampton Wanderers, Stan Cullis had won the FA Cup. He had been the youngest manager ever to win the FA Cup. He had been just thirty-two years old. In 1954, Wolverhampton Wanderers had won the First Division Championship. They had won it again in 1958 and they had retained it in 1959. The next year, Wolverhampton Wanderers had won the FA Cup again. That year, they had also been runners-up in the First Division, losing to Burnley Football Club by just one point. Just one point. Two points and they would have won the Double. The first Double since Aston Villa in 1897. Stan Cullis had won three Championships and two FA Cups. Yesterday, the directors of Wolverhampton Wanderers Football Club had sacked Stan Cullis. In the night and in the silence. In his chair. Bill turned to the inside back page of the paper. The page of results, the page of tables. And Bill looked down at the First Division table. Bill looked down the First Division table for the Champions of England. A long, long way down. On Saturday 12 September, 1964, the Champions of England were seventeenth in the First Division.

Seventeenth. This season, this new season, the Champions of England had played seven games. They had won two and they had drawn one. And they had lost four games. At Blackburn Rovers and at Leeds, at Sheffield Wednesday and at Leicester. Again. In the night and in the silence. In his chair. Bill let the pages of the paper fall to the floor. And Bill picked up his diary from the arm of his chair. His diary of dates, his diary of fixtures. Bill opened the diary to the next date and Bill stared down at the next fixture. On Saturday 19 September, 1964, Liverpool Football Club would play Everton. At home,

at Anfield.

. . .

After the whistles, all of the whistles. Along the corridor, into the dressing room. Bill slammed the door, Bill locked the door. Bill turned to face the players of Liverpool Football Club. The tops of their heads, the fall of their shoulders. Their necks and their backs. And Bill said, Look up. Look up at me! Into my face and into my eyes. Look up at me now. You parcel of rogues! You pack of scoundrels! You're a disgrace. Every single one of you. A disgrace and a menace. A disgrace to this club and a menace to our supporters. Stealing their money and killing their dreams. A parcel of thieves, a pack of murderers. That's what you are. Thieves and murderers. And you should be in prison. Every one of you, every single one of you. In prison. That's where you belong. Because I saw men crying today. Grown men crying on the Kop, crying today because of you. And I cannot blame them, I do not blame them. Spending their money, their hard-earned money. To watch you, watching you play like that. Losing like that, four–nil. Four–nil at home, at home to Everton. Everton of all teams. Everton! I'd be crying, too. If I wasn't so angry, if I wasn't so furious. I tell you, if you ever play for Liverpool Football Club again, the next game you play, you better win five–nil. Five–nil! And the next time they come here, the next time Everton Football Club come here, here to Anfield, you better beat them five–nil, too. Five–nil! Or you will never play for Liverpool Football Club again. I tell you that now. Not one of you. Never again. If you ever play like that again. Now get out, get out! Every one of you, every single one of you. Because I cannot look at you, I cannot look at you any more. Because I'm ashamed of you. I am ashamed to be your manager. And I never thought, never thought in my worst nightmares, never thought I'd ever feel that, never thought I'd ever say that. So get out, get out now! While there are still some folk about. Folk who supported you, the folk who paid your wages today. Get out there now, walk among them now. And let them tell you what they think of you, what they think of Liverpool Football Club losing four–nil at home, at Anfield, to Everton. Because I tell you, what I've said will be nothing compared to what they say. Nothing. So get up, get out! Get up and get out there now. And walk among those people. And listen to those people. Listen to their words and remember their words. And remember those people.


## 17. A RED GLOW IN THE SKY

On the morning of Sunday 20 September, 1964, Liverpool Football Club were twenty-first in the First Division. The Champions of England second from the bottom of the table. Under the stands, among the boots. The dirty boots, the hanging boots. Bill Shankly, Bob Paisley, Reuben Bennett, Joe Fagan and Albert Shelley knew this was going to be a long season. The longest season in the history of Liverpool Football Club. A long and tiring season. Bill Shankly, Bob Paisley, Reuben Bennett, Joe Fagan and Albert Shelley knew their preparations for this season, this long and tiring season, had not been ideal, had not been what they wanted. The players of Liverpool Football Club had returned from their tour of the United States exhausted. Many of the players of Liverpool Football Club had now won the recognition of their countries. Many of the players of Liverpool Football Club were now in their national teams. Selected and capped. Playing more games, many more games. Training with different managers, listening to different voices. Being distracted, getting exhausted. Exhausted and injured. Injured and finished. Under the stands, among the boots. The dirty boots, the hanging boots. Bill Shankly, Bob Paisley, Reuben Bennett, Joe Fagan and Albert Shelley knew some players would have to step down, down to the reserves. Players like Alan A'Court and Ronnie Moran. That some players would not want to step down, that some players would want a transfer. Players like Alan A'Court. Under the stands, among the boots. The dirty boots, the hanging boots. Bill Shankly, Bob Paisley, Reuben Bennett, Joe Fagan and Albert Shelley knew some players would have to step up, up from the reserves. They knew some players would be able to step up, up to the first team. Players like Bobby Graham, Chris Lawler, Tommy Smith and Gordon Wallace. They knew other players would struggle, struggle to step up. Players like Philip Ferns, Alan Hignett, Thomas Lowry, Willie Molyneux and John Sealey. Under the stands, among the boots. The dirty boots, the hanging boots. Bill Shankly, Bob Paisley, Reuben Bennett, Joe Fagan and Albert Shelley knew they would need still more players, need to bring in still more players. Players like Phil Chisnall. From Manchester United. Players like Geoff Strong. From Arsenal. Under the stands, among the boots. The dirty boots, the hanging boots. Bill Shankly, Bob Paisley, Reuben Bennett, Joe Fagan and Albert Shelley knew there would have to be these changes, have to be these experiments. That these changes, that these experiments, would make consistency difficult, would make stability elusive. That there would be ups and there would be downs. Before consistency, before stability. In a long season, the longest season in the history of Liverpool Football Club. Bill Shankly, Bob Paisley, Reuben Bennett, Joe Fagan and Albert Shelley knew there would be ups and downs. Many more ups

and downs, ups and

downs.

. . .

On Saturday 26 September, 1964, one week after Everton Football Club had come to Anfield, Liverpool. One week after Everton Football Club had beaten Liverpool Football Club four–nil at Anfield, Liverpool. Aston Villa Football Club came to Anfield, Liverpool. That afternoon, thirty-eight thousand, nine hundred and forty folk came, too. In the sixth minute, Bobby Graham scored. In the thirty-sixth minute, Ian Callaghan scored. In the fifty-sixth minute, Roger Hunt scored. In the sixty-fourth minute, Graham scored again. And in the eighty-sixth minute, Graham scored again. And Liverpool Football Club beat Aston Villa five–one. At home, at Anfield. On Wednesday 7 October, 1964, Sheffield United came to Anfield, Liverpool. That evening, thirty-seven thousand, seven hundred and forty-five folk came, too. In the thirty-first minute, Roger Hunt scored. In the fifty-third minute,

Hunt scored again. And in the fifty-ninth minute, Bobby Graham scored. And Liverpool Football Club beat Sheffield United three–one. At home, at Anfield. Three days after that, Liverpool Football Club travelled to St Andrews, Birmingham. And Liverpool Football Club drew nil–nil with Birmingham City. Three days later, Leicester City Football Club came to Anfield, Liverpool. That evening, forty-two thousand, five hundred and fifty-eight folk came, too. That evening, Liverpool Football Club lost one–nil to Leicester City. Again.

Four days later, West Ham United came to Anfield, Liverpool. That afternoon, thirty-six thousand and twenty-nine folk came, too. In the seventh minute, Ian St John scored. In the twenty-seventh minute, Roger Hunt scored. But that afternoon, Liverpool Football Club drew two-all with West Ham United. One week later, Liverpool Football Club travelled to the Hawthorns, Birmingham. And Liverpool Football Club lost three–nil to West Bromwich Albion.

On Saturday 31 October, 1964, Manchester United came to Anfield, Liverpool. That afternoon, fifty-two thousand, four hundred and two folk came, too. But Liverpool Football Club lost two–nil to Manchester United. At home, at Anfield. That evening, Manchester United were top of the First Division. That evening, Liverpool Football Club were eighteenth in the First Division. That evening, under the stands, among the boots. The dirty boots and the hanging boots. Bill Shankly, Bob Paisley, Reuben Bennett, Joe Fagan and Albert Shelley knew this was a long, hard season. The longest and the hardest season in the history of Liverpool Football Club. A season of ups and downs. Home and away, ups

and downs. Ups and

downs.

. . .

Bill Shankly and Bob Paisley had been to Wembley. Bill Shankly and Bob Paisley had seen England play Belgium. Bill Shankly and Bob Paisley had seen the Belgians murder the English. Bill Shankly and Bob Paisley knew England had been lucky to draw against Belgium. The Belgium side had included seven players from Royal Sporting Club Anderlecht of Brussels. Heylens, Cornelis, Plaskie, Puis, Jurion, Verbiest and Van Himst. Royal Sporting Club Anderlecht were Liverpool Football Club's next opponents in the

European Cup. In the First Round proper of the European Cup. Over two legs, home and away. The first leg at home, at Anfield. Bill Shankly and Bob Paisley were concerned, Bill Shankly and Bob Paisley were worried. Bill Shankly and Bob Paisley went to Brussels. Bill Shankly and Bob Paisley watched Royal Sporting Club Anderlecht play Standard Liège. Bill Shankly and Bob Paisley watched Royal Sporting Club Anderlecht murder Standard Liège. Bill Shankly and Bob Paisley were not only worried. Bill Shankly and Bob Paisley were frightened. Bill Shankly and Bob Paisley were scared.

After the flight back from Belgium, on the way back from the airport. In the car, at the wheel. Bob Paisley was thinking out loud, Bob Paisley saying, Van Himst is the problem, Boss. The problem for us. The problem for Big Ron. Van Himst plays behind their front man. You never see him, never see him until it's too late. That is the danger, that is the threat. The threat to us, Boss. The threat . . .

You're right, said Bill Shankly. You're exactly right, Bob. And so Ron will need help. A lot of help. But they mark man-for-man. And that can be a weakness. If we can exploit it. If we can confuse and deceive them. If we can trick them like Leicester City tricked us. Then we can beat them. Then we can win. But we will need to deceive them. We'll need to fool them. To make them not believe their own eyes, to make them doubt their own eyes. So it all comes down to appearance, Bob. All down to appearance . . .

In the car, at the wheel. Bob Paisley nodded. And Bob Paisley said, Yes, Boss. If we can . . .

Oh, we can, laughed Bill Shankly. We can, Bob. Pull over here!

In the car, at the wheel. Bob Paisley pulled over. And Bill Shankly jumped out of the car. Bob Paisley watched Bill Shankly go into a sporting-goods shop. Bob Paisley watched Bill Shankly come back out of the sporting-goods shop. Bill Shankly had a big bin liner stuffed full of something in his arms. Bill Shankly opened the boot of the car. Bill Shankly put the big bin liner stuffed full of something into the boot of the car. Bill Shankly closed the boot. Bill Shankly got back into the car. Bill Shankly looked at his watch –

Forget my house, Bob. Drop me at the ground.

Bob Paisley shrugged, Bob Paisley nodded. Bob Paisley turned the car around, Bob Paisley drove to the ground. And Bob Paisley dropped Bill Shankly at the ground, at Anfield.

. . .

After the training, after their bath. In the dressing room, in their suits. Ron Yeats and Ian St John heard the footsteps in the corridor outside. The fast steps, the heavy steps. Ron Yeats and Ian St John saw the dressing-room door fly open. Bill Shankly in the doorway, Bill Shankly with a big bin liner –

Strip off, Ron!

Ron Yeats looked at Bill Shankly. Ron Yeats looked at Ian St John. Ron Yeats shrugged. Ron Yeats stood up. Ron Yeats stripped off. And Ron Yeats stood in the middle of the dressing room. Naked.

Bill Shankly took a shirt off a peg on the dressing-room wall. A red shirt. Bill Shankly opened the big bin liner. Bill Shankly took a pair of shorts out of the big bin liner. A pair of red shorts. Bill Shankly handed the red shirt and the red shorts to Ron Yeats –

Put these on, son.

Ron Yeats put on the shorts. The red shorts. Ron Yeats put on the shirt. The red shirt.

Ian St John opened up his kit bag. Ian St John took out a pair of socks. A pair of red socks. Ian St John handed the socks to Bill Shankly. And Bill Shankly smiled –

Oh yes. Yes . . .

Bill Shankly handed the red socks to Ron Yeats. And Ron Yeats put on the socks. The red socks. And Ron Yeats stood in the middle of the dressing room, the Anfield dressing room. In red.

Now your boots, said Bill Shankly. Put on your boots, Ron. And follow me. Follow me, son . . .

Ron Yeats put on his boots. And Ron Yeats followed Bill Shankly out of the dressing room. Down the corridor, onto the pitch,

the Anfield pitch. And Ron Yeats stood on the pitch, the Anfield pitch. And Bill Shankly looked at Ron Yeats –

On the pitch, the Anfield pitch. In his red shirt. In his red shorts. In his red socks. Bill Shankly walked around Ron Yeats. On the pitch, the Anfield pitch. Bill Shankly clapped,

Bill Shankly laughed –

Jesus Christ, son. You look awesome. You look terrifying, son. You look gigantic, you look massive. You look seven foot tall, man!

You'll scare the living daylights out of Anderlecht. You'll scare them to death, son. All the way back to Belgium!

. . .

On Wednesday 25 November, 1964, Royal Sporting Club Anderlecht came to Anfield, Liverpool. That night, forty-four thousand, five hundred and sixteen folk came, too.

Before the whistle, the first whistle. In the dressing room, on the bench. Bill Shankly put a hand on Gordon Milne's knee. And Bill Shankly squeezed it tight –

When we have the ball, you come out and play with it, son. Just like you always do. Forwards like you always do, son. But when they have the ball, you pick up Van Himst. Wherever he goes, whatever he does, you follow him and you stick with him, son. Wherever he goes, whatever he does, you mark him out of the game.

Before the whistle, the first whistle. In the dressing room, on the bench. Bill Shankly put a hand on young Tommy Smith's knee. And Bill Shankly squeezed it tight –

Forget that number on the back of your shirt, Tommy. Forget that number ten tonight. Tonight I want you to be Ron's right leg, Tommy. To win every ball, to find a red shirt. Out to the wings if you can, Tommy. To Callaghan or to Thompson. But I don't want to see you over the halfway line, Tommy. Not tonight. Not tonight, Tommy.

Before the whistle, the first whistle. In the dressing room, on the benches. The players of Liverpool Football Club looked at Bill Shankly. Bill Shankly looking from player to player. From Lawrence to Lawler, Lawler to Byrne, Byrne to Milne, Milne to Yeats, Yeats to Stevenson, Stevenson to Callaghan, Callaghan to Hunt, Hunt to St John, St John to Smith and from Smith to Thompson. From player to player, red player to red player. In red. Ten players in red, from head to toe. In red, all in red. Bill Shankly nodding, Bill Shankly smiling –

I know Peter and Gordon played against some of this lot at Wembley, said Bill Shankly. And Bob and me, we saw them play the other Sunday. And so I'm not going to lie to you, boys. I'm not going to lie. They have a couple of good players. A couple of very handy lads. So we'll need to be on our toes. On our toes tonight, boys. But they are not a good team. Don't let us kid ourselves. They're not in our league, boys. They'd never be Champions of England. Never in a million years. And I'll tell you another thing, they'll never have played anywhere like here before. Anywhere like Anfield, boys. Because there's nowhere like Anfield. Nowhere like this crowd, like our crowd. And when our crowd see you tonight, boys. Dressed like this, dressed in red. All in red. They are going to go berserk, boys. Berserk! And when Anderlecht hear them, hear them roar. And when Anderlecht see you, see you in red. Anderlecht of Belgium are going to wish they'd brought a spare kit with them, boys. Because they're going to shit their pants. They're going to shit their bloody pants, boys!

In the tenth minute, Lawrence threw the ball to Byrne. In red, all in red, Byrne passed to Thompson. In red, all in red, Thompson passed to Smith. In red, all in red, Smith passed to Hunt. In red, all in red, Hunt shot. And Trappeniers parried the ball. The ball bounced to St John. And in red, all in red, St John scored. In red, all in red. In the forty-third minute, St John wrested the ball from Verbiest. In red, all in red, St John slipped the ball through to Hunt. And in red, all in red, Hunt scored. In red, all in red. In the fiftieth minute, Byrne took a free kick on the left in red, all in red. The ball arched over to Yeats. And in red, all in red, Yeats glanced the ball into the corner of the goal. And in red, all in red, Liverpool Football Club beat Royal Sporting Club Anderlecht three–nil. In red, all in red. At home,

at Anfield. Bill Shankly danced around the dressing room. From player to player, red player to red player. Bill Shankly patted their backs, Bill Shankly shook their hands. All of their backs and all of their hands. Smiling and laughing –

Do you know who I've just seen, boys? Just seen out there in that corridor? I've just seen Mister Herrera, boys. The manager of Internazionale of Milan. And do you know what he told me, boys? Do you know what Mister Herrera of Internazionale just said to me? He said he hopes he does not meet us until the final, boys. Until the final of the European Cup. That's what he just told me, boys. What Mister Herrera of Internazionale of Milan just said to me. And I know why he said that, boys. I know why. Because when you took to that pitch tonight, boys. You were like a burning fire. A red fire, boys. It was like an oven out there tonight. And you looked like giants in that oven, boys. Red giants. And you played like giants, boys. Red giants. Because Anderlecht are a great team, boys. Anderlecht are one of the best teams I have ever seen. But you swept them aside, boys. You swept them aside like a fire. Like a red fire, boys. Red hot you were. Red hot, boys. Every one of you. Every single one of you, boys. Like the red heat of revolution. That is what you were tonight, boys. The Red Heat of a Revolution. The Red Heat of a Revolution that is only just beginning, boys. A Red Revolution. A Red Revolution that will never end, boys! A revolution without end, boys . . .

. . .

In the winter-time. In the ice and in the snow. Liverpool Football Club travelled to Belgium. And Liverpool Football Club knocked Anderlecht out of the European Cup. They travelled to Burnley. And they beat Burnley Football Club. They beat Blackburn Rovers, they beat Sunderland Football Club. They beat Sheffield Wednesday and they beat Blackpool Football Club. They knocked West Bromwich Albion out of the FA Cup. They knocked out Stockport County and they knocked out Bolton Wanderers –

In the winter-time. In the ice and in the snow. Liverpool Football Club drew with FC Cologne in the Second Round of the European Cup. Away. And Liverpool Football Club drew with Leicester City in the Sixth Round of the FA Cup –

In the winter-time. In the ice and in the snow. On Wednesday 10 March, 1965, Leicester City came to Anfield, Liverpool. That evening, fifty-three thousand, three hundred and twenty-four folk came, too. Fifty-three thousand, three hundred and twenty-four folk to watch Liverpool Football Club play Leicester City in the Sixth Round replay of the FA Cup. For a place in the semi-final, in the semi-final of the FA Cup. The Cup that Liverpool Football Club had never won, the Cup that some folk said was cursed. Jinxed. That some folk said Liverpool Football Club would never win. In the seventy-second minute, Chris Lawler took a free kick. Lawler found Ron Yeats. Yeats found Roger Hunt. And Hunt found the net. And Liverpool Football Club beat Leicester City one–nil. At home, at Anfield. One week after that, FC Cologne came to Anfield, Liverpool. Forty-eight thousand, four hundred and thirty-two folk came, too. Forty-eight thousand, four hundred and thirty-two folk to watch Liverpool Football Club play FC Cologne in the second leg of the Second Round of the European Cup. Another cup Liverpool Football Club had never won, a tournament

Liverpool Football Club had never played in before. But Liverpool Football Club drew nil–nil with FC Cologne. Again. Liverpool Football Club and FC Cologne would have to play another game, another match. On neutral ground, on foreign soil –

On Wednesday 24 March, 1965, Liverpool Football Club travelled to the Stadion Feyenoord in Rotterdam, Holland. Fifty-odd thousand folk came, too. Fifty-odd thousand mainly German folk. In the twenty-second minute, Ian St John scored. In the thirty-seventh, Roger Hunt scored. But then Thielen scored for FC Cologne. And then Loehr scored for FC Cologne. And after ninety minutes of this match, after two hundred and seventy minutes of this tie, Liverpool Football Club and FC Cologne were still drawing. And after extra time, after one hundred and twenty minutes of this match, after three hundred minutes of this tie, Liverpool Football Club and FC Cologne were still drawing. Still tied. And so after three hundred minutes, after the final whistle. The captain of Liverpool Football Club walked to the centre of the field, the centre circle. And the captain of FC Cologne walked to the centre of the field, the centre circle. Reporters followed them, photographers followed them. The captains stood in the centre of the field, in the centre circle. The referee took a chip from his pocket. A gambler's chip. One side red, one side white. The referee asked Ron Yeats which side of the chip he wanted. And Ron Yeats said red. He wanted the red side. The referee said he would now throw the chip in the air. Into the night, into the dark. And then the chip would fall onto the ground, into the mud. If it landed red-side up, Liverpool Football Club would be in the semi-final of the European Cup. If it landed white-side up, FC Cologne would be in the semi-final of the European Cup. In the centre of the field, in the centre circle, the referee flicked the chip into the air. Into the night, into the dark. The lights of the cameras flashed. On their benches, the players, the officials and the staff of Liverpool Football Club and FC Cologne blinked. In the lights. The players, the officials and the staff followed the chip. Into the night, into the dark. Up and then down. Down onto the ground, down into the mud. The captains stared down at the ground, down at the mud. Down at the chip, the gambler's chip. In the ground, in the mud. On its side. The chip had landed on its side. The gambler's chip. Stuck in the mud, on its side. The referee bent down.

The referee picked up the chip. The gambler's chip. The referee wiped the chip. The gambler's chip. The referee flicked the chip back into the air. Into the night, into the dark. The lights flashed again. Again, on their benches, the players, the officials and the staff of Liverpool Football Club and FC Cologne blinked. In the lights. Again, the players, the officials and the staff followed the chip. Into the night, into the dark. Up and then down. Down onto the ground, down into the mud. The captains stared down at the ground, down at the mud. And Ron Yeats leapt up. Up into the night, up

into the lights. In

red, all in red.

The players, the officials and the staff of Liverpool Football Club ran towards the centre of the field, towards the centre circle, towards Ron Yeats. Ron Yeats –

his arms raised,

raised in

red, all in red. But Bill Shankly did not run to the centre of the pitch, to the centre circle. Bill Shankly got up from the bench. Slowly. Bill Shankly walked down the touchline to the coach of FC Cologne. Bill Shankly shook his head, Bill Shankly stuck out his hand –

That's no way to settle a game, said Bill Shankly. No way to win a match. Not on the toss of a coin. Not for your team. I have to be honest, tonight you were the better team, sir.

. . .

Three days after Liverpool Football Club had knocked FC Cologne out of the European Cup on the toss of a coin. Three days after Liverpool Football Club had played one hundred and twenty minutes of football, Liverpool Football Club travelled to Villa Park, Birmingham. That afternoon, sixty-seven thousand, six hundred and eighty-six folk came, too. Liverpool folk and London folk. Sixty-seven thousand, six hundred and eighty-six folk to watch Liverpool Football Club play Chelsea Football Club in the semi-final of the FA Cup –

Before the whistle, the first whistle. In the dressing room, the Liverpool dressing room at Villa Park, Birmingham. Bill Shankly took a brochure from his pocket. A brochure for the FA Cup Final. A brochure printed by Chelsea Football Club. Bill Shankly held up the brochure. The Chelsea Cup Final brochure. Bill Shankly made sure every player, every player of Liverpool Football Club, could see this brochure, this Chelsea Cup Final brochure –

That mob from London think they have already won this game, said Bill Shankly. Already won this match. That mob think we are drained, that mob think we are exhausted. Already beaten. They think they have won the game, they think they have won the match. That mob think they are already in the final. Already at Wembley. Because that London mob are arrogant, because that London mob are ignorant. But that London mob know nothing. Nothing about Liverpool Football Club! Because we are never drained, we are never exhausted. Not you boys and not our supporters. Never! And so Liverpool Football Club are never beaten. Never beaten!

On Saturday 27 March, 1965, at Villa Park, Birmingham, the supporters of Liverpool Football Club were not drained. The supporters of Liverpool Football Club were not exhausted. They sang and they roared. And out on the pitch, the players of Liverpool Football Club heard their songs, they heard their roars. And the players of Liverpool Football Club were no longer drained, no longer exhausted. Neither mentally nor physically. The players of Liverpool Football Club attacked and attacked and attacked. The players of Liverpool Football Club defended and defended and defended. The players of Liverpool Football Club ran and ran and ran. And the players of Chelsea Football Club could only stand and watch. They watched and they waited. They waited for the players of Liverpool Football Club to run themselves into the ground. Into the pitch. To lie prostrate upon the pitch. Drained and exhausted, exhausted and beaten. But still the players of Liverpool Football Club attacked and attacked and attacked. Still the players of Liverpool Football Club defended and defended and defended. For ten minutes. For twenty minutes. For thirty minutes. For forty minutes. For fifty minutes. Still the players of Liverpool Football Club ran and ran and ran. And after sixty minutes, Stevenson found Thompson with a long cross-field pass. Thompson dummied Hinton and Murray. Thompson cut between Hinton and Murray. In a flash, in the space, Thompson shot. And Thompson scored. And the supporters of Liverpool Football Club cheered, the supporters of Liverpool Football Club roared. And again the players of Liverpool Football Club attacked and attacked and attacked. Again the players of Liverpool Football Club defended and defended and defended. For seventy minutes. Again the players of Liverpool Football Club ran and ran and ran. And just before the eightieth minute, Harris upended St John in the Chelsea penalty area. The referee blew his whistle. The referee pointed to the penalty spot. Stevenson grabbed the ball. Stevenson placed the ball on the penalty spot. Stevenson stepped back. Stevenson stepped up. Stevenson shot. And Stevenson scored. And Liverpool Football Club beat Chelsea Football Club two–nil. The players of Liverpool Football Club not drained, the players of Liverpool Football Club not exhausted. They were jubilant and they were triumphant. And never beaten. The supporters of Liverpool Football Club sang, *Ee-aye-addio, we're going to win the Cup . . .*

After the whistle, the final whistle. Tommy Docherty, the manager of Chelsea Football Club, walked down the touchline to Bill Shankly. Tommy Docherty shook hands with Bill Shankly. And Tommy Docherty said, I don't understand it, Bill. You had a hard game in midweek. I just don't understand it, Bill. All our boys were fit and fresh. But today you were fitter and you were fresher, Bill. You were by far the better side. Congratulations, Bill. Congratulations.

Thank you, said Bill Shankly. And then Bill Shankly smiled. Bill Shankly took out the brochure from his coat pocket. And Bill Shankly handed the brochure to Tommy Docherty.

Tommy Docherty looked down at the brochure. The Chelsea brochure for the FA Cup Final. Tommy Docherty shook his head. And Tommy Docherty said, What's this, Bill? What on earth is this?

Just a wee souvenir for you, said Bill Shankly. A little something for you to remember us by, Tommy. A Cup Final souvenir.


## 18. THE WORLD TURNED UPSIDE DOWN

In the house, in their hall. The letters never stopped coming. The first post and the second post. The letters always coming. The letters asking for tickets. Cup Final tickets. And Bill answered them all. Bill apologised to them all. In the house, at their door. The callers never stopped knocking. Early in the morning, late in the evening. The callers always knocking. The callers begging for tickets. Cup Final tickets.

And Bill answered them all. Bill apologised to them all. In the house, in their hall. The telephone never stopped ringing. Early in the morning, late in the evening. The telephone always ringing. The calls pleading for tickets. Cup Final tickets. And Bill answered them all. Bill apologised to them all. And in the house, in their hall. The telephone was still ringing. But now Bill had to go. The telephone still ringing. Bill put on his coat. The telephone still ringing. Bill put on his hat. The telephone still ringing. Bill opened the front door. The telephone still ringing. Bill stepped outside. The telephone still ringing. Bill closed the door. The telephone still ringing. Bill walked down the drive. In the street, children spotted him. The children called out to him. Bill waved at them. The children asked Bill for tickets. Cup Final tickets. And Bill apologised to them. Bill got into his car. Bill drove down the West Derby Road. On the pavements, people spotted him. People waved at him. Bill waved back. People begged Bill for tickets. Cup Final tickets. And Bill apologised to them. Bill turned onto Belmont Road. Again, people waved at him. Again, Bill waved back. Again, people pleaded with Bill for tickets. Cup Final tickets. And again, Bill apologised to them. Bill turned into Anfield Road. Again, there were crowds of people. In the car park. Bill parked his car. Bill got out of his car. The crowds of people saw Bill. The crowds of people rushed to Bill. The crowds of people asked Bill for tickets. Cup Final tickets. They begged and they pleaded. Bill pushed through the crowds of people. And Bill apologised. Bill apologised and Bill apologised. And Bill went inside Anfield. The telephones ringing. Bill went up the stairs. The telephones ringing. Bill went down the corridor. The telephones ringing. Bill tapped on the office door. The telephones ringing. The office door of the club secretary. The telephones ringing. Bill opened the door. The telephones ringing. Bill saw the camp bed in the corner. The telephones ringing. Bill saw the bags of mail standing on the floor. The telephones ringing. The bags and bags of mail. The telephones ringing. Bill saw the stacks of letters on the desk. The telephones ringing. The stacks and stacks of letters. The telephones ringing. And Bill looked at Jimmy McInnes. The telephones ringing. Jimmy sat behind his desk. The telephones ringing. Among the letters. The telephones ringing. The stacks and stacks of letters. The telephones ringing. And Bill saw the circles under the eyes of Jimmy

163

McInnes. The telephones ringing. The black, dark circles under Jimmy's eyes. The telephones ringing. Bill picked up one of the phones on Jimmy's desk. And Bill said, Yes, what do you want, sir?

Did you get my letter, asked the voice on the other end of the line, the voice with a thick Birmingham accent. The letter I sent to you? The one I sent to you weeks ago now. Weeks ago . . .

What letter was that, sir?

For tickets. For the final. From Birmingham.

In Jimmy's office, down Jimmy's phone. Bill shouted, From Birmingham? Birmingham? I've got hundreds of friends, hundreds of relatives, all asking me for tickets, sir. But not one of them is getting a ticket. Not one of them. The tickets we've got are going to the Kop. To the boys on the Kop. To the boys who have supported us, week in and week out. That's where our tickets are going, sir. To the Kop. To the boys on the Spion Kop. The Liverpool boys.

But I was born in Liverpool . . .

Then you should have stayed here! You should never have moved to Birmingham. You should never have left Liverpool, sir.

And Bill put down the phone. The telephones still ringing. Bill looked at Jimmy. The telephones ringing. The circles under the eyes of Jimmy McInnes. The telephones ringing. The black and dark circles. The telephones ringing. And Bill smiled. The telephones ringing. And Bill said, I see you're still the most popular man at Anfield, Jimmy. Still the most popular man at Liverpool Football Club . . .

No, I'm not, said Jimmy McInnes. I'm definitely the most unpopular man at Liverpool Football Club, Bill.

Bill smiled again. The telephones ringing. And Bill said, No, Jimmy. No. I know you try to make as many people happy as you can, Jimmy. I know you try. I know you do . . .

Yes, said Jimmy McInnes. I try, Bill. I really do try. But I can't.

Bill picked up a phone on the desk. Bill put down the phone again. But the telephone started ringing again. And Bill said, But at least you try, Jimmy. At least you try to make the people happy.

. . .

In the studio, the BBC studio. On the radio, on *Desert Island Discs*. Because Liverpool Football Club had reached the final of the FA Cup, because Liverpool Football Club would play Leeds United in the final. Roy Plomley asked Bill which eight records he would take with him if Bill was cast away on a desert island. And Bill chose *My Love Is Like a Red, Red Rose*, sung by Kenneth McKellar. Bill chose *When the Saints Go Marching In*, sung by Danny Kaye and Louis Armstrong. Bill chose *The Last Rose of Summer*, sung by Sydney MacEwan and Robinson Cleaver. Bill chose *Danny Boy*, sung by Jim Reeves. Bill chose *Étude in E major, Op. 10/3*, composed by Frédéric Chopin, played by Claudio Arrau. Bill chose *Because You're Mine*, sung by Mario Lanza. Bill chose *The English Rose*, sung by Webster Booth. And finally, Bill chose *You'll Never Walk Alone*, sung by Gerry and the Pacemakers. Then Roy Plomley asked Bill which book he would take with him if Bill was cast away on a desert island. And Bill chose *Life of Robert Burns*, by John Stuart Blackie. And then Roy Plomley asked Bill what luxury item he would take with him if Bill was cast away on a desert island. Bill smiled, Bill laughed –

And Bill said, A football.

. . .

On the bus, the Liverpool bus. On their way, up Wembley Way. With a bus behind them, an empty bus behind them. Just in case. Nothing left to chance. No shocks and no surprises. Everything planned, everything prepared. On their bus, their Liverpool bus. On their way, up Wembley Way. At the front of their bus, in his seat. Bill looked out through the window. Into a sea of red, into a world of red. Red scarves and red flags, red banners and red songs. Everywhere Bill looked, everywhere Bill turned. Bill saw red –

A Red Sea and a Red World.

And on the bus, the Liverpool bus. On their way, up Wembley Way. Bill stood up at the front, Bill turned up the radio. Bill *on* the radio, Bill on *Desert Island Discs*. And Bill shouted down the bus, Can you hear these songs, boys? These are all great songs. Great Scottish songs, boys. Great Liverpool songs –

Great red songs, boys . . .

In their dressing room, their Wembley dressing room. Bill saw the players of Liverpool Football Club smiling, listening to the songs of Frankie Vaughan. And Bill heard the players of Liverpool Football Club laughing, listening to the jokes of Jimmy Tarbuck. The players smiling, the players laughing. The players relaxed, the players ready.

Ready for the game, ready for the final. The game now minutes away, the final now moments away. Bill walked into the centre of their dressing room, their Wembley dressing room. But Bill did not close the door, the dressing-room door. Bill stood with his back to the door, the open door. And Bill looked from player to player. From Tommy Lawrence to Chris Lawler. From Chris to Gerry Byrne. From Gerry to Geoff Strong. From Geoff to Ronnie Yeats. From Ronnie to Willie Stevenson. From Willie to Ian Callaghan. From Cally to Roger Hunt. From Roger to Ian St John. From the Saint to Tommy Smith. From Tommy to Peter Thompson. And Bill pointed out of the dressing room, the Liverpool dressing room, across the corridor, the Wembley corridor, to the other dressing room, the Leeds dressing room. And Bill said, Look, boys. Look! They have had their door shut for the past hour. And listen, boys. Listen! They are silent in there. Silent as the grave. Because they are frightened, boys. Frightened of this occasion. Frightened of this opportunity. But look at you, boys. Look at all of you. You are bouncing. You are smiling. Because you are enjoying this occasion. You are relishing this opportunity. Because this is what you were born to do. This is what you've worked your whole lives for. The opportunity to win the Cup. The opportunity to make history. And to make the supporters of Liverpool Football Club happy. So enjoy it, boys. Enjoy it! Because this will be the greatest day of your lives . . .

And then in their dressing room, their Wembley dressing room. Bill heard the buzzer, the Wembley buzzer. And Bill led the players of Liverpool Football Club down the tunnel, the Wembley tunnel, out onto the pitch, the Wembley pitch, and out into a sea of red, a world of red. LI-VER-POOL. A sea so deafening, a world so bright that the whole of London, the whole of England heard that sea and saw that world. LI-VER-POOL. On their radios and on their televisions. LI-VER-POOL. People might have read about the supporters of Liverpool Football Club, but today, on their televisions, live on their televisions, in black and white, now people saw the supporters of Liverpool Football Club. LI-VER-POOL. Their scarves and their flags, their banners and their songs. LI-VER-POOL. Now people saw the supporters of Liverpool Football Club and now people heard the supporters of Liverpool Football Club. LI-VER-POOL. This sea of red, this world of red. LI-VER-POOL. In black and white. LI-VER-POOL.

166

And Bill knew people would never forget Liverpool Football Club. LI-VER-POOL. Their sea of red, their world of red. LI-VER-POOL. Not black, not white. LI-VER-POOL. But red, all in red. Their LI-VER-POOL, their LI-VER-POOL, their LI-VER-POOL . . .

In red, all in red. On the first of May –

On the bench, the Wembley bench. Bill looked out at the pitch, the Wembley pitch. Its damp turf, its holding turf. And Bill watched Gerry Byrne go into a challenge with Bobby Collins. Bobby Collins went over the top on Gerry Byrne. Gerry Byrne fell on the pitch, Gerry Byrne lay on the turf. And on their bench, their Wembley bench. Bill turned to Bob. Bob jumped up from his seat, Bob picked up his bag. And Bob ran onto the pitch, across the turf. Bob knelt down beside Gerry Byrne. On the pitch, on the turf. In agony, in pain. Gerry Byrne pointed to his ankle. Bob put his hand on the ankle of Gerry Byrne. Bob felt the ankle bones of Gerry Byrne. Bob opened up his bag, Bob took out a can. And Bob sprayed the ankle of Gerry Byrne with ice. Then Bob helped Gerry Byrne to his feet. In agony and in pain. Bob heard the shoulder bones of Gerry Byrne grind. In agony and in pain. Bob sprayed the right shoulder of Gerry Byrne with ice. And then Bob patted Gerry Byrne on his cheek. In agony and in pain. Gerry Byrne nodded. And Bob ran back across the turf, back off the pitch. Bob sat back down on the bench beside Bill. And Bill turned to Bob –

I could hear Gerry's bones, whispered Bob. His bones, Boss. I think Gerry's collarbone is gone. It's gone, Boss . . .

His coat stuck to his jacket. His jacket stuck to his shirt. His shirt stuck to his vest. His vest stuck to his skin. Bill nodded. And Bill stared back out across the pitch, the Wembley pitch. Its damp turf, its holding turf. In the grey light now, in the slow rain now. For forty-five minutes. Forty-five dour minutes. Across the pitch, across the turf. In the grey-light and in the slow-rain. For ninety minutes. Ninety hard, hard minutes. On the Wembley pitch, on the Wembley turf. In the grey-light and in the slow-rain. Into extra time. On the damp turf, the holding turf. In the grey-light and in the slow-rain. In extra time. His coat stuck to his jacket. His jacket stuck to his shirt. His shirt stuck to his vest. His vest stuck to his skin. Bill watched Stevenson pass to Byrne. In agony and in pain. Byrne crossed to Hunt. Hunt headed the ball. And Hunt scored. In the grey-light, in the slow-rain. In the ninety-third minute. The players of Liverpool Football Club were winning. *Ee-aye-addio, we're going to win the Cup.* And the supporters of Liverpool Football Club were singing. *We're going to win the Cup.* In a sea of red, in a world of red. *Ee-aye-addio, we're going to win the Cup.* But nine minutes later. On the damp turf, the holding turf. In the grey-light and in the slow-rain. His coat stuck to his jacket. His jacket stuck to his shirt. His shirt stuck to his vest. His vest stuck to his skin. Bill watched Bremner score for Leeds. The sea white now, the world white now. But in the grey-light, in the slow-rain. Bill could still hear the supporters of Liverpool Football Club. The supporters of Liverpool Football Club now singing. *Walk on, walk on, with hope in your heart.* In the grey-light and in the slow-rain. *And you'll never walk alone.* Smith passed to Callaghan. *You'll never walk alone.* Callaghan crossed to St John. *A-lone.* St John headed the ball. *You'll never walk alone.* And St John scored. LI-VER-POOL! The supporters of Liverpool Football Club turning the world red again. LI-VER-POOL! Forever red, forever LI-VER-POOL. Liverpool Football Club had beaten Leeds United two–one. LI-VER-POOL, LI-VER-POOL, LI-VER-POOL. In the grey-light and in the slow-rain. LI-VER-POOL, LI-VER-POOL, LI-VER-POOL! On the damp Wembley pitch, on the holding Wembley turf. Liverpool Football Club had won the FA Cup for the first time. On the first of May, nineteen sixty-five –

For the first time. In history,

in their history.

His coat stuck to his jacket. His jacket stuck to his shirt. His shirt stuck to his vest. His vest stuck to his skin. Bill got up from the bench. The Liverpool bench. Bill walked down the touchline. The Wembley touchline. And Bill shook the hand of Don Revie. The Leeds United manager. And then Bill walked across the pitch. The Wembley pitch. Bill went from player to player. From Sprake to Reaney, Reaney to Bell, Bell to Bremner, Bremner to Charlton, Charlton to Hunter, Hunter to Giles, Giles to Storrie, Storrie to Peacock, Peacock to Collins, Collins to Johanneson. Bill patted their backs, Bill shook their hands. And then Bill turned. Bill turned and Bill walked across the turf. The Wembley turf. Towards the supporters of Liverpool Football Club. Towards their scarves and their flags, towards their banners and their songs. *Ee-aye-addio, we've won the Cup.* And Bill stopped on the pitch, the Wembley pitch. Bill stood on the turf, the Wembley turf. Before this sea of red, before this world of red. *We've won the Cup.* His coat stuck to his jacket. His jacket stuck to his shirt. His shirt stuck to his vest. His vest stuck to his skin. Bill clenched his fists, Bill raised his arms. In triumph and in gratitude. Before the crowd and in the crowd, before her sea and in her world. In victory and in thanks. *Ee-aye-addio, we won the Cup!* For her sea of red,

in her world of red.

. . .

On the train from London to Liverpool, from Euston to Lime Street. In their carriage, in his seat. Bill looked across the table at Ness. Ness had been at Wembley Stadium. Ness had been at the Cup Final. It had been the first time Ness had ever seen Liverpool Football Club play. And Ness had seen Liverpool Football Club win the Cup. The first time Liverpool Football Club had ever won the FA Cup. The Cup under their table now, at his feet now. Bill smiled at Ness. Ness smiled back at Bill. And in their carriage, in his seat. Bill closed his eyes. And Bill felt the wheels of the train beneath him again. Turning, turning. Their movement and their rhythm. Round and round. Movement and rhythm. Forward, always forward. And in his mind, in his eyes. Bill saw the players of Liverpool Football Club walking up the steps at Wembley. In red. In his mind, in his eyes. Bill saw Ronnie collecting the Cup from the Queen. The Queen in red. In his mind, in his eyes. Bill saw Ronnie lifting the Cup aloft, showing the Cup to the supporters of Liverpool Football Club. In red. In his mind, in his ears. Bill heard the roar of the crowd. In red. That roar that had shook the earth, that had raised the dead. In red, all in red. Resurrected in red, all in red. In their carriage, in his seat. Bill opened his eyes. Again. Bill tapped the Cup with the toe of his shoe. The Cup still there. Under their table, at his feet. In the carriage, on the train, The train back to Lime Street, the train back to Liverpool. The FA Cup coming to Liverpool Football Club. For the very first time. In history, in their history. To *LI-VER-POOL, LI-VER-POOL, LI-VER-POOL . . .*

At Lime Street Station, Liverpool. Bill and Ness and the players and the staff of Liverpool Football Club got off the train. And Bill could not believe his eyes. Everywhere Bill looked, Bill saw faces. The faces of people. Everywhere Bill turned, Bill saw people. People cheering, people clapping. And Bill could not believe his ears. People shouting, people singing. Fifty thousand people cheering and clapping, fifty thousand people shouting and singing. All singing, singing –

*LI-VER-POOL, LI-VER-POOL, LI-VER-POOL . . .*

At the station, Bill and Ness and the players and the staff of Liverpool Football Club boarded the bus. The bus to take them to the Town Hall. And still Bill could not believe his eyes. Everywhere Bill looked, Bill saw more faces. More faces of people. People lining the streets, people thronging the roads. Everywhere Bill turned, Bill saw more people. People hanging off hoardings, people dangling off lamp posts. And still Bill could not believe his eyes. On Castle Street, on Dale Street. People in dangerous places, people risking their lives. For a glimpse of the Cup. One hundred thousand people cheering and clapping, one hundred thousand people shouting and singing –

*LI-VER-POOL, LI-VER-POOL, LI-VER-POOL . . .*

At the Town Hall, Bill and Ness and the players and the staff of Liverpool Football Club got off the bus. Bill and Ness and the players and the staff of Liverpool Football Club walked up the Town Hall steps. Bill and Ness and the players and the staff of Liverpool Football Club walked out onto the Town Hall balcony. And Bill blinked. And blinked. And blinked again. Bill just could not believe his eyes. Across the square, across the city. Everywhere Bill looked, there were people. Bill just could not believe his ears. Everywhere Bill turned, there were people. Two hundred and fifty thousand people. Two hundred and fifty thousand people cheering. Two hundred and fifty thousand people clapping. Two hundred and fifty thousand people shouting. Two hundred and fifty thousand people singing. All singing –

*LI-VER-POOL, LI-VER-POOL, LI-VER-POOL. LI-VER-POOL, LI-VER-POOL, LI-VER-POOL. LI-VER-POOL,*

*LI-VER-POOL, LI-VER-POOL . . .*

Bill fought back tears, Bill struggled to breathe. Ness gripped his arm, Ness squeezed his hand –

I never knew until now, whispered Ness, until today, how much football meant to the people of Liverpool. But you knew, love. You always knew what it meant to the people of Liverpool . . .

*LI-VER-POOL, LI-VER-POOL . . .*

Bill shook his head. And Bill said, No, love. I didn't know. I only dreamt, I only imagined. But *now* I know, love . . .

*LI-VER-POOL* . . .

Now I know. But I know we have not finished, love. I know we have just begun. I know this is just the start, love.

. . .

At Anfield, in the dressing room. Three days after, just three days after Liverpool Football Club had won the FA Cup. Two hours before the match, still two hours before Liverpool Football Club would play Internazionale of Milan in the first leg of the semi-final of the European Cup. Bill could already hear the fifty-two thousand and eighty-two folk inside Anfield, Liverpool. Bill could already hear them singing, Bill could already hear them chanting. *We want to see the Cup! We want to see the Cup! Ee-aye-addio, we want to see the Cup* . . .

And in the dressing room, before the kick-off. Bill had an idea. Bill and Bob went to find Gordon Milne and Gerry Byrne. Gordon Milne with his knee still damaged, Gerry Byrne with his arm in a sling. Gordon would not be playing tonight and Gerry would not be playing tonight. But Gordon and Gerry had played their parts. And Gordon and Gerry still had a part to play. Bill and Bob brought Gordon and Gerry back to the dressing room. Bill told Gordon and Gerry to wait in the dressing room, Bill told Gordon and Gerry to hide behind the dressing-room door. And then Bill looked at his watch. Bill smiled. And Bill went out of the Liverpool dressing room. Bill went out into the corridor. Bill knocked on the door of the other dressing room. The Internazionale of Milan dressing-room door. Mister Herrera, the manager of Internazionale of Milan, opened the door. Bill smiled. Bill pointed at his watch. And Bill said, It's time to go, Mister Herrera. It's time your team went out there. Out there onto the pitch, sir.

Thank you, said Mister Herrera.

Bill went back into the Liverpool dressing room. Bill closed the dressing-room door. Bill looked around the dressing room. From Lawrence to Lawler, Lawler to Moran, Moran to Strong, Strong to Yeats, Yeats to Stevenson, Stevenson to Callaghan, Callaghan to Hunt, Hunt to St John, St John to Smith, Smith to Thompson. And Bill raised his finger in the air. Bill put his finger to his ear. And Bill said, Listen, boys. Just listen to this . . .

And on the benches, the Liverpool benches. The players of

Liverpool Football Club listened to the sound of studs. The studs of boots. The boots of the players of Internazionale of Milan walking out of their dressing room, down the corridor and down the steps, out onto the pitch, the Anfield pitch, and into a wall of whistles, into a chorus of *Go back to I-ta-lee, Go back to I-ta-lee, GO BACK TO I-TA-LEE!*

In the dressing room, the Liverpool dressing room. Bill turned to Gordon Milne and Gerry Byrne. Gordon with his damaged knee, Gerry with his broken collarbone. And Bill picked up the FA Cup. Bill handed the FA Cup to Gordon and Gerry. And Bill said, The people want to see the FA Cup, boys. The people are desperate to see the Cup. So you two boys show them the Cup. Parade the Cup, boys. And you make sure everybody in this ground sees this Cup. Everybody on every side of this ground. Make sure you go to the Anfield Road end first. And then down to the Kop. To the boys on the Kop . . .

Ron Yeats stood up. Ron Yeats led the players of Liverpool Football Club out of their dressing room, down the corridor and down the steps, out onto the pitch, the Anfield pitch, into a wall of applause, into a chorus of *LI-VER-POOL, LI-VER-POOL, LI-VER-POOL . . .*

And then behind Ron Yeats, behind the players of Liverpool Football Club, out of the dressing room, down the corridor and down the steps, out onto the pitch, the Anfield pitch, came Gordon Milne and Gerry Byrne, one hobbling and one limping, carrying the FA Cup, parading the FA Cup, around the ground, around the stadium, from one end to the other, from the Anfield Road end to the Spion Kop end, to applause so intense, to cheers so piercing, that the very earth shook, the very world shook. *WE'VE WON THE CUP! WE'VE WON THE CUP! EE-AYE-ADDIO, WE'VE WON THE CUP . . .*

And on the pitch, the Anfield pitch, the players of Internazionale of Milan stood and stared, their legs shaking with fear, their eyes blinking in terror. Red fear,

red terror. In the centre of this sea of noise, in the middle of this world of red. The referee blew his whistle. St John kicked off. Smith passed to Strong. Strong passed to Callaghan. Callaghan crossed to Hunt. And Hunt turned. Hunt hit the ball on the volley. In the fourth minute, the volley from the edge of the penalty area. The volley into the top of the net. *LI-VER-POOL, LI-VER-POOL, LI-VER-POOL.* But now Internazionale of Milan began to find their feet. And now they began to find the ball. Corso found space down the left. Corso found Peiró. Peiró found Mazzola. And Mazzola found the net. *Walk on, walk on, with hope in your heart.* In the thirty-fourth minute, a free kick on the edge of the Internazionale of Milan penalty area. *And you'll never walk alone.* Callaghan feinted to shoot, Callaghan hopped over the ball. *You'll never walk alone.* Stevenson passed to St John. *A-lone.* Callaghan slid the ball past Sarti. *You'll never walk alone.* Into the net, into the goal. *LI-VER-POOL, LI-VER-POOL, LI-VER-POOL.* In the fortieth minute, Lawler passed to Callaghan. Callaghan passed back to Lawler. Lawler beat one man, Lawler beat a second, Lawler beat a third. And Lawler hit the ball. With his left foot. Hit the ball and shot. Into the net, into the goal. *LI-VER-POOL, LI-VER-POOL, LI-VER-POOL.* Into the goal that was not a goal. The goal disallowed. Bedlam, cacophony. *LI-VER-POOL, LI-VER-POOL, LI-VER-POOL.* In the seventy-fifth minute, Thompson passed to Callaghan. Callaghan headed on to Smith. Smith inside to Hunt. Hunt shot. Sarti parried the ball. The ball loose, loose to St John. And St John shot. Into the net, into the goal. And *LI-VER-POOL, LI-VER-POOL, LI-VER-POOL* Football Club had beaten Internazionale of Milan three–one. Internazionale of Milan. The European Champions. The Intercontinental Cup Champions. Internazionale of Milan dazed, Internazionale of Milan shell-shocked. In a sea of noise, in a world of red. Mister Herrera got up from the bench. Slowly. Mister Herrera walked down the touchline. The Anfield touchline. And Mister Herrera shook Bill's hand –

We've been beaten before, said Mister Herrera. But tonight we were defeated. Defeated. So congratulations, Mr Shankly.

Bill smiled. And Bill said, Thank you, sir.

Mister Herrera looked around the ground, the Anfield ground. Mister Herrera stared up at the Kop, the Spion Kop –

But I'll see you again, said Mister Herrera. I'll see you soon, Mr Shankly. In Italy. In Milan. At the San Siro.

. . .

In the house, in their hall. The telephone was ringing. And ringing. Always ringing. In the front room, in his chair. Bill put down his paper again. The accolades and the praise. The accolades for the night before, the praise for the night before. Bill looked across at Ness. Ness looked up from her paper. From her crossword. And Ness smiled at Bill. And Bill said, Aye, no doubt it'll be for me, love . . .

Well, I'll put the kettle on, said Ness. I'll make us a cup of tea.

Bill smiled, Bill nodded. Bill went out into the hall, Bill picked up the telephone. Bill listened to the voice on the line –

And Bill dropped the phone –

Bill ran to the door, Bill ran to the car. Bill drove to the ground, Bill ran into the stadium. The telephones ringing. Bill ran up the stairs. The telephones ringing. Bill ran down the corridor. The telephones ringing. Bill banged on the office door. The telephones ringing. The office door of the club secretary. The telephones ringing. Bill pushed open the door. The telephones ringing. Bill saw the bags of mail standing on the floor. The telephones ringing. The bags and bags of mail. The telephones ringing. Bill saw the camp bed in the corner. The telephones ringing. Bill saw the stacks of letters on the desk. The telephones ringing. The stacks and stacks of letters. The telephones ringing. Jimmy not at his desk. The telephones ringing. Among the letters. The telephones ringing. The stacks and stacks of letters. The telephones ringing. Jimmy not in his office. Bill turned around, Bill ran again. Back down the corridor, back down the stairs. Out of the building and around the ground. To the back of the Kop, to the Archway turnstile. And Bill stopped. At the back of the Kop, at the Archway turnstile. Bill saw Arthur Riley. Bill saw the policemen. Bill saw the ambulance. Bill saw the stretcher. And Bill saw the blanket. Under the blanket, the shape of a body. On the stretcher, in the ambulance. By the turnstile, under the Kop. The body of Jimmy McInnes. And then Bill saw his wife. Jimmy's wife.

. . .

In the drive, in the car. Bill turned off the engine. Bill got out of the car. Bill walked up the drive. Bill opened the front door. Bill went into the house. Bill shut the door. Bill walked down the hall. Bill went into the front room. And Bill saw Ness. Ness on her feet. Ness looking at Bill. Her hands to her mouth. Ness looking at Bill. And Bill said, It's Jimmy, love. He's dead, love.

Dead? How? When?

This morning, love. He hanged himself. Under the Kop.

. . .

In the drive, in the car. In the night. Bill turned off the engine.

In the night. Bill got out of the car. In the night. Bill walked up the drive. In the night. Bill unlocked the front door of the house. In the night. Bill opened the door. In the night. Bill stepped into the house. In the dark. Bill closed the door. In the dark. Bill put down his case in the hallway. In the dark. Bill walked down the hallway to the kitchen. In the dark. Bill sat down at the table. In the dark. Bill put his hand in his pocket. In the dark. Bill took out the chip. The red and white chip. In the dark. Bill stared down at the chip. The red and white chip. In the dark. Bill turned the chip in his fingers. The red and white chip. In the dark. The happiest day of his life. That day on the balcony of Liverpool Town Hall. The best night of his life. That night Liverpool Football Club had beaten Internazionale of Milan at Anfield. The worst night of his life. The night Internazionale of Milan beat Liverpool Football Club at the San Siro, the night Internazionale of Milan knocked Liverpool Football Club out of the European Cup. The saddest day of his life. The day he had stood beneath the Spion Kop. The day they had found Jimmy McInnes. By the Archway turnstile. Hanging under the Kop. The saddest days and the happiest days, the worst days and the best. In the dark. Bill turned the chip again. The red and white chip. And again. The red side and the white side. Two sides, two sides. There were always two sides. Two sides

to every coin, two sides

to every story.


## 19. AFTER THE WAR, BEFORE THE WAR

The 1964–65 season had been a long season. The longest season in the history of Liverpool Football Club. A hard season and a tiring season. A season of ups and a season of downs. In the 1964–65 season, Liverpool Football Club had finished seventh in the First Division. But Liverpool Football Club had reached the semi-finals of the European Cup and Liverpool Football Club had won the FA Cup. For the first time in the history of Liverpool Football Club. It had been a long season. But it had been a good season. And it should have been a happy season. But no one was happy.

In the summer of 1965, at the start of the pre-season training.

The players of Liverpool Football Club were not happy. The players of Liverpool Football Club had complaints. The players of Liverpool Football Club had grievances.

The directors of Liverpool Football Club had promised every player of Liverpool Football Club a bonus of one thousand pounds if Liverpool Football Club won the FA Cup. The players of Liverpool Football Club had won the FA Cup. The players of Liverpool Football Club expected to each receive their bonus of one thousand pounds, plus their basic wage of thirty-five pounds, less tax. The players of Liverpool Football Club also expected to receive a crowd bonus. Home or away, the players of Liverpool Football Club always received a crowd bonus. One hundred thousand folk had come to Wembley Stadium on Saturday 1 May, 1965. One hundred thousand folk had seen Liverpool Football Club win the FA Cup. And so the players of Liverpool Football Club expected to receive a crowd bonus. Plus their one thousand pounds for winning the Cup, plus their basic wage, less tax. The directors of Liverpool Football Club paid the players of Liverpool Football Club their bonus for winning the FA Cup, plus their basic wage, less tax. But the directors of Liverpool Football Club said Wembley Stadium was neither home nor away. The directors of Liverpool Football Club said Wembley Stadium was a neutral ground. The directors of Liverpool Football Club refused to pay the players of Liverpool Football Club a crowd bonus. And so the players of Liverpool Football Club were not happy. The players of Liverpool Football Club had complaints. The players of Liverpool Football Club had grievances. Complaints about their wage structure, grievances about their salaries. The players of Liverpool Football Club knew their wages were amongst the lowest in the First Division. The players of Liverpool Football Club contacted the secretary of the Players' Association. The secretary of the Players' Association came to Anfield, Liverpool, to assist the players of Liverpool Football Club in their negotiations with the directors of Liverpool Football Club. The secretary of the Players' Association told the local press, the Liverpool press, I deny as emphatically as possible the rumour being put about that the players of Liverpool Football Club are seeking a basic wage of one hundred pounds a week. Their basic wage, far from being in three figures, has not even been half that sum.

Bill Shankly nodded. But Bill Shankly was not happy. Bill Shankly didn't like money. He didn't want to talk about money, he didn't even like to think about money. Bill Shankly knew you needed a roof over your head. A decent roof. Food on your table and clothes on your back. Decent food and decent clothes. For you and for your family. Bill Shankly believed the wages from your work should provide you with a roof. With food and with clothes. A decent roof. Decent food and decent clothes. For you and for your family. But Bill Shankly believed you had to earn your wage. You had to earn that roof over your head. The food on your table and the clothes on your back. That then you would cherish that roof. That food and those clothes. Because you had earned that roof. That food, those clothes. Bill Shankly believed anything else, anything more, was a luxury. Bill Shankly believed a luxury was something you had not earned. Something you had not worked for. Bill Shankly knew such luxuries were also a distraction. A distraction from your work. Bill Shankly didn't like distractions. He didn't want to talk about distractions, he didn't want to even think about distractions –

It would be a pity if differences of this sort were to create unease where no uneasiness has existed in the past, said Bill Shankly. And if these differences, if this unease, were to create distractions. Distractions from our work.

. . .

On Saturday 14 August, 1965, Liverpool Football Club travelled to Old Trafford, Manchester. That afternoon, forty-eight thousand, five hundred and two folk came, too. Manchester folk and Liverpool folk. Forty-eight thousand, five hundred and two folk to watch the winners of the Football League play the winners of the FA Cup for the Charity Shield. There were floating banners in the stands, boisterous chorales to the roofs of the stands. In the thirty-eighth minute, Willie Stevenson scored. In the eighty-sixth minute, Ron Yeats scored. But Herd had scored, too. And Best had scored, too. And the Charity Shield was shared between the winners of the Football League and the winners of the FA Cup. And thirteen thousand pounds was raised for charity. Charity.

That Saturday morning, before the match, the directors of Liverpool Football Club had announced that all the players of

Liverpool Football Club had signed new contracts for the coming season. That the players of Liverpool Football Club had no more complaints, the players of Liverpool Football Club had no more grievances. That the players of Liverpool Football Club were happy. And Bill Shankly was happy –

I would like to pay tribute to the chairman, the president and the board of Liverpool Football Club, said Bill Shankly. They have given the players of Liverpool Football Club one of the finest deals I have ever known in the game. One of the best deals in the game. And so now everybody is happy. There are no more differences, there is no more unease. And no more distractions. Only work now. Only work!

. . .

On Saturday 21 August, 1965, Liverpool Football Club travelled to Filbert Street, Leicester, for their first League game of the 1965–66 season. In the thirty-fifth minute, Roger Hunt scored. In the fifty-third minute, Geoff Strong scored. And in the eightieth minute, Hunt scored again. And Liverpool Football Club beat Leicester City three–one. Away from home, away from Anfield. It was a good start. But only a start. Four days later, Sheffield United came to Anfield, Liverpool. That evening, forty-seven thousand, two hundred and fifty-nine folk came, too. But Liverpool Football Club lost one–nil. At home, at Anfield, in their first home game of the 1965–66 season. One week later, Liverpool Football Club travelled to Bramall Lane, Sheffield. And Liverpool Football Club drew nil–nil with Sheffield United. Liverpool Football Club then beat Blackpool Football Club away, Liverpool Football Club then beat West Ham United five–one away. And Liverpool Football Club then beat Fulham Football Club. At home, at Anfield. Liverpool Football Club then drew one-all with West Ham United. Three days later, Liverpool Football Club travelled to White Hart Lane, London. And Liverpool Football Club lost two–one to Tottenham Hotspur. That evening, Liverpool Football Club had played eight games. They had won four games, they had drawn two games. And they had lost two games. That evening, Liverpool Football Club had nine points. That evening, Liverpool Football Club were eighth in the First Division. It was not a good start, it was not a bad start. It was just a start. Just the start.

. . .

On Saturday 25 September, 1965. In the dressing room, on the benches. In their kits and in their boots. The players of Liverpool Football Club heard the footsteps in the corridor. Fast and heavy. Bill Shankly walked into the dressing room. Bill Shankly closed the door. Bill Shankly looked around the room. From player to player. From Lawrence to Strong, Strong to Byrne, Byrne to Milne, Milne to Yeats, Yeats to Stevenson, Stevenson to Callaghan, Callaghan to Hunt, Hunt to St John, St John to Smith and from Smith to Thompson –

Everybody here today in this room, said Bill Shankly. Everybody here today in this ground. Everybody in this city, everybody in the world. They all know what happened the last time this mob came here. Nobody in this room, nobody in this ground, nobody in this city, nobody in the world, has forgotten what happened that day. They all remember and you all remember. And you all remember the things I said to you that day, the things the people in this ground said to you that day. Well, today, you have the chance to answer me, to answer those people. At last. You can answer us all back, boys. But you all know there can only be one answer. There is only one answer. Five–nil –

Five–nil, boys.

In the thirty-fourth minute, Tommy Smith scored. In the forty-ninth minute, Roger Hunt scored. In the fifty-second minute, Willie Stevenson scored. In the seventy-third minute, Hunt scored again. And in the eighty-ninth minute, with only one minute remaining, Ian St John scored. And a supporter of Liverpool Football Club jumped out of the Kop. The Spion Kop. The supporter of Liverpool Football Club ran onto the pitch. The Anfield pitch. The supporter of Liverpool Football Club gave a handbag to Gordon West, the Everton keeper. And the supporters of Liverpool Football Club laughed. The supporters of Liverpool Football Club roared. And the players of Everton Football Club stood on the pitch with their hands on their hips. The players of Everton Football Club shook their heads. And the manager of Everton Football Club walked down the touchline. The manager of Everton Football Club shook his head. And then Harry Catterick shook the hand of Bill Shankly. And Harry Catterick said, I am stunned, Bill. I am simply stunned. I do not know what to say. I do not understand it. Last week, you lost two–one at Tottenham. Last week, you were rubbish. Everybody said so, everybody told me. But today, you won five–nil. Today, you were brilliant, Bill. Simply brilliant.

Thank you, said Bill Shankly. Thank you, Harry. But you're wrong. You're wrong again, Harry. Last week, we were brilliant, too. Last week, we were better than we were today. Much, much better. Last week, we should have murdered Tottenham six–nil. Last week, we should have given them a drubbing. So this was coming to someone. And that someone was Everton. That someone was you, Harry . . .

After the whistle, the final whistle. In the dressing room, on the benches. Still in their kits, still in their boots. The players of Liverpool Football Club heard the footsteps in the corridor. Bouncing, dancing. Bill Shankly waltzed into the dressing room, around the dressing room. From player to player. Patting their backs, shaking their hands –

You were magnificent, boys. Magnificent. Every one of you, boys. Every single one of you. I could not have asked for more. The crowd could not have asked for more. You have answered back every comment, every question, with a magnificent display of total, team football. From the back to the front, from the left to the right. Every one of you, boys. Every single one of you. Magnificent. I tell you, boys. That is one of the best displays of football I have ever seen in my life. And no one here today will have seen a better display, a better example of team football in this country since the war. Playing like that, playing like you can, we will be the Champions again. We will win the Cup again. And we will win the Cup Winners' Cup, too. We can win them all, boys. We can win them all! So now you go out there tonight, boys. With your heads held high. And you walk among the people of this city. And you listen to what those people will tell you. Because to a man, they will tell you the same as I'm telling you now, boys. You are the best team in England since the war.

## 20. DEAR PEOPLE

His jacket stuck to his shirt. His shirt stuck to his vest. His vest stuck to his skin. His skin stretched and his muscles taut. Bill opened his eyes again. And Bill tried to shift in his seat. His skin burning, his muscles straining. Bill could not shift in his seat. Burning, straining.

Bill tried to move his hands. His hands locked tight around the armrest of his seat. His knuckles white. Bill forced open the fingers of his right hand. Bill raised his right arm. Bill brought his right hand over to the left sleeve of his jacket. Bill pulled up the left sleeve of his jacket. Bill stared down at his watch. The aeroplane shuddered. Again. Bill gripped the armrests of his seat. The aeroplane dipped. Again. Bill closed his eyes. And again. Bill tried not to think of the last time he had sat on a plane. The last time he had flown to Italy. The things that happened in Italy, the things that happened in Milan. *Addio!* The klaxons and the trumpets, the rockets and the flares. *Addio!* Their fireworks and their smoke bombs, their arrogance and their hostility. *Addio!* It had been one long carnival of hate, it had been one dark charade of corruption. *Addio!* A very long, dark night, a very long, bad night. *Addio!* Filled with potions and filled with spells. *Addio!* And now Bill was coming back to Italy, now Liverpool Football Club were flying to Turin. Another city of potions, another city of spells.

In their hotel in Turin, in the dining room. The players of Liverpool Football Club finished their meals, the players of Liverpool Football Club went up to their rooms. An early night tonight, before the game tomorrow. Tomorrow, the players of Liverpool Football Club would play Juventus Football Club at the Stadio Comunale in the preliminary round of the European Cup Winners' Cup.

In their hotel in Turin, in the dining room. The waiters cleared away their plates, the waiters cleared away their glasses. The waiters leaned against the bar, the waiters looked at their watches. And then the waiters looked at Bill, Bob, Joe and Reuben. Their plates clean, their glasses empty. Bill laughed. And Bill said, Tommy Finney is always telling me about the day he played here for England at their Stadio Comunale. Tommy always says it was the finest all-round team performance of his England career. In front of fifty-eight thousand people, in ninety-degree temperatures. He says the people had to bring umbrellas to shield themselves from the sun. It was that hot. And that Italian team were hot, too. You all remember them. That team. They were the best team in the world then. The world champions. The Olympic champions. And the crowd were expecting them to put on a show. All fifty-eight thousand of them. With their umbrellas. Expecting them to hammer England. Humiliate them and murder them.

In revenge for the war. That's what they wanted. That crowd. Those fifty-eight thousand folk, with their umbrellas. They wanted revenge. But Tommy says Frank Swift was brilliant that day. They all were. Don Howe, Neil Franklin, Henry Cockburn, Stan Matthews. Magnificent. All of them. Mortensen scored the first, I think. Lawton got another. And then Tommy scored two, scored them like this –

Bill jumped up from his chair, Bill ripped off his jacket. Bill stood between the tables and the chairs. Bill looked one way, Bill looked another. In their hotel, in the dining room. Bill looked for the ball, Bill saw the ball. Bill turned to hit the ball, Bill struck it. And Bill said, One on the volley from a cross from Wilf Mannion . . .

Bill stepped back. In their hotel, in the dining room. Bill looked for the ball again, Bill saw the ball again. Bill struck it again. And Bill said, And the other like that, in from close range . . .

Bill sat back down at the table. And Bill said, And Tommy was playing on the left that day. That was the first time they'd found a way to play Tommy and Matthews in the same side. Tommy says the Italians didn't know what had hit them. That they started arguing amongst themselves. Because they weren't used to losing, you see. Seven of them played for that Torino side that won all those consecutive titles. You all remember them. That side that were killed in the air crash a year later. Terrible, terrible. But can you imagine that forward line? Matthews, Mortensen, Lawton, Mannion and Tommy. Jesus Christ! What a team that was, what a game that must have been. Like a different game, in a different world. It's all back to front and inside out now. Now it's the defenders who score the goals. Not the forwards. That's the new game, that's the new world. It's a game for defenders now. That's the secret, boys. And that's what we'll be up against tomorrow. A team of defenders.

. . .

In the dressing room, the Anfield dressing room. Before the whistle, the first whistle of the return leg. Bill shook his head again. And Bill said, One goal. That's all they got. One goal. And from their full-back. One goal. And we all know that's all they wanted. One goal. And that's all they got. That one goal. That's all they wanted and that's all they've got. One goal. And so they've come here today. With that goal, that one goal. Determined to hang onto that goal, that one

182

goal. To keep that goal, that one goal. And to take that goal, that one goal. In their suitcases, their fancy suitcases. Back to Turin, back to Italy. With their goal, their one goal. That's their plan, their only plan. But they're in for a surprise, boys. They're in for a shock. Because how many folk do you think there were? Last week, in Turin? Five thousand, ten thousand? Nobody. There was nobody there! Not like today, not like tonight. Tonight there are fifty thousand folk here! Fifty thousand folk inside Anfield tonight. Fifty thousand folk here to watch you prise open their fancy, flash suitcases, their grubby, little hands. Fifty thousand folk here to watch you take that one goal from Juventus Football Club and to send them packing back to Turin, back to Italy. With nothing in their cases, with nothing in their hands . . .

On the bench, the Anfield bench. Among the banners, among the songs. The red banners and the red songs. Bill watched a sea of incessant movement, Bill watched a world of strong meat. The red movement, the red meat. The free kick by Stevenson out on the left. The free kick finding Strong. Strong streaking in from the right, Strong out-leaping the whole field. Heading the ball square to Lawler. A defender to a defender. Coming in fast to dive forward, diving forward to the ball. Into the net, into a goal. In a sea of incessant movement, in a world of strong meat. Red movement, red meat. The lazy back-heel from Del Sol. Lawler robbing Del Sol, Lawler feeding Callaghan. Callaghan crossing, St John rising. The ball coming loose, the ball coming back. Back out to Strong. A defender at the edge of their penalty area, a defender with a rocket for a shot. Into the net, into a goal. In a sea of incessant movement, in a world of strong meat. The red movement and the red meat. Among the banners, among the songs. The red banners and the red songs. Juventus Football Club had nothing to hold onto, nothing to protect. Juventus Football Club had been beaten from the back, beaten by two goals from two defenders. Juventus Football Club had been beaten at their own game. Liverpool Football Club had learnt their lesson. And Liverpool Football Club had taught Juventus Football Club a lesson –

The pupil now the master.

. . .

Under the stands, among the boots. Bill, Bob, Reuben, Joe and Albert each had a piece of paper in their hands. On the piece of paper was a list, a list of names: Alf Arrowsmith, John Bennett, Phil Chisnall, Roy Evans, Bobby Graham, Brian Hall, Alan Hignett, Geoff Long, Thomas Lowry, Ted McDougall, Grant McCulloch, Kevin Marsh, William Molyneux, Ronnie Moran, John Ogston, Steve Peplow, Ian Ross, John Sealey, Ken Walker and Gordon Wallace. The names of players, the players in the Liverpool Football Club reserve team –

Bill saw the reserves play as often as he could. Bill had seen the reserves play seven times this season. But Bill had not seen the reserves play since Monday 20 September, when the reserves had drawn three-all with Wolverhampton Wanderers reserves –

Under the stands, among the boots. Bill, Bob, Reuben, Joe and Albert discussed each player in the reserve team. Their strong points and their weak points. Bill, Bob, Joe, Reuben and Albert discussed every game the reserve team had played. The good points and the bad points. The reserve team had played seventeen matches this season. They had won six games and they had drawn six games. And they had lost five. They had scored twenty-eight goals and they had conceded twenty-one goals. Phil Chisnall was the leading scorer in the reserve team with five goals. Bill put down the piece of paper. And Bill said, How about Ronnie Moran? How's Ronnie doing?

He's doing very well, said Joe. Training as hard as ever, playing as well as ever. And he's helping the younger lads, too. With a word here and with a word there. Showing them how it's done, showing them what it takes, Boss. Helping them, teaching them.

Bill smiled. And Bill said, That's good to hear, Joe. That's great to hear. It's what I hoped you'd say, what I thought you'd say. But you never know, you can never tell. It's a terrible thing when you have to step down, down from the first team. We all know it is. We've all been there. There's nothing worse in football. Nothing worse in life. The feeling your best days are behind you, the knowledge you're on the way down. On the way down and on the way out. To the knacker's yard, to the glue factory. I wouldn't wish it on any man, not on any man. That feeling, that knowledge. But it comes to us all, it comes to us all. In the end, Joe. In the end.

. . .

Down the corridor, the Anfield corridor. Bill tapped on the office door. The office door of the club secretary. Bill opened the door. Bill saw the bags of mail standing on the floor. The bags and bags of mail. Bill glanced at the corner of the office. The corner where a camp bed had once stood. No camp bed in the corner now. Only more bags of mail. More bags and bags of mail. Bill looked at the desk. Bill saw the stacks of letters on the desk. The stacks and stacks of letters. And Bill saw the new club secretary sat behind the desk. Among the letters. The stacks and stacks of letters. Bill smiled at Peter Robinson. And Bill said, It's getting late, Peter. You should get off home. Home to your family. And leave all that for tomorrow . . .

Peter Robinson looked up from his typewriter. From the stacks and stacks of letters. And Peter Robinson smiled –

I will, said Peter Robinson. I will soon, Bill. I'll just finish off these last few letters and then I'll be off.

Bill said, That's good, Peter. Are there any letters for me?

Only two, said Peter Robinson. Only two.

Then let me have them, Peter. And I'll get them done now.

Peter Robinson pointed at two bags of mail. Two big bags of mail in the corner. In the corner where a camp bed had once stood. And Peter Robinson laughed –

Only two bags, said Peter Robinson. Those two bags over there.

Bill laughed. Bill went over to the corner. The corner where a camp bed had once stood. And Bill picked up the two bags. The two big bags of mail. Bill carried the bags over to the door. Bill turned back to Peter Robinson. Bill smiled. And Bill said, Jesus Christ. These are heavy bags. I best be making a start on them now. But you make sure you get off home soon, Peter. You promise me you won't stay all night now. Promise me you'll go home soon, Peter . . .

I will, said Peter Robinson. I promise.

Bill smiled. And Bill said, Well, I'll be checking. So you make sure you do, Peter. Make sure you do . . .

I will, Bill, I will. Goodnight, Bill. Goodnight.

And goodnight to you, Peter. Goodnight . . .

In his office, his Anfield office. Bill closed the door behind him. Bill put down the two bags of mail beside his desk. Bill sat down in his chair behind his desk. Bill reached down to the first bag of mail. Bill opened the bag. Bill put his hand inside the bag. Bill took out a letter. Bill opened the letter. Bill read the letter. And Bill smiled. Bill put down the letter on his desk. Bill opened the top drawer of his desk. Bill took out a piece of paper. Across the top of the piece of paper were three big words. In bold, in red. **LIVERPOOL FOOTBALL CLUB.** Below these three words were five more words. In italics, in red: *and Athletic Grounds Co. Ltd.* Bill closed the top drawer of his desk. Bill threaded the piece of paper into his typewriter. Bill turned the platen knob. And then Bill began to type:

**Dear People, Received your letter, thanks very much indeed. Also thanks for the invitation to your son Robert's birthday party on the 26th of next month, which is the night before we play Leeds United. In actual fact the players, the trainers and myself will be in special preparation for this vital game. I am sure you will understand how important it is, especially Robert, who is a member of the greatest place on earth 'THE KOP'. We all wish Robert the best of luck on his Birthday. Yours sincerely,**

Bill stopped typing. Bill took the letter out of his typewriter. Bill put down the letter on his desk. Bill put his hand inside his jacket pocket. Bill took out his pen. His red pen. Bill unscrewed the top of his pen. Above the word **Manager**, Bill signed the letter *B. Shankly*. Bill put down his pen on the desk. Bill opened the top drawer of his desk. Bill took out an envelope. Bill closed the drawer of his desk. Bill picked up his pen. His red pen. Bill addressed the envelope. Bill put down his pen. Bill picked up the letter. Bill folded it. Bill put the folded letter into the envelope. Bill brought the letter up to his mouth. Bill stuck out his tongue. Bill licked the two gummed strips on the underside of the back flap of the envelope. Bill put down the envelope on his desk. Bill pressed down the palm of his hand on the envelope. Bill picked up the envelope. Bill put it to one side of his desk. Bill reached down to the first bag of mail again. Bill put his hand inside the bag again. Bill took out another letter. Bill opened the letter. Bill read the letter. And Bill smiled. Bill put down the letter on his desk. Bill opened the top drawer of his desk. Bill took out another piece of paper. Bill closed the drawer of his desk. Bill threaded the piece of paper into his typewriter. Bill turned the platen knob. And Bill began to type. Again. Bill began to type. To type and to type and to type. To type and to type and to type. To type and to type and to type. Letter after letter after letter. Letter after letter after letter. Letter after letter after letter –

To type and to type and to type. To type and to type and to type. Letter after letter after letter. Letter after letter after letter –

To type and to type and to type. Letter after letter after letter.

. . .

In the house, in their front room. The lights on the Christmas tree blinked on and off in the corner. On and off, on and off. In the quiet house, their warm room. Bill had just lost again at Scrabble. Ness was putting away the tiles, the racks and the board. Bill looked at his watch. Bill smiled. And Bill said, I think I'll just give Don a quick ring, love. Just to wish him and his family a merry Christmas.

It's a bit late, said Ness. Don't you think he'll be in bed, love?

Bill shook his head. And Bill said, Not Don, love. No. I know Don, I know Don. He'll be fretting and worrying about the game tomorrow. He'll be a glad of a chat. He'll be glad of a call, will Don.

Well, I'm going up, love. So try to keep your voice down.

I will, love. I will. Goodnight, love. Goodnight.

Bill picked up his address book from the arm of the chair. Bill went out into the hallway. Bill switched on the hall light. Bill found Don Revie's number in his address book. Bill picked up the receiver. Bill dialled Don's number. Bill listened to the phone ring. And ring. And ring. And then Bill heard Don say, Hello? Hello? Who is it?

And Bill said, It's me, Don. Only me. It's Bill. Only Bill. I just thought I'd give you a quick ring before the game, before the match tomorrow. Oh, it'll be a great game, Don. A great game. A big crowd, too, Don. A very big crowd. They'll be wanting to see a repeat of the Cup Final. Well, our lot will be. Not your lot, I suppose. But I hope you are as ready as we are, Don. Because we are ready for you. I can tell you that, Don. Tell you that for nothing. And I tell you another thing, Don. I'll tell you this. I think we are a better side now than we were last season. To be very honest with you, Don. And not to be arrogant, Don. Just to be honest with you. I think we are going to walk the League. And the Cup. And the Cup Winners' Cup. That's my feeling, Don. That's my feeling. Because I tell you, Don. I think this is the finest side in England since the war. The very finest. I don't know what you think, Don? But I can't see a weakness in us. Not one. From the back to the front. I think we have it all. And we are improving. Improving all the time. Every game. That's the incredible thing to me,

Don. The wonder of this team to me. I think I've seen the best of them. But no, Don. Oh no! The next game, the next match. They are even better. Better than the last game, the last match. Much, much better. I know Tommy Lawrence has his critics. But for me, Don. For me, he is the finest keeper in the League. I'm sure you agree, Don. I'm sure you agree with me. And the younger boys we have. Lawler and Smith. I tell you, Don. I tell you. Those two would walk into any side there has ever been. Any side. And make that side a better side. A much, much better side. And then when you combine that youth and that enthusiasm with the age and with the wisdom of the likes of Gerry Byrne and Gordon Milne, Ronnie Yeats and Willie Stevenson. Well, it's not fair, is it, Don? Let's be honest, Don. It's just not fair on the other teams. On other sides. And as for the front four. Well, what can I say, Don? What more can I say? Really, truly, what words are there left to say about those four? Callaghan, Hunt, St John and Thompson. Yes, there might well be individuals who are as talented. *Individually*. There might be, yes. Perhaps. Your Jimmy Greaves, your Denis Law. But come on, Don. Come on, man. As a *team*. Well, there is not a better balance, not a better combination. Not a better team than this Liverpool team. And we both know that's what it's about, Don. What this game is all about. *Teams*. The balance and the combination. Not the individual, not the superstar. Because this is a team game, a team sport, is it not, Don? Is it not? It's about how you play as a team. Not as an individual. With a good game here and a good game there. It's about the team. Week in, week out. Game after game, match after match. How the team plays. And so I tell you, Don. I tell you this. I have simply not seen a better team than this one. This Liverpool team. Not with my eyes. Not in my lifetime. Well, Don. I won't keep you. I won't keep you up. I'll see you tomorrow, Don. I'll see you at Anfield. So you sleep well, Don. Sleep well. Goodnight, Don. Goodnight . . .

On the bench, the Anfield bench. In bitter air, in biting wind. Bill heard the carols, the Christmas carols. Fifty-three thousand, four hundred and thirty folk singing carols, Christmas carols. To thaw the air, to warm the wind. To boil the air, to burn the wind. But on the ground, the frozen-solid ground, on the pitch, the rock-hard pitch. There was no cheer, no Christmas cheer. And there was no goodwill, no seasonal goodwill. There was only battle and there was only fight.

Body against body, man against man. Red man against white man. In bitter air, in biting wind. Bone and muscle, earth and leather. Grinding bone and straining muscle, white earth and black leather. In bitter air, in biting wind. Minute after minute. In the fourteenth minute, Reaney hit the ball straight at Lawrence. Lawrence beat the ball away. Yeats ground bone, Yeats crossed earth. Lorimer strained muscle, Lorimer found leather. In bitter air, in biting wind. Lorimer shot. And Lorimer scored. And in bitter air, in biting wind. Leeds United Association Football Club beat Liverpool Football Club one–nil. It was the first defeat for Liverpool Football Club in ten matches, the first defeat since Saturday 23 October, 1965. And in the bitter air, in the biting wind. Bill walked down the touchline. The Anfield touchline. Bill shook Don Revie's hand. Bill half smiled. And Bill said, Well, never say I never give you anything for Christmas, Don. Merry Christmas to you, Don. And I'll be seeing you tomorrow, Don. Tomorrow . . .

On their bench, their bench at Elland Road. Across the bone-hard ground, over the sand-coated pitch. The black ice and the driving snow. Bill watched and Bill waited. And in the forty-eighth minute, Thompson turned. Thompson beat his man. Thompson fed Hunt. Hunt jumped Charlton's tackle. Hunt reached the byline. Exact and precise, low and diagonal. Hunt passed to Milne. Milne shot. And Milne scored. And Liverpool Football Club beat Leeds United Association Football Club one–nil. Away from home, away at Elland Road. And across the bone-hard ground, over the sand-coated pitch. The black ice and the driving snow. The only voices were the Liverpool voices. Rising from the banks, reaching into the sky. Into the sky, the black, winter sky. Red voices, germinal voices. Holy voices . . .

On their bus, their Liverpool bus. Through the streets, the Leeds streets. Bill stared out through the window, the bus window. At these streets, these Leeds streets. And on these streets, these Yorkshire streets. Bill saw some boys, three young lads. Red scarves around their necks, thin coats upon their backs. Their white faces to the road, the deserted road, their blue thumbs to the sky, the empty sky. And on their bus, their Liverpool bus. Bill stood up. And Bill called down to the driver, Pull up. Pull up!

The driver stopped the bus. The driver opened the doors. And Bill got off the bus. And Bill called to the boys, Climb on board, lads.

Climb on board! We'll take you home, boys. We'll take you home.

Bill brought the boys onto the bus. Bill made space for the boys on the bus. Bill got them sandwiches. Sandwiches from the players. Bill got them autographs. Autographs from the players. Bill asked the boys about the game. Bill asked the boys about the team. Bill asked the boys what they thought about the game. Bill asked the boys what they hoped for the team. Bill listened to the boys. Bill listened to them. All the way back to Liverpool, all the way back home. And when their bus, their Liverpool bus, reached the city centre, the Liverpool city centre. Bill checked the boys had enough money now. Enough money now to get to their homes, their Liverpool homes –

Thank you, said the boys. Thank you for everything . . .

Bill shook his head. And Bill said, No, boys. No. You don't have to thank me, boys. You have nothing to thank me for. It's me who should be thanking you, boys. Thanking you for travelling all the way to Leeds today. In the ice and in the snow. Wearing your red scarves, your Liverpool scarves. To support Liverpool Football Club. So I thank *you*, boys. I thank *you*. For supporting Liverpool Football Club. Because we could do nothing without you, boys –

We would be nothing without you.


## 21. THE OLD ENEMY

On Saturday 1 January, 1966, Manchester United came to Anfield, Liverpool. That New Year's Day, fifty-three thousand, nine hundred and seventy folk came, too. That New Year's Day, the gates were locked hours before kick-off. Hundreds of folk, thousands of folk, locked outside Anfield, Liverpool. Hundreds of folk, thousands of folk, among the policemen, the mounted policemen. Refusing to disperse, refusing to go home. Hundreds of folk, thousands of folk already home. Outside Anfield, inside Anfield. In one voice, just one word: LI-VER-POOL. Over and over, in one voice, again and again, just one word. One red word: LI-VER-POOL, LI-VER-POOL, LI-VER-POOL –

The word ignited the air, the word scorched the wind. But within the first two minutes of the game, Gregg cleared high and far into the air. Law sniffed and chased the wind. Law beat Yeats to the ball, Law dodged Byrne in the tackle, Law sidestepped Lawrence at his heels, Law shot. And Law scored. But the word did not retreat. The word did not surrender. LI-VER-POOL, LI-VER-POOL, LI-VER-POOL. Now the word tore through muscle, now the word drilled through bone. LI-VER-POOL, LI-VER-POOL, LI-VER-POOL. And a shot from Hunt. And a shot from Stevenson. And a shot from St John. And a shot from Smith. All rained down on Gregg beneath his crossbar. There was no shelter from the word. There was no respite from the word. LI-VER-POOL, LI-VER-POOL, LI-VER-POOL. In the thirty-ninth minute, Byrne passed to Smith. Smith shrugged off two tackles. Smith took four more strides. And Smith shot. From twenty-five yards out. Fast and hard and low. In off the post. Smith scored. LI-VER-POOL, LI-VER-POOL, LI-VER-POOL. But the word was not finished. The word was not satisfied. LI-VER-POOL, LI-VER-POOL, LI-VER-POOL. The word insatiable, the word voracious. LI-VER-POOL, LI-VER-POOL, LI-VER-POOL. In the last two minutes of the game, St John shot again. Gregg saved again. The ball flew back out of the ruck. Byrne drove the ball back into the ruck. And Milne diverted the ball. Into the net, into a goal. LI-VER-POOL, LI-VER-POOL, LI-VER-POOL. The word triumphant, the word victorious. On New Year's Day, 1966, Liverpool Football Club had thirty-six points. That New Year's Day, Liverpool Football Club were first in the First Division.

. . .

On Saturday 22 January, 1966, Chelsea Football Club came to Anfield, Liverpool. That afternoon, fifty-four thousand and ninety-seven folk came, too. Fifty-four thousand and ninety-seven folk to watch Liverpool Football Club play Chelsea Football Club in the Third Round of the FA Cup. In the second minute, Roger Hunt scored. But in the seventh minute, Osgood equalised. And in the sixty-seventh minute, Tambling scored. And Liverpool Football Club lost two–one to Chelsea Football Club. In silence. The holders of the FA Cup had let go of the Cup. And in silence. Chelsea Football Club took the FA Cup back to London with them. Back to Lancaster Gate, to the headquarters of the Football Association –

For safe keeping.

After the Cup, out of the cup. Bill Shankly closed the dressing-room door. The home dressing-room door. Bill Shankly looked around the dressing room. The Liverpool dressing room. From player to player. From Lawrence to Lawler, Lawler to Byrne, Byrne to Milne, Milne to Yeats, Yeats to Stevenson, Stevenson to Callaghan, Callaghan to Hunt, Hunt to St John, St John to Smith and from Smith to Thompson. Bill Shankly nodded and Bill Shankly smiled –

I know you are all disappointed, boys. I know you are all hurt. I can see it in your faces, boys. In every one of your faces. But what is done is done, boys. What is lost is lost. And so you must not let that disappointment, you must not let that hurt, devour your belief and eat your confidence. Because you are still the best side I have ever seen play, boys. You are still the finest team in England since the war. And so you must believe in yourselves and believe in each other, boys. You must have confidence in yourselves and in each other. And then you will win again, boys. And again and again. That is the only answer to disappointment, that is the only way to deal with hurt. To win, boys. And to win and win again. Until you have won the League. Until Liverpool Football Club are the Champions again. That is the only answer now, boys. That is the only way now. To win and win again, boys. And to be Champions. Champions again, boys!

. . .

After, later. Liverpool Football Club beat Leicester City one–nil and Liverpool Football Club beat Blackburn Rovers four–one. Then they beat Sunderland Football Club four–nil and then they beat Blackpool Football Club four–one.

On Saturday 26 February, 1966, Liverpool Football Club travelled to Craven Cottage, London. Fulham Football Club were bottom of the First Division. Liverpool Football Club were top of the First Division. That afternoon, thirty-one thousand, six hundred and twenty-six folk came, too. Thirty-one thousand, six hundred and twenty-six folk to watch bottom versus top. Last play first. That afternoon, Ian St John punched Mark Pearson. St John hit Pancho Pearson with a left hook. St John was sent off. And that afternoon, Liverpool Football Club lost two–nil to Fulham Football Club. Away from home, away from Anfield. The bottom had beaten the top, the last had beaten the first.

. . .

After the dismissal, after the defeat. At Lancaster Gate, in

London. At the headquarters of the Football Association. Bill Shankly and Ian St John walked past the FA Cup. The FA Cup on display, in safe keeping. Bill Shankly and Ian St John sat down in the corridor at Lancaster Gate. Bill Shankly in his best suit and red tie, Ian St John in his best suit and red tie –

Come!

Bill Shankly and Ian St John stood up. Bill Shankly and Ian St John adjusted their red ties. Bill Shankly and Ian St John stepped through the door, into the room. And the head of the FA Disciplinary Panel said, Sit down, Shankly. Sit down, St John.

Bill Shankly and Ian St John walked down to two chairs at the end of a long table. Bill Shankly and Ian St John sat down in the two chairs at the end of the long table. Bill Shankly and Ian St John looked up the long table at the members of the Disciplinary Panel. And the head of the Disciplinary Panel said, Well then, what do you have to say for yourselves? In answer to the charge of violent conduct?

Plenty, said Bill Shankly. Because I have evidence to present to you which I believe will prove the innocence of my player. Evidence that will exonerate him. This evidence is on film. And so, as you are aware, I have arranged to show you a film. To prove the innocence of my player. And to exonerate him of the charge against him.

The head of the Disciplinary Panel said, Go on then, Shankly, show us this little film of yours then.

Bill Shankly got up from his chair at the end of the long table. Bill Shankly walked over to the wall. Bill Shankly switched off the lights. Bill Shankly walked over to the projector. Bill Shankly started the projector. And Bill Shankly showed his little film. His film which showed Mark Pearson of Fulham Football Club pulling the hair of Ian St John of Liverpool Football Club. His film which showed Ian St John turning around and punching Mark Pearson. His film which showed Ian St John hitting Pancho Pearson with a left hook. His film which then showed Ian St John being ordered off the field of play.

After his film, Bill Shankly stopped the projector. Bill Shankly walked back over to the wall. Bill Shankly switched back on the lights. But Bill Shankly did not sit back down in his chair at the end of the long table. Bill Shankly paced the room. The courthouse –

As you can clearly see, said Bill Shankly. See as clear as day.

My player was clearly provoked by the ungentlemanly and unsporting behaviour and conduct of the other player, of the Fulham player. And as I am sure you will all agree, such behaviour, such conduct has no place in the game, in the modern game of football. My player was clearly provoked. My player then simply reacted. And so the charge against him is unfair. The suspension unjust. The most unfair and most unjust in the history of the world. Because my player is an innocent man. The most innocent man in the history of the world!

The members of the Football Association Disciplinary Panel looked down the long table at Bill Shankly and Ian St John. The members of the Football Association Disciplinary Panel shook their heads. And the head of the Football Association Disciplinary Panel said, The Football Association will not tolerate violent conduct on the football pitch. The charge is justified. The suspension stands –

Close the door on your way out, Shankly.

Bill Shankly and Ian St John walked back to the door. Bill Shankly and Ian St John stepped through the door, into the corridor. Bill Shankly and Ian St John closed the door behind them. Bill Shankly and Ian St John walked down the corridor, past the FA Cup, into the street. Bill Shankly and Ian St John stood on the pavement outside the headquarters of the Football Association. And Ian St John said, I am sorry, Boss. I am very sorry . . .

And so you should be, said Bill Shankly. Next time you make sure you get your retaliation in first. When the referee is not about. So the other feller knows *you* are about. And then he'll keep away from you. Because he won't fancy another taste. Another taste of that retaliation. So just remember, son. Always get your retaliation in first.

. . .

On Monday 28 February, 1966, Liverpool Football Club flew to Brussels, Belgium. Then Liverpool Football Club flew to Cologne, West Germany. Then Liverpool Football Club flew to Budapest, Hungary. To the City of Football, the home of Honvéd Football Club. Honvéd Football Club were the Hungarian Army football team. Ferenc Puskás, Sándor Kocsis, József Bozsik, Zoltán Czibor, László Budai, Gyula Lóránt and Gyula Grosics had all once played for Honvéd Football Club. These players had been the nucleus of the Mighty Magyars. In 1953, the Mighty Magyars beat England 6–3 at

Wembley Stadium. In 1954, the Mighty Magyars beat England 7–1 at the Népstadion, Budapest. On Tuesday 1 March, 1966, Liverpool Football Club came to the Népstadion, the People's Stadium, to play Honvéd Football Club in the first leg of the Second Round of the European Cup Winners' Cup. That evening, sixteen thousand, one hundred and sixty-three folk came, too. Under giant floodlights, before an electric scoreboard. In a stadium that could seat one hundred thousand folk. To a constant chorus of shrill whistles, against a talented but inexperienced Honvéd side. On a perfect pitch, in an all-white strip. Liverpool Football Club drew nil–nil with Honvéd Football Club in Budapest, Hungary. The City of Football.

One week later, Honvéd Football Club travelled to Anfield, Liverpool. To another City of Football, to the New City of Football. That evening, fifty-four thousand, six hundred and thirty-one folk came, too. In the twenty-eighth minute, Callaghan won a corner. The corner was cleared. Thompson crashed the clearance against the post. And Lawler headed home the rebound. In the forty-seventh minute, Callaghan won another corner. Callaghan took a short corner to Thompson. Thompson crossed the ball. The ball eluded a line of Honvéd defenders. But at the end of the line, from the sharpest of angles, St John headed home the ball. And Liverpool Football Club beat Honvéd Football Club two–nil in the second leg of the Second Round of the European Cup Winners' Cup. That night, Liverpool Football Club were through to the semi-final of the European Cup Winners' Cup. In the semi-final of the European Cup Winners' Cup, Liverpool Football Club would play the Celtic Football Club. Away and then home. Folk had hoped this tie might be the final, folk had dreamt this tie might be the final. But it was still a dream tie. The tie all of Britain had been hoping for, the tie all of Britain had been dreaming of. The tie Bill Shankly had been dreaming of, the tie Bill Shankly had been praying for. One of his dreams, one of his prayers. His many dreams, his many prayers.

. . .

On Thursday 14 April, 1966, Liverpool Football Club travelled to Parkhead, Glasgow. That night, seventy-six thousand, four hundred and forty-six folk came, too. Seventy-six thousand, four hundred and forty-six folk to watch the leaders of the Scottish First Division play the leaders of the English First Division in the first leg of the semi-final of the European Cup Winners' Cup. Seventy-six thousand, four hundred and forty-six folk to watch the Celtic Football Club versus Liverpool Football Club. At Parkhead, in Glasgow. Seventy-six thousand, four hundred and forty-six folk in full voice, in full cry. Their war cry: CEL-TIC! CEL-TIC! CEL-TIC! CEL-TIC! CEL-TIC! CEL-TIC! CEL-TIC! CEL-TIC! CEL-TIC! CEL-TIC! CEL-TIC! CEL-TIC! CEL-TIC! CEL-TIC! CEL-TIC!

CEL-TIC! CEL-TIC! CEL-TIC!

CEL-TIC! CEL-TIC!

CEL-TIC!

Before the whistle, the first whistle. In their dressing room, their dressing room at Parkhead. Bill Shankly closed door. The dressing-room door shaking. Bill Shankly looked around the dressing room. The Liverpool dressing room trembling. Bill Shankly looked from player to player. From Lawrence to Lawler, Lawler to Byrne, Byrne to Milne, Milne to Yeats, Yeats to Stevenson, Stevenson to Callaghan, Callaghan to Chisnall, Chisnall to St John, St John to Smith and from Smith to Thompson. Bill Shankly saw the fear in their eyes, Bill Shankly heard the terror in their ears –

CEL-TIC! CEL-TIC! CEL-TIC!

CEL-TIC! CEL-TIC!

CEL-TIC!

Don't be afraid, said Bill Shankly. Don't be afraid, boys. You have nothing to fear. Nothing to fear, boys. This is paradise. Football paradise, boys! This is what we dream of, this is what we pray for. Playing at Parkhead, playing in paradise. So enjoy it. Enjoy it, boys. This taste of Parkhead, this taste of paradise. Because remember. Remember, boys. This is only one half of paradise, only one half. Five days from now, Celtic Football Club will be sat in the away dressing room at Anfield. And they will be shaking and they will be trembling. Five days from now, Celtic Football Club will be playing in our paradise. At Anfield. In our paradise, boys . . .

CEL-TIC! CEL-TIC! CEL-TIC!

CEL-TIC! CEL-TIC!

CEL-TIC!

In the fifty-second minute, Murdoch hammered the ball low

along the Liverpool goal line. At the left-hand post, Chalmers back-heeled the ball to Lennox. And Lennox stabbed the ball into the net, into a goal. And the whole of paradise, the whole of Parkhead cried out, CEL-TIC! CEL-TIC! CEL-TIC! CEL-TIC! CEL-TIC! CEL-TIC!
CEL-TIC! CEL-TIC! CEL-TIC! CEL-TIC! CEL-TIC!
CEL-TIC! CEL-TIC! CEL-TIC! CEL-TIC!
CEL-TIC! CEL-TIC! CEL-TIC!
CEL-TIC! CEL-TIC!
CEL-TIC!

After the whistle, the final whistle. Bill Shankly walked down the touchline. The Parkhead touchline. Bill Shankly shook the hand of Jock Stein, the manager of the Celtic Football Club –

Well done, John. Well played. Though I am sure you had your groundsman polish the pitch before the game. But well played, John. Well done. And we'll see you next Tuesday . . .

Jock Stein laughed. And Jock Stein said, Thank you, Bill. And yes, I'll see you next Tuesday. In England, Bill. In England.

No, you won't, said Bill Shankly. You'll see me at Anfield, John. And Anfield is not in England. Anfield is in Liverpool. And Liverpool is not in England. Liverpool is in a different country, John. In a different country, in a different league.

. . .

On Tuesday 19 April, 1966, the Celtic Football Club came to Anfield, Liverpool. In the mud and in the rain. That night, fifty-four thousand, two hundred and eight folk came, too. Liverpool folk and Glasgow folk. In the mud and in the rain, in the steam and in the sweat. Thousands and thousands of Glasgow folk. With their banners and with their flags. Their green and white banners, their green and white flags. With their voice, with their cry. Their war cry: CEL-TIC –
CEL-TIC! CEL-TIC! CEL-TIC! CEL-TIC!
CEL-TIC! CEL-TIC! CEL-TIC!
CEL-TIC! CEL-TIC!
CEL-TIC!

And the Spion Kop saw the supporters of the Celtic Football Club. Their green and white banners, their green and white flags. And the Spion Kop heard the supporters of the Celtic Football Club. Their voice, their cry. Their war cry: CEL-TIC! CEL-TIC! CEL-TIC!

And the Spion Kop shouted, RANGERS! RANGERS! RANGERS! And the Spion Kop sang, *GO BACK TO IRE-LAND, GO BACK TO IRE-LAND, GO BACK TO IRE-LAND . . .*

The Spion Kop heaving, the Spion Kop surging. Body crushing against body, body clambering over body. In their steam and in their sweat. The Spion Kop falling onto the pitch, the Anfield pitch. The Spion Kop flowing up to the touchline, the Anfield touchline. In the mud and in the rain. In one voice, in one cry,

full voice and full cry, one word,

one cry; one war cry –

ATTACK!

And in the eye of this hurricane of fury, in the centre of this storm of sound. In the mud and in the rain, in the steam and in the sweat. The players of Liverpool Football Club attacked and attacked and attacked. But the players of the Celtic Football Club built a fortress on the pitch, the Anfield pitch. And defended and defended and defended. But in the fury and in the sound, in the mud and in the rain, in the steam and in the sweat, the Liverpool attack was ceaseless, the Liverpool onslaught endless. And in the sixty-first minute, Smith burst out of midfield. Three Celtic defenders took him down. Smith won a free kick. Smith took the free kick. From twenty-five yards out. Smith shot. And Smith scored. LI-VER-POOL, LI-VER-POOL, LI-VER-POOL. And before the players of the Celtic Football Club could get off their knees, before the players of the Celtic Football Club could find their feet. In the sixty-seventh minute, Stevenson passed to Milne. Milne passed to Thompson. Left to right. Thompson dummied. Thompson flicked on to Callaghan. Callaghan boxed in. Callaghan found an inch. Callaghan crossed. Strong leapt, Strong rose. With a damaged cartilage, on an injured leg. Strong headed the ball. Into the net, into a goal. LI-VER-POOL, LI-VER-POOL, LI-VER-POOL. EASY! EASY! EASY! But in the fury and in the sound, in the mud and in the rain, in the steam and in the sweat. In the eighty-eighth minute, Murdoch swept a ball over to McBride. McBride knocked the ball down. From five yards behind Yeats, Lennox reached the ball first. Lennox shot. And Lennox scored. Into the net, into a goal. An away goal, a goal that would count double. That would send Celtic through, into the final of the European Cup Winners' Cup at Hampden Park,

Glasgow. But the flag was up, the goal disallowed. Lennox offside. And now bottles and cans rained down onto the pitch, the Anfield pitch, from the supporters of the Celtic Football Club, from the back of the Anfield Road end, onto their fellow fans, the fans at the front, glass arrows into hair, metal blades into skin. And the Spion Kop laughed, HOOLIGANS! HOOLIGANS! HOOLIGANS! The Spion Kop sang, *BEHAVE YOURSELVES, BEHAVE YOURSELVES, BEHAVE YOURSELVES*. But the referee stopped the game. And the police took to the pitch. Until order was restored, until glass was removed. The bottles and the cans. And then the referee started the game. The referee looked at his watch. And the referee blew his whistle, his final whistle. And in the fury and in the sound, in the mud and in the rain, through the steam and through the sweat. The referee and the linesmen ran for cover. Down the tunnel, into their dressing room. They fled.

After that whistle. That final whistle, that last whistle. Bill Shankly walked down the touchline. The Anfield touchline. Bill Shankly walked up to Jock Stein. Bill Shankly held out his hand towards Jock Stein. And Jock Stein looked down at Bill Shankly's hand. Jock Stein shaking with fury, Jock Stein trembling with rage. And Jock Stein hissed, That was never offside, Bill. Bobby Lennox was onside. That was clearly a goal, Bill. A perfectly good goal. You never beat us, Bill. The referee beat us. You never beat us, Bill!

I understand, John. I understand how you feel. And I'm sorry, John. I'm sorry you feel that way. I really am, John. But cheer up. Cheer up, John. If you and me go out there now, onto that pitch now. If you and me collect up all those empty bottles off the pitch. And if you and me return all those empties. We'll be rich, John. Rich!

Jock Stein shook his head. And Jock Stein said, You're already rich, Bill. You don't need anything more. Not tonight, Bill. You've already got everything you wanted. You've got everything now, Bill.

. . .

Eleven days after, eleven days later. The players of Chelsea Football Club formed a guard of honour on the pitch, the Anfield pitch. And the players of Chelsea Football Club applauded the players of Liverpool Football Club onto the pitch, the Anfield pitch. And on the pitch, the Anfield pitch. In the forty-eighth minute, Roger Hunt scored. And in the sixty-ninth minute, Hunt scored again. And the players of

Liverpool Football Club beat the players of Chelsea Football Club two–one. At home, at Anfield. The players of Liverpool Football Club ran a lap of honour around the pitch, the Anfield pitch. The players of Liverpool Football Club paraded the trophy around the ground, the red papier-mâché trophy around the ground, the Anfield ground. The crowd all clapping, the crowd all cheering. Around the ground, the Anfield ground. The crowd all singing, all singing. Around the ground, the Anfield ground. All singing, all in one voice. Around the ground, the Anfield ground. In one voice, the fifty-three thousand, seven hundred and fifty-four folk inside the ground, the Anfield ground today. In one voice, the one million, two hundred and thirty-three thousand, one hundred and thirty-seven folk who had come to the ground, the Anfield ground this season. In one voice, all singing, in one red voice, all singing, *SHANK-LEE, SHANK-LEE, SHANK-LEE,*

*SHANK-LEE, SHANK-LEE,*

*SHANK-LEE . . .*

Across the pitch, the Anfield pitch. Before the Kop, the Spion Kop. Bill Shankly lifted his arms, Bill Shankly raised his hands. To touch her, to hold her. And Bill Shankly looked up into the faces, the thousands of faces, Bill Shankly stared back into their eyes, their thousands of eyes. To cherish and to keep her. Their happy faces, their smiling eyes. To never let her go. And then before the Kop, the Spion Kop. Bill Shankly lowered his arms, Bill Shankly joined his hands. Together, together. In prayer and in thanks –

For paradise, a red paradise,

on earth, red earth,

this paradise

on earth –

First in the First Division, top of the top division. Liverpool Football Club had sixty-one points. Liverpool Football Club had played forty-two League games. Tommy Lawrence had played in all of those games. Gerry Byrne had played in all of those games. Ron Yeats had played in all of those games. Ian Callaghan had played in all of those games. Tommy Smith had played in all of those games. Ian St John had played in forty-one of those games and Willie Stevenson had played in forty-one of those games. Chris Lawler had played in forty of those games and Peter Thompson had played in forty of those games. Roger Hunt had played in thirty-seven of those games. Gordon Milne had played in twenty-eight of those games. Geoff Strong had played in twenty-two of those games. Alf Arrowsmith had played in five of those games. And Bobby Graham had played in one of those games. Liverpool Football Club had used only fourteen players in their forty-two League games. They had won seventeen games at home and they had won nine games away from home. They had drawn two games at home and they had drawn seven games away from home. They had lost two games at home and they had lost five games away from home. They had scored fifty-two goals at home and they had scored twenty-seven goals away from home. They had conceded fifteen goals at home and they had conceded nineteen goals away from home. And Liverpool Football Club were the Football League Champions. Again. Liverpool Football Club were the Champions of England. And Liverpool Football Club had not finished, their season not over,

not yet.

. . .

On Thursday 5 May, 1966, Liverpool Football Club came to Hampden Park, Glasgow, to play Ballspiel-Verein Borussia 1909 e.V. Dortmund in the final of the European Cup Winners' Cup. Liverpool Football Club had never reached the final of a European cup before. That night, forty-one thousand, six hundred and fifty-seven folk came, too. In the rain. The sheets and sheets of rain. Just forty-one thousand, six hundred and fifty-seven folk in a stadium that could hold over one hundred and thirty thousand folk. That night, Hampden Park was barely a third full. And of those forty-one thousand, six hundred and fifty-seven folk, twenty-five thousand were Liverpool folk. The rest were German folk, or Scottish folk. And the rest wanted Borussia Dortmund to win. The rest wanted Liverpool Football Club to lose –

Before the whistle, the first whistle. In their dressing room, their dressing room at Hampden Park. Bill Shankly looked from player to player. From Lawrence to Lawler, Lawler to Byrne, Byrne to Milne, Milne to Yeats, Yeats to Stevenson, Stevenson to Callaghan, Callaghan to Hunt, Hunt to St John, St John to Smith and from Smith to Thompson. Bill Shankly smiling, Bill Shankly laughing –

Did you hear, boys? Did you hear what happened in the night?

Some of our lads, some of our supporters. They scaled the walls, the Hampden Park walls. They scaled the Hampden walls and they painted the goalposts red. They painted them red, boys. It's taken the ground staff all day to get the red paint off. To paint them posts white again. Well, I can tell you. I can tell you, boys. They needn't have bothered. They needn't have wasted their energy. Because tonight you are going to paint them goals red again. Paint them red again, boys. Because I've seen this lot play, this German team play. And I have to say. I have to tell you, boys. This lot would be hard pushed to hold a place in our league. They would struggle. They really would struggle, boys. I mean, Northampton Town would give them a game. And Northampton Town have been relegated. But I think Northampton Town could beat this lot. I really believe that. I really do, boys. So I think you're going to murder them. Absolutely murder them, boys. And paint them goals red again. Paint them red again! So I've only one word for you. One piece of advice for you tonight, boys –

ATTACK!

In the night. The Glasgow night. In the rain. The sheets and sheets of Glasgow rain. The players of Liverpool Football Club attacked and attacked and attacked. And in the night. The Glasgow night. In the rain. The sheets and sheets of Glasgow rain. The players of Borussia Dortmund defended and defended and defended. But in this night. This Glasgow night. In this rain. These sheets and sheets of Glasgow rain. The players of Borussia Dortmund began to soak up the night, soak up the rain. They soaked up the attacks and they soaked up the pressure. And in the night. The Glasgow night. In the rain. The sheets and sheets of Glasgow rain. The players of Borussia Dortmund began to grow, they began to flower. Tilkowski. Cyliax. Redder. Kurrat. Paul. Assauer. Libuda. Schmidt. Held. Sturm. And Emmerich. In the night. The Glasgow night. In the rain. The sheets and sheets of Glasgow rain. Growing and flowering, faster and stronger. With economy, but with sophistication. With strength, but with finesse. And in the night. The Glasgow night. In the rain. The sheets and sheets of Glasgow rain. In the sixty-third minute, Sigfried Held passed to Lothar Emmerich. Lothar Emmerich lifted a pass back to Held. Over the head of Ron Yeats, behind the back of Ron Yeats. Held met the pass. And Held volleyed the pass. Into the net, into a goal. In the night. The

Glasgow night. In the rain. The sheets and sheets of Glasgow rain. In the sixty-eighth minute, Peter Thompson ran yard after yard down the right. Peter Thompson beat man after man on the right. Peter Thompson reached the byline. The linesman raised his flag. The referee ignored the linesman. Peter Thompson crossed. Roger Hunt met the cross. Roger Hunt shot. And Roger Hunt scored. And the linesman lowered his flag. In the night. The Glasgow night. In the rain. The sheets and sheets of Glasgow rain. The players of Borussia Dortmund complained, the players of Borussia Dortmund protested. But the referee just shook his head. And the referee pointed to the centre spot. And in the night. The Glasgow night. In the rain. The sheets and sheets of Glasgow rain. The supporters of Liverpool Football Club roared. And some supporters of Liverpool Football Club ran onto the pitch, the Hampden Park pitch. And the police chased some supporters of Liverpool Football Club off the pitch. The police arrested some supporters of Liverpool Football Club. And in the night. The Glasgow night. In the rain. The sheets and sheets of Glasgow rain. The referee blew his whistle. For full time, for extra time. But in the night. The Glasgow night. In the rain. The sheets and sheets of Glasgow rain. In the one hundred and seventh minute, Sigfried Held passed to Lothar Emmerich. Emmerich passed back to Held. Tommy Lawrence came out to the edge of his penalty area, out towards Held. Held with the ball at his feet. Tommy Lawrence dived at the feet of Held. And Held shot. The ball rebounded off Tommy Lawrence. Thirty-five yards. The ball came to Reinhard Libuda. Thirty-five yards out. Libuda curved a slow, dropping shot over Tommy Lawrence. In the night. The Glasgow night. Over Tommy Lawrence, towards the unguarded goal. In the rain. The sheets and sheets of Glasgow rain. Ronnie Yeats ran, Ronnie Yeats lunged. The ball hit the post. Ronnie Yeats lurched, Ronnie Yeats dived. And the ball hit his chest. The ball and Ronnie Yeats over the line. Into the net, into a goal. And in the night. The Glasgow night. In the rain. The sheets and sheets of Glasgow rain. Ballspiel-Verein Borussia 1909 e.V. Dortmund beat Liverpool Football Club two–one. In the night. The Glasgow night. Ballspiel-Verein Borussia 1909 e.V. Dortmund became the first German side to win a European trophy. And in the rain. The sheets and sheets of Glasgow rain. The players of Borussia Dortmund collected the European Cup Winners' Cup.

And some supporters of Liverpool Football Club booed the German side. The players of Borussia Dortmund paraded the European Cup Winners' Cup around Hampden Park, Glasgow. And some supporters of Liverpool Football Club threw bottles at the German side. The players of Borussia Dortmund ran a lap of honour around Hampden Park, Glasgow. And some supporters of Liverpool Football Club were arrested for breaches of the peace. Some of the supporters of Liverpool Football Club didn't like losing. Some of the supporters of Liverpool Football Club were bad losers. Very, very bad losers –

We were beaten by a team of frightened men, said Bill Shankly. Frightened men who scored two flukes. It was their plan from the start, simply to keep us in subjection. They had no real attacking plan. No plan of attack. Only of subjection. Only of theft. And so yes, they won. They might have won. But they stole it.

They stole it through luck –

Because if Roger Hunt and Tommy Smith had been fully fit tonight, we would have won easily. We would have murdered them. Because I am quite sincere when I say to you, they are the worst team we have met in this competition this season. The very worst team we have ever met. In any competition, in any season –

So they were just lucky.


## 22. THE DIGNITY OF LABOUR

At the airport, Speke airport. The morning after the night before, lost morning after lost night before. Bill and the players and the staff and the officials of Liverpool Football Club got off the plane. The Liverpool plane, the losers' plane. In silence. The Lord Mayor of Liverpool was there to greet them. The Lord Mayor of Liverpool and four supporters. In silence. Bill and the players and the staff and the officials of Liverpool Football Club got on the bus. The Liverpool bus, the losers' bus. In silence. Bill and the players and the staff and the officials of Liverpool Football Club got off the bus. In the car park, the deserted car park at Anfield Road. In silence. Bill and the players and the staff and the officials of Liverpool Football Club got into their cars. In silence. Bill and the players and the staff and the officials of

Liverpool Football Club drove back to their homes. Down empty roads, along silent streets. In their losers' cars, to their losers' homes.

In the drive, in the car. Bill turned off the engine. Bill got out of the car. Bill walked up the drive. Bill opened the front door of the house. Bill stepped into the house. Bill closed the door. Bill put down his suitcase in the hall. Bill walked into the kitchen. Bill said hello to Ness. Bill kissed her on her cheek. And Bill said, I'll just take my case up, love. And sort out my stuff. I'll be back down in a bit . . .

OK, love, said Ness. I'll put the kettle on.

Bill walked back out into the hall. Bill picked up his suitcase. Bill walked up the stairs. Bill went into the bedroom. Bill put down his case on the carpet. Bill walked over to the window. And Bill stared through the glass, through the trees. Into the morning, into Bellefield. Their season not finished, their season not over. Through the glass and through the trees. Bill could see the players of Everton Football Club practising, Bill could hear the players of Everton Football Club preparing. Through the glass and through the trees. Practising for success, preparing for victory. Excited and optimistic. In just over a week, Everton Football Club would travel to Wembley Stadium. And Everton Football Club would play Sheffield Wednesday in the final of the FA Cup. In the bedroom, at the window. Bill believed Everton would be successful. And Bill hoped Everton would be victorious. For the people, the people of Liverpool. But now Bill closed the window. Now Bill drew the curtains. And then Bill walked over to the bed. Bill sat down on the bed. Bill closed his eyes. And Bill put his fingers in his ears. It was going to be a long summer,

a very, very long summer,

this summer of 1966.

. . .

In the bedroom, on their bed. Bill took his fingers out of his ears. And Bill opened his eyes. Bill had had enough of listening to national anthems. Bill had had enough of watching negative football. Now Bill got up from the bed. Now Bill walked over to the window. And Bill pulled back the curtains. Bill opened the windows. And Bill felt the warm summer breeze. Bill smelt the warm summer air. The Liverpool breeze, the Liverpool air. And Bill looked out through the glass, out through the trees. Into the morning, into the day. Into the summer, into the autumn. The winter and the spring. Into the new season, the Liverpool season. And Bill smiled, Bill smiled.

. . .

On the bench, their bench at Goodison Park. Bill watched Ron Yeats, the captain of Liverpool Football Club, parade the Football League trophy around the ground, the Goodison ground. Bill watched Brian Labone, the captain of Everton Football Club, parade the FA Cup around the ground, the Goodison ground. Together. And then Bill watched Roger Hunt of Liverpool Football Club and Ray Wilson of Everton Football Club parade the Jules Rimet trophy around the ground, the Merseyside ground. Together. And then nine minutes later, Bill watched Roger Hunt pass to Ian Callaghan. Callaghan pass to Peter Thompson. Thompson pass back to Hunt. And Hunt score for *Li-ver-pool, Li-ver-pool, Li-ver-pool.* And then for the next eighty-one minutes, Bill watched Liverpool Football Club harry and hound Everton Football Club for every ball. *Li-ver-pool, Li-ver-pool, Li-ver-pool.* Bill watched Liverpool Football Club run Everton Football Club ragged. *Li-ver-pool, Li-ver-pool, Li-ver-pool.* And Bill listened to the supporters of Liverpool Football Club shout, *How did they win the Cup? How did they win the Cup?* Bill listened to the supporters of Liverpool Football Club sing, *Show them the way to go home, they are tired and they want to go to bed.* And Bill watched Liverpool Football Club beat Everton Football Club one–nil. And Bill watched the players of Liverpool Football Club parade the Charity Shield around the ground, the Goodison ground. And Bill smiled.

In the tunnel, the Goodison tunnel. After the game, after the parade. Joe Mercer shook Bill's hand. Joe Mercer had played for Everton Football Club. Joe Mercer had played for Arsenal Football Club. Joe Mercer had managed Sheffield United. Joe Mercer had managed Aston Villa. Now Joe Mercer was the manager of Manchester City Football Club –

For the first time in years, said Joe Mercer, I have seen a team, I have seen a side which I wasn't good enough to play in, Bill . . .

Bill smiled again. And Bill said, Don't say that, Joe. Please never say that. But thank you, Joe. Thank you. And you know I'm not a man for fortune-telling, Joe. Not a man for predictions. But I cannot believe there is a side that can come close to this Liverpool side, Joe. I cannot see another team who can touch this Liverpool team. Not in England and not in Europe. Not this season, Joe. Not this season.

. . .

In his office, at his desk. Bill read the letters. The hundreds of letters, the hundreds of signatures. Bill studied the petitions. The hundreds of petitions, the thousands of signatures. Bill picked up the bags of letters. Bill gathered up the piles of petitions. Bill walked up the stairs, the Anfield stairs. Bill knocked on the door of the board-room, the Anfield boardroom. And Bill waited.

Come, said the voice.

Bill opened the door. Bill stepped inside the room.

Have a seat, Mr Shankly, said the directors of Liverpool Football Club. Please have a seat.

Bill walked to the end of the long table. With his bags of letters, with his piles of petitions. Bill did not sit down in a chair at the end of the long table. Bill looked up the long table at the directors of Liverpool Football Club. And Bill waited.

Now what can we do for you today, Mr Shankly?

Bill picked up the bags of letters. Bill emptied the bags of letters onto the long table. The hundreds of letters. Bill picked up the petitions. Bill threw the petitions down onto the long table. The thousands of signatures. And Bill said, You can read these letters. You can count these signatures. That's what you can do for me today.

The directors of Liverpool Football Club stared down at the letters. The hundreds of letters. The directors of Liverpool Football Club stared down at the petitions. The thousands of signatures. And the directors of Liverpool Football Club shook their heads –

We have made our decision, Mr Shankly.

Bill picked up one of the petitions from the long table. And Bill said, This is a petition from the workers at the Ford car factory in Halewood. This is a petition signed by over ten thousand workers at the Ford car factory. This is a petition that demands you reconsider the ban on television cameras inside Anfield. A petition that says if you do not reconsider the ban on television coverage, then these ten thousand workers will boycott all Liverpool matches. A petition that shows how strongly folk feel about this ban.

The directors of Liverpool Football Club looked down the long table, across the letters, across the petitions. And the directors of Liverpool Football Club shook their heads again –

You know our reasons, Mr Shankly. The reasons behind our decision to ban television cameras from the ground. We are worried about attendances. We are worried about gate receipts. Very worried.

Bill shook his head. And Bill said, But almost every game we play is sold out. The gates are often locked hours before kick-off. Had we the room, had we the space, we could have double the crowd, sell double the tickets. If we had the room, if we had the space.

But we haven't the room, we haven't the space, said the directors of Liverpool Football Club. So we cannot have double the crowd. And so we cannot sell double the tickets.

Bill said, But I have said it before. I've told you before. A hundred times before, a thousand times before. We could build a new stadium. A bigger stadium. A stadium for the future. For all the people. So all the people can watch Liverpool Football Club. Not just the people of Liverpool, not just the people of Merseyside. If people see Liverpool Football Club, the supporters we have, the players we have, then people will want to come to Liverpool Football Club. From all over the country, from all over the world. To support Liverpool Football Club, to be part of Liverpool Football Club. But for that to happen, for that to be reality, then people need to be able to see Liverpool Football Club. On television. Then people will see what a team we are, what a club we are. And then the people will come. From all across the country, from all corners of the world. They will come to Liverpool, they'll come to Anfield –

From near and from far.

. . .

Again. The aeroplane shuddered. This season, this new season, Liverpool Football Club had played eleven games. They had won five of those games and they had drawn four of those games. And they had lost two of those games. Again. The aeroplane dipped. Liverpool Football Club were seventh in the First Division. Shuddering and dipping. Again. Bill gripped the armrests of his seat. And again. Bill closed his eyes. Bill hated aeroplanes, Bill hated travelling. But Bill had to fly, Bill had to travel. If Bill wanted to win the European Cup. Bill had to fly, Bill had to travel. And Bill wanted to win the European

Cup. More than anything else. Bill wanted to win the one cup that no British team had ever won before. More than anything. The one cup no British manager had ever won before. His jacket stuck to his shirt. His shirt stuck to his vest. His vest stuck to his skin. Bill felt the aeroplane begin to descend. And Bill smiled. Two weeks ago, Fotbal Club Petrolul Ploieşti of Romania had come to Anfield, Liverpool. That night, forty-four thousand, four hundred and sixty-three folk had come, too. Under a cold harvest moon, in a thin veil of mist. Liverpool Football Club were all in red, Fotbal Club Petrolul Ploieşti all in yellow. A field of tulips and a field of daffodils. Under a cold harvest moon and under the Anfield floodlights. Fotbal Club Petrolul Ploieşti had never played under floodlights before. Fotbal Club Petrolul Ploieşti had never played at Anfield before. And under the Anfield floodlights. Under the cold harvest moon, in the thin veil of mist. Fotbal Club Petrolul Ploieşti had massed nine men on the edge of their own penalty area. And Fotbal Club Petrolul Ploieşti had defended and defended and defended. But Liverpool Football Club had attacked and attacked and attacked. Under the cold harvest moon, in the thin veil of mist. For ten minutes, for twenty minutes. For thirty minutes, for forty minutes. For fifty minutes, for sixty minutes. And under the cold harvest moon, in the thin veil of mist. In the seventy-first minute, out on the left, Willie Stevenson had hoisted a long, diagonal cross. Ian St John had risen to the ball. St John had headed the ball. And St John had scored. Under a cold harvest moon, in a thin veil of mist. In the eightieth minute, Bobby Graham's centre had been diverted by Dragomar to Ian Callaghan. Callaghan had struck the ball on the volley. With his right foot, in off the far post. Callaghan had scored. And under that cold harvest moon, in that thin veil of mist. Liverpool Football Club had beaten Fotbal Club Petrolul Ploieşti of Romania two–nil in the first leg of the First Round of the European Cup. The home leg, the Anfield leg. On the plane, in his seat. Bill heard the aeroplane lowering its wheels. Bill heard the wheels touching the ground. And Bill opened his eyes. Again. Bill released his grip. A little.

In the hotel in Ploieşti, Prahova County, Romania. In the room, on the threadbare carpet. Bill put down his suitcase. Bill walked over to the bed. Bill pulled back the covers on the bed. Bill picked up the pillow. Bill looked under the pillow. Bill knelt down on the carpet. Bill looked under the bed. Bill went over to the desk and the chair. Bill picked up the chair. Bill carried the chair to the centre of the room. Bill took off his shoes. Bill stood on the chair. Bill stared up at the light bulb hanging from the ceiling. And on the chair, in his socks. Bill whispered to the ceiling, I know you are listening. I know you are watching. Don't think I don't know, don't think I don't know . . .

In the hotel, in the dining room. Bill looked around the room. From Lawrence to Lawler, Lawler to Milne, Milne to Smith, Smith to Yeats, Yeats to Stevenson, Stevenson to Callaghan, Callaghan to Hunt, Hunt to St John, St John to Strong and from Strong to Thompson. Bill looked at the plates of food on the table in front of them. Bill looked at the glasses of water in front of them. The forks in their hands, the glasses at their lips. And Bill shouted, Stop, boys. Stop! Put down your forks, put down your glasses. Do not eat a morsel! Do not drink a mouthful! That stuff is contaminated –

That stuff is poisoned!

Bill turned to the waiter. Bill asked for the hotel manager. The manager appeared. Bill walked up to the manager. Bill stared into his eyes. And Bill said, Where are the cans of baked beans I gave you? Where are the bottles of Coca-Cola I ordered from you?

We have cooked the baked beans, said the manager. And your players have eaten them. But I'm sorry, sir. We have no Coca-Cola. This is Romania, sir. This is not America. We have no Coca-Cola.

Bill's eyes were locked on the manager's eyes. And Bill said, I do not believe you. Not a word you are saying, sir!

The manager shifted his weight from foot to foot. Right to left. The manager shifted his eyes. Left to right –

I'm sorry, said the manager again. But we have no Coca-Cola.

Bill turned. Bill walked out of the dining room. Down a corridor, into the kitchen. Bill opened cupboards, Bill opened doors. And Bill found a tray of Coca-Cola. A tray of Coca-Cola all wrapped in plastic. Bill picked up the tray. Bill marched out of the kitchen. Down the corridor, into the dining room. Bill put down the tray of Coca-Cola on the dining-room table. Bill ripped off the plastic. Bill went from table to table. Bill went from player to player. A bottle of Coca-Cola for every Liverpool player. And Bill said, There you are, boys. There you go. Go on, boys. Go on. Drink up, boys. Drink up!

Bill turned again. Bill spied the manager. The hotel manager walking backwards out of the dining room. Bill caught the manager. And Bill said, And where do you think you are going? You are a cheat and you are a liar. Telling my boys, telling me, there was no Coca-Cola. When we had ordered Coca-Cola and we had paid for Coca-Cola. You should be ashamed of yourself. You are a disgrace to International Socialism. You are a disgrace to your party. An absolute disgrace. And I am going to report you. Report you to the Kremlin, sir!

Bill turned back to the players. And Bill said, This is abroad, boys. This is Europe. Never forget that, always remember that. So it is always a conspiracy, boys. Always a war of nerves . . .

In the car park of the Ploieşti Municipal Stadium in Ploieşti, in Prahova County, in Romania. Bill and the players and the staff of Liverpool Football Club got off their bus. Bill and the players and the staff of Liverpool Football Club went inside the Ploieşti Municipal Stadium. Bill and the players and the staff of Liverpool Football Club walked into the dressing room at the Ploieşti Municipal Stadium, the away dressing room. Bill and the players and the staff of Liverpool Football Club looked around the dressing room at the Ploieşti Municipal Stadium, the away dressing room. Bill and the players and the staff of Liverpool Football Club saw the mud and the puddles on the floor of the dressing room. Bill and the players and the staff of Liverpool Football Club saw the bloody bandages and the soiled towels on the benches of the dressing room. The old strips of Elastoplast, the cold cups of tea. Bill and the players and the staff of Liverpool Football Club opened the door to the toilets in the dressing room at the Ploieşti Municipal Stadium. Bill and the players and the staff of Liverpool Football Club smelt the piss and the shit. Bill and the players and the staff of Liverpool Football Club saw the piss on the floor and the shit in the toilets. And Bill told the players and the staff of Liverpool Football Club to go back out to their bus in the car park of the Ploieşti Municipal Stadium. And then Bill found the officials of Fotbal Club Petrolul Ploieşti. And Bill said, The toilets have not been cleaned. The dressing room has not been cleaned. It is a disgrace. And it is degrading. And if the dressing room is not cleaned, if the toilets are not disinfected, then we will go back to Liverpool. We will go back home. And we will report you, report Fotbal Club Petrolul

Ploieşti, report you to UEFA and to FIFA and to the world . . .

Fifteen minutes later, Bill and the players and the staff of Liverpool Football Club got back off their bus again. Bill and the players and the staff of Liverpool Football Club went back into the dressing room, the away dressing room again. The clean dressing room, the disinfected toilets. And now the players of Liverpool Football Club changed into their kits and into their boots. And then the players and the staff of Liverpool Football Club sat down on the benches in the dressing room, the away dressing room.

Ten minutes before kick-off, the lights went out in the dressing room, the away dressing room. For ten minutes, Bill and the players and the staff of Liverpool Football Club sat in the dark and waited for the kick-off. And waited –

After thirty-six minutes, in a vicious game, Moldoveanu scored. After fifty minutes, in a vicious game, Roger Hunt equalised. After fifty-nine minutes, in a vicious game, Boc scored. And then Dridea scored. And after eighty-nine minutes, in a vicious game, Dridea was through again, certain to score again. But in the eighty-ninth minute, in this vicious game, Yeats tackled Dridea. And Dridea did not score again. But on Wednesday 12 October, 1966, at the Ploieşti Municipal Stadium, in a vicious game, Fotbal Club Petrolul Ploieşti beat Liverpool Football Club three–one. In the First Round of the European Cup, Fotbal Club Petrolul Ploieşti and Liverpool Football Club had drawn the tie three-all. In the European Cup, away goals did not count double. In the First Round of the European Cup, Fotbal Club Petrolul Ploieşti and Liverpool Football Club would have to play another match, another game. At a neutral ground,

on foreign soil. On the bench, their bench at the Heysel Stadium, in Brussels, in Belgium. Bill watched and Bill waited. And after thirteen minutes, Roger Hunt put Ian St John through. And St John scored. And after forty-three minutes, Peter Thompson beat three men. Thompson passed to St John. St John passed to Geoff Strong. Strong shot. And the ball rebounded off a defender. But Thompson got to the ball first. Thompson shot. And Thompson scored. And at a neutral ground, on foreign soil, Liverpool Football Club beat Fotbal Club Petrolul Ploieşti two–nil in the First Round play-off of the European Cup. And Liverpool Football Club were through to the

Second Round of the European Cup.

. . .

Before the house, on their doorstep. In the night and in the silence. Bill unlocked the front door. In the night and in the silence. Bill opened the door. In the night and in the silence. Bill stepped into the house. In the dark and in the silence. Bill closed the door. In the dark and in the silence. Bill put down his suitcase in the hallway. In the dark and in the silence. Bill walked down the hallway to the kitchen. In the dark and in the silence. Bill switched on the light. In the kitchen, at their table. Bill sat down. In the kitchen, at their table. Bill looked around the room. In the kitchen, at their table. Bill saw the cooker and the fridge. In the kitchen, at their table. Bill saw the kettle and the pans. In the kitchen, at their table. Bill saw the cups and the plates. In the kitchen, at their table. Bill smelt the air, Bill felt the warmth. The air of their house, the warmth of their home. And Bill smiled. Bill smiled.


## 23. TOTAL FOOTBALL

On Saturday 29 October, 1966, Liverpool Football Club travelled to the Victoria Ground, Stoke. And Liverpool Football Club lost two–nil to Stoke City Football Club. That evening, the Champions of the Football League were ninth in the First Division.

On Saturday 5 November, 1966, Nottingham Forest came to Anfield, Liverpool. That afternoon, forty thousand, six hundred and twenty-four folk came, too. In the sixteenth minute, Geoff Strong scored. In the sixty-second minute, Roger Hunt scored. In the seventy-third minute, Peter Thompson scored. And two minutes later, Hunt scored again. And Liverpool Football Club beat Nottingham Forest four–nil. At home, at Anfield. Four days afterwards, Burnley Football Club came to Anfield, Liverpool. That evening, fifty thousand, one hundred and twenty-four folk came, too. In the fourth minute, Chris Lawler scored. In the eighty-ninth minute, Peter Thompson scored. And Liverpool Football Club beat Burnley Football Club two–nil. At home, at Anfield. Three days later, Liverpool Football Club travelled to St James' Park, Newcastle. In the twenty-second minute, Ian St

John scored. In the sixty-fifth minute, Roger Hunt scored. And Liverpool Football Club beat Newcastle United two–nil. That evening, Chelsea Football Club had twenty-three points. And Chelsea Football Club were first in the First Division. That evening, the Champions of the Football League had twenty-one points. The Champions second in the First Division.

On Saturday 19 November, 1966, Leeds United came to Anfield, Liverpool. That afternoon, fifty-one thousand and fourteen folk came, too. In the forty-third minute, Chris Lawler scored. In the fifty-seventh minute, Peter Thompson scored. In the seventy-fifth minute, Geoff Strong scored. In the eighty-third minute, Ian St John scored. And in the eighty-ninth minute, Strong scored again. And Liverpool Football Club beat Leeds United five–nil. At home, at Anfield. Don Revie tried to walk down the touchline. The Anfield touchline. Don Revie tried to shake the hand of Bill Shankly. And Don Revie said, That first goal, just before the interval, that was a lucky goal, Bill. And then after your second goal, we were too brazen, we were too cavalier. Too intent on chasing the game, too intent on winning the match. So your last three goals, Bill. The last three Liverpool goals. They give an unrealistic look to the actual game, an untrue picture of the actual match. Five–nil is no real reflection of the game. Five–nil is no true reflection of either Leeds United or Liverpool. And so I have to say, Bill. I have to say we were unlucky, very unlucky today. And you were lucky, very lucky today . . .

Lucky, said Bill Shankly. You think we were lucky? Well, I think you need your eyes testing, Don. That was not luck you saw today, that was the finest side in England since the war you saw. The very finest! You were not beaten by bad luck, Don. You were beaten by the best team in England. The best-ever team in England. And in Europe, Don. In Europe.

. . .

On Wednesday 7 December, 1966, Liverpool Football Club arrived at the Olympic Stadium, Amsterdam. In the fog, the heavy, wet blanket of fog. From out across the North Sea, in across the city. Clinging to their clothes, sticking to their skin. Bill Shankly and Rinus Michels, the manager of Amsterdamsche Football Club Ajax NV, the referee, his linesmen and the UEFA observer walked down one tunnel.

And then down another tunnel. A one-hundred-foot tunnel of unbreakable glass. To stop bottles hitting the players as they walked out onto the pitch. Bill Shankly, Rinus Michels, the referee, the linesmen and the UEFA observer walked out onto the pitch. There were coils of barbed wire around the pitch. To stop Dutch 'Provos' from invading the pitch. Bill Shankly, Rinus Michels, the referee, the linesmen and the UEFA observer stood in the centre circle of the pitch. No one could see the coils of barbed wire around the pitch. No one could see anything. The heavy, wet blanket of fog had smothered the Olympic Stadium, Amsterdam. Now it smothered Bill Shankly, Rinus Michels, the referee, the linesmen and the UEFA observer. It wrapped them in its heavy, wet blanket. Smothering them and blinding them –

I cannot see a thing, said Bill Shankly. Not a single thing! This game cannot be played. The match should be postponed. I am worried we'll not get home. The airport is already closed. I don't know how we'll get home. We have to play Manchester United at Old Trafford on Saturday. It is a crucial game for us, a vital match for us. I do not want us to be delayed. I do not want us to be unprepared. So this game should be called off. The match postponed. Until next week . . .

The referee stared into the fog, the heavy, wet blanket of fog. The referee nodded. And the referee said, If we can see from goal to goal, then the game can go ahead. But I cannot see from goal to goal, so the game cannot go ahead. The match must be postponed. But the forecast is for the fog to clear, the fog to lift. And so we can play the match tomorrow. Back here, tomorrow night . . .

You what, said Bill Shankly. I told you, we cannot hang around. We cannot wait another day in Amsterdam. We have to play United, Manchester United, on Saturday. It is a crucial game, it is a vital match. We have to get back home tonight, back home to Liverpool tonight . . .

But the UEFA observer shook his head. And the UEFA observer said, There is a different rule in Holland. In Holland, if you can see from the halfway line to the goal, then the game can still be played. That is the rule in Holland. And I can see from here in the centre circle to each goal. So the match need not be postponed. The game can still be played. And played tonight –

Before the whistle, the first whistle. In the dressing room, the away dressing room at the Olympic Stadium in Amsterdam. Bill

Shankly looked around the room. The Liverpool dressing room. From player to player. From Lawrence to Lawler, Lawler to Graham, Graham to Smith, Smith to Yeats, Yeats to Stevenson, Stevenson to Callaghan, Callaghan to Hunt, Hunt to St John, St John to Strong and from Strong to Thompson –

The game is not being postponed, said Bill Shankly. The match is being played. Well, more fool them, boys. More fool them, I say. This lot could not hold a candle to us if they could see us. So they are going to need a thousand candles out there tonight. Because who has ever heard of Ajax Football Club, boys? No one I know. Two seasons ago, this lot were almost relegated. Into the Dutch toilet. And that's what I thought Ajax was, boys. A detergent for cleaning your toilet. My only worry tonight, my only fear tonight, is how on earth we are going to get out of here, boys. How we are going to get back home. We've got United on Saturday, boys. So I don't want you stuck in airports. I want you rested, boys. I want you ready. So once the game is done, boys. Once this match is won. Make sure you get back here sharpish, boys. And let's be getting back. Getting back and getting home, boys . . .

After the whistle, the first whistle. On the bench, their bench in the Olympic Stadium, Amsterdam. Bill Shankly, Bob Paisley, Joe Fagan and Reuben Bennett stared out into the fog, the heavy, wet blanket of fog. They could hear the crowd. The sixty-five thousand people inside the Olympic Stadium, Amsterdam. But they could not see the crowd. The sixty-five thousand people inside the Olympic Stadium, Amsterdam. In the fog, the heavy, wet fog. They could barely see the halfway line on the pitch before them. But in the third minute, white-shirted Dutchmen appeared like ghosts before them. From out of the fog, the heavy, wet fog. Swart saw Groot, Swart passed to Groot. Groot saw De Wolf, Groot crossed to De Wolf. De Wolf saw the ball, De Wolf saw the net. And De Wolf saw the goal. De Wolf headed the ball. Into the net, into a goal. In the fog, the heavy, wet fog. On the bench, their bench in the Olympic Stadium, Amsterdam. Bill Shankly, Bob Paisley, Joe Fagan and Reuben Bennett heard the clapping. But still they could see nothing, still nothing but ghosts. And in the sixteenth minute, the ghosts appeared again. Out of the fog, the heavy, wet fog. Swart saw Nuninga, Swart passed to

Nuninga. Nuninga saw the ball, Nuninga saw the net. And Nuninga shot. Lawrence saw the ball, Lawrence blocked the shot. Cruyff saw the ball, Cruyff saw the net. And Cruyff shot into the net, into a goal. In the fog, the heavy, wet fog. Again on the bench, their bench in the Olympic Stadium, Amsterdam. Again Bill Shankly, Bob Paisley, Joe Fagan and Reuben Bennett heard the clapping. And now they heard the cheering. But in the fog, the heavy, wet fog. They still had not seen a thing. But Bill Shankly had heard enough. In the fog, the heavy, wet fog. Bill Shankly got off the bench. In the fog, the heavy, wet fog. Bill Shankly stepped over the line. In the fog, the heavy, wet fog. Bill Shankly crossed the line onto the pitch. In the fog, the heavy, wet fog. Bill Shankly walked up to Tommy Smith. And Tommy Smith jumped out of his skin. In the fog. Tommy Smith could not believe his eyes –

Go find Geoff, said Bill Shankly. And go find Willie. Get them back here, Tommy. Get them back here now. It's time for a meeting, Tommy. Time for a little team meeting . . .

In the fog, the heavy, wet fog. Tommy Smith ran off to find Geoff Strong and Willie Stevenson. And in the fog, the heavy, wet fog. Tommy Smith came back with Geoff Strong and Willie Stevenson –

Jesus Christ, said Bill Shankly. You're playing like lunatics. Like madmen, boys. There's another game to come. Another match at Anfield. Jesus Christ, boys. It's not even half-time. And we're losing two–nil. So let's just take two–nil, boys. Let's take that back home. So batten down them hatches. And don't go giving away any more goals!

In the fog, in the heavy, wet fog. Bill Shankly walked back off the pitch. Bill Shankly crossed back over the line. Bill Shankly went back to the bench. Bill Shankly sat back down on the bench. But in the fog, the heavy, wet fog. Bill Shankly still could barely see the half-way line on the pitch before him. But in the thirty-eighth minute, Bill Shankly saw the ghosts again. Out of the fog, the heavy, wet fog. Cruyff saw the ball, Cruyff took the ball. Yeats saw Cruyff, Yeats took Cruyff. Swart took the free kick. The ball rebounded off the Liverpool defenders. Cruyff saw the ball, Cruyff shot. The ball rebounded off the Liverpool defenders. Nuninga saw the ball, Nuninga saw the net. And Nuninga shot. Into the net, into a goal. And on the bench, their bench in the Olympic Stadium, Amsterdam. Bill Shankly, Bob Paisley, Joe Fagan and Reuben Bennett heard the clapping. They heard the cheering. And now they heard the chanting. *Ha-ha, Liverpool! Ha-ha, Liverpool! Ha-ha, Liverpool!* But in the forty-second minute, the ghosts were not finished. In the fog, the heavy, wet fog. Nuninga saw the ball again, Nuninga saw the goal again. And Nuninga shot. Into the net again, into a goal again. And in the fog, the heavy, wet fog. On the bench, their bench in the Olympic Stadium, Amsterdam. Bill Shankly, Bob Paisley, Joe Fagan and Reuben Bennett heard the clapping. They heard the cheering and they heard the chanting. The chanting and the laughing. *Ha-ha, Liverpool! Ha-ha, Liverpool! Ha-ha, Liverpool!* And in the seventy-sixth minute, still the ghosts would not rest. In the fog, the heavy, wet fog. Groot won a free kick. Another free kick. Groot saw the net. Groot hit the free kick into the net. And on the bench, their bench in the Olympic Stadium, Amsterdam. Bill Shankly, Bob Paisley, Joe Fagan and Reuben Bennett heard only laughter. *Ha-ha! Ha-ha! Ha-ha!* Only laughter in the fog, the heavy wet, fog. The heavy, wet laughter. *Ha-ha! Ha-ha! Ha-ha!* In the last minute, the very last minute. Lawler scored for Liverpool Football Club. But in the fog, the heavy, wet fog. In the fog and in the laughter. *Ha-ha! Ha-ha! Ha-ha!* Liverpool Football Club had lost five–one to Amsterdamsche Football Club Ajax NV. *Ha-ha! Ha-ha! Ha-ha!* One, two, three, four, five–one.

After the whistle, the final whistle. Back down the tunnel, behind the wire. Back in the dressing room, their away dressing room. Out of the fog, the heavy, wet fog. The fog and the laughter. Bill Shankly shook his head again. And Bill Shankly cursed –

Haphazard play, boys. Very haphazard. That's what that was, boys. And that has cost us dear. Very, very dear, boys. But that's not to say they are not much better than I'd heard. Much, much better than I'd heard. They are a good side, boys. A very good team. And that wee lad, Cruyff. He is some player, boys. He is a real class act. So let's be under no illusions, boys. Let's make no mistake. We have a job on our hands next week, boys. A very tough task. But we can turn it around, boys. And we will turn it around. When they come to Anfield, boys. Where there will be no fog. And where there'll be no hiding place, boys. No hiding place. For them or for us, boys.

. . .

Three days afterwards, on Saturday 10 December, 1966, Liverpool Football Club travelled to Old Trafford, Manchester. That afternoon, sixty-five thousand, two hundred folk came, too. Manchester folk and Liverpool folk. For the first time, there were closed-circuit television cameras with zoom lenses trained on the terraces behind both goals of Old Trafford, Manchester. On Manchester folk and on Liverpool folk. For the first time, police worked from screens at a central control point and kept in contact by radio with constables on the ground. But that afternoon, there were no causes for alarm. There were no outbreaks of disturbance at Old Trafford, Manchester. When the reigning League Champions played the present League leaders, there was only virtuosity playing method. The virtuosity of Best versus the method of Milne. In the fifteenth minute, Milne saw St John drifting to the left. Milne passed to St John drifting to the left. St John shot. And St John scored. In the twentieth minute, Best had the ball. Under severe pressure, Best floated free. All balance and all control. Best shot. And Best scored. In the thirtieth minute, Yeats hooked up Ryan in the penalty area. Best put the ball on the penalty spot. Best shot. And Best scored again. In the forty-fifth minute, Milne saw Lawler. Milne passed to Lawler. Lawler passed to Strong. Strong passed to St John. St John passed to Hunt. The ball went out for a corner. Callaghan took the corner. St John took down the ball. His back to the goal. St John swivelled, St John turned. St John shot. And St John scored again. And that afternoon, the reigning League Champions and the present League leaders drew two-all at Old Trafford, Manchester. Method drew with virtuosity. Virtuosity first in the First Division, method third in the First Division.

After the whistle, the final whistle. Matt Busby walked down the touchline at Old Trafford. Matt Busby shook Bill Shankly's hand. And Matt Busby said, That must have been quite some game in Amsterdam, Bill. They must be quite some side, must this Ajax of Amsterdam. You'll have your work cut out for you on Wednesday night, Bill. To beat this Ajax of Amsterdam.

Bill Shankly shook his head –

No, Matt. No. We were beaten by the fog in Amsterdam, Matt. We were never beaten by Ajax in Amsterdam. They are used to playing in the fog, Matt. And so that helped them to win. But there'll be no fog at Anfield on Wednesday night, Matt. And so this tie is by no means over. Because I know we'll score four on Wednesday night,

Matt. I know that for a fact. In fact, I think we might even score eight.

Matt Busby smiled. Matt Busby laughed. And Matt Busby said, Well, it's no crime to believe in Father Christmas, Bill. I just hope you've got a chimney big enough at Anfield . . .

. . .

Before the game, the return game against Ajax of Amsterdam. Bill Shankly had told the milkman Liverpool Football Club would beat Ajax of Amsterdam five–nil. Bill Shankly had told the postman Liverpool Football Club would beat Ajax of Amsterdam six–nil. Bill Shankly had told the children in the street Liverpool Football Club would beat Ajax of Amsterdam seven–nil. Bill Shankly had told the newspaper reporters, the local reporters and the national reporters, Liverpool Football Club would beat Ajax of Amsterdam five–nil, six–nil, seven–nil or even eight–nil. Bill Shankly had told everyone he'd met, anyone who'd listen, Liverpool Football Club would beat Ajax of Amsterdam five–nil, six–nil, seven–nil or even eight–nil. And in the dressing room, their Anfield dressing room. Bill Shankly told Tommy Lawrence, Chris Lawler, Gordon Milne, Tommy Smith, Ron Yeats, Willie Stevenson, Ian Callaghan, Roger Hunt, Ian St John, Geoff Strong and Peter Thompson the same thing. The very same thing –

Eight–nil, said Bill Shankly. Because I know you can, I know we can. Because the people here tonight, the fifty-five thousand people here tonight. They know you can, they believe you can –

And they believe you will, boys!

On Wednesday 14 December, 1966, there was no fog at Anfield, Liverpool. But there was mist and there was steam. The mist from the Mersey, the steam from the stands. The stands aglow, the Spion Kop on fire. A cauldron of passions, a furnace of emotions. Exploding and roaring. LI-VER-POOL, LI-VER-POOL, LI-VER-POOL. The Spion Kop swaying, the Spion Kop surging. On fire and aglow. In the mist and in the steam. In the push and in the crush. One hundred folk were treated by the ambulance services at Anfield. Thirty folk were taken to hospital. And in the push and in the crush. In the mist and in the steam. In this cauldron, in this furnace. In the fourth minute, Thompson crashed a shot against the crossbar. In the next fifteen minutes, Ajax of Amsterdam hit the post twice. And in the first half, Liverpool Football Club had a goal disallowed. But then in the fiftieth minute, Keizer threaded the ball through to Nuninga, Nuninga threaded the ball through to Cruyff. Cruyff flying, Cruyff gliding. With a final touch, the briefest of touches. The ball in the net, the ball a goal. Ten minutes later, St John found Hunt. And Hunt found the net. And a goal. But in the seventieth minute, Keizer again threaded the ball through to Nuninga, Nuninga again threaded the ball through to Cruyff. Cruyff not flying, Cruyff not gliding. Cruyff dancing now, Cruyff waltzing now. With a final stroke, the briefest of strokes. The ball in the net again, the ball a goal again. In the eighty-eighth minute, Thompson passed to St John. St John passed to Hunt. And Hunt scored again. And on the night, Liverpool Football Club drew two-all with Amsterdamsche Football Club Ajax NV. But in the tie, Liverpool Football Club had lost seven–three to Amsterdamsche Football Club Ajax NV. And Amsterdamsche Football Club Ajax NV had knocked Liverpool Football Club out of the European Cup –

Out of Europe and out of the Cup –

Out, out. Out, out –

That night, eight clubs went through to the quarter-finals of the European Cup. The Celtic Football Club of Scotland. CSKA Red Flag of Bulgaria. Dukla Prague of Czechoslovakia. Fudbalski klub Vojvodina of Yugoslavia. Internazionale of Italy. Linfield Football Club of Northern Ireland. Real Madrid of Spain. And Amsterdamsche Football Club Ajax NV of Holland. But not Liverpool Football Club of England. No Liverpool, no England. Not tonight, not now –

After the whistle, that final, final whistle. In the corridors and the tunnels, the Anfield corridors and the Anfield tunnels. Bill Shankly raged and Bill Shankly ranted. Against defensive football, against negative football. Against European football, against foreign football. And against luck. Against the luck of the Dutch. But in the corridors and in the tunnels, the Anfield corridors and the Anfield tunnels. No one was listening to Bill Shankly. In the corridors,

in the tunnels. No one was there.

No one but Bill.

## 24. THE MORTAL AND THE IMMORTAL

In the drive, in the car. Bill switched off the headlights. In the night, in the mist. Bill switched on the headlights. In the drive, in the car. On and then off, off and then on. In the night and in the mist. Bill could not forget Amsterdam. In the drive, in the car. Bill could not forget Ajax. The headlights off, the headlights on. Bill knew Ajax of Amsterdam were one of the best sides he had ever seen play. In the night and in the mist. Bill knew Ajax of Amsterdam were going to be one of the best teams in Europe. The headlights off, the headlights on. Bill knew Ajax of Amsterdam had played a type of football he had never seen before. In the drive, in the car. Bill knew it was not defensive football, Bill knew it was not negative football. And Bill knew it was not lucky football. In the night and in the mist. Bill knew it was simple football, Bill knew it was team football. On and off, off and on. Simple team football, total team football. In the drive, in the car. The type of football Bill had seen in his dreams. In the night and in the mist. Bill switched off the headlights. In the drive, in the car. Bill closed his eyes. In the night and in the mist.

In his dreams, only in his dreams.

. . .

In the house, in their front room. Bill had shaved. Bill had washed. And Bill had dressed. Bill had eaten his breakfast. Bill had drunk his tea. And Bill had read the newspaper. In the front room, in his chair. Bill looked at his watch. It was seven o'clock. Bill took out his address book. Bill went out into the hall. Bill opened his address book. Bill picked up the telephone. Bill dialled the number. The number of a guest house in Blackpool. Bill listened to the phone ring. And ring and ring. Bill heard the landlady answer. Bill asked to speak to Emlyn. Bill waited for the landlady to fetch Emlyn. Bill heard Emlyn stammer. Bill heard Emlyn stutter. Bill heard Emlyn say –

Hello, Mr Shankly? Hello, sir? Good morning, Mr Shankly. Good morning, sir. How are you, Mr Shankly? How are you, sir?

And Bill said, I'm very well. Thank you, son. But I'm always very well, son. So how are you, son? How are you today? I know you are having a tough season, son. I know it must not be easy for you. Your first season, son. The season Blackpool are having. With Ron

Suart resigning and Stan Mortensen coming in. But I want you to know I am watching you, son. I haven't forgotten you. So you bide your time, son. And soon you'll be with us. With Liverpool Football Club, son. The greatest football club there is. So I want you to look after yourself, son. I want you to take good care of yourself . . .

Thank you, Mr Shankly, said Emlyn Hughes. Thank you, sir. And I am looking after myself, Mr Shankly. I am taking good care of myself, sir. Thank you, Mr Shankly . . .

That's what I want to hear, son. That's what I want to hear. And so what are you doing, son? What are you doing now?

Well, I'm having my breakfast, sir, said Emlyn Hughes.

That's good, son. That's very good. It's the most important meal of the day, son. Your breakfast. You don't want to be missing your breakfast. Good boy. Good lad.

I never do, sir, said Emlyn Hughes. I never miss my breakfast.

And so what do you eat, son? What are you eating for your breakfast today then?

Well, laughed Emlyn Hughes. I'm eating the Mrs Williams Special. The special Mrs Williams always makes us. Fried egg, bacon and some black pudding. Her full English special, sir . . .

Bill stammered, Bill stuttered. And Bill said, You what? Are you mental, son? Are you insane? That stuff will make you fat, that stuff will make you lazy. Make you stupid, son! A glass of orange juice and a slice of toast. That's all you need for your breakfast, son. A glass of orange and a slice of toast. To keep you lean, to keep you hungry. When you play for Liverpool Football Club, when you play for the greatest football club there is, you need to be lean, you need to be hungry, son. Now pass this phone to that woman, son. Let me speak to her now. I want you lean, son. I want you hungry. Lean and hungry for Liverpool Football Club, son.

. . .

In the front room, in his chair. Bill dropped the newspaper. As soon as he had read the headline. Bill put on his coat, Bill put on his hat. As quickly as he could. Bill drove to Filbert Street, Leicester. As fast as he could. Bill met the directors of Leicester City Football Club. As soon as they could. Bill talked with the directors of Leicester City Football Club. Bill shook hands with the directors of Leicester City

Football Club. Bill met Gordon Banks. As soon as he could. Bill talked with Gordon Banks. Bill shook hands with Gordon Banks. Bill travelled back to Anfield, Liverpool. As fast as he could. Bill met the directors of Liverpool Football Club. As soon as they could. And Bill said, I have met the directors of Leicester City Football Club. I have talked with the directors of Leicester City Football Club. I have shaken hands with the directors of Leicester City Football Club. I have met Gordon Banks. I have talked with Gordon Banks. I have shaken hands with Gordon Banks. And so the deal is done. The feat accomplished.

In the boardroom, the Anfield boardroom. The directors of Liverpool Football Club looked down the long table at Bill –

But how much do Leicester City want for Banks, Mr Shankly? How much must we pay for Gordon Banks?

Just sixty thousand pounds.

Sixty thousand pounds, repeated the directors of Liverpool Football Club. *Just* sixty thousand pounds? For a goalkeeper?

Bill nodded. And Bill said, Yes. Just sixty thousand pounds. But not just sixty thousand pounds for just any old goalkeeper. No. For the best goalkeeper in the country. The best goalkeeper in the world . . .

But you are always saying we already have the best goalkeeper in the country, Mr Shankly. You are always saying Tommy Lawrence is the best goalkeeper in the world . . .

Bill nodded again. And Bill said, Yes. Tommy Lawrence *was* the best goalkeeper in the country. But Tommy Lawrence is not the best goalkeeper in the country any more. Gordon Banks is the best goalkeeper in the country now. And not only in the country. In the world. You all know Gordon Banks has a World Cup winner's medal. A World Cup winner's medal!

Yes, we all know Gordon Banks has a World Cup winner's medal, Mr Shankly. But sixty thousand pounds is still a lot of money for a goalkeeper. No football club has ever paid sixty thousand pounds for a goalkeeper . . .

Bill shook his head. And Bill said, But this is not just any goalkeeper. This is the best goalkeeper in the country we are talking about. This is the best goalkeeper in the world. With Gordon Banks in our side, with Gordon Banks in this Liverpool team, we will save twenty goals a season, at least twenty goals a season. And if we can save twenty goals a season, if Gordon Banks saves us twenty goals a season, then there will no stopping us, no stopping Liverpool Football Club. Sixty grand is a bargain. An absolute bargain!

Sixty thousand pounds is not a bargain, said the directors of Liverpool Football Club. Not for a goalkeeper. We think sixty thousand pounds is robbery, Mr Shankly. For a goalkeeper. It's absolute robbery, Mr Shankly . . .

Bill stammered, Bill stuttered. And Bill said, You what? Are you all mental? Are you all insane? Sheffield Wednesday paid Stoke City seventy-five thousand pounds for John Ritchie. Tottenham Hotspur paid Blackburn Rovers ninety-five thousand pounds for Mike England. Chelsea paid Aston Villa one hundred thousand pounds for Tony Hateley. And need I remind you, that mob across the park, they paid one hundred and twelve thousand pounds for Alan Ball. One hundred and twelve thousand pounds! And so how on earth, how in God's name, is sixty thousand pounds robbery for Gordon Banks? For the best goalkeeper in the world? How is that robbery?

John Ritchie is not a goalkeeper, said the directors of Liverpool Football Club. John Ritchie is a striker. Mike England is not a goalkeeper, Mike England is a defender. Tony Hateley is not a goalkeeper, Tony Hateley is a striker. And Alan Ball is not a goalkeeper, Alan Ball is a midfielder. But Gordon Banks is a goalkeeper. Just a goalkeeper. And we will not pay sixty thousand pounds for a goalkeeper, Mr Shankly. We simply will not pay.

Bill looked down the long table at the directors of Liverpool Football Club. Bill shook his head. And Bill said, Well, I will tell you this. Without a better goalkeeper, without Gordon Banks, Liverpool Football Club will not win the League again. And so Liverpool Football Club will not play in the European Cup again. And so Liverpool Football Club will not win the European Cup. Not ever. Not without a better keeper. Not without Gordon Banks.

. . .

On the bench, their bench at Goodison Park. Bill was watching, watching with the sixty-four thousand, eight hundred and fifty-one folk inside Goodison Park, watching with the forty thousand, one hundred and forty-nine folk inside Anfield, the forty thousand, one hundred and forty-nine folk watching on closed-circuit

225

television, on eight giant screens, inside Anfield –

Watching, watching –

On the bench, their bench at Goodison Park. In a gale of paper, in a tunnel of noise. Bill watched Everton Football Club harry Liverpool Football Club, Bill watched Everton Football Cub hound Liverpool Football Club. And in the last minute of the first half, Bill watched Yeats fail to clear. Bill watched Milne pass back to Lawrence, Husband harrying Lawrence. Bill watched Lawrence fail to collect the ball, Husband hounding Lawrence. Bill watched Lawrence fail to gather the ball, Alan Ball collecting the ball on the byline, Alan Ball gathering the ball on the byline. And from the byline, from the most difficult of angles, Bill watched Alan Ball hook the ball over Tommy Lawrence and into the net, into a goal. The only goal, the only difference. In a gale of paper, in a tunnel of noise. Bill knew Alan Ball was the difference between Everton Football Club and Liverpool Football Club. The only difference and the only reason. In a gale of paper, in a tunnel of noise. Bill knew Alan Ball was the reason Everton Football Club beat Liverpool Football Club one–nil in the Fifth Round of the FA Cup. In a gale of paper, in a tunnel of noise. The only reason Liverpool Football Club were out of the FA Cup. Out of another cup. Out, out –

Again.

. . .

In the boardroom, the Anfield boardroom. Bill looked down the long table at the directors of Liverpool Football Club. And Bill said, You would not give me the money to buy Alan Ball from Blackpool. Everton bought Alan Ball from Blackpool. You would not give me the money to buy Howard Kendall from Preston North End. Everton bought Howard Kendall from Preston. You would not give me the money to buy Gordon Banks from Leicester City. Stoke City bought Gordon Banks from Leicester. But today I hope you will give me the money to buy Emlyn Hughes from Blackpool Football Club.

And how much do the directors of Blackpool Football Club want for Hughes, asked the directors of Liverpool Football Club.

Bill said, Sixty-five thousand pounds. But Emlyn Hughes is not a goalkeeper. Emlyn Hughes is a defender. But Emlyn Hughes could also be a midfielder. He is versatile and he is talented. Very, very versatile and very, very talented. And I tell you this. I believe he will play for England. I believe he will be the captain of England. I believe he can be the captain of Liverpool Football Club. I believe he can be a rock for Liverpool Football Club. A great, great captain and a great, great rock. A rock on which we can build. For a great future and for great success. With this boy in our side, with this boy in our team.

The directors of Liverpool Football Club nodded. And the directors of Liverpool Football Club smiled –

You have sold this boy to us, Mr Shankly. And so we agree to your request. We will pay Blackpool Football Club sixty-five thousand pounds for Hughes, Mr Shankly.

Bill raised his eyebrows. Bill sighed. And Bill said, Thank you.

The directors of Liverpool Football Club smiled again. And the directors of Liverpool Football Club picked up a piece of paper from the long table. And the directors of Liverpool Football Club passed the piece of paper all the way down the long table to Bill –

There was one other thing, Mr Shankly. Just one other thing. We'd like to offer you this, Mr Shankly. This is a new contract. A new five-year contract for you, Mr Shankly.

Bill looked down at the piece of paper. And Bill said, But I have a contract. And I still have one year left on my contract.

The directors of Liverpool Football Club nodded again. The directors of Liverpool Football Club smiled again –

We know, Mr Shankly. We know you do. But we also know how very important you are to Liverpool Football Club. How very, very important you are, Mr Shankly. So we do not want you to feel any doubt, Mr Shankly. We do not want you to feel any uncertainty. Any doubt at all, any uncertainty at all. So we would like to offer you a new contract, a new five-year contract now. For your peace of mind, Mr Shankly. Your own peace of mind . . .

Bill looked back up from the piece of paper. Bill looked back down the long table at the directors of Liverpool Football Club. And Bill said, Thank you, gentlemen. Thank you very much. I appreciate your concern for my peace of mind. And I appreciate your commitment to me. And so I will take this contract home with me today. And I will consider this contract. I'll consider it very carefully.

. . .

At the ground or at their house. In the office or in their kitchen. At his desk or at their table. With the papers and with his books. His books of names, his books of notes. With the glue and with the scissors. Bill kept turning the pages, Bill kept turning the pages. The pages of the papers, the pages of his books. His books of names and his books of notes. Backwards and forwards, forwards and backwards. Liverpool Football Club were third in the First Division, Liverpool Football Club were second in the First Division, Liverpool Football Club were third in the First Division. Backwards and forwards, forwards and backwards. Third and then fourth, fourth and then fifth. Backwards and backwards, backwards and backwards,

backwards and backwards.

. . .

In the house, in their hallway. Bill put down the telephone. Bill stood in the hallway. Bill looked at the front door, Bill looked at the cupboard door. Inside the cupboard was his coat, inside the cupboard was his hat. But Bill walked back into the front room. Bill sat back down in his armchair. Bill looked over at Ness. And Bill smiled.

Who was that, asked Ness. On the phone, love?

Bill said, It was the chairman of Aston Villa.

Oh, said Ness. And what did he want, love?

He wanted me to pop down for a chat.

Where is Aston Villa, asked Ness.

They are in Birmingham.

Oh, said Ness again. I've never been to Birmingham. What kind of place is Birmingham? Is it a big place?

Bill said, Yes. It's a very big city.

Well, are you going, asked Ness. To Birmingham?

No, love. I don't think I am. Not today.

Ness stood up. And Ness smiled –

That's good, love. Well, I'll go and put the kettle on then. I'll make us both a nice cup of tea. How about that, love?

Bill smiled again. And Bill said, That sounds great, love. Thank you. Thank you very much, love.

Ness got up from her chair. Ness went out into the kitchen. Bill could hear her filling the kettle. Bill could hear her lighting the cooker. And Bill could hear one of their girls upstairs. Playing her records.

And Bill could hear the kids outside. Playing their games. And in their home, in his chair. Bill closed his eyes. And in his mind, in his ears. Bill could hear the crowd. The Anfield crowd, the Spion Kop. Now all Bill could hear was *LI-VER-POOL, LI-VER-POOL, LI-VER-POOL.*

. . .

In the boardroom, the Anfield boardroom. Before the press, the local press. At the table, the long table. The directors of Liverpool Football Club sat down. And Bill sat down. The directors of Liverpool Football Club smiled. And Bill said, I am not playing with words when I say Liverpool Football Club have the most loyal supporters in the world. The greatest supporters in the world. And that is my challenge, to care for them. That is my challenge, to look after them. Because if the supporters of Liverpool Football Club are happy, then the players of Liverpool Football Club are happy, and if the players are happy, then the club is successful. That is the only sort of dividend I seek for my labours. That is the only reward I want. To make the supporters happy, to make the people happy. And I have never cheated the supporters, I have never cheated the people. And I never will, I never will. They deserve the best. Because they are the best. And no man, no man alive, can give more, can strive harder to give them the best, to make them happy. That is all I seek to do. That is all I try to do . . .

And so come what may, whether or not I am still associated with Liverpool Football Club after that time, that time this contract ends, my wife and I will spend the rest of our days in Liverpool. We have been made to feel at home here. We like the place and we like the people. And so we can see no reason for going elsewhere . . .

This is our home. Our home.

. . .

At home, at Anfield. Later that afternoon, that last afternoon of the 1966–67 season, Blackpool Football Club came to Anfield, Liverpool. And that afternoon, that last afternoon, twenty-eight thousand, seven hundred and seventy-three folk came, too. Just twenty-eight thousand, seven hundred and seventy-three folk. Blackpool Football Club had already been relegated from the First Division. And in the twenty-first minute, Peter Thompson scored. But that afternoon, that last afternoon, Liverpool Football Club lost three–one to Blackpool Football Club. At home, at Anfield. That afternoon, that last afternoon of the season, Liverpool Football Club were fifth in the First Division. And Liverpool Football Club were Champions no more.

. . .

In Portugal, in Lisbon. In the Estádio Nacional, in his seat. In the sun, the scalding sun. Bill watched Craig tackle Cappellini inside the Celtic penalty area. Bill watched Cappellini fall to the ground inside the Celtic penalty area. Bill watched the German referee point to the penalty spot inside the Celtic penalty area. Bill watched Mazzola send Simpson the wrong way in the Celtic goal. Bill watched the ball hit the back of the Celtic goal. In the Estádio Nacional, in his seat. In the sun, the scalding sun. Bill watched Auld hit the bar. Bill watched Gemmell shoot. Bill watched Sarti save. Bill watched Johnstone head the ball towards the goal. Bill watched Sarti tip the ball over the bar. Bill watched Gemmell shoot again. Bill watched Sarti save again. In the sun, the scalding sun. At the end of the first half, Bill watched Jock Stein harangue the referee, the German referee. Bill watched Jock Stein harangue Helenio Herrera, the manager of Internazionale of Milan. In the Estádio Nacional, in his seat. In the sun, the scalding sun. At the start of the second half, Bill watched the players of the Celtic Football Club wait for the players of Internazionale of Milan. In the sun, the scalding sun. In the heat, the eighty-five-degree heat. In the Estádio Nacional, in his seat. In the sun, the scalding sun. Bill watched Sarti save. Bill watched Sarti save and save again. In the sun, the scalding sun. In the sixty-second minute, Bill watched Gemmell scream for the ball. Bill watched Craig square the ball to Gemmell. Bill watched Gemmell shoot. And Bill watched Gemmell score. In the sun, the scalding sun. Bill watched justice prevail. Bill watched Murdoch shoot. Bill watched Chalmers turn the shot into the net. In the Estádio Nacional, in his seat. In the sun, the scalding sun. Bill watched the supporters of the Celtic Football Club pour down the marble terraces. Ready. Bill watched the supporters of the Celtic Football Club mass around the perimeter moat. Ready. And in the Estádio Nacional, in his seat. In the sun, the scalding sun. Bill heard the whistle, the final whistle. The Celtic Football Club had beaten Internazionale of Milan two–one. The Celtic Football Club had won the European Cup. The Celtic Football Club were the first British team to win the European Cup. Jock Stein the first British manager to win the European Cup. Not Matt Busby. And not Bill Shankly –

His jacket stuck to his shirt. His shirt stuck to his vest. His vest stuck to his skin. Bill had tears in his eyes. Tears on his cheeks now. The collar of his shirt, the silk of his tie –

His Liverpool tie. His red,

red Liverpool tie. In the dressing room, the Celtic dressing room. Bill patted Jock Stein's back, Bill shook Jock Stein's hand. And Bill said, Congratulations, John. Congratulations. I could not be happier for you, John. I could not be happier. You have won the League. You have won the Scottish Cup. You have won the Scottish League Cup. You have won the Glasgow Cup. And now you have won the European Cup. All in one season, John. All in the same season!

And so now you are immortal, John.

Now you are immortal.

Immortal, John.


## 25. WE DO NOT LIVE ON MEMORIES

After the season. The season of loss. Before the season. The season of hope. In the summer. The summer of love. Bill Shankly, Bob Paisley, Joe Fagan and Reuben Bennett were not on their holidays. In the board-room. The boardroom at Anfield. Bill Shankly, Bob Paisley, Joe Fagan and Reuben Bennett were about their work. The books were spread out over the long table. The books of names, the books of notes. The sheets of paper piled up on the long table. The sheets of names, the sheets of dates. Bill Shankly, Bob Paisley Joe Fagan and Reuben Bennett going through every page of every book, every sheet of every paper. Every player and every game. Bill Shankly, Bob Paisley, Joe Fagan and Reuben Bennett discussing every page, studying every sheet. They analysed every player, they evaluated every game. The games that had been, the season that had been. The season of loss –

In the 1966–67 season, Liverpool Football Club had played forty-two League games. They had won twelve games at home, at Anfield, and they had won seven games away, away from Anfield. They had drawn seven games at home and they had drawn six games away. They had lost two games at home, at Anfield, and they had lost eight games away, away from Anfield. They had scored thirty-six goals at home, at Anfield, and they had scored twenty-eight goals away, away from Anfield. They had conceded seventeen goals at home, at Anfield, and they had conceded thirty goals away from home, away from Anfield. In the 1966–67 season, Liverpool Football Club had finished with fifty-one points. And Liverpool Football Club had finished fifth in the First Division. Leeds United had fifty-five points. Tottenham Hotspur had fifty-six points. And Nottingham Forest had fifty-six points, too. Manchester United Football Club had sixty points. Manchester United had finished first in the First Division. Manchester United were the Champions of England. The new Champions.

The season before, Liverpool Football Club had finished first in the First Division. Liverpool Football Club had been the Champions of England. The season before, Liverpool Football Club had scored seventy-nine goals and they had conceded thirty-four. Home and away. In the 1966–67 season, Liverpool Football Club had scored sixty-four goals and they had conceded forty-seven. Home and away. Manchester United Football Club had scored eighty-four goals and they had conceded forty-six. Home and away.

In the new season, the season to come, Bill Shankly, Bob Paisley, Joe Fagan and Reuben Bennett knew Liverpool Football Club would need to score more goals. A lot more goals.

Twenty-one more goals.

Bill Shankly had heard Tony Hateley was unhappy. Bill Shankly knew Tony Hateley had played one hundred and thirty-one times for Notts County Football Club. Bill Shankly knew Tony Hateley had scored seventy-seven goals for Notts County Football Club. Bill Shankly knew Tony Hateley had played one hundred and twenty-seven times for Aston Villa Football Club. Bill Shankly knew Tony Hateley had scored sixty-eight goals for Aston Villa Football Club. Bill Shankly knew Tony Hateley had played twenty-seven times for Chelsea Football Club. Bill Shankly knew Tony Hateley had scored six goals for Chelsea Football Club. Only six goals. Bill Shankly knew why Tony Hateley was unhappy. Bill Shankly didn't like to think of any man being unhappy. Not when he could be happy. Not when he could be playing for Liverpool Football Club. Not when he could be scoring goals for Liverpool Football Club. Twenty-one goals for Liverpool Football Club. Home and away. At least twenty-one goals, for Liverpool Football Club.

. . .

After his summer holidays, back in the boardroom. Sidney Reakes said, But ninety-six thousand pounds is much more than we have ever paid for any footballer, Mr Shankly. Much, much more.

I know, said Bill Shankly. And I know it is a huge amount of money. And you know how much I dislike spending such huge amounts of money. But these are the amounts of money we have to spend these days. This is the world we have to live in these days. And we can dream of a different world, we can wish for a better world. We can still strive for that world, we can still work towards that world. That different world, that better world. But we still have to live in this world, we cannot only live in history. What has been done has been done. But what has been done is history now. Now we need to turn the page and to write a new page. And I believe this man is the player to help us turn the page, to let us write that new page. A new page of history, a new page of success. Because the supporters of Liverpool Football Club have been weaned on success. And the supporters of Liverpool Football Club deserve success. Anything less would be an insult. An insult to the supporters of Liverpool Football Club. And an insult to the people of Liverpool . . .

Sidney Reakes said, You make a very powerful case, Mr Shankly. As usual. A very persuasive case, Mr Shankly. And I will present your case to the board. And then I will get back to you, Mr Shankly. Now was there anything else? Anything else I can do for you today, Mr Shankly?

Yes, said Bill Shankly. There was one other thing. One small thing. I'd also like eighteen thousand pounds to buy Ray Clemence from Scunthorpe Football Club . . .

Ray who?

. . .

Last season, Geoff Twentyman had called Bill Shankly. Geoff Twentyman had told Bill Shankly about a young lad called Ray Clemence. Ray Clemence was the goalkeeper for Scunthorpe United. In the Third Division. Eight times, Bill Shankly had travelled to the Old Showground, Scunthorpe. Eight times on a Friday night at a quarter to seven, Bill Shankly had sat in the stand at the Old Showground, Scunthorpe. Eight times, Bill Shankly had watched Ray Clemence play in goal for Scunthorpe United at the Old Showground, Scunthorpe. In the Third Division, on a Friday night. Eight times, because Bill Shankly had wanted to see Ray Clemence stop a shot with his left hand. Eight times, because Bill Shankly had wanted to see Ray Clemence stop a shot with his right hand. Eight times, because Bill Shankly had wanted to see Ray Clemence cut out a cross from the left. Eight times, because Bill Shankly had wanted to see Ray Clemence cut out a cross from the right. Eight times, because Bill Shankly had wanted to see Ray Clemence save with his left hand. Eight times, because Bill Shankly had wanted to see Ray Clemence save with his right hand. Eight times, because Bill Shankly had wanted to see Ray Clemence kick with his left foot. Eight times, because Bill Shankly had wanted to see Ray Clemence kick with his right foot. Eight times, because Ray Clemence was a goalkeeper. Eight times, because Ray Clemence was left-footed. Eight times, because Bill Shankly wanted to make sure Ray Clemence was not left-handed. Eight times, because Bill Shankly did not like left-handed goalkeepers. Eight times, because Bill Shankly thought left-handed goalkeepers were short of balance. Eight times, until Bill Shankly was certain Ray Clemence was not left-handed. Eight times, until Bill Shankly was convinced. Now Bill Shankly was certain. Now Bill Shankly was convinced. Ray Clemence was the best goalkeeper he had ever seen. Ever –

In the summer of 1967. At the doors to Anfield. Ray Clemence shook Bill Shankly's hand. Hard. With his right hand. Hard.

Follow me, said Bill Shankly. Follow me, son . . .

And Ray Clemence followed Bill Shankly into the dressing rooms, the Anfield dressing rooms. And Bill Shankly smiled –

These are the best dressing rooms in the world, son . . .

Ray Clemence followed Bill Shankly out onto the pitch, the Anfield pitch. Bill Shankly knelt down. Bill Shankly touched the grass, the Anfield grass. And Bill Shankly smiled again –

Feel that, son. Feel that grass. That is the best grass in the world, son. The finest playing surface in the world . . .

Ray Clemence followed Bill Shankly down to the Kop end. Bill Shankly looked up at the Kop, the empty Kop –

That is the Kop, son. The Spion Kop. That is where the finest supporters in the world stand, son. The greatest people in the world. Every game, every match. With those supporters behind you, with those people supporting you, you cannot lose, son. You cannot lose.

Ray Clemence followed Bill Shankly to his office. Ray Clemence sat down. Bill Shankly passed Ray Clemence a contract –

If you carry on improving the way you are doing, then you will be in our first team within a year, son. And you will be the best goalkeeper in the land, the best goalkeeper in the world. Playing for the best team in the land, the best team in the world, son. And you'll be playing for England, too. I believe that, son. In fact, I know that.

Ray Clemence looked down at the contract in his hand. And then Ray Clemence looked back up at Bill Shankly. And Ray Clemence said, I want to sign, Mr Shankly. I want to play for Liverpool Football Club. But Tommy Lawrence is a great goalkeeper. Tommy Lawrence is the first-team goalkeeper. Now I am playing first-team football. If I sign, I'll be playing in the reserves . . .

Yes, said Bill Shankly. Tommy Lawrence is a great goalkeeper. You are right, son. And yes, you will be playing in the reserves. You are right again, son. But Tommy Lawrence is almost thirty-one years old. Tommy Lawrence won't be the first-team goalkeeper for very much longer. And you will be learning from Tommy. And you will be improving, son. And remember, Liverpool reserves are not just any team. Liverpool reserves are the second-best team in the land, son. The only team better than the Liverpool reserve team is the Liverpool first team. So you will be learning and you will be improving, son. And then you will be ready to play for the first team. Ready to play for the best team in the world, son. You will be ready . . .

Ray Clemence took the pen from Bill Shankly. And Ray Clemence signed the contract with Liverpool Football Club. Ray Clemence shook hands with Bill Shankly. Ray Clemence followed Bill Shankly out of his office. Down the corridor, in the corridor. Bill Shankly opened a door. The door to the toilets. Ray Clemence followed Bill Shankly into the toilets. The Anfield toilets. Bill Shankly opened a cubicle door. Ray Clemence followed Bill Shankly into the cubicle. Bill Shankly lifted the lid on the toilet. Bill Shankly flushed the toilet. Bill Shankly looked at his watch. Bill Shankly laughed –

Look at that, son. Look at the flush. Look at that toilet, son. That toilet refills in fifteen seconds. We have everything here, son. And everything we have is the best. Remember that, son. Everything we have here is the best. Only the very best, son.

. . .

On Saturday 19 August, 1967, Liverpool Football Club travelled to Maine Road, Manchester. Manchester City missed a penalty. And Liverpool Football Club drew nil–nil with Manchester City in the first game of the 1967–68 season. Three days afterwards, Arsenal Football Club came to Anfield, Liverpool. That evening, fifty-two thousand and thirty-three folk came, too. In the first fifteen minutes, Liverpool Football Club had seven headers or shots. In the twenty-third minute, Tommy Smith passed to Tony Hateley. Hateley passed to Roger Hunt. And Hunt scored. In the seventy-fifth minute, Liverpool Football Club won a corner. Ron Yeats shot. Furnell parried. And Hunt scored again. And Liverpool Football Club beat Arsenal Football Club two–nil. At home, at Anfield. The Spion Kop cheered and the Spion Kop clapped. The Spion Kop shouted and the Spion Kop sang, *We are the Greatest, the Greatest . . .*

On Saturday 26 August, 1967, Newcastle United came to Anfield, Liverpool. That afternoon, fifty-one thousand, eight hundred and twenty-nine folk came, too. In the eighth minute, Tony Hateley scored his first goal for Liverpool Football Club. In the thirtieth minute, Emlyn Hughes scored. In the forty-first minute, Roger Hunt scored. In the forty-seventh minute, Hateley scored his second goal for Liverpool Football Club. In the seventy-fifth minute, Hateley scored his third goal for Liverpool Football Club. And in the eighty-seventh minute, Hunt scored again. And Liverpool Football Club beat Newcastle United six–nil. At home, at Anfield. And the Spion Kop roared, *We're going to win the League. We're going to win the League . . .*

Two days later, Liverpool Football Club travelled to Highbury, London. Liverpool Football Club had not lost to Arsenal Football Club in the last thirteen matches they had played against Arsenal Football Club. That afternoon, Liverpool Football Club lost two–nil to Arsenal Football Club. Away from home, away from Anfield.

. . .

Geoff had no job. Geoff had just five pounds in his pocket.

Geoff was planning to use that five pounds, his last five pounds, to travel to Liverpool. Geoff was planning to ask for a job at Ford's in Halewood, Liverpool. That morning, just before Geoff left, the telephone rang. Geoff picked up the phone. And Geoff said, Hello?

Hello, said Bill Shankly. How are you, Geoff?

Geoff Twentyman had first met Bill Shankly in March, 1949. In March, 1949, Bill Shankly was appointed as the manager of Carlisle United. Geoff Twentyman was a player at Carlisle United. Bill Shankly liked Geoff. Geoff left Carlisle United for Liverpool Football Club. But Bill Shankly had kept in touch with Geoff. And Geoff had told Tom Williams, the chairman of Liverpool Football Club, many stories about Bill Shankly. In December, 1959, Bill Shankly had come to Liverpool Football Club. And Geoff had left Liverpool Football Club. But Bill Shankly had still kept in touch with Geoff. Geoff had gone into management. Geoff had managed Morecombe. Geoff had managed Hartlepools United. Hartlepools United had sacked Geoff. Hartlepools United appointed Brian Clough as their new manager. Hartlepools United gave Geoff and his family one month's notice on the house they were living in. Hartlepools United owned the house they were living in. Hartlepools United needed the house for their new manager. For Brian Clough and his family. Geoff and his family moved back to Carlisle. Geoff tried to get a job in football. Geoff could not get a job in football. Bill Shankly thought that was a tragedy. A tragedy for the man. Bill Shankly thought that was a waste. A waste for football. But Bill Shankly had kept in touch with Geoff. And Geoff had kept in touch with football. Geoff still watched games. Geoff still watched players. And Geoff still called Bill Shankly. Geoff still talked to Bill Shankly about the games he had seen. The players he had seen. Players like Ray Clemence. But Geoff had had to get a job as a van driver. But then Geoff had lost his job as a van driver. Now Geoff had no job. That morning, the telephone rang –

Norman Lowe has just resigned as our chief scout, said Bill Shankly. Would you like to be our new chief scout? Would you like to come and work with me, Geoff? To work for Liverpool Football Club?

Yes, said Geoff. I would. Thank you, Bill.

. . .

On Saturday 2 September, 1967, Liverpool Football Club

travelled to the Hawthorns, Birmingham. In the sixth minute, Tony Hateley scored. And in the fifty-eighth minute, Roger Hunt scored. And Liverpool Football Club beat West Bromwich Albion two–nil. Away from home, away from Anfield. Three days afterwards, Liverpool Football Club travelled to the City Ground, Nottingham. In the fifty-first minute, Emlyn Hughes scored. And Liverpool Football Club beat Nottingham Forest one–nil.

On Saturday 9 September, 1967, Chelsea Football Club came to Anfield, Liverpool. In high summer sunshine. That afternoon, fifty-three thousand, eight hundred and thirty-nine folk came, too.

Before the whistle, the first whistle. Bill Shankly walked into the dressing room. The home dressing room. Bill Shankly closed the dressing-room door. The Anfield dressing-room door. Bill Shankly looked around the dressing room. The Liverpool dressing room. From player to player. From Lawrence to Lawler, Lawler to Byrne, Byrne to Smith, Smith to Yeats, Yeats to Hughes, Hughes to Callaghan, Callaghan to Hunt, Hunt to Hateley, Hateley to St John and from St John to Thompson. And Bill Shankly smiled –

In the last eight years, boys. In our last thirty-two League games against London clubs. Only West Ham United have ever won at Anfield, boys. And that was back in 1963. And that was a fluke, boys. A bloody fluke. Hateley here will tell you all how much London clubs hate coming here. Hate coming to Liverpool, hate coming to Anfield. A cup of tea is all we give a London club when they come here, boys. It is a tradition. An Anfield tradition, boys. We give London nothing when they come to Liverpool. Nothing but a cup of tea, boys.

In the high summer sunshine, on a hard, fast surface. Liverpool Football Club were all attack, Liverpool Football Club all power. In the high summer sunshine, on the hard, fast surface. Callaghan danced down one wing, Thompson weaved down the other. In the high summer sunshine, on the fast, hard surface. Hughes had hunger, Smith had thirst. In the high summer sunshine, on the fast, hard surface. Hateley took the weight off Hunt, Hateley made the space for Hunt. In the high summer sunshine, on the hard, fast surface. Bonetti saved, Bonetti saved and Bonetti saved again. In the high summer sunshine, on the fast, hard surface. After thirty-seven minutes, Harris hooked up Hateley in the Chelsea penalty area. Smith put the ball on the Chelsea penalty spot. And Smith put the ball in the back of the Chelsea net. In the high summer sunshine, on the fast, hard surface. At the beginning of the second half, when Bonetti took his place with his back to the Kop, the Spion Kop applauded him. But in the high summer sunshine, on the hard, fast surface. Ninety seconds later, Hughes crossed the ball. Hateley dived for the ball. A human rocket, a human torpedo. Hateley's head met the ball. And the ball hit the back of the net. The Chelsea net. In the high summer sunshine, on the hard, fast surface. Ninety seconds later, Thompson crossed the ball. Hateley brushed between two defenders. A human rocket, a human torpedo. Hateley's head met the ball. The ball hit the back of the net. The Chelsea net. And in the high summer sunshine, on the fast, hard surface. Liverpool Football Club beat Chelsea Football Club three–one. In the high summer sunshine, on the hard, fast surface. Tony Hateley had made his point against his former club. And Liverpool Football Club had served their notice on all the other clubs. That evening, Tottenham Hotspur had eleven points. That evening, Liverpool Football club had eleven points, too. But that evening, Liverpool Football Club were first in the First Division. On goal average. First again.

One week afterwards, Liverpool Football Club travelled to the Dell, Southampton. In the thirtieth second, Southampton Football Club scored. In the tenth minute, Tommy Smith put the ball on the Southampton penalty spot. But Smith put the ball wide of the Southampton goal. And Liverpool Football Club lost one–nil to Southampton Football Club. Away from home, away from Anfield. That evening, Tottenham Hotspur still had eleven points. But now Sheffield Wednesday had eleven points, Manchester City had eleven points and Arsenal Football Club had eleven points, too. Liverpool Football Club still had eleven points, too. And that evening, Liverpool Football Club were first in the First Division. Still. On goal average.

On Tuesday 19 September, 1967, Liverpool Football Club came to the Malmö Stadium, Malmö, Sweden, to play Malmö Fotbollförening in the first leg of the First Round of the Inter-Cities Fairs Cup. Liverpool Football Club had never played in the Inter-Cities Fairs Cup before. In the ninth minute, Tony Hateley scored. In the eightieth minute, Hateley scored again. And Liverpool Football Club beat Malmö Fotbollförening two–nil in the first leg of the First Round of the Inter-Cities Fairs Cup.

Five days later, Everton Football Club came to Anfield, Liverpool. That afternoon, fifty-four thousand, one hundred and eighty-nine folk came, too. In the seventy-eighth minute, Roger Hunt scored. And Liverpool Football Club beat Everton Football Club one–nil. That evening, Sheffield Wednesday had thirteen points and Arsenal Football Club had thirteen points. And Liverpool Football Club had thirteen points, too. That evening, Liverpool Football Club were first in the First Division. Still. On goal average.

One week afterwards, Stoke City came to Anfield, Liverpool. That afternoon, fifty thousand, two hundred and twenty folk came, too. In the thirty-eighth minute, Peter Thompson scored. In the fifty-fifth minute, Tommy Smith scored another penalty. And Liverpool Football Club beat Stoke City two–one. That month, Liverpool Football Club had played six League games. They had won five of those games and they had lost one of those games. Lawrence, Lawler, Byrne, Smith, Yeats, Hughes, Callaghan, Hunt, Hateley, St John and Thompson had played in all six games. The same eleven players in all six games.

. . .

At the end of the month. At the end of the corridor. In his office. Bill Shankly and Joe Fagan were talking about the reserve team. The reserve team had played ten games. They had won four, drawn five and lost one. They had scored fifteen goals and conceded seven.

How is Clemence doing, asked Bill Shankly.

Joe Fagan said, Not bad, Boss. Not bad.

But not good, asked Bill Shankly. Not good enough for the first team yet? Is that what you are saying, Joe?

Joe Fagan shook his head. And Joe Fagan said, Not yet, Boss. Not yet. But he will be, Boss. He will be. He'll be a great goalkeeper. If we give him the help, Boss. And if we give him the time . . .

Aye, said Bill Shankly. It's always a question of time, is it not? Knowing when is the right time. The right time to bring a player on. To give him his chance. His moment. That beautiful moment, that wonderful time. When everything is before him. All to come for him. But then there is that other time. The time to let a player go. To give him his cards. That horrible moment, that terrible time. When

240

everything is behind him. All gone for him. Aye, it's always a question of time, Joe. Always a question of time . . .

. . .

On Wednesday 4 October, 1967, Malmö Fotbollförening of Sweden came to Anfield, Liverpool. That evening, thirty-nine thousand, seven hundred and ninety-five folk came, too. Thirty-nine thousand, seven hundred and ninety-five folk to watch Liverpool Football Club play Malmö Fotbollförening in the second leg of the First Round of the Inter-Cities Fairs Cup. In the twenty-eighth minute, Ron Yeats scored. In the thirty-sixth minute, Roger Hunt scored. And Liverpool Football Club of England beat Malmö Fotbollförening of Sweden two–one in the second leg of the First Round of the Inter-Cities Fairs Cup. At home, at Anfield.

Three days afterwards, Liverpool Football Club travelled to Filbert Street, Leicester. In the twenty-seventh minute, Ian St John scored. But Liverpool Football Club lost two–one to Leicester City. One week later, West Ham United came to Anfield, Liverpool. That afternoon, forty-six thousand, nine hundred and fifty-one folk came, too. In the fifteenth minute, Ian St John scored. In the thirty-eighth minute, St John scored again. And in the sixty-eighth minute, Tommy Smith scored. And Liverpool Football Club beat West Ham United three–one. At home, at Anfield.

On Tuesday 24 October, 1967, Liverpool Football Club travelled to Turf Moor, Burnley. In the eighty-second minute, Chris Lawler scored. And Liverpool Football Club drew one-all with Burnley Football Club. Away from home, away from Anfield.

Four days afterwards, Sheffield Wednesday Football Club came to Anfield, Liverpool. That afternoon, fifty thousand, three hundred and ninety-nine folk came, too. In the tenth minute, Chris Lawler scored. And Liverpool Football Club beat Sheffield Wednesday one–nil. At home, at Anfield. That evening, Liverpool Football Club had twenty points. And Liverpool Football Club were still first in the First Division. That month, Liverpool Football Club had played five games. They had won three, drawn one and lost one. Lawrence, Lawler, Byrne, Smith, Hughes, Callaghan, Hunt, Hateley, St John and Thompson had played in all five games. Yeats had played in four of the five games. And Strong had played in the other game.

That season, Liverpool Football Club still had twenty-eight more League games to come. Twenty-eight more games to play.

## 26. NOW BRINGS A SMILE, NOW BRINGS A TEAR

In the drive, in the car. In the night. Bill turned off the engine. Bill got out of the car. Bill walked up the drive. Bill unlocked the front door. Bill opened the door. Bill stepped into the house. In the dark. Bill closed the door. Bill took off his hat. Bill took off his coat. Bill hung up his hat. Bill hung up his coat. Bill went into the front room. Bill switched on the light. Bill walked over to his armchair. Bill picked up the pile of newspapers from beside his armchair. Bill carried the pile of newspapers into the kitchen. Bill put down the pile of newspapers on the table. Bill walked back into the front room. Bill went over to the bookcase. Bill opened the small cupboard at the side of the bookcase. Bill took a scrapbook, a pair of scissors and a tin of glue out of the cupboard. Bill closed the cupboard door. Bill switched off the light. Bill walked back into the kitchen. Bill switched on the light. Bill put down the scrapbook, the pair of scissors and the tin of glue on the table. Bill sat down at the table. Bill picked up the first newspaper on the pile. Bill turned the pages of the newspaper. Bill picked up the pair of scissors. Bill cut out the reports of every game. Not only the reports about the games Liverpool Football Club had played. The reports about every game every football club had played. Bill opened the tin of glue. Bill stuck the reports into the scrapbook. Not only the reports about the games Liverpool Football Club had played. The reports about every game every football club had played. In the kitchen, at the table. In the night and in the silence. Bill kept turning the pages of the newspapers. Bill kept picking up his scissors. Bill kept cutting out the reports. Bill kept sticking the reports in the scrapbook. In the kitchen, at the table. Bill stopped turning the pages. In the night and in the silence. Bill stared down at one page. Tommy Docherty, the manager of Chelsea Football Club, had received a twenty-eight-day suspension from all football activity following incidents on the club's goodwill tour of Bermuda in June. Bill turned to the next page. Tommy Docherty had resigned as manager of Chelsea Football Club. Bill turned to the next page. On Saturday 7 October, 1967, Leeds United had beaten Chelsea Football Club seven–nil. In the kitchen, at the table. Bill shook his head. Bill knew Tommy. Tommy had played for Preston North End. Bill liked Tommy. Bill thought what had happened to Tommy was a tragedy. A tragedy for Tommy. Bill thought what had happened to Tommy was a waste. A waste for Chelsea Football Club. In the night and in the silence. Bill shook his head again. And Bill turned the pages again. In the kitchen, at the table. Bill stopped turning the pages again. In the night and in the silence. Bill stared down at another page. On Sunday 8 October, 1967, Clement Attlee had died. Bill stood up. Bill walked back into the front room. Bill switched on the light again. Bill went back over to the bookcase again. Bill opened the small cupboard at the side of the bookcase again. Bill took another scrapbook out of the small cupboard. Bill turned the pages of the scrapbook. Bill came to the pages of cuttings from January, 1965. The pages of cuttings about the funeral of Winston Churchill. The cuttings and the photographs. In the night and in the silence. Bill stared down at one photograph. The photograph of Clement Attlee at the funeral of Winston Churchill. Clement Attlee standing, frozen in St Paul's Cathedral. Clement Attlee standing, frail in St Paul's Cathedral. In the night and in the silence. Bill closed the pages of the scrapbook. Bill put the scrapbook back in the small cupboard at the side of the bookcase. Bill closed the door. Bill switched off the light again. Bill walked back into the kitchen again. Bill sat back down again. In the kitchen, at the table. Bill stared down at the pages of obituaries of Clement Attlee. In the night and in the silence. Bill shook his head. Bill had admired Clement Attlee. Bill had respected Clement Attlee. And Bill had voted for Clement Attlee. Bill thought what had happened to Clement Attlee was a tragedy. A tragedy for the man. Bill thought what had happened to Clement Attlee was a waste. A waste for the country. In the kitchen, at the table. Bill shook his head again. In the night and in the silence.

. . .

On the bench, the Anfield bench. In the night and in the noise. Bill watched Hughes pass to St John. St John run to the left, St John run to the right. St John shoot. And St John score. Bill watched St John cross. Hateley fly in. And Hateley score. Bill watched Smith put

243

the ball on the penalty spot. And Smith put the ball in the net. Nine minutes later, Bill watched Hunt score. One minute afterwards, Bill watched Thompson score. And one minute later, Bill watched Hunt score again. And then Callaghan score. And then Callaghan score again. And on the bench, the Anfield bench. In the night and in the noise. The red night, the red noise. Bill heard the Spion Kop clap, Bill heard the Spion Kop cheer. And Bill heard the Spion Kop sing, *God help United, God help United, God help. . .*

On the touchline, the Anfield touchline. Albert Sing, the manager of TSV 1860 München, shook Bill's hand –

I have never seen a display of attacking football like that, said Albert Sing. The only thing I can think to compare it to is the great Hungarian Golden Team of Puskás, Kocsis, Bozsik and Hidegkuti. And so I only hope my own boys have learnt a lesson. A lesson in how to play football, in how football should be played. And I also hope someone makes a film loop of all those eight goals, those eight beautiful goals, to show to every school in England and every school in Europe. To show every boy in England and every boy in Europe. Because that is how football should be played, Mr Shankly. That is how all boys should play football. So congratulations, Mr Shankly . . .

Bill said, Thank you, Herr Sing. Thank you very much, sir.

Bill walked down the touchline. The Anfield touchline. Bill walked down the tunnel. The Anfield tunnel. Bill walked into the dressing room. The home dressing room. Bill looked around the dressing room. The Liverpool dressing room. From player to player. From Tommy Lawrence to Chris Lawler, Chris to Gerry Byrne, Gerry to Tommy Smith, Tommy to Ron Yeats, Ronnie to Emlyn Hughes, Emlyn to Ian Callaghan, Cally to Roger Hunt, Roger to Tony Hateley, Tony to Ian St John and from the Saint to Peter Thompson. And Bill smiled. And Bill said, Well played, boys. Well played.

. . .

In the front room, in his chair. Bill stared down at his book. His book of names, his book of notes. Bill could hear the rain falling on their house. Bill closed his book. His book of names, his book of notes. Bill could hear the wind blowing around their house. Bill picked up his diary off the arm of the chair. His diary of dates, his diary of fixtures. Bill listened to the rain. And Bill stared down at the dates. Bill listened to the wind. And Bill stared down at the fixtures. The rain and the wind. On Saturday 6 October, 1967, Ian Ure of Arsenal Football Club had brought down Denis Law of Manchester United. Denis Law had taken a swing at Ian Ure. Denis Law had been sent off. The newspapers had predicted that Denis Law would be suspended for six months. Denis Law had been suspended for six weeks. Denis Law would miss nine games. Bill knew Manchester United would miss Denis Law. Bill closed his diary. His diary of dates, his diary of fixtures. In the front room, in his chair, Bill listened to the rain falling on their house. Bill listened to the wind blowing around their house. The rain falling on all the houses, the wind blowing around all the houses. And Bill smiled again.

. . .

In the dressing room. The home dressing room. Bill took a piece of paper from his jacket pocket. Bill unfolded the piece of paper. And Bill said, Listen to this, boys. Just listen to this: Stepney, Dunne, Burns, Crerand, Foulkes, Sadler, Fitzpatrick, Kidd, Charlton, Best and Aston. That's Manchester United today, boys. That's their team today. No Denis Law, boys. And no Norbert Stiles. Now I know you'd beat Manchester United even if Law and Stiles were playing, boys. I know you would. So I have no doubts at all, boys. No doubts at all that you will murder this Manchester United team today. Absolutely bloody murder them. Worse than you did to the Germans on Tuesday. I know that, boys. I know that. Because this is their reserve team, boys. A second-string side. And I know Matt will be nervous, boys. I know Matt will be shitting bricks. Bringing a reserve team to Anfield, boys. Fielding a second-string side against Liverpool Football Club.

On the bench, the Anfield bench. Bill watched George Best dodge every challenge, George Best elude every tackle. Bill watched George Best spin threads, George Best weave webs. With artistry and with craft, with bravery and with strength. Bill watched Best dance, Bill watched Best sing. And score and score again. And on the bench, the Anfield bench. Bill watched Liverpool Football Club slip and slip again. Liverpool Football Club no longer first in the First Division. Manchester United first in the First Division. Again. Liverpool Football Club second. Again. Second best. Again.

In the dressing room. The home dressing room. Bill said, That boy Best is turning into some player, lads. Into some player. But this is just one game in a long season, lads. A very long season. And we will play them again, lads. We will play them again on April the sixth. And so remember that date, boys. Remember that date. Because on April the sixth we will go there, boys. We will go to Old Trafford and we will beat them. And if I'm not mistaken, boys. If I am not wrong. That will be the game, boys. That will be the match that decides the Championship, boys. That decides who will be first and who will be second. So remember that date, boys –

Remember that date.

. . .

On the runway, the Budapest runway. In the aeroplane, the Liverpool aeroplane. Bill listened to the engines of the plane start. Bill listened to the engines of the plane stop. Liverpool Football Club had come to the City of Football again. Liverpool Football Club had come to the Népstadion again. But Liverpool Football Club had not played Honvéd Football Club. Liverpool Football Club had played Ferencvárosi Torna Club in the first leg of the Third Round of the Inter-Cities Fairs Cup. In 1965, Ferencvárosi Torna Club had beaten AS Roma, Athletic Bilbao, Manchester United and Juventus. In 1965, Ferencvárosi Torna Club had won the Inter-Cities Fairs Cup. In 1966, Ferencvárosi Torna Club had reached the quarter-finals of the European Cup. In 1967, Flórián Albert of Ferencvárosi Torna Club had been named as the European Footballer of the Year. Nine players of the Hungarian national team played for Ferencvárosi Torna Club. Ferencvárosi Torna Club were a very good side. Ferencvárosi Torna Club were a great team. And Ferencvárosi Torna Club had beaten Liverpool Football Club one–nil at the Népstadion. In a game that had been brought forward to one o'clock in the afternoon because snow was falling. Falling and falling. Heavier and heavier. And still falling, still falling. Heavier, still heavier. On the runway, the Budapest runway. In the aeroplane, the Liverpool aeroplane. Bill was not thinking about the game. Bill was thinking about the snow. And Bill was thinking about Matt again. Bill heard the ground crew clearing the snow from the runway. Bill heard the ground crew clearing the ice from the wings of the plane. And Bill thought about Tommy Curry. On the runway, the Budapest runway. In the aeroplane, the Liverpool aeroplane. Bill listened to the engines start again. Bill listened to the engines of the plane stop again. And Bill thought about the twenty-three people who had died that day in Munich. On the runway, the Budapest runway. In the aeroplane, the Liverpool aeroplane. Bill heard the ground crew clear the snow from the runway again. Bill heard the ground crew clear the ice from the wings of the plane again. And Bill could not stop thinking about that day in February, 1958. On the runway, the Budapest runway. In the aeroplane, the Liverpool aeroplane. Bill listened to the engines of the plane start for a third time. And Bill thought about Ness. Bill felt the plane begin to move. Bill thought about the girls. Bill felt the plane begin to pick up speed. Bill closed his eyes. Bill felt the plane shake. Bill gripped the armrest of his seat. Bill felt the plane shudder. His coat stuck to his jacket. His jacket stuck to his shirt. His shirt stuck to his vest. His vest stuck to his skin. His eyes closed and his knuckles white. Bill prayed. Bill felt the plane begin to leave the ground. And Bill prayed and Bill prayed, like he had prayed and prayed that day in February, 1958. And Bill felt the plane begin to climb. Like he had never prayed for anything before. To climb and climb. Jesus. Bill hated flying. Above the ice and above the snow. Christ. Bill hated travelling. Bill felt the plane begin to level off. Jesus. Bill hated Europe. Christ. Bill hated abroad. And now Bill felt the plane begin to cruise. But Bill did not relax his grip. Bill did not open his eyes. Not until the plane was on the ground again. Not until his feet were on the ground again. His grip tight, his eyes closed. Until Bill was back in Liverpool. Until Bill was home again.

. . .

On the bench, the Anfield bench. In the snow, the heavy snow. On the hard and treacherous ground. Bill shivered and Bill watched. Liverpool Football Club precise, Liverpool Football Club swift. Bill shivered and Bill watched Hateley send the ball, the orange ball, through to Hunt. And Reaney reach the ball first. But Reaney could only nudge the orange ball. In the snow, the heavy snow. On the hard and treacherous ground. Reaney lost his balance, Reaney lost his footing. And Reaney lost the orange ball. In the snow, the heavy snow. On the hard and treacherous ground. Hunt found the ball. And Hunt found the net. And a goal. On the bench, the Anfield bench. In the snow, the heavy snow. On the hard and treacherous ground. Bill not shivering now, Bill just watching now, watching Sprake collect a pass from Charlton. The players of Liverpool Football Club falling back to defend, the players of Leeds United pushing forward to attack. Sprake holding the ball in his hands, Sprake preparing to throw the orange ball out to Cooper. In the snow, the heavy snow. On the hard and treacherous ground. On the right of his own goal, Sprake shaped to throw the ball to Cooper. Then Sprake seemed to have his doubts. Now Sprake seemed to change his mind. Sprake brought the orange ball back towards his chest. Sprake lost his grip on the ball. In the snow, the heavy snow. On the hard and treacherous ground. The orange ball curled up out of his arms. The ball swept up into the air. And in the snow, the heavy snow. On the hard and treacherous ground. The orange ball dropped into his goal. And in the snow, the heavy snow. On the hard and treacherous ground. There was silence. Then cheers. And then laughter. In the snow, the heavy snow. On the hard and treacherous ground. At half-time, over the tannoy, the Anfield tannoy, the announcer, the Anfield announcer, played *Careless Hands* by Des O'Connor. And the Spion Kop laughed. And the Spion Kop sang along to *Careless Hands*. In the snow, the heavy snow. On the hard and treacherous ground. *Careless Hands* . . .

. . .

In the front room, in his armchair. In the night and in the silence. Bill blinked. Bill rubbed his eyes. And Bill put down his book. His book of names, his book of notes. Bill got up from his chair. Bill switched off the light in the front room. Bill walked into the kitchen. Bill switched on the light. Bill went to the drawer. Bill opened the drawer. Bill took out the tablecloth. Bill closed the drawer. Bill walked over to the table. Bill spread the cloth over the table. Bill walked over to another drawer. Bill opened the drawer. Bill took out the cutlery. The spoons, the forks. And the knives. Bill closed the drawer. Bill walked back over to the table. Bill laid four places at the table. Bill went to the cupboard. Bill opened the cupboard door. Bill took out the crockery. The bowls and the plates. Bill walked back over to the table. Bill put a bowl and a plate in each of the four places. Bill walked back to the cupboard. Bill took out four glasses. Bill closed the cupboard door. Bill walked back to the table. Bill put a glass in each of the four places. Bill walked to another cupboard. Bill opened the door.

Bill took out the salt and pepper pots. Bill closed the cupboard door. Bill walked back to the table. Bill put the salt and pepper pots on the table. Bill went to the pantry. Bill opened the pantry door. Bill took out a jar of honey and a jar of marmalade. Bill walked back to the table. Bill put the jar of honey and the jar of marmalade on the table. Bill walked over to the refrigerator. Bill opened the refrigerator door. Bill took out the butter dish. Bill walked back over to the table. Bill put the butter dish down in the centre of the table. Bill walked back over to the refrigerator. Bill took out a bottle of fresh orange juice. Bill closed the refrigerator door. Bill walked back over to the table. Bill poured orange juice into each of the four glasses. Bill put the bottle down on the table. In the night and in the silence. Bill walked over to the wall. Bill switched off the kitchen light. And in the night and in the silence. Bill heard Ness cough upstairs. In their bed, in her sleep. Bill heard her cough again. In the night and in the silence. Bill switched on the kitchen light again. In the night and in the silence. Bill looked at the kitchen table. Bill stared at the four places. And Bill shook his head. In the night and in the silence. Bill walked back over to the table. Bill picked up two spoons. Two forks. And two knives. Bill put them back in the drawer. Bill picked up two bowls and two plates. Bill put them back in the cupboard. Bill walked back over to the table. Bill picked up one of the glasses of orange juice. Bill poured the orange juice back into the bottle of orange juice. Bill picked up another of the glasses of orange juice. Bill poured the orange juice back into the bottle of orange juice. Bill took the two empty glasses over to the sink. Bill washed up the two dirty glasses. Bill dried up the two glasses. Bill put them back in the cupboard. Bill walked back over to the wall. Bill switched off the light again. And in the night and in the silence. Bill heard Ness cough again. In their bed, in her sleep. In the night and in the silence. Bill switched on the kitchen light again. In the night and in the silence. Bill looked at the kitchen table again. Bill stared at the two places. And in the night and in the silence. Bill fought back tears,

Bill struggled to breathe.

## 27. A KICK IN THE BALLS

On Saturday 16 December, 1967, Manchester City came to Anfield, Liverpool. That afternoon, fifty-three thousand, two hundred and sixty-eight folk came, too. Fifty-three thousand, two hundred and sixty-eight folk to watch second play third. In the first half, Manchester City could and should have won. In the second half, Liverpool Football Club could and should have won. And in the fiftieth minute, Roger Hunt scored. But that afternoon, Liverpool Football Club drew one-all with Manchester City. At home, at Anfield. Bill Shankly shook hands with Joe Mercer. Bill Shankly nodded. And Bill Shankly smiled –

Well played, Joe. Very well played indeed. And if I'm not mistaken, Joe. If I am not wrong. This is going to be a three-horse race, Joe. A three-horse race. So I just hope your lads have got the legs for it, Joe. And I hope your lads have got the stomach for it, too.

Joe Mercer smiled, too. And Joe Mercer said, Thank you, Bill. Thank you very much. And the same to you, Bill. The same to you and your lads. Their legs and their stomachs.

. . .

One week afterwards, Liverpool Football Club travelled to St James' Park, Newcastle. In the forty-third minute, Ian St John scored. But Liverpool Football Club drew one-all with Newcastle United. One-all again. Three days later, on Boxing Day, 1967, Liverpool Football Club travelled to Highfield Road, Coventry. Coventry City were fighting for their lives, their very lives, at the bottom of the First Division, at the very foot of the table. In the thirteenth minute, Ian Callaghan crossed the ball to the far post. Tony Hateley turned the ball back at the far post. And Roger Hunt scored. In the thirtieth minute, Ian St John fouled Lewis. Lewis went down. The referee blew his whistle. The referee spoke to St John. St John walked away. Lewis got up. Lewis followed St John. Lewis spoke to St John. St John felled Lewis with a right hook. And the referee sent St John off. And from the free kick, Coventry City equalised. And Liverpool Football Club drew one-all with Coventry City. One-all. Again. Another draw.

After the whistle, after the dismissal. In the dressing room. The away dressing room. Bill Shankly looked at Ian St John. And Bill Shankly shook his head. And Bill Shankly cursed –

What the hell were you thinking, son?

He grabbed my goolies, Boss!

The cheating bastard. The dirty bastard. But you know they're going to throw the book at you now, son? They're going to suspend you, like they did to Denis Law?

I know, Boss. I know. And I'm sorry, Boss. I'm sorry . . .

Too late for sorry now, son. Too late. You get yourself into Anfield first thing tomorrow, son. You meet me there. First thing.

First thing. Ian St John knocked on the door of the treatment room at Anfield. Ian St John opened the door of the treatment room. Ian St John walked into the treatment room. And Ian St John saw Bill Shankly and Bob Paisley waiting in the treatment room –

Take off your trousers, said Bill Shankly. And take off your underpants. And then lie down there on that table, son.

Ian St John took off his shoes. Ian St John loosened his belt. Ian St John unzipped his trousers. Ian St John took off his trousers. Ian St John took off his underpants. And then Ian St John laid down on the table in the treatment room at Anfield.

Bill Shankly and Bob Paisley walked over to the table. Bill Shankly and Bob Paisley stared down at the testicles of Ian St John. And Bill Shankly shook his head –

There's not a bruise on you, son. Not a single scratch.

But he grabbed them, Boss. He twisted them, Boss. Twisted and bloody squeezed them, Boss. It fucking hurt, Boss.

I believe you, said Bill Shankly. I believe you, son. That man is depraved. That man is perverted, son. The football field is no place for a man like that. A depraved man and a perverted man. And I'm going to make sure everybody knows. The whole world knows, son. Knows what a depraved and perverted man he is. I will not rest . . .

And Bill Shankly turned to Bob Paisley –

Get to work, Bob. Do your worst.

Bob Paisley opened up his medicine bag. Bob Paisley took out a piece of cloth. Bob Paisley took out a bottle of iodine. Bob Paisley took out a tin of boot polish. Bob Paisley opened the bottle. Bob Paisley dabbed the piece of cloth with iodine. Bob Paisley smeared the iodine across the genitals of Ian St John. And Ian St John giggled. Bob Paisley opened the tin. Bob Paisley dabbed the piece of cloth with boot polish. Bob Paisley smeared the boot polish over the genitals of Ian St John. And Ian St John laughed. And Ian St John said, I hope this is giving you as much pleasure as it's giving me, Bob.

Shut your dirty mouth, said Bill Shankly. I'll have no depraved talk here, son. I'll have no perverted talk at Anfield.

Bob Paisley put down his cloth. And Bob Paisley and Bill Shankly stared down at the testicles of Ian St John. The black and purple testicles of Ian St John. And Bill Shankly smiled –

Good job, Bob. Great work, Bob.

Thank you very much, Bill.

Bill Shankly nodded. Bill Shankly turned to Ian St John –

Stay there, son. And don't you move a muscle. I'll be back in a minute, son. Back in just a minute . . .

And Ian St John stayed where he was. On the treatment table. Naked from the waist down. His testicles black and purple.

There were voices in the corridor, there were footsteps in the corridor. Lots of voices and lots of footsteps. And then the door to the treatment room opened. And Bill Shankly led in the reporters and the photographers. Bill Shankly ushered the reporters and the photographers into the treatment room. Bill Shankly gathered the reporters and the photographers around the treatment table. Around the black and purple testicles of Ian St John –

Look at them, said Bill Shankly. Just look at them, boys. It's a disgrace. An outrage! So I want to the world to know the truth. And I want the world to see the truth. I want pictures, boys. On all the front pages. All your front pages, boys!

The reporters and the photographers stared down at the testicles of Ian St John. The black and purple testicles of Ian St John. And the reporters and the photographers shook their heads. And the reporters and the photographers said, We can't take pictures of that, Bill. We can't print pictures of that. It's disgusting, Bill. It's horrible . . .

Well, take some pictures anyway, said Bill Shankly. Because I want copies. And I want them quick, boys. I need them for tomorrow.

The next day. Bill Shankly and Ian St John sat down in the corridor at Lancaster Gate, London, at the headquarters of the Football Association. Bill Shankly was in his best suit and red tie. Ian St John was in his best suit and red tie.

Come!

Bill Shankly and Ian St John stood up. Bill Shankly and Ian St John adjusted their red ties. Bill Shankly and Ian St John opened the door. Bill Shankly and Ian St John stepped inside the room.

Sit down, Shankly. Sit down, St John.

Bill Shankly helped Ian St John limp down to two chairs at the end of a long table. Bill Shankly and Ian St John sat down in the two chairs at the end of the long table. Ian St John grimaced. Ian St John stifled a scream. And Bill Shankly and Ian St John looked up the long table at the members of the Disciplinary Panel.

The head of the Disciplinary Panel shook his head. The head of the Disciplinary Panel said, This is the third time you have come before us, St John. This is the third time you have sat in that chair, St John. The third time for violent conduct, St John. The third time and the last time, St John. We made an example of Denis Law. We set a precedent with Law. We suspended him for six weeks. And so you are suspended for six weeks, St John.

Bill Shankly touched his red tie. Bill Shankly nodded. And Bill Shankly nodded again –

The example you made of Denis Law was the correct one, sir. The precedent you set was the right one to set. And the press are right to label that man a thug and an animal. But this man here is no animal, this man here is no thug. What happened to Ian St John is very different, sir. It is beyond the pale. And it has no place on the football field, sir. No place in our beautiful game. No place at all, sir . . .

What are you talking about, Shankly? Your player violently attacked another player. Your player is the same as Law.

Bill Shankly shook his head. Bill Shankly picked up his briefcase. Bill Shankly opened his briefcase. Bill Shankly took out three photographs from his briefcase. And Bill Shankly passed the photographs up the long table to the Disciplinary Panel –

I hope you have strong stomachs, gentlemen. Because what you will see in these photographs will surely turn your stomachs. This is the documentary proof, the forensic evidence of the barbarous and outrageous attack that was inflicted upon this man here. An attack on his very manhood. An assault on his unborn children. The heinous and scandalous assault that provoked him into an act of self-defence. Sheer self-defence. And while he knows now, in the cold light of day, he should not have reacted as he did. While he knows now, with the benefit of hindsight, that two wrongs do not make a right. And while he now readily apologises for his act of self-defence. While he now is utterly contrite. Still I would beseech you, gentlemen. Still I would implore you. Not to tar this man with the same brush as the likes of Denis Law. Not to equate an act of self-defence with such acts of mindless thuggery. And to let this man walk free today. Free of any suspension. Free to play his football . . .

The members of the Football Association Disciplinary Panel looked down at the three photographs of the testicles of Ian St John. The black and purple testicles of Ian St John. The members of the Football Association Disciplinary Panel shifted in their seats. The members of the Football Association Disciplinary Panel turned pale. Their hands to their mouths, their mouths behind their hands. The members of the Football Association Disciplinary Panel whispered among themselves. And then the head of the Disciplinary Panel looked down the long table at Bill Shankly and Ian St John. And the head of the Disciplinary Panel said, The obligatory three-match suspension for violent conduct on the field of football still stands. However, in this case, in the face of this evidence, there will be no further suspension. No six-week suspension.

Thank you, said Bill Shankly. Thank you, gentlemen.

The head of the Football Association Disciplinary Panel said, But I sincerely hope we will not see either of you again for a very long time. Or your photographs. Now close the door on your way out.

Bill Shankly helped Ian St John to his feet. Bill Shankly helped Ian St John limp past the long table back to the door. Bill Shankly opened the door for Ian St John. Bill Shankly and Ian St John stepped out into the corridor. Bill Shankly and Ian St John closed the door behind them. Bill Shankly and Ian St John walked down the corridor, out of Lancaster Gate, and into the street. And on the pavement outside the headquarters of the Football Association. Bill Shankly looked at Ian St John. And Bill Shankly shook his head –

What did I say to you the last time we were standing here, son? What did I tell you the last time we were standing here?

I'm sorry, Boss, said Ian St John. I'm sorry . . .

Well, this is the last time I'm going to tell you, son. Make sure you get your retaliation in first. When the referee is not about. So the other feller knows *you* are about. And then he'll not be fiddling with your goolies. Fondling your testicles. So remember –

Always get your retaliation in first, son.

. . .

On Saturday 6 January, 1968, West Bromwich Albion came to Anfield, Liverpool. That afternoon, fifty-one thousand and ninety-two folk came, too. In the third minute, Geoff Strong scored. In the fifty-seventh minute, Roger Hunt scored. In the sixty-seventh minute, Hunt scored again. And in the seventy-ninth minute, Hunt scored again. And Liverpool Football Club beat West Bromwich Albion four–one. At home, at Anfield. That evening, Manchester United had thirty-seven points. Liverpool Football Club had thirty-five points. Leeds United had thirty-three points. And Manchester City had thirty-two points.

Three days afterwards, Ferencvárosi Torna Club of Budapest, Hungary, came to Anfield, Liverpool. In the ice and in the snow. That night, forty-six thousand, eight hundred and ninety-two folk came, too. In the ice and in the snow. Forty-six thousand, eight hundred and ninety-two folk to watch Liverpool Football Club play Ferencvárosi Torna Club in the second leg of the Third Round of the Inter-Cities Fairs Cup. In the ice and in the snow. This was Liverpool Football Club's thirteenth European game at Anfield. And in the ice and in the snow. Liverpool Football Club were all sweat, Liverpool Football Club were all toil. But with the ice in the air, with the snow on the ground. Ferencvárosi Torna Club were hard in the tackle, Ferencvárosi Torna Club were subtle on the ball. In the ice and in the snow. Ferencvárosi Torna Club pulled Liverpool Football Club in all directions, Ferencvárosi Torna Club stretched Liverpool Football Club in every direction. In the ice and in the snow. In the twentieth minute, Katona passed to Rákosi, Rákosi passed to Juhász, Juhász passed to Varga, Varga flicked to Branikovics. And Branikovics scored. And in the ice and in the snow. Liverpool Football Club lost one–nil to Ferencvárosi Torna Club. At home, at Anfield. And at the whistle, the final whistle. In the ice and in the snow. The Spion Kop acknowledged Ferencvárosi Torna Club. Their tactics and their technique. And the Spion Kop applauded Ferencvárosi Torna Club. In the ice and in the snow. From the pitch, the Anfield pitch. In the ice and in the snow. Liverpool Football Club were out of the Inter-Cities Fairs Cup. Liverpool Football Club were out of Europe. Leeds United were still in the Inter-Cities Fairs Cup. Leeds United were still in Europe. Manchester United were still in the European Cup. Manchester United were still in Europe. But Liverpool Football Club were still second in the First Division. Liverpool Football Club could still win the League Championship. And Liverpool Football Club could still win the FA Cup. The League and the Cup. The Double –

On Saturday 27 January, 1968, Liverpool Football Club travelled to Dean Court, Bournemouth. And Liverpool Football Club of the First Division drew nil–nil with Bournemouth Football Club of the Third Division in the Third Round of the FA Cup. Three days afterwards, Bournemouth Football Club came to Anfield, Liverpool. That evening, fifty-four thousand and seventy-five folk came, too. In the thirty-third minute, Tony Hateley scored. In the forty-fourth minute, Peter Thompson scored. In the fifty-first minute, Roger Hunt scored. And in the seventy-third minute, Chris Lawler scored. And Liverpool Football Club beat Bournemouth Football Club four–one in the Third Round replay of the FA Cup.

Four days later, Liverpool Football Club came to Goodison Park, Liverpool. That afternoon, sixty-four thousand, four hundred and eighty-two folk came, too. But that afternoon, Liverpool Football Club lost one–nil to Everton Football Club. Away from home, away from Anfield. That evening, Liverpool Football Club had thirty-six points. Leeds United had thirty-eight points. And Manchester United had forty-one points. And that evening, Liverpool Football Club were third in the First Division.

On Wednesday 12 February, 1968, Liverpool Football Club travelled to Stamford Bridge, London. That night, Liverpool Football Club were bereft of ideas, Liverpool Football Club were drained of power. That night, Liverpool Football Club lost three–one to Chelsea Football Club. And it could have been more, it should have been a rout. Four days afterwards, Liverpool Football Club travelled to Fellows Park, Walsall. And Liverpool Football Club of the First Division drew nil–nil with Walsall Football Club of the Third Division in the Fourth Round of the FA Cup. Two days later, Walsall Football Club came to

Anfield, Liverpool. In the fog, the heavy fog. Thirty-nine thousand, one hundred and thirteen folk came, too. In the fog, the heavy fog. Thirty-nine thousand, one hundred and thirteen folk to try to watch Liverpool Football Club play Walsall Football Club in the Fourth Round replay of the FA Cup. In the fog, the heavy fog. In the twenty-fourth minute, Liverpool Football Club scored. And in the fog, the heavy fog. The Spion Kop asked, *We want to know who scored?* And through the fog, the heavy fog. The Annie Road end answered, *Hateley scored.* And in the fog, the heavy fog. The Spion Kop sang, *Thank you very much.* In the fog, the heavy fog. In the thirty-third minute, Liverpool Football Club scored again. *We want to know who scored again?* In the fog, the heavy fog. *Hateley scored again.* In the fog, the heavy fog. *Thank you very much.* And a minute later, Liverpool Football Club scored again. *We want to know who scored again?* In the fog, the heavy fog. *Strong scored.* In the fog, the heavy fog. *Thank you very much.* And in the fog, the heavy fog. In the sixty-fourth and seventy-first minutes, Hateley scored and scored again. And Liverpool Football Club beat Walsall Football Club five–two in the Fourth Round replay of the FA Cup –

*Thank you very much . . .*

On Saturday 9 March, 1968, Liverpool Football Club travelled to White Hart Lane, London. That afternoon, fifty-four thousand and five folk came, too. Fifty-four thousand and five folk to watch Tottenham Hotspur play Liverpool Football Club in the Fifth Round of the FA Cup. Tottenham Hotspur were the holders of the FA Cup. Tottenham Hotspur had already beaten Manchester United in the FA Cup. Tottenham Hotspur were the favourites to win the FA Cup. But that afternoon, there was lightning on the terraces, there was thunder on the pitch. Invention versus effort, precision versus strength. In the fifty-first minute, Gilzean flicked the ball forward to Greaves. And Greaves accelerated. Like lightning. Greaves found that extra pace, Greaves found that extra space. Between Yeats and Hughes. From twelve yards out. Greaves shot. Like thunder. And Greaves scored. Three minutes later, Lawler robbed the ball from Mackay. Lawler passed the ball to St John. St John lobbed the ball diagonally from right to left. And Hateley rose to meet the ball. Hateley headed the ball. And Hateley scored. And Liverpool Football Club drew one-all with

Tottenham Hotspur in the Fifth Round of the FA Cup –

Three days afterwards, Tottenham Hotspur came to Anfield, Liverpool. That evening, fifty-three thousand, six hundred and fifty-eight folk came, too. Tottenham Hotspur had not won at Anfield in fifty-six years. In the twenty-third minute, Roger Hunt scored. And in the eightieth minute, Tony Hateley was brought down in the Tottenham penalty area. Tommy Smith put the ball on the Tottenham penalty spot. But Smith did not put the ball in the Tottenham net. Jennings saved the penalty. But the referee said Tottenham Hotspur had twelve players on the pitch. The referee said Mackay had not yet left the pitch when Jones came on. The referee said the penalty should be retaken. And Smith put the ball on the Tottenham penalty spot again. And this time Jennings did not save. This time Smith put the ball in the Tottenham net. Two minutes from the end of the match, from the final whistle, Jones scored for Tottenham. But it did not matter. It did not count. Tottenham Hotspur still had not won at Anfield for fifty-six years.

Four days later, Liverpool Football Club beat Burnley Football Club. One week later, Liverpool Football Club beat Sheffield Wednesday. That evening, Liverpool Football Club had forty-three points. And Manchester City had forty-three points, too. Manchester United had forty-five points. And Leeds United had forty-five points, too. That evening, Leeds United were first in the First Division. On goal average. Liverpool Football Club were fourth.

On Saturday 30 March, 1968, Liverpool Football Club travelled to the Hawthorns, Birmingham. That afternoon, fifty-three thousand and sixty-two folk came, too. Fifty-three thousand and sixty-two folk to watch West Bromwich Albion play Liverpool Football Club in the Sixth Round of the FA Cup. To watch two balls end up on the roof of the stand. To watch Liverpool Football Club win their first corner in the fifty-seventh minute. To watch Liverpool Football Club blatantly play for a draw. To watch Liverpool Football Club get what they blatantly played for. To watch Liverpool Football Club draw nil–nil with West Bromwich Albion in the Sixth Round of the FA Cup. Nil–nil again. Another replay again.

On Saturday 6 April, 1968, Liverpool Football Club travelled to Old Trafford, Manchester. In the opening minutes, Yeats made errors.

Hughes made mistakes. And in the third minute, Best romped away from Yeats and Hughes. And Best scored. But six minutes later, Yeats headed the ball against the Manchester United post. And then Yeats headed the ball again. And this time the ball crossed the line. Ten minutes later, Hateley combined with Hunt. And Hunt scored. And Liverpool Football Club beat Manchester United two–one. Away from home, away from Anfield. The players of Liverpool Football Club had remembered that date. But that evening, Liverpool Football Club were still fourth in the First Division.

Two days afterwards, West Bromwich Albion came to Anfield, Liverpool. That evening, fifty-four thousand, two hundred and seventy-three folk came, too. Fifty-four thousand, two hundred and seventy-three folk to cheer and to chant, to shout and to sing. And to split open the sky. The clear and starlit Anfield sky. In the twenty-fourth minute, Peter Thompson was obstructed. Thompson won a free kick. Ian St John took the free kick. St John floated the ball in from right to left. Ron Yeats hurtled into the West Bromwich Albion penalty area, Yeats tore through the West Bromwich Albion defence. And Yeats headed the ball. The ball hit the crossbar. Yeats stretched for the rebound. Yeats could not reach the rebound. But Hateley reached the rebound. Hateley struck the ball. And the ball struck the back of the net. And the Spion Kop roared. The Spion Kop ripped open the sky. The clear and starlit Anfield sky. But in the sixty-eighth minute, Fraser passed the ball to Brown. Brown crossed the ball. Astle rose to head the ball. And Astle scored. And under the clear and starlit Anfield sky, Liverpool Football Club drew one-all with West Bromwich Albion in the Sixth Round replay of the FA Cup. There would have to be another match, another replay. On neutral ground, on Manchester soil.

On Good Friday, 1968, Sheffield United came to Anfield, Liverpool. That Friday, fifty thousand, four hundred and twenty-two folk came, too. In the thirty-second minute, Roger Hunt scored. But Currie scored for Sheffield United. And Reece scored for Sheffield United. And Liverpool Football Club lost two–one to Sheffield United. At home, at Anfield. Liverpool Football Club still only had forty-five points. Liverpool Football Club still only fourth in the First Division. The next day, the very next day, Sunderland Football Club came to

Anfield, Liverpool. That day, forty thousand, three hundred and fifty folk came, too. In the eighteenth minute, Roger Hunt scored. And in the seventy-first minute, Hunt scored again. And Liverpool Football Club beat Sunderland Football Club two–one. At home, at Anfield. Liverpool Football Club now had forty-seven points. But Liverpool Football Club were still only fourth in the First Division. Two days later, on Easter Monday, 1968, Liverpool Football Club travelled to Bramall Lane, Sheffield. But Gerry Byrne did not travel. Tommy Smith did not travel. Tony Hateley did not travel. And Peter Thompson did not travel. Peter Wall travelled. Alf Arrowsmith travelled. Bobby Graham travelled. And Geoff Strong travelled. And in the thirty-fourth minute, Geoff Strong scored. But Sheffield United scored, too. And Liverpool Football Club drew one-all with Sheffield United. Away from home, away from Anfield.

Three days afterwards, Liverpool Football Club travelled to neutral ground, to Manchester soil. To Maine Road, Manchester. To play West Bromwich Albion in the second Sixth Round replay of the FA Cup. For a place in the semi-final of the FA Cup. That evening, fifty-six thousand folk came, too. This was the ninth FA Cup tie Liverpool Football Club had played this season. This season, over four hundred thousand folk had watched Liverpool Football Club play in the FA Cup. But that evening, on neutral ground, on Manchester soil, in a constant drizzle, a Manchester drizzle, the ball was always up in the drizzle, the Manchester drizzle, the ball never on the ground, the Manchester soil. The Liverpool balls hit high, looking for the head of Hateley. The West Brom balls hit high, looking for the head of Astle. And in the seventh minute, a West Brom ball found the head of Astle. And Astle found the net. In the fortieth minute, a Liverpool ball found the head of Hateley. And Hateley found the net. But in the sixtieth minute, a West Brom ball found the feet of Clive Clark. And Clive Clark found the net. And Liverpool Football Club were out of the FA Cup. After nine games, after nine matches. Liverpool Football Club were out of the Cup –

Out, out.

Two days later, just two days later, Liverpool Football Club travelled to Upton Park, London. And Liverpool Football Club lost one–nil to West Ham United.

On Saturday 27 April, 1968, Fulham Football Club came to Anfield, Liverpool. That afternoon, thirty-two thousand, three hundred and seven folk came, too. Just thirty-two thousand, three hundred and seven folk. In the twenty-ninth minute, Ian Callaghan scored. In the fortieth minute, Roger Hunt scored. In the forty-ninth minute, Hunt scored again. And in the fifty-sixth minute, Tony Hateley scored. And Liverpool Football Club beat Fulham Football Club four–one. At home, at Anfield. Two days later, Tottenham Hotspur came to Anfield, Liverpool. That evening, forty-one thousand, six hundred and eighty-eight folk came, too. In the ninth minute, Mackay came forward from his own penalty area with the ball. Mackay found Robertson with the ball. Robertson found Gilzean with the ball. Gilzean found Greaves with the ball. And Greaves found the net with the ball. In the thirty-eighth minute, Peter Thompson crossed. Tony Hateley jumped for the ball, Tony Hateley headed the ball. And Tony Hateley scored. And Liverpool Football Club drew one-all with Tottenham Hotspur. At home, at Anfield. That night, Liverpool Football Club had fifty-one points. And Leeds United had fifty-one points, too. Manchester United had fifty-four points. And Manchester City had fifty-four points, too. That night, Manchester City were first in the First Division. On goal average. Liverpool Football Club fourth in the First Division. On goal average. But Manchester City and Manchester United had only two games left to play. Liverpool Football Club still had three more games to play. Three more games to play, three more games to win –

On Saturday 4 May, 1968, Liverpool Football Club travelled to Elland Road, Leeds. That afternoon, forty-four thousand, five hundred and fifty-three folk came, too. In the fifteenth minute, Jones scored. And for the next sixty-nine minutes, Leeds United were beating Liverpool Football Club. But in the eighty-fourth minute, Chris Lawler latched on to a poor clearance by Harvey. And Lawler scored. And one minute later, Bobby Graham scored. And Liverpool Football Club beat Leeds United two–one. Away from home, away from Anfield. That day, Manchester City beat Tottenham Hotspur and Manchester United beat Newcastle United. That evening, Liverpool Football Club had fifty-three points. Manchester United had fifty-six points and Manchester City had fifty-six points, too. Manchester City were still first in the First Division. On goal average. Liverpool Football Club now third in the First Division. But Manchester City and Manchester United had only one last game to play. Liverpool Football Club still had two more games to play. If Manchester City and Manchester United each lost their last game and if Liverpool Football Club won each of their last two games, then Liverpool Football Club would be the Champions of England –

On Saturday 11 May, 1968, Nottingham Forest came to Anfield, Liverpool. That afternoon, thirty-eight thousand, eight hundred and fifty folk came, too. For the last home game of the season. Just thirty-eight thousand, eight hundred and fifty folk. In the thirty-fourth minute, Ian St John scored. In the thirty-sixth minute, Tony Hateley scored. And in the forty-first minute, Hateley scored again. In the fifty-fifth minute, Roger Hunt scored. And in the seventy-first minute, Hunt scored again. And in the eighty-fourth minute, Hateley scored again. His third goal of the match, his twenty-seventh goal of the season. And Liverpool Football Club beat Nottingham Forest six–one. But it didn't matter. It didn't count. That day, Manchester United lost two–one to Sunderland. But it didn't matter. It didn't count either. That day, Manchester City beat Newcastle United four–three. That evening, Manchester City were first in the First Division. And that evening, Manchester City were the Champions of England.

. . .

On Wednesday 15 May, 1968, Manchester United travelled to the Santiago Bernabéu Stadium in Madrid, Spain, to play Real Madrid in the second leg of the semi-final of the European Cup. If Manchester United beat Real Madrid, then Manchester United would be in the final of the European Cup. That evening, Liverpool Football Club travelled to the Victoria Ground, Stoke. Bill Shankly walked into the dressing room. The away dressing room. Bill Shankly looked around the dressing room. The Liverpool dressing room. From player to player. From Lawrence to Lawler, Lawler to Wall, Wall to Smith, Smith to Yeats, Yeats to Strong, Strong to Callaghan, Callaghan to Hunt, Hunt to Hateley, Hateley to St John and from St John to Thompson. And Bill Shankly swallowed. And Bill Shankly swallowed again. Bill Shankly coughed. And Bill Shankly coughed again –

If we win tonight, boys. Then we will overtake Manchester United. And then we will be the runners-up in the Football League.

262

We will finish second. And so we will be the second-best team in the Football League, boys. The second best . . .

On Wednesday 15 May, 1968, Manchester United came from three–one down at half-time to draw three–three with Real Madrid in the second leg of the semi-final of the European Cup. Manchester United had won the tie four–three on aggregate. Manchester United had reached the final of the European Cup. That night, in the fifty-eighth minute, Roger Hunt scored his thirtieth goal of the season. But that night, Liverpool Football Club lost two–one at Stoke City. That night, that season, after forty-two games, Liverpool Football Club finished third in the First Division –

Not first, not second –

Third best.


## 28. THE CROSSES AND THE MARKS

At the Estadio Insular, in the Canary Islands, Liverpool Football Club played UD Las Palmas in a post-season friendly. And Liverpool Football Club drew one-all with UD Las Palmas. That night, in the bar of their hotel in the Canary Islands, the players and the staff of Liverpool Football Club watched the final of the European Cup on the television. That night, the players and the staff of Liverpool Football Club watched Manchester United beat SL Benfica four–one after extra time. That night, the players and the staff of Liverpool Football Club watched Manchester United become the first English team to win the European Cup. And that night, on the television in the bar of the hotel, Bill watched Matt on the pitch, the Wembley pitch. Bill watched Matt surrounded by his players on the pitch, the Wembley pitch. And Bill saw the look in Matt's eyes. The memories in Matt's eyes. And Bill knew what this meant to Matt. Bill knew Matt had set his heart on this. Bill wanted to call Matt, Bill wanted to congratulate Matt. And Bill tried to stand. Bill tried to get to his feet. His shirt stuck to his vest. His vest stuck to his skin. But in the bar, the hotel bar, Bill could not stand. Bill could not get to his feet. His shirt stuck to his vest. His vest stuck to his skin. Bill fought back tears. Bill struggled to breathe.

In his room, his hotel room. Not in his bed, his hotel bed. Bill paced and Bill paced. Bill thinking and Bill thinking. Bill knew failure could become habitual, defeat become routine. Routine and familiar. Familiar and accepted. Accepted and permanent. Permanent and imprisoning. Imprisoning and suffocating. Bill knew failure carried chains. Chains to bind you. You and your dreams. To bind you and your dreams alive. Bill knew defeat carried spades. Spades to bury you. You and your hopes. To bury you and your hopes alive. Bill knew you had to fight against failure. With every bone in your body. Bill knew you had to struggle against defeat. With every drop of your blood. You had to fight against failure, you had to struggle against defeat. For your dreams and for your hopes. For you and for the people. To fight and to struggle. For the dreams of the people,

for the hopes of the people.

. . .

In the car park, the Anfield Road car park. In the sunshine, the July sunshine. On the first day of training. In his sweater and in his tracksuit bottoms. Bill waited for the players of Liverpool Football Club. In their kits, their training kits. Bill greeted every player. Bill shook their hands, Bill patted their backs. Bill asked after their families, Bill asked after their holidays. And then Bob, Joe, Reuben and Ronnie Moran joined Bill and the players in the car park at Anfield. And in the sunshine, the July sunshine. They all walked out to Melwood. Then Bill and the players jogged once around the training pitch. Then Bill and the players passed the ball back and forth, in pairs, back and forth to each other for twenty minutes. Then Bill and the players jogged once more around the training pitch. And then Bill, Bob, Joe, Reuben, Ronnie and the players all walked back to Anfield.

In the car park, the Anfield car park. In the sunshine, the July sunshine. On the second day of training. Bill, Bob, Joe, Reuben, Ronnie and the players all jogged out to Melwood. Then Bill and the players ran once around the training pitch. Then Bill and the players passed the ball back and forth, in threes, back and forth to each other for thirty minutes. Then Bill and the players ran once more around the training pitch. And then Bill, Bob, Joe, Reuben, Ronnie and the players all jogged back to Anfield.

In the car park, the Anfield car park. In the sunshine, the July sunshine. On the third day of training. Bill, Bob, Joe, Reuben, Ronnie and the players all ran out to Melwood. Then Bill and the players ran twice around the training pitch. Then Bill and the players passed the ball back and forth, in fours, back and forth to each other for forty minutes. Then Reuben blew his whistle. And Bill gathered the players in the middle of the training pitch. Bill, Bob, Joe, Reuben and Ronnie divided the thirty players into six groups of five. And Bill said, Right, lads. Enough running. We're going to play some football. We're going to play some five-a-sides . . .

In the car park, the Anfield car park. In the sunshine, the July sunshine. In the second week of training. In his sweater and in his tracksuit bottoms. Bill waited for the players of Liverpool Football Club. In their kits, their training kits. Bill greeted every player. Bill shook their hands, Bill patted their backs. Bill asked after their families, Bill asked after their weekends. And then Bob, Joe, Reuben and Ronnie joined Bill and the players in the car park at Anfield. Then Bill, Bob, Joe, Reuben, Ronnie and the players all climbed on the bus to Melwood. And when the players arrived at Melwood, when the players got off the bus, the players saw the boxes on the training pitch. And the players groaned, the players laughed. And Bill and the players ran twice around the training pitch. Then Bill and the players passed the ball back and forth, in pairs, back and forth for twenty minutes. Then Bill and the players went into the boxes. In pairs. Balls came over the top into the boxes. One player tried to hit the ball first time, the other tried to hit the same ball on the rebound. First time. Ball after ball. Every second, another ball. Into the box. Every second for one minute. Ball after ball. Then for two minutes. Then for three minutes. Again and again. Ball after ball. Every second. Shot after shot. Every second. Inside the box. In pairs, in turn. Pair after pair, player after player. Then Reuben blew his whistle. Bill gathered the players in the middle of the training pitch. And Bill said, Right, lads. Enough exercises. We're going to play some football. Some five-a-sides . . .

And that was the second week of training. And the third. And the fourth. And the fifth. They did not practise set pieces, they did not practise corners. And they did not practise free kicks. They practised passing. Always forward, always faster. Faster and faster, for five weeks. Always forward. And always to a red shirt,

always to a red shirt,

a red shirt. Bill training, always training. Bill playing, always playing. With hunger and with passion. In amongst the players, in amongst the team. Bill training, Bill playing. Bill watching and Bill listening. Watching for hunger and listening for passion. Hunger for the red shirt, passion for the red shirt –

The hunger and the passion –

For the shirt, the red shirt. And Bill watched Tommy Smith square up to Emlyn Hughes. Bill watched Bob pull them apart. Bill watched Ian St John square up to Tony Hateley. And Bill watched Bob pull them apart –

And Bill smiled.

. . .

At Maine Road, Manchester. In the stands, in his seat. Bill watched Manchester City play West Bromwich Albion in the 1968 Charity Shield. Manchester City were the Champions of the Football League. West Bromwich Albion were the winners of the FA Cup. In the stands, in his seat. Bill watched West Bromwich Albion try to keep the ball in the air. Bill watched Manchester City keep the ball on the ground. And Bill watched Manchester City beat West Bromwich Albion six–one in the 1968 Charity Shield. And in the stands, in his seat. Bill stood up. Bill left the ground. And Bill drove back to Anfield. Bill went into his office. Bill shut the door. Bill took off his hat, Bill took off his jacket. Bill sat down at his desk. And Bill took out his book. His book of names, his book of notes. Bill took out his pen. His red pen. And in the office, at his desk. Bill began to write in his book. His book of names, his book of notes. In the office, at his desk. Bill stopped writing. Bill put down his pen. His red pen. Bill took out his diary. His diary of dates, his diary of fixtures. And Bill stared down at the first date in his diary, the first fixture of the season. The new season. In the office, at his desk. Bill sat back in his chair. Bill closed his eyes. And then Bill opened his eyes. Bill leaned forward. Bill picked up his book. His book of names, his book of notes. Bill turned to the last page. The last page of names, the last page of notes. Bill picked up his pen. His red pen. Bill drew a line through one name on the page. The last name on the last page. *Hateley*. And then Bill wrote a name on the page. A new name on the last page. *Graham*. Bill put down his pen. His red pen. Bill closed his book. His book of names, his book of notes. In his office, at his desk. Bill sat back in his chair again. Bill closed his eyes again. And Bill waited.

. . .

In the dressing room. The home dressing room. Bill looked from player to player. From Lawrence to Lawler, Lawler to Wall, Wall to Smith, Smith to Yeats, Yeats to Hughes, Hughes to Callaghan, Callaghan to Hunt, Hunt to Graham, Graham to St John and from St John to Thompson. And Bill said, Last season, on the first day of last season, we went to Maine Road and we drew nil–nil with this lot. And then, when they came here, we drew one-all. So last season, Manchester City took two points from us. Home and away. Last season, Manchester City finished with three points more than us. Just three points. But we finished third and they finished first. And they were the Champions and we were not. We were nothing, we were nowhere. So if you are thinking this is just the first game of the season. Just the first match of forty-two League matches this season. If you are thinking to drop a point today, to even lose two points today, it doesn't matter. That there will be other games, forty-one other games. Well, if there is any man in this room thinking thoughts like that, then that man has no place in this room. No place in this team. Because a point dropped today is a point lost forever. And every point lost is a point that costs you. Because that point lost today could be the point that costs you the title. That gives them the title. That condemns you to second best. To third best. Or even worse. And that's not good enough. That's never good enough. Not for Liverpool Football Club. Not for the people who support Liverpool Football Club. The only thing that is good enough for Liverpool Football Club, for the people who support Liverpool Football Club, is to win every game, to take two points from every match. From all forty-two matches. And then to be Champions. Because that is the only thing good enough. For Liverpool Football Club. And for the people who support Liverpool Football Club –

To be Champions again.

On the bench, the Anfield bench. In the first game of the season, in the second minute of the match, Bill watched Manchester City score. But in the twenty-fourth minute of the first match of the season, Graham equalised. And in the seventy-third minute of the first match of the season, Thompson scored. And Liverpool Football Club beat Manchester City two–one. At home, at Anfield. In the first match of the 1968–69 season –

On the bench, the bench at the Dell. In the second game of the season, Bill watched Southampton Football Club score. And score again. And Liverpool Football Club lost two–nil. Away from home, away from Anfield –

On the bench, the bench at Highbury. In the third game of the season, Bill watched the players of Liverpool Football Club harry and harry and harry. Run and run and run. But in the thirtieth minute of the third match of the season, Sammels sent Radford through. And Radford slotted the ball home. But still the players of Liverpool Football Club harried and harried and harried. Ran and ran and ran. And in the fiftieth minute of the third match of the season, Thompson dribbled through three players. Thompson passed inside to Hunt. And Hunt scored. But then on the bench, the bench at Highbury, Bill watched the sun disappear. And the sky turn black. With thunder and with lightning. And then the rain came. And the rain swept thousands from the terraces. And the rain turned the pitch into a cauldron. But still the players of Liverpool Football Club harried and harried and harried. Ran and ran and ran. Under a black sky, in the pouring rain. But then the whistle came, the final whistle. And the game was drawn, only drawn. And in that first week of the 1968–69 season, in the first three games of this new season, Liverpool Football Club had won once, drawn once and lost once. In the first week of the 1968–69 season, in the first three games of the new season, Liverpool Football Club had dropped three points. Three points lost forever. It was a bad start to the 1968–69 season, a very bad start to the new season –

The new season same as the old season.

. . .

In the house, in their bed. Bill heard Ness cough. In her sleep, in their bed. Bill opened his eyes. And Bill saw the darkness. Bill got out of the bed. Bill went down the stairs. Bill went into the front room. Bill switched on the light. Bill sat down in his armchair. Bill picked up his book. His book of names, his book of notes. And Bill turned the pages. The pages of names, the pages of notes. To the last page of names, to the last page of notes. And Bill picked up his pen. His red pen. And Bill drew a line through one name on the page. The last page.

*Graham*. And then Bill wrote a name on the page. The last page. *Hateley*. And Bill put down his pen. His red pen. Bill closed his book. His book of names, his book of notes. In the front room, in his armchair. Bill heard Ness cough again upstairs. In their bed, in her sleep. And in the darkness. Bill waited for the dawn,

Bill waited for the light.

. . .

On the bench, the bench at Elland Road. In the sunshine, the late and rare Yorkshire sunshine. Bill watched Jackie Charlton and Ronnie Yeats cast long shadows, Mick Jones and Tony Hateley cast long shadows. And on the bench, the bench at Elland Road. In the thirtieth minute, Bill watched Billy Bremner strike a long, steepling pass towards the silhouettes of Mick Jones and Ronnie Yeats. And Ronnie Yeats came to meet the pass, to block the pass. Yeats kicking out towards the pass, towards the ball. But Yeats kicked out into the air, into the shadows. And Jones met the pass, Jones touched on the pass. Past Tommy Lawrence. Lawrence groping after the ball, Lawrence sprawling on the floor. And Jones touched the pass again. Jones struck the pass. And Jones scored. And in the sunshine, the late and rare Yorkshire sunshine. Leeds United were beating Liverpool Football Club one–nil. But in the sunshine, the late and rare Yorkshire sunshine, still Liverpool Football Club passed the ball long towards Hateley. Still Liverpool Football Club passed the ball high to Hateley. But Charlton met every ball, Charlton blocked every pass. And in the sunshine, the late and rare sunshine, Jackie Charlton put Tony Hateley's head on the block. And in the sunshine, the late and rare Yorkshire sunshine. Liverpool Football Club lost one–nil to Leeds United. And that evening, Leeds United had eleven points and Arsenal Football Club had twelve points. Arsenal Football Club were first in the First Division. That evening, Liverpool Football Club had eight points. Liverpool Football Club seventh in the First Division. That evening, Liverpool Football Club were nowhere.

. . .

In the house, in their bed. Bill heard Ness cough. Again. In her sleep, in their bed. And Bill opened his eyes. Again. Bill saw the darkness. Again. Bill got out of the bed. Again. Bill went down the stairs. Again. Bill went into the front room. Again. Bill switched on the light. Again. Bill sat down in his armchair. Again. Bill picked up his book. His book of names, his book of notes. And again. Bill turned the pages. The pages of names, the pages of notes. To the last page of names, to the last page of notes. Again. Bill picked up his pen. His red pen. Again Bill drew a line through one name on the page. The last page. *Hateley*. Again. Bill put down his pen. His red pen. And in the front room, in his chair. Bill closed his eyes. Again. In his armchair, in his mind. Bill saw the goals. Again. The twenty-seven goals Hateley had scored last season. The goal he had scored this season. And again. In the front room, in the chair. Bill opened his eyes. Again. Bill picked up his pen. Again. His red pen. And again. Bill wrote a name on the page. Again. The name on the page. *Hateley*. Bill put down his pen. Again. His red pen. Again. Bill closed his eyes. Again. In the armchair, in his mind. Bill saw the long passes. The high balls. The passes never met. Again. The balls never controlled. And again. Bill opened his eyes. Again. Bill picked up his pen. Again. His red pen. And again. Bill drew a line through that name on that page again. Again. That last name on that last page. *Hateley*. Again and again. Bill drew line after line. Red line after red line. Through that name on that page. That last name and that last page. Again and again. Until the name was gone, until the page was gone. And then Bill put down his pen. His red pen. And Bill closed his book. His book of names, his book of notes. And in the front room, in his armchair. Again. Bill heard Ness cough upstairs. Again. In their bed, in her sleep. And again. In the darkness. Bill waited for the dawn. Again. Bill waited for the light.

. . .

On the bench, the Anfield bench. In the second minute, Bill watched Ron Yeats score. In the fourth minute, Bill watched Tommy Smith score a penalty. And then in the tenth minute, Bill watched Alun Evans score his first goal for Liverpool Football Club. On his debut, his Anfield debut. Liverpool Football Club had sold Tony Hateley to Coventry City for eighty thousand pounds. And Liverpool Football Club had bought Alun Evans from Wolverhampton Wanderers for one hundred thousand pounds. Alun Evans was nineteen years old. No football club had ever paid one hundred thousand pounds for a teenager. It was a British transfer record for a teenager. Liverpool Football Club had never paid one hundred thousand pounds for anyone.

It was a club record. And on the bench, the Anfield bench. Two minutes later, Bill watched Ian Callaghan score. And Liverpool Football Club beat Leicester City four–nil. At home, at Anfield. And on the touchline, the Anfield touchline. Bill shook the hand of Matt Gillies, the manager of Leicester City –

After those first fifteen minutes, said Matt Gillies, I thought you were going to put us to the sword, Bill. I was sure you would score six or seven. Even ten or eleven. I thought you were going to humiliate us, Bill. Humiliate me . . .

Bill shook his head. And Bill said, Don't say that, Matt. Please don't say that. I would never try to humiliate any man, Matt. Especially not you . . .

On the bench, the bench at Molineux, Wolverhampton. In the early autumn sunshine, Bill watched the red of Liverpool Football Club and the gold of Wolverhampton Wanderers burn and glow on the green, green grass. And in the fifteenth minute, Bill watched the long, gentle parabola of Roger Hunt's shot ricochet off the foot of Parkin. And Hunt score. And in the twenty-fifth minute, Bill watched Peter Thompson sidestep his man. And Thompson shoot. And the ball flash in off the post. And in the thirtieth minute, Bill watched a pass from Hunt send Alun Evans clear. And Evans shoot. And Evans score against his old club. And in the sixty-third minute, Bill watched a flick from Hunt find the head of Evans. And Evans dive. And Evans score again. And in the seventy-fourth minute, Bill watched Ian Callaghan cross to Hunt. And Hunt score again. And in the eightieth minute, Bill watched Evans pass to Thompson. And Thompson shoot. And Thompson score again. And in the early autumn sunshine, the red of Liverpool Football Club beat the gold of Wolverhampton Wanderers six–nil. Away from home, away from Anfield. And on the touchline, the touchline at Molineux. Bill shook the hand of Ronnie Allen, the manager of Wolverhampton Wanderers –

I knew we should never have sold Alun Evans, said Ronnie Allen. Especially not to you, Bill. Especially not to Liverpool Football Club. That was the most crushing performance I have ever seen by an away team at Molineux, Bill. That anyone has ever seen. We were annihilated, Bill. We were humiliated . . .

Bill shook his head. And Bill said, Thank you, Ronnie. Thank

271

you very much. But please don't say you were humiliated, Ronnie. Please never say that. Yes, we were the better team today, Ronnie. But we never lost respect for you. We never tried to humiliate you, Ronnie. We simply wanted to win.

. . .

On the bench, the Anfield bench. Bill and forty-nine thousand, five hundred and sixty-seven folk watched Liverpool Football Club play Athletic Club Bilbao in the second leg of the First Round of the Inter-Cities Fairs Cup. Athletic Club Bilbao had won the first leg two–one. Everyone thought Athletic Club Bilbao would come to defend their two–one lead. But everyone thought wrong. Athletic Club Bilbao came to attack. And in the thirty-second minute, Uriarte made an opening for Argoitia. Argoitia dribbled. Argoitia sidestepped Tommy Smith's sliding tackle. And Argoitia scored. And the Kop was silent. The Spion Kop stunned. But not for long. Not for long. The Kop found its voice. And the Spion Kop roared again. And in the seventy-eighth minute, Ian St John took a free kick. And Ronnie Yeats met the free kick. Yeats nodded the ball back into the middle of the penalty area. And Chris Lawler met the nod. And Lawler scored. And the Kop roared. The Spion Kop roared. And roared again. And in the eighty-seventh minute, Emlyn Hughes shot. And Hughes scored. And Liverpool Football Club beat Athletic Club Bilbao two–one in the second leg of the First Round of the Inter-Cities Fairs Cup. Both teams had won two–one at home. Both teams had scored an away goal. The tie tied at three–three. But there was no extra time. There were no replays. There were no third matches. There was only the toss of a coin. And the referee called the two captains to the centre of the field, the centre circle. The referee took a coin from his pocket. One side heads, one side tails. The referee turned to Ron Yeats. The referee asked the home captain to call it. And Yeats called it. In the centre of the field, the centre circle. The referee flicked the coin up into the air. Up into the night. And the lights of the cameras flashed. And the eyes of the crowd, the Anfield crowd, the forty-nine thousand, five hundred and sixty-seven pairs of eyes, Anfield eyes, followed the coin. Up into the night, up into the dark. Up and then down again. Down onto the ground, the Anfield ground. And the referee and the two captains stared down at the ground, the Anfield ground. And the captain of

Athletic Club Bilbao leapt up into the night,

the Anfield night –

In the dressing room, the Anfield dressing room. Bill walked up to Ron Yeats. And Bill said, What did you call, son?

Heads, said Ron Yeats.

Jesus Christ! You fool, you idiot. You never call heads. Everybody knows that. You never call heads!

But you told me never to call tails, said Ron Yeats. You said I should always call heads, Boss.

Bill shook his head. And Bill said, What day of the week is it today, son? What day is today?

It's Wednesday.

Exactly. And whose day of the week is Wednesday, son?

I don't know whose day it is, Boss.

Jesus Christ! Don't you know anything, son? Wednesday is the Devil's day. The Devil's day, son. Hence the phrase, Wednesday's child is full of woe. I presume you have heard that phrase before, son?

Yes, Boss. I have.

Well, that phrase comes from the fact that Wednesday is the Devil's day. And what does the Devil have? Sticking out of his arse?

A tail.

Exactly. A tail. So you always call tails on the Devil's day. Everybody knows that, son. You always call tails on a Wednesday.

. . .

In the house, in their hallway. Bill closed the front door. In the dark. Bill walked down the hallway to the kitchen. In the dark. Bill switched on the light. Bill sat down at the table. And Bill put his hand in his pocket. In the kitchen, at the table. Bill took out a coin. Bill stared down at the coin. And Bill turned the coin in his fingers. The two sides of the coin. In the kitchen, at the table. Bill flicked the coin up. Up into the air, down onto the floor. And Bill stared down at the coin on the floor. The kitchen floor. Tails. In the kitchen, at the table. Bill bent down. And Bill picked up the coin from the floor. In the kitchen, at the table. Again. Bill flicked the coin up. Up into the air, down onto the floor. Again. Bill stared down at the coin on the floor. Tails. Again. In the kitchen, at the table. Bill bent down. Again. Bill picked up the coin from the floor. In the kitchen, at the table. Again.

273

Bill flicked the coin up. Up into the air, down onto the floor. Again. Bill stared down at the coin on the floor. Tails. Again. Bill bent down. Bill picked up the coin. Again. In the kitchen, at the table. Bill stared at the coin in his fingers. Again. Bill turned the coin in his fingers. Again and again. The two sides of the coin. Again and again,

the two sides. In the kitchen, at the table. Bill knew people did not need chance. Bill knew people did not need luck. Yes, people wanted success. Yes, people wanted victory. But not by chance,

not through luck. The name of your father or the name of your school. People wanted success through their effort, people wanted victory through their work. Not the toss of a coin,

the roll of a dice. Through their effort and through their work. Their communal effort, their collective work.


## 29. THE BIG HAMMER AND THE MAGIC WAND

Three days after losing to Athletic Club Bilbao on the toss of a coin, Liverpool Football Club travelled to Turf Moor, Burnley. In the twentieth minute, Roger Hunt scored. And in the thirty-fifth minute, Hunt scored again. In the sixty-second minute, Peter Thompson scored. And in the eighty-seventh minute, Geoff Strong scored. And Liverpool Football Club beat Burnley Football Club four–nil. Away from home, away from Anfield. In their last five League matches, Liverpool Football Club had scored eighteen goals and they had conceded none. That evening, Leeds United had eighteen points, Arsenal Football Club had eighteen points and Liverpool Football Club had eighteen points, too. But that evening, Liverpool Football Club were first in the First Division. On goal average.

On Tuesday 8 October, 1968, Everton Football Club came to Anfield, Liverpool. That evening, fifty-four thousand, four hundred and ninety-six folk came, too. Fifty-four thousand, four hundred and ninety-six folk to watch the one hundredth League meeting of Liverpool Football Club and Everton Football Club. The one hundredth League derby. But for the first half-hour of the one hundredth League derby, Liverpool Football Club were completely eclipsed, completely outplayed by Everton Football Club. By Kendall.

By Harvey. And by Ball. By move after move, by pass after pass, by shot after shot. One shot crossed the line, into the goal. But the goal was disallowed for offside. Another shot hit the bar. Another shot rebounded off Lawrence but stuck on the line. The ball refusing to cross the line. But in the sixty-sixth minute, Morrissey swung in a high ball. And Royle nodded the high ball back into the jaws of the goal. And Ball met the high ball in the jaws of the goal. And Ball nodded the high ball down the throat of the goal. But the supporters of Liverpool Football Club refused to accept defeat. And so the players of Liverpool Football Club refused to accept failure. And in the seventy-fifth minute, Ian St John was fouled on the edge of the Everton penalty area. And Tommy Smith stepped up to take the free kick. Smith struck the free kick. And West did not move in his goal. And the ball flew past West into the goal. And the one hundredth League derby was drawn –

One-all.

Four days afterwards, Manchester United came to Anfield, Liverpool. That afternoon, fifty-three thousand, three hundred and ninety-two folk came, too. Fifty-three thousand, three hundred and ninety-two folk to watch Liverpool Football Club play the European Champions. Two weeks before, the European Champions had travelled to the Estadio Alberto J. Armando, in Buenos Aires, in Argentina, to play Estudiantes de La Plata in the first leg of the 1968 Intercontinental Cup. Nobby Stiles had been sent off. And Marcos Conigliaro had scored. And Estudiantes de La Plata had beaten the European Champions one–nil. In four days, Estudiantes de La Plata would come to Old Trafford, Manchester, to play the European Champions in the second leg of the 1968 Intercontinental Cup. But the European Champions were struggling. Struggling to find any form in the League, struggling to cope with injuries to the team. Burns was out injured. Dunne was out injured. Sadler was out injured. Kidd was out injured. Best was out injured. And Law was out injured. The European Champions were struggling to name a team to play Liverpool Football Club. The European Champions had asked the Football League to postpone the game against Liverpool Football Club. The Football League had refused to postpone the game. And in the fourteenth minute, Ian St John scored. And in the eighty-second minute, Alun

Evans scored. And Liverpool Football Club beat the European Champions two–nil. At home, at Anfield. Bill Shankly walked down the touchline. The Anfield touchline. Bill Shankly shook Sir Matt Busby's hand. Bill Shankly looked into Sir Matt Busby's face. And Bill Shankly saw a drained man. Bill Shankly saw an old man. A man whose dreams of winning the European Cup had sustained him. Day in, day out. A man whose hopes of winning the European Cup had propelled him. Day in, day out. A man whose dreams had rescued him from grief, a man whose hopes had saved him from tragedy. Day in, day out. A man whose dreams had been realised, a man whose hopes had been attained. That night, last May. A man whose dreams had now deserted him, a man whose hopes had now left him. Drained and old –

I'm very sorry, said Bill Shankly. I am very sorry that this game had to be played today, Matt. Liverpool Football Club supported your request for a postponement. Because I know you would have done the same for us, Matt. So we were very disappointed that the Football League refused your request. We were very sorry that the game had to be played today, Matt . . .

Sir Matt Busby nodded. And Sir Matt Busby said, I know, Bill. I know. And thank you, Bill. Thank you for your support. And for the support of Liverpool Football Club. Thank you very much, Bill.

And I want you to know we are all hoping you win on Wednesday night, Matt. We are all hoping you thrash the Argentinians on Wednesday night. Hoping and praying, Matt . . .

Sir Matt Busby nodded. And Sir Matt Busby said, Thank you, Bill. Thank you very much . . .

Four days later, Estudiantes de La Plata came to Old Trafford, Manchester. Sixty-three thousand, four hundred and twenty-seven folk came, too. Sixty-three thousand, four hundred and twenty-seven folk and Bill Shankly. In the seventh minute, Juan Ramón Verón scored. In the eighty-eighth minute, George Best punched José Hugo Medina in the face. George Best pushed Néstor Togneri to the ground. And the referee sent off George Best and José Hugo Medina. And George Best spat at José Hugo Medina. And police and officials had to escort George Best and José Hugo Medina from the pitch. And some of the Old Trafford crowd threw coins at José Hugo Medina. And in the eighty-ninth minute, Willie Morgan scored for Manchester United. But it didn't count, it didn't matter. The game was drawn one-all. And Estudiantes de La Plata had won the 1968 Intercontinental Cup two–one on aggregate. And there was fighting on the pitch. After the final whistle. There were punches thrown on the pitch. After the final whistle. The players of Estudiantes de La Plata tried to run a lap of honour around the Old Trafford pitch. But some of the Old Trafford crowd threw coins and bottles at the players of Estudiantes de La Plata. And the players of Estudiantes de La Plata ran for cover, down the tunnel, onto their plane. And after that whistle, that final whistle. In the stand, the Old Trafford stand. Bill Shankly stared down at the pitch, the Old Trafford pitch. At the coins and at the bottles. The anger and the hate. People against people,

man against man.

On Saturday 19 October, 1968, Liverpool Football Club travelled to White Hart Lane, London. In the thirty-seventh minute, Tommy Lawrence saved from Jenkins. And Lawrence cleared. Roger Hunt chased the clearance. Hunt caught the clearance. Hunt side-stepped Mullery. Hunt wrong-footed Beal. And Hunt shot. And Hunt scored. But just before half-time, Greaves found an extra foot of pace, Greaves found an extra yard of space. And Greaves met a cross from Gilzean. And Greaves scored. In the fifty-fifth minute, Lawrence dived at the feet of Pearce on the edge of the Liverpool penalty area. The linesman raised his flag. The linesman said Lawrence had handled the ball outside the Liverpool penalty area. Lawrence argued with the linesman. Lawrence said only his body had crossed the line. The linesman disagreed. Lawrence argued with the referee. Lawrence said the ball and his hands had not crossed the line. The referee disagreed. The referee awarded a free kick to Tottenham Hotspur on the edge of the Liverpool penalty area. The referee marched the Liverpool wall back ten paces into the Liverpool penalty area. Venables stood over the ball with Greaves and Mullery. Venables feinted to take the free kick. The Liverpool wall moved forward to block the free kick. The referee blew his whistle. The referee marched the Liverpool wall back ten paces. The referee spoke to the Liverpool players. The referee warned the Liverpool players not to move forward until he had blown his whistle. Again, Venables feinted to take the free kick. Again, the Liverpool wall moved forward to block the free kick. Again, the referee blew his whistle. Again, the referee marched the Liverpool wall back ten paces. Again, the referee spoke to the Liverpool players. Again, the referee warned the Liverpool players not to move forward until he had blown his whistle. But as the referee was speaking to the Liverpool players, as the referee was warning the Liverpool players, Greaves took the free kick. Greaves bent the free kick around the Liverpool wall. And Greaves scored. And the referee blew his whistle. And the players of Liverpool Football Club looked at the referee. But the referee pointed to the centre of the pitch, to the centre circle. The referee awarded a goal to Tottenham Hotspur. And the players of Tottenham Hotspur celebrated. And the terraces erupted. In anger and in hate. And the police moved onto the terraces. In anger and in hate. And the police marched away some of the supporters of Liverpool Football Club. In anger and in hate. Just before full time, Collins bowled over Alun Evans in the Tottenham penalty area. And the players of Liverpool Football Club looked to the linesman. But the linesman did not raise his flag. The linesman shook his head. And the players of Liverpool Football Club looked at the referee. But the referee shook his head. The referee did not award a penalty to Liverpool Football Club. And Liverpool Football Club lost two–one at White Hart Lane, London. And again, the terraces erupted. In anger and in hate. And again, the police moved onto the terraces. In anger and in hate. And again, the police marched away some of the supporters of Liverpool Football Club. In anger and in hate –

People against people, man against man.

One week afterwards, Newcastle United came to Anfield, Liverpool. That afternoon, forty-five thousand, three hundred and twenty-three folk came, too. In the twenty-third minute, Alun Evans scored. And in the eighty-fifth minute, Peter Thompson scored. And Liverpool Football Club beat Newcastle United two–one. At home, at Anfield. That evening, Leeds United had twenty-three points, Everton Football Club had twenty-three points and Liverpool Football Club had twenty-three points, too. But that evening, Liverpool Football Club were still first in the First Division –

On goal average.

On Saturday 2 November, 1968, Liverpool Football Club travelled to the Hawthorns, Birmingham. That day, Liverpool Football

Club did not score. That day, Liverpool Football Club drew nil–nil with West Bromwich Albion. Away from home, away from Anfield. That day, Everton Football Club beat Sunderland Football Club two–nil. That evening, Leeds United had twenty-four points and Liverpool Football Club had twenty-four points, too. But that evening, Everton Football Club had twenty-five points. That evening, Everton Football Club were first in the First Division.

One week afterwards, Chelsea Football Club came to Anfield, Liverpool. That afternoon, forty-seven thousand, two hundred and forty-eight folk came, too. In the fifth minute, Birchenall scored for Chelsea Football Club. In the twenty-fifth minute, Bonetti failed to hold a shot from Tommy Smith. And Ian Callaghan pounced. And Callaghan scored. Three minutes later, Houseman toppled over Chris Lawler in the Chelsea penalty area. The referee awarded a penalty to Liverpool Football Club. Smith put the ball on the penalty spot. Smith struck the ball. And Smith scored. That day, Liverpool Football Club beat Chelsea Football Club two–one. At home, at Anfield. That day, Leeds United drew at Tottenham Hotspur and Everton Football Club drew at Ipswich Town. That evening, Liverpool Football Club were first in the First Division. Again –

On goal average.

On Saturday 16 November, 1968, Liverpool Football Club beat Sheffield Wednesday two–one. Away from home, away from Anfield. That day, Everton Football Club beat Queens Park Rangers and Leeds United beat Coventry City. One week later, Coventry City came to Anfield, Liverpool. That afternoon, forty-four thousand, eight hundred and twenty folk came, too. In the thirty-sixth minute, Geoff Strong scored. And in the eighty-third minute, Ian Callaghan scored. And Liverpool Football Club beat Coventry City two–nil. That day, Everton Football Club lost two–one at Elland Road, Leeds. That evening, Leeds United had twenty-nine points and Liverpool Football Club had thirty points. That evening, Liverpool Football Club were still first in the First Division. But not by goal average. By points, a point –

A single point.

One week later, Liverpool Football Club travelled to the City Ground, Nottingham. And in the twenty-fourth minute, Roger Hunt scored. His two hundred and thirty-third League goal for Liverpool

Football Club. Roger Hunt had equalled the club record set by Gordon Hodgson. And Liverpool Football Club beat Nottingham Forest one–nil. Away from home, away from Anfield. That day, Leeds United drew with Chelsea Football Club and Everton Football Club beat Leicester City seven–one. That evening, Leeds United had thirty points and Everton Football Club had thirty points, too. That evening, Liverpool Football Club had thirty-two points. That evening, Liverpool Football Club were still first in the First Division. But not by a single point. By two points.

That evening, Leicester City Football Club announced the resignation of Matt Gillies. Matt Gillies had played for Leicester City Football Club one hundred and three times. Matt Gillies had been the captain of Leicester City. Matt Gillies had captained Leicester City to the Second Division Championship in the 1953–54 season. And then Matt Gillies had been appointed as the manager of Leicester City Football Club. Matt Gillies had been the manager of Leicester City Football Club for ten years. Matt Gillies had managed Leicester City to two FA Cup finals. Matt Gillies had managed Leicester City to two League Cup finals. And in 1964, Leicester City had won the League Cup. But that evening, Matt Gillies said, Too many people think the Big Hammer is the Magic Wand for success in football. I am afraid that a lot of what goes on during play makes me cringe. I am often appalled at what I see and I want no part in thuggery and gamesmanship that reaches the point of cheating. I have no new job waiting for me but I may stay in the game. I have laid down my burden and I want time to consider the future.

Three days afterwards, Southampton Football Club came to Anfield, Liverpool. That evening, forty-five thousand, five hundred and twenty-seven folk came, too. And in the fourteenth minute, Ian Callaghan scored. And Liverpool Football Club beat Southampton Football Club one–nil. At home, at Anfield. Four days later, West Ham United came to Anfield, Liverpool. That afternoon, forty-eight thousand, six hundred and thirty-two folk came, too. In the forty-fourth minute, Emlyn Hughes scored. In the forty-seventh minute, Peter Thompson scored. And Liverpool Football Club beat West Ham United two–nil. At home, at Anfield. That day, Leeds United beat Sheffield Wednesday and Arsenal Football Club beat Everton Football

Club. That evening, Everton Football Club had thirty points and Leeds United had thirty-two points. That evening, Liverpool Football Club had thirty-six points. That evening, Liverpool Football Club were still first in the First Division. By four points.

On Saturday 14 December, 1968, Liverpool Football Club travelled to Old Trafford, Manchester. That afternoon, fifty-five thousand, three hundred and fifty-four folk came, too. Fifty-five thousand, three hundred and fifty-four folk to watch the current European Champions play the current First Division leaders. The current European Champions were still struggling. The current European Champions were fifteenth in the First Division. Struggling to find any form, struggling to cope with injuries. But today, Burns was back. Today, Dunne was back. Today, Sadler was back. Today, Kidd was back. Today, Best was back. And today, Law was back. And today, Law scored. And that day the current European Champions beat the current First Division leaders one–nil. Bill Shankly shook Sir Matt Busby's hand. Bill Shankly looked into Sir Matt Busby's face. And Bill Shankly saw a man still drained. Bill Shankly saw a man still old. A man in need of dreams, a man in need of hopes –

Fresh dreams and new hopes –

Well played, said Bill Shankly. Very well played indeed, Matt. I think you might just have turned the corner. And I hope you have, Matt. And so I wish you all the best for the rest of the season . . .

Sir Matt Busby shook his head. And Sir Matt Busby said, Thank you, Bill. Thank you very much. And I hope you are right, Bill. I really hope you are right. But I think the corner is still a long way off. Still a very long way off for us. But I think this season could be yours, Bill. Yours or Don's. I can't see anyone else winning the League this season, Bill. I think it's down to you or Don. And so I hope it's you, Bill. I really hope it's you who wins the League this season . . .

One week later, Tottenham Hotspur came to Anfield, Liverpool. That afternoon, forty-three thousand, eight hundred and forty-three folk came, too. At home, at Anfield. Liverpool Football Club had won twenty-five of twenty-six possible points in the season so far. At home, at Anfield. Liverpool Football Club were invincible in the season so far. At home, at Anfield. Liverpool Football Club pounded and pounded away. At home, at Anfield. Jennings saved from Alun Evans.

At home, at Anfield. Jennings saved from Peter Thompson. At home, at Anfield. Jennings saved from Roger Hunt. At home, at Anfield. Jennings saved from Ian St John. At home, at Anfield. Jennings saved from Ian Callaghan. At home, at Anfield. Still Liverpool Football Club pounded and pounded away. And at home, at Anfield. In the seventieth minute, Tommy Smith robbed Mullery. At home, at Anfield. Smith fed Emlyn Hughes. At home, at Anfield. Friends advanced ahead of him, foes retreated before him. And at home, at Anfield. Hughes shot and Hughes scored. And at home, at Anfield. Liverpool Football Club beat Tottenham Hotspur one–nil. At home, at Anfield. Liverpool Football Club had thirty-eight points. And Leeds United had thirty-five points. And that evening, Liverpool Football Club were still first in the First Division. By three points. Still first,

at Christmas. *I think this season could be yours, Bill.* In the 1962–63 season, Everton Football Club had been first in the First Division at Christmas. And Everton Football Club had won the Championship. *I think this season could be yours, Bill.* In the 1964–65 season, Manchester United had been first in the First Division at Christmas. And Manchester United had won the Championship. *I think this season could be yours, Bill.* In the 1965–66 season, Liverpool Football Club had been first in the First Division at Christmas. And Liverpool Football Club had won the Championship. *I think this season could be yours, Bill.* In the 1966–67 season, Manchester United had been first in the First Division at Christmas. And Manchester United had won the Championship. *I think this season could be yours, Bill.* But in the 1963–64 season, Blackburn Rovers had been first in the First Division at Christmas. And Blackburn Rovers had not won the Championship. Liverpool Football Club had won the Championship. *Yours or Don's.* And last season, Manchester United had been first in the First Division at Christmas. But Manchester United had not won the Championship. Manchester City had won the Championship. *Yours or Don's. Yours or Don's . . .*

On Boxing Day, 1968, Burnley Football Club came to Anfield, Liverpool. That afternoon, fifty-two thousand, five hundred and fifteen folk came, too. In the forty-third minute, Chris Lawler scored. But Burnley Football Club scored, too. And Liverpool Football Club drew one-all with Burnley Football Club. At home, at Anfield. Nine days later, Doncaster Rovers came to Anfield, Liverpool. That afternoon, forty-eight thousand, three hundred and thirty-three folk came, too. Forty-eight thousand, three hundred and thirty-three folk to watch Liverpool Football Club play Doncaster Rovers of the Fourth Division in the Third Round of the FA Cup. In the seventieth minute, Roger Hunt scored. In the eighty-fourth minute, Ian Callaghan scored. And Liverpool Football Club beat Doncaster Rovers of the Fourth Division two–nil in the Third Round of the FA Cup. At home,

at Anfield. One week afterwards, West Bromwich Albion came to Anfield, Liverpool. That afternoon, forty-seven thousand, five hundred and eighty-seven folk came, too. In the eighty-third minute, Peter Thompson scored. And Liverpool Football Club beat West Bromwich Albion one–nil. At home, at Anfield. That evening, Everton Football Club had thirty-seven points and Arsenal Football Club had thirty-seven points, too. That evening, Leeds United had thirty-nine points and Liverpool Football Club had forty-one points. That evening, Liverpool Football Club were still first in the First Division.

On Saturday 18 January, 1969, Liverpool Football Club travelled to Stamford Bridge, London. Bill Shankly did not like London. Bill Shankly hated London. Bill Shankly walked into the dressing room. The away dressing room. Bill Shankly looked around the dressing room. The Liverpool dressing room. From player to player. From Lawrence to Lawler, Lawler to Strong, Strong to Smith, Smith to Yeats, Yeats to Hughes, Hughes to Callaghan, Callaghan to Hunt, Hunt to Evans, Evans to St John and from St John to Thompson. And Bill Shankly shook his head –

People tell me Liverpool Football Club have not won a League match in London since December, 1966. People tell me Liverpool Football Club cannot win a League match in London. So people tell me Liverpool Football Club cannot win the League. That Liverpool Football Club are not good enough to win the League. Because Liverpool Football Club cannot win a match in London. But I tell those people that is rubbish. Utter rubbish, boys. I tell those people Liverpool Football Club were robbed by the rain at Arsenal back in August. I tell those people Liverpool Football Club were robbed by the referee at Tottenham in October. I tell those people Liverpool Football

Club will win the League. Because I tell those people Liverpool Football Club will not lose again in London. That Liverpool Football Club will win every game in London from now on. And win the League. So don't you contradict me today, boys. Don't you make me look a liar to those people. Those ignorant people, boys. Those ignorant London people . . .

After the whistle, the first whistle. In the swirling, London wind. Just before half-time, Ian Callaghan scored. But the goal was disallowed. Alun Evans offside. But in the swirling, London wind. In the sixty-fifth minute, Hughes of Chelsea dropped a shot from Peter Thompson of Liverpool. And Roger Hunt of Liverpool pounced on the loose ball. And Hunt of Liverpool stabbed at the loose ball. And Hunt of Liverpool scored. His two hundred and thirty-fourth League goal for Liverpool Football Club. Roger Hunt had beaten the club record set by Gordon Hodgson. And in the swirling, London wind. In the seventy-second minute, Hunt broke free. Hunt passed to Thompson. Thompson crossed. And Evans scored. But in the swirling, London wind. Now Chelsea Football Club woke up. And Tambling scored. In the swirling, London wind. Webb shot. But Ron Yeats cleared the ball off the goal line. And in the swirling, London wind. Liverpool Football Club beat Chelsea Football Club two–one. Away from home, away from Anfield. In the swirling, London wind. Liverpool Football Club had won in London for the first time since December, 1966.

After the whistle, the final whistle. Bill Shankly took his hat off the back of the door of the away dressing room at Stamford Bridge. Bill Shankly put on his hat. Bill Shankly pulled the brim of his hat down low. And Bill Shankly stepped out of the away dressing room. In the corridor at Stamford Bridge, the gentlemen of the London sporting press were waiting for Bill Shankly. And Bill Shankly was waiting for them. Bill Shankly ready for them. His jaw jutting, his finger jabbing. His eyes darting and his mouth moving –

Who can catch Liverpool Football Club now? Who will stop us now, gentlemen? You mark my words. Liverpool Football Club will be Champions. We will be Champions again, gentlemen. Because no one can catch Liverpool Football Club now. No one can stop us now. You mark my words, gentlemen. And so you come back to me in May and then you'll see. Then you'll see. Because I'm never wrong, gentlemen. I'm never wrong.


## 30. WITH ONE FOOT IN EDEN

In the house, in their front room. Bill had heard the news and Bill had seen the reports. In the car, at the wheel. Bill could not believe his ears, Bill could not believe his eyes. On the road, the road to Manchester. Bill still could not believe his ears, Bill still could not believe his eyes. In the car park, the car park at Old Trafford. Bill would not believe it. Bill refused to believe it. In the office, the office at Old Trafford. Bill would not believe it until he had heard it from the man himself. Until he had seen the man himself. And Bill had asked, Why, Matt? Why?

I've had enough, Bill. And so I've resigned. I've quit.

But you're not a quitter, Matt. You can't resign.

But I have, Bill. Because I've had enough.

Enough of what, Matt? Enough of football? But football is your life, Matt. Football is all there is. You know that, Matt . . .

Yes, I know that, Bill. But I've had enough of it, enough of football. It has been a burden to me. A burden I have wanted, yes. But the burden has been demanding. The burden has been great. It has weighed me down. And it has tired me out. And now I'm too drained to go on. I am too old to go on. It's time for a younger man to pick up the burden. It is time for a younger man to carry the weight, Bill.

Bill shook his head. And Bill said, But who, Matt? Who? Who can pick up that burden? Who can carry that weight, Matt? Do you have a man in mind? A younger man in mind, Matt?

Well, that's the problem, Bill. The biggest problem. Because if they bring in a new man, if they bring in a man from outside. Then that man will want his own staff. Just as I did twenty-three years ago. And then what will become of my staff? Of Jimmy Murphy? Of Jack Compton? Of Johnny Aston? Of Joe Armstrong? Of Wilf McGuinness? These men who have been with me through everything. These men who have been with me through so much. Through all the joy and through all the agony. And so I cannot see them just pushed aside, Bill. I cannot see them just thrown away. I cannot, Bill. I cannot . . .

But that is what will happen, Matt. If you go, if you leave. That is what will happen to them, Matt. They will be pushed aside. They will be thrown away, Matt . . .

No, said Matt. I won't let that happen. And the chairman and the board agree. And so we have all agreed that I will stay on as general manager. But there will also be a team manager. A manager who will take the training every day. A manager who will pick the team every game. But I will still be here to help lessen the other demands on him, to help him carry the other burdens. And so we will promote a man from within. To be the man who takes the training, the man who picks the team. And he will be his own man. But I will still be here to guide him. I will still be here to help him. And then we'll be able to continue all the work we have done. And we will be able to preserve all the work we have done. That is the plan. My plan . . .

But who, Matt? Who? Who do you have in mind?

Wilf, said Matt. Wilf McGuinness. But not just yet. Not with the position the team are in now, not the way things are now. It wouldn't be fair, it wouldn't be right. So I will put things right, I will sort things out. And then we'll make Wilf chief coach and see how things go. But I've said nothing to him. I've said nothing to anyone.

Well, I hope you're right, Matt. I really do. I really hope things work out the way you hope. The way you've planned them, Matt. I really do. And I pray they do, Matt. For you and for Manchester United. But mainly for you, Matt. Especially for you . . .

Thank you, Bill. Thank you very much. It's not been an easy decision to make. It's been the hardest decision of my life. But it comes to us all. It comes to us all, Bill. Because things do not go on forever. Things do not last forever, Bill. We are none of us immortal. None of us immortal, Bill . . .

. . .

In the house, in their kitchen. Bill got up from the table. Bill picked up the plates. Bill walked over to the sink. Bill put the plates in the sink. Bill walked back over to the kitchen table. Bill picked up the salt and pepper pots. Bill put them in the cupboard. Bill walked back over to the table. Bill took the cloth off the table. Bill walked over to the back door. Bill opened the back door. Bill stepped outside. Bill stood on the step. Bill shook the cloth. Bill stepped back into the kitchen. Bill closed the door. Bill folded up the tablecloth. Bill put it in the drawer. Bill walked back over to the sink. Bill turned on the taps. Bill squeezed washing-up liquid into the sink. Bill turned off the taps. Bill picked up the scrubbing brush. Bill washed up the plates, Bill washed up the pans. Bill washed up the knives and forks. Bill put them on the draining board. Bill pulled out the plug. Bill dried his hands. Bill picked up the tea towel. And Bill dried up the pans. Bill dried up the plates. Bill dried up the knives and forks. Bill put the pans in one cupboard. Bill put the plates in another. And Bill put the knives and forks in the drawer. Bill walked back over to the sink. Bill picked up the dishcloth. Bill wiped down the draining board. Bill turned on the taps again. Bill rinsed the dishcloth under the taps. Bill turned off the taps. Bill squeezed the water out of the dishcloth. Bill put the dish-cloth down next to the bottle of washing-up liquid. Bill turned around. Bill looked round the kitchen. Bill turned back to the sink. Bill bent down. Bill opened the cupboard under the sink. Bill took out a bucket from under the sink. Bill bent back down. Bill opened a box under the sink. Bill took out a Brillo pad from the box. Bill closed the cupboard door. Bill picked up the bucket. Bill put the bucket in the sink. Bill turned the taps on again. Bill filled the bucket half full. Bill turned off the taps. Bill took the bucket and the Brillo pad over to the cooker. Bill put down the bucket in front of the cooker. Bill opened the oven door. Bill looked inside the oven. Bill could see the dirt. Bill could smell the fat. Bill knelt down on the kitchen floor. Bill unbuttoned the cuffs of his shirt. Bill rolled up the sleeves of his shirt. Bill picked up the Brillo pad. Bill sank the Brillo pad into the bucket of water. Bill pulled the Brillo pad back up, out of the water. Bill squeezed the water from the Brillo pad. The wet, steel wool. Bill squeezed it tighter. Bill put his hand inside the oven. Into the dirt, amongst the fat. In the kitchen, on the floor. On his knees. Bill began to scrub. Liverpool Football Club had lost two–nil to Nottingham Forest. On his knees. Bill began to scour. At home, at Anfield. On his knees. Bill began to clean. Liverpool Football Club were no longer first in the First Division. On his knees, to clean and clean again. Liverpool Football Club were now second in the First Division. On his knees, on his knees. Leeds United now first in the First Division. Among the dirt,

among the fat. On his knees.

. . .

On the bench, the Anfield bench. Bill watched Shilton save from Ian St John. And Shilton save from Peter Thompson. And in the thirty-first minute, Bill watched Glover cross a high ball in from the left. Ron Yeats jumped and Lochhead jumped. But Yeats did not meet the ball. Lochhead met the ball. Lochhead headed the ball. And Lochhead scored. And in the fortieth minute, Bill watched Sjöberg handle the ball in the Leicester City penalty area. The referee blew his whistle. The referee awarded a penalty to Liverpool Football Club. Tommy Smith put the ball on the penalty spot. Smith struck the ball. And Shilton saved from Smith. And on the bench, the Anfield bench. Bill watched Shilton save from Chris Lawler. Shilton save from Emlyn Hughes. And Shilton save from Ian Callaghan. And on the bench, the Anfield bench. Bill turned to Bobby Graham. And Bill told Graham to warm up. And in the seventieth minute, Bill stood up. And on the touchline, the Anfield touchline. Bill gesticulated at Ronnie Yeats. Bill called over Ronnie. Bill spoke to Ronnie. And Yeats nodded. And on the pitch, the Anfield pitch. Yeats walked towards Roger Hunt. And Yeats spoke to Hunt. But Hunt shook his head. And Hunt walked away. And on the touchline, the Anfield touchline. Bill cursed. And Bill gesticulated at the referee. Bill called over the referee. Bill spoke to the referee. And the referee nodded. And on the pitch, the Anfield pitch. The referee walked towards Roger Hunt. The referee spoke to Hunt. And now Hunt looked up at the Kop. The Spion Kop. And Hunt looked up into the sky. The Anfield sky. And Hunt felt the ground beneath his feet move. The Anfield ground. And Hunt felt the world turn upside down. The Anfield world. And Hunt walked slowly across the pitch. The Anfield pitch. And Hunt walked towards the touchline. The Anfield touchline. And Hunt took off his shirt. His Liverpool shirt. And Hunt threw his Liverpool shirt into the dug-out. The Anfield dug-out. And Hunt ran down the tunnel. The Anfield tunnel. Into the darkness. The darkness. And in the ninetieth minute, the referee blew his whistle. The final whistle. And Liverpool Football Club were out of the FA Cup. Liverpool Football Club had lost one–nil to Leicester City in the Fifth Round replay of the FA Cup. At home,

at Anfield. Bill walked down the tunnel. The Anfield tunnel. Bill walked into the dressing room. The Liverpool dressing room. The

Liverpool dressing room silent, the Liverpool dressing room waiting. Bill walked up to Roger Hunt. Roger Hunt sat silent, Roger Hunt sat waiting. And Bill looked down at Roger Hunt. Bill handed Roger Hunt his shirt. His Liverpool shirt. And Bill said, I thought you were more of a sportsman than to ever do something like that, son.

The shirt in his hands. The Liverpool shirt in his hands. Roger Hunt looked up at Bill. The tears in his tears –

And I thought you had more respect for me. After all the games I have played for you, after all the goals I have scored for you. I thought you had more respect for me than to take me off, than to substitute me. At home, at Anfield. In front of our own people, in front of our own supporters. I would never have believed you would do such a thing. I would have never believed you *could* do such a thing. I was shocked and I was hurt, Boss . . .

Bill saw the shirt in the hands of Roger Hunt. The Liverpool shirt. And Bill saw the tears in the eyes of Roger Hunt. And Bill sat down beside Roger Hunt. And Bill put his arm around the shoulders of Roger Hunt. And Bill said, I believe you are one of the greatest centre-forwards I have ever seen, son. I believe you have played in some of the greatest games I have ever seen. I believe you have scored some of the greatest goals I have ever seen. But it is not about me. And it is not about you. You did not play in those games for me. You did not score those goals for me. You played in those games for Liverpool Football Club. For the team. And for the supporters of Liverpool Football Club. For the people. And so you scored those goals for Liverpool Football Club. For the team. And for the supporters of Liverpool Football Club. For the people. Not for me, son. And not for you. Every single decision we make, every single thing we do, is for Liverpool Football Club. For the team. And for the supporters of Liverpool Football Club. For the people. Not for you, not for me. For the team, for the people.
. . .

In the house, in their bedroom. In the dark and in the silence. Bill stared up at the ceiling. The bedroom ceiling. And Bill saw the tables on the ceiling. The bedroom ceiling. Bill saw the standings on the ceiling. The bedroom ceiling. Bill knew if Leeds United lost their last two games. Their game against Liverpool Football Club and their game against Nottingham Forest. And if Liverpool Football Club won their last three games. Their game against Leeds United, their game against Manchester City and their game against Newcastle United. Then Liverpool Football Club would be the Champions of England. In their house, in the bedroom. Bill knew Liverpool Football Club had to beat Leeds United tomorrow night. But Bill knew Leeds United could lose tomorrow night and still be the Champions of England. If Leeds United drew with Nottingham Forest. Leeds United would still be the Champions of England. In the dark and in the silence. Bill knew it was out of his hands. It was out of his hands. And in the dark,

and in the silence. Bill cursed his hands,

his empty, empty hands.

. . .

On the bench again, the Anfield bench again. On a Monday night, the last Monday night in April. In a madhouse of electric noise that hammered the senses. Bill watched Bremner win the toss. And Bremner choose to make Liverpool Football Club play towards the Spion Kop in the first half. It was a gamble, it was a risk. And in a madhouse of electric noise that hammered the senses. From the first minute, Liverpool Football Club attacked and attacked. In a madhouse of electric noise that hammered the senses. From the very back to the front, from Tommy Lawrence to Chris Lawler, Lawler to Geoff Strong, Strong to Tommy Smith, Smith to Ronnie Yeats, Yeats to Emlyn Hughes, Hughes to Ian Callaghan, Callaghan to Bobby Graham, Graham to Alun Evans, Evans to Ian St John and from St John to Peter Thompson. In a madhouse of electric noise that hammered the senses. The players of Leeds United were rattled, the players of Leeds United were shaken. The challenges rash and the tackles fierce. Tommy Smith needed treatment. Tommy Lawrence needed treatment. Terry Cooper needed treatment. Gary Sprake needed treatment. And Mick Jones needed treatment. But in the madhouse of electric noise that hammered the senses. The players of Leeds United began to find their feet, the players of Leeds United began to find their rhythm. And to defend and to defend. From the very front to the back, from Gray to Giles, Giles to Jones, Jones to Madeley, Madeley to O'Grady, O'Grady to Hunter, Hunter to Charlton, Charlton to Bremner, Bremner to Cooper, Cooper to Reaney and from Reaney to Sprake. In a madhouse of electric noise that hammered the senses. The white cliffs repelled the red waves. The shot from Ian Callaghan and the header from Alun Evans. The white cliffs stood and the red waves broke. In a madhouse of electric noise that hammered the senses. For minute after minute, long minute after long minute. In the seventy-second minute, Ian St John lobbed the ball into the penalty area. The ball found Alun Evans in the penalty area. Evans unmarked. The goal unguarded. The goal at his mercy. Evans shot and Evans missed. And in the madhouse of electric noise that hammered the senses. Hammered and hammered, hammered and hammered. The long minutes became short minutes, the short minutes became dying minutes. In the madhouse of electric noise that hammered the senses. Hammered and hammered. The dying minutes, the last minute. Hammered. The last minute, the last seconds. And hammered. The last seconds, the last second. Hammered. And in that last second, Bill watched the referee put his whistle to his lips. And the referee blew his whistle. And in the madhouse of electric noise that had hammered the senses. Liverpool Football Club had drawn nil–nil with Leeds United. And Leeds United had got their point. Their last point. And Leeds United were the Champions of England for the first time in the history of Leeds United Association Football Club. But the players of Leeds United Association Football Club did not leap into the air. The Anfield air. The players of Leeds United Association Football Club did not jump for joy into the night. The Anfield night. The players of Leeds United Association Football Club stood upon the pitch. The Anfield pitch. Their backs bent in half, their hands upon their thighs. Gasping for air, panting for breath. Until slowly, one by one, man by man, the players of Leeds United Association Football Club realised what they had done, knew what they had achieved. And the players of Leeds United Association Football Club raised their heads. And the players of Leeds United Association Football Club raised their arms. In salute and in victory. And they walked with heads held high, they strode with arms raised high, towards their own supporters, the supporters of Leeds United Association Football Club. In salute and in victory. In victory.

On the touchline, the Anfield touchline. Bill shook the hand of Don Revie. And Bill said, Congratulations, Don. Congratulations. You are a great team, Don. A great team. And you are worthy and deserving champions, Don. Champions of England.

Thank you, said Don Revie. Thank you, Bill. You cannot know what your words mean. What your praise means to me. Thank you for your words, Bill. Thank you for your praise . . .

Bill nodded. And Bill said, Now lead your team, Don. Lead your team to the Kop. So the Spion Kop can applaud you, Don. So the Spion Kop can salute you, too.

Don Revie walked onto the pitch. The Anfield pitch. Don Revie went up to his players. The players of Leeds United. And Don Revie led the players of Leeds United down the pitch. The Anfield pitch. Towards the Kop. The Spion Kop. And there was silence. Sudden silence, momentary silence. And then there was applause. From the Kop. There were cheers. From the Spion Kop. And the Spion Kop hailed the new Champions of England, the Spion Kop saluted Leeds United Association Football Club. In their victory.

In the tunnel, the Anfield tunnel. Bill picked up a crate. A crate of champagne. Bill went into the dressing room. The away dressing room. And Bill put down the crate of champagne on a bench in the away dressing room. The Champions' dressing room. And then Bill walked out of the away dressing room. The Champions' dressing room. And Bill walked into the home dressing room. The silent dressing room. And Bill heard the studs of the Leeds United players coming down the tunnel. The Anfield tunnel. Bill heard the songs of the Leeds United players. The songs of celebration. The champagne corks and the champagne toasts. The toasts to victory. And Bill looked around the dressing room. The losers' dressing room. From player to player. These players who had given everything, these players who had won nothing. And Bill looked at Bob Paisley, Reuben Bennett, Joe Fagan and Ronnie Moran. These men who had given everything, these men who had won nothing. And Bill had no words.

But Emlyn Hughes had words. And Hughes jumped up –

Come on, lads. Come on! Why the long faces? Why the sad frowns? We still finished above Everton. Ha! We still finished second, lads. Ha! We're still the runners-up. Ha! I don't think runners-up is to be sneezed at, lads. Ha! I don't think second place is so bad . . .

Bill stared at Emlyn Hughes. Bill held out his hands towards Hughes. And Bill said, Look at my hands, son. Look at these hands. What do you see in these hands, son? What do you see?

Nothing, said Emlyn Hughes. Nothing, Boss.

Bill nodded. And Bill said, You get nothing for coming second, son. Because if you are second, you *are* nothing. You are nowhere –

First is first. Second is nowhere.

. . .

In the drive, in the car. Bill switched off the headlights. In the night, the last night. Bill switched on the headlights. In the drive, in the car. On and then off, off and then on. In the night, the last night. Bill remembered every run. Every kick. Every pass. Every tackle. Every shot. In the drive, in the car. In the night, the last night. Every run, every kick, every pass, every tackle and every shot of every game. Every single game of the season. The headlights off, the headlights on. Liverpool Football Club had played forty-two League games this season. Liverpool Football Club had lost six, drawn eleven and won twenty-five of those forty-two games. Liverpool Football Club had conceded twenty-four goals and scored sixty-three goals in those forty-two games. And Liverpool Football Club had finished the season with sixty-one points. Sixty-one points, sixty-three goals and forty-two games. In the drive, in the car. In the night, the last night. The headlights on, the headlights off. Every run, every kick, every pass, every tackle and every shot of every game. Every single game of those forty-two games. And in the drive, in the car. In the night, that last night. Bill fought back tears. Forty-two games, sixty-three goals. Bill struggled to breathe. And sixty-one points –

For nothing, for nowhere.


## 31. SMALL STEPS

In the summer of 1969, Bill Shankly did not take a holiday. Bob Paisley did not take a holiday. Joe Fagan did not take a holiday. Reuben Bennett did not take a holiday. And Ronnie Moran did not take a holiday. In the summer of 1969, Bill Shankly worked. Bob Paisley worked. Joe Fagan worked. Reuben Bennett worked. And Ronnie Moran worked. In the boardroom and in the offices, in the darkness and in the shadows. Through the books of names, through the books of notes. The sheets of names, the sheets of dates. The names of players and the dates of games. The reports on every player, the reports on every game. Every first-team player and every first-team game, every reserve-team player and every reserve-team game. They debated every player, they discussed every game. They analysed and they evaluated. In the boardroom and in the offices, in the darkness and in the shadows. In the summer of 1969, there were no days off –

And no complacency. Complacency was born of self-congratulation, complacency was born of self-satisfaction. Arrogance and contempt. There was no complacency. No days off,

no nights off. Every evening. Bill Shankly got in his car. Or in Reuben's car. Or in Geoff's car. Every evening. They drove. Every evening. North, south, east or west. Every evening. They drove and they discussed. The game they would see, the players they would see. Laughing and joking. Every evening. They watched a football game. Every evening. A friendly game or a testimonial game. A reserve-team match or an amateur-team match. And then, every evening. Bill Shankly got back into his car. Or into Reuben's car. Or into Geoff's car. Every evening. They drove back home. Every evening. North, south, east or west. Every evening. They drove and they discussed. The game they had seen, the players they had seen. Laughing and joking. Every evening. Every evening of every day of every week of every month of every year. Every year,

every evening.

. . .

In the summer of 1969, Liverpool Football Club did not go on a pre-season tour. In the summer of 1969, Liverpool Football Club stayed at home, at Anfield. In the summer of 1969, Liverpool Football Club began their pre-season training ten days earlier than usual. Because the 1969–70 season would start ten days earlier than usual. Because of the World Cup, in Mexico, in 1970. Liverpool Football Club would have to start training earlier, Liverpool Football Club would have to start training harder. In the summer of 1969, outside Anfield, in the car park, in his tracksuit and in his sweater. Bill Shankly waited for the players. Bill Shankly greeted the players. Bill Shankly shook their hands. Bill Shankly patted their backs. He asked after their summer holidays, he asked after their families. Bill Shankly laughing, Bill Shankly joking. In the summer of 1969, the players got on the bus. Bob Paisley, Joe Fagan, Reuben Bennett and Ronnie Moran got on the bus. And Bill Shankly got on the bus. Bill Shankly laughing, Bill Shankly joking. In the summer of 1969, they all travelled to Melwood. Some people smiling, some people not. In the summer of 1969, they all got off the bus. Some smiling and some not. In the summer of 1969, the players ran round the training pitch at Melwood. And Bill Shankly ran round the training pitch at Melwood. Bill Shankly laughing, Bill Shankly joking. In the summer of 1969, the players heard the whistle. And the players split into their groups. The players lifted weights. The players skipped. The players jumped. The players did squats. The players did abdominal exercises. The players sprinted. And Bill Shankly heard the whistle. Bill Shankly lifted weights. Bill Shankly skipped. Bill Shankly jumped. Bill Shankly did squats. Bill Shankly did abdominal exercises. Bill Shankly sprinted. Bill Shankly laughing, Bill Shankly joking. In the summer of 1969, the players heard the whistle again. And the players passed the ball. The players dribbled with the ball. The players headed the ball. The players chipped the ball. The players controlled the ball. The players tackled. And Bill Shankly heard the whistle, too. Bill Shankly passed the ball. Bill Shankly dribbled with the ball. Bill Shankly headed the ball. Bill Shankly chipped the ball. Bill Shankly controlled the ball. Bill Shankly tackled. Bill Shankly laughing, Bill Shankly joking. In the summer of 1969, the players heard the whistle again. And the players went between the training boards. The players moving, the ball moving. Playing the ball against one board. Then taking the ball, controlling the ball. Turning with the ball, dribbling with the ball. Up to the other board. In just ten touches. Playing the ball against the other board. Then pulling the ball down, turning again and dribbling again. Back down to the first board. In just ten touches. And Bill Shankly heard the whistle again, too. Bill Shankly went between the training boards. Bill Shankly moving, the ball moving. Bill Shankly playing the ball against one board. Then taking the ball, controlling the ball. Bill Shankly turning with the ball, dribbling with the ball. Up to the other board. In just ten touches. Bill Shankly playing the ball against the other board. Then pulling the ball down, turning again and dribbling again. Back down to the first board. In just ten touches. Bill Shankly laughing, Bill Shankly joking. In the summer of 1969, the players heard the whistle yet again. And the players went inside the sweat box. Ball after ball. Into the box. Every second, another ball. For one minute. Then for two minutes. Then for three minutes. Ball after ball, into the box. And Bill Shankly heard the whistle yet again, too. Bill Shankly went into the sweat box. Ball after ball. Into the box. Every second, another ball. For one minute. Then for two minutes. Then for three minutes. Bill Shankly laughing, Bill Shankly joking. In the summer of 1969, the players heard the whistle. And they played three-a-sides. Three-a-sides then five-a-sides. Five-a-sides then seven-a-sides. Seven-a-sides then eleven-a-sides. And Bill Shankly heard the whistle, too. And Bill Shankly played three-a-sides. Three-a-sides then five-a-sides. Five-a-sides then seven-a-sides. Seven-a-sides then eleven-a-sides. Bill Shankly laughing, Bill Shankly joking. In the summer of 1969, the players ran one last time around the training pitch. And Bill Shankly ran one last time around the training pitch. Bill Shankly laughing, Bill Shankly joking. And then, in the summer of 1969, the players got back on the bus. Bob Paisley, Joe Fagan, Reuben Bennett and Ronnie Moran got back on the bus. And Bill Shankly got back on the bus. Bill Shankly laughing, Bill Shankly joking. In the summer of 1969, they all travelled back to Anfield. More people smiling now, still some people not. In the summer of 1969, they all got off the bus. More smiling now and still some not. In the summer of 1969, the players went into Anfield. And Bill Shankly went into Anfield. Bill Shankly laughing, Bill Shankly joking. In the dressing rooms, the players took off their boots, the players took off their tracksuits. And in the dressing rooms, Bill Shankly took off his boots, Bill Shankly took off his sweater and his tracksuit. Bill Shankly laughing, Bill Shankly joking. The players went into the baths. And Bill Shankly went into the baths. Bill Shankly laughing, Bill Shankly joking. The players washed and changed. And Bill Shankly washed and changed. Bill Shankly laughing, Bill Shankly joking. The players said goodbye. And Bill Shankly said goodbye. Bill Shankly still laughing, Bill Shankly still joking. The players went out to their bigger cars. The players went back to their bigger houses. Some smiling and some not. But Bill Shankly did not go out to his car. His same car. Bill Shankly did not go back to his house. His same house. Bill Shankly not laughing now, Bill Shankly not joking now. Bill Shankly looking, Bill Shankly listening. Always looking, always listening. Looking for complacency, listening for satisfaction. Complacency with the way things were, satisfaction with the way things were. Always learning. Learning who had become complacent with the way things were, learning who had become satisfied with the way things were. Because Bill Shankly was working. Always working. Day after day. Day in and day out. Always

working, always

working.

. . .

On Saturday 9 August, 1969, the first Saturday of the new season, Chelsea Football Club came to Anfield, Liverpool. That afternoon, forty-eight thousand, three hundred and eighty-three folk came, too. Forty-eight thousand, three hundred and eighty-three folk to watch the first game of the new season. In the twenty-sixth minute of the first game of the new season, Chris Lawler scored. In the forty-ninth minute of the first game of the new season, Ian St John scored. In the sixtieth minute of the first game of the new season, Geoff Strong scored. And in the eighty-third minute of the first game of the new season, St John scored again. And in the first game of the new season, Liverpool Football Club beat Chelsea Football Club four–one. At home, at Anfield. Three days afterwards, Manchester City Football Club came to Anfield, Liverpool. That evening, fifty-one thousand, nine hundred and fifty-nine folk came, too. Fifty-one thousand, nine hundred and fifty-nine folk to watch the second game of the new season. In the second minute of the second game of the new season, St John scored. But in the second game of the new season, Tommy Smith scored an own goal. And in the second game of the new season, Bowyer scored for Manchester City. And in the second game of the new season, Liverpool Football Club were losing. At home, at Anfield. But in the eighty-third minute of the second game of the new season, Roger Hunt scored. And in the second game of the new season, Liverpool Football Club were drawing. At home, at Anfield. But in the eighty-eighth minute of the second game of the new season, St John scored again. And in the second game of the new season, Liverpool Football Club beat Manchester City three–two. At home, at Anfield.

On Saturday 16 August, 1969, Liverpool Football Club travelled to White Hart Lane, London, for the third game of the new season. In the sunshine, the shirt-sleeved summer sunshine, the players of Tottenham Hotspur Football Club were tanned, but flabby. In the sunshine, the shirt-sleeved summer sunshine, the players of Liverpool Football Club were pale, but toned. And in the second minute of the third game of the new season, Emlyn Hughes sent Roger Hunt on his way. But Hughes did not stand and watch Hunt on his way. Hughes followed Hunt, giant stride after giant stride. And Hunt shot. But Hunt did not score. The ball rebounded off Jennings. But there was Hughes. And Hughes did score. In the sunshine, the shirt-sleeved summer sunshine. In the thirty-seventh minute of the third game of the new season. Chris Lawler passed to Ian Callaghan. But Lawler did not stand and watch Callaghan. Lawler followed Callaghan. And Callaghan shot. But Callaghan did not score. The ball deflected off Jennings. And there was Lawler. And Lawler scored. And in the sunshine, the shirt-sleeved summer sunshine. In the third game of the new season, Liverpool Football Club beat Tottenham Hotspur two–nil. Away from home, away from Anfield.

Four days afterwards, Liverpool Football Club travelled to Maine Road, Manchester, for the fourth game of the new season. In the forty-fourth minute of the fourth game of the new season, Bobby Graham scored. And in the eightieth minute of the fourth game of the new season, Graham scored again. And in the fourth game of the new season, Liverpool Football Club beat Manchester City two–nil. Away from home, away from Anfield. And that evening, Liverpool Football Club had played four games of the new season and Liverpool Football Club had won all four of their games of this new season. But Liverpool Football Club were only second in the First Division. Wolverhampton Wanderers and Everton Football Club had also won all four of their games of the new season. And Everton Football Club were first in the First Division. On goal average. In the new season, after four games, after four victories, home and away, Liverpool Football Club were only second. Again.

On Saturday 23 August, 1969, Burnley Football Club came to Anfield, Liverpool. That afternoon, fifty-one thousand, one hundred and thirteen folk came, too. In the thirty-sixth minute, Tommy Smith scored a penalty. In the forty-ninth minute, Ian Callaghan crossed the ball. Bobby Graham met the ball. And Graham scored. And Liverpool

Football Club were beating Burnley Football Club two–nil. At home, at Anfield. But then Thomas shot from twenty-five yards out. And Thomas scored. And then Yeats hit a ball into the sky in his own penalty area. And everyone stood and everyone watched. The ball going up, the ball coming down. Everybody standing, everybody watching. Casper head the ball. And Casper score. And now Liverpool Football Club were drawing two-all with Burnley Football Club. At home, at Anfield. And then Dobson glanced home a third goal for Burnley Football Club. And Liverpool Football Club were losing three–two. At home, at Anfield. But in the seventy-seventh minute, Smith scored again. And Liverpool Football Club drew three–three with Burnley Football Club. At home, at Anfield.

Four days afterwards, Liverpool Football Club travelled to Selhurst Park, London. In the thirty-sixth minute, Emlyn Hughes scored. In the seventy-third minute, Roger Hunt scored. And in the eighty-second minute, Peter Thompson scored. And Liverpool Football Club beat Crystal Palace three–one. Away from home, away from Anfield. And that evening, Liverpool Football Club and Everton Football Club both had eleven points. That evening, Everton Football Club were still first in the First Division and Liverpool Football Club still second in the First Division. Again.

On Saturday 30 August, 1969, Liverpool Football Club travelled to Hillsborough, Sheffield. And in the forty-second minute, Chris Lawler scored. But Sheffield Wednesday scored, too. And Liverpool Football Club drew one-all with Sheffield Wednesday. Away from home, away from Anfield. That day, Everton Football Club did not draw. That day, Everton Football Club won. And that evening, Everton Football Club were still first in the First Division. But not on goal average. On points.

Four days afterwards, Liverpool Football Club travelled to Vicarage Road, Watford, to play Watford Football Club in the Second Round of the Football League Cup. In the sixth minute, Slater scored an own goal for Watford Football Club. In the seventy-fifth minute, Ian St John scored for Liverpool Football Club. And Liverpool Football Club beat Watford Football Club of the Second Division two–nil. Away from home, away from Anfield. Three days later, Coventry City came to Anfield, Liverpool. That afternoon, forty-eight thousand, three hundred and thirty-seven folk came, too. Coventry City were fourth in the First Division and Liverpool Football Club were second in the First Division. In the thirty-seventh minute, Ian St John scored. And in the eighty-ninth minute, Geoff Strong scored. And Liverpool Football Club beat Coventry City Football Club two–one. At home, at Anfield. That day, Derby County beat Everton Football Club two–one.

On Tuesday 9 September, 1969, Sunderland Football Club came to Anfield, Liverpool. That evening, forty-six thousand, three hundred and seventy folk came, too. In the twelfth minute, Geoff Strong scored. And in the thirty-fourth minute, Tommy Smith scored. And Liverpool Football Club beat Sunderland Football Club two–nil. At home, at Anfield. That evening, Liverpool Football Club had sixteen points. That evening, Derby County had fourteen points. And Everton Football Club had thirteen points. That evening, Liverpool Football Club were first in the First Division.


## 32. WINTER: A DIRGE

In the bedroom, at their window. Bill stared out through the glass, up beyond the trees. Into the night, into the sky. And up at the moon. Men had designed rockets. Men had built rockets. Men had travelled in rockets. And everybody had stood and everybody had watched. Men land on the moon. Men walk on the moon. Men plant a flag on the moon. Everybody standing, everybody watching. The ball going up, the ball coming down. Just standing, just watching. The flag on the moon, the ball in the goal. In their bedroom, at the window. Bill heard footsteps on the stairs. The bedroom door open. And Ness cough –

There you are, love. What are you doing, standing in the dark? Draw the curtains, love. It's dark now. It's getting late, love.

Bill smiled. And Bill said, I know, love. I know.

Bill knew if you listened carefully. If you listened closely. There was always the sound of chains. Always the sound of knives. And always the sound of spades. At your back, in your shadow. The sound of chains rattling. The sound of knives sharpening. The sound of spades digging. Rattling, sharpening and digging –

And ticking. The clock ticking.

. . .

On the touchline, the touchline at Old Trafford. Bill shook the hand of Wilf McGuinness. And Bill said, Well played, Wilf. Well played. And I wish you all the best for the rest of the season, Wilf.

Thank you, Mr Shankly. And the same to you, sir . . .

Bill nodded. And Bill looked up into the stand, the Main Stand at Old Trafford. And Bill saw Matt. Matt still looking old, Matt still looking drained. Exhausted and not smiling –

Bill not smiling. Liverpool Football Club not first in the First Division now. Liverpool Football Club third in the First Division –

On the bench, the Anfield bench. In the first minute, Bill watched Evans score. In the tenth minute, Lawler score. In the twenty-fourth minute, Smith score. In the thirty-sixth minute, Graham score. In the thirty-eighth minute, Evans score again. In the fifty-sixth minute, Alec Lindsay score. On his debut. In the sixty-seventh minute, Smith score again. In the sixty-ninth minute, Thompson score. In the seventy-sixth minute, Callaghan score. In the eighty-second minute, Graham score again. And on the bench, the Anfield bench. Bill was smiling now. Liverpool Football Club had beaten Dundalk Football Club ten–nil in the first leg of the First Round of the Inter-Cities Fairs Cup –

On the bench, the bench at Maine Road. Bill watched Doyle score for Manchester City. Bill watched Evans equalise. Bill watched Young score for Manchester City. Bill watched Graham equalise. But then Bill watched Bowyer score for Manchester City. And Manchester City had knocked Liverpool Football Club out of the Football League Cup. And Bill was not smiling now –

On the bench, the bench at the Hawthorns. Bill stared out at the players of Liverpool Football Club. But Bill did not see Ron Yeats. Yeats was injured. And Bill did not see Ian St John. St John was injured. Bill saw Larry Lloyd. And Bill saw Phil Boersma. And Bill saw West Bromwich Albion Football Club tear Liverpool Football Club apart. Lawrence save from Suggett. Lawrence save from Hope. Lawrence save from Brown. Lawrence save from Hegan. And Lawrence save from Suggett again. But then the ball fell to Astle. And Lawrence did not save from Astle. And Astle scored. But in the twenty-fifth minute, Thompson passed to Hunt. And Hunt crossed. Graham met the cross from Hunt. And Graham nodded the cross into the goal. But in the second half, from thirty yards out, Hegan shot. And Hegan scored. And Liverpool Football Club were losing two–one. And the long minutes became short minutes. Again. Bill heard the crowd whistling. The short minutes become dying minutes. Again. The crowd whistling, still whistling. But in the ninety-seventh minute, Hughes passed to Hunt on the edge of the penalty area. The crowd whistling, still whistling and whistling. And Hunt shot. And Hunt scored. And with the last kick of the game, Liverpool Football Club drew two-all with West Bromwich Albion. And Bill saw some of the crowd run onto the pitch. Onto the field. And one of the crowd punched the referee in his face. And the police came onto the pitch. And the police escorted the referee from the pitch. From the field,

down the tunnel.

. . .

In Newcastle, in the hotel. In the dining room, in his chair. Bill watched the players eat their steak and chips. Bill watched the players eat their tinned fruit and cream. Tommy Lawrence. Chris Lawler. Geoff Strong. Tommy Smith. Ron Yeats. Emlyn Hughes. Ian Callaghan. Phil Boersma. Bobby Graham. Alun Evans. Peter Thompson. And the Saint. Bill heard the players joking, Bill heard the players laughing. And in the lounge, in his chair, Bill watched the players playing cards. Tommy Lawrence. Chris Lawler. Geoff Strong. Tommy Smith. Ron Yeats. Emlyn Hughes. Ian Callaghan. Phil Boersma. Bobby Graham. Alun Evans. Peter Thompson. And the Saint. Bill heard the players joking. Bill heard the players laughing. And in the lobby, by the lift. Bill heard the players say goodnight. Bill watched the players go upstairs. Tommy Lawrence. Chris Lawler. Geoff Strong. Tommy Smith. Ron Yeats. Emlyn Hughes. Ian Callaghan. Phil Boersma. Bobby Graham. Alun Evans. Peter Thompson. And the Saint. The players still joking, the players still laughing. And in his room, on the bed. Bill threw his book onto the floor. His book of names, his book of notes. And Bill stood up. And in his room, on the carpet. Bill paced and Bill paced. And Bill thought and Bill thought. About the players, all the players. About Tommy Lawrence. About Chris Lawler. About Geoff Strong. About Tommy Smith. About Ron Yeats. About Emlyn Hughes. About Ian Callaghan. About Phil Boersma. About Bobby Graham. About Alun Evans. About

Peter Thompson. And about the Saint. The games he had played and the runs he had made. The tackles he had made and the balls he had won. The passes he had played and the goals he had scored. On the Friday night, the night before the game. In Newcastle, in the hotel. In his room, his tiny hotel room. Bill paced and Bill paced. Bill thought and Bill thought. And Bill worried and Bill worried. He thought about the Saint and he worried about the Saint. About what he would do with the Saint, about what he would say to the Saint. And Bill paced and he paced. And Bill thought and he thought. And Bill worried and he worried. His jacket stuck to his shirt. The sound of the chains. His shirt stuck to his vest. The sound of the knives. His vest stuck to his skin. The sound of the spades. Until night became morning, until Friday became Saturday. The day here,

the game here.

. . .

In the office, at his desk. Bill heard the footsteps coming down the corridor. The angry footsteps. Bill heard the two short knocks upon the door. The angry knocks. And Bill saw the Saint burst into the office. And the finger in his face –

Why didn't you tell me I wasn't playing, asked Ian St John. Why didn't you say something to me? To my face?

You weren't in the dressing room when I read out the team. If you had been in the dressing room when I read out the team, you would have heard. You would have heard then.

But you could have told me on the Friday night, said Ian St John. At the hotel, before the game. You could have told me at breakfast. On Saturday morning, before the game. You could have told me any time before the game. Any time . . .

Yes, I would have told you before the game. I would have told you in the dressing room before the game. If you'd been in the dressing room before the game. But you weren't in the dressing room before the game. I don't know where you were. But you were not there.

I'd just nipped out to give some tickets to some mates. I was only gone a minute. But you'd already decided. You'd already written it on the team sheet. That's how I heard about it. Not from you. From Jackie Milburn. In the bloody lobby. Looking at the team sheet. Hearing it from Jackie fucking Milburn. Not from you . . .

Because you weren't in the dressing room. You would have heard it from me, if you'd been in the dressing room before the game. But you weren't in the dressing room . . .

That's not the bloody point. That's not what I fucking mean. You should have taken me to one side. You should have told me to my face. Just you and me. That's what you should have done . . .

Why? I've never done that with anyone before.

But I've never been dropped before. I've never been left out of the team before. This has never happened to me before. And then to hear it like I did. In the bloody lobby, from a fucking stranger. I thought I deserved something better than that. After all we've been through, how long we've known each other. Doesn't that mean anything to you? Don't I mean anything to you? After all these years? After all these games? Doesn't it mean anything?

Bill shook his head. And Bill said, Those games were for Liverpool Football Club. Those games you played, those things you did. They were all for the club. Not for me . . .

Ian St John fought back tears. Ian St John struggled to breathe. Ian St John swallowed –

I know they were for Liverpool Football Club. But they were also for you. Because you believed in me. That is why I came here. Because of you. Because of your belief in me. That is why I did the things I did. For Liverpool Football Club. Because of you. Yes, I did all those things for Liverpool Football Club. But every one of those things was also for you. To thank you. For your belief in me. And for your faith in me. Those things were all for you. All for you, Boss.

Bill opened his mouth. Bill closed his mouth. Bill looked up at the clock on the wall. Bill looked down at the watch on his arm. And then Bill stood up. And Bill said, It's almost time for training, son. We're going to be late. Come on, son. Let's go . . .

Ian St John did not move –

Saturdays have always been the best days of my life, whispered Ian St John. But last Saturday was the worst day of my life. And these have been the happiest days of my life. Here at Liverpool, here with you. But those days are gone now, aren't they? They are finished now.

Bill looked up at the clock on the wall again. Bill looked down at the watch on his arm again. Bill shook his head. And Bill said, No, son. No. Not yet. But it comes to us all, son. And so you have to be prepared. You have to be ready, son. Because you have to decide how you will deal with it. Will it be with grace and with dignity? Or will it be with anger and with bitterness? But only you can decide that –

Only you can know that, son.

. . .

On the bench, the bench at the Baseball Ground. Bill was not smiling. Bill was worried. Last season, Derby County had been first in the Second Division. And Derby County had been promoted. This season, Derby County were third in the First Division. And everybody was talking about Derby County. Everybody talking about their manager. Bill had admired Brian Clough as a player. Bill had tried to buy Brian Clough as a player. And Bill admired Brian Clough as a manager. Bill admired the things he had achieved with Derby County. The players he had bought, the way they played the game. And on the bench, the bench at the Baseball Ground. Bill knew this would not be an easy game for Liverpool Football Club. But Bill knew there were no easy games for Liverpool Football Club. And Bill was right –

In the thirteenth minute, Hinton came flying down the right. Past Thompson. Past St John. Past Graham. Past Hunt. Past Callaghan. Past Hughes. And Hinton passed to McGovern. And McGovern shot. Past Yeats. Past Smith. Past Strong. Past Lawler. And past Lawrence. Forty-five seconds later, O'Hare sidestepped Yeats. O'Hare flicked the ball to Hector. And Hector scored. But the supporters of Liverpool Football Club inside the Baseball Ground sang, *No surrender! No surrender! No surrender!* But Mackay passed to McFarland. And McFarland passed to Carlin. And Carlin passed to Durban. And Durban passed to McGovern. And McGovern passed to Hector. And Hector passed to Hinton. Again and again and again. And in the second half, McGovern passed to Durban. And Durban passed to Hinton. And Hinton crossed for Hector. And Hector dived and Hector scored. And in the sixty-eighth minute, Hector sidestepped Strong again. And Hector passed to Durban. And Durban passed to O'Hare. And O'Hare back-heeled the ball into the net. But the linesman had raised his flag. And the referee disallowed the goal. But one minute later, Durban passed to Hector. Hector rolled the ball to O'Hare. And O'Hare scored. And Derby County beat Liverpool Football Club four–

nil. It was Liverpool Football Club's worst defeat in six years. And it could have been worse, it should have been worse. It could have been eight–nil, it should have been eight–nil –

On the touchline, the touchline at the Baseball Ground. Bill shook the hand of Brian Clough. And Bill said, Well played. Very well played indeed, son. On this form, you could beat anyone. On this form, you could win the League . . .

Brian Clough smiled. And Brian Clough thanked Bill. And then Brian Clough started talking. Talking and talking. But Bill was not listening. Bill had heard enough. Bill had seen enough.

. . .

In the corridor. The Anfield corridor. Bill opened the dressing-room door. The home dressing-room door. Bill looked around the dressing room. The Liverpool dressing room. From player to player. From Lawrence to Lawler, Lawler to Strong, Strong to Smith, Smith to Yeats, Yeats to Hughes, Hughes to Callaghan, Callaghan to Hunt, Hunt to Graham, Graham to St John and from St John to Thompson. And Bill said, Last week we were outplayed and we were outclassed by Derby County. Last week we were humiliated by Derby County. We have been written off in the press. We've been told we are past it. We've been told we are yesterday's men. Old horses fit only for the knacker's yard. Fit only for the glue factory. People have said we need to make changes. People have said we need new players. Fresh legs and young blood. But I believe every man should have the chance to answer his critics. I believe every man deserves that chance. And so I have not listened to what those people say, to what the critics say. Because I will not believe what those people say, what those critics say. Until you have had the chance to prove them wrong, to make them eat their words. Until I have seen with my own eyes whether or not you can answer your critics. Until I have seen with my own eyes whether or not you can prove them wrong. In front of your own people, in front of the supporters of Liverpool Football Club . . .

Bill walked out of the dressing room. The home dressing room. Bill walked down the corridor. The Anfield corridor. Bill walked down the steps. The Anfield steps. Bill walked down the touchline. The Anfield touchline. Bill sat down in the dug-out. The home dug-out. And Bill watched Liverpool Football Club play Wolverhampton

Wanderers. At home, at Anfield. Bill watched Tommy Lawrence try and try. Bill watched Chris Lawler try and try. Bill watched Geoff Strong try and try. Bill watched Tommy Smith try and try. Bill watched Ron Yeats try and try. Bill watched Emlyn Hughes try and try. Bill watched Ian Callaghan try and try. Bill watched Roger Hunt try and try. Bill watched Bobby Graham try and try. Bill watched Ian St John try and try. Bill watched Peter Thompson try and try. For ninety minutes. Bill watched them try and try.

In the dressing room, the home dressing room. Bill looked around the dressing room. The Liverpool dressing room. From player to player. From Lawrence to Lawler, Lawler to Strong, Strong to Smith, Smith to Yeats, Yeats to Hughes, Hughes to Callaghan, Callaghan to Hunt, Hunt to Graham, Graham to St John and from St John to Thompson. And Bill said, Well played, boys. Well played. I know how hard you all tried, boys. I could see how hard you all tried. And we didn't deserve to draw, boys. We deserved to win today. And if they gave goals for effort. If they gave points for graft. Then we would have won. And we would always win. So well played, boys. Well played. And thank you, boys.

Thank you.

. . .

In his seat, in the stands at the Estádio do Bonfim, in Setúbal, in Portugal, Bill watched Vitória Futebol Clube of Setúbal play Futebol Clube do Porto. And Bill did not like what he saw. Vitória Futebol Clube of Setúbal beat Futebol Clube do Porto five–nil. Three days later, on the bench at the Estádio do Bonfim, Bill watched Liverpool Football Club play Vitória Futebol Clube of Setúbal in the first leg of the Second Round of the Inter-Cities Fairs Cup. And again, Bill did not like what he saw. In the fortieth minute, on a greasy surface, Cardoso shot. The ball hit the crossbar. The ball rebounded to Tomé. And Tomé scored. And in the seventy-ninth minute, on a greasy surface, Liverpool Football Club won their first corner of the game. But that was all they won. On Wednesday 12 November, 1969, on a greasy surface, Liverpool Football Club lost one–nil to Vitória Futebol Clube of Setúbal in the first leg of the Second Round of the Inter-Cities Fairs Cup. Away from home,

away from Anfield. On the bench, the bench at Elland Road. In the mud. In the twentieth minute, Bill watched Strong trip up Bremner in the penalty area. And the referee blew his whistle. The referee awarded a penalty to Leeds United. And Giles scored the penalty. In the mud. In the thirty-first minute, Bill watched Yeats head the ball into the Leeds goalmouth. And the ball stuck in the Leeds goalmouth. In the mud. Sprake bent down to pick up the ball. The ball at his feet. In the mud. The ball between his fingers, the ball through his fingers. In the mud. The ball through his legs and the ball in net. And the supporters of Liverpool Football Club inside Elland Road cheered. And the supporters of Liverpool Football Club inside Elland Road laughed. And the supporters of Liverpool Football Club inside Elland Road sang *Careless Hands*. In the second half, Bill watched the referee blow his whistle again. And the referee awarded a penalty to Leeds United again. In the mud. Giles took the penalty again. But Lawrence saved the penalty. And Liverpool Football Club drew one-all with Leeds United. In the mud. Don Revie marched down the touchline. The Elland Road touchline. Shaking his head, wringing his hands –

By, you were lucky today, said Don Revie. We should have won. And we should have won easily, Bill.

Bill shook his head, too. Bill smiled. And Bill said, And well played to you, too, Don. Well played indeed. But we'll see you again in March, Don. Back at our place –

On a decent pitch,

on some grass. Back at Anfield. Four days later. On the bench. Bill and forty-one thousand, six hundred and thirty-three folk were watching Liverpool Football Club play Vitória Futebol Clube of Setúbal in the second leg of the Second Round of the Inter-Cities Fairs Cup. Everyone thought Vitória Futebol Clube of Setúbal would come to protect what they had. Everyone thought Vitória Futebol Clube of Setúbal would come to defend their one–nil advantage. Everyone thought wrong. Vitória Futebol Clube of Setúbal had not come to defend. Vitória Futebol Clube of Setúbal had come to attack. Attack and attack. And in the twenty-third minute, Lawler looked at the ball and waited for Yeats to go to the ball. But Yeats did not go to the ball. Yeats looked at the ball and waited for Lawler to go to the ball. But Lawler did not go to the ball. Guerreiro went for the ball. And Lawrence went for Guerreiro. And Lawrence brought down Guerreiro in the Liverpool penalty area. And the referee blew his whistle. The referee awarded a penalty to Vitória Futebol Clube of Setúbal. Wagner took the penalty. And Wagner scored the penalty. But now, finally, finally, Liverpool Football Club attacked. Attacked and attacked. And Vital saved from Thompson. And Vital saved from Graham. And Vital saved from Peplow. And in the second half, Bill took off Peplow and brought on Hunt. And Bill took off Graham and brought on Evans. And again, Liverpool Football Club attacked and attacked. But Vitória Futebol Clube of Setúbal broke quickly. Tomé sprinted down the left flank. Tomé crossed. Strong rose to defend the cross. And Strong met the cross. But Strong headed the cross into his own goal. And Liverpool Football Club were losing two–nil on the night and three–nil on aggregate. But still Liverpool Football Club attacked and attacked. And in the sixtieth minute, Hunt shot. And Carriço punched the ball off the line. And the referee blew his whistle. The referee awarded a penalty. And Smith took the penalty. And Smith scored the penalty. And still Liverpool Football Club attacked and attacked. And Vital saved from Callaghan. And Vital saved from Evans. And Vital saved from Hunt. And Vital saved from Strong. And Vital saved from Lawler. But in the eighty-eighth minute, Evans shot and Vital did not save. Evans scored. And still Liverpool Football Club attacked and attacked. And in the ninetieth minute, Hunt turned. And Hunt shot and Hunt scored. His two hundred and eighty-sixth goal for Liverpool Football Club. And Liverpool Football Club beat Vitória Futebol Clube of Setúbal three–two. But Liverpool Football Club would not be in the Third Round of the Inter-Cities Fairs Cup. Liverpool Football Club had drawn the tie three–three on aggregate. And Liverpool Football Club lost the tie on away goals scored. And Liverpool Football Club were out of the Inter-Cities Fairs Cup. Out,

out. Again. On the bench, the Anfield bench. In silence. In the thirtieth minute, Bill watched Robertson score for Arsenal Football Club. And Liverpool Football Club lose one–nil to Arsenal Football Club. At home, at Anfield. In silence. For the first time that season, Liverpool Football Club had been beaten at home,

at Anfield. In silence. In the office, at his desk. Bill stared down at his book. His book of names, his book of notes. At all his books. His many books of names, his many books of notes. And Bill heard the wind. Blowing around the ground. And Bill heard the winter. Howling around the ground. And at the desk, in his chair. Bill opened his diary. His diary of dates, his diary of fixtures. And Bill stared down at the next date. The next fixture. Next week, next Saturday. Liverpool Football Club would travel across the park. And Liverpool Football Club would play Everton Football Club. Everton Football Club had not lost at home, at Goodison, all season. Liverpool Football Club had not won away, away from Anfield, since August. Everton Football Club were first in the First Division. And Liverpool Football Club were third in the First Division. Third in the First Division and out of the Fairs Cup. People said Liverpool Football Club had no chance of beating Everton Football Club. People said Everton Football Club would easily beat Liverpool Football Club. The wind blowing around the ground. *Easy.* The winter howling around the ground. *Easy.* Bill closed his eyes. *Easy! Easy! Easy . . .*

On the bench, the bench at Goodison Park. In the forty-seventh minute, Bill watched Ian Callaghan pull the ball back from the byline. *Easy.* Callaghan passed for Emlyn Hughes. *Easy.* Hughes beat six defenders and the goalkeeper to the ball. *Easy.* Hughes bundled the ball across the line and into the Everton goal. *Easy.* In the fifty-fourth minute, Bill watched Peter Thompson round his man. *Easy.* Thompson crossed. *Easy.* Brown rose to defend the cross, Brown met the cross. But Brown headed the cross into his own goal. *Easy.* And on the bench, the bench at Goodison Park, Bill heard the supporters of Liverpool Football Club inside Goodison Park cheer. And the supporters of Liverpool Football Club inside Goodison Park chant, *Easy! Easy! Easy!* And in the seventy-fourth minute, Bill watched Bobby Graham beat Hurst to the ball. *Easy.* Graham ran from the halfway line towards West. *Easy.* Graham rounded West. *Easy.* Graham tapped the ball into the back of the empty net. And again on the bench, the bench at Goodison Park, Bill heard the supporters of Liverpool Football Club inside Goodison Park cheer. And again the supporters of Liverpool Football Club inside Goodison Park chanted, *Easy! Easy! Easy!* And Liverpool Football Club beat Everton Football Club three–nil. *Easy! Easy! Easy!* Away from home, away from Anfield. *Easy! Easy! Easy!*

*Easy! Easy! Easy! . . .*

On the bench, the Anfield bench. Bill and forty-seven thousand, six hundred and eighty-two folk were watching Liverpool Football Club play Manchester United. Manchester United were still struggling, Wilf McGuinness still struggling. One month ago, Manchester United had been beaten four–nil by Manchester City. *Easy*. One week ago, Manchester United had been beaten two–nil by Chelsea Football Club. *Easy*. Early in the first half, Bill watched Manchester United win a corner. Charlton took the corner. Ronnie Yeats met the corner. And Yeats sliced the corner into his own net. *Easy*. In the twenty-fifth minute, Bill watched Ian Callaghan shoot. Stepney could not hold the shot. Stepney dropped the shot. And Emlyn Hughes equalised. *Easy*. But early in the second half, Bill watched Hughes give away a needless corner with a reckless back pass. *Easy*. Charlton took the corner. Ure met the corner. And Ure scored. *Easy*. And later in the second half, Bill watched Charlton shoot again. And the shot hit the crossbar. The shot fell to Morgan. Morgan unmarked, Morgan free. Free to shoot and free to score. *Easy*. And seven minutes from the end of the second half, Bill watched Charlton shoot again. And Charlton score. *Easy*. And Liverpool Football Club had lost four–one to Manchester United. At Anfield, at home. On Saturday 13 December, 1969. Tomorrow would be the tenth anniversary of the appointment of Bill Shankly as manager of Liverpool Football Club. Ten years, two League Championships and one FA Cup. Ten years and beaten four–one by Manchester United. At home, at Anfield. Ten years and third in the First Division. Ten years and nowhere,

nowhere and nothing. Nothing but the sound of chains rattling, knives sharpening and spades digging. At your back, in your shadow. Rattling, sharpening, digging. And ticking. The clock ticking. No matter what you knew. No matter what you believed. No matter what you did. The clock ticking, always ticking. Binding you, stabbing you and burying you. In the wasteland, in the wilderness. No matter what you knew. No matter what you believed. No matter what you did. There was always, already the wasteland. There was always, already

the wilderness. The wasteland and the wilderness of the clock. The clock ticking, always ticking. But the directors of Liverpool Football Club wanted to hold a dinner for Bill. The directors of Liverpool Football Club wanted to throw a party for Bill. On his anniversary. To make speeches, to give toasts. To pop corks and to fill glasses. For his anniversary. But Bill did not want a dinner. Bill did not want a party. To listen to speeches, to listen to toasts. To corks pop and to glasses clink. Bill only wanted cups –

FA Cups, League Championship cups and European Cups. That was all Bill wanted. Cups. In the wasteland. Another cup, one more cup. In the wilderness. A cup,

a grail. The grail.


## 33. INTO THE DUSTBIN OF HISTORY

On Tuesday 16 December, 1969, Liverpool Football Club sold Roger Hunt to Bolton Wanderers. After four hundred and ninety-two games. After two hundred and eighty-six goals. And ten years. Four days later, Liverpool Football Club should have travelled to Highfield Road, Coventry. But Liverpool Football Club did not travel to Highfield Road, Coventry. The game was postponed. That day, Derby County did travel to Goodison Park, Liverpool. And that day, Everton Football Club beat Derby County one–nil. That evening, Everton Football Club had thirty-nine points. Leeds United had thirty-eight points. And Liverpool Football Club had thirty points. On Christmas Day, 1969, Everton Football Club were first in the First Division.

On Boxing Day, 1969, Liverpool Football Club travelled to Turf Moor, Burnley. In the twenty-sixth minute, Ian Ross scored. In the thirty-ninth minute, Bobby Graham scored. In the forty-fourth minute, Chris Lawler scored. In the fifty-second minute, Peter Thompson scored. And in the sixtieth minute, Ian Callaghan scored. And Liverpool Football Club beat Burnley Football Club five–one. Away from home, away from Anfield. But that day, Everton Football Club also won. And that day, Everton Football Club still had nine more points than Liverpool Football Club.

The next day, Sheffield Wednesday should have come to Anfield, Liverpool. But Sheffield Wednesday did not come to Anfield, Liverpool. The game was postponed. That day, Everton Football Club did travel to Elland Road, Leeds. And that day, Everton Football Club lost two–one to Leeds United. But that evening, Everton Football Club were still first in the First Division. And that evening, Liverpool

Football Club were fourth in the First Division. Still only fourth.

On Saturday 3 January, 1970, Liverpool Football Club should have travelled to Highfield Road, Coventry, to play Coventry City in the Third Round of the FA Cup. But Liverpool Football Club did not travel to Highfield Road, Coventry. The game was postponed. But four days later, Liverpool Football Club did travel to Highfield Road, Coventry, to play Coventry City in the Third Round of the FA Cup. In the twenty-seventh minute, Martin scored for Coventry City Football Club. But three minutes later, Bobby Graham scored for Liverpool Football Club. And then Lawrence saved from Martin. And then Lawrence saved from Mortimer. And Lawrence was outstanding. Lawrence was unbeatable. And Liverpool Football Club drew one-all with Coventry City in the Third Round of the FA Cup –

On Monday 12 January, 1970, Coventry City came to Anfield, Liverpool. That evening, fifty-one thousand, two hundred and sixty-one folk came, too. Fifty-one thousand, two hundred and sixty-one folk to watch Liverpool Football Club play Coventry City in the Third Round replay of the FA Cup. And in the thirty-ninth minute of the Third Round replay of the FA Cup, Ross scored. In the fifty-fourth minute, Thompson scored. In the seventy-second minute, Graham scored. And Liverpool Football Club beat Coventry City three–nil in the Third Round replay of the FA Cup. At home, at Anfield. And Liverpool Football Club were in the Fourth Round of the FA Cup.

On Saturday 24 January, 1970, Wrexham Football Club came to Anfield, Liverpool. That afternoon, fifty-four thousand and ninety-six folk came, too. Fifty-four thousand and ninety-six folk to watch Liverpool Football Club of the First Division play Wrexham Football Club of the Fourth Division in the Fourth Round of the FA Cup. In the twenty-fourth minute, Smith of Wrexham Football Club of the Fourth Division scored. And at half-time in the Fourth Round of the FA Cup, Liverpool Football Club of the First Division were losing one–nil to Wrexham Football Club of the Fourth Division. But in the fifty-first minute, Bobby Graham scored. And in the fifty-ninth minute, Ian St John scored. And in the seventy-third minute, Graham scored again. And Liverpool Football Club of the First Division beat Wrexham Football Club of the Fourth Division three–one in the Fourth Round of the FA Cup. At home, at Anfield. And Liverpool Football

Club were in the Fifth Round of the FA Cup.

On Saturday 7 February, 1970, Leicester City Football Club came to Anfield, Liverpool. That afternoon, fifty-three thousand, seven hundred and eighty-five folk came, too. Fifty-three thousand, seven hundred and eighty-five folk to watch Leicester City play Liverpool Football Club in the Fifth Round of the FA Cup. Last season, Leicester City had reached the final of the FA Cup. But Leicester City had lost the final one–nil to Manchester City. And Leicester City had also been relegated. Leicester City were now in the Second Division. On Saturday 7 February, 1970, Leicester City of the Second Division did not score. And Liverpool Football Club of the First Division did not score. And Liverpool Football Club drew nil–nil with Leicester City in the Fifth Round of the FA Cup –

Four days afterwards, Liverpool Football Club travelled to Filbert Street, Leicester, to play Leicester City in the Fifth Round replay of the FA Cup. This was the seventh meeting and the third replay between Liverpool Football Club and Leicester City in the FA Cup since 1963. In nine hours of cup football, there had been only three goals. But on the last three occasions, the winner had gone on to Wembley, on to the final. After this replay, the winner would face Watford Football Club of the Second Division in the Sixth Round of the FA Cup. People were saying this could be Liverpool Football Club's season. People were saying this could be Liverpool Football Club's chance. For redemption,

for salvation. Their best chance, their only chance. On a frozen pitch, in inches of sand. In the twenty-first minute, Peter Thompson was tackled. Hard. Thompson fell, Thompson hurt. Hard. And on the frozen pitch, in the inches of sand. Thompson did not get back up. And Evans came on for Thompson. And on the frozen pitch, in the inches of sand. Liverpool Football Club were all fingers and thumbs. Error after error, mistake after mistake. On the frozen pitch, in the inches of sand. In the fifty-third minute, Lochhead put Glover through. And Glover shot. But the shot hit the bar. And on the frozen pitch, in the inches of sand. In the sixty-fourth minute, Tommy Smith passed to Bobby Graham. Graham passed to Ian Callaghan. Callaghan crossed for Chris Lawler. Lawler flicked on the cross. And Alun Evans turned the flick past Shilton. On the frozen pitch, in the inches of sand. The ball in the goal, the ball in the net. The Leicester City goal, the Leicester City net. But on the frozen pitch, in the inches of sand. Liverpool Football Club were still all fingers and thumbs. Still error after error, still mistake after mistake. And on the frozen pitch, in the inches of sand. In the eightieth minute, Farrington had only Lawrence to beat. To beat and to score. To score and to equalise. But on the frozen pitch, in the inches of sand. Lawrence dived at the feet of Farrington. And Farrington did not beat Lawrence. He did not score, he did not equalise. Lawrence saved at the feet of Farrington. And on the frozen pitch, in the inches of sand. In the ninetieth minute, Ian St John passed to Graham. Graham passed to Evans. And Evans shot and Evans scored. And on the frozen pitch, in the inches of sand. All fingers and all thumbs. Error after error. Mistake after mistake. Liverpool Football Club beat Leicester City Football Club two–nil in the Fifth Round replay of the FA Cup. Away from home, away from Anfield. And Liverpool Football Club of the First Division would now play Watford Football Club of the Second Division in the Sixth Round of the FA Cup. And inside Filbert Street, the supporters of Liverpool Football Club sang, *Ee-aye-addio, we're going to win the Cup! We're going to win the Cup. Ee-aye-addio, we're going to win the Cup!*

On Saturday 21 February, 1970, Liverpool Football Club came to Vicarage Road, Watford, to play Watford Football Club in the Sixth Round of the FA Cup. That afternoon, thirty-four thousand and forty-seven folk came, too. Thirty-four thousand and forty-seven folk to watch Liverpool Football Club of the First Division play Watford Football Club of the Second Division. Watford Football Club of the bottom of the Second Division. And before the whistle, the first whistle. The supporters of Liverpool Football Club inside Vicarage Road sang *Ee-aye-addio, we're going to win the Cup! We're going to win the Cup! Ee-aye-addio, we're going to win the Cup!* Over and over. The supporters of Liverpool Football Club sang, *Ee-aye-addio, we're going to win the Cup! We're going to win the Cup! Ee-aye-addio, we're going to win the Cup!* Again and again. The supporters of Liverpool Football Club sang, *Ee-aye-addio, we're going to win the Cup! We're going to win the Cup. Ee-aye-addio, we're going to win the Cup!*

But on Saturday 21 February, 1970, the players of Watford

Football Club were quicker off the mark. The players of Watford Football Club were harder in the tackle. They were more assured on the ball, they were more certain in possession. More steady in defence and more penetrative in attack. And Lugg of Watford Football Club moved effortlessly up and down the right wing. Time and time again. Lugg of Watford Football Club effortlessly beat Liverpool player after Liverpool player. Time and time again. Yeats not assured, Yeats not certain. And his uncertainty was contagious. From Liverpool player to Liverpool player. Uncertainty spread. From Yeats to Lawrence, Lawrence to Lawler, Lawler to Wall, Wall to Strong, Strong to Hughes, Hughes to Callaghan, Callaghan to Ross, Ross to Evans, Evans to St John and from St John to Graham. Their every touch uncertain, their every pass uncertain. And in the sixty-third minute of the Sixth Round of the FA Cup, again Lugg effortlessly moved up the right wing. And again Lugg effortlessly beat Liverpool player after Liverpool player. And Lugg effortlessly crossed. And Endean effortlessly rose over Lawler. And Endean effortlessly beat Lawler to the cross. And Endean effortlessly headed the ball past Lawrence into the goal. And into the net. The Liverpool goal, the Liverpool net. But for the next thirty minutes of the Sixth Round of the FA Cup, for the last thirty minutes of the Sixth Round of the FA Cup, the supporters of Liverpool Football Club sang and they sang. They roared and they roared. They screamed and they screamed. And for the next thirty minutes of the Sixth Round of the FA Cup, for the last thirty minutes of the Sixth Round of the FA Cup, the bench of Liverpool Football Club shouted and they shouted. They roared and they roared. They screamed and they screamed. But in the ninetieth minute of the Sixth Round of the FA Cup, the referee looked at his watch. In the ninetieth minute of the Sixth Round of the FA Cup, the referee raised his whistle towards his mouth. In the ninetieth minute of the Sixth Round of the FA Cup, the referee put the whistle to his lips. In the ninetieth minute of the Sixth Round of the FA Cup, the referee breathed in. In the ninetieth minute of the Sixth Round of the FA Cup, the referee breathed out. And in the ninetieth minute of the Sixth Round of the FA Cup, the referee blew his whistle –

The final whistle –

And Watford Football Club had beaten Liverpool Football

Club one–nil in the Sixth Round of the FA Cup. And the players of Watford Football Club jumped into the air. And the supporters of Watford Football Club ran onto the pitch. And the players of Liverpool Football Club fell to their knees. In silence. And the supporters of Liverpool Football Club fell to their knees. In silence. As the players of Watford Football Club sang, *Ee-aye-addio, we're going to win the Cup! We're going to win the Cup! Ee-aye-addio, we're going to win the Cup!* As the supporters of Watford Football Club sang, *Ee-aye-addio, we're going to win the Cup! We're going to win the Cup! Ee-aye-addio, we're going to win the Cup!* As the whole of Watford sang, *Ee-aye-addio, we're going to win the Cup! We're going to win the Cup! Ee-aye-addio, we're going to win the Cup!*

And after that whistle, that final, final whistle. In the dug-out. The dug-out at Vicarage Road. Bill Shankly tried to stand. Bill Shankly tried to get to his feet. His coat stuck to his jacket. His jacket stuck to his shirt. His shirt stuck to his vest. His vest stuck to his skin. And in the dug-out. The dug-out at Vicarage Road. Bill Shankly finally stood up. Bill Shankly finally got to his feet. His coat still stuck to his jacket. His jacket still stuck to his shirt. His shirt still stuck to his vest. His vest still stuck to his skin. Bill Shankly walked down the touchline. The Vicarage Road touchline. Bill Shankly went into the dressing room. The away dressing room. Bill Shankly looked around the dressing room. The Liverpool dressing room. Bill Shankly looked from player to player. From Lawrence to Lawler, Lawler to Wall, Wall to Strong, Strong to Yeats, Yeats to Hughes, Hughes to Callaghan, Callaghan to Ross, Ross to Evans, Evans to St John and from St John to Graham. His coat stuck to his jacket. His jacket stuck to his shirt. His shirt stuck to his vest. His vest stuck to his skin. Bill Shankly looked into their eyes. Bill Shankly looked into their hearts. And Bill Shankly opened his mouth. Bill Shankly tried to speak. But Bill Shankly could not speak. Bill Shankly had no words. In their eyes, in their hearts. They knew and Bill Shankly knew. The old were dying and the new could not be born. His coat stuck to his jacket. His jacket stuck to his shirt. His shirt stuck to his vest. His vest stuck to his skin. Bill Shankly knew there was nothing more to say. There were no more words. No other words. All redemption gone,

all salvation lost.

．．．

One week afterwards, Derby County came to Anfield, Liverpool. That day, forty-three thousand, five hundred and ninety-four folk came, too. But that day, Tommy Lawrence did not come to Anfield, Liverpool. And that day, Ron Yeats did not come to Anfield, Liverpool. And that day, Ian Ross did not come to Anfield, Liverpool. And that day, Ian St John did not come to Anfield, Liverpool. That day, Tommy Smith was no longer injured. Tommy Smith was fit again. So that day, Tommy Smith came to Anfield, Liverpool. And that day, Peter Thompson was no longer injured. Peter Thompson was fit again. So that day, Peter Thompson came to Anfield, Liverpool. And so did Ray Clemence. And so did Doug Livermore. And so did Chris Lawler, Peter Wall, Geoff Strong, Emlyn Hughes, Ian Callaghan, Alun Evans and Bobby Graham. That day, Liverpool Football Club made four changes to the side that lost one–nil to Watford Football Club the week before. But that day, Liverpool Football Club still lost two–nil to Derby County. At home, at Anfield. Liverpool Football Club still lost. And that night, Liverpool Football Club were ninth in the First Division.

Three days later, Liverpool Football Club travelled to Highfield Road, Coventry. But Tommy Lawrence did not travel to Highfield Road, Coventry. And Ian St John did not travel to Highfield Road, Coventry. And that night, Coventry City scored twice. But in the thirty-eighth minute, Emlyn Hughes scored. In the sixty-fifth minute, Alun Evans scored. And in the seventy-second minute, Evans scored again. And that night, Liverpool Football Club beat Coventry City three–two. And that night, Liverpool Football Club were fifth in the First Division. But that night, Liverpool Football Club were still nowhere. Liverpool Football Club still lost.

On Saturday 7 March, 1970, Leeds United Association Football Club came to Anfield, Liverpool. That afternoon, fifty-one thousand, four hundred and thirty-five folk came, too. Fifty-one thousand, four hundred and thirty-five folk to watch fifth play first. But that afternoon, fifth failed to score and first failed to score. And that afternoon, fifth drew nil–nil with first. And that evening, first were still first. And fifth were still fifth.

Four days afterwards, Liverpool Football Club travelled to the Dell, Southampton. But Tommy Lawrence did not travel to the Dell,

Southampton. And Ian St John did not travel to the Dell, Southampton. In the forty-third minute, Alun Evans scored. And Liverpool Football Club beat Southampton Football Club one–nil. Away from home, away from Anfield. Three days later, Liverpool Football Club travelled to Highbury, London. Again, Tommy Lawrence did not travel to Highbury, London. And again, Ian St John did not travel to Highbury, London. In the eighty-third minute, Ron Yeats scored. But that afternoon, Arsenal Football Club scored once. And Arsenal Football Club scored again. And Liverpool Football Club lost two–one to Arsenal Football Club. Away from home, away from Anfield. That afternoon, Chelsea Football Club beat Watford Football Club five–one in the semi-final of the FA Cup. And Leeds United drew nil–nil with Manchester United in the other semi-final of the FA Cup.

Two days later, Sheffield Wednesday came to Anfield, Liverpool. That evening, thirty-one thousand, nine hundred and thirty-one folk came, too. Just thirty-one thousand, nine hundred and thirty-one folk. And not Tommy Lawrence. And not Ian St John. In the fiftieth minute, Chris Lawler scored. In the sixty-third minute, Ron Yeats scored. And in the eighty-eighth minute, Bobby Graham scored. And Liverpool Football Club beat Sheffield Wednesday three–nil. At home, at Anfield. In front of just thirty-one thousand, nine hundred and thirty-one folk.

On Saturday 21 March, 1970, Everton Football Club came to Anfield, Liverpool. This time, fifty-four thousand, four hundred and ninety-six folk came, too. And Ian St John. That morning, Everton Football Club were first in the First Division. Again. That morning, Liverpool Football Club were fifth in the First Division. Still. And that afternoon, Everton Football Club outclassed Liverpool Football Club. *Easy!* That afternoon, Everton Football Club outplayed Liverpool Football Club. *Easy!* Alan Ball ran the Everton midfield, Alan Ball overran the Liverpool midfield. *Easy!* Joe Royle outmuscled the Liverpool defence, Joe Royle outjumped the Liverpool defence. And Joe Royle scored. *Easy!* And Alan Whittle scored. *Easy!* And Everton Football Club beat Liverpool Football Club two–nil. At their home, at Anfield. *Easy! Easy! Easy!* And that evening, Everton Football Club had fifty-seven points. Everton Football Club were first in the First Division. And that evening, Liverpool Football Club had forty-three points. And Liverpool Football Club were nowhere –

*In the wasteland, in the wilderness . . .*

Three days afterwards, Ipswich Town came to Anfield, Liverpool. That evening, twenty-nine thousand, five hundred and forty-eight folk came, too. Just twenty-nine thousand, five hundred and forty-eight folk. And not Tommy Lawrence. And not Ron Yeats. And not Ian St John. In the thirty-second minute, Ian Callaghan scored. And in the forty-third minute, Tommy Smith scored a penalty. And Liverpool Football Club beat Ipswich Town two–nil. At home, at Anfield. In front of twenty-nine thousand, five hundred and forty-eight folk. Just twenty-nine thousand, five hundred and forty-eight folk.

On Saturday 28 March, 1970, Liverpool Football Club travelled to Upton Park, London. Tommy Lawrence did not travel to Upton Park, London. Ron Yeats did not travel to Upton Park, London. And Ian St John did not travel to Upton Park, London. That afternoon, Ray Clemence, Chris Lawler, Roy Evans, Tommy Smith, Larry Lloyd, Emlyn Hughes, Peter Thompson, Doug Livermore, Alun Evans, Ian Callaghan and Bobby Graham travelled to Upton Park, London. That afternoon, Ian Callaghan played in the centre of midfield. That afternoon, Ian Callaghan struggled in the centre of midfield. That afternoon, Alun Evans led the line. That afternoon, Alun Evans struggled to lead the line. And that afternoon, Liverpool Football Club lost one–nil to West Ham United. Away from home, away from Anfield. That afternoon, Everton Football Club beat Chelsea Football Club five–two. And that evening, Everton Football Club were five points clear of Leeds United at the top of the First Division.

Two days later, Liverpool Football Club travelled to Molineux, Wolverhampton. Again, Tommy Lawrence did not travel to Molineux, Wolverhampton. And again, Ian St John did not travel to Molineux, Wolverhampton. But Ron Yeats did travel to Molineux, Wolverhampton. And so did Ray Clemence, Chris Lawler, Tommy Smith, Larry Lloyd, Emlyn Hughes, Ian Callaghan, Doug Livermore, Alun Evans, Bobby Graham and Peter Thompson. And this time, Ian Callaghan played on the right of midfield. And this time, Ian Callaghan did not struggle. And Alun Evans still led the line. And Alun Evans still struggled to lead the line. But in the forty-third minute, Lawler scored. And Liverpool Football Club beat Wolverhampton Wanderers one–nil.

Away from home, away from Anfield. That afternoon, Leeds United lost four–one to Derby County and Everton Football Club beat Stoke City one–nil. And that evening, Everton Football Club needed just one more win, just two more points, to be the Champions of England –

On Wednesday 1 April, 1970, West Bromwich Albion came to Goodison Park, Liverpool. That evening, fifty-eight thousand, five hundred and twenty-three folk came, too. In the nineteenth minute, Harvey shot. And the shot was blocked. But Whittle controlled the rebound. Whittle shot. And Whittle scored. In the sixty-fifth minute, Harvey pounced on a loose ball in midfield. First Harvey went one way, dragging the defenders this way. Then Harvey went the other way, dragging the defenders that way. The defenders left, the defenders standing. Harvey shot. And Harvey scored. And Everton Football Club were the Champions of England. For the seventh time, the Champions of England. And the supporters of Everton Football Club cheered. And the supporters of Everton Football Club sang, *Ever-ton, Ever-ton, Ever-ton.* And the supporters of Everton Football Club ran onto the pitch. The Goodison pitch. And the supporters of Everton Football Club sang *We Shall Not Be Moved.* And the supporters of Everton Football Club watched Alan Ball and the players of Everton Football Club parade the Football League trophy around the pitch. The Goodison pitch. And the supporters of Everton Football Club sang, *We are the Champions, Champions, Champions! We are the Champions, Champions, Champions! We are the Champions,*
*Champions, CHAMPIONS!*

And after the celebrations, after the champagne. Alan Ball said, The average age of this Everton side is twenty-four. Just twenty-four years old! So I can see five great seasons ahead. At least five great seasons ahead of us. This team is certain to go better. We have lots of skill and every player works hard for each other. So with that behind us, how can we fail? Who can catch us –

Who can stop us?


## 34. LOW SPIRITS AND BLUE DEVILS

In the house, in their front room. In his armchair, on the edge of his armchair. Bill stared at the television. Thirteen million, one hundred and forty-five thousand, one hundred and twenty-three folk had voted for the Conservative Party. Twelve million, two hundred and eight thousand, seven hundred and fifty-eight folk had voted for the Labour Party. The Conservative Party had won three hundred and thirty seats in the House of Commons. The Labour Party had won two hundred and eighty-eight seats in the House of Commons. And the Conservative Party had won the 1970 General Election. Edward Heath, the Member of Parliament for Bexley in Kent, who had been born in Broadstairs and who supported Burnley Football Club, would be the Prime Minister of the United Kingdom. Harold Wilson, the Member of Parliament for Huyton in Liverpool, who had been born in Huddersfield and who supported Huddersfield Town Football Club, would no longer be the Prime Minister of the United Kingdom. In his armchair, on the edge of his armchair. Bill tried to stand. Bill tried to get back on his feet. Bill knew you had to stand. You had to get back on your feet. Bill knew if you did not stand. If you did not get back on your feet. Then you were finished. You were dead. And the people who supported you. The people who believed in you. They were finished, too. They were dead, too. And so Bill knew you had to stand. You had to get back on your feet. For the people, for the people. You always had to stand. You always had to get back on your feet. And Bill stood. Bill got back on his feet. And Bill walked over to the television. Bill switched off the television. And Bill walked over to the window. Bill drew back the curtains. In the front window, in the morning light. Bill stared out through the glass, out at the street. The boys in the street, the boys with their ball. Their ball at their feet, their ball in the air. Bill saw the ball in the air, Bill saw the clouds in the sky. The promise of rain, the threat of storms. The drops of rain in the air, the spits of rain on the window, And Bill turned away from the window. Bill walked out of the front room. Bill walked down the hall. Bill went out of the front door. Bill went into the street. And Bill said, Come on, boys. Come on then, lads. Let's have a quick game. One last game,

before it pours.

. . .

In the house, in their front room. Bill did not watch the World Cup on the television. And Bill did not go to television studios. Bill did not sit on panels and talk about the World Cup in television studios. Bill went to work. And Bob Paisley, Reuben Bennett, Joe Fagan and Ronnie Moran went to work, too. Every day. They worked. Every day. They talked. Every day. They analysed. Every day. They discussed. The games Liverpool Football Club had played last season. The players who had played for Liverpool Football Club last season. The first-team players and the reserve-team players. The first team had played forty-two games; they had won twenty, drawn eleven and lost eleven of those forty-two games. They had scored sixty-five goals and they had conceded forty-two goals. They had gained fifty-one points and they had finished fifth in the First Division. The reserve team had played forty-two games, too; they had won twenty-eight, drawn twelve and lost two of those forty-two games. They had scored eighty-nine goals and they had conceded twenty goals. They had gained sixty-eight points and they had finished first in the Central League. Bill, Bob Reuben, Joe and Ronnie analysed every one of those games the first team had played, every one of those games the reserve team had played. Every day. Bill, Bob, Reuben, Joe and Ronnie discussed every player who had played for the first team in those games, every player who had played for the reserve team in those games. Every day. They analysed and they discussed. Who would be stepping down and who would be stepping up. Every day. Analysing and discussing. Every day. Who would be leaving and who would be staying. Every day. Who would be going and who would be coming. Every day. The old players and the new players. Liverpool Football Club had bought Jack Whitham from Sheffield Wednesday for fifty-seven thousand pounds; Liverpool Football Club had bought Steve Heighway from Skelmersdale United. Every day. Who would not be playing and who would be playing. Every day. In the season to come, in the games to come. Every day. Analysing and discussing. Every day. The season to come and the games to come. Every day. Bill, Bob, Reuben, Joe and Ronnie worked. Every day. Until they were prepared,

until they were ready.

. . .

At the stadium, in the office. At his desk, in his chair. Bill stared down at his book. His book of names, his book of notes. The last page of names, the last page of notes. And Bill read aloud the names on the page: Clemence, Lawler, Ross, Smith, Lloyd, Hughes, Callaghan, Evans, Graham, McLaughlin and Thompson. Bill put the book to one side. The book of names, the book of notes. Bill stood up. Bill walked over to the shelves. The shelves of books. The shelves of names and the shelves of notes. Bill took a book from the shelf. Another book of names, another book of notes. The names from last season, the notes from last season. Old names and old notes. Bill turned to the first page of the last season. The first page of names from the first game of last season. And Bill read aloud the names on the page: Lawrence, Lawler, Strong, Smith, Yeats, Hughes, Callaghan, Hunt, Graham, St John and Thompson. Bill closed the book. The book from last season. The book of old names, the book of old notes. Bill put it back on the shelf. The shelf of names, the shelf of notes. Old names and old notes. Bill walked back to his desk. Bill sat back down. At his desk, in his chair. Bill stared back down at the book on his desk. Again. The book of names, the book of notes. New names and new notes. The names for the new season, the notes for this season. The last page of names, the last page of notes. And again. Bill read aloud the names on the page: Clemence, Lawler, Ross, Smith, Lloyd, Hughes, Callaghan, Evans, Graham, McLaughlin and Thompson. Bill swallowed. Bill knew five of the names on the first page of the new season were not the same as five of the names on the first page of last season. Five new names for five old names. At his desk, in his chair. Bill swallowed again. Bill knew Liverpool Football Club had finished fifth in the First Division. Last season, in the old season. Bill knew Liverpool Football Club had finished nowhere. Last season, in the old season. Bill closed the book. The book of names, the book of notes. The book of new names, the book of new notes. At his desk, in his chair. Bill closed his eyes. His old eyes. Bill was sick of finishing nowhere. In the last seasons, in the old seasons. Sick of finishing nowhere, sick of winning nothing –

Sick and bloody tired.

. . .

On the bench, the bench at Turf Moor. Bill watched Liverpool Football Club beat Burnley Football Club two–one. On the bench, the bench at Bloomfield Road. Bill watched Liverpool Football Club draw nil–nil with Blackpool Football Club. On the bench, the Anfield bench.

Bill watched John McLaughlin score his first goal for Liverpool Football Club on his home debut for Liverpool Football Club. John McLaughlin was eighteen years old. And Bill watched Liverpool Football Club beat Huddersfield Town four–nil. On the bench, the Anfield bench. Bill watched Ray Clemence jump to catch a header. Clemence misjudge the header. The header drop over Clemence. And into the net. And Bill watched Liverpool Football Club draw one-all with Crystal Palace Football Club. On the bench, the bench at the Hawthorns. Bill watched Liverpool Football Club draw one-all with West Bromwich Albion. On the bench, the Anfield bench. Bill watched Liverpool Football Club draw one-all with Manchester United. On the bench, the bench at Field Mill. Bill watched Liverpool Football Club draw nil–nil with Mansfield Town of the Third Division in the Second Round of the Football League Cup. On the bench, the bench at St James' Park. Bill watched Liverpool Football Club draw nil–nil with Newcastle United. Another draw,

another bloody draw.

On the bench, the Anfield bench. Bill watched Liverpool Football Club beat Ferencvárosi Torna Club of Budapest, Hungary, one–nil in the first leg of the First Round of the Inter-Cities Fairs Cup. On the bench, the Anfield bench. Bill watched Liverpool Football Club beat Nottingham Forest three–nil. On the bench, the Anfield bench. Bill watched Liverpool Football Club beat Mansfield Town of the Third Division three–two after extra time in the replay of the Second Round of the Football League Cup. And in the dressing room. The Liverpool dressing room. Bill looked from player to player. From Clemence to Lawler, Lawler to Lindsay, Lindsay to Smith, Smith to Lloyd, Lloyd to Hughes, Hughes to Hall, Hall to Evans, Evans to Graham, Graham to McLaughlin and from McLaughlin to Heighway. And Bill smiled. And Bill said, Well played, boys. Well played indeed. And you have learnt a lesson tonight, boys. A few very important lessons. You've learnt to never underestimate any team you play, boys. And you've learnt never to surrender any game you play. You have learnt to always keep trying, boys. To always keep struggling. To never give in and to never give up. That's what I saw out there today, boys. I saw you never give in and never give up. And so I am proud of you, boys. Very, very proud of you. Of the way you learnt those lessons and of the way you played tonight . . .

On the bench, the bench at the Dell. Bill watched Alec Lindsay score. An own goal. And Bill watched Liverpool Football Club lose one–nil to Southampton Football Club. It was Liverpool Football Club's first defeat of the 1970–71 season. On the bench, the bench in the Nep Stadium in Budapest, Hungary. Bill watched Liverpool Football Club beat Ferencvárosi Torna Club of Budapest, Hungary, two–one on aggregate in the First Round of the Inter-Cities Fairs Cup. On the bench, the Anfield bench. Bill watched Liverpool Football Club beat Chelsea Football Club one–nil. On the bench, the bench at the County Ground. Bill watched Trollope sprint thirty yards down the wing. And Trollope crossed the ball. The ball dropped at the feet of Rogers. Rogers moved across the face of the goal. The Liverpool goal. Rogers took Clemence with him across the goal. And Rogers shot. And Rogers scored. Two minutes later, Bill watched Dangerfield pass to Rogers. And again Rogers moved across the face of the goal. The Liverpool goal. Again Rogers took Clemence with him. And again Rogers shot. And again Rogers scored. And on the bench, the bench at the County Ground. Bill watched Liverpool Football Club of the First Division lose two–nil to Swindon Town of the Second Division in the Third Round of the Football League Cup. And in the dressing room. The away dressing room. Bill looked from player to player. From Ray Clemence to Chris Lawler, from Chris to Alec Lindsay, from Alec to Tommy Smith, from Tommy to Larry Lloyd, from Larry to Emlyn Hughes, from Emlyn to Brian Hall, from Brian to Alun Evans, from Alun to Steve Heighway, from Steve to Doug Livermore and from Doug to Jack Whitham. And Bill saw the sadness. The wounds of sadness. And Bill saw the hurt. The wounds of hurt. Bill saw the wounds. And Bill felt the fear. Their wounds and their fear. And Bill smiled. And Bill said, There will always be times when we get beaten, boys. There will always be times when we lose. But the important thing is what we take away from that beating, what we learn when we lose, boys. Because we'll always learn more from a defeat than a victory. Remember that, boys. Remember that. And learn it, boys. And I'll see you all tomorrow. First thing tomorrow, boys –

Bright and early, bright and early.

On the bench, the bench at White Hart Lane. Bill watched

Liverpool Football Club lose one–nil to Tottenham Hotspur. On the bench, the Anfield bench. Bill watched Liverpool Football Club beat Burnley Football Club two–nil. On the bench, the Anfield bench. Bill watched Liverpool Football Club beat Fotbal Club Dinamo Bucureşti of Romania three–nil in the first leg of the Second Round of the Inter-Cities Fairs Cup. On the bench, the bench at Portman Road. Bill watched Liverpool Football Club lose one–nil to Ipswich Town. On the bench, the Anfield bench. Bill watched Liverpool Football Club beat Wolverhampton Wanderers two–nil. On the bench, the bench in the Twenty-third of August Stadium in Bucharest, Romania. Bill watched Liverpool Football Club beat Fotbal Club Dinamo Bucureşti of Romania four–one on aggregate in the Second Round of the Inter-Cities Fairs Cup. On the bench, the bench at the Baseball Ground, Bill watched Liverpool Football Club draw nil–nil with Derby County. Again. Another draw. Again. Draw

after draw after
fucking
draw.

. . .

At the stadium, in the office. The glue on the desk, the scissors in his hands. Bill stared down at the League table. Down and down the League table. That evening, Liverpool Football Club had played fifteen League games in the 1970–71 season. Liverpool Football Club had won six, drawn six and lost three of those fifteen games. They had scored seventeen goals and they had conceded seven goals. That evening, Liverpool Football Club had eighteen points. And that evening, Liverpool Football Club were eighth in the First Division. Not first, not second, not third,

not even fifth –
Eighth.

At the stadium, in the office. At the desk, in the chair. Bill knew it was not acceptable. Bill knew it was not good enough. Not for Liverpool Football Club. Not for the supporters of Liverpool Football Club. But Bill knew what the problem was. And Bill knew what had to be done. At the desk, in the chair. Bill picked up the telephone. And Bill phoned Huddersfield Town. Bill told Huddersfield Town he wanted to buy Frank Worthington. Huddersfield Town agreed to sell

Frank Worthington to Liverpool Football Club. Frank Worthington came to Anfield. Frank Worthington had a medical at Anfield. Frank Worthington failed the medical at Anfield. Frank Worthington went back to Huddersfield Town. At the stadium, in the office. At the desk, in the chair. Bill picked up the telephone again. Bill phoned Cardiff City. Bill told Cardiff City he wanted to buy John Toshack. Cardiff City agreed to sell John Toshack to Liverpool Football Club. John Toshack came to Anfield. John Toshack had a medical at Anfield. John Toshack passed the medical at Anfield. Liverpool Football Club paid Cardiff City one hundred and ten thousand pounds for John Toshack. It was a club record. And at his desk,

in his chair. Bill smiled.

. . .

On the bench, the Anfield bench. Bill and fifty-three thousand, seven hundred and seventy-seven Merseyside folk were watching Liverpool Football Club play Everton Football Club. Everton Football Club were eleventh in the First Division. But Everton Football Club were still the Champions of England. In the first half, the pace was relentless, the challenges unflinching, the game breathless and the game raw. In the second half, Morrissey tackled Tommy Smith. Morrissey won the tackle and Morrissey won the ball. Morrissey passed to Whittle. And Whittle lobbed the ball over the head of Clemence. Over his head, into the net. The Liverpool net, the Liverpool goal. Minutes later, Ball passed to Morrissey. Morrissey passed to Ball. Ball crossed. Larry Lloyd lost the cross. Royle found the cross. And Royle headed the cross into the net. The Liverpool net, the Liverpool goal. And Liverpool Football Club were losing two–nil to Everton Football Club. At home, at Anfield. But in the sixty-ninth minute, Steve Heighway slipped past Hurst on the left. Heighway cut inside from the left. And Heighway shot through four defenders into the net. The Everton net, the Everton goal. And five minutes later, again Heighway came down the left. Heighway crossed from the left. John Toshack met the cross from the left. Toshack found the cross. And Toshack headed the cross into the net. The Everton net, the Everton goal. His first goal for Liverpool Football Club. And Anfield erupted. With noise. And Anfield exploded. With sound. Deafening noise and thunderous sound. And in the eighty-fourth minute, Toshack

328

nodded on a cross to Chris Lawler. And Lawler turned. And Lawler shot. And Lawler scored. In a maelstrom of noise, in a riot of sound. Liverpool noise and Liverpool sound. Liverpool Football Club beat Everton Football Club three–two. At home, at Anfield. In the red noise, in the red sound. LI-VER-POOL, LI-VER-POOL –

LI-VER-POOL!

. . .

Before the house, on their step. In the night and in the silence. Bill unlocked the front door. In the night and in the silence. Bill opened the door. In the night and in the silence. Bill stepped into the house. In the dark and in the silence. Bill walked down the hallway to the kitchen. In the dark and in the silence. Bill switched on the kitchen light. In the kitchen, at the table. Bill sat down. In the silence. Bill closed his eyes. In the kitchen, at the table. In his ears and in his mind. Bill heard the crowd. The Anfield crowd. *LI-VER-POOL*. In the kitchen, at the table. In his ears and in his mind. Bill heard the Kop. The Spion Kop. *LI-VER-POOL*. In the kitchen, at the table. In his ears and in his mind. Bill heard the voices of the Kop, the dreams of the Spion Kop. *LI-VER-POOL*. In the kitchen, at the table. Bill heard Ness cough upstairs. In their bed, in her sleep. In the kitchen, at the table. Bill opened his eyes. And Bill heard Ness cough again. And the clock upon the wall ticking. Ticking and ticking. In the kitchen, at the table. The watch upon his arm ticking. Ticking and ticking. Always ticking, already ticking. And in the kitchen, at the table. Bill put his fingers in his ears. In the kitchen, at the table. His fingers in his ears.

In the night and in the silence,

his fingers in his ears. Bill knew you had to be patient. Even if by nature you were impatient. Impatient for success, impatient for victory. Impatient to give the people success, impatient to give the people victory. Even if others around you were telling you what had to be done. Even if others around you were telling you what needed to be done. Bill knew you still had to be patient in your methods. You still had to be patient in your ways. You had to be a patient, impatient man.

A very patient, impatient man.

## 35. IN THE LEAGUE OF STRUGGLE

On Saturday 28 November, 1970, Liverpool Football Club travelled to Highbury, London. But Ian Callaghan did not travel to Highbury, London. Ian Callaghan was injured. And Peter Thompson did not travel to Highbury, London. Peter Thompson was injured. And Alun Evans did not travel to Highbury, London. Alun Evans was injured. And Bobby Graham did not travel did to Highbury, London. Bobby Graham was injured. On Saturday 28 November, 1970, Arsenal Football Club were second in the First Division. And Liverpool Football Club were sixth in the First Division. And on Saturday 28 November, 1970, Liverpool Football Club struggled against Arsenal Football Club. Clemence struggled, Lawler struggled, Lindsay struggled, Smith struggled, Lloyd struggled, Hughes struggled, Hall struggled, Toshack struggled, Heighway struggled, McLaughlin struggled and Ross struggled. And in the sixty-sixth minute, Graham of Arsenal Football Club volleyed past Clemence. Into the net, into the goal. And minutes later, Radford of Arsenal Football Club went up for a ball. And Radford found the ball. And the ball found the net. And the goal. And Liverpool Football Club lost two–nil to Arsenal Football Club. Away from home, away from Anfield. Bill Shankly walked down the touchline. The Highbury touchline. And Bill Shankly shook the hand of Bertie Mee, the manager of Arsenal Football Club –

Well played, Bertram. Very well played indeed. I thought we might have got a draw out of you, Bertram. But oh no. Not today . . .

Thank you, William, said Bertie Mee. Thank you very much. But you gave us a game and a half, William. You have some promise and you have some talent. In those young lads you have coming through, William. Some real promise and some real talent . . .

Thank you, Bertram. Thank you very much. And you are not wrong, Bertram. You are not wrong. And they are improving all the time. Because they are learning all the time. Every game they play. They are getting better. Better and better. And so mark my words. You mark my words, Bertram. You have not seen the best of these boys yet. And you've not heard the last of them. Not yet. Not by a long chalk, Bertram. Not by a very long chalk . . .

One week afterwards, Leeds United came to Anfield, Liverpool.

That day, fifty-one thousand, three hundred and fifty-seven folk came, too. Leeds United were first in the First Division. And Liverpool Football Club were seventh in the First Division. And Liverpool Football Club struggled against Leeds United. Clemence struggled, Lawler struggled, Lindsay struggled, Smith struggled, Lloyd struggled, Hughes struggled, Hall struggled, McLaughlin struggled, Heighway struggled, Toshack struggled and Thompson struggled. And in the fiftieth minute, Cooper belted down the wing. Cooper crossed. Madeley met the cross. And Madeley scored. But the supporters of Liverpool Football Club did not surrender. They kept cheering and they kept singing. And so the players of Liverpool Football Club did not surrender. They kept struggling and they kept trying. Harder. Clemence struggled and Clemence tried. Harder. Lawler struggled and Lawler tried. Harder. Lindsay struggled and Lindsay tried. Harder. Smith struggled and Smith tried. Harder. Lloyd struggled and Lloyd tried. Harder. Hughes struggled and Hughes tried. Harder. Hall struggled and Hall tried. Harder. McLaughlin struggled and McLaughlin tried. Harder. Heighway struggled and Heighway tried. Harder. Toshack struggled and Toshack tried. Harder. And Thompson struggled and Thompson tried. Harder and harder. And Liverpool Football Club won a free kick. Tommy Smith took the free kick. Smith floated the free kick towards the far post. The Leeds far post. And there was John Toshack. In the air, the Anfield air. At the far post. To meet the free kick. To head the free kick. Into the net and into the goal. And the supporters of Liverpool Football Club cheered. The supporters of Liverpool Football Club sang. And the supporters of Liverpool Football Club roared. Roared for more. More and more. And Liverpool Football Club attacked and attacked. Harder and harder. For the next thirty minutes. The supporters of Liverpool Football Club roared and the players of Liverpool Football Club attacked. More and more, harder and harder. But Leeds United defended. For the last thirty-five minutes. They defended and they defended. And Liverpool Football Club drew one-all with Leeds United. At home, at Anfield. Bill Shankly walked down the touchline. The Anfield touchline. Bill Shankly shook the hand of Don Revie. And Bill Shankly smiled –

Well defended, Don. Very well defended. I thought we were going to beat you, Don. I really did. I thought we would win . . .

Not a chance, Bill. Not a chance. You were lucky today, Bill. Very lucky. We should have beaten you, Bill. We should have won.

Well, I don't know what game you were watching, Don. I really don't. But my advice to you, Don. My advice if you want to win a game of football. Would be to attack, Don. And not simply to defend.

Three days later, in a land of darkness, in a land of power cuts, Liverpool Football Club travelled to Easter Road, Edinburgh, to play Hibernian Football Club in the first leg of the Third Round of the Inter-Cities Fairs Cup. And in a land of darkness, in a land of power cuts, Liverpool Football Club attacked and attacked. Away from home, away from Anfield. And in a land of darkness, in a land of power cuts. In the seventy-fifth minute, John Toshack scored. And Liverpool Football Club beat Hibernian Football Club one–nil in the first leg of the Third Round of the Inter-Cities Fairs Cup. Away from home, away from Anfield. In a land of darkness, in a land of power cuts.

On Saturday 12 December, 1970, in a land still in darkness, in a land still of power cuts, Liverpool Football Club travelled to Upton Park, London. And because of the darkness, because of the power cuts, the game between Liverpool Football Club and West Ham United kicked off thirty minutes early, at half past two. Because of the darkness, because of the power cuts. But in the darkness, among the power cuts, in the twenty-seventh minute, Jack Whitham scored for Liverpool Football Club. His first goal for Liverpool Football Club. And in the darkness, among the power cuts, in the forty-third minute, Phil Boersma scored for Liverpool Football Club. And in the darkness, among the power cuts, Liverpool Football Club beat West Ham United two–one. Away from home, away from Anfield. One week later, Liverpool Football Club travelled to Leeds Road, Huddersfield. But Liverpool Football Club did not score. And Huddersfield Town did not score. And Liverpool Football Club drew nil–nil with Huddersfield Town. Away from home, away from Anfield. Bill Shankly walked down the touchline. The Leeds Road touchline. And Bill Shankly shook the hand of Ian Greaves, the manager of Huddersfield Town –

Well played, Ian. Well played. And I wish you all the best, Ian. All the very best for the rest of the season. I know you have a battle on your hands, Ian. But I hope it is a battle you win. I really do, Ian. I really do. Because I've always said Huddersfield Town belong in the

First Division, Ian. In the First Division. And I admire the job you have done, Ian. The success you have brought to Huddersfield Town.

Ian Greaves smiled. And Ian Greaves said, Thank you, Bill. Thank you very much. It means a lot to us. It really does . . .

Three days afterwards, Hibernian Football Club came to Anfield, Liverpool. That night, thirty-seven thousand, eight hundred and fifteen folk came, too. Thirty-seven thousand, eight hundred and fifteen folk to watch Liverpool Football Club play Hibernian Football Club in the second leg of the Third Round of the Inter-Cities Fairs Cup. In the twenty-third minute, Emlyn Hughes sent Steve Heighway through the middle. Heighway racing, Heighway accelerating. Leaving Hibernian standing, leaving Hibernian watching. And Heighway shot. And Heighway scored. And in the fiftieth minute, Phil Boersma crossed the ball from the right. Hibernian standing, Hibernian watching. The cross drop over the Hibernian keeper, the cross drop into the Hibernian net. And Liverpool Football Club beat Hibernian Football Club three–nil on aggregate in the Third Round of the Inter-Cities Fairs Cup.

Four days later, on Boxing Day, 1970, in blizzards and in ice, Stoke City came to Anfield, Liverpool. That afternoon, in the blizzards and in the ice, forty-seven thousand, one hundred and three folk came, too. But in the blizzards and in the ice, Liverpool Football Club did not score. And Stoke City did not score. And in the blizzards and in the ice, Liverpool Football Club drew nil–nil with Stoke City. At home, at Anfield. It was Liverpool Football Club's tenth draw of the season, their sixth nil–nil draw of the season. And that evening, in the blizzards and in the ice, Liverpool Football Club had twenty-six points. And Liverpool Football Club were seventh in the First Division. In the blizzards and in the ice, Liverpool Football Club were still lost, Liverpool Football Club still missing –

Still nowhere.

On Saturday 2 January, 1971, Aldershot Football Club of the Fourth Division came to Anfield, Liverpool. That afternoon, forty-five thousand and five hundred folk came, too. Forty-five thousand and five hundred folk to watch Liverpool Football Club play Aldershot Football Club of the Fourth Division in the Third Round of the FA Cup. At home, at Anfield. Bill Shankly walked into the dressing room.

The home dressing room. Bill Shankly looked around the dressing room. The Liverpool dressing room. From Clemence to Lawler, Lawler to Boersma, Boersma to Smith, Smith to Lloyd, Lloyd to Hughes, Hughes to Hall, Hall to McLaughlin, McLaughlin to Heighway, Heighway to Toshack and from Toshack to Callaghan. And Bill Shankly took a piece of paper from his coat pocket. And Bill Shankly read out the names on the piece of paper –

Dixon, Walden, Walker, Joslyn, Dean, Giles, Walton, Brown, Howarth, Melia and Brodie. That is the Aldershot team, boys. That is who you are playing today. Now you'll all recognise one of those names, boys. The name of Jimmy Melia. And you all know Jimmy played two hundred and eighty-six times for Liverpool Football Club and scored seventy-nine goals for Liverpool Football Club. Two hundred and eighty-six times, boys. And seventy-nine goals. And so Jimmy knows everything there is to know about Liverpool Football Club, boys. But today Jimmy is the captain of Aldershot Football Club. And Jimmy will have told his teammates all there is to know about Liverpool Football Club. He will have told them about you and he will have told them about the crowd. About what they can expect when they play Liverpool Football Club, when they come to Anfield. And he will be settling their nerves, telling them they have nothing to lose. That this is the biggest game of their lives, the greatest day of their careers. Telling them to go out there and enjoy the game, telling them to go out there and savour the day. But we know very little about the other players of Aldershot Football Club. About Dixon, Walden, Walker, Joslyn, Dean, Giles, Walton, Brown, Howarth and Brodie. All we know is that they are in the Fourth Division. But that means nothing today, boys. Because this is not the League. This is the Cup, boys. But the expectation is still on us, boys. The pressure is on us. But I tell you this, boys. I tell you this: if we treat those players with the same respect we would treat the players of Manchester United. The players of Leeds United. And if we play like we would play against Manchester United. Against Leeds United. Then I know we will win. If we struggle and if we try. We will win, boys. We will win. Because we play for Liverpool Football Club. Because we are Liverpool Football Club. And this is Anfield. And we treat every player who comes to Anfield with respect. Every team that comes to Anfield with respect. Because we are not complacent, boys. But we are not afraid either. And that is how we win, boys. With respect. And with graft. And with skill, boys. That is how we win . . .

On Saturday 2 January, 1971, in the Third Round of the FA Cup, in the twenty-eighth minute, John McLaughlin scored. And Liverpool Football Club beat Aldershot Football Club of the Fourth Division one–nil in the Third Round of the FA Cup. At home, at Anfield. And the players of Liverpool Football Club shook hands with the players of Aldershot Football Club. And the supporters of Liverpool Football Club applauded the players of Aldershot Football Club. And then the supporters of Liverpool Football Club sang, *Ee-aye-addio, we're going to win the Cup. We're going to win the Cup. Ee-aye-addio, we're going to win the Cup . . .*

That same day, that same Saturday. Sixty-six men and boys had woken up. In their beds. Those sixty-six men and boys had eaten their breakfasts and their lunches with their families. In their kitchens. Those sixty-six men and boys had joked and talked with their families. In their homes. Those sixty-six men and boys had said goodbye to their families. See you later. In their halls. Those sixty-six men and boys had walked out of their doors, walked out of their houses and caught a bus, caught a train. In the mist. Those sixty-six men and boys had gone to see a football match between Rangers and Celtic at Ibrox Stadium, in Glasgow, in Scotland. In the mist. The sixty-six men and boys had paid at the turnstiles to Ibrox Stadium. In the mist. The sixty-six men and boys had stood and watched the football match between Rangers and Celtic. In the mist. The sixty-six men and boys had seen Celtic score, had seen Rangers equalise, and had heard the final whistle. In the mist. The sixty-six men and boys had made their way to the top of the terracing, made their way to stairway thirteen. In the mist. The sixty-six men and boys felt the crowd getting tighter and tighter at the top of stairway thirteen. In the mist. The sixty-six men and boys felt the weight of the people behind them. In the mist. The sixty-six men and boys felt themselves being carried over the top of the stairs. In the mist. The sixty-six men and boys felt their feet begin to leave the ground. In the mist, on the stairs. The sixty-six men and boys began to fall forward. In the mist, on the stairs. The sixty-six men and boys felt the crowd stop moving but the pressure increase. In the mist, on the stairs. And increase. In the mist, on the stairs. And increase. In the mist, on the stairs. The sixty-six men and boys heard the cries and the screams around them. In the mist, on the stairs. The sixty-six men and boys heard the cries and the screams stop. In the mist, on the stairs. The sixty-six men and boys heard the silence, only the silence. In the mist, on the stairs. The sixty-six men and boys felt the breath begin to leave their bodies. In the mist, on the stairs. The sixty-six men and boys felt the life being squeezed out of them. In the mist, on the stairs. The sixty-six men and boys felt the life leave them. In the mist, on the stairs. The sixty-six dead men, boys and one young woman were lifted from the stairway. In the mist. The sixty-six dead men, boys and one young woman were carried down the terracing. In the mist. The sixty-six dead men, boys and one young woman were laid on the edge of the pitch. In a row. In the mist. The black-and-white mist. The sixty-six dead men, boys and one young woman who had gone to see a game of football on Saturday 2 January, 1971. In the mist. The black-and-white mist. In a row. In the mist. The black-and-white mist. The sixty-six dead men, boys and one young woman who had been crushed and asphyxiated under the weight of thousands of other bodies in stairway thirteen at Ibrox Stadium, in Glasgow, in Scotland. In the mist. The black-and-white mist. In the evening, that Saturday evening. In their house, in their front room. Bill Shankly tried to get to his feet. Bill Shankly tried to stand. To walk to the television, to turn off the television. The pictures. The black-and-white pictures. His jumper stuck to his shirt. His shirt stuck to his vest. His vest stuck to his skin. Bill Shankly could not get to his feet. Bill Shankly could not stand. And Bill Shankly turned to his wife. Bill Shankly tried to speak. To find the words. The words for his wife. The words for Jock. The words for Willie Waddell, the manager of the Rangers Football Club. The words for the people of Glasgow. The people of Scotland. But Bill Shankly could not speak. Bill Shankly could not find the words. That evening, that Saturday evening. In their house, in their front room. There were no words. There were only pictures. Black-and-white pictures. Pictures and silence,

silence and tears.

. . .

On Saturday 9 January, 1971, Blackpool Football Club came to

Anfield, Liverpool. That day, forty-two thousand, nine hundred and thirty-nine folk came, too. In the thirty-eighth minute, Steve Heighway scored. But Blackpool Football Club scored, too. And Blackpool Football Club scored again. And in the eighty-second minute Blackpool scored again. An own goal. And Liverpool Football Club drew two-all with Blackpool Football Club. At home, at Anfield. Another draw. Three days afterwards, Manchester City came to Anfield, Liverpool. That night, forty-five thousand, nine hundred and eighty-five folk came, too. But Liverpool Football Club did not score. And Manchester City did not score. And Liverpool Football Club drew nil–nil with Manchester City. At home, at Anfield. Another draw. Another goalless draw. Four days later, Liverpool Football Club travelled to Selhurst Park, London. And again Liverpool Football Club did not score. But Crystal Palace did score. And Liverpool Football Club lost one–nil to Crystal Palace. Away from home,

away from Anfield.

On Saturday 23 January, 1971, Swansea City came to Anfield, Liverpool. That afternoon, forty-seven thousand, two hundred and twenty-nine folk came to Anfield, too. Forty-seven thousand, two hundred and twenty-nine folk to watch Liverpool Football Club play Swansea City of the Third Division in the Fourth Round of the FA Cup. And that afternoon, in the first half of the Fourth Round tie of the FA Cup, Liverpool Football Club did not score. But in the fifty-third minute, John Toshack scored. And in the seventy-sixth minute, Ian St John came on for Ian Callaghan. And in the eighty-fifth minute, Ian St John scored. His one hundred and eighteenth goal for Liverpool Football Club in his four hundred and twenty-fifth appearance for Liverpool Football Club. And in the eighty-seventh minute, Chris Lawler scored. And Liverpool Football Club beat Swansea City of the Third Division three–nil in the Fourth Round of the FA Cup. At home, at Anfield. The supporters of Liverpool Football Club applauded the players of Swansea City. And then the supporters of Liverpool Football Club sang, *Ee-aye-addio, we're going to win the Cup —*

*We're going to win the Cup. Ee-aye-addio,*
*we're going to win the Cup . . .*

. . .

On the Monday morning. The Monday morning after the game,

the Monday morning before the training. Ian St John knocked on the door to the office of Bill Shankly. Ian St John opened the door to the office. And Ian St John said, Bob said you wanted to see me, Boss?

Yes. I had a call from George Eastham last week.

George Eastham? How is George?

George sounds very well, said Bill Shankly. He is out in South Africa now. George is in Cape Town. He's managing a side out there called Cape Town Hellenic . . .

That's nice for George. That's nice for him. And I hope he's having a nice time out there. But what's that got to do with me, Boss?

George wanted to know if I would let him speak to you.

Speak to me? Speak to me about what, Boss?

Speak to you about you going out there.

Out where?

Out to South Africa, said Bill Shankly. Out to Cape Town.

Ian St John looked across the desk at Bill Shankly. Ian St John stared at Bill Shankly. And Ian St John said nothing.

George is offering you a hundred quid a week, said Bill Shankly. The same money as you are on here. But George also wants you to be player–coach. And I know you've been to Lilleshall and got your whatever-it-is-they-call-it these days . . .

My FA coaching certificate.

Yes, said Bill Shankly. That thing. And so I thought you might be interested. I thought you might want to have a chat with George. To listen to what he has to say . . .

Ian St John stared at Bill Shankly. And Ian St John smiled.

Bill Shankly picked up a scrap of paper off his desk. And Bill Shankly handed the scrap of paper to Ian St John –

That's his number. Give him a call.

Ian St John took the scrap of paper from Bill Shankly's hand. Ian St John looked down at the telephone number on the scrap of paper. Then Ian St John looked back up at Bill. And Ian St John said, Do you know when I realised I was finished here? It was not that day at Newcastle when you dropped me. It was not that day. And it was not the Monday after, when I came to see you here in this office. Not that day either. It was when I went to the snooker room to get my Christmas present from the club. The turkey you give us every year as

338

a thank you. And I went to the table I usually go to. And I picked up a turkey. A big one. A good one. Like I usually do. Like I've always done. And that bloke Bill Barlow. Your assistant club secretary or whatever-it-is-you-call-him these days. That bastard said, The birds on this table are for first-team players. Your bird is over there. On the table for reserve-team players. And I turned around and I looked at the turkeys over there. The little ones. The shit ones. And that was when I realised I was finished here. After I had played four hundred and twenty-four times for Liverpool Football Club. After I had scored one hundred and seventeen goals for Liverpool Football Club. That was when I knew. When your little bloody lap dog gave me a tiny fucking budgie for my Christmas turkey. That was when I knew I was finished at this club. But I still played for you on Saturday. And I still scored for you on Saturday. Didn't I, Boss? For you. For you, Boss . . .

It comes to us all, said Bill Shankly. It happens to us all, son.

Yes, I know it does. I'm not stupid. But it didn't have to come like that. It didn't have to happen like this. Not like this.

. . .

On Saturday 30 January, 1971, Arsenal Football Club came to Anfield, Liverpool. That afternoon, forty-three thousand, eight hundred and forty-seven folk came, too. Arsenal Football Club were second in the First Division. And Liverpool Football Club were eighth in the First Division. But that afternoon, Liverpool Football Club did not struggle against Arsenal Football Club. Clemence did not struggle, Lawler did not struggle, Yeats did not struggle, Smith did not struggle, Lloyd did not struggle, Hughes did not struggle, Boersma did not struggle, McLaughlin did not struggle, Heighway did not struggle, Toshack did not struggle and Hall did not struggle. And in the fourth minute, Ron Yeats passed to Steve Heighway. Heighway raced down the wing, Heighway accelerated down the wing. And Heighway crossed. Brian Hall met the cross, Hall headed the cross. Towards the goal, towards the net. And John Toshack helped the ball. Into the net and into a goal. And in the fiftieth minute, Emlyn Hughes rolled a free kick short to Tommy Smith. And Smith shot. And Smith scored. And Liverpool Football Club beat Arsenal Football Club two–nil. At home, at Anfield. Bill Shankly walked down the touchline. Bill Shankly shook the hand of Bertie Mee. And Bill Shankly smiled –

Well played, Bertram. Very well played indeed. I told my boys we'd be lucky to draw with you, Bertram. But no . . .

Thank you, William. Thank you very much. But you are a liar, William. And a bloody good liar. You never told those boys of yours they were going to draw. Never in a month of Sundays. You have never sent out a team to play for a draw. I know that. And you know that, William. And you also know what a team they are becoming. They are fulfilling their promise and they are fulfilling your belief. You must be very proud of them, William. Very proud indeed . . .

Thank you, Bertram. Thank you very much. And yes, I am proud. Very proud of them, Bertram. But you've still not seen the best of these boys yet. And so you've still not heard the last of them. Not by a long chalk, Bertram. Not by a very, very long chalk . . .

One week afterwards, Liverpool Football Club travelled to Elland Road, Leeds. Leeds United were first in the First Division. And Liverpool Football Club were sixth in the First Division. And in the second minute, Reaney went up for the ball. And Sprake went up for the ball. And Reaney and Sprake collided. And the ball fell to the ground. The Elland Road ground. And there was John Toshack. On the ground. The Elland Road ground. To tap the ball. The loose ball. Into the net and into a goal. And the supporters of Liverpool Football Club cheered. But the supporters of Leeds United roared. Roared for vengeance. And Leeds United attacked and attacked. For the next eighty-eight minutes. The supporters of Leeds United roared and the players of Leeds United attacked. But Liverpool Football Club defended. For the last eighty-eight minutes. They defended and they defended. And Liverpool Football Club beat Leeds United one–nil. Away from home, away from Anfield. Bill Shankly walked down the touchline. And Bill Shankly shook Don Revie's hand –

Well played, Don. I thought you were going to beat us. Or draw at least, Don. I wasn't sure we could hang on. I really wasn't.

Don Revie shook his head. And Don Revie said, You were lucky today, Bill. Very, very lucky. But to be honest, you are always lucky, Bill. I think you live a charmed life. Because for the life of me I don't know how you won that match, Bill. We battered you. And we should have beaten you, Bill. We should have thrashed you. Murdered you, Bill. We should have murdered you. Two, three, four–nil . . .

Well, I think what you saw today, Don, was a lesson in defending. Great defending. Pure and simple, Don. We did our attacking early on. And then we defended, Don. From the back to the front, from the front to the back. So that's how we beat you, Don. By great defending. It wasn't a matter of luck, Don. There was no question of luck about it. It was heroic defending, Don. Plain and simple. But all the best to you, Don. And good luck in the Cup next week. Good luck to you, Don . . .

On Saturday 13 February, 1971, Southampton Football Club came to Anfield, Liverpool. That day, fifty thousand, two hundred and twenty-six folk came, too. Fifty thousand, two hundred and twenty-six folk to watch Liverpool Football Club play Southampton Football Club in the Fifth Round of the FA Cup. In the twenty-ninth minute, Steve Heighway raced down on the left, Heighway accelerated down the left. Heighway switched from one foot to the other. And Heighway crossed. Brian Hall met the cross. And Hall headed the cross. Towards the goal, towards the net. And there was Chris Lawler. Up from the back, down by their goal. And Lawler reached out a foot towards the ball. And Lawler stabbed the ball. Into the net, into a goal. And Liverpool Football Club beat Southampton Football Club one–nil in the Fifth Round of the FA Cup. At home again, at Anfield again. The supporters of Liverpool Football Club cheered. The supporters of Liverpool Football Club sang. And the supporters of Liverpool Football Club roared, *We're going to win the Cup! We're going to win the Cup! EE-AYE-ADDIO, WE'RE GOING TO WIN THE CUP!*

. . .

After the whistle, the final whistle. After the crowds had gone and after the players had gone. After everybody had gone, everyone gone. In the office, at his desk. Bill Shankly was answering letters. Again. Bill Shankly heard the telephone ringing. Again. Bill Shankly stopped typing. And Bill Shankly picked up the telephone –

Bill Shankly speaking. What can I do for you?

Hello, Bill. It's Andy, said Andy Beattie. How are you, Bill?

Bill Shankly had played with Andy Beattie at Preston North End. Andy Beattie had then gone into management. Andy Beattie had managed Barrow. Then Stockport County. And then Huddersfield Town. Andy Beattie had appointed Bill Shankly as his assistant manager at Huddersfield Town. But Huddersfield Town had been relegated. And Andy Beattie had resigned. And Bill Shankly had become the manager of Huddersfield Town. Andy Beattie had left management. And Andy Beattie had become a sub-postmaster in Preston. Bill Shankly had thought that was a tragedy, Bill Shankly had thought that was a waste. But Andy Beattie had not been a sub-postmaster for long. Andy Beattie had gone back into management. Andy Beattie had managed Carlisle United. Then Andy Beattie had managed Nottingham Forest. Then Plymouth Argyle. And then Andy Beattie had been appointed as caretaker manager of Wolverhampton Wanderers. But Wolverhampton Wanderers had been relegated. And Andy Beattie had resigned. Andy Beattie had become a scout for Brentford. Then Andy Beattie had been appointed as general manager of Notts County. Then Andy Beattie had been appointed as assistant manager at Sheffield United. And then Andy Beattie had done some scouting for Walsall. Now Andy Beattie did some scouting for Liverpool Football Club. A word here with Geoff Twentyman, a word there with Geoff. About this player or that player. A call to Bill Shankly here, a call to Bill there. About this player or that player –

I am very well, thank you. And how are you, Andy?

I am well, too. Thank you, Bill . . .

And so who have you seen now, Andy? Who are we missing? Who should we be signing now? Go on, Andy. Let's be knowing . . .

You already know, Bill. This lad I keep telling you about. This lad Keegan at Scunthorpe. I've told Geoff about him, too. But I know you've not seen him, Bill. I know you've not. I know no one has . . .

And how would you know that, Andy? How do you know . . .

Because if you'd seen him, you'd have signed him, Bill. On the day, on the night. You'd have already signed him, Bill . . .


## 36. CHRIST IS WITH THE RED GUARDS

On the bench, the bench at Goodison Park. Bill and fifty-six thousand, eight hundred and forty-six folk were watching Liverpool Football Club play Everton Football Club. Liverpool Football Club were sixth in the First Division. And Everton Football Club were twelfth in the

First Division. But Everton Football Club were still the Champions of England. And Everton Football Club were still in the FA Cup. But that day Everton Football Club did not score. And Liverpool Football Club did not score. And Liverpool Football Club drew nil–nil with Everton Football Club. Away from home, away from Anfield. Nil–nil. Again. And that evening, Everton Football Club were still twelfth in the First Division. And Liverpool Football Club were now fifth in the First Division. But still only fifth, in the League –

In the League, still nowhere.

On the bench, the Anfield bench. Bill and fifty-four thousand, seven hundred and thirty-one folk were watching Liverpool Football Club play Tottenham Hotspur in the Sixth Round of the FA Cup. Bill and fifty-four thousand, seven hundred and thirty-one folk watching move after move, from flank to flank, pass after pass, from flank to flank. Bill and fifty-four thousand, seven hundred and thirty-one folk watching and waiting for that one touch of flair or that one tiny error. But on Saturday 6 March, 1971, there were no touches of flair and there were no tiny errors. And Liverpool Football Club drew nil–nil with Tottenham Hotspur in the Sixth Round of the FA Cup. At home, at Anfield. There would have to be a replay. Away from home, away from Anfield. That afternoon, Everton Football Club were playing Colchester United in the Sixth Round of the FA Cup. Colchester United had beaten Leeds United in the Fifth Round of the FA Cup. But Colchester United did not beat Everton Football Club. Everton Football Club beat Colchester United five–one. And Everton Football Club were in the semi-finals of the FA Cup. The following Monday lunchtime, in the draw for the semi-final of the FA Cup, Everton Football Club were drawn to play the winners of the Sixth Round replay between Tottenham Hotspur and Liverpool Football Club.

On the bench, the Anfield bench. Bill and forty-five thousand, six hundred and sixteen folk were watching Liverpool Football Club of England play Fußball-Club Bayern München e.V. of West Germany in the first leg of the quarter-final of the Inter-Cities Fairs Cup. In the thirtieth minute, Alun Evans shot. And Evans scored. Ten minutes later, Müller shot. But Müller did not score. Ray Clemence saved. His only save of the game. In the forty-ninth minute, Liverpool Football Club won a free kick. Alec Lindsay took the free kick. Chris Lawler nodded down the free kick. And Evans hooked the ball into the goal, into the net. In the seventy-third minute, Emlyn Hughes broke from midfield. And Hughes shot. The shot charged down. But there was Evans. And Evans shot and Evans scored again. His third goal, a hat-trick. And Liverpool Football Club beat Fußball-Club Bayern München e.V. of West Germany three–nil in the first leg of the quarter-final of the Inter-Cities Fairs Cup.

On the bench, the bench at White Hart Lane. Bill was watching Liverpool Football Club play Tottenham Hotspur in the Sixth Round replay of the FA Cup. For a place in the semi-final, the semi-final against Everton Football Club. That night, thousands had been turned away from White Hart Lane. That night, hundreds sat on the touchline at White Hart Lane. To watch a match of incredible energy, to watch a match of incredible speed. In the twenty-fifth minute, Liverpool Football Club won a free kick. Alec Lindsay took the free kick. And John Toshack leapt for the free kick. Higher than every man in the Tottenham Hotspur penalty area. Toshack leapt and Toshack met the free kick. Toshack headed the free kick square towards the far post. Alun Evans dived for the ball at the far post. To touch the ball. Past the post, into the goal. And Evans missed the ball. But Steve Heighway found the ball. Heighway touched the ball. Past the post, into a goal. But still the supporters of Tottenham Hotspur roared and roared. And now Tottenham Hotspur came at Liverpool Football Club. On and on. Again and again. They came and they came. And Ray Clemence saved from Mullery. His body arching upwards. Clemence saved from Chivers. His body arching downwards. Clemence saved from Pratt. His body arching to the left. And Clemence saved from Perryman. His body arching to the right. Clemence saved and saved again. And Liverpool Football Club beat Tottenham Hotspur one–nil in the Sixth Round replay of the FA Cup. Away from home, away from Anfield. Liverpool Football Club were through to the semi-final of the FA Cup. Through to play Everton Football Club. For a place in the final, the final of the FA Cup. And the supporters of Liverpool Football Club cheered. The supporters of Liverpool Football Club sang. And the supporters of Liverpool Football Club roared, *We're going to win the Cup! We're going to win the Cup! EE-AYE-ADDIO,*
*WE'RE GOING TO WIN THE CUP!*

. . .

Before the house, on their doorstep. Bill unlocked the front door. In the night and in the silence. Bill opened the door. In the night and in the silence. Bill stepped into the house. In the dark and in the silence. Bill put down his suitcase in the hallway. In the dark and in the silence. Bill walked down the hallway to the kitchen. In the dark and in the silence. Bill switched on the kitchen light. And Bill went to the drawer. Bill opened the drawer. Bill took out the tablecloth. Bill closed the drawer. Bill walked over to the table. Bill spread the cloth over the table. Bill walked over to another drawer. Bill opened the drawer. Bill took out the cutlery. The spoons. The forks. And the knives. Bill closed the drawer. Bill walked back over to the table. Bill laid two places at the table. Bill went to the cupboard. Bill opened the cupboard door. Bill took out the crockery. The bowls and the plates. Bill walked back over to the table. Bill put a bowl and a plate in each of the two places. Bill walked back to the cupboard. Bill took out two glasses. Bill closed the cupboard door. Bill walked back to the table. Bill put a glass in each of the places. Bill walked to another cupboard. Bill opened the door. Bill took out the salt and pepper pots. Bill closed the cupboard door. Bill walked back to the table. Bill put the salt and pepper pots on the table. Bill went to the pantry. Bill opened the pantry door. Bill took out a jar of honey and a jar of marmalade. Bill walked back to the table. Bill put the jar of honey and the jar of marmalade on the table. Bill walked over to the refrigerator. Bill opened the refrigerator door. Bill took out the butter dish. Bill walked back over to the table. Bill put the butter dish down in the centre of the table. Bill walked back over to the refrigerator. Bill took out a bottle of fresh orange juice. Bill closed the refrigerator door. Bill walked back over to the table. Bill poured orange juice into both of the glasses. Bill put the bottle down on the table. And in the kitchen, at the table. Bill sat down. In the night and in the silence. Bill wanted to close his eyes, Bill wanted to sleep. But in the kitchen, at the table. Bill could not close his eyes, Bill could not sleep. In the night and in the silence. In his eyes, in his mind. Bill saw the saves Clemence had made. In his eyes, in his mind. Bill saw the tackles Lawler had made. The tackles Lindsay, Smith, Lloyd and Hughes had made. The tackles they had made and the passes they had made. In his eyes, in his mind. Bill saw the runs

345

and the passes Thompson had made. The runs and the passes Heighway had made. The runs and the passes for Evans, Toshack and Hall. The moves Evans, Toshack and Hall had made, the balls Evans, Toshack and Hall had played. The tackles and the passes they had all made. The runs they had all made and the balls they had all played. The football they had played. They had all played. And in the kitchen, at the table. Bill could not close his eyes, Bill could not sleep. In the night and in the silence. Bill could only think of the games to come. The victories to come. Not to dream, not to hope. And not to pray. To anticipate and to expect. And to believe. To believe in redemption,
to believe in salvation. At last, at last –
Bill believed again. At last,
at last. Bill believed
again.
. . .

On the bench, the bench at the Sechzger Stadion, Munich. Three days before the semi-final of the FA Cup. Bill watched Liverpool Football Club play Fußball-Club Bayern München e.V. of West Germany in the second leg of the quarter-final of the Inter-Cities Fairs Cup. But Brian Hall did not start the game. Steve Heighway did not start the game. And Peter Thompson did not start the game. Bill had rested Hall, Heighway and Thompson. Ian Callaghan, John McLaughlin and Ian Ross started the game. And in the seventy-fifth minute, Ian Ross scored. Minutes later, Schneider equalised for Fußball-Club Bayern München e.V. of West Germany. But it didn't count, it didn't matter. Liverpool Football Club of England beat Fußball-Club Bayern München e.V. of West Germany four–one on aggregate in the quarter-final of the Inter-Cities Fairs Cup. And Liverpool Football Club were through to the semi-final of the Inter-Cities Fairs Cup. Through to another semi-final,
for a place in another final,
a European final.
. . .

On the bench, the bench at Old Trafford. Bill and sixty-two thousand, one hundred and forty-four Merseyside folk were watching Liverpool Football Club play Everton Football Club in the semi-final of the FA Cup. The last time Liverpool Football Club had played

Everton Football Club in the semi-final of the FA Cup, Bob Paisley had scored for Liverpool Football Club. And Liverpool Football Club had beaten Everton Football Club. And Liverpool Football Club had reached the final of the FA Cup. But that afternoon, history was not the only thing against Everton Football Club. Four days before, Everton Football Club had played Panathinaikos of Greece in the European Cup. Panathinaikos of Greece had spat in the faces of the players of Everton Football Club. Panathinaikos of Greece had tried to gouge out the eyes of the players of Everton Football Club. Panathinaikos of Greece had stuck their fingers in the eyes of the players of Everton Football Club. And Panathinaikos of Greece had knocked Everton Football Club out of the European Cup. Everton Football Club had returned from Greece beaten. Beaten and dejected. Dejected and ill. That afternoon, Harry Catterick, the manager of Everton Football Club, did not come to Old Trafford, Manchester. That afternoon, Harry Catterick was ill. Harry Catterick had caught bronchitis in Greece. People said history was against Everton Football Club. And people said the omens were against Everton Football Club. But Bill did not believe the past dictated the present. And Bill did not believe in omens. Good omens or bad omens. And in the eleventh minute, Royle passed to Morrissey. Morrissey crossed from the left. Ray Clemence came for the cross. Clemence misjudged the cross. The cross fell to Whittle. Whittle flicked on the cross. Ball met the flick. And Ball shot and Ball scored. But the supporters of Liverpool Football Club did not fall silent. They did not surrender. The Stretford End awash with banners, a sea of red. Liverpool red. The Stretford End a crescendo of noise, a chorus of song. Red songs, Liverpool songs. And the players of Liverpool Football Club did not surrender. The players of Liverpool Football Club kept coming and coming, attacking and attacking. But at half-time in the semi-final of the FA Cup, Everton Football Club were beating Liverpool Football Club –

And in the dressing room. The Liverpool dressing room. Bill looked from player to player. From Clemence to Lawler, Lawler to Lindsay, Lindsay to Smith, Smith to Lloyd, Lloyd to Hughes, Hughes to Callaghan, Callaghan to Evans, Evans to Heighway, Heighway to Toshack and from Toshack to Hall. And Bill said, Come on, boys. Come on. You're playing too many high balls, boys. Keep the ball on the grass, the ball on the pitch. Where football is meant to be played, boys. Where God wants it played. On the grass and on the pitch, boys. You'd need a ladder to get to some of these balls. So come on, boys. Come on. Play to your strengths, boys. Play to your talents. On the grass and on the pitch, boys. And so keep the ball down. On the grass and on the pitch, boys. Where it belongs. Where God wants it played, boys. And where I want it played!

Back on the bench, the bench at Old Trafford. Five minutes into the second half of the semi-final of the FA Cup, Bill watched Brian Labone pull up. His hamstring tight, his game finished. And five minutes later, Bill watched Tommy Smith pass long down the left to Steve Heighway. On the ground. Heighway raced down the left, Heighway accelerated down the left. On the ground. Faster and faster. Turning past Brown, turning past Wright. On the ground. Heighway passed to Alun Evans. On the ground. Evans shot and Evans scored. And the supporters of Liverpool Football Club roared and roared. Louder, still louder. And the players of Liverpool Football Club came and came. Attacked and attacked. Harder, still harder. And fifteen minutes later, Evans crossed from the left. Rankin jumped and John Toshack jumped. Rankin partially touched the ball and Rankin partially cleared the ball. But the ball fell to Brian Hall. On the ground. Hall hooked the ball. Into the net and into a goal. And Liverpool Football Club beat Everton Football Club two–one in the semi-final of the FA Cup. Liverpool Football Club were in the final of the FA Cup. And on the Stretford End, awash with banners, in a sea of red, the supporters of Liverpool Football Club cheered. The supporters of Liverpool Football Club sang. And the supporters of Liverpool Football Club roared, *We're going to win the Cup! We're going to win the Cup! Ee-aye-addio, we're going to win the Cup!* Again and again. They cheered and they cheered. Again and again. They sang and they sang. Again and again. They roared and they roared, *WE'RE GOING TO WIN THE CUP! WE'RE GOING TO WIN THE CUP! EE-AYE-ADDIO, WE'RE GOING TO WIN THE CUP!*

. . .

In the house, in their hall. The letters started coming again. The first post and the second post. The letters always coming. The letters asking for tickets. Cup Final tickets. And Bill answered them all. Bill apologised to them all. And in the house, at their door. The callers started knocking again. Early in morning, late in the evening. The callers always knocking. The callers begging for tickets. Cup Final tickets. And Bill answered them all. Bill apologised to them all. And in the house, in their hall. The telephone ringing. Early in the morning, late in the evening. The telephone always ringing. The calls pleading for tickets. Cup Final tickets. And Bill answered them all. Bill apologised to them all. In the house, in their hall. The telephone still ringing. Bill put on his coat. In the house, in their hall. The telephone still ringing. Bill opened the front door. In the house, in their hall. The telephone still ringing. Bill put on his hat. And Bill stepped outside. Bill closed the door. The telephone still ringing. Bill walked down the drive. In the street, children spotted him. The children called out to him. Bill waved at them. And the children asked him for tickets. Cup Final tickets. And Bill apologised to them. And Bill got into his car. Bill drove down the West Derby Road. On the pavements, people spotted him. People waved at him. And Bill waved back. People begged him for tickets. Cup Final tickets. And Bill apologised to them. Bill turned onto Belmont Road. Again. People waved at him. Again. Bill waved back. Again. People pleaded for tickets. Cup Final tickets. Again. Bill apologised to them. Bill turned into the car park at Anfield Road. There were crowds of people in the car park at Anfield Road. Among the builders, among the scaffolding. Bill parked his car. And Bill got out of his car. The crowds of people saw Bill. The crowds of people rushed to Bill. And the crowds of people asked Bill for tickets. Cup Final tickets. They begged and they pleaded. Bill pushed through the crowds of people. And Bill apologised. And he apologised and he apologised. And Bill went inside Anfield. The telephones ringing. Bill went up the stairs. The telephones ringing. Bill went down the corridor. The telephones ringing. Bill opened his office door. The telephones ringing. Bill went into his office. The telephone on his desk ringing. Bill took off his hat. The telephone ringing. Bill hung up his hat. The telephone ringing. Bill took off his coat. The telephone ringing. Bill hung up his coat. The telephone ringing. Bill walked around the bags of mail standing on the floor. The telephone ringing. The bags and bags of mail. The telephone ringing. The mountain of bags and bags of mail. The telephone ringing. Bill sat down at his desk. The telephone ringing. Bill picked up the telephone on his desk. And Bill said, Bill Shankly speaking. What can I do for you?

Hello, said Andy Beattie. It's only me, Bill. And I am sorry to bother you. Because I know how busy you must be, Bill. I know it must be like Piccadilly bloody Circus. But I need to talk to you about this boy Keegan. This young lad at Scunthorpe. Now I know you've not seen him yet. I know you've probably been too busy. You've not had the time. But others have seen him now, Bill. And I'm hearing talk of offers from Preston. Whispers that Leeds might be in for him . . .

Bill stood up. The phone in his hand. And Bill said, You what? You're joking, Andy? You're kidding me? Not Leeds, Andy?

Yes, said Andy Beattie. Leeds. That's what I'm hearing, Bill. The whisper I'm hearing. This lad is a talent, Bill. A real talent. You know me, Bill. I wouldn't be bothering you. Not with everything you've got on, Bill. If I didn't believe this boy was the one. The best I've seen, Bill. He's better than Denis. The best I've ever seen, Bill . . .

Right then, Andy. Right then. Either me, Bob or Reuben will be over to see him. I promise you, Andy. I promise . . .

You won't regret it, said Andy Beattie. I promise you that, Bill. Because this lad is the future. The future of Liverpool Football Club.

I believe you, Andy. I believe you. And thanks again, Andy. Thanks again. And you take care now, Andy. You take care.

Bill put down the telephone. Bill sat back down in his chair. Bill picked up his diary from the desk. His diary of dates, his diary of fixtures. The telephone started to ring again. Bill put down his diary. His diary of dates, his diary of fixtures. The telephone ringing. Bill picked up the *FA Yearbook*. The telephone ringing. Bill turned to the fixtures at the back of the yearbook. The telephone ringing. Bill put down the yearbook. The telephone ringing. Bill stood up. The telephone ringing. Bill walked round the bags of mail standing on the floor. The telephone ringing. The bags and bags of mail. The telephone ringing. The mountain of bags and bags of mail. The telephone ringing. Bill opened his office door. The telephone ringing. Bill walked out of his office. The telephone ringing. Bill walked down the corridor. The telephones ringing, all the telephones ringing. Bill tapped on the door to the boot room. Bill opened the door to the boot room. And Bill saw Bob, Joe, Reuben and Ronnie sat on the empty, upturned beer crates.

Among the scrubbed and hanging boots. No telephones here. And Bill said, Right then, who fancies a wee trip to Scunthorpe?

. . .

On the bench, the Anfield bench. Bill and fifty-two thousand, five hundred and seventy-seven folk were watching Liverpool Football Club play Leeds United in the first leg of the semi-final of the Inter-Cities Fairs Cup. The last time fifty-two thousand, five hundred and seventy-seven folk could come to Anfield, Liverpool, this season. Because of the alterations to Anfield, because of the improvements to Anfield. If Liverpool Football Club beat Leeds United, if Liverpool Football Club reached the final of the Inter-Cities Fairs Cup, then the home leg of the final would have to be played at Goodison Park. Because of the alterations to Anfield, because of the improvements to Anfield. But on Wednesday 14 April, 1971, Liverpool Football Club were not yet in the final of the Inter-Cities Fairs Cup. And that night, Bremner won the toss. And Bremner elected to defend the Kop end in the first half. And so in the first half, the players of Liverpool Football Club attacked the Kop end, the players of Liverpool Football Club surged towards the Spion Kop end. Brian Hall and Steve Heighway sharp and searching. And in front of the Kop end, Sprake saved from Larry Lloyd. In front of the Spion Kop end, Sprake saved from Heighway. But the players of Leeds United attacked, too. And Madeley shot. But Ray Clemence turned the shot over the bar. The Liverpool bar. In the seventeenth minute, Ian Callaghan crossed. Alun Evans went for the cross. But Evans missed the cross. And in an instant, Leeds United attacked again. And Clarke beat Clemence. The ball in the net, the ball in the goal. But the goal was disallowed. And again the players of Liverpool Football Club attacked the Kop end, again the players of Liverpool Football Club surged towards the Spion Kop end. And in front of the Kop end, Sprake saved from Chris Lawler. Sprake saved from Lindsay. And Sprake saved from Heighway. But again in an instant, Leeds United attacked. Giles passed to Bremner. Bremner passed to Madeley. Madeley shot. But Clemence saved the shot. And at half-time in the home leg of the semi-final of the Inter-Cities Fairs Cup, Liverpool Football Club were drawing nil–nil with Leeds United Association Football Club. Early in the second half, John Toshack crossed the ball. And Sprake met the cross. But Sprake dropped the ball. The ball loose. On the ground. The Anfield ground. At the feet of Evans. Evans unmarked. The ball before him and the goal before him. The ball at his feet, the goal at his mercy. The goal unguarded, the goal open. Evans shot. And the ball hit the post. And the supporters of Liverpool Football Club gasped. The supporters of Liverpool Football Club groaned. And then the supporters of Liverpool Football Club wept. In the sixty-seventh minute, Bremner won a free kick for Leeds United. Giles took the free kick. Giles shot into the Liverpool penalty area. Towards the Kop. And Bremner leapt into the air. The Anfield air. Bremner flung himself at the ball. Through the air, the Anfield air. Bremner flicked on the free kick. In front of the Spion Kop. Into the net and into a goal. In front of the Kop. And Jack Charlton sprinted the length of the pitch. The Anfield pitch. Jack Charlton picked up Billy Bremner. In front of the Spion Kop. Jack Charlton lifted Billy Bremner into the air. The Anfield air. But the supporters of Liverpool Football Club did not fall silent. The supporters of Liverpool Football Club did not surrender. And the players of Liverpool Football Club did not fall to their knees. The players of Liverpool Football Club did not surrender. And on the touchline, the Anfield touchline. Bill took off Callaghan and Evans. And Bill sent on Bobby Graham and Peter Thompson. And the supporters of Liverpool Football Club roared and roared. And the players of Liverpool Football Club attacked and attacked. And the players of Liverpool Football Club caged Leeds United into their own half. They penned them into their penalty area. And Toshack shot. But Sprake saved from Toshack. And Lloyd shot. But Hunter cleared the shot off the line. And Heighway put Emlyn Hughes through. The ball at the feet of Hughes. But Charlton took the ball from his feet. And the game from Liverpool Football Club. And Liverpool Football Club lost one–nil to Leeds United in the first leg of the semi-final of the Inter-Cities Fairs Cup. The home leg, the Anfield leg. And on the touchline. The Anfield touchline. Bill shook the hand of Don Revie. And Bill said, Well played, Don. Well defended as usual. But never say it's me with the charmed life, Don. Never say it's me who leads a charmed life. That would be you, Don. You with the charmed life. You tonight, Don.

Don Revie looked up at the sky. The Anfield sky. Don Revie looked down at the ground. The Anfield ground. And Don Revie frowned. And Don Revie shook his head –

Well, it would be about time . . .

On the bench, the bench at Elland Road. For ninety minutes, Bill watched the players of Liverpool Football Club attack and attack and attack. Shoot and shoot and shoot. And for ninety minutes, Bill watched the players of Leeds United defend and defend and defend. Block after block after block. For ninety minutes, Liverpool Football Club could not score. And Liverpool Football Club drew nil–nil with Leeds United in the second leg of the semi-final of the Inter-Cities Fairs Cup. Away from home, away from Anfield. Liverpool Football Club were out of the Inter-Cities Fairs Cup. And on the touchline, the touchline at Elland Road. Bill shook the hand of Don Revie. And Bill said, Congratulations, Don. Congratulations. And I hope you go on and win this cup. I really do, Don. I really mean that.

Don Revie looked up at the sky. The Yorkshire sky. And then Don Revie looked down at the ground. The Yorkshire ground –

Thank you, Bill. Thank you very much. That's very kind of you, Bill. That's very generous of you. Thank you, Bill . . .

Bill shrugged. And Bill said, But I'll tell you this, Don. If you're hoping to win this cup, then you'll have to try and attack –

On the bench, the Anfield bench. Bill and thirty-eight thousand, four hundred and twenty-seven folk were watching Liverpool Football Club play Southampton Football Club in the last League game of the 1970–71 season. Among the building work, among the scaffolding. In the thirtieth minute, Emlyn Hughes scored. And Liverpool Football Club beat Southampton Football Club one–nil in the last League game of the season. At home, at Anfield. Among the building work and among the scaffolding. The supporters of Liverpool Football Club applauded the players of Liverpool Football Club. And the supporters of Liverpool Football Club saluted the manager of Liverpool Football Club. And the supporters of Liverpool Football Club sang, *We're going to win the Cup! We're going to win the Cup! Ee-aye-addio, we're going to win the Cup!* They sang and they roared, *EE-AYE-ADDIO, WE'RE GOING TO WIN THE CUP! WE'RE GOING TO WIN THE CUP! EE-AYE-ADDIO, WE'RE GOING TO WIN THE CUP!*

. . .

In the temporary office. Because of the alterations to Anfield, because of the improvements to Anfield. Bill picked up the telephone. Again. And Bill said, Bill Shankly speaking. What can I do for you?

Hello, Bill. It's me, Bob. I'm at Scunthorpe with Reuben. We're watching this lad Keegan. And we should sign him. Immediately, Bill. Now. Tonight. This very minute . . .

And Bill said, Thanks, Bob. That's all I wanted to hear. All I wanted to know, Bob. Thank you very much.

Bill put down the telephone. Bill picked up the telephone again. And Bill dialled a number. Bill listened to the telephone on the other end of the line ring. Bill listened to the voice on the other end of the line. And then Bill said, Good evening, Mr Roberts. And I'm very sorry to call you at home, at this hour. But I want us to buy this boy Keegan from Scunthorpe United. I want us to sign him now. Tonight. This very night. This very minute . . .

In the temporary office, the very next day. Bill put down the telephone on his desk. Again. And Bill got up from his desk. The telephone ringing again. Bill walked around the bags and bags of mail. The telephone ringing. The mountain of bags and bags of mail. The telephone ringing. Bill went out of his temporary office. The telephone still ringing. Bill walked down the corridor. The telephones ringing, all the telephones ringing. Bill opened the door. The telephones still ringing. And Bill saw this boy Keegan. This boy Keegan sat on a dustbin outside Anfield. Among the building work, among the scaffolding. Bill shook hands with this boy Keegan. And Bill said, Welcome to Anfield, son. Now for your medical . . .

Kevin Keegan got off the dustbin. Kevin Keegan followed Bill across the car park. Through the building work, through the scaffolding. Kevin Keegan got into Bill's car. And Bill drove this boy Keegan to the surgery of the doctor of Liverpool Football Club. Bill not looking at the road, Bill looking at this boy Keegan. Bill saying, You'll like it here, son. You'll love it here. The best club in the country, the best supporters in the land, son. The players we have, the Kop we have. The best in the world, son . . .

At the doctor's, in the surgery. Bill watched this boy Keegan have his medical. Bill watched this boy Keegan pass his medical. And then Bill said, Right, back to Anfield. Back to my office, son. So you can sign your contract. So you can join Liverpool Football Club.

In the temporary office. Bill looked across his desk at this boy Keegan. And Bill said, We can offer you forty-five pounds a week, son.

Kevin Keegan looked down at the contract on the desk. Kevin Keegan looked down at the pen on the contract on the desk. And Kevin Keegan looked away. Kevin Keegan shifted in his seat.

Is something wrong, son? Something on your mind?

Well, to be honest with you, said Kevin Keegan, I'm on thirty-five pounds a week now at Scunthorpe, sir. And so I was hoping for a little bit more. But I hope you don't think I'm being cheeky or greedy, sir. I hope you don't think I'm being ungrateful. But my father always tells me I should try to better myself, sir. If I can, whenever I can.

And what does your father do, son? What's his job?

He was a miner, said Kevin Keegan. But he cannot work now. Because of his bronchitis. Because of the dust.

Bill looked at this boy Keegan. And Bill nodded. And Bill said, Well, you do right to listen to him, son. Because that man knows graft. That man knows work, son. And so I can offer you fifty pounds.

Kevin Keegan smiled. Kevin Keegan picked up the pen –

Thank you, sir. Thank you very, very much.

Bill leant across the desk. Bill put his hand on the contract. And Bill said, But remember this, son. If you do it for Liverpool Football Club, if you do it for the supporters of Liverpool Football Club. Then you will never have to ask me for another rise again.

Kevin Keegan nodded. Kevin Keegan signed the contract. Kevin Keegan shook hands with Bill. And Bill gave Kevin Keegan a list of landladies and digs. Bill told Kevin Keegan to report for training tomorrow. And Bill told Kevin Keegan he'd be travelling with Liverpool Football Club to Wembley. To watch the Cup Final. And then Bill gave Kevin Keegan two tickets for the Cup Final. For his family. His father. And Bill said, But don't lose them, son. These tickets are like gold. And so don't be selling them either!

Bill watched Kevin Keegan bounce out of his office, his temporary office. And Bill walked over to the filing cabinet. Bill switched on the radio. Bill walked back over to his desk. Bill sat back down at his desk. And Bill began to answer letters from the bags and bags of mail. The mountain of bags and bags of mail. And Bill listened to the match on the radio as he typed. The match between Tottenham

Hotspur and Arsenal Football Club. And Bill listened to Arsenal Football Club beat Tottenham Hotspur one–nil. Bill listened to Arsenal Football Club become Champions of England. For a record eighth time. And Bill stopped typing. Bill picked up the telephone on his desk. The telephone which had been lying on his desk, off the hook. And Bill dialled White Hart Lane, London. And Bill asked to be put through to the dressing room. The away dressing room, the Arsenal dressing room. And Bill said, Hello, Bertram. It's only me. It's only Bill. Just to say congratulations, Bertram. Just to say well done. Very well done indeed. I could not be more happy for you, Bertram. More pleased . . .

Thank you, said Bertie Mee. Thank you very much, Bill. It's the greatest moment of my life. And to win it with a goal, Bill. And not a draw. It's just the best feeling in the world, Bill. And I know the North did not think we could do it. But we showed you, Bill. We showed the North. And this is just what we needed, Bill. Before Saturday. The very thing we needed. Before the final, Bill . . .

Bill smiled. And Bill said, Well, enjoy it, Bertie. Enjoy it while it lasts. Because you'll get a much tougher game on Saturday, Bertie. I can promise you that. I promise you that.

. . .

On their bus, their Liverpool bus. On their way, up Wembley Way. With a bus behind them, an empty bus behind them. Just in case. Just like before. Nothing left to chance. No shocks and no surprises. Everything planned, everything prepared. On their bus, their Liverpool bus. On their way, up Wembley Way. At the front of their bus, in his seat. Bill looked out through the window. Into a sea of red, into a world of red. Just like before. Red scarves and red flags, red banners and red songs. Everywhere Bill looked, everywhere Bill turned. Just like before. A Red Sea, a Red World. Just like before.

And on their bus, their Liverpool bus. On their way, up Wembley Way. Bill stood up at the front. Bill put on a cassette tape. Bill turned up the volume. So everyone on their bus, their Liverpool bus, could hear the cassette tape. The cassette tape of Bill on the radio. On *Desert Island Discs*, six years before. And Bill stood in the centre of the bus. In the middle of the aisle. And Bill said, Just listen to these songs, boys. These are all great songs. Great, great Scottish songs, boys. And great, great Liverpool songs . . .

And on their bus, their Liverpool bus. The players of Liverpool Football Club listened. The young players of Liverpool Football Club listened to the songs on the tape. And the players of Liverpool Football Club smiled. The young players of Liverpool Football Club smiled at Bill Shankly. As Bill stood in the centre of the bus. In the middle of the aisle. His lips moving and his arms moving. And when the cassette tape came to the last song, Bill turned up the volume as high as it would go. So everyone on their bus, their Liverpool bus, could hear the last song on the cassette tape. So everyone outside their bus, out on Wembley Way, could hear this last song. And Bill sang along to this last song on the cassette tape. And the players of Liverpool Football Club sang along to this last song on the cassette tape. The young players and the old players. Bill waving his arms, Bill shouting, Come on, boys. Come on! I can't hear you, boys. I can't hear you! And the players of Liverpool Football Club raised their voices. In chorus, as one. All the players of Liverpool Football Club singing –

*You'll never walk alone . . .*

In their dressing room, their Wembley dressing room. Bill looked from player to player. From Ray Clemence to Chris Lawler. From Chris to Alec Lindsay. From Alec to Tommy Smith. From Tommy to Larry Lloyd. From Larry to Emlyn Hughes. From Emlyn to Ian Callaghan. From Cally to Alun Evans. From Alun to Steve Heighway. From Steve to John Toshack. From John to Brian Hall. And from Brian to Peter Thompson. Peter in the number-twelve shirt. And Bill smiled. And then Bill said, Six years ago, Tommy and Chris and Cally and Peter were sat here in this dressing room, waiting to play in the Cup Final. For the first time. And I've sat in here twice myself as a player, waiting to play in the Cup Final. And so those of us who've been here before, who've sat in here before, waiting to play in the final, we know what it's like the first time you sit in here, waiting to play in the final. And we know it's the worst part. The waiting. It's hell. We know. But we also know it's worth it. The waiting. This hell. Because once you get out there, boys. Onto that pitch, onto that turf. It's heaven, boys. It's paradise. It's everything you've ever dreamt of, boys. Everything you've worked for. This is it, boys. The chance to win the Cup. The opportunity to make history, boys. And to make the supporters of Liverpool Football Club happy. So enjoy it, boys. Enjoy it. Because you're going to experience heaven on earth, boys. You are going to know paradise on earth. So let's get going, boys . . .

And in their dressing room, their Wembley dressing room. The buzzer sounded, the Wembley buzzer. And Bill led the players of Liverpool Football Club down the tunnel, the Wembley tunnel, onto the pitch, the Wembley pitch, and out into a sea of red, a world of red. LI-VER-POOL. The sea so deafening, the world so loud that the whole of London, the whole of England, heard that sea again, saw that world again. LI-VER-POOL. On their radios and on their televisions. Their colour televisions. LI-VER-POOL. People heard the supporters of Liverpool Football Club and people saw the supporters of Liverpool Football Club. LI-VER-POOL. Their scarves and their flags, their banners and their songs. LI-VER-POOL. Their red scarves and their red flags, their red banners and their red songs. LI-VER-POOL. Their sea of red, their world of red. LI-VER-POOL. And Bill knew people would always remember the supporters of Liverpool Football Club. LI-VER-POOL. Their sea of red, their world of red. LI-VER-POOL. Always remember. LI-VER-POOL, LI-VER-POOL, LI-VER-POOL.

On the bench, the Wembley bench. Bill looked out at the pitch, the Wembley pitch. The players of Liverpool Football Club wearing all red, the players of Arsenal Football Club wearing yellow and blue. But on the bench, the Wembley bench. His jacket already stuck to his shirt. His shirt already stuck to his vest. His vest already stuck to his skin. Bill felt the heat. The punishing Wembley heat. And Bill knew that pitch, that Wembley pitch, would be a sapping pitch, a sapping Wembley pitch. But in the first half, Bill watched Liverpool Football Club attack. And Wilson save. In the heat, the punishing Wembley heat, on the pitch, the sapping Wembley pitch. Bill watched Arsenal Football Club counter-attack. And Ray Clemence save. In the heat, the punishing Wembley heat, on the pitch, the sapping Wembley pitch. Attack and counter-attack, counter-attack and attack. Back and forth, forth and back. In the heat, the punishing Wembley heat, on the pitch, the sapping Wembley pitch. In the second half, Arsenal Football Club attacked again. And Clemence saved from Kennedy. In the heat, the punishing Wembley heat, on the pitch, the sapping Wembley pitch. Liverpool Football Club counter-attacked. And Wilson saved from

John Toshack. In the heat, the punishing Wembley heat, on the pitch, the sapping Wembley pitch. In the sixty-fourth minute, Kelly replaced Storey for Arsenal Football Club. In the heat, the punishing Wembley heat, on the pitch, the sapping Wembley pitch. In the sixty-seventh minute, Bill replaced Alun Evans with Peter Thompson. And in the heat, the punishing Wembley heat, on the pitch, the sapping Wembley pitch. Liverpool Football Club attacked again. And McLintock cleared the ball. In the heat, the punishing Wembley heat, on the pitch, the sapping Wembley pitch. Arsenal Football Club counter-attacked. And Clemence saved from Kennedy. And George Graham hit the bar. And Alec Lindsay cleared off the goal line. The Liverpool goal line. But in the heat, the punishing Wembley heat, on the pitch, the sapping Wembley pitch. Liverpool Football Club attacked. And Wilson saved from Steve Heighway. And Wilson saved from Thompson. And Wilson saved from Brian Hall. In the heat, the punishing Wembley heat, on the pitch, the sapping Wembley pitch. After ninety minutes, the referee blew his whistle for extra time. In the heat, the punishing Wembley heat, on the pitch, the sapping Wembley pitch. In the first period of extra time, Emlyn Hughes passed to Thompson. Thompson passed to Heighway. Heighway accelerated down the left, Heighway raced down the left. Heighway came in from the left, Heighway came to the edge of the penalty area. And Heighway shot and Heighway scored. And in the heat, the punishing Wembley heat, on the pitch, the sapping Wembley pitch. Liverpool Football Club were beating Arsenal Football Club one–nil in the first period of extra time in the final of the FA Cup. In the heat, the punishing Wembley heat, on the pitch, the sapping Wembley pitch. Two minutes later, Wilson saved from Toshack. But in the heat, the punishing Wembley heat, on the pitch, the sapping Wembley pitch. In the one hundred and first minute of extra time, Radford kicked the ball over his own head. Back into the penalty area, the Liverpool penalty area. The ball loose, loose among the bodies. The bodies and the feet. And the feet of Kelly found the ball. The loose ball over the line. Into the net and into a goal. And in the heat, the punishing Wembley heat, on the pitch, the sapping Wembley pitch. Liverpool Football Club were drawing one-all with Arsenal Football Club. In the heat, the punishing Wembley heat, on the pitch, the sapping Wembley pitch. Two minutes later, Clemence saved from Kelly. And Clemence saved from Radford. In the heat, the punishing Wembley heat, on the pitch, the sapping Wembley pitch. In the seventh minute of the second period of extra time, in the one hundred and eleventh minute of the final of the FA Cup, Radford passed to Charlie George. George on the edge of the penalty area, the Liverpool penalty area. And George shot and George scored. And George fell to the ground, the Wembley ground. On his back, his arms outstretched. And in the heat, the punishing Wembley heat, on the pitch, the sapping Wembley pitch. Arsenal Football Club were beating Liverpool Football Club two–one in the second period of extra time. And in the heat, the punishing Wembley heat, on the pitch, the sapping Wembley pitch. In the one hundred and twentieth minute of the final of the FA Cup, the referee blew his whistle. And Arsenal Football Club had won the FA Cup. Arsenal Football Club had done the Double. They had won the League and they had won the Cup.

On the bench, the Wembley bench. His jacket melted into his shirt. His shirt melted into his vest. His vest melted into his skin. His eyes drained of colour and his face carved with lines. Bill got up from the bench. The Liverpool bench. Bill walked down the touchline. The Wembley touchline. And Bill shook the hand of Bertie Mee. And then Bill walked across the pitch. The Wembley pitch. Bill went from player to player. From Wilson to Rice. From Rice to McNab. From McNab to Storey. From Storey to McLintock. From McLintock to Simpson. From Simpson to Armstrong. From Armstrong to Graham. From Graham to Radford. From Radford to Kennedy. From Kennedy to George. And from George to Kelly. And Bill shook their hands. Bill congratulated them all. And then Bill turned. Bill turned and Bill walked across the turf. The Wembley turf. Towards the supporters of Liverpool Football Club. Towards their scarves and their flags, towards their banners and their songs. And Bill stopped on the pitch. The Wembley pitch. Bill stood on the turf. The Wembley turf. Before the sea of red, before the world of red. His jacket stuck to his shirt. His shirt stuck to his vest. His vest stuck to his skin. His eyes filling with colour again. The lines leaving his face again. And Bill raised his arms. Bill put his hands together. And Bill applauded the supporters of Liverpool Football Club. For their sea of red, their world of red. And the supporters of Liverpool Football Club applauded the players of

Arsenal Football Club, they saluted the players of Arsenal Football Club. And the supporters of Liverpool Football Club applauded the players of Liverpool Football Club, they saluted the players of Liverpool Football Club. And then the supporters of Liverpool Football Club cheered. The supporters of Liverpool Football Club sang. And the supporters of Liverpool Football Club roared, one word, the same word. Over and over, again and again,

one word: *Shank-lee! Shank-lee . . .*

*SHANK-LEE!*

. . .

On the balcony of the St George's Hall. Bill could not believe his eyes. Everywhere Bill looked, he saw faces. The faces of people. Two hundred and fifty thousand people, five hundred thousand people. People smiling, people happy. And Bill could not believe his ears. People cheering, people clapping. People shouting, people singing. Two hundred and fifty thousand people, five hundred thousand people all cheering and all clapping, all shouting and all singing –

*LI-VER-POOL, LI-VER-POOL,*

*LI-VER-POOL . . .*

And Bill stepped forward. Bill opened his arms. And the people, the two hundred and fifty thousand people, the five hundred thousand people, all fell silent. And Bill said, Ladies and gentlemen. Yesterday at Wembley. We may have lost the Cup. But you, the people. Have won everything. You have won over the public in London. You have even won over the policemen in London. And it's questionable if even Chairman Mao of China could have arranged such a show of strength as you have shown yesterday and today . . .

And the people, the two hundred and fifty thousand people, the five hundred thousand people, they all cheered and they all clapped, they all shouted and they all sang, *LI-VER-POOL, LI-VER-POOL, LI-VER-POOL, LI-VER-POOL, LI-VER-POOL, LI-VER-POOL,*

*LI-VER-POOL, LI-VER-POOL,*

*LI-VER-POOL . . .*

And Bill fought back tears. Bill struggled to breathe. And again Bill opened his arms. And again the people, the two hundred and fifty thousand people, the five hundred thousand people, all fell silent. And Bill said, Since I came to Liverpool. And to Anfield. I have drummed it into our players. Time and again. That they are privileged to play for you. And if they didn't believe me then –

They believe me now.


## 37. A PARTY OF A NEW TYPE

Two months after Liverpool Football Club had finished fourth in the First Division. Two months after Liverpool Football Club had lost the final of the FA Cup. The chairman, the directors and the manager of Liverpool Football Club held a press conference at Anfield, Liverpool. A press conference to announce changes at Anfield, Liverpool –

Bob Paisley was promoted from senior trainer to assistant manager. Joe Fagan was promoted from reserve-team trainer to first-team trainer. Ronnie Moran was promoted from looking after the junior teams to looking after the reserve team. Tom Saunders was appointed to look after the junior teams and the club's youth policy. And Reuben Bennett was officially given the role of assessing players recommended by the scouts of Liverpool Football Club and of assessing the opponents of Liverpool Football Club; the job and the title of 'special duties in conjunction with the manager' –

And, said Eric Roberts, the new chairman of Liverpool Football Club, Mr Shankly was offered a five-year contract. But Mr Shankly has decided to settle for three years. However, Mr Shankly also knows he has a further option on his contract when this new one expires in May, 1974. Because Mr Shankly knows that the job is his for as long as he wants it. And we hope, and we pray, he will continue to want it for a very, very long, long time . . .

I have always said, said Bill Shankly, I am happy to go on working here. Here at Anfield, here in Liverpool. Because the happiest and hardest days of my life have been spent here. Here at Anfield, here in Liverpool. Only Celtic and Rangers in their pomp could begin to compare with Liverpool Football Club. But I don't think I'll be going back to Scotland. And so I see no reason why I should even think of going to another football club. And so contracts do not matter to me . . .

And retirement is something I rarely consider. For me, football is my life. Provided I can still do my job satisfactorily and as long as I feel able to carry on. It seems silly to me to say you are such and such an age and therefore you are too old to carry on working and you must retire. It's that old motto: you are as young as you feel you are. And that will always be one of my yardsticks. And whenever I come round to thinking about retirement, I will base my decision on two things: how I feel. And also my means. Because, basically, any man must go on working until he has earned enough to live independently. A lot of publicity is given to the high salaries to be earned in football. Not only by the players but by the managers. But there is not a lot said about the vast tax that has to be paid. The higher a person's income, the more severely he is taxed, with surtax and then supertax following the normal levels of income tax. These taxes mean that someone earning one hundred pounds a week, in fact, receives little more than fifty pounds in his pay packet. As a result, it is only when you reach the age when you begin to consider retirement that you realise the benefit and the value of the pension schemes and the like that have been introduced into football in the last ten years. But there are not many men in football today who can say they have made enough to retire. So much for my means! But as far as feeling my age is concerned, I'm feeling perfectly fit and ready to go on for years yet. I train every day and do nothing that is likely to jeopardise my health. I don't smoke. And the only time I drink is for medicinal purposes. When a drop of Scotch will keep out the cold and do me good. As a result, I feel fit and younger than most people of my age. And so I feel I am able to continue working as manager of Liverpool Football Club as long as Liverpool Football Club are willing to have me . . .

Football management, though, can be a soul-destroying profession. But I think I am about to achieve what I set out to do when I took over almost twelve years ago . . .

It was in the autumn of 1959 that I was given the opportunity of taking over another Second Division club, Liverpool Football Club. There was not much more money in it for me. And so that was not why I accepted the offer from Liverpool Football Club. What attracted me to Liverpool Football Club was the potential of the support. For me, the support given to Rangers and Celtic has always been unequalled. But here at Anfield, here in Liverpool, I felt there was the potential support to rival even those two great clubs. That was the main reason I took the job. So I felt my job, my challenge, was to wake up the support that was lying dormant. Here at Anfield, here in Liverpool. That they only needed a good team to make them the finest supporters in the country. And I think the supporters of Liverpool Football Club have proved that over the last twelve years. In fact, I know they have!

So when I arrived, my first job, my first challenge, was to get Liverpool Football Club out of the Second Division and to win respect for Liverpool Football Club, at home and abroad. Next was the ground. Because when I first came here, the place was a disgrace. But at the beginning of the new season, the new main stand will be open. It will be a place fit for a king. It will mean that three sides of the ground have been completely rebuilt. And on the fourth side, the Kop end – which must never be rebuilt – we have made improvements. We are trying to build a fortress here. An impregnable fortress. And a bastion. A bastion of invincibility. Because the fans are worthy of that. And we are nearly there. Because my last challenge is to build another team, a new team. And last season. With a team of boys, a team of mere boys. We had the greatest average attendance in the League. That is the greatest tribute to those supporters. And we reached the Cup Final. With a team of boys, a team of mere boys. And so I think we are nearly there now. I think the end is in sight now. . . .

But for me, personally, the end is not in sight yet. Retirement is not yet something I have considered. While I feel as fit and able as I do, I shall go on as manager of Liverpool Football Club. Here at Anfield, here at Liverpool. We live on strength, not weakness. Because there is nothing for anybody who does not give one hundred per cent. We have too many good players around. Our motto is pro-Liverpool, anti-nobody. And so now we are going for the big stuff. The real meat. And the League, and the Cup, and the European Cup will do for a start!

. . .

In the summer of 1971. After the walking and after the jogging. Outside Anfield, in the car park. In his tracksuit, in his sweater. Bill Shankly waited for the players, Bill Shankly greeted the players. Bill Shankly shook their hands and Bill Shankly patted their backs. He asked after their weekends, he asked after their families. Bill Shankly laughing, Bill Shankly joking. And then Bob Paisley, Joe Fagan, Reuben Bennett, Ronnie Moran and Tom Saunders joined Bill Shankly and the players in the car park at Anfield. Then Bob Paisley, Joe Fagan, Reuben Bennett, Ronnie Moran, Tom Saunders, Bill Shankly and the players all climbed on the bus to Melwood. Bill Shankly joking, Bill Shankly laughing. Everybody laughing, everybody joking. And then they all got off the bus at Melwood. Bill Shankly and the players ran round the training pitch at Melwood. Bill Shankly laughing, Bill Shankly joking. Everybody joking and everybody laughing. Bill Shankly and the players heard the whistle. Bill Shankly and the players split into their groups. And they lifted weights. They skipped. They jumped. They did squats. They did abdominal exercises. And they sprinted. Bill Shankly joking, Bill Shankly laughing. Bill Shankly and the players heard the whistle again. And they passed the ball. They dribbled with the ball. They headed the ball. They chipped the ball. They controlled the ball. They tackled. Bill Shankly laughing, Bill Shankly joking. Bill Shankly and the players heard the whistle again. And they went between the training boards. Playing the ball against one board. Then taking the ball, controlling the ball. Turning with the ball, dribbling with the ball. Up to the other board. In just ten touches. Playing the ball against the other board. Then pulling the ball down, turning again and dribbling again. Back down to the first board. In just ten touches. Bill Shankly joking, Bill Shankly laughing. Bill Shankly and the players heard the whistle again. Bill Shankly and the players went inside the sweat box. Ball after ball. Into the box. Every second, another ball. For one minute. Then for two minutes. Then for three minutes. Ball after ball, into the box. Bill Shankly laughing, Bill Shankly joking. Bill Shankly and the players heard the whistle. And they played three-a-sides. Three-a-sides then five-a-sides. Five-a-sides then seven-a-sides. Seven-a-sides then eleven-a-sides. Bill Shankly joking, Bill Shankly laughing. And then Bill Shankly and the players ran one last time around the training pitch. Bill Shankly laughing, Bill Shankly joking. And then Bob Paisley, Joe Fagan, Reuben Bennett, Ronnie Moran, Tom Saunders, Bill Shankly and the players all got back on the bus to Anfield. Bill Shankly still joking, Bill Shankly still laughing. Everybody laughing, everybody joking. And then they all got off the bus. Still joking and still laughing. They all went into Anfield. Bill Shankly laughing, Bill Shankly joking. In the dressing rooms, Bill Shankly and the players took off their boots, the players took off their tracksuits. Joking and laughing. Bill Shankly and the players went into the baths. Joking and laughing. Bill Shankly went into the baths. Bill Shankly laughing, Bill Shankly joking. Bill Shankly and the players washed and changed. Still joking, still laughing. And then Bill Shankly said goodbye to the players –

See you tomorrow, boys. Bright and early, lads. So don't be up late, boys. Don't be staying up all hours now, lads . . .

Bill Shankly still laughing, Bill Shankly still joking. The players went out to their cars. The players went back to their houses. Everybody smiling, everybody happy. Bill Shankly did not go out to his car. Bill Shankly did not go back to his house. But Bill Shankly was still smiling, Bill Shankly still happy. Because Bill Shankly had been looking, Bill Shankly had been listening. Always looking, always listening. And Bill Shankly had liked what he had seen, Bill Shankly had liked what he had heard. The players laughing, the players joking. But the players training, the players working. Hard. And Bill Shankly liked what he had learnt. Everybody smiling, everybody happy. But everybody working. Hard, together. Happy in their work. Together. Happy and prepared. Together. Happy and ready. Together –

The way it should be, the way it had to be –

The Anfield way. Together.

. . .

On Saturday 7 August, 1971, Liverpool Football Club travelled to Filbert Street, Leicester. That afternoon, twenty-five thousand, one hundred and four folk came, too. Twenty-five thousand, one hundred and four folk to watch the 1971 FA Charity Shield between Leicester City and Liverpool Football Club. Arsenal Football Club had won the Football League and the FA Cup. Arsenal Football Club had done the Double. But Arsenal Football Club did not want to play in the 1971 FA Charity Shield. Arsenal Football Club had gone to Holland to play Feyenoord of Rotterdam instead. Leeds United had finished second in the First Division. But Leeds United did not want to play in the 1971 FA Charity Shield. So the Football Association invited the Second Division Champions to play the FA Cup runners-up in the 1971 FA Charity Shield. And in the fifteenth minute of the 1971 FA Charity Shield, Fern passed to Whitworth. And Whitworth tapped the ball into the net and into a goal. And the Second Division Champions beat the FA Cup runners-up in the 1971 Charity Shield.

Three days afterwards. At Melwood, behind closed doors. The Liverpool first team played the Liverpool reserve team. It was always the last pre-season game before the start of the season. The new season, the real season. That day, Kevin Keegan played for the first team. And Alun Evans and Bobby Graham played for the reserve team. That day, Kevin Keegan scored a hat-trick for the Liverpool first team. That day, the Liverpool first team beat the Liverpool reserve team seven–one. At Melwood, behind closed doors.

Four days later, Nottingham Forest came to Anfield, Liverpool. That afternoon, fifty-one thousand, four hundred and twenty-seven folk came, too. Fifty-one thousand, four hundred and twenty-seven folk to watch the first game of the 1971–72 season. At home, at Anfield. Tommy Smith led out Ray Clemence, Chris Lawler, Alec Lindsay, Larry Lloyd, Emlyn Hughes, Peter Thompson, Steve Heighway, John Toshack, John McLaughlin and Kevin Keegan to the centre of the pitch, the Anfield pitch. The players of Liverpool Football Club stood in the centre circle, in the centre of the pitch. The Anfield pitch. And the players of Liverpool Football Club turned and waved to every part of the stadium. The Anfield stadium. And then the players of Liverpool Football Club turned and faced the Kop. The Spion Kop. And the players of Liverpool Football Club waved at the Kop. The Spion Kop. And the Kop, the Spion Kop roared –

*LI-VER-POOL, LI-VER-POOL, LI-VER-POOL . . .*

And before he had kicked a ball for Liverpool Football Club, before he had kicked one single ball at Anfield, the Kop, the Spion Kop, chanted, *Ke-vin Kee-gan, Ke-vin Kee-gan, Ke-vin Kee-gan . . .*

And a man leapt from the Kop, from the Spion Kop. And the man ran across the pitch, the Anfield pitch. And the man came up to Kevin Keegan. And the man kissed Kevin Keegan on his lips. And then the man fell to his knees on the pitch. The Anfield pitch. And the man kissed the grass. The Anfield grass. Before the Kop, the Spion Kop. And then the man stood back up. And the man ran back across the pitch, the Anfield pitch. Back to the Kop, to the Spion Kop.

And in the twelfth minute of his first game for Liverpool Football Club, a cross from Thompson came to Keegan. Keegan six yards from the goal. Keegan met the cross. And Keegan shot. But the ball skimmed off the top of his boot. And the ball bobbled towards the goal. Towards the keeper on the goal line. The Nottingham Forest goal line. The two full-backs on the goal line. But the ball kept bobbling. And the ball bobbled over the feet of one of the full-backs. Over the line and into the net. Into a goal. And in the twelfth minute of his first game for Liverpool Football Club, on his Anfield debut, Kevin Keegan had scored for Liverpool Football Club. Three minutes later, Keegan was fouled in the penalty area. The Nottingham Forest penalty area. Smith took the penalty. And Smith scored the penalty. And in the fifty-fifth minute, Hughes scored. And Liverpool Football Club beat Nottingham Forest three–one. At home, at Anfield.

Three days afterwards, Wolverhampton Wanderers came to Anfield, Liverpool. That night, fifty-one thousand, eight hundred and sixty-nine folk came, too. And in the seventh minute, John Toshack scored. In the twenty-seventh minute, Steve Heighway scored. And in the eighty-ninth minute, Tommy Smith scored another penalty. In the last minute, the very last minute. Liverpool Football Club beat Wolverhampton Wanderers three–two. At home, at Anfield. Four days later, Liverpool Football club travelled to St James' Park, Newcastle. In the tenth minute, Emlyn Hughes scored. In the fifteenth minute, Smith missed a penalty. In the seventy-fifth minute, Keegan scored. But it didn't matter, it didn't count. Malcolm Macdonald scored for Newcastle United. Malcolm Macdonald scored again for Newcastle United. And Malcolm Macdonald scored again for Newcastle United. And Liverpool Football Club lost three–two to Newcastle United. Away from home, away from Anfield. Three days later, Liverpool Football Club travelled to Selhurst Park, London. And in the fifty-seventh minute, John Toshack scored. And Liverpool Football Club beat Crystal Palace one–nil. Away from home, away from Anfield.

On Saturday 28 August, 1971, Leicester City came to Anfield, Liverpool. That afternoon, fifty thousand, nine hundred and seventy folk came, too. In the twenty-fifth minute, Steve Heighway scored. In the thirty-fifth minute, Kevin Keegan scored. And in the seventy-first minute, a shot deflected off Toshack, into his own goal. But it didn't matter, it didn't count. Liverpool Football Club beat Leicester City three–two. At home, at Anfield. And that night, in the first month of the new season, Liverpool Football Club had played five games.

They had won four of those games and they had lost one of those games. That night, Sheffield United had nine points. Manchester United had eight points. And Liverpool Football Club had eight points, too. That night, Liverpool Football Club were third in the First Division. It was not a perfect start. But it was not a bad start.

. . .

Every morning, every day. Bill Shankly trained with the players of Liverpool Football Club and Bill Shankly watched the players of Liverpool Football Club. And every morning, every day. Bill Shankly trained with Kevin Keegan and Bill Shankly watched Kevin Keegan. Bill Shankly could not keep his eyes off Kevin Keegan. The way Kevin Keegan trained. The way Kevin Keegan worked. All the players of Liverpool Football Club trained hard, all the players of Liverpool Football Club worked hard. But this was different, this was something else. This boy was different, this lad was something else. And Bill Shankly did not quite know what it was. Bill Shankly did not quite know what he had. Because Bill Shankly had not come across a player like Kevin Keegan before. Bill Shankly had not seen a player like Kevin Keegan before. Kevin Keegan was not a naturally gifted footballer. He did not have natural control, he did not have natural touch. He did not even look like a footballer. But Kevin Keegan was a footballer. A footballer unlike any other Bill Shankly had ever seen. Kevin Keegan was small, but Kevin Keegan was strong. And he was willing to learn and he was willing to work. Every morning, every day. Reuben Bennett was building up the boy's stamina. Every morning, every day. Joe Fagan was improving the lad's technique. Every morning, every day. Bob Paisley was building up the boy's knowledge. And every morning, every day. The lad was taking it all on board. The stamina. The technique. And the knowledge. Every morning, every day. Kevin Keegan was absorbing everything he heard. Everything he saw. And every morning, every day. Kevin Keegan was getting better and better. And every morning and every day. Bill Shankly saw him. Every morning, every day. Bill Shankly watched him. And Bill Shankly knew they were getting closer to building the perfect footballer. Bill Shankly knew they were getting closer to creating the perfect footballer for Liverpool Football Club. This boy who would be the spark, the new spark. This lad who would ignite Liverpool Football Club, the new Liverpool Football Club.

. . .

On Wednesday 1 September, 1971, the new Liverpool Football Club travelled to Maine Road, Manchester. That night, for the first time that season, the new Liverpool Football Club did not score. But Mellor scored for Manchester City. And the new Liverpool Football Club lost one–nil to Manchester City. Away from home, away from Anfield. Three days later, the new Liverpool Football Club travelled to White Hart Lane, London. And Keegan ran and Keegan ran. And Keegan leapt over this tackle and Keegan leapt over that tackle. But in the eleventh minute, Kinnear took a corner kick for Tottenham Hotspur. And Gilzean headed on the corner kick for Chivers. And Chivers had time to wander across the goalmouth. All the time in the world. To wander across the goalmouth with the ball at his feet. All the time in the world. To put the ball into the back of the net. And into a goal. But still Keegan ran and Keegan ran. Still Keegan leapt over this tackle, still Keegan leapt over that tackle. But in the fifty-seventh minute, Coates passed to Knowles. Knowles crossed for Peters. And Peters met the cross. And Peters headed the cross past Clemence. Into the net and into another goal. And the new Liverpool Football Club lost two–nil to Tottenham Hotspur. Away from home, away from Anfield.

On Tuesday 7 September, 1971, Hull City came to Anfield, Liverpool. That night, thirty-one thousand, six hundred and twelve folk came, too. Thirty-one thousand, six hundred and twelve folk to watch the new Liverpool Football Club play Hull City of the Second Division in the Second Round of the Football League Cup. But that night, Tommy Smith did not play. Smith was injured. And Ian Callaghan did not play. Callaghan was injured. And John Toshack did not play. But Toshack was not injured. Toshack was dropped. And Peter Thompson did not play. Thompson not injured, either. Thompson dropped, too. In the thirty-fourth minute, Chris Lawler scored. Four minutes later, Alec Lindsay scored. And in the fifty-fourth minute, Brian Hall scored a penalty. And the new Liverpool Football Club beat Hull City of the Second Division three–nil in the Second Round of the Football League Cup. At home, at Anfield. Four days later, Southampton Football Club came to Anfield, Liverpool. That afternoon, forty-five thousand, eight hundred and seventy-eight folk came, too. And Ian Callaghan played. And John Toshack played.

And in the thirty-second minute, Toshack scored. And the new Liverpool Football Club beat Southampton Football Club one–nil. At home, at Anfield. That evening Sheffield United had fourteen points. And Sheffield United were first in the First Division. That evening, the new Liverpool Football Club had ten points. And the new Liverpool Football Club were seventh in the First Division.

On Wednesday 15 September, 1971, the new Liverpool Football Club came to the Stade de Charmilles, in Geneva, in Switzerland, to play Servette Football Club of Geneva in the first leg of the First Round of the European Cup Winners' Cup. That night, Tommy Smith did not play. Smith still injured. And that night, Kevin Keegan did not play. Keegan had complained of severe pains in the bones of his left foot. Keegan was injured. And that night, Dörfel scored for Servette Football Club of Geneva. And Neneth scored for Servette Football Club of Geneva. And in the eighty-first minute, Chris Lawler scored for the new Liverpool Football Club. But that night, the new Liverpool Football Club lost two–one to Servette Football Club of Geneva in the first leg of the First Round of the European Cup Winners' Cup. Away from home, away from Anfield. Three days afterwards, the new Liverpool Football Club travelled to Elland Road. And again Tommy Smith did not play. Smith still injured. And again Kevin Keegan did not play. Keegan still injured. And the new Liverpool Football Club lost one–nil to the old Leeds United. Away from home, away from Anfield.

On Saturday 25 September, 1971, Manchester United came to Anfield, Liverpool. That afternoon, fifty-five thousand, six hundred and thirty-four folk came, too. Fifty-five thousand, six hundred and thirty-four folk and Kevin Keegan. Keegan injected with cortisone. Injected with enough cortisone to play against Manchester United. Manchester United were second in the First Division. The new Liverpool Football Club seventh in the First Division. In the eighth minute, Ian Callaghan shot. And the shot hit Bobby Graham's leg. The shot deflected off Graham's leg. Past Stepney. Into the net and into a goal. And in the twenty-fourth minute, Graham shot. And the shot hit Brian Hall's back. The shot deflected off Hall's back. Past Stepney. Into the net and into another goal. And at half-time, the new Liverpool Football Club were beating Manchester United two–nil. But in the eighth minute of the second half, Best dragged the defenders of Liverpool Football Club across the penalty area. The Liverpool penalty area. And Best clipped the ball back across the penalty area. The Liverpool penalty area. And Law touched on the ball. With the side of his foot. From point-blank range. Into the net and into a goal. And in the seventy-second minute, Best passed to Charlton. And Charlton shot. Into the net and into another goal. But minutes later, Emlyn Hughes shot. Into the penalty area. The Manchester United penalty area. And the shot hit the hand of James. In the penalty area. The Manchester United penalty area. But the referee did not blow his whistle. The referee did not award a penalty. And the ball ran loose from the hand of James. The ball loose at the feet of Graham. And Graham shot. Into the net and into a goal. But the linesman had raised his flag. The linesman said Graham was offside. And the referee blew his whistle. The referee shook his head. And the referee disallowed the goal. And the players of Liverpool Football Club protested. But still the referee shook his head. Still the referee disallowed the goal. And the supporters of Liverpool Football Club howled at the referee. And the supporters of Liverpool Football Club wailed at the referee. But the new Liverpool Football Club drew two-all with Manchester United. At home, at Anfield. Bill Shankly walked down the touchline. The Anfield touchline. Bill Shankly shook the hand of Frank O'Farrell –

That was either a penalty or a goal, said Bill Shankly. We should have had either a penalty or a goal. You must agree we have been robbed. You must agree you've been very lucky, Frank . . .

Frank O'Farrell shook his head. And Frank O'Farrell said, It was never a penalty, Bill. And Graham was clearly offside. So I don't agree you were robbed, Bill. In fact, I think you were very lucky to get a draw. I think we were the ones who were robbed. The way we played in the second half. It was men against boys. Men against boys, Bill.

Bill Shankly shook his head. And Bill Shankly walked away. Down the touchline. The Anfield touchline. Down the tunnel. The Anfield tunnel. Into the darkness. Into the evening –

That evening, some of the supporters of Liverpool Football Club threw bottles and bricks at the Manchester United team bus. That evening, some of the supporters of Liverpool Football Club broke the windows of the Manchester United team bus. That evening, some of the players of Manchester United were injured by broken glass. And that evening, Sheffield United were still first in the First Division. And Manchester United still second in the First Division. Derby County third, Manchester City fourth, Leeds United fifth, Arsenal Football Club sixth and Tottenham Hotspur seventh. That evening, the new Liverpool Football Club were eighth in the First Division. The new Liverpool Football Club still nowhere –

Still bloody nowhere –

Still not even close, not even fucking close.


## 38. RED YOUTH UNDER DIFFICULT CIRCUMSTANCES

In the house, in their kitchen. Bill got up from the table. Bill picked up the plates. Ness got up from the kitchen table. Ness walked out of the kitchen. Bill put the plates in the sink. Bill walked back over to the kitchen table. Ness went into the front room. Ness sat down in her chair. Bill picked up the salt and pepper pots. Bill put them in the cupboard. Ness picked up her packet of cigarettes from the arm of the chair. Ness lit a cigarette. Bill walked back over to the table. Bill took the cloth off the table. Bill walked over to the back door. Bill opened the back door. Bill stepped outside. Bill stood on the step. Bill shook the cloth. Bill stepped back into the kitchen. Bill closed the door. Bill folded up the tablecloth. Bill put it in the drawer. Ness finished her cigarette. Ness stubbed out her cigarette. Bill walked back over to the sink. Bill turned on the taps. Bill squeezed washing-up liquid into the sink. Bill turned off the taps. Bill picked up the scrubbing brush. Bill washed up the plates. Bill washed up the pans. Bill washed up the knives and forks. Bill put them on the draining board. Bill pulled out the plug. Bill dried his hands. Ness picked up the newspaper and her pen. Ness turned to the crossword. Bill picked up the tea towel. Bill dried up the pans. Bill dried up the plates. Bill dried up the knives and forks. Bill put the pans in one cupboard, Bill put the plates in another. Bill put the knives and forks in the drawer. Ness put down her pen. Ness lit another cigarette. Bill walked back over to the sink. Bill picked up the dishcloth. Bill wiped down the draining board. Bill turned on the taps again. Bill rinsed the dishcloth under the taps. Bill turned off the taps. Bill squeezed the water out of the dishcloth. Bill put the dishcloth down next to the bottle of washing-up liquid. Bill turned around. Bill looked round the kitchen. Ness finished her cigarette. Ness stubbed out her cigarette. Bill turned back to the sink. Bill bent down. Bill opened the cupboard under the sink. Bill took out a bucket from under the sink. Bill bent back down. Bill opened a box under the sink. Bill took out a Brillo pad from the box. Bill closed the cupboard door. Bill picked up the bucket. Bill put the bucket in the sink. Bill turned the taps on again. Bill filled the bucket half full. Bill turned off the taps. Ness put her pen in her mouth. Ness stared down at the crossword. Bill took the bucket and the Brillo pad over to the cooker. Bill put the bucket down in front of the cooker. Bill opened the oven door. Bill looked inside. Bill saw the darkness. Bill smelt the fat. Bill knelt down on the kitchen floor. Bill unbuttoned the cuffs of his shirt. Bill rolled up the sleeves of his shirt. Bill picked up the Brillo pad. Bill sank the Brillo pad into the bucket of water. Bill pulled the Brillo pad back up, out of the water. Bill squeezed the water from the Brillo pad. The wet, steel wool. Bill squeezed it tighter. Bill put his hand inside the oven. Into the darkness. Amongst the fat. Ness put down her pen again. Ness lit another cigarette. In the kitchen, on his knees. Bill began to scrub. On his knees, Bill began to scour. Bill began to clean. To clean, and to clean, and to clean. And Bill heard Ness begin to cough. To cough, and to cough, and to cough. On his knees, Bill knew flesh aged. Flesh strained and flesh tore. In the damp. Bill knew bones aged. Bones fractured and bones broke. In the dry. Bodies aging. Bit by bit. Older and older, weaker and weaker. Bodies dying. Bit by bit. Hour by hour, day by day. In the damp and in the dry. Bill knew that was the battle. That was the war. The battle against age, the war against death. The battle you could not win, the war you could never win. But the battle you must try to fight. Hour by hour. The war you must try to win. Day by day. In the damp and in the dry. On his knees, Bill knew you had to fight against age. Hour by hour, day by day. In the damp and in the dry. On his knees, Bill knew you had to try to beat death. You had to try, you had to try.

. . .

On the bench, the Anfield bench. Bill and thirty-eight thousand, five hundred and ninety-one folk were watching the new Liverpool

Football Club play Servette Football Club of Geneva in the second leg of the First Round of the European Cup Winners' Cup. Tommy Smith was playing and Kevin Keegan was playing. Tommy Smith injected with cortisone and Kevin Keegan injected with cortisone. In the twenty-seventh minute, Emlyn Hughes scored. And in the sixtieth minute, Steve Heighway scored. But Kevin Keegan was limping, Kevin Keegan was struggling. And in the seventy-first minute, Bill took off Kevin Keegan. And Bill sent on John Toshack. In the eightieth minute, Tommy Smith tackled Barriquand of Servette Football Club of Geneva. And Tommy Smith won the ball. But Barriquand's studs raked down the right shin of Tommy Smith. And the referee blew his whistle. And the referee awarded a free kick to Liverpool Football Club. Tommy Smith got up. Tommy Smith took the free kick. And Tommy Smith kept on playing, Tommy Smith kept on running. But the players of Servette Football Club of Geneva were not playing. The players of Servette Football Club of Geneva were staring at the right shin of Tommy Smith and now the players of Liverpool Football Club were staring at the right shin of Tommy Smith. And Tommy Smith looked down at his right shin. His red sock. His Liverpool sock. Torn in two. The red sock. The Liverpool sock flapping loose. The support bandage and the surgical tape ripped apart. The bandage and the tape. Loose. The skin torn and the skin ripped. Loose. And red. And black. Red and black with blood and mud. Red and black. And white. White with bone. The white bone of his shin poking through the torn skin. Through the ripped skin. And now the referee was staring at the right shin of Tommy Smith. The referee white with shock. The referee blowing his whistle. Pointing to the bench, pointing to the tunnel. And in the eighty-fourth minute, Bill took off Tommy Smith. And Bill sent on Ian Ross. And the new Liverpool Football Club beat Servette Football Club of Geneva two–nil in the second leg of the First Round of the Cup Winners' Cup. Three–two on aggregate. At home,

at Anfield. The thirty-eight thousand, five hundred and ninety-one folk had all gone home. But Tommy Smith had not gone home. And Joe Fagan had not gone home. Tommy Smith and Joe Fagan were in the treatment room at Anfield. Joe Fagan told Tommy Smith to lie down on the physio bench. Joe Fagan took off the right boot of

Tommy Smith. Joe Fagan stared down at the right foot. The right shin. The right leg of Tommy Smith. And Joe Fagan shook his head –

We best wait for the doc, said Joe Fagan.

John Reid, one of the club doctors of Liverpool Football Club, came into the treatment room. John Reid looked down at the right foot. The right shin. The right leg of Tommy Smith –

That's the worst cut I've ever seen outside of theatre, said John Reid. We best wait for my brother Bill to get here, Tommy.

Bill Reid, the brother of John Reid and the other club doctor at Liverpool Football Club, came into the treatment room. Bill Reid looked down at the right foot. The right shin. The right leg of Tommy Smith. And Bill Reid shook his head –

Fucking hell, Tommy.

On his back, on the bench. In pain. In the treatment room, at Anfield. In fear. Tommy Smith looked up at the two doctors –

What are you going to do, docs?

I'm going to clean it up, said John Reid. And then I'm going to try and stitch it up, Tommy.

Try? What do you mean try? Either you can or you can't . . .

Well, I'm not going to lie to you, Tommy, said John Reid. It's not going to be easy and it's not going to be pleasant . . .

John Reid took out a pair of scissors. And John Reid cut away the red sock. The Liverpool sock. From the right shin of Tommy Smith. And John Reid cleaned up the right shin and the right ankle of Tommy Smith. And then John Reid took out a needle. A giant needle. And John Reid stared down at the right shin of Tommy Smith. And John Reid brought down the needle towards the right shin of Tommy Smith. But then John Reid took away the needle. John Reid wiped his brow on the back of his hand. And John Reid turned to his brother –

Go get Tommy a brandy, Bill. And go get one for me, too. A bloody large one, Bill. Bloody large ones for the both of us.

On his back, on the bench. In pain. In the treatment room, at Anfield. In fear. Tommy Smith waited for Bill Reid to return. And Bill Reid returned with two brandies. Tommy Smith declined his brandy. John Reid drank both brandies. And then John Reid picked up the needle again. The giant needle again. And John Reid stuck the giant needle into the right shin of Tommy Smith. And John Reid filled the wound in the right shin of Tommy Smith with penicillin. And then John Reid began to stitch. To try to stitch –

Have you washed your hands, John Reid asked Joe Fagan. Are they clean, Joe? Your hands?

No, doc. Not very.

Never mind. Just put your finger on the knots, Joe. So I can tighten them, will you? Put your fingers there. And keep them there.

Joe Fagan put his fingers on the knots in the stitches in the right shin of Tommy Smith. And Joe Fagan looked away from the stitches in the right shin of Tommy Smith. Joe Fagan looked up at the ceiling.

There you go, said John Reid. All done, Tommy. All done.

On the bench, in the treatment room. Tommy Smith raised himself up on his elbows. And Tommy Smith looked down at his right shin. At the stitches in his right shin. The stitches and the knots –

Are you sure that's right, asked Tommy Smith. Those are big gaps between the stitches. There must be an inch between each stitch.

Well, I'll pack the gaps with some more penicillin. How about I do that for you, Tommy? Will that make you feel better, Tommy?

On his back, on the bench. In the treatment room, at Anfield. Tommy Smith nodded. And Tommy Smith stared up at the ceiling.

Joe Fagan patted Tommy Smith on his shoulder –

I'll be back in a minute, Tommy. I'll give you a lift home.

Joe Fagan walked out of the treatment room at Anfield. And Joe Fagan saw Bill Shankly. Bill Shankly pacing up and down in the corridor outside the treatment room at Anfield –

And Bill said, How is he, Joe?

It's bad. It's very bad, Bill. Tommy's going to be out for quite some time. Quite a long time, Bill . . .

. . .

In the house, in their front room. In the night and in the silence. Bill threw his book onto the carpet. His book of names, his book of notes. The names of injured players, the notes on their injuries. And in the night and in the silence. Bill cursed. And cursed again. Bill remembered when Tommy Smith had severed his kneecap against Vitoria Setúbal two seasons ago. And Bill remembered how Liverpool Football Club had struggled without Tommy Smith two seasons ago. Without his drive, without his leadership. And Bill knew Liverpool

377

Football Club were going to struggle again. Without his drive and without his leadership. In the front room, in his chair. Bill picked up his book from the carpet. His book of names, his book of notes. Bill opened the book again. The book of names, the book of notes. The names of injured players, the notes on their injuries. Kevin Keegan was injured, too. Pains in his left foot, the bones of his left foot. But no one seemed to know how. No one seemed to know why. But in the night and in the silence. Bill knew Liverpool Football Club struggled without Kevin Keegan. Without his spark, without his fire. Bill knew Liverpool Football Club needed that spark, Bill knew Liverpool Football Club needed that fire. And in the night and in the silence. Bill was determined not to lose that spark. Bill was determined not to lose that fire. That spark and that fire. In the front room, in his chair. Bill closed his book. His book of names, his book of notes. Bill put the book down on the arm of his chair. And Bill stood up. In the night and in the silence. Bill heard Ness cough upstairs. In their bed, in her sleep. And cough again. And in the night and in the silence. Bill sat back down in his chair. And Bill coughed, too.

. . .

In the corridor, the Anfield corridor. Kevin Keegan knocked on the door of the treatment room. Kevin Keegan opened the door of the treatment room. Kevin Keegan limped into the treatment room. Kevin Keegan saw Bill Shankly and Bob Paisley standing in the treatment room. Bill Shankly and Bob Paisley waiting for Kevin Keegan –

Bill coughed. And Bill said, Take off your trousers, take off your socks. And lie down on that table, son. And let's be having a look at you. Let's be getting to the bottom of this, son . . .

Kevin Keegan took off his shoes. Kevin Keegan loosened his belt. Kevin Keegan unzipped his trousers. Kevin Keegan took off his trousers. Kevin Keegan took off his socks. And Kevin Keegan lay down on the treatment table at Anfield.

Bill and Bob walked over to the treatment table. Bill and Bob stared down at the left foot of Kevin Keegan. Bill shook his head. Bob shook his head. And Bill said, There's not a bruise on you, son. Not a single mark. What the hell is wrong with you, lad? What on earth is it?

I don't know, said Kevin Keegan. But I know I can't play on it. It hurts when I walk, Boss. Let alone when I run. Or when I kick a ball.

Bill said, But there's no bruise and there's no swelling, son. So it wasn't a tackle. It can't have been from a tackle now, can it?

No, said Kevin Keegan. I don't think so.

And you've not gone over on your ankle, have you, son?

No, said Kevin Keegan again.

And you've not been skiing or anything daft like that, have you, son? Not behind our backs. Without telling us? Nipping off to the slopes? For a quick turn on the slopes, son?

No, laughed Kevin Keegan. Not in Liverpool, Boss.

Bill shook his head. And Bill said, It's no laughing matter, son. I'm just trying to get to the bottom of what's bloody wrong with you.

I'm sorry, said Kevin Keegan. But I've not been skiing.

What about a bike? You been riding a bike, son?

No, said Kevin Keegan. I've got a car. I drive.

What kind of car, son?

A Capri.

A Capri? The last time I looked you had a Cortina?

Well, I bought a new Capri . . .

When?

A couple of weeks ago, said Kevin Keegan.

Bill said, A brand-new one?

Yes, said Kevin Keegan.

Bill looked at Bob. Bill shook his head. Bob shook his head. And Bill said, Well, that'll be it. It'll be your fancy new car. I bet the clutch is stiff. And you've been pressing down on it too hard. And so that's how you've done your foot in. Jesus Christ. You fool, you bloody idiot. More money than sense. That's you, son. That's you . . .

It can't be the car, said Kevin Keegan. It can't be.

Oh, and so now you know better than me, do you? Well, I'm telling you, it's your car. Your fancy new car, son. Because we've seen it before. Too many times before. And so you won't be driving that car again, son. And you'll be coming to Stoke and you'll be playing against Stoke. So get your trousers on, son. And get yourself on that bus. I've had enough of your bloody malingering . . .

Kevin Keegan sat up on the treatment table. Kevin Keegan got off the treatment table. Kevin Keegan pulled on his trousers. Tears in his eyes, hurt in his throat. Kevin Keegan looked at Bill Shankly –

I'm not malingering, Boss. It hurts when I walk. So I'm not going to Stoke, Boss. Because I can't play. I'm going home!

Bill and Bob watched Kevin Keegan limp barefoot out of the treatment room. Bill and Bob listened to Kevin Keegan slam the door on his way out of the treatment room. And Bob looked at Bill. Bill winked at Bob. And Bill said, Let him go, Bob. Let him go. He'll be back, Bob. He'll be back. But be sure to take that car off him when he does come back. Be sure to take his bloody car.

. . .

On the bench, the bench at the Victoria Ground. Bill watched Ray Clemence try his hardest for Liverpool Football Club. Bill watched Chris Lawler try his hardest for Liverpool Football Club. Bill watched Alec Lindsay try his hardest for Liverpool Football Club. Bill watched Ian Ross try his hardest for Liverpool Football Club. Bill watched Larry Lloyd try his hardest for Liverpool Football Club. Bill watched Emlyn Hughes try his hardest for Liverpool Football Club. Bill watched Brian Hall try his hardest for Liverpool Football Club. Bill watched John McLaughlin try his hardest for Liverpool Football Club. Bill watched Steve Heighway try his hardest for Liverpool Football Club. Bill watched Bobby Graham try his hardest for Liverpool Football Club. And Bill watched Ian Callaghan try his hardest for Liverpool Football Club. But Bill saw no drive. Bill saw no leadership. And Bill saw no spark. Bill saw no fire. And Bill saw no goals. And on the bench, the bench at the Victoria Ground. Bill watched Liverpool Football Club draw nil–nil with Stoke City –

On the bench, the Anfield bench. Bill and forty-eight thousand, four hundred and sixty-four folk watched Ray Clemence try his hardest for Liverpool Football Club. They watched Chris Lawler try his hardest for Liverpool Football Club. They watched Alec Lindsay try his hardest for Liverpool Football Club. They watched Ian Ross try his hardest for Liverpool Football Club. They watched Larry Lloyd try his hardest for Liverpool Football Club. They watched Emlyn Hughes try his hardest for Liverpool Football Club. They watched Peter Thompson try his hardest for Liverpool Football Club. They watched Brian Hall try his hardest for Liverpool Football Club. They watched Steve Heighway try his hardest for Liverpool Football Club. They watched Bobby Graham try his hardest for Liverpool Football Club.

And they watched Ian Callaghan try his hardest for Liverpool Football Club. But still they saw no drive. They saw no leadership. And still they saw no spark. Still they saw no fire. And again they saw no goals. And again they saw Liverpool Football Club draw nil–nil. Again. Nil–nil with Chelsea Football Club. At home,

at Anfield. In the office, at his desk. In the night and in the silence. Bill looked down at the paper. The pink evening paper. And Bill looked down at the table. The League table. And Bill saw the standings. The First Division standings. Liverpool Football Club had played twelve games. Liverpool Football Club had thirteen points. And Liverpool Football Club were ninth in the First Division. And in the office, at his desk. Bill put down the paper. The pink evening paper. And in the night and in the silence. Bill picked up the glue. The pot of glue. Bill picked up the scissors. The pair of scissors. And Bill coughed. Bill coughed

again. On the bench, the bench at the City Ground. Bill was watching the new Liverpool Football Club play Nottingham Forest. Bill watching Tommy Smith, Bill watching Kevin Keegan. Bill watching drive and leadership, Bill watching spark and fire. And in the fifth minute, Emlyn Hughes scored. In the sixty-fifth minute, Steve Heighway scored. And in the seventy-eighth minute, Smith scored a penalty. And the new Liverpool Football Club beat Nottingham Forest three–two. And on the bench, the bench at the City Ground. Bill smiled. And then Bill coughed. Bill coughed again. And

again. On the bench, the Anfield bench. Bill and forty-two thousand, nine hundred and forty-nine folk were watching the new Liverpool Football Club play Fußball-Club Bayern München e.V. of West Germany in the first leg of the Second Round of the European Cup Winners' Cup. But the new Liverpool Football Club did not score. And Fußball-Club Bayern München did not score. And the new Liverpool Football Club drew nil–nil with Fußball-Club Bayern München in the first leg of the Second Round of the European Cup Winners' Cup. Bill coughing,

coughing and coughing. On the bench, the Anfield bench. Bill and forty-one thousand, six hundred and twenty-seven folk were watching the new Liverpool Football Club play Huddersfield Town. And again, they saw drive and leadership. Again, they saw spark and fire. And in the fifty-seventh minute, Tommy Smith scored. And in the eightieth minute, Alun Evans scored. And the new Liverpool Football Club beat Huddersfield Town two–nil. Bill smiling. But Bill coughing, still coughing. On the bench, the bench at Upton Park. Bill watched the new Liverpool Football Club play West Ham United in the Third Round of the Football League Cup. And there was drive and there was leadership. But again there was no spark. And again there was no fire. Again Kevin Keegan had not travelled. Again Kevin Keegan was injured. And the new Liverpool Football Club lost two–one to West Ham United in the Third Round of the Football League Cup. Away from home, away from Anfield. Without the spark and without the fire. Bill was not smiling. But Bill was coughing again. Again and again. Bill could not stop

coughing. In the house, in their bedroom. Bill was coughing and Bill was sweating. In the house, in their kitchen. Bill took a nip of Scotch. But Bill was still coughing, Bill was still sweating. Coughing and coughing, sweating and sweating. And in the house, in their hall. Ness put her hand on Bill's forehead –

You're burning up, love. You're on fire. You should go back to bed. Or at least see the doctor . . .

Bill shook his head. Bill smiled. And Bill said, I'll be fine, love. I'll be fine. It's only a wee cough and a cold, love.

And Bill picked up his hat. Bill put on his hat. Bill coughed. And Bill said, I'll see you tonight, love . . .

And Bill went out of the front door. Bill coughing. Bill went down the drive. Bill sweating. Bill got into the car. Coughing, sweating. Bill drove to work. Coughing and sweating. Bill pulled into the car park at Anfield. Bill coughing. Bill parked the car. Bill sweating. Bill got out of the car. Coughing, sweating. Bill walked across the car park. Coughing and sweating. Bill went into the stadium. Bill coughing. Bill went down the corridor. Bill sweating. Bill went up the stairs. Coughing, sweating. Bill went into his office. Coughing and sweating. Bill took off his hat. Bill coughing. Bill hung up his hat. Bill sweating. Bill walked around the bags of mail. Coughing, sweating. The mountain of bags and bags of mail. Coughing and sweating. Bill sat down at his desk. Bill coughing. Bill reached into the first bag of mail on top of the mountain of bags and bags of mail. Bill sweating.

Bill took out a letter. Coughing, sweating. Bill opened the letter. Coughing and sweating. Bill read the letter. Twice. Bill coughing. And then a third time. Bill seeing double. Bill sweating. Bill put down the letter. Coughing, sweating. Bill opened the top drawer of his desk. Coughing and sweating. Bill took out a piece of paper. Bill coughing. Bill closed the top drawer of his desk. Bill sweating. Bill threaded the piece of paper into his typewriter. Coughing, sweating. Bill turned the platen knob. Coughing and sweating. And Bill began to type. Bill coughing. To type and to type. Bill sweating. Coughing, sweating. Coughing and sweating. Bill stopped typing. But Bill could not stop coughing. Bill looked at his watch. Bill could not stop sweating. Bill got up from his desk. Coughing, sweating. Bill picked up his bag from the floor. Coughing and sweating. Bill walked around the bags of mail. Bill coughing. The mountain of bags and bags of mail. Bill sweating. Bill went out of his office. Coughing, sweating. Bill walked down the corridor. Coughing and sweating. Bill saw someone walking down the corridor towards him. Maybe two people. Three people –

Are you all right, asked John Reid. You look terrible, Bill. What's wrong with you, man? Come with me . . .

On the bench. Bill coughing. In the treatment room. Bill sweating. Bill felt the stethoscope cold on his chest. Coughing, sweating. Bill felt the thermometer cold in his mouth –

You've got the flu, said John Reid. Very, very bad flu, Bill. And possibly also tonsillitis. And so you need to go back home, man. Back to your bed. And you need to go now, Bill . . .

On the bench. Coughing and sweating. In the treatment room. Bill coughed again. Bill shook his head. Sweating, Bill said, But I've got training, doc. And I'm late enough as it is . . .

Don't talk daft, said John Reid. You can't train, Bill. Not like this, in this condition. You'll bloody kill yourself, man.

On the bench. Coughing, sweating. In the treatment room. Coughing and sweating. Bill shook his head again. And Bill said, I've never missed a day's training in my life, doc. Not one. Never in my life. What will the players say, doc? What will the players think? If I go back home. Back to my bed. What will the players think . . .

If you go down to the changing rooms like this, said John Reid. If you get on the bus like this, Bill. Then you'll infect the whole bloody team, man. The whole team will get what you've got.

Still coughing and still sweating. Bill still shaking his head. Bill said, And then there's the game. I've only ever missed one match. I wasn't even ill. I went to watch Cologne. And we drew one–one with Stockport County in the Cup. Stockport bloody County . . .

Bill, Bill, said John Reid. If you go near the team, then we'll have no bloody team. And it'll be because of you, Bill. Because you refused to go home. All because of you. So go home –

And go home now, man!

. . .

In the house, in their bedroom. Coughing, sweating. In the bed, on his back. Still coughing and still sweating. Bill was listening to the radio. Bill was listening to the commentary from Bramall Lane, Sheffield. And in the bed, on his back. Bill heard Kevin Keegan score. But Sheffield United scored, too. And the new Liverpool Football Club drew one-all with Sheffield United. Away from home, away from Anfield. Coughing, sweating. Bill heard the football scores on the radio. And on his back, in his head. Bill worked out the standings in the table. Coughing and sweating. Bill knew Manchester United were first in the First Division. And Derby County were second. Manchester City third. Leeds United fourth. Sheffield United fifth. Arsenal Football Club sixth. And on his back, in his head. Bill knew Liverpool Football Club were seventh in the First Division. And Bill got up. Coughing, sweating. Bill got dressed. Coughing and sweating, sweating and coughing –

Bill went back to work. On the bench, the bench at the Sechzger Stadion in Munich. Against the advice of his doctor. Coughing, sweating. Against the orders of his doctor. Coughing and sweating. On the bench, the bench at the Sechzger Stadion. Bill watched the new Liverpool Football Club play Fußball-Club Bayern München in the second leg of the Second Round of the European Cup Winners' Cup. And in the twenty-fourth minute, coughing and sweating, Bill watched Müller score for Fußball-Club Bayern München. And three minutes later, still coughing and still sweating, Bill watched Müller score again for Fußball-Club Bayern München. And in the thirty-seventh minute, coughing and sweating, Bill watched Alun Evans score for the new Liverpool Football Club. But it didn't matter, it didn't count. In the seventy-fifth minute, still coughing and still sweating, still sweating and still coughing. Bill watched Höneß score a third goal for Fußball-Club Bayern München. And the new Liverpool Football Club had lost three–one to Fußball-Club Bayern München in the second leg of the Second Round of the European Cup Winners' Cup. Away from home, away from Anfield. The new Liverpool Football Club were out of the European Cup Winners' Cup. Coughing, sweating. Out of Europe,

again. Sweating and coughing.

. . .

Before the house, on their doorstep. In the night, still coughing. Bill unlocked the front door of the house. In the night, still sweating. Bill opened the door. In the night, still coughing. Bill stepped into the house. In the dark, still sweating. Bill closed the door. In the dark, still coughing. Bill put down his suitcase in the hallway. In the dark, still sweating. Bill walked down the hallway to the kitchen. In the dark, coughing. Bill went into the kitchen. In the dark, sweating. Bill sat down at the table. In the dark, coughing. His coat stuck to his jacket. His jacket stuck to his shirt. His shirt stuck to his vest. His vest stuck to his skin. In the dark, sweating. Bill put his head down on the table. In the dark. Coughing, sweating. Bill closed his eyes. In the dark. Coughing and sweating. Bill knew it was always easier to give up. To throw in the towel. And surrender. To the chains, to the knives, to the spades. To take your comfort in past glories, to dine out on past victories. To abandon the present to other men, to leave the future to younger men. And to let the grass grow, and to let the wind blow. As you took your comfort, as you ate your dinner. Suffocating under your blankets, choking on your dinner. In the wasteland and in the wilderness. Choking and suffocating. Your limbs bound, your throat cut, your body buried. Choking on your own blood, suffocating in your own grave. As the grass grew and the wind blew. In the wasteland, in the wilderness. In the kitchen, at the table. In the dark. Coughing, sweating. Coughing and sweating. Bill knew you could never give up. Never throw in the towel. And never surrender. To the chains, to the knives, to the spades. To the grass and to the wind. And in the kitchen, at the table. In the dark. Bill opened his eyes. In the night. Bill stood up. Bill got to his feet. Bill knew you could never give up –

You could never, ever give up –
Never, ever give up.


## 39. A COUNTRY MILE

On Saturday 6 November, 1971, Arsenal Football Club came to
Anfield, Liverpool. That afternoon, forty-six thousand, nine hundred
and twenty-nine folk came, too. But that afternoon, Kevin Keegan did
not come. Keegan was injured again. And in the fifth minute, the ball
fell between Tommy Smith and Chris Lawler. And Smith left it for
Lawler and Lawler left it for Smith. And Kennedy came between
Smith and Lawler. Kennedy shot. And Kennedy scored. But the
supporters of Liverpool Football Club did not give up. And so the players
of Liverpool Football Club did not give up. And in the forty-first
minute, Smith rolled a free kick square to Emlyn Hughes. And Hughes
shot. And Hughes scored. In the fifty-fifth minute, Smith chipped the
ball through to Ian Callaghan. And Callaghan saw Wilson off his line.
And Callaghan lobbed the ball over Wilson. Into the net and into a
goal. Twenty minutes later, Kennedy shot. Ray Clemence knocked the
shot down. Down into the path of Smith. Smith running back to cover,
Smith colliding with the ball. Falling with the ball. Into the net and
into the goal. His own net, his own goal. But again the supporters of
Liverpool Football Club did not give up. And so again the players of
Liverpool Football Club did not give up. And in the eighty-seventh
minute, Hughes passed to John Toshack. Toshack passed to Ian Ross.
Ross shot. And Ross scored. And the new Liverpool Football Club
beat Arsenal Football Club three–two. At home, at Anfield.

One week afterwards, the new Liverpool Football Club came to
Goodison Park, Liverpool. That afternoon, fifty-six thousand, five
hundred and sixty-three Merseyside folk came, too. But again Kevin
Keegan did not come. Keegan still injured. And without that spark,
without that fire. The new Liverpool Football Club lost one–nil to
Everton Football Club. Away from home,

away from Anfield. On Saturday 20 November, 1971, the new
Liverpool Football Club travelled to Highfield Road, Coventry. But
again Kevin Keegan did not travel. Keegan still injured. And Larry

Lloyd did not travel. Lloyd now injured. And John Toshack did not travel. Toshack now injured, too. But Jack Whitham travelled with the new Liverpool Football Club to Highfield Road, Coventry. And in the eightieth minute, Whitham scored. And in the eighty-ninth minute, Whitham scored again. And the new Liverpool Football Club beat Coventry City two–nil. Away from home, away from Anfield.

One week later, West Ham United came to Anfield, Liverpool. That afternoon, forty-three thousand, three hundred and ninety-nine folk came, too. But not Keegan. Not Lloyd. And not Toshack. But in the sixty-ninth minute, Emlyn Hughes scored. And the new Liverpool Football Club beat West Ham United one–nil. At home, at Anfield.

On Saturday 4 December, 1971, the new Liverpool Football Club travelled to Portman Road, Ipswich. That day, Kevin Keegan did travel with the new Liverpool Football Club. And Keegan did play for the new Liverpool Football Club. But still there was no spark, still there was no fire. And no goals. And the new Liverpool Football Club drew nil–nil with Ipswich Town. Away from home, away from Anfield. One week afterwards, Derby County came to Anfield, Liverpool. That afternoon, forty-four thousand, six hundred and one folk came, too. But still no Lloyd and still no Toshack. But Keegan came and Whitham came. And in the fourteenth minute, Whitham scored. And in the forty-fourth minute, Whitham scored again. And in the fifty-third minute, Whitham scored a third. A hat-trick. And the new Liverpool Football Club beat Derby County three–two. At home, at Anfield. That evening, Manchester United had thirty-three points. Manchester United still first in the First Division. Manchester City were second. Leeds United third. And Derby County fourth. That evening, the new Liverpool Football Club had twenty-seven points. That evening, the new and battered, bruised and wounded Liverpool Football Club were fifth in the First Division. Despite their injuries, against the odds. The new Liverpool Football club were moving up –

Up the League, up the table.

Two days after Christmas Day, 1971, the new Liverpool Football Club travelled to the Hawthorns, Birmingham. West Bromwich Albion had lost their last seven games. West Bromwich Albion were bottom of the First Division. Last in the League. And fighting for their lives. And on Monday 27 December, 1971, Brown scored for West Bromwich Albion. And the new Liverpool Football Club lost one–nil to West Bromwich Albion. Away from home, away from Anfield. Five days later, on New Year's Day, 1972, Leeds United came to Anfield, Liverpool. That New Year's Day, fifty-three thousand, eight hundred and forty-seven folk came, too. Leeds United were third in the First Division. But Liverpool Football Club had not lost at home, at Anfield, for thirty-four League games, not since March 1970. And in the first half, the supporters of Liverpool Football Club roared and roared and roared. And the players of the new Liverpool Football Club attacked and attacked and attacked. And the players of the old Leeds United defended and defended and defended. And Sprake saved from Hughes. And Keegan hit the post. And then Whitham found himself in front of the goal. The Leeds goal, an open goal. With the ball at his feet. And the Leeds goal yawning. And Whitham shot. But the Leeds goal was no longer open, the Leeds goal no longer yawning. There was Madeley. On the goal line. The Leeds goal line. To clear the ball and to save the day. The day for Leeds United. And in the fifty-eighth minute, Giles played a free kick out wide to Madeley on the right. Madeley nodded the ball back across the goal. And with a flick of his head, Clarke headed the ball into the net and into a goal. Twenty minutes later, Lorimer won the ball in a tackle. Lorimer passed the ball to Clarke. Clarke passed the ball to Jones. Jones shot. And Jones scored. And on New Year's Day, 1972, the new Liverpool Football Club lost two–nil to the old Leeds United. At home, at Anfield. Bill Shankly walked down the touchline. The Anfield touchline. And Bill Shankly shook the hand of Don Revie –

Well played, Don. Very well played, indeed. And thank Christ we won't have to play you again this season, Don . . .

That night, Manchester United had thirty-five points. Manchester United still first in the First Division. But Leeds United had thirty-five points, too. And Leeds United were second in the First Division. Manchester City third. Derby County fourth. Sheffield United fifth. Wolverhampton Wanderers sixth. Tottenham Hotspur seventh. Arsenal Football Club eighth. That night, the new Liverpool Football Club had twenty-eight points. That night, the new Liverpool Football Club were ninth in the First Division –

Ninth. Only ninth.

One week afterwards, the new Liverpool Football Club travelled to Filbert Street, Leicester. And for the fourth League game in a row, the fourth League match in succession, the new Liverpool Football Club did not score. But Leicester City did score. And the new Liverpool Football Club lost one–nil to Leicester City. Away from home, away from Anfield.

On Saturday 15 January, 1972, the new Liverpool Football Club travelled to the Manor Ground, Oxford, to play Oxford United of the Second Division in the Third Round of the FA Cup. And they travelled with spark, and they travelled with fire. And they played with spark, and they played with fire. And in the forty-seventh minute, Kevin Keegan scored. And in the eighty-first minute, Keegan scored again. Three minutes later, Alec Lindsay scored. And the new Liverpool Football Club beat Oxford United three–nil in the Third Round of the FA Cup. Away from home, away from Anfield. But two days later, on the Monday lunchtime, the new Liverpool Football Club were drawn to play Leeds United in the Fourth Round of the FA Cup. At home, at Anfield.

On Saturday 22 January, 1972, the new Liverpool Football Club travelled to Molineux, Wolverhampton. But in a dour game, in a miserable game, the new Liverpool Football Club could not score. They did not score. And the new Liverpool Football Club drew nil–nil with Wolverhampton Wanderers. Away from home, away from Anfield. That night, the new Liverpool Football Club were tenth in the First Division. Tenth. And the next morning, in the Sunday papers, people wrote that Liverpool Football Club were a faded side, a jaded side. A team going backwards, a team in retreat. That morning, in the papers. People wrote off Liverpool Football Club –

One week afterwards, Bill Shankly walked into the dressing room. The Anfield dressing room. Bill Shankly looked around the dressing room. The Liverpool dressing room. From player to player. From Clemence to Lawler, Lawler to Lindsay, Lindsay to Smith, Smith to Lloyd, Lloyd to Hughes, Hughes to Keegan, Keegan to Ross, Ross to Heighway, Heighway to Toshack and from Toshack to Callaghan. And Bill Shankly put his hand in his pocket. His coat pocket. Bill Shankly took out some cuttings. Newspaper cuttings. And Bill Shankly read from the cuttings –

You are a faded side. You are a jaded side. A team going backwards. A team in retreat. That is what people are saying about Liverpool Football Club, boys. That is what people are writing about Liverpool Football Club. But I know they are lying, boys. I know they are wrong. And I know today you are going to expose them as the liars they are, boys. You are going to show them they are wrong. Wrong about you, boys. And wrong about Liverpool Football Club. And I know the forty thousand people who have come here today do not believe them either, boys. Because I know the supporters of Liverpool Football Club believe in you. They believe in you, boys . . .

In the thirty-eighth minute, Chris Lawler scored. In the sixty-sixth minute, Chris Lawler scored again. In the seventy-second minute, Ian Callaghan scored. And in the eighty-second minute, Kevin Keegan scored. And the new Liverpool Football Club beat Crystal Palace four–one. At home, at Anfield.

One week later, Leeds United came back to Anfield, Liverpool. In the rain. That afternoon, fifty-six thousand, five hundred and ninety-eight folk came, too. In the rain. Fifty-six thousand, five hundred and ninety-eight folk to watch the new Liverpool Football Club play the old Leeds United in the Fourth Round of the FA Cup. In the rain. The biggest crowd inside Anfield for nine years, the gates closed fifty minutes before kick-off. And sixteen minutes after kick-off, in the rain, Chris Lawler met a clearance from Bates. Lawler headed the ball down to John Toshack. Toshack on the edge of the penalty area. The Leeds penalty area. Sprake raced out towards Toshack. Toshack passed wide to Steve Heighway. Heighway eight yards from the goal. The Leeds goal. The Leeds goal gaping, the Leeds goal yawning. But Heighway miskicked the ball. The ball fell to Kevin Keegan. And Keegan shot. But the Leeds goal was no longer gaping, the Leeds goal no longer yawning. And the shot was cleared, the Leeds line cleared. And now Leeds United broke, now Leeds United attacked. In the rain. Lorimer breaking, Lorimer attacking. Lorimer lobbed the ball over Ray Clemence. But Clemence threw himself back, back after the lob. And Clemence saved. And then saved from Clarke. In the rain. And then again from Lorimer. And in the rain, Sprake saved from Lloyd. And in the rain, in the ninetieth minute, the referee blew his whistle. And Bill Shankly walked down the touchline. The Anfield touchline. In the rain.

Bill Shankly shook the hand of Don Revie –

And so we'll have to play each other again, Don. After all. And so I'll see you soon, Don . . .

On Wednesday 9 February, 1972, the new Liverpool Football Club travelled to Elland Road to play the old Leeds United in the Fourth Round replay of the FA Cup. On the day of a Proclamation of Emergency. In a State of Emergency. Because the National Union of Mineworkers were on strike. Because the stocks of coal were falling. The kick-off brought forward to half past two in the afternoon. Because the Electricity Board could not guarantee there would lighting in the evening. Lighting for the floodlights, lighting for the ground. Because the power used for floodlights was not essential. Because football was not essential. In a State of Emergency. Ten thousand supporters of Liverpool Football Club travelled to Elland Road, Leeds. In a State of Emergency. Forty-five thousand, eight hundred and twenty-one folk came to Elland Road. In a State of Emergency. Hundreds were locked out of Elland Road. In a State of Emergency. Folk standing on the roof of the Old Peacock pub. In a State of Emergency. In the second minute of the Fourth Round replay of the FA Cup, Emlyn Hughes brought down Clarke. In a State of Emergency. In the thirteenth minute, Ian Callaghan passed to Steve Heighway. Heighway passed to Hughes. Hughes shot. And Hughes missed. In a State of Emergency. In the twenty-second minute, Bremner passed to Cooper. Cooper passed to Giles. Giles passed to Madeley. Madeley passed to Bremner. Bremner still breaking forward, Bremner still thrusting forward. Bremner twisting and Bremner turning. Bremner flipped the ball to Clarke. Chris Lawler bearing down on Clarke, Tommy Smith bearing down on Clarke, Larry Lloyd bearing down on Clarke, and Ray Clemence coming out towards Clarke. But Clarke flipped the ball over Clemence. Into the net and into a goal. In a State of Emergency. In the second half, Sprake saved from Callaghan. And Sprake saved from Bobby Graham. But in a State of Emergency. In the sixty-third minute, Giles passed to Clarke. Clarke out on the touchline. Clarke by the halfway flag. Clarke began to run. Lloyd went for Clarke. Clarke skipped over Lloyd. Clarke still running, Clarke still coming. Running at Clemence, coming at Clemence. And with a slight turn, with a sudden turn. Clarke left Clemence on the ground. The

Elland Road ground. Clarke shot. And Clarke scored. And in a State of Emergency. The new Liverpool Football Club lost two–nil to the old Leeds United in the Fourth Round replay of the FA Cup. Away from home, away from Anfield. In a State of Emergency. Bill Shankly walked down the touchline. The Elland Road touchline. Bill Shankly shook the hand of Don Revie. And Bill Shankly shook his head –

Well played, Don. Very well played indeed. But you have to admit, Don. You have to say, there was not much in it. Not much but two clever goals, Don. Two very clever goals . . .

Don Revie smiled. And Don Revie said, It was a great game, Bill. A great game. And we could never relax, Bill. Because you always give us a game. A very hard game. But at least now you won't have to play us again, Bill. Not this season . . .

On Saturday 12 February, 1972, Liverpool Football Club travelled to Leeds Road, Huddersfield. In a State of Emergency. There was no heating in shops, there was no heating in offices. Offices and factories working for only three days a week. Heating allowed for only one room in a house, lighting allowed for only one room in a house. The kick-off of all football matches brought forward to half past two. To conserve energy, to save power. And in this State of Emergency. In the seventy-third minute, Jack Whitham scored. And Liverpool Football Club beat Huddersfield Town one–nil. Away from home, away from Anfield. In a State of Emergency. Liverpool Football Club had thirty-three points. Liverpool Football Club eighth in the First Division. Eighth.

One week afterwards, Sheffield United came to Anfield, Liverpool. In a State of Emergency. Forty-two thousand and five folk came, too. In a State of Emergency. In the forty-second minute, John Toshack scored. And in the eighty-second minute, Toshack scored again. And in a State of Emergency. Liverpool Football Club beat Sheffield United two–nil. At home, at Anfield. In a State of Emergency. Liverpool Football Club had thirty-five points. Liverpool Football Club sixth in the First Division. Sixth.

On Saturday 26 February, 1972, Manchester City came to Anfield, Liverpool. That Saturday afternoon, there was no longer a State of Emergency. The Proclamation of Emergency had been lifted. The National Union of Mineworkers had won. The National Union of

Mineworkers would return to work on Monday. And that Saturday afternoon, fifty thousand and forty-seven folk came to Anfield, Liverpool, to watch Liverpool Football Club play Manchester City. Manchester City first in the First Division. In the thirty-seventh minute, Larry Lloyd scored. In the fifty-third minute, Kevin Keegan scored. And in the sixty-fifth minute, Bobby Graham scored. And Liverpool Football Club beat Manchester City three–nil. At home, at Anfield. That evening, Liverpool Football Club had thirty-seven points. Liverpool Football Club fifth in the First Division. Fifth.

One week later, Everton Football Club came to Anfield, Liverpool. That afternoon, fifty-three thousand, nine hundred and twenty-two Merseyside folk came, too. But Harry Catterick did not come. The manager of Everton Football Club was recovering from a heart attack. And in the first minute, Wright scored an own goal. And in the sixty-sixth minute, McLaughlin scored a second own goal. And in the seventy-fourth minute, Chris Lawler scored for Liverpool Football Club. And in the eighty-seventh minute, Emlyn Hughes scored for Liverpool Football Club. And Liverpool Football Club beat Everton Football Club four–nil. At home, at Anfield. That evening, Liverpool Football Club had thirty-nine points. Liverpool Football Club fourth in the First Division. Fourth.

On Saturday 18 March, 1972, Newcastle United came to Anfield, Liverpool. That afternoon, forty-three thousand, eight hundred and ninety-nine folk came, too. Forty-three thousand, eight hundred and ninety-nine folk and Malcolm Macdonald –

In the tunnel. The Anfield tunnel. At the top of the stairs. The Anfield stairs. Malcolm Macdonald looked up at the sign on the wall. The new sign on the old wall. And Malcolm Macdonald laughed, This is Anfield, eh? Well, we've come to the right ground then, lads. That's very helpful. At least we know where we are.

You think it's funny, do you, asked Bill Shankly. Well, you'll find out soon enough where you are, son . . .

In the ninth minute, Chris Lawler scored. In the twenty-second minute, Kevin Keegan scored. In the thirty-ninth minute, John Toshack scored. In the sixty-third minute, Emlyn Hughes scored. And in the eighty-first minute, Steve Heighway scored. And Liverpool Football Club beat Newcastle United five–nil. At home, at Anfield.

That evening, Liverpool Football Club had forty-two points. Liverpool Football Club were still fourth in the First Division. Still fourth.

On Saturday 25 March, 1972, Liverpool Football Club travelled to the Dell, Southampton. And in the fifty-second minute, John Toshack scored. And Liverpool Football Club beat Southampton Football Club one–nil. Away from home, away from Anfield. That evening, Manchester City had fifty points. Manchester City were first in the First Division. Derby County had forty-seven points. Derby County were second. Leeds United had forty-six points. Leeds United third. And Liverpool Football Club had forty-four points. Liverpool Football Club fourth in the First Division. Still fourth.

Three days afterwards, Stoke City came to Anfield, Liverpool. That evening, forty-two thousand, four hundred and eighty-nine folk came, too. And Ritchie scored a goal for Stoke City. The first goal Liverpool Football Club had conceded in seven games. But Burrows scored an own goal. And in the fifty-third minute, Kevin Keegan scored for Liverpool Football Club. And Liverpool Football Club beat Stoke City two–one. At home, at Anfield.

On Saturday 1 April, 1972, West Bromwich Albion came to Anfield, Liverpool. That afternoon, forty-six thousand, five hundred and sixty-four folk came, too. In the thirty-first minute, Tommy Smith scored a penalty. And in the fifty-eighth minute, Chris Lawler scored. And Liverpool Football Club beat West Bromwich Albion two–nil. At home, at Anfield. That afternoon, Derby County beat Leeds United. And Stoke City beat Manchester City. And that evening, Derby County had fifty-one points. And Derby County were first in the First Division. Manchester City had fifty points. Manchester City were second. Leeds United had forty-eight points. Leeds United third. And Liverpool Football Club had forty-eight points. Liverpool Football Club were still fourth in the First Division. Still fourth. But just three points behind Derby County. Just three points off first.

Two days afterwards, Bill Shankly walked into the dressing room. The away dressing room. Bill Shankly looked around the dressing room. From player to player. From Clemence to Lawler, Lawler to Lindsay, Lindsay to Smith, Smith to Lloyd, Lloyd to Hughes, Hughes to Keegan, Keegan to Hall, Hall to Heighway, Heighway to Toshack and from Toshack to Callaghan –

Bill Shankly took out eleven plastic men from his jacket pocket. Bill Shankly put the eleven plastic men on the table in the middle of the dressing room. Bill Shankly stared down at the eleven plastic men on the table. Bill Shankly picked them back up. The plastic men. Bill Shankly held them up. One by one. These plastic men –

Alex Stepney. Rubbish. Tommy O'Neil. Rubbish. Tony Dunne. Rubbish. Martin Buchan. Rubbish. Steve James. Rubbish. Alan Gowling. Rubbish. Willie Morgan. Rubbish. Ian Storey-Moore. Rubbish. Expensive rubbish. Overpriced rubbish . . .

Bill Shankly walked over to the bin in the corner of the dressing room. Bill Shankly dropped the eight plastic men into the bin. Bill Shankly walked back over to the table in the middle of the dressing room. Bill Shankly stared down at the three plastic men left on the table in the middle of the dressing room –

One of these men is a drunkard. One of these men is a cripple. And one of these men is a pensioner. Now are you telling me, boys. Are you telling me you can't go out there and beat a drunkard, a cripple and a pensioner? Are you telling me you can't go out there and beat these three men, boys . . .

In the sixtieth minute, Chris Lawler scored. Two minutes later, John Toshack scored. And in the eighty-fourth minute, Emlyn Hughes scored. And Liverpool Football Club beat Manchester United three–nil. Away from home, away from Anfield. Bill Shankly walked down the touchline. The Old Trafford touchline. Bill Shankly shook the hand of Frank O'Farrell. And Bill Shankly smiled –

Bad luck, Frank. Hard luck. But at least today you can't claim you were robbed, Frank. At least today everybody saw you were murdered. The way we played today. The way we murdered you today, Frank. It was men against men. I'm sure you'll agree, Frank. My young men against your very old men . . .

That night, Derby County had fifty-one points. Derby County were first in the First Division. But that night, Liverpool Football Club had fifty points. And Liverpool Football Club were second in the First Division. Second. Liverpool Football Club had taken twenty-two points from their last twelve games. Liverpool Football Club had scored twenty-seven goals in those last twelve games and Liverpool Football Club had conceded just two goals in those last twelve games.

And Liverpool Football Club were just one point behind Derby County. Just one point off first. First.

On Grand National Day, Coventry City came to Anfield, Liverpool. And that lunchtime, fifty thousand and sixty-three folk came, too. Fifty thousand and sixty-three folk and Ray Clemence, Chris Lawler, Alec Lindsay, Tommy Smith, Larry Lloyd, Emlyn Hughes, Kevin Keegan, Brian Hall, Steve Heighway, John Toshack and Ian Callaghan. The same eleven players who had started the last eight games for Liverpool Football Club. And that lunchtime, in the twenty-first minute, Keegan scored. In the sixty-seventh minute, Smith scored a penalty. And in the eighty-fifth minute, Toshack scored. And Liverpool Football Club beat Coventry City three–one. At home, at Anfield. And that lunchtime, Liverpool Football Club were first in the First Division. First. And that lunchtime, the supporters of Liverpool Football Club sang, *We're going to win the League! We're going to win the League! Ee-aye-addio, we're going to win the League . . .*

Later that afternoon, Manchester City beat West Ham United. Derby County beat Sheffield United. And Leeds United beat Stoke City. And that evening, Derby County had fifty-four points. Derby County were first again in the First Division. And Leeds United had fifty-three points. Leeds United second in the First Division. And Liverpool Football Club had fifty-two points. Liverpool Football Club third in the First Division. But Liverpool Football Club had played one match less than Derby County. And Liverpool Football Club had a game in hand. A game to come. More games to come –

One week afterwards, Liverpool Football Club travelled to Upton Park, London. In the ninth minute, Ian Callaghan passed the ball to Kevin Keegan. Keegan floated the ball to Chris Lawler. Lawler flicked on the ball to John Toshack. And Toshack swept the ball into the net. And into a goal. And in the forty-sixth minute, Steve Heighway robbed Moore. Heighway took six strides. And Heighway shot. Into the net and into another goal. And Liverpool Football Club beat West Ham United two–nil. Away from home, away from Anfield. And that evening, Derby County had fifty-six points. Derby County still first in the First Division. Manchester City had fifty-five points. Manchester City second. And Liverpool Football Club had fifty-four points. Liverpool Football Club still third in the First Division. But

Liverpool Football Club still had played one game less than Derby County and Manchester City. Liverpool Football Club still had a game in hand. Still a game to come –

A match to come –

On Saturday 22 April, 1972, Ipswich Town came to Anfield, Liverpool. That afternoon, fifty-four thousand, three hundred and sixteen folk came, too. Fifty-four thousand, three hundred and sixteen folk to watch the last home game of the season. And in the thirty-ninth minute of the last home game of the season, Steve Heighway passed to Kevin Keegan. Keegan crossed for John Toshack. And Toshack headed home the ball. Into the net, into a goal. And in the sixty-sixth minute of the last home game of the season, Emlyn Hughes shot. And Toshack deflected the shot. Into the net and into another goal. And in the last home game of the season, Liverpool Football Club beat Ipswich Town two–nil. At home, at Anfield. Liverpool Football Club had won their eighth straight match. Over one million people had paid at the gates to watch Liverpool Football Club this season. Liverpool Football Club had the highest average gate in the First Division this season. And the supporters of Liverpool Football Club sang, *We're going to win the League! We're going to win the League! Ee-aye-addio, we're going to win the League!* And the Spion Kop roared, *WE'RE GOING TO WIN THE LEAGUE! WE'RE GOING TO WIN THE LEAGUE! EE-AYE-ADDIO, WE'RE GOING TO WIN THE LEAGUE!* And the players of Liverpool Football Club ran to the Kop end. And the players of Liverpool Football Club thanked the Spion Kop. And the Spion Kop sang, *Li-ver-pool, Li-ver-pool, Li-ver-pool.* And Bill Shankly walked across the pitch. The Anfield pitch. And Bill Shankly stood before the Kop. And Bill Shankly thanked the Spion Kop. And the Spion Kop roared, *SHANK-LEE –*

*SHANK-LEE, SHANK-LEE . . .*

That afternoon, Manchester City beat Derby County. Manchester City had fifty-seven points. Manchester City were first in the First Division. But Manchester City had played all forty-two games of their season. Their season finished, their season over. Liverpool Football Club had fifty-six points and Derby County had fifty-six points, too. But Liverpool Football Club were second in the First Division. On goal average. And Liverpool Football Club still had two games in hand over Manchester City. And Liverpool Football Club still had one game in hand over Derby County. Derby County had only one more game, only one more game to play –

On May Day, 1972, Liverpool Football Club travelled to the Baseball Ground, Derby. Early in the first half, Hector shot. And Ray Clemence tipped the shot onto the bar. Early in the second half, Kevin Keegan beat Todd. With a change of direction, with a clever back-heel. Keegan crossed for John Toshack. A perfect cross. A perfect cross that needed only the slightest of touches from Toshack. The slightest of touches to find the net, to find a goal. But Toshack could not find the slightest of touches. And Toshack could not find the net, not find a goal. And in the sixty-second minute, Gemmill passed to Durban. Durban dummied and left the ball for McGovern. For McGovern to shoot. And for McGovern to score. And Liverpool Football Club lost one–nil to Derby County. Away from home, away from Anfield. And now Derby County had fifty-eight points. Now Derby County were first in the First Division. But Derby County had played all forty-two games of their season. Their season finished, their season over. But Liverpool Football Club still had a game to come. And Leeds United still had a game to come. And if Liverpool Football Club won their game to come. And if Leeds United lost their game to come. Then Liverpool Football Club would win the League. On goal average. Liverpool Football Club would be Champions. And Brian Clough walked down the touchline. The touchline at the Baseball Ground. Brian Clough shook the hand of Bill Shankly. And Brian Clough said, Of course, I hope you lose, Mr Shankly. And I hope Leeds lose, too. And I hope we'll be the Champions. Of course I do. Of course I do. But if we are not to be the Champions. Then I hope it'll be you, Mr Shankly. And not Leeds. I hope it will be you, Mr Shankly, sir . . .

On Saturday 6 May, 1972, Leeds United beat Arsenal Football Club one–nil in the one hundredth FA Cup Final. The Centenary Cup Final. Leeds United had won the FA Cup for the first time in the history of Leeds United Association Football Club. Two days later, Leeds United travelled to Molineux, Wolverhampton, and Liverpool Football Club travelled to Highbury, London. But in the mud, the Highbury mud. There were no favours from the players of Arsenal Football Club, the beaten finalists in the FA Cup. And in the first half,

Emlyn Hughes shot. And the shot dipped. Dipped behind Barnett. And hit the bar. The Arsenal bar. And in the first half, Hughes shot again. And Barnett dived. And Barnett saved. And in the second half, the supporters of Liverpool Football Club inside Highbury knew Leeds United were losing to Wolverhampton Wanderers. And now the players of Liverpool Football Club knew Leeds United were losing to Wolverhampton Wanderers. But in the mud, the Highbury mud. There were still no favours from the players of Arsenal Football Club. And in the mud, the Highbury mud. Still the beaten finalists of the FA Cup were not tiring. And Radford crossed. And Kennedy rose to meet the cross. To head the cross. Against the post. And the supporters of Liverpool Football Club inside Highbury shouted, *Li-ver-pool, Li-ver-pool, Li-ver-pool.* And the supporters of Liverpool Football Club inside Highbury roared, *LI-VER-POOL! LI-VER-POOL! LI-VER-POOL!* From the first minute to the last. And in the last minute of the last game of the season, Hughes shot. And the shot flew across the goalmouth. The Arsenal goalmouth. And Kevin Keegan slipped the shot back to John Toshack. And Toshack sent the ball into the net and into a goal. And the players of Liverpool Football Club leapt into the air. The Highbury air. And the supporters of Liverpool Football Club inside Highbury jumped into the air. The Highbury air. Dancing and cheering. In the Highbury air. But the linesman had raised his flag. And the referee blew his whistle. The goal disallowed. Toshack offside. And in the mud, the Highbury mud. Liverpool Football Club drew nil–nil with Arsenal Football Club. Away from home, away from Anfield. Derby County were the Champions of England –

With their feet up, on their holidays.


## 40. THE SOLEMN LEAGUE AND COVENANT

On the bus, their Liverpool bus. Back to Anfield, back to Liverpool. There was silence. And there were even tears. And in the silence. Among the tears. Bill stared out through the window of the bus, their Liverpool bus. Into the darkness. And into the night. Bill knew Liverpool Football Club had been the masters of their own fate. In the darkness, in the night. Bill knew Liverpool Football Club had been the engineers of their own failure. In the silence. And among the tears. Bill remembered the points dropped. The points lost. The chances missed. The opportunities spurned. The decisions that had gone against Liverpool Football Club. And the injuries to Liverpool Football Club. Bill remembered them all. And Bill smiled. In the darkness, in the night. Bill remembered Liverpool Football Club had been tenth in the First Division in February. And out of the Cup. Three cups. But in the silence. Among the tears. Bill remembered the points gained. The points won. The chances taken. The opportunities seized. The way the players of Liverpool Football Club had played. The way they had played as a team. In the darkness, in the night. Bill knew this was just the beginning. This was only the start. The real beginning, the true start. And on the bus, their Liverpool bus. Back to Anfield, back to Liverpool. In the darkness. And in the night. In the silence,

among the tears. Bill smiled

again. In the shadows of the big room at Anfield, Liverpool. Bill smiled. Bill, Bob, Reuben, Joe, Ronnie and Tom were working. Every day, all through the summer. They were working. Every day, through the summer. They were talking. Every day, that summer. They were analysing and they were discussing. The games Liverpool Football Club had played last season. The season Liverpool Football Club had finished third in the First Division. The season Liverpool Football Club had lost the Football League Championship by one single point. The season Liverpool Football Club had gained fifty-seven points. Not fifty-eight points. The season Liverpool Football Club had won seventeen games at home, at Anfield, and seven games away, away from Anfield. The season Liverpool Football Club had drawn three games at home, at Anfield, and six games away, away from Anfield. The season Liverpool Football Club had lost one game at home, at Anfield, and eight games away, away from Anfield. The season Liverpool Football Club had scored forty-eight goals at home, at Anfield, and sixteen away, away from Anfield. The season Liverpool Football Club had conceded sixteen goals at home, at Anfield, and fourteen away, away from Anfield. In the shadows of the big room at Anfield, Liverpool. Bill, Bob, Reuben, Joe, Ronnie and Tom analysed and discussed the players who had played for Liverpool Football Club last season. Every player. Phil Boersma. Ian Callaghan.

Ray Clemence. Alun Evans. Bobby Graham. Brian Hall. Steve Heighway. Emlyn Hughes. Kevin Keegan. Chris Lawler. Alec Lindsay. Larry Lloyd. John McLaughlin. Ian Ross. Tommy Smith. Peter Thompson. Phil Thompson. John Toshack. And Jack Whitham. The first-team players and the reserve-team players. Steve Arnold. Derek Brownbill. Phil Dando. Roy Evans. Chris Fagan. Edward Flood. John Higham. James Holmes. Robert Johnston. Kevin Kewley. Frank Lane. Graham Lloyd. Hughie McAuley. Stephen Marshall. Dave Rylands. John Waddington. And John Webb. In the shadows of the big room at Anfield, Liverpool. Bill, Bob, Reuben, Joe, Ronnie and Tom analysed and discussed every player who had played for the first team and every player who had played for the reserve team. Every day, all through the summer. They were analysing and they were discussing. Who would be stepping down and who would be stepping up. Every day, through the summer. Analysing and discussing. Every day, that summer. Who would be leaving and who would be staying. Every day, every single day. Who would be going and who would be coming . . .

. . .

In the office, at his desk. Bill put down the folder. Bill had first heard about Peter Cormack from his brother Bob. Bob had been the manager of Hibernian Football Club. And Bob had raved and raved about Peter Cormack. Peter Cormack had played one hundred and eighty-two games and scored seventy-five goals for Hibernian Football Club. In June, 1966, Bill had watched Peter Cormack play for Scotland at Hampden Park against Brazil. That day, Scotland had drawn one-all with Brazil. And Bill had liked what he had seen. Bill had liked Peter Cormack. But after Bob had resigned as the manager of Hibernian Football Club, Peter Cormack had been sold to Nottingham Forest for eighty thousand pounds. Bill had watched Peter Cormack every time Liverpool Football Club played Nottingham Forest. Bill had studied Peter Cormack. Bill knew Peter Cormack had scored twenty goals in his eighty-six games for Nottingham Forest. Bill also knew Peter Cormack had not really settled at Nottingham Forest. Bill did not like to think of any man being unsettled. Last season, Nottingham Forest had been relegated from the First Division. Bill did not like to think of any man being relegated. But Bill knew Peter Cormack was for sale.

In the boardroom, the Anfield boardroom. Bill looked up the

long table at the chairman and the directors of Liverpool Football Club. And Bill said, One hundred and ten thousand pounds.

One hundred and ten thousand pounds, exclaimed the chairman and the directors of Liverpool Football Club. For Peter Cormack? That is a lot of money, Mr Shankly. For a player who has never settled, who has never fulfilled his potential . . .

Bill stared up the long table at the chairman and the directors of Liverpool Football Club. And Bill said, This player will settle at Anfield, gentlemen. And this player will not only fulfil his potential, he will help fulfil the potential of this team. This team we are building. This team that should have been Champions last season. This team that were denied the Championship by one raised flag and one lost point. One lost point because of the injuries we suffered last season. Because of the lack of players we had last season. I need this player so that never happens to Liverpool Football Club again.

We can understand your frustration, said the chairman and the directors of Liverpool Football Club. And we share your frustration, Mr Shankly. And that is the reason we agreed to pay Tranmere Rovers twenty-five thousand pounds for Trevor Storton. To add cover for injuries, to add depth to the squad. But one hundred and ten thousand pounds is a lot of money, Mr Shankly. For cover and for depth.

Bill brought down his fists on the long table. And Bill said, I am not asking for one hundred and ten thousand pounds for a player who will cover for injuries. I'm not asking for one hundred and ten thousand pounds to add depth to the squad. I am asking for it because I believe this player is worth one hundred and ten thousand pounds. To our team and to this club. Worth every single penny to Liverpool Football Club. This is what I believe, gentlemen –

Because this is what I know.

Of course, we appreciate how strongly you feel, said the chairman and the directors of Liverpool Football Club. But this is still a lot of money, Mr Shankly. And so we will need to discuss the matter further, to consider it further . . .

Bill stood up at the end of the long table. And Bill shouted up the long table, This might be a hobby to you. To all of you. To sit around and to discuss at your leisure. Over a cigar and over a drink. But this is my life. My bloody life. And so you either give me the money now. Or you find yourselves a new bloody manager. Because I will not see this team finish third again. I refuse to see our supporters runners-up again. Always the bloody bridesmaids,

always fucking second best.

. . .

On the bench, the Anfield bench. In the sunshine, the bright August sunshine. Bill and fifty-five thousand, three hundred and eighty-three folk were watching the first home game of the 1972–73 season. And in the sunshine, the bright August sunshine, in the third minute, they watched Brian Hall score. But in the bright August sunshine, in an ill-tempered match, they watched Larry Lloyd go up for the ball. And Wyn Davies go up for the ball. And in the bright August sunshine, in this ill-tempered match, Lloyd and Davies clashed in the air, the Anfield air. And in the bright August sunshine, in the ill-tempered match, the referee sent off Larry Lloyd and Wyn Davies. But in the bright August sunshine, in this ill-tempered match, in the eighty-fourth minute, Ian Callaghan scored. And Liverpool Football Club beat Manchester City two–nil. At home,

at Anfield. On the bench, the Anfield bench. In the evening, the hot August night. Bill and fifty-four thousand, seven hundred and seventy-nine folk were watching Liverpool Football Club play Manchester United. And in the twelfth minute, they watched John Toshack score. And in the twentieth minute, they watched Steve Heighway score. And Liverpool Football Club beat Manchester United two–nil. At home, at Anfield –

On the bench, the bench at Selhurst Park. Bill watched Liverpool Football Club play Crystal Palace. And in the forty-fifth minute, in the last minute of the first half, Bill watched Steve Heighway get caught dawdling on the ball, Heighway caught napping, Heighway robbed of the ball. And from that ball, that robbed and stolen ball, Bill watched Anthony Taylor score. And in the seventy-fifth minute, Bill watched Emlyn Hughes equalise. And Liverpool Football Club drew one-all with Crystal Palace. Away from home, away from Anfield. A point dropped, a point lost. The first point dropped, the first point lost. And on the bench, the bench at Selhurst Park. Bill stood up, Bill got to his feet. And Bill walked down the touchline. The touchline at Selhurst Park. Bill walked down the tunnel. The tunnel at Selhurst

Park. Bill walked into the dressing room. The away dressing room. And Bill looked from player to player. From Clemence to Lawler, Lawler to Lindsay, Lindsay to Smith, Smith to Lloyd, Lloyd to Hughes, Hughes to Keegan, Keegan to Hall, Hall to Toshack, Toshack to Callaghan and from Callaghan to Heighway. And Bill held his tongue. For now. Bill said nothing.

In the pavilion, the pavilion at Melwood. Every Monday, after the game on the Saturday. Every Monday, after the training was finished. Bill and the players and the staff of Liverpool Football Club discussed the last game, the match on the Saturday. Their strengths and their weaknesses. The reasons they had won or the reasons they had lost. The reasons they had drawn. That Monday, after that Saturday. After that draw. In the pavilion, the pavilion at Melwood. Bill looked around the room. From player to player. And then Bill stopped looking around the room. From player to player. And Bill stared at one player. Bill stared at Steve Heighway. And Bill said, It was you, Steve Heighway. It was you who cost us a point. You who lost us one point. One point which might be the reason we are not Champions in April. The reason we finish nowhere again. Because you dawdled on the ball, because you were robbed of the ball. Because after you had been robbed, because after you had lost the ball. You did not chase back after the man, you did not run back after the ball. You made no attempt to make right your wrong. You just stood there. And you just watched. Watched him play a one-two. And watched him score. Because of you, Steve Heighway. Because of you. Have you no legs, son? No legs to chase after him? To help out your team, son?

I'm not a defender, said Steve Heighway. It's not my job.

Not your job? You play for a team, son. You work for a team. What would you do if you saw your neighbour's house on fire? Would you just say, I'm not a fireman? It's not my job? Is that what you'd say? Or would you fetch a bucket of water? To help him put out his fire? To help him save his house? What would you do, son?

What are you talking about, asked Steve Heighway. I don't know what you mean, what you're asking me . . .

I'm asking you a simple question. You've been to university, son. You've got a bloody degree. So you tell me, would you help your neighbour if his house was on fire? Or would you just stand and just watch and just say, It's not my job? I'm asking you a simple question, son. And so I want you to give me an answer. A straight answer, son.

I'll give you an answer, said Steve Heighway. When you ask me a sensible question. A sensible answer to a sensible question . . .

Bill turned to Tommy Smith. Bill turned to Chris Lawler. And Bill shouted, Get him out of here. Out of my sight. Take him away. Before I set bloody fire to him.

. . .

On the bench, the bench at Stamford Bridge. In the third minute, Bill watched Steve Heighway cross to John Toshack. And Toshack met the cross. And Toshack scored. Ten minutes later, from thirty yards out, Bill watched Ian Callaghan shoot. And Callaghan scored. And Liverpool Football Club beat Chelsea Football Club two–one. Away from home, away from Anfield –

On the bench, the Anfield bench. In the forty-fourth minute, Bill and fifty thousand, four hundred and ninety-one folk watched John Toshack score again. In the sixty-second minute, they watched Ferguson score an own goal. And two minutes later, they watched Emlyn Hughes score. And Liverpool Football Club beat West Ham United three–two –

On the bench, the bench at Filbert Street. In the eighth minute, Bill watched John Toshack score again. And in the sixteenth minute, Bill watched Toshack score again. But in the six minutes before half-time, Bill watched Weller score twice for Leicester City. And in the second half, Bill watched Weller score again for Leicester City. And Liverpool Football Club lost three–two to Leicester City. Away from home, away from Anfield. That night, Arsenal Football Club had ten points. And Arsenal Football Club were first in the First Division. Everton Football Club had nine points. Tottenham Hotspur had nine points. And Liverpool Football Club had nine points, too. That night, Liverpool Football Club were fourth in the First Division. On goal average. Not second, not even third best. Fourth, fourth, fourth.

On the bench, the bench at the Baseball Ground. On his fifty-ninth birthday, Bill was watching Liverpool Football Club play Derby County. And Bill was watching Peter Cormack play for Liverpool Football Club. Peter Cormack making his debut for Liverpool Football Club. But that day, on his birthday, Bill was not watching Ray

Clemence play for Liverpool Football Club. Ray Clemence was injured. That day, on his birthday, Bill was watching Frankie Lane play for Liverpool Football Club. Frankie Lane making his debut for Liverpool Football Club. Against Derby County, against the Champions of England. Derby County eighteenth in the First Division, the Champions struggling in the First Division. And on his birthday, in the sixteenth minute, Bill watched Kevin Keegan pass to John Toshack. And Toshack scored again. But then, Bill watched Hinton cross for Derby County. A long cross. And Bill watched Frankie Lane catch the cross for Liverpool Football Club. The long cross. And Lane held the ball in his arms. And Lane stepped back. The ball in his arms. His feet over the line. The goal line. And into the goal. An own goal. A needless own goal. And on his birthday, in the eighty-seventh minute, Bill watched Nish pass to O'Hare. And O'Hare scored. And on his birthday, Bill watched Liverpool Football Club lose two–one to Derby County. Away from home, away from Anfield. Brian Clough walked down the touchline. The touchline at the Baseball Ground. Brian Clough shook Bill's hand. And Brian Clough smiled –

That was bad luck, Mr Shankly. Very bad luck. But I said all we needed to get going, to get our season going, was a little bit of luck. And that's what we got today. A little bit of luck . . .

On the bench, the bench at Brunton Park. Bill watched Liverpool Football Club play Carlisle United in the Second Round of the Football League Cup. But again, Ray Clemence did not travel. Ray Clemence still injured. And so again, Frankie Lane played for Liverpool Football Club. In the forty-second minute, Bill watched Kevin Keegan score. But in the seventy-second minute, Bill watched O'Neill score, too. And Liverpool Football Club drew one-all with Carlisle United in the Second Round of the Football League Cup. Away from home, away from Anfield –

On the bench, the Anfield bench. In the twenty-eighth minute, Bill and forty-three thousand, three hundred and eighty-six folk watched Emlyn Hughes shoot. And his shot hit the post. The shot rebounded off the post onto the body of Parkes and the ball rebounded off the body of Parkes. Into the net and into a goal. In the seventy-sixth minute, Bill and the forty-three thousand, three hundred and eighty-six folk watched Kevin Keegan pass to Steve Heighway. And Heighway passed to Peter Cormack. And Cormack shot. And Cormack scored. His first goal for Liverpool Football Club. On his home debut, his Anfield debut. Four minutes later, they watched Tommy Smith take a penalty. Twice. And Smith scored for Liverpool Football Club. And in the eighty-fourth minute, they watched Heighway take a free kick. And Keegan met the free kick. And Keegan headed the free kick. Into the net and into another goal. And Liverpool Football Club beat Wolverhampton Wanderers four–two. At home, at Anfield. That evening, Everton Football Club had thirteen points. And Everton Football Club were first in the First Division. Everton Football Club unbeaten. Tottenham Hotspur had twelve points. Tottenham Hotspur second in the First Division. Arsenal Football Club, Liverpool Football Club, Ipswich Town and Leeds United all had eleven points. Liverpool Football Club still fourth in the First Division. On goal average –

Still fourth, fourth, fourth, fourth –

On the bench, the Anfield bench. Bill and thirty-three thousand, three hundred and eighty folk were watching Liverpool Football Club play Eintracht Frankfurt of West Germany in the first leg of the First Round of the UEFA Cup. In the twelfth minute, they watched Kevin Keegan score. And in the seventy-fifth minute, they watched Emlyn Hughes score. And Liverpool Football Club beat Eintracht Frankfurt of West Germany two–nil in the first leg of the First Round of the UEFA Cup. At home, at Anfield –

On the bench, the bench at Highbury. In the fifteenth minute, Bill watched the linesman collapse with torn knee ligaments. And the game stopped, the match was suspended. Twenty minutes later, Jimmy Hill, the head of LWT Sport, appeared on the touchline. Dressed in black and holding a flag. The game restarted, the match continued. And Ray Clemence saved from Radford. And saved from Graham. And saved from Ball. And John Toshack hit the post. But no one scored. And Liverpool Football Club drew nil–nil with Arsenal Football Club. Away from home, away from Anfield –

On the bench, the Anfield bench. Bill and twenty-two thousand, one hundred and twenty-eight folk were watching Liverpool Football Club play Carlisle United in the replay of the Second Round of the Football League Cup. Early on, John Toshack was injured. And Bill took off Toshack. Bill sent on Phil Boersma. And in the thirty-seventh minute, Kevin Keegan scored. Two minutes later, Boersma scored. In the seventieth minute, Tommy Smith missed a penalty. But three minutes later, Chris Lawler scored. And ten minutes later, Boersma scored again. And in the eighty-sixth minute, Steve Heighway scored. And Liverpool Football Club beat Carlisle United five–one in the replay of the Second Round of the Football League Cup. At home,

at Anfield. On the bench, the Anfield bench. In the twenty-eighth minute, Bill and forty-two thousand, nine hundred and forty folk watched Phil Boersma score again. In the thirty-first minute, they watched Alec Lindsay score. In the thirty-third minute, they watched Steve Heighway score. In the fifty-first minute, they watched Peter Cormack score. In the fifty-third minute, they watched Tommy Smith miss another penalty. But in the fifty-fourth minute, they watched Kevin Keegan score a penalty. And Liverpool Football Club beat Sheffield United five–nil. At home, at Anfield. That afternoon, there was fighting on the terraces at White Hart Lane, London. There was fighting on the streets outside the City Ground, Nottingham. But that evening, Liverpool Football Club had fourteen points. And Tottenham Hotspur had fourteen points, too. But Liverpool Football Club had scored twenty-two goals and Liverpool Football Club had conceded ten goals. And so that evening, Liverpool Football Club were first in the First Division. On goal average –

First. First. First –

Top.

. . .

In the drive, in the car. Bill turned off the engine. In the night and in the silence. Bill got out of the car. Bill walked up the drive. And Bill opened the front door. In the dark and in the silence. Bill took off his hat. Bill hung up his hat. And Bill went down the hall. In the dark and in the silence. Bill went into the kitchen. Bill switched on the light. And Bill went to the drawer. Bill opened the drawer. Bill took out the tablecloth. And Bill closed the drawer. Bill walked over to the table. Bill spread the cloth over the table. And Bill walked over to another drawer. Bill opened the drawer. Bill took out the cutlery. The spoons. The forks. And the knives. And Bill closed the drawer. Bill walked back over to the table. Bill laid two places at the table. And Bill went to the cupboard. Bill opened the cupboard door. Bill took out the crockery. The bowls and the plates. And Bill walked back over to the table. Bill put a bowl and a plate in each of the two places. Bill walked back to the cupboard. And Bill took out two glasses. Bill closed the cupboard door. Bill walked back to the table. And Bill put a glass in each of the places. Bill walked to another cupboard. Bill opened the door. And Bill took out the salt and pepper pots. Bill closed the cupboard door. Bill walked back to the table. And Bill put the salt and pepper pots on the table. Bill went to the pantry. Bill opened the pantry door. And Bill took out a jar of honey and a jar of marmalade. Bill walked back to the table. Bill put the jar of honey and the jar of marmalade on the table. And Bill walked over to the refrigerator. Bill opened the refrigerator door. Bill took out the butter dish. And Bill walked back over to the table. Bill put the butter dish down in the centre of the table. Bill walked back over to the refrigerator. And Bill took out a bottle of fresh orange juice. Bill closed the refrigerator door. Bill walked back over to the table. And Bill put down the bottle of orange juice on the table. In the night and in the silence. Bill sat down at the table. In the kitchen, at the table. Bill closed his eyes. But in his mind, in his eyes. Bill saw the saves Ray Clemence had made. Bill saw the blocks and the tackles Chris Lawler had made. The blocks and tackles Alec Lindsay had made. The blocks and tackles Tommy Smith had made. The blocks and tackles Larry Lloyd had made. The passes they all had made. The passes and the runs Emlyn Hughes had made. The passes and the runs Kevin Keegan had made. The passes and the runs Peter Cormack had made. The passes and the runs Steve Heighway had made. The passes and the runs Phil Boersma had made. The passes and the runs Ian Callaghan had made. The passes and the runs they all had made, the blocks and the tackles they all had made. From the back to the front, from the front to the back. Again and again, over and over. Never stopping, never tiring. With the ball and without the ball, without the ball and with the ball. Never tiring, never stopping. Over and over, again and again. From the front to the back, from the back to the front. And in the kitchen, at the table. In the night and in the silence. In his mind, in his ears. Bill heard the crowd. The Anfield crowd. The Kop. The Spion Kop. Never stopping, never tiring. Always shouting, always singing, *Li-ver-pool, Li-ver-pool, Li-ver-pool.* Never stopping, never tiring. Always supporting, always believing in *Li-ver-pool,*

*Li-ver-pool, Li-ver-pool.* And in the kitchen, at the table. Bill opened his eyes. Bill smiled. And Bill stood up. Bill walked over to the kitchen wall. Bill switched off the kitchen light. But in the dark and in the silence. Bill heard Ness cough upstairs. In their bed, in her sleep. Bill heard Ness coughing and coughing. Bill switched on the light again. Bill walked over to the cupboard. And Bill took out a glass. Bill walked over to the sink. Bill filled the glass with water. And Bill walked back over to the kitchen wall. Bill switched off the light. In the dark and in the silence. Bill walked up the stairs. Bill went into their bedroom. And Bill walked around their bed. Bill put down the glass of water on the table beside their bed. Beside his wife. And in the dark and in the silence. Ness said, Thank you, love. Thank you.

. . .

On the bench, the bench at the Waldstadion, in Frankfurt, in West Germany. Bill was watching Liverpool Football Club play Eintracht Frankfurt in the second leg of the First Round of the UEFA Cup. But in the fifty-seventh minute, Bill took off Tommy Smith. Because he was hurt, because he was injured. And in the fifty-seventh minute, Bill sent on Trevor Storton. And Liverpool Football Club did not score. But Eintracht Frankfurt did not score either. And Liverpool Football Club beat Eintracht Frankfurt two–nil on aggregate in the First Round of the UEFA Cup. Away from home,

away from Anfield. On the bench, the bench at Elland Road. Bill was watching Liverpool Football Club play Leeds United. Last season, Leeds United had beaten Liverpool Football Club home and away in the Football League. And last season, Leeds United had knocked Liverpool Football Club out of the Cup, too. And on the bench, the bench at Elland Road, in the thirtieth minute, Bill watched Clarke back-head the ball to Jones. And Jones scored. But ten minutes later, Bill watched Liverpool Football Club win a corner. And Phil Boersma took the corner. And Larry Lloyd headed the corner. Into the net and into a goal. In the sixty-fifth minute, Bill watched Charlton cut out a pass for Lindsay. But Charlton lost his feet. And Charlton lost the ball. Phil Boersma found the ball. Boersma jumped over the tackle from Hunter. And Boersma shot. Into the net and into another goal. And now Charlton went up. Charlton now a forward. And Clarke scored. But the linesman raised his flag. For offside. And the referee disallowed the goal. For offside. And then Ray Clemence pushed a shot over the bar. Tipped it over the bar. And then Bremner shot. And Bremner's shot clipped the post. The wrong side of the post. And Liverpool Football Club held on. They held on. And Liverpool Football Club beat Leeds United two–one. Away from home,

away from Anfield. On the bench, the bench at the Hawthorns. In the sixty-sixth minute, Bill watched Hartford score for West Bromwich Albion. And in the eighty-sixth minute, Bill watched Steve Heighway equalise for Liverpool Football Club. And Liverpool Football Club drew one-all with West Bromwich Albion in the Third Round of the Football League Cup. Away from home, away from Anfield. There would have to be a replay. Another replay –

On the bench, the Anfield bench. Bill and fifty-five thousand, nine hundred and seventy-five Merseyside folk were watching Liverpool Football Club play Everton Football Club. And in the opening minutes, they watched Clemence drop the ball in his own six-yard box. Clemence lost the ball. And Royle found the ball in the six-yard box. The Liverpool six-yard box. And Royle shot. But Larry Lloyd was on the line. The Liverpool goal line. And Lloyd cleared the ball off the line. The Liverpool goal line. But in the sixtieth minute, Johnson passed to Royle. Royle passed to Connolly. And Connolly passed to Kendall. Kendall in front of the goal. The Liverpool goal. The goal open, the goal yawning. Kendall shot. And Kendall missed. The open goal, the yawning goal. And in the seventy-seventh minute, Alec Lindsay passed to Steve Heighway. Heighway hoisted the ball. From the left, to the right. And the ball dropped. By the post, the Everton post. And there was Peter Cormack. Cormack headed. And Cormack scored. And Liverpool Football Club beat Everton Football Club one–nil. At home, at Anfield. That evening, Everton Football Club had fifteen points. And Tottenham Hotspur had sixteen points and Arsenal Football Club had sixteen points, too. But that evening, Liverpool Football Club had eighteen points. And Liverpool Football Club were first in the First Division. Not on goal average. On points. Two points. First in the First Division by two points –

And with a game in hand.

. . .

In the kitchen, at the sink. In the night and in the silence. In his pyjamas and in his slippers. Bill filled another glass with water. Bill walked back over to the kitchen wall. And Bill switched off the light again. In the dark and in the silence. Bill walked back up the stairs. Bill went back into their bedroom. And Bill walked around their bed. Bill put down the glass of water on the table beside the bed. Beside his wife. And Ness looked up at Bill. And Ness smiled up at Bill –

Thank you, love. Thank you. But I'm sorry, love . . .

In the bedroom, by their bed. In the night and in the silence. Bill said, I wish you'd see the doctor, love. I really wish you'd go.

But it's nothing, love. It's just a cough. A little cough.

But it's getting no better, love. It's getting worse.

In the night and in the silence. Ness did not reply. Ness had closed her eyes again. In the night and in the silence. Bill walked back around their bed. Bill got back into their bed. In the dark and in the silence. Bill stared up the ceiling. Their bedroom ceiling. And in the dark, and in the silence. Bill said his prayers again.


## 41. THIS IS YOUR LIFE

Three days after Liverpool Football Club had beaten Everton Football Club one–nil. At home, at Anfield. West Bromwich Albion came to Anfield, Liverpool, to play Liverpool Football Club in the replay of the Third Round of the Football League Cup. That evening, twenty-six thousand, four hundred and sixty-one folk came, too. In the fifty-first minute, Robertson of West Bromwich Albion shot from the edge of the penalty area. And the shot glanced off Kevin Keegan. And the shot arced over Ray Clemence. Into the net and into a goal. In the sixty-second minute, Emlyn Hughes shot from the edge of the penalty area. And Latchford knocked the shot down. But the shot still bobbled over the line and into a goal. And the replay of the Third Round of the Football League Cup went into extra time. And in the last minute of extra time, in the one hundred and twentieth minute of the match, the two hundred and tenth minute of the tie, Alec Lindsay crossed into the penalty area. And there was Keegan. To meet the cross, to head the cross. Into the net and into a goal. And Liverpool Football Club beat West Bromwich Albion two–one in the last minute of extra time in the replay of the Third Round of the Football League Cup. At home, at Anfield. Four days later, Liverpool Football Club travelled to the Dell, Southampton, and Liverpool Football Club drew one-all with Southampton Football Club. Away from home, away from Anfield. But that evening, Liverpool Football Club were still first in the First Division. By one point, just one point. But still with a game in hand.

On Saturday 21 October, 1972, Stoke City came to Anfield, Liverpool. That afternoon, forty-five thousand, six hundred and four folk came, too. Forty-five thousand, six hundred and four folk and Tommy Smith. Tommy Smith no longer hurt, Tommy Smith no longer injured. But in the thirty-fourth minute, Hurst hit the bar. The Liverpool bar. And Greenhoff met the rebound. Greenhoff headed the rebound into the net and into a goal. In the sixty-sixth minute, Banks carried the ball more than the permitted four steps. And from the free kick, the indirect free kick, Smith rolled the ball to Emlyn Hughes. And Hughes shot. And Hughes scored. And in the ninetieth minute, the last minute of the match, Ian Callaghan shot into the penalty area. And the shot deflected off Skeels' face. Into the net and into a goal. And Liverpool Football Club beat Stoke City two–one. At home, at Anfield. In the last minute of the match, the very last minute.

Three days afterwards, Athletic Union of Constantinople Football Club of Greece came to Anfield, Liverpool. That evening, thirty-one thousand, nine hundred and six folk came, too. Thirty-one thousand, nine hundred and six folk to watch Liverpool Football Club of England play Athletic Union of Constantinople of Greece in the first leg of the Second Round of the UEFA Cup. In the ninth minute, Ian Callaghan won a corner. Emlyn Hughes passed to Steve Heighway. Heighway shot hard and low across the goalmouth. And Phil Boersma met the shot. Boersma touched the shot over the line and into a goal. Twenty minutes later, Kevin Keegan shot. And the shot rebounded back to Peter Cormack. Cormack shot. And Cormack scored. But in the fifty-ninth minute, Hughes was hurt. Hughes injured. And Phil Thompson came on for Hughes. And in the seventy-eighth minute, Tommy Smith scored a penalty. And Liverpool Football Club beat Athletic Union of Constantinople of Greece three–nil in the first leg of the Second Round of the UEFA Cup. At home, at Anfield.

On Saturday 28 October, 1972, Liverpool Football Club

travelled to Carrow Road, Norwich. But Emlyn Hughes did not travel to Carrow Road. Hughes still hurt, Hughes still injured. Phil Thompson travelled to Carrow Road. In the eighteenth minute, Peter Cormack scored. But Norwich City scored, too. And Liverpool Football Club drew one-all with Norwich City. Away from home, away from Anfield. But that evening, Liverpool Football Club were still first in the First Division. And still with a game in hand.

Three days afterwards, Leeds United came to Anfield, Liverpool. That evening, forty-four thousand, six hundred and nine folk came, too. Forty-four thousand, six hundred and nine folk to watch Liverpool Football Club play Leeds United in the Fourth Round of the Football League Cup. And John Toshack headed wide. And Peter Cormack shot wide. And Harvey saved from Kevin Keegan. But Liverpool Football Club kept coming, Keegan kept coming. And in the thirty-first minute, Steve Heighway robbed Clarke. Heighway crossed for Keegan. Keegan jumped for the cross, Keegan headed the cross. And Keegan scored from the cross. But eight minutes later, Gray took a corner. Jones jumped for the corner. And Jones headed the corner. Into the net and into a goal. And in the second half, after thirteen minutes, Gray passed to Clarke. Clarke passed to Lorimer. Lorimer shot. And Lorimer scored. And Liverpool Football Club were losing to Leeds United. And again Harvey saved from Toshack. But again Liverpool Football Club kept coming, Toshack kept coming. And in the eightieth minute, Emlyn Hughes pushed the ball through to Toshack. Toshack shot. And Toshack scored. And Liverpool Football Club drew two-all with Leeds United in the Fourth Round of the Football League Cup. At home, at Anfield. There would have to be another replay. Another game, always another game –

On Saturday 4 November, 1972, Chelsea Football Club came to Anfield, Liverpool. That afternoon, forty-eight thousand, three hundred and ninety-two folk came, too. In the thirty-third minute, Emlyn Hughes beat Webb to the ball. Hughes faster, Hughes hungrier. And Hughes passed to Kevin Keegan. Keegan fast, Keegan hungry. But Keegan did not shoot. Keegan passed to Toshack. Toshack shot. And Toshack scored. And in the fiftieth minute, Keegan won the ball again. Keegan still fast, Keegan still hungry. Keegan passed to Toshack. But Keegan kept running. Fast and hungry. Toshack crossed.

Keegan met the cross. Fast and hungry. Keegan headed the cross. Into the net and into a goal. And five minutes later, Steve Heighway found Toshack again. And Toshack scored again. And Liverpool Football Club beat Chelsea Football Club three–one. At home, at Anfield. That evening, Arsenal Football Club had twenty-one points and Leeds United had twenty-one points, too. But Liverpool Football Club had twenty-four points. Liverpool Football Club first in the First Division. Not by one point. Not by two points. Liverpool Football Club were first in the First Division by three points.

Three days afterwards, Liverpool Football Club came to the Nikos Goumas Stadium, in Athens, in Greece, to play Athletic Union of Constantinople in the second leg of the Second Round of the UEFA Cup. On a pleasant, sunny afternoon. Against a backdrop of mountains and white houses. In front of fanatical, hysterical supporters. Athletic Union of Constantinople attacked and attacked. And Emlyn Hughes headed off the line. The Liverpool goal line. And Ray Clemence saved. And Clemence saved again. And in the eighteenth minute, Tommy Smith rolled a free kick to Hughes. Hughes shot. The shot hit the inside of the post. The shot flew across the face of the goal. And into the net. But then Hughes fell on the ball in his own penalty area. Hughes touched the ball with his hand in his own penalty area. And Athletic Union of Constantinople won a penalty. And Nikolaidis scored the penalty. As afternoon turned to evening, as the mountains darkened. The houses black now. In front of fanatical, hysterical supporters. Again. Athletic Union of Constantinople attacked and attacked. But in the forty-fourth minute, Hughes won the ball in midfield. Hughes ran with the ball. Hughes passed to Kevin Keegan. Keegan passed back to Hughes. Hughes shot. And Hughes scored. But in the seventieth minute, Heighway was hurt. Heighway injured. And Phil Boersma came on for Heighway. And in the eighty-seventh minute, Smith passed to Keegan. Keegan crossed. And Boersma tapped the cross. Into a goal. And in the night. Before the silent mountains, in the muted stadium. Liverpool Football Club beat Athletic Union of Constantinople three–one in the second leg of the Second Round of the UEFA Cup. Away from home, away from Anfield.

On Saturday 11 November, 1972, Liverpool Football Club travelled to Old Trafford, Manchester. Liverpool Football Club were first in the First Division and Manchester United were last in the First Division. That afternoon, fifty-three thousand, nine hundred and forty-four folk came to Old Trafford, Manchester, to watch top versus bottom. Some of them in gangs, some of them in mobs. Inside the ground and outside the ground. There were policemen with dogs, there were policemen on horses. Supporters herded towards the turnstiles, supporters pushed through the turnstiles. And there were stampedes and there were crushes. Men flattened, children flattened. In the streets and on the terraces. Things fell apart, people fell apart. And on the pitch, the Old Trafford pitch, things fell apart, people fell apart. MacDougall handled the ball. But the referee waved play on. And MacDougall shot. Ray Clemence half stopped the shot. But Davies pounced. And Davies scored. And then O'Neil crossed the ball. And MacDougall beat Chris Lawler to the ball. And MacDougall scored. And Liverpool Football Club lost two–nil to Manchester United. Away from home, away from Anfield. That evening, there was fighting. Fighting in department stores, fighting at the stations. And fighting on the trains. But that evening, Liverpool Football Club were still top of the First Division. Manchester United still bottom.

. . .

High above the battles, high above the fighting. In his office, in his director's office. Sir Matt Busby put down his cup of tea. And Sir Matt Busby said, Well, it's not easy, Bill. And I try to keep out of Frank's way. To not interfere, to not meddle. As much as I can, Bill. To not be seen to be interfering, to not be seen to be meddling. But of course I hear things, Bill. I hear whispers. And things seem to have gone sour in the dressing room. I know things have gone sour in the dressing room. And I know he should be buying . . .

So why don't you step in, asked Bill Shankly. Why don't you say something, Matt? Before it's too late . . .

Sir Matt Busby shook his head. And Sir Matt Busby said, But it's not that easy, Bill. Not that easy at all. I don't want to undermine the man. I don't want to be accused of that. So I'm in a difficult position. A very difficult position. And it's not a position I'd recommend to anyone. Not to you, Bill. Not when your time comes.

Oh, my time is a way off yet, laughed Bill Shankly. So don't you be wasting your worries on me, Matt . . .

Sir Matt Busby looked across his desk at Bill Shankly. Sir Matt Busby stared at Bill Shankly. And then Sir Matt Busby said, Are you sure about that, Bill? Are you certain? If you don't mind me saying, I do think you look tired, Bill. I do think you look drained. And it worries me, Bill. You worry me . . .

I'm fine, said Bill Shankly. Really I am. But thank you, Matt. Thank you. It's just been a very hard week. We were in bloody Athens on Tuesday. Then straight back here to face your lot. So it's been a very tough week. But you know how it is, Matt. You know how it is.

Sir Matt Busby nodded. And Sir Matt Busby said, And Ness? And the girls? They're all well, I hope, Bill?

The girls are great, said Bill Shankly. I don't see enough of them or the grandkids. There's never enough time. But you know how it is, Matt. That's football for you . . .

Sir Matt Busby nodded again. And Sir Matt Busby asked again, And Ness? How is Ness, Bill?

Well, she's had a bad cough, said Bill Shankly. And she's had it for a while now. And I wish she'd cut down on the cigarettes. Because they're not helping. Not helping at all. But she says she smokes two packs every time we play. That's the only way she can cope with the stress. With the worry. Every time we play. But I wish she'd ease up, Matt. And I wish she'd go to the doctors. But what can I do, Matt? She's like me. You'd have to drag her kicking and screaming to the doctors. That's the only way she'll go, Matt . . .

Sir Matt Busby smiled. And Sir Matt Busby said, Well, then maybe you should, Bill. Drag her kicking and drag her screaming. If that's what it takes, Bill. Maybe you should . . .

. . .

On Saturday 18 November, 1972, Newcastle United came to Anfield, Liverpool. That afternoon, forty-six thousand, one hundred and fifty-three folk came, too. In the fifth minute, Peter Cormack scored. In the thirty-fifth minute, Alec Lindsay scored. In the forty-eighth minute, John Toshack scored. And Liverpool Football Club beat Newcastle United three–two. At home, at Anfield.

Four days afterwards, Liverpool Football Club travelled to Elland Road to play Leeds United in the replay of the Fourth Round of the Football League Cup. And Chris Lawler cleared off the line from Charlton. And Jones shot wide of the post. And Bremner shot over the bar. But Leeds United kept coming, Bremner kept coming. And midway through the second half, Tommy Smith took the ball off the toes of Bremner in the penalty area. But Smith took the toes of Bremner, too. The referee awarded a penalty to Leeds United. And Giles took the penalty. But Giles missed the penalty. And in the last minute, the last minute of normal time, the very last minute before extra time, Charlton conceded a corner. And Kevin Keegan jumped for the corner. Keegan leapt. And Keegan outjumped everyone for the corner. Keegan outleapt everyone. And Keegan met the corner. Keegan headed the corner. Into the net and into a goal. And Liverpool Football Club beat Leeds United one–nil in the replay of the Fourth Round of the Football League Cup. Away from home, away from Anfield. In the last minute, the very last minute.

On Saturday 25 November, 1972, Liverpool Football Club travelled to White Hart Lane, London. And in the dressing room. The away dressing room at White Hart Lane. Bill Shankly looked from player to player. From Clemence to Lawler, Lawler to Lindsay, Lindsay to Smith, Smith to Lloyd, Lloyd to Hughes, Hughes to Keegan, Keegan to Cormack, Cormack to Heighway, Heighway to Toshack and from Toshack to Callaghan –

To win anything. Anything at all these days. Then you have to beat Leeds United. You have to beat Chelsea. You have to beat Arsenal. And you have to beat Spurs. And you've beaten Leeds United. And you've beaten Chelsea. And so now you have to beat Spurs, boys. You have to beat them today. Here at White Hart Lane, boys. If we are to win anything. But I know you can, boys. And so I know you will. I know you can and I know you will . . .

In the twenty-eighth minute, Kevin Keegan passed to Steve Heighway. Heighway feinting one way, Heighway swerving the other way. The Tottenham defence going one way, the Tottenham defence leaving the other way open. And Heighway chipped the ball over Jennings. Into the net and into a goal. In the fortieth minute, Peter Cormack played a short corner to Ian Callaghan. Callaghan crossed the ball. Keegan jumped and Keegan leapt. On spring heels. To meet the cross, to head the ball. Into the net and into a goal. And Liverpool Football Club beat Tottenham Hotspur two–one. Away from home, away from Anfield. That evening, Arsenal Football Club had twenty-five points. Leeds United had twenty-six points. And Liverpool Football Club had twenty-eight points. That evening, Liverpool Football Club were still first in the First Division. First, by two points.

Four days afterwards, in the ice and in the snow, Liverpool Football Club came through Checkpoint Charlie to the Sportforum Hohenschönhausen to play Berliner Fußball Club Dynamo of East Berlin, East Germany, in the first leg of the Third Round of the UEFA Cup. But Tommy Smith did not travel. Smith was injured. Trevor Storton travelled. And in the last minute of the first half, the very last minute of the first half, in the ice and in the snow, Brillat crashed into Kevin Keegan. Keegan hurt, Keegan injured. And Brian Hall came on for Keegan. But in the ice and in the snow, Liverpool Football Club held on. Liverpool Football Club prevailed. In the ice and in the snow. Liverpool Football Club drew nil–nil with Berliner Fußball Club Dynamo of East Berlin the first leg of the Third Round of the UEFA Cup. Away from home, away from Anfield.

On Saturday 2 December, 1972, Birmingham City came to Anfield, Liverpool. That afternoon, forty-five thousand, four hundred and seven folk came, too. But not Tommy Smith. Smith still injured. And in the thirteenth minute, Taylor scored for Birmingham City. And in the twenty-first minute, Hope scored for Birmingham City. In the thirty-second minute, Alec Lindsay scored. But ten minutes later, Latchford scored for Birmingham City. One minute later, Peter Cormack scored. But at half-time, Liverpool Football Club were losing three–two to Birmingham City. At home, at Anfield. But ten minutes into the second half, Lindsay equalised. And in the seventy-seventh minute, John Toshack scored. And Liverpool Football Club had come back from three–one down to beat Birmingham City four–three.

Two days later, just two days later, Tottenham Hotspur came to Anfield, Liverpool. That evening, forty-eight thousand, six hundred and seventy-seven folk came, too. Forty-eight thousand, six hundred and seventy-seven folk to watch Liverpool Football Club play Tottenham Hotspur in the Fifth Round of the Football League Cup. In the fifty-fourth minute, Pearce sent a corner over the penalty area. To the far post. The Liverpool far post. And there was Peters. At the far post. The Liverpool far post. And Peters scored. But in the seventy-eighth minute, Emlyn Hughes cut in from the left. And with his left foot, from an impossible angle, Hughes shot. And Hughes scored. And Liverpool Football Club drew one-all with Tottenham Hotspur in the Fifth Round of the Football League Cup. At home, at Anfield. There would have to be yet another replay. Yet another game –

Two days later, just two days later, Liverpool Football Club travelled to White Hart Lane to play Tottenham Hotspur in the replay of the Fifth Round of the Football League Cup. And on a rain-lashed pitch, under a sky lit by lightning, a night deafened by thunder, Tottenham Hotspur scored three goals in the first fifteen minutes. And on a rain-lashed pitch, under a sky lit by lightning, a night deafened by thunder, in the eighty-fifth minute, Ian Callaghan scored. But it didn't matter, it didn't count. On a rain-lashed pitch, under a sky lit by lightning, a night deafened by thunder, Liverpool Football Club had lost three–one to Tottenham Hotspur in the replay of the Fifth Round of the Football League Cup. Away from home, away from Anfield. Liverpool Football Club drenched, Liverpool Football Club soaked. Drained

and exhausted –

Three days later, Liverpool Football Club travelled to the Hawthorns, Birmingham. But Tommy Smith did not travel. And Kevin Keegan did not travel. Phil Thompson travelled and Phil Boersma travelled. And in the twenty-first minute, Boersma scored. But West Bromwich Albion scored, too. And Liverpool Football Club drew one-all with West Bromwich Albion. Away from home, away from Anfield. Another draw, another draw.

Four days later, Berliner Fußball Club Dynamo of East Berlin came to Anfield, Liverpool. That evening, thirty-four thousand, one hundred and forty folk came, too. Thirty-four thousand, one hundred and forty folk to watch Liverpool Football Club play Berliner Fußball Club Dynamo of East Berlin in the second leg of the Third Round of the UEFA Cup. But again Tommy Smith did not come. And again Kevin Keegan did not come. Again Phil Thompson came and again Phil Boersma came. And in the first minute, Peter Cormack passed to Steve Heighway. And Heighway shot. The shot straight at Lihsa. Lihsa unable to hold the shot. The ball loose. And there was Boersma. Boersma racing in from the left. To gather up the loose ball. To shoot.

And to score. But then a neat chip from Netz found Schulenberg. Schulenberg jumped the tackle from Alec Lindsay, Schulenberg passed back to Netz. Netz shot. And Netz scored. An away goal. A dangerous goal. But in the twenty-fifth minute, Heighway shot again. And the shot hit Brillat. The shot cannoned off Brillat. Into the net and into a goal. And in the fifty-sixth minute, Cormack took a free kick. And John Toshack met the free kick. And Toshack scored. And Liverpool Football Club beat Berliner Fußball Club Dynamo of East Berlin three–one in the second leg of the Third Round of the UEFA Cup. At home, at Anfield.

On Saturday 16 December, 1972, Liverpool Football Club travelled to Portman Road, Ipswich. In the twenty-fourth minute, Steve Heighway scored. But Ipswich Town scored, too. And Liverpool Football Club drew one-all with Ipswich Town. Away from home, away from Anfield. Another draw.

One week afterwards, Coventry City came to Anfield, Liverpool. That afternoon, forty-one thousand, five hundred and fifty folk came, too. In the sixth minute, John Toshack scored. And in the twenty-second minute, Toshack scored again. And Liverpool Football Club beat Coventry City two–nil. At home, at Anfield.

On Boxing Day, 1972, Liverpool Football Club travelled to Bramall Lane, Sheffield. In the twenty-seventh minute, Phil Boersma scored. In the fiftieth minute, Chris Lawler scored. And in the eighty-first minute, Steve Heighway scored. And Liverpool Football Club beat Sheffield United three–nil. Away from home, away from Anfield. And that evening, that Boxing Day evening, Leeds United had thirty-three points. Arsenal Football Club had thirty-four points. And Liverpool Football Club had thirty-six points. That evening, that Boxing Day evening, Liverpool Football Club were still first in the First Division. Still first, by two points.

On Saturday 30 December, 1972, Crystal Palace came to Anfield, Liverpool. That afternoon, that last Saturday afternoon of 1972, fifty thousand, eight hundred and sixty-two folk came, too. In the sixty-sixth minute, Peter Cormack scored. And Liverpool Football Club beat Crystal Palace one–nil. At home, at Anfield. And that Saturday evening, that last Saturday evening of 1972, Leeds United were still third in the First Division. Arsenal Football Club still second in the First Division. And Liverpool Football Club were still first in the First Division. Still first,

by two points.

. . .

After their training. At Melwood. After their baths. At Anfield. Bill Shankly and the players and the staff of Liverpool Football Club went upstairs for their lunch. Bill Shankly and the players and the staff ate their steak and chips. Bill Shankly and the players and the staff ate their tinned fruit and cream. And then Bill Shankly and the players and the staff went back out into the car park. Bill Shankly and the players and the staff got back on the bus. Bill Shankly and the players and the staff went to Lime Street Station on the bus. Bill Shankly and the players and the staff got off their bus at Lime Street Station. And Bill Shankly and the players and the staff got onto the front coach of the Liverpool Pullman at Lime Street Station. Bill Shankly and the players and the staff sat on the train to London. Bill Shankly with his book. His book of names, his book of notes. The players with their cards. Their packs of cards, their schools of cards. All the way to London, all the way to Euston Station. And then Bill Shankly and the players and the staff stood up. Bill Shankly and the players and the staff put on their coats. Bill Shankly and the players and the staff picked up their bags. Bill Shankly and the players and the staff got off the Liverpool Pullman at Euston Station. Bill Shankly and the players and the staff stepped onto Platform Three at Euston Station. And now Bill Shankly saw the lights. The bright lights. Bill Shankly saw the cameras. The television cameras. Bill Shankly saw the microphone. The television microphone. And Bill Shankly saw the book. The red book –

Bill Shankly, said Eamonn Andrews –

This is your life . . .


## 42. WE KNOW NEITHER THE DAY, NOR THE HOUR

On the bench, the bench at Upton Park. In the seventy-fifth minute, Bill watched Emlyn Hughes pass to Steve Heighway. Heighway took the pass on his chest, Heighway killed the pass with his chest. Heighway wrong-footed McDowell and Heighway crossed for Kevin

Keegan. Keegan jumped, Keegan leapt. On spring heels. Keegan headed the ball. Into the net and into the goal. The winning goal.

In the dressing room, the away dressing room at Upton Park. Bill pulled the brim of his trilby down low. Bill stepped into the corridor at Upton Park. And Bill grinned at the gentlemen of the London sporting press. And Bill said, What you gentlemen saw today, what you were lucky enough to watch, what you were privileged enough to witness, was total commitment. Total dedication. Total enthusiasm. Total self-belief. And total skill. And so that is what I call 'Total Football', gentlemen. Total Liverpool football.

. . .

On the bench, the bench at Turf Moor. Bill watched Liverpool Football Club play Burnley Football Club in the Third Round of the FA Cup. Burnley Football Club were top of the Second Division, Liverpool Football Club top of the First Division. And on the bench, the bench at Turf Moor, Bill watched John Toshack have chance after chance. But Toshack missed chance after chance. And Liverpool Football Club did not score. And Burnley Football Club did not score. And Liverpool Football Club drew nil–nil with Burnley Football Club in the Third Round of the FA Cup. Away from home, away from Anfield. Another draw, another bloody draw. There would have to be another replay, another bloody replay. Another game,

another bloody game.

. . .

In the office, at his desk. With his glue and with his scissors. Bill put down the newspaper. And Bill put on his thinking cap –

In the week before Christmas, the chairman and the directors of Manchester United had sacked Frank O'Farrell. And the chairman and the directors of Manchester United had appointed Tommy Docherty as their new manager. Bill knew Tommy, Bill liked Tommy. Bill hoped Tommy would do well. And Bill had wished Tommy good luck. Before he was appointed as the manager of Manchester United, Tommy had been the manager of the Scottish national team. Tommy had been bringing new players into the Scottish national team, young players. Players like Kenny Dalglish, players like Lou Macari. Bill knew Tommy would have to bring new players to Manchester United, young players. Players like Lou Macari. Lou Macari played for the

Celtic Football Club. But Bill knew Lou Macari was not happy playing for the Celtic Football Club. Not happy playing for Jock Stein. Lou Macari wanted more money to play for the Celtic Football Club. And Jock Stein would not pay him more money to play for the Celtic Football Club. Lou Macari had had enough of the Celtic Football Club. And Lou Macari had had enough of Jock Stein. And Jock Stein had had enough of Lou Macari. Jock had called Bill. And Jock had told Bill that Lou Macari was unhappy. That Lou Macari wanted away. Away from Celtic, away from Scotland. Bill had seen Lou Macari play for the Celtic Football Club and for the Scottish national team. And Bill had liked what he had seen. Bill liked Lou Macari. Jock told Bill he would sell Lou Macari to Liverpool Football Club if Bill wanted Lou Macari. Bill did want Lou Macari. Bill thought Lou Macari was just the player they needed. Just the player they needed to stay first in the First Division. Just the player they needed to guarantee they finished the season first in the First Division. Champions of England –

And so how much do Celtic want for Macari, asked the chairman of Liverpool Football Club. How much are they asking?

Two hundred thousand pounds. And before you say another word. I know two hundred thousand pounds is a lot of money. But this player is still only twenty-three years old. Just twenty-three years old. And this player has already scored fifty-seven goals in just one hundred games. And he has scored many of those goals as a substitute. And many of those goals have been vital goals. Winning goals. I believe this player has that knack. That magic knack of getting vital goals. Vital goals that win vital matches. Goals that win cups, goals that win trophies. Goals that win championships . . .

Very well, said the chairman of Liverpool Football Club. If you believe this is the player we need. The player we need to secure the League. And if the Celtic Football Club are willing to sell Lou Macari for two hundred thousand pounds. Then we will give you the money to buy him, Mr Shankly.

Back in the office, back at his desk. Bill phoned Jock Stein. And then Bill phoned Lou Macari. Bill invited Lou Macari down to Liverpool, down to Anfield, to watch Liverpool Football Club play Burnley Football Club in the replay of the Third Round of the FA Cup. And Lou Macari came down to Liverpool, down to Anfield. Lou

Macari was the guest of honour of Liverpool Football Club. Lou Macari sat in the stands with the chairman and the directors of Liverpool Football Club. That night, fifty-six thousand, one hundred and twenty-four folk were in the stands at Anfield, Liverpool, too. And Lou Macari watched John Toshack score twice. And Peter Cormack score once. And Lou Macari watched Liverpool Football Club beat Burnley Football Club three–nil in the replay of the Third Round of the FA Cup. And after the game, after the match, Bill invited Lou Macari down to his office. And Bill put a contract down on his desk in front of Lou Macari. And Bill put a pen on top of the contract in front of Lou Macari. And Bill said, After what you have seen tonight, son. After what you have heard tonight. The team you have seen and the supporters you have heard. I'm certain I do not need to convince you to sign for Liverpool Football Club, son. I am sure you need no more persuading. I am certain you are already convinced. I am sure you are already persuaded. This team is as good as the one you are leaving, these supporters as great as the ones you are leaving. And I've always said this city is very similar to Glasgow, son. So I think you'll find Liverpudlians very similar to Glaswegians. In their humour and in their warmth. And so you'll feel at home, son. Very much at home.

Lou Macari looked down at the pen on top of the contract on the desk. And then Lou Macari looked up at Bill Shankly –

It's a very big move for me, Mr Shankly. And so I would be very grateful if you'd give me a little bit more time to think about it and to talk it over with my family, sir.

Bill nodded. And Bill said, Of course, son. Of course. You should always talk things over with your family. But you tell them from me. You tell them from Bill Shankly, that we will look after you, son. And so I'll see you tomorrow. First thing tomorrow, son. Bright and early. After you've had a good chat with your family, son. And after you've had a good night's sleep. I'll see you with a pen and I'll see you with your boots, son . . .

In the office, at his desk. Bright and early. Bill waited for Lou Macari. And Bill waited and Bill waited. But Lou Macari did not come back to Anfield, Liverpool. Not with his pen and not with his boots. Lou Macari went to Old Trafford, Manchester. With his pen and with his boots. Lou Macari signed for Manchester United. Manchester

United and Tommy Docherty. And in the office, at his desk. Bill cursed. And Bill cursed. Bill picked up the telephone. Bill phoned Jock Stein. And Bill said, What the hell happened with Macari, John?

Manchester gold, said Jock Stein. That's what happened, Bill.

So how much have they offered you for him, John?

The same as you, said Jock Stein. But apparently they have offered the boy double the wages you were offering him . . .

Double the wages? They must be desperate.

I am sorry, said Jock Stein. I'm very sorry for all the trouble he's caused you, Bill. And I'm sorry for any embarrassment the greedy little bastard might have caused you, too . . .

Bill laughed. And Bill said, You've nothing to apologise to me for, John. To be honest, the boy has probably made the right choice. After all, United can give him something I could never have given him. Something more than bloody money . . .

You what, said Jock Stein. What on earth can Manchester United give him that Liverpool could not have given him, Bill?

First-team fucking football, John. That's what.

. . .

On the bench, the Anfield bench. Bill and forty-five thousand, nine hundred and ninety-six folk were watching Liverpool Football Club play Derby County. In the twenty-third minute, they watched John Toshack score. But they also watched Davies score for Derby County. And Liverpool Football Club drew one-all with Derby County. At home, at Anfield. Another draw. But the first draw at home this season, the first point dropped at Anfield this season. The only point dropped at home, the only point lost at Anfield. And that evening, Liverpool Football Club were still first in the First Division –

Still first, by two points.

On the bench, the bench at Molineux. Bill watched Emlyn Hughes score an own goal. And in the seventeenth minute, Bill watched Kevin Keegan equalise. But then Bill watched Richards score for Wolverhampton Wanderers. And Liverpool Football Club lost two–one to Wolverhampton Wanderers. Away from home, away from Anfield. That evening, Liverpool Football Club were still first in the First Division. But by just one point –

Just one point.

On the bench, the Anfield bench. Bill and fifty-six thousand, two hundred and ninety-six folk were watching Liverpool Football Club play Manchester City in the Fourth Round of the FA Cup. But that afternoon, they did not see Liverpool Football Club score. And they did not see Manchester City score. And Liverpool Football Club drew nil–nil with Manchester City in the Fourth Round of the FA Cup. At home, at Anfield. Yet another draw. Yet another

replay. Yet another

game –

On the bench, the bench at Maine Road. Bill was watching the forty-sixth game Liverpool Football Club had played this season, their eighteenth cup tie of the season. And on a night of sweeping rain, on a sodden field, Bill watched Towers pass to Donachie. Donachie passed to Lee. Lee shot. And Ray Clemence pushed the shot away. But the ball fell to Bell. Bell shot. And Bell scored. And then on this night of sweeping rain, on this sodden field, Bill watched Summerbee float a free kick over the Liverpool defence. Bell touched the free kick on to Booth. Booth shot. And Booth scored. And on this night of sweeping rain, on this sodden pitch, Liverpool Football Club lost two–nil to Manchester City in the replay of the Fourth Round of the FA Cup. Away from home, away from Anfield. In their forty-sixth game of the season, their eighteenth cup tie of the season. Liverpool Football Club had been drenched again, Liverpool Football Club soaked again. Liverpool Football Club drained –

Drained and exhausted. On the bench, the Anfield bench. Bill and forty-nine thousand, eight hundred and ninety-eight folk were watching Liverpool Football Club play Arsenal Football Club. Arsenal Football Club were second in the First Division. Arsenal Football Club just one point behind Liverpool Football Club. Just one point. That was all there was between first and second. Between Liverpool Football Club and Arsenal Football Club. And in the first half, Bill and the forty-nine thousand, eight hundred and ninety-eight folk watched Liverpool Football Club attack and attack. And Kevin Keegan shot. And Keegan missed by inches. And now they watched Arsenal Football Club attack and attack. And Ray Clemence saved from Radford. And at half-time, there was nothing to choose between Liverpool Football Club and Arsenal Football Club. Nothing to choose but one point. And in the second half, Bill and forty-nine thousand, eight hundred and ninety-eight folk watched Liverpool Football Club attack and attack again. And Ian Callaghan shot. And Callaghan missed by inches. And Wilson saved from Brian Hall. And now they watched Arsenal Football Club attack and attack again. And Armstrong charged into the penalty area. Alec Lindsay hooked up Armstrong. The referee blew his whistle. The referee awarded a penalty to Arsenal Football Club. Ball took the penalty. And Ball scored the penalty. And seven minutes later, Radford charged towards the penalty area. Radford skipped past Clemence. Clemence out of his area. And Radford shot. Into the net, the empty net. And into a goal. And Liverpool Football Club lost two–nil to Arsenal Football Club. At home, at Anfield. That evening, Arsenal Football Club had forty-two points. And Liverpool Football Club had forty-one points. That evening, Arsenal Football Club were first in the First Division. And Liverpool Football Club were second in the First Division –

Second again. Second best again,
the bridesmaid again. Always
the bridesmaid, never
the bride.

. . .

In the house, in their hallway. In the night and in the silence. Bill took off his coat, Bill took off his hat. Bill hung up his coat and Bill hung up his hat. And in the dark and in the silence. Bill heard Ness cough. Not upstairs, downstairs. In the dark and in the silence. Bill went into the front room. Bill switched on the light. And Bill saw Ness. In her chair. And Bill said, What are you doing down here, love? Sat in the dark, love? Are you OK, love? Why are you not upstairs, love? Why are you not in your bed, love? Are you OK, love?

I'm sorry, said Ness. I must have nodded off, love. I'm sorry, I'm sorry. I'm very sorry, love . . .

In the front room, in her chair. Ness tried to stand. To get to her feet. But Ness sat back down. Back down in her chair –

I'm sorry, love. I'm sorry . . .

Bill put his hand on Ness. Bill felt her forehead. And Bill said, Christ, love. You're burning up, love. I'm calling the doctor, love. Stay still, love. Stay there, love . . .

Bill ran out into the hall. Bill picked up the telephone. Bill rang the doctor. Bill called the doctor out. And then Bill went back into the front room. Bill sat down beside Ness. Bill held her hand. And Bill waited for the doctor to come. The doctor came. The doctor looked at Ness. The doctor listened to her chest. The doctor took her temperature. And then the doctor went out into the hall. The doctor picked up the telephone. The doctor rang the hospital. The doctor asked for an ambulance. Bill stayed sat beside Ness. Bill held her hand. And Bill waited for the ambulance to come. The ambulance came. The ambulance staff looked at Ness. The ambulance staff carried Ness out to the ambulance. The ambulance staff put Ness into the back of the ambulance. Bill got into the back of the ambulance. Bill sat beside Ness in the back of the ambulance. Bill held her hand. Bill squeezed her hand. And the ambulance took Ness to the hospital. The ambulance staff carried Ness out of the ambulance. The ambulance staff took Ness into the hospital. The nurses helped Ness into a wheelchair. The nurses wheeled Ness upstairs into a ward. The nurses lifted Ness onto a bed. The nurses helped Ness undress. The nurses helped Ness settle into her bed. Her hospital bed. Ness lay in her bed. Her hospital bed. And Ness looked at Bill sat beside her bed. Her hospital bed –

I'm sorry, said Ness. I'm sorry about all this . . .

Please stop saying sorry, love. It's me who should be saying sorry to you, love. Me who should have been home sooner . . .

Ness shook her head. And Ness smiled –

Did you win, asked Ness. Today?

No, love. We lost two–nil.

Ness shook her head again. And Ness closed her eyes –

I'm sorry, said Ness again. I'm sorry, love.

Bill stood up. Bill leant over the bed. Bill kissed Ness on her forehead. And Bill said, It doesn't matter, love. It doesn't matter. You just rest, love. You just sleep now, love . . .

Ness opened her eyes again. And Ness smiled at Bill.

Bill sat back down in the chair beside the bed. Beside his wife. Bill reached back over to the bed. Back over to Ness. And Bill took her hand. Bill held her hand. Bill squeezed her hand –

Bill would not let it go.

And Ness smiled again. And Ness closed her eyes again.

Beside the bed, the hospital bed. Beside his wife, beside his Ness. In the night and in the silence. The long night and the long silence. Bill knew nothing. Nothing but Ness. Ness and work.

That was all Bill knew. Ness and work.

That was all. All there was.

Ness and work.

. . .

In the corridor, the Anfield corridor. Outside the office, the office of Bill Shankly. On the Monday morning, the Monday morning after Liverpool Football Club had lost two–nil to Arsenal Football Club. The Monday morning after Phil Thompson had not played against Arsenal Football Club. Phil Thompson was standing in the corridor outside the door to the office of Bill Shankly. Phil Thompson was rehearsing the words he would say to Bill Shankly. Phil Thompson was getting things straight in his mind. Ronnie Moran had told Phil Thompson he thought Phil would be playing on Saturday against Arsenal Football Club. But Phil Thompson had not played on Saturday against Arsenal Football Club. Ronnie Moran had told Phil Thompson he thought Phil should have played on Saturday against Arsenal Football Club. Ronnie Moran had said, You should go and see the Boss, lad. You should go and ask him why you didn't play on Saturday. Why he left you out. It's important you see him, lad. It's important you ask him. The Boss will think more of you if you go and see him. If you go and ask him, lad . . .

In the corridor, in front of the door. The door to Bill Shankly. Rehearsing the words in his head, getting them straight in his mind. His mind racing, his heart beating. Phil Thompson saw the door fly open. And Phil Thompson saw Bill Shankly. In the corridor, outside his office. Bill said, Hello, son. How are you today? You well, son?

Phil Thompson swallowed and Phil Thompson stammered –

Well, I was hoping I might have a word with you, Boss . . .

Then step inside, son. And sit yourself down . . .

Bill held open the door for Phil Thompson. Phil Thompson stepped into the office. Bill closed the door. And Bill said, Sit down, son. Sit down. Don't be standing on ceremony now, son. And now you tell me what's on your mind, son. Come on now. Don't keep me guessing, son. Don't be keeping me in suspense now . . .

430

Phil Thompson sat down in front of the desk. Phil Thompson stared across the desk at Bill Shankly. Phil Thompson swallowed again, Phil Thompson cleared his throat. And Phil Thompson stammered –

I was just wondering why didn't I play on Saturday, Boss?

Bill leapt back up onto his feet. And Bill shouted, Play? Why didn't you play? You are asking me why you didn't play? Jesus Christ, son. You should be thanking me you didn't play. I wouldn't play you in the same team as that load of rubbish: Clemence, Lawler, Lindsay, Smith, Lloyd, Hughes, Keegan, Hall, Boersma, Toshack and Callaghan. Jesus Christ. Every one of them is crap. Every one of them a has-been. They are the past. But you are the future, son. The future. How old are you, son? Eighteen years old? Jesus Christ. And you're asking me why you didn't play? Jesus Christ. You are going to play for this club for the next ten years. You are the future of this club, son. A future captain of this club. A future captain of England, son. Jesus Christ. Now be off with you, son. Get out of here. Before I change my mind, son. Before I make you train with the reserves. Before I make you play for the reserves again. Go on, get out. Out with you . . .

. . .

In the ward, in the chair. Beside the bed, beside his wife. In the evening and in the silence. Bill reached across the blankets. Back over to his wife, back over to Ness. Bill took her hand. Bill held her hand.

Ness opened her eyes. Ness turned her face to Bill –

You're never still here? Have you nothing better to do, love?

Bill smiled. Bill shook his head. And Bill said, No, love.

Ness smiled again. And Ness closed her eyes again.

In the ward, in the chair. Beside the bed, beside his wife. In the evening and in the silence. The nurse came to tell Bill it was time he should go home. And Bill stood up. Bill leant over the bed. Bill kissed Ness on her forehead. And Bill whispered, I'll see you tomorrow, love. I'll see you tomorrow. You sleep well now, love. You sleep well.

Bill walked out of the ward. Bill walked down the stairs. And Bill walked out of the hospital. Bill got to his car. Bill got into his car. And Bill drove home. In the night and in the silence. Bill pulled into the drive. Bill got out of his car. And Bill went up the drive. In the night and in the silence. Bill took out his key. Bill unlocked the front door. And Bill opened the door. In the dark and in the silence. Bill took off his hat, Bill took off his coat. And Bill hung up his coat and hat. In the dark and in the silence. Bill went down the hall. Bill went into the kitchen. And Bill switched on the light. In the night and in the silence. Bill went to the drawer. Bill opened the drawer. And Bill took out the tablecloth. Bill closed the drawer. Bill walked over to the table. And Bill spread the cloth over the table. Bill walked over to another drawer. Bill opened the drawer. And Bill took out the cutlery. The spoon. The fork. And the knife. Bill closed the drawer. Bill walked back over to the table. And Bill laid one place at the table. Bill went to the cupboard. Bill opened the cupboard door. And Bill took out the crockery. The bowl and the plate. Bill walked back over to the table. Bill put the bowl and the plate on the table. And Bill walked back to the cupboard. Bill took out a glass. Bill closed the cupboard door. And Bill walked back to the table. Bill put the glass on the table. Bill walked to another cupboard. And Bill opened the door. Bill took out the salt and pepper pots. Bill closed the cupboard door. And Bill walked back to the table. Bill put the salt and pepper pots on the table. Bill went to the pantry. And Bill opened the pantry door. Bill took out a jar of honey. Bill walked back to the table. And Bill put the jar of honey on the table. Bill walked over to the refrigerator. Bill opened the refrigerator door. And Bill took out the butter dish. Bill walked back over to the table. Bill put the butter dish down in the centre of the table. And Bill walked back over to the refrigerator. Bill took out a bottle of fresh orange juice. Bill closed the refrigerator door. And Bill walked back over to the table. Bill put down the bottle of orange juice on the table. And in the night and in the silence. In the kitchen, at the table. Bill stared down at the spoon. The fork and the knife. The bowl and the plate. The glass on the table. And in the night and in the silence. In the kitchen, at the table. Bill knelt down. Bill put his hands together. Bill closed his eyes. And Bill said a prayer. Over and over,

the same prayer. The one prayer.

. . .

On the bench, the bench at Maine Road. In the forty-third minute, Bill watched Summerbee float a free kick over the Liverpool defence. And Booth met the free kick. Booth headed the free kick. Into the net and into a goal. In the sixty-ninth minute, Bill watched Tommy Smith argue with the referee. And the referee sent Smith off for dissent. In the seventy-fourth minute, Bill took off Steve Heighway. And Bill sent on Brian Hall. One minute later, Bill watched Alec Lindsay take a free kick. And Hall touched on the free kick to Boersma. Boersma spun, Boersma turned. Boersma shot and Boersma scored. And Liverpool Football Club drew one-all with Manchester City. Away from home, away from Anfield. Another draw. That afternoon, Arsenal Football Club beat Leicester City. Arsenal Football Club had forty-four points now. And Liverpool Football Club had forty-two points. That evening, Arsenal Football Club were still first in the First Division. And Liverpool Football Club were still second in the First Division. But not by one point. Now by two points –

On the bench, the bench at Anfield. In the sixty-seventh minute, Bill and forty-three thousand, eight hundred and seventy-five folk watched Steve Heighway score. And in the eightieth minute, they watched Kevin Keegan score. And Liverpool Football Club beat Ipswich Town two–one. At home,

at Anfield. On the Friday morning. The Friday morning before Liverpool Football Club would play Everton Football Club. Away from home, away from Anfield. Brian Hall was standing in the corridor outside the door to the office of Bill Shankly. Brian Hall was fed up, Brian Hall was frustrated. Fed up with being in and out of the team, frustrated at being the twelfth man. Brian Hall had had enough. He had rehearsed the words he would say to Bill Shankly, he had got the words straight in his mind. Brian Hall knocked on the door to the office of Bill Shankly. Brian Hall opened the door –

And Bill looked up from his desk. Up from his typewriter. And Bill said, Hello, son. How are you today? Sit yourself down, son . . .

Thank you, said Brian Hall. But I'd rather stand, Boss.

Bill shrugged. And Bill said, Suit yourself, son. So what's on your mind, son? Come on now. Don't be keeping me guessing now . . .

I've decided I want a transfer, Boss . . .

Bill leapt to his feet. And Bill shouted, A transfer? Jesus Christ, son. But you're playing tomorrow. Jesus Christ, son. What will we do?

I'm playing, asked Brian Hall.

Of course you're playing. Jesus Christ, son. I'm not going to leave my best player out. Not when we're playing bloody Everton. No bloody way. Jesus Christ, son. What's wrong with you? A transfer?

Jesus Christ. Now be off with you, son. Get out of here. Before I change my mind, son. Go on, get out . . .

On the bench, the bench at Goodison Park. In the eightieth minute, Bill and fifty-four thousand, two hundred and sixty-nine Merseyside folk watched Emlyn Hughes score. And eight minutes later, they watched Hughes score again. And Liverpool Football Club beat Everton Football Club two–nil. Away from home, away from Anfield. That evening, Arsenal Football Club had forty-five points. And Liverpool Football Club had forty-six points. That evening, Liverpool Football Club were first again in the First Division. First again, by one point. One point and with a game in hand –

On the bench, the Anfield bench. Bill and thirty-three thousand, two hundred and seventy folk were watching Liverpool Football Club play Sportgemeinschaft Dynamo Dresden of East Germany in the first leg of the Fourth Round of the UEFA Cup. In the twenty-fifth minute, they watched Brian Hall pass to Steve Heighway. And Heighway passed to Phil Boersma. Boersma crossed for Hall. And Hall headed the cross. Into the net and into a goal. In the sixtieth minute, they watched Heighway shoot. And the shot was saved. But the ball fell to Boersma. Boersma shot. And again the shot was saved. But again the ball fell to Boersma. Again Boersma shot. And Boersma scored. And Liverpool Football Club beat Sportgemeinschaft Dynamo Dresden two–nil in the first leg of the Fourth Round of the UEFA Cup. At home,

at Anfield. On the bench, the Anfield bench. In the thirty-seventh minute, Bill and forty-one thousand, six hundred and seventy-four folk watched Tommy Smith roll a free kick to Brian Hall. And Hall crossed the ball. The ball came back to Hall. Hall crossed the ball again. Larry Lloyd met the cross. And Lloyd headed the cross. Into the net and into a goal. One minute later, they watched Phil Boersma pass to John Toshack. And Toshack shot. The shot blocked on the line. But there was Kevin Keegan. And Keegan shot. And Keegan scored. And Liverpool Football Club were beating Southampton Football Club two–nil. At home, at Anfield. But in the forty-fourth minute, Larry Lloyd and Emlyn Hughes misjudged a long free kick from Steele. The long free kick floating behind Lloyd and Hughes. Channon behind Lloyd and Hughes. And Channon headed the ball over Ray Clemence. Into the net and into a goal. And in the sixty-first minute, Lloyd and

Clemence went up for the same ball. Lloyd and Clemence misjudged the ball. The ball falling to Gilchrist. And Gilchrist shot. Into the open goal, into the yawning net. And Liverpool Football Club were drawing two-all with Southampton Football Club. But at home, at Anfield. The supporters of Liverpool Football Club did not surrender. The Spion Kop did not surrender. The Kop called, the Spion Kop roared. For victory. And in the eighty-seventh minute, Phil Boersma crossed for Keegan. Keegan jumped, Keegan leapt. On spring heels. Keegan met the ball. And Keegan headed the ball. Into the net and into a goal. The winning goal. And the Kop cheered, the Spion Kop celebrated. Victory. That evening, Arsenal Football Club had forty-eight points and Liverpool Football Club had forty-eight points, too. But Liverpool Football Club were still first in the First Division. On goal average.

On the bench, the bench at the Victoria Ground. Bill watched Liverpool Football Club play Stoke City. And Bill did not see Liverpool Football Club score. But Bill did see Stoke City score. An own goal. And Liverpool Football Club beat Stoke City one–nil. Away from home, away from Anfield. Thanks to an own goal. Liverpool Football Club were still first in the First Division. Not on goal average –

On points again. By two points again –

First, still first.

. . .

In the hospital, on the ward. By her bed, her hospital bed. The doctors said Ness was over the worst. The doctors said Ness could go back home. But the doctors said Ness would still need to rest. And to take things easy. Bill knew Ness did not like to rest. And to take things easy. Bill worried that Ness would not rest. And not take things easy. And Bill was worried because he had to go away. Away to Germany, away to Dresden. Bill knew his daughters would take care of Ness. His daughters would look after Ness. And their friends and their neighbours. But Bill was still worried. Bill did not want to go away. Away to Germany, away to Dresden. Bill wanted to stay at home, to stay in Liverpool. To take care of Ness, to look after Ness.

Ness shook her head. And Ness smiled –

But it's what you do, love. It's your work. So you have to go, love. And you have not to be worrying about me . . .

But I do worry. I worry I should be here. Here with you . . .

Ness shook her head again –

You have to go, love. It's your job. The job that puts the food on our table, love. And keeps the roof over our head. It's your work . . .

I know, love. I know it's my job. I know it's my work. But it keeps me from you. From taking care of you, from looking after you. And that's not right, love. That cannot be right . . .

But the girls will take care of me, love. The girls will look after me. So there's no need for you to be here, love. Under my feet.

Perhaps not this time. But what about the next time? There's never a time when I'm here. Never a time when I'm not at work. I've never been here. Here when you needed me, here when I should have been. I know I have neglected you. I know I have, love . . .

Now you're talking rubbish, laughed Ness. A load of old rubbish, love. I've never once felt neglected in my life. Believe me, love. Never once. But I do worry about *you*. I worry about the strain of it all on you. The long days and the long nights. The days away and the nights away. I do worry about that. Because I worry about you, love. Because I know you don't do things by half. I know it's not in your nature. And I wouldn't have it any other way. Have you any other way, love. But that doesn't stop me worrying. About the strain of it all on you. That's what I worry about, love. I worry about you.

I know that, love. I know that. But the doctors don't want you worrying. And I don't want you worrying, love. Because that's no good for you. No good for you at all, love. No good . . .

Well, a fine pair we are, laughed Ness. You worrying about me and me worrying about you. A fine pair of worriers we are, love.

I know that, love. I know that. But the day has surely got to come when we can stop all our worrying. The day has got to come when we can start enjoying ourselves, love . . .

Ness put her arms around Bill. And Ness smiled –

And what day would that be, love . . .

When will that day come?

. . .

On the bench, the bench at the Rudolf Harbig Stadium, in Dresden, in East Germany. Bill watched Liverpool Football Club play Sportgemeinschaft Dynamo Dresden in the second leg of the Fourth Round of the UEFA Cup. In the fifty-third minute, Bill watched Alec

Lindsay cross. And Kevin Keegan met the cross with his right foot. Keegan hammered the ball with his right foot. Into the net and into a goal. And Liverpool Football Club beat Sportgemeinschaft Dynamo Dresden one–nil in the second leg of the Fourth Round of the UEFA Cup. Away from home, away from Anfield.

On the bench, the Anfield bench. In the fiftieth minute, Bill and forty-two thousand, nine hundred and ninety-nine folk watched Chris Lawler score. Five minutes later, they watched Emlyn Hughes score. And in the eighty-eighth minute, they watched Brian Hall score. And Liverpool Football Club beat Norwich City three–one. At home, at Anfield. That evening, Arsenal Football Club had fifty points and Liverpool Football Club had fifty-two points. And that evening, Liverpool Football Club were still first in the First Division –

On the bench, the Anfield bench. On Grand National Day, at lunchtime. Bill and forty-eight thousand, four hundred and seventy-seven folk were watching Liverpool Football Club play Tottenham Hotspur. Bill and forty-eight thousand, four hundred and seventy-seven folk watching Jennings save from Peter Cormack. Jennings save from Hall. Jennings save from Hughes. Jennings save a penalty from Keegan. And Jennings save a penalty from Smith. And Gilzean score for Tottenham Hotspur. But in the seventieth minute, they watched Kevin Keegan score for Liverpool Football Club. And Liverpool Football Club drew one-all with Tottenham Hotspur. At home, at Anfield. That evening, Liverpool Football Club were still first in the First Division. But by one point, just one point –

But with a game in hand.

On the bench, the bench at St Andrew's. Bill watched Tommy Smith score. But Bill watched Birmingham City score. And score again. And Bill watched Emlyn Hughes get sent off. And Liverpool Football Club lost two–one to Birmingham City. Away from home, away from Anfield. That evening, Liverpool Football Club were still first in the First Division. Still by one point, by just one point –

But now with no game in hand.

On the bench, the Anfield bench. Again, Bill was watching Liverpool Football Club play Tottenham Hotspur. Bill and forty-eight thousand, six hundred and seventy-seven folk watching Liverpool Football Club play Tottenham Hotspur in the first leg of the semi-final of the UEFA Cup. And in the seventeenth minute, they watched Tommy Smith take a free kick. And the free kick rebounded to Lindsay. Lindsay shot. And Lindsay scored. And Liverpool Football Club beat Tottenham Hotspur one–nil in the first leg of the semi-final of the UEFA Cup. At home, at Anfield.

On the bench, the Anfield bench. In the fourteenth minute, Bill and forty-three thousand, eight hundred and fifty-three folk watched Steve Heighway get brought down in the penalty area. And the referee awarded a penalty. Kevin Keegan took the penalty. And Keegan scored the penalty. And Liverpool Football Club beat West Bromwich Albion one–nil. At home, at Anfield. That evening, Liverpool Football Club were still first in the First Division. But not by one point. By two points, by two points again.

On the bench, the bench at Highfield Road. In the thirty-sixth minute, Bill watched Phil Boersma score. And in the sixtieth minute, Bill watched Boersma score again. And Liverpool Football Club beat Coventry City two–one. Away from home,

away from Anfield. On the bench, the bench at St James' Park. In the high wind and in the lashing rain, in the twenty-fourth minute, Bill watched Peter Cormack cross the ball. And Kevin Keegan hit the ball. Into the net and into a goal. But then Bill watched Tudor score for Newcastle United. And Tudor score again. And in the high wind and in the lashing rain, Liverpool Football Club lost two–one to Newcastle United. Away from home, away from Anfield.

On the bench, the Anfield bench. Two days later, just two days later. In driving rain and in howling wind. The gates closed one and a half hours before the kick-off. In driving rain and in howling wind, Bill and fifty-five thousand, seven hundred and thirty-eight folk were watching Liverpool Football Club play Leeds United. And in the driving rain and in the howling wind, in the forty-seventh minute, they watched Harvey touch a free kick from Tommy Smith over the bar. And in the driving rain, the howling wind, they watched Brian Hall take the corner. Chris Lawler went up for the ball. Larry Lloyd went up for the ball. Phil Thompson went up for the ball. But the ball fell to Peter Cormack. Cormack shot. And Cormack scored. And in the driving rain and in the howling wind, the Spion Kop sang, *We're going to win the League! We're going to win the League! Ee-aye-addio, we're going to win the League!* And in the driving rain and in the howling wind, in the eighty-fifth minute, Cormack dribbled to the left of the byline. And Cormack crossed. Harvey cut out the cross. But the ball ran loose. Loose to Kevin Keegan. Keegan wheeling in, Keegan wriggling free. Keegan shot. And Keegan scored. And in the driving rain and in the howling wind, Liverpool Football Club beat Leeds United two–nil. At home, at Anfield. In the driving rain, in the howling wind. The Spion Kop roared, *WE'RE GOING TO WIN THE LEAGUE! WE'RE GOING TO WIN THE LEAGUE! EE-AYE-ADDIO, WE'RE GOING TO WIN THE LEAGUE!* And in the driving rain and in the howling wind, the players of Leeds United formed an avenue to the tunnel. The Anfield tunnel. In the driving rain, in the howling wind, the players of Leeds United applauded the players of Liverpool Football Club from the pitch. The Anfield pitch. That evening, Arsenal Football Club had fifty-five points. And Liverpool Football Club had fifty-nine points. But Arsenal Football Club still had two more games to play. And Liverpool Football Club had just one more game to play. Just one last game. And Bill knew if Liverpool Football Club lost that one last game. And if Arsenal Football Club won their last two games. And scored seven goals in those last two games. Then Arsenal Football Club would be the Champions of England. But Bill knew if Liverpool Football Club did not lose their last game. If they won or if they drew. Their last game against Leicester City. At home, at Anfield. Then Bill knew Liverpool Football Club would be the Champions of England. The Champions again –

Champions at last.

On the bench, the bench at White Hart Lane. Two days later, just two days later. Bill watched Liverpool Football Club play Tottenham Hotspur in the second leg of the semi-final of the UEFA Cup. And in the forty-eighth minute, Bill watched Chivers take a throw-in. And Gilzean flicked on the throw-in to Peters. And Peters side-footed the ball past Ray Clemence. Into the net and into a goal. But seven minutes later, Bill watched Kevin Keegan pounce on a loose ball from England. And Keegan passed to Steve Heighway. Heighway shot. And Heighway scored. An away goal, a dangerous goal. And then Bill watched Peters ride three tackles. And Peters shot. The shot hit the bar. And Pratt headed wide the rebound. But then Bill watched

Coates cross. And Peters met the cross. Peters shot. And Peters scored. And Tottenham Hotspur had beaten Liverpool Football Club two–one in the second leg of the semi-final of the UEFA Cup. But Liverpool Football Club had won the tie. Liverpool Football Club had won the semi-final. On away goals. Away from home, away from Anfield. Liverpool Football Club were in the final of the UEFA Cup –

A European final.

. . .

On the bench, the Anfield bench. Bill and fifty-six thousand, two hundred and two folk were watching the last home game of the season, the very last game of the season. Bill and fifty-six thousand, two hundred and two folk who knew Liverpool Football Club needed only one point to be crowned Champions of England. Just one point, one last point. And for ninety minutes, Bill and fifty-six thousand, two hundred and two folk watched Clemence, Lawler, Lindsay, Smith, Lloyd, Hughes, Keegan, Boersma, Thompson, Heighway, Callaghan and then Hall attack and attack. But Liverpool Football Club did not score. And for ninety minutes, Bill and fifty-six thousand, two hundred and two folk watched Clemence, Lawler, Lindsay, Smith, Lloyd, Hughes, Keegan, Boersma, Thompson, Heighway, Callaghan and then Hall defend and defend. But Leicester City did not score. And in the ninetieth minute, the referee looked at his watch. The referee put his whistle to his lips. And the referee blew his whistle. Liverpool Football Club had drawn nil–nil with Leicester City. And Liverpool Football Club had their point. Their one point, their one last point. And Liverpool Football Club were Champions of England. At home, at Anfield. Liverpool Football Club were crowned Champions again, Champions at last. And on this day, this coronation day. The supporters of Liverpool Football Club erupted, the supporters of Liverpool Football Club exploded. With joy and with relief. In applause and in song. In praise and in celebration. And the players of Liverpool Football Club paraded the Football League trophy around the ground. The Anfield ground. All four sides of the ground. The Anfield ground. And all four sides of the ground applauded and sang. In praise and in celebration. And on the bench, the Anfield bench. His jacket stuck to his shirt. His shirt stuck to his vest. His vest stuck to his skin. Bill stood up, Bill got to his feet. And Bill walked across the pitch. The Anfield pitch. And Bill stood before the Kop. The Spion Kop. His jacket stuck to his shirt. His shirt stuck to his vest. His vest stuck to his skin. Bill put his hands together. Not in prayer, but in thanks. In thanks to the Kop. The Spion Kop –

And the Spion Kop threw their scarves down towards Bill. Their red scarves. Raining down on Bill. In thanks. All of their scarves. Their red scarves. And Bill picked up their scarves. All of their scarves. Their red scarves. And Bill tied one scarf around his neck. One red scarf. And Bill held up another scarf. Another red scarf. In his arms. A scarf. A red scarf. Aloft. His arms aloft,

in thanks.

. . .

Before the house, on their doorstep. In the evening and in the silence. Bill opened the door, Bill stepped into the house. Into the hall. And there was Ness. In the house, in their home –

Well done. Well done, love.

Thank you, love.

I've got the kettle on. It's almost boiled. So sit yourself down, love. You must be exhausted . . .

Bill nodded. And Bill followed Ness into the kitchen. His jacket still stuck to his shirt. His shirt still stuck to his vest. His vest still stuck to his skin. Bill sat down at the table. The kitchen table. The scarf still around his neck –

The red scarf.

Ness waited for the kettle to boil. Ness poured the boiling water into the teapot. Ness waited for the tea to stand. Ness walked over to the refrigerator. Ness took out the jug of milk. Ness poured the milk into the two mugs. The two Liverpool mugs. Ness put the milk jug down. Ness picked up the teapot. Ness poured the tea into the two mugs. The two Liverpool mugs. And then Ness carried the two mugs over to the table. Ness put one mug down on the table in front of Bill. And Bill saw her hand. Her fingers and her nails. And Bill reached out to Ness. Bill took her hand, Bill held her hand. And Bill said, Look at your nails, love. What have you been doing, love?

I was a bit worried, laughed Ness.

Bill shook his head. And Bill said, I'm sorry, love. I'm sorry I make you so worried. Every day, every game . . .

Don't be sorry, said Ness. Be happy, be pleased. Happy you've another game, love. A final . . .

. . .

In the dressing room, the Anfield dressing room. Bill looked from player to player. The sixteen players in the Liverpool dressing room. The sixteen players desperate to play for Liverpool Football Club in the first leg of the final of the UEFA Cup against Borussia VfL 1900 Mönchengladbach e.V. of West Germany. At home, at Anfield. Bill took out a piece of paper from the pocket of his coat. And Bill said, Our team will be Clemence, Lawler, Lindsay, Smith, Lloyd, Hughes, Keegan, Cormack, Hall, Heighway and Callaghan. And our substitutes will be Lane, Thompson, Storton, Boersma and Toshack.

And in the dressing room, the Anfield dressing room. Tommy Smith stood up. And Tommy Smith led out the players of Liverpool Football Club. Into the rain, the heavy rain. There were pools of water standing on the pitch. The Anfield pitch. But at half past seven, the match kicked off. In the ceaseless, heavy rain. The players could not kick the ball further than two yards. In the ceaseless, heavy and torrential rain. The pools of water became lakes of water. The ball not moving, the ball stuck. The lakes of water now a sea. And at eight o'clock, the referee took the players off the field. And in the ceaseless, heavy and torrential rain. The Spion Kop sang, *Ee-aye-addio, we're not going home! We're not going home! Ee-aye-addio, we're not going home!* But twenty minutes later, the match was abandoned. Abandoned and postponed until tomorrow evening. And in the ceaseless, heavy and torrential rain. Bill walked down the touchline. The Anfield touchline. Bill walked into the dressing room. The home dressing room. Bill looked from player to player. From drenched and sodden player to drenched and sodden player. And Bill said, Get yourselves bathed, boys. Get yourselves changed. And get yourselves away to your homes, away to your beds, boys. And I'll see you all back here tomorrow.

. . .

In the corridor, the Anfield corridor. The morning after the match had been abandoned. The match postponed. John Toshack knocked on the door to the office of Bill Shankly. John Toshack took a deep breath. And John Toshack opened the door –

In the office, at his desk. Bill looked up from his desk. Up from his typewriter. And Bill said, Hello, son. How are you today, son?

Actually, I'm not very well, said John Toshack.

I'm sorry to hear that, son. What's the matter with you?

I'll tell you what's the matter with me, said John Toshack. You're the matter with me, Boss! But I'll say this for you, Boss. You must be the luckiest man alive. You've gone out at home in a European final playing just two men up because Bob bloody Paisley and Joe bloody Fagan told you the bloody Germans would attack. But the Germans fooled Bob and Joe. The Germans kidded you all. And so you were bloody lucky the game was abandoned. Because you'd never have beaten them, Boss. Not playing like that. You'd have been lucky to win a bloody corner. Let alone the match. You'd never have won. Not playing like that. Not with that team. You'd have been lucky to get a draw. A bloody draw. At home. In a European final. And if you play like that tonight. Play that same team tonight. That's all you'll get, Boss. A bloody draw. And I tell you. They'll be laughing all the way back to Germany. Because they know they'll slaughter you back at their place. Back in Germany. They know they'll bloody slaughter you!

Bill stared at John Toshack. And Bill said, Finished?

No, said John Toshack. I haven't finished. I have one last question for you, Boss. I want to know who picks the team. Is it you, Boss? Or is it Bob bloody Paisley and Joe bloody Fagan? I want to know who picks the team here. Is it you, Boss?

Bill leapt to his feet. And Bill shouted, Who the hell do you think you're talking to? Who the hell do you think you are? Coming in here, shouting the odds. Jesus Christ. Get out of here, you cheeky bastard. Go on, get out. Get out with you . . .

Don't worry, said John Toshack. I'm going. But I'm not coming back. Because you can stuff your bloody team!

Bill watched John Toshack storm out of the office. Bill heard John Toshack slam the door of the office. And Bill smiled. Bill walked around his desk. Around the bags and bags of mail. And Bill went out of the office. Bill went down the corridor. Bill went down to the boot room. And Bill saw Bob, Joe, Reuben and Ronnie sat on the empty, upturned beer crates, among the scrubbed and hanging boots. And Bill sat down in the boot room. Among the scrubbed and hanging boots. And Bill said, Morning, boys. How are you all today, boys? I hope you're all dried off? Jesus Christ, eh? What a night. I thought that rain would never end. I thought it would never stop. It was like something out of the Bible. Like Noah and his flood, it was . . .

Yes, laughed Bob. It was. But the pitch will be fine for tonight, Bill. Heavy but fine enough.

Bill smiled. And Bill said, That's great, Bob. Great news. And so what about the Germans, eh? What did you think of them, boys?

I think they thought we'd attack more than we did, said Joe. I think they thought we might play Phil Boersma from the start. Or even Tosh. And so I think they'd set themselves up to defend. And then to try and nick a goal. And so I think that's why they brought in Surau for Michallik. That was a bit of a surprise . . .

Bill nodded. And Bill said, Aye. We didn't expect them to do that. Not from what we'd said, not from what they'd said. I thought they would push more for a goal. I didn't think they'd be so defensive. Not from what we'd all said . . .

Yes, said Bob again. And I wouldn't be surprised if they don't bring Michallik back in tonight. And attack a bit more . . .

Bill said, Aye. I am sure you are right, Bob. I am sure they will. But I think we should, too. Because their defence are not that tall. Not that tall at all. They are much smaller than I thought . . .

Yes, said Bob. You're right. So what are you thinking, Bill?

I'm thinking we should make a change . . .

And Bill stood up. Bill walked out of the boot room. Bill walked back down the corridor. Bill went back into the office. Around the bags and bags of mail. And Bill sat down at his desk. Bill picked up his address book. Bill turned the pages of his address book. Bill picked up the telephone. Bill dialled a number. And Bill said, Hello, son. Are you not in your bed yet?

No, said John Toshack. I've only just got back home.

Well, get to your bloody bed, son. Don't be dilly-dallying. Because you'll need your rest, son. You're playing tonight . . .

. . .

In the dressing room, the Anfield dressing room. Bill looked from player to player. The sixteen players in the Liverpool dressing room. The sixteen players desperate to play for Liverpool Football Club in the first leg of the final of the UEFA Cup against Borussia VfL

444

1900 Mönchengladbach e.V. of West Germany. At home, at Anfield. Bill took out a piece of paper from the pocket of his coat. And Bill said, There'll just be the one change to our team tonight, boys. And so our team will be Clemence, Lawler, Lindsay, Smith, Lloyd, Hughes, Keegan, Cormack, Toshack, Heighway and Callaghan. And the substitutes will be Lane, Thompson, Storton, Boersma and Hall . . .

And in the dressing room, the Anfield dressing room. Brian Hall stood up. Brian Hall stared at Bill Shankly. Brian Hall shook his head, Brian Hall cursed. And Brian Hall walked out of the dressing room. Brian Hall slammed the dressing-room door. And the players looked at Bill Shankly. The staff looked at Bill Shankly. And Bill said, Let him go. Let him calm down. The boy is disappointed. The boy is hurt. Disappointed he's not playing, hurt he is on the bench. And so the boy has reacted like he has done. But I would expect the same reaction from every one of you boys. If you were not playing, if you were on the bench. Because you should be disappointed, you should be hurt. If you're not playing for Liverpool Football Club in a European final. If you've not the chance to be part of history. And to do something no Liverpool player has ever done before. To win a European trophy. And to do something no English player has ever done before. To win the League and to win a European trophy. In one season, in the same season . . .

In the twenty-first minute, Chris Lawler crossed. John Toshack met the cross. Toshack headed the cross down for Kevin Keegan. Keegan diving for the ball, Keegan lunging for the ball. And Keegan headed the ball. Into the net and into a goal. Four minutes later, Lindsay crossed. And Bonhof handled the cross in the penalty area. The referee blew his whistle. The referee awarded a penalty. Keegan took the penalty. But Kleff saved the penalty. In the twenty-ninth minute, Rupp passed to Wimmer. Wimmer passed to Heynckes. Heynckes passed to Dammer. And Dammer shot. But the shot hit the post. In the thirty-third minute, Emlyn Hughes crossed. Toshack met the cross. Toshack headed the cross down for Keegan. And Keegan shot. Into the net and into a goal. In the sixtieth minute, Heynckes passed to Wimmer. And Wimmer shot. But the shot went over the bar. Two minutes later, Keegan took a corner. Larry Lloyd met the corner. And Lloyd headed the corner. Into the net and into a goal. In the sixty-fifth minute, Steve Heighway fouled Jensen in the penalty area. The referee blew his whistle. The referee awarded a penalty. Heynckes took the penalty. But Ray Clemence saved the penalty. And Liverpool Football Club beat Borussia VfL 1900 Mönchengladbach e.V. of West Germany three–nil in the first leg of the final of the UEFA Cup. At home, at Anfield. Bill walked down the touchline. The Anfield touchline. And Bill shook the hand of Hennes Weisweiler, the coach of Borussia VfL 1900 Mönchengladbach –

Well played, said Hennes Weisweiler. Well played to you and to Liverpool Football Club, Mr Shankly. You are easily the best team we have ever played. You are full of power, you are full of strength. But you are also very attractive when you attack. Very skilful. And so I can't say I fancy our chances now. I think our chances of winning the trophy have disappeared. So congratulations to you, Mr Shankly . . .

Bill shook his head. And Bill said, Thank you, sir. Thank you very much. It was a fantastic match. A high-class game. An international-class game. Because you played very well, too. And so I cannot say it was a case of what you did wrong. It was more a case of what we did right. And the most important thing for us is that we did not give a goal away. That was the most important thing we did right. But you are a great side, sir. And so I make no predictions for the second leg. Because I know it's only half-time –

Still only half-time.

. . .

In the dressing room. The away dressing room at the Bökelberg-stadion in Mönchengladbach, in West Germany. Bill looked from player to player. The sixteen players in the Liverpool dressing room. The sixteen players desperate to play for Liverpool Football Club in the second leg of the final of the UEFA Cup. Away from home, away from Anfield. Bill took out a piece of paper from the pocket of his tracksuit. His red tracksuit. And Bill said, There'll be no change to our team tonight, boys. It'll be the same team who won three–nil at Anfield. And so our team will be Clemence, Lawler, Lindsay, Smith, Lloyd, Hughes, Keegan, Cormack, Toshack, Heighway and Callaghan. And the substitutes will be the same. The substitutes will be Lane, Thompson, Storton, Boersma and Hall . . .

But from the first whistle of the game, from the very first kick of the match, Borussia Mönchengladbach attacked and attacked Liverpool Football Club. Again and again, they came and they came at Liverpool Football Club. And in the twentieth minute, the heavens opened. With a flash of lightning, with a clap of thunder. The German heavens fell down upon Liverpool Football Club. Rain. Cold rain. Cold and heavy rain. Cold and heavy, ceaseless and torrential rain falling down on Liverpool Football Club. And in the thirtieth minute, Rupp cut out a pass from Ian Callaghan to Larry Lloyd. Rupp pounced on the pass. Rupp pulled the ball back for Heynckes to hammer. Into the net and into a goal. And ten minutes later, Netzer played a long ball down the left to Rupp. Rupp beat two Liverpool players. And again Rupp pulled the ball back for Heynckes. And again Heynckes hammered the ball. From the edge of the penalty area. Into the net and into the goal. And in the first half of the second leg of the final of the UEFA Cup, Liverpool Football Club had been completely outplayed. And completely outclassed. And Liverpool Football Club were losing two–nil to Borussia Mönchengladbach. Away from home, away from Anfield. On the bench, the bench in Bökelbergstadion. Bill stood up, Bill got to his feet. And Bill walked down the touchline. Down the tunnel. Into the dressing room. The away dressing room. And Bill looked from player to player to player. From drenched and sodden player to drenched and sodden player. And Bill said, I tell you what, boys. By, they are a good side. And by, they've played well. But I'll tell you something else, boys. As they walked off just now. As they came down this tunnel. I looked into their eyes, boys. Into all of their eyes. And I'll you this, boys. I'll tell you this: they've gone, boys. They've given it their best shot. And they have shot their bolt, boys. They've nothing left to give. The tank is empty, boys. They're done. You mark my words, boys. That lot are done. So come on, boys. Come on now. Because we're almost there, boys –

We're almost home . . .

But from the start of the second half, from the very first kick of the second half, Borussia Mönchengladbach attacked and attacked Liverpool Football Club. Again and again, they came and they came at Liverpool Football Club. And on the bench, the bench in Bökelberg-stadion. Bill stood up again, Bill got to his feet again. And Bill began to pace the touchline. To pace and to prowl. Turning to look up at the supporters of Liverpool Football Club. To point up at the supporters of Liverpool Football Club. To stare up into the eyes of the supporters of Liverpool Football Club. Knowing *they* knew this was the greatest test Liverpool Football Club had ever faced. But knowing they *believed* this was a test Liverpool Football Club would pass. Knowing they believed. Knowing they believed victory would come,

believing victory would come,

victory would come,

victory –

And now the supporters of Liverpool Football Club were scaling the perimeter of the pitch, the supporters of Liverpool Football Club swarming onto the pitch. Dancing for joy, jumping for joy. Patting the players of Liverpool Football Club on their backs, hoisting the players of Liverpool Football Club onto their own backs. And the officials of UEFA carried a large table onto the pitch. The officials of UEFA placed the huge UEFA Cup on the table. And Tommy Smith stepped out of the carnival of supporters of Liverpool Football Club. Tommy Smith picked up the huge UEFA Cup. And Tommy Smith held aloft the huge UEFA Cup. And the players of Liverpool Football Club reached out and touched the UEFA Cup. They held the UEFA Cup. And the supporters of Liverpool Football Club reached out and touched the UEFA Cup. And they held the UEFA Cup, too. The players and the supporters of Liverpool Football Club . . .

In the dressing room. The away dressing room. Drenched in rain, soaked in sweat. Bill sat on the bench. Drenched in rain and soaked in sweat. Bill listened to the joy of the players of Liverpool Football Club. Drenched in rain, soaked in sweat. Bill listened to the joy of the supporters of Liverpool Football Club. Drenched in rain and soaked in sweat. Bill heard the studs coming down the tunnel. Drenched in rain, soaked in sweat. Bill watched the dressing-room door open. Drenched in rain and soaked in sweat. Tommy Smith carried the huge UEFA Cup into the dressing room. Drenched in rain, soaked in sweat. Tommy Smith handed the huge UEFA Cup to Bill –

Here you are, Boss. There you go. It's all yours, Boss.

Drenched in rain, soaked in sweat. Bill shook his head. Bill smiled. And Bill said, No, Tommy. It's all ours . . .

. . .

At the airport, at Speke Airport. In the morning, at half past two in the morning. Bill and the players and the staff of Liverpool Football Club got off the plane from Germany. And Bill could not believe his eyes. Everywhere he looked, he saw faces. The faces of people. Everywhere. There were hundreds, there were thousands. Hundreds and thousands of people at the airport, at Speke Airport. In the morning, at half past two in the morning. The people waiting to greet the players and the staff of Liverpool Football Club, the people waiting to cheer the players and the staff of Liverpool Football Club. The people smiling, the people happy. And Bill could not believe his ears. The people all cheering and clapping, the people all shouting and singing, *LI-VER-POOL, LI-VER-POOL, LI-VER-POOL . . .*

And the next evening there was a parade. A parade through the streets of Liverpool. On an open-top bus, on the top deck of the bus. With their two cups, with their two trophies. From Anfield to the centre of the city, to the heart of the city from Anfield. On the open-top bus, on the top deck of the bus. Again. Bill could not believe his eyes. Everywhere he looked, he saw faces. The faces of people. Everywhere. There were hundreds. There were thousands. Hundreds *of* thousands of people. The people smiling, the people happy. From Anfield to the centre of the city, to the heart of the city from Anfield. Again. Bill could not believe his ears. The people all cheering and clapping, the people all shouting and singing, *LI-VER-POOL,*
*LI-VER-POOL, LI-VER-POOL . . .*

On William Brown Street. Bill got off the bus with the players and the staff of Liverpool Football Club. On William Brown Street. Bill walked up the steps to the front of the Picton Library with the players and the staff of Liverpool Football Club. Before the Corinthian columns of the Picton Library. Bill stood with the players and the staff of Liverpool Football Club and their families. And before the Corinthian columns of the Picton Library. Bill still could not believe his eyes. Everywhere Bill looked, Bill saw more faces. The faces of more people. Everywhere. More and more people. Hundreds of thousands more people. More smiling people, more happy people. And before the Corinthian columns of the Picton Library. Bill still could not believe his ears. These hundreds of thousands of smiling people all cheering and all clapping, these hundreds of thousands of happy people all shouting and all singing, *LI-VER-POOL, LI-VER-POOL, LI-VER-POOL . . .*

And on William Brown Street. Before the Corinthian columns of the Picton Library. With the players and with the staff of Liverpool Football Club and their families. Between the two cups, between the two trophies. Again. Bill fought back tears. Again. Bill struggled to breathe. And again. Bill stepped forward. Again. Bill opened his arms. And again. The people, the hundreds of thousands of people, all fell silent. *Just like that.* They all fell silent. All silent, all waiting –

Ladies and gentlemen. This is the greatest day of my career. The happiest day of my life. I have known nothing like it as a player or a manager. Because you are the greatest fans in the world. We have won for you. And that is all we are interested in, winning for you. And the reason we have won is because we believe in you and you believe in us. And it's your faith and your interest that have won us something. Thank God you are all here. Thank God we are all here. Thank you. You don't know how much we love you. Thank you . . .

And the people, the hundreds of thousands of people, all cheered and clapped, they all shouted and sang –

*SHANK-LEE, SHANK-LEE –*

*SHANK-LEE . . .*

On William Brown Street. Before the Corinthian columns of the Picton Library. With the players and with the staff of Liverpool Football Club and their families. Between the two cups, between the two trophies. Bill turned to Ness. Bill took her hand. Bill held her hand. Bill squeezed her hand. And Bill said, Thank you, love. Thank you.

Ness looked up at Bill. And Ness smiled at Bill –

Is this the day, love? Is this the day?


## 43. AFTER THE TRIUMPHS, BEFORE THE TRIUMPHS

In the summer of 1973, in the second week of July. In the pavilion, the pavilion at Melwood. Bill Shankly, Bob Paisley, Joe Fagan, Reuben Bennett, Ronnie Moran and Tom Saunders stood before the players of Liverpool Football Club. And Bill Shankly looked around the pavilion.

The pavilion at Melwood. From player to player. From Phil Boersma to Derek Brownbill, from Derek to Ian Callaghan, from Ian to Ray Clemence, from Ray to Peter Cormack, from Peter to Roy Evans, from Roy to Brian Hall, from Brian to Steve Heighway, from Steve to Emlyn Hughes, from Emlyn to Kevin Keegan, from Kevin to Frankie Lane, from Frankie to Chris Lawler, from Chris to Alec Lindsay, from Alec to Larry Lloyd, from Larry to Hughie McAuley, from Hughie to John McLaughlin, from John to Dave Rylands, from Dave to Tommy Smith, from Tommy to Peter Spiring, from Peter to Trevor Storton, from Trevor to Peter Thompson, from Peter to Phil Thompson, from Phil to John Toshack, from John to Alan Waddle and from Alan to John Webb. Bill Shankly nodded. And Bill Shankly smiled –

Thanks for last year. Thank you very much, boys. Your medals and your plaques are in that box over there in the corner. But now forget them. Because now we start again. And we start again at the bottom. The very bottom. So come on now, boys –

Come on. Let's get it going, boys . . .

. . .

In the summer of 1973, at the end of the second week of July. In the corridor, the Anfield corridor. Emlyn Hughes knocked on the door to the office of Bill Shankly. And Emlyn Hughes opened the door.

Bill Shankly looked up from his desk. Up from his typewriter –

Hello, Emlyn. How are you today, son? Sit yourself down . . .

Thank you, Boss. And how are you, Boss? Are you well, Boss? And how are your family, Boss? Are they all well, Boss?

They are all very well, Emlyn. Thank you, son. And how about you and your family, Emlyn? Are they are all well, son? And your father, Emlyn? How is your father, son?

He's very well, Boss. Thank you, Boss. But it was actually something my dad said that made me want to have a word, Boss.

Oh? And what was that, son? What did he say?

Well, we were talking, Boss. Me and my dad, Boss. About my new contract. And so we were talking about my future, Boss. Me and my dad. Because you know I always talk to him about everything, Boss. You and him. You are the two people I always talk to, Boss. And he knows, and you know, how much I love playing for this club. And playing for you, Boss. And how I'd never want to play for anyone else. Not for Manchester United or Arsenal or any of them clubs that have been sniffing around, Boss. Like they always do. I wouldn't want to, Boss. Especially not now, not after the season we've just had. But the thing is, Boss. The thing is, I'm playing for England now. And I love playing for England, Boss. And I want to be the captain of England, Boss. It's my dream. It's been my dream for as long as I can remember, Boss. And so me and my dad were talking about it. About me being captain of England, Boss. But my dad said he doesn't think I'll ever be captain of England. Not if I'm not even captain of Liverpool, Boss. My dad thinks it'll never happen. If I'm not even captain of my own club, Boss. He thinks I'll never be captain of England. But he thinks it might happen if I was at Manchester United. Or at Arsenal. Or Leeds. Or even Everton, Boss. He thinks if I was playing for any of them. Then I'd be captain, Boss –

And then the captain of England . . .

Bill Shankly leapt to his feet –

So you're saying to me, son. You're telling me, unless I make you captain of Liverpool Football Club, then you're off, son. Off to play for Manchester United. Arsenal or Leeds. Or even bloody Everton. Is that what you're saying, son? Is that what you're telling me?

No, Boss, no. Not at all, Boss. No, Boss. I'd never do that, Boss. But I'm confused, Boss. Confused about what to do, Boss. About whether to give up on my dream or not, Boss. I mean, you told me, Boss. You told me when I first came here I was a future captain of Liverpool, Boss. And a future captain of England, Boss. And I believed you, Boss. I believed you and so did my dad, Boss . . .

So now you're calling me a liar, are you?

No, Boss, no. Not at all, Boss. No, Boss. I'd never do that, Boss. After my own father, Boss. You are the man I respect most, Boss . . .

So what are you saying, son? What are you asking me?

I'm just asking you if I should forget my dream, Boss? My dream of captaining England, Boss. That's all, Boss. I just want to know if I should give up even thinking about it, Boss. Because I know *you* know how much it means, Boss. You told me the thing you wanted most was to play for Scotland, Boss. And how proud you were the day you captained Scotland. At Hampden, against England . . .

Bill Shankly sat back down behind his desk –

Aye, the day you beat us three–one.

I'm sorry about that, Boss. But at least you can always say you captained your country, Boss. You had that honour, sir –

It was not just a dream for *you* . . .

. . .

In the summer of 1973, at the start of the third week of July. In the car park, the Anfield Road car park. Tommy Smith had changed into his training gear. Tommy Smith was standing in the car park with the other players of Liverpool Football Club. Tommy Smith was about to get on the bus. The bus to take him and the other players of Liverpool Football Club out to Melwood. Out to training. Tommy Smith laughing, Tommy Smith joking. In the car park, the Anfield Road car park. In his tracksuit and in his sweater. Bill Shankly walked towards the players of Liverpool Football Club. Bill Shankly greeted the players. Bill Shankly shook their hands, Bill Shankly patted their backs. Bill Shankly asked after their weekends, Bill Shankly asked after their families. Bill Shankly laughing and Bill Shankly joking. Bill Shankly turned to Tommy Smith. Still smiling, still smiling –

Morning, Tommy. Morning, son. How are you today, Tommy? And can I have a word, son? A quick word, Tommy?

Tommy Smith nodded. And Tommy Smith followed Bill Shankly back into the stadium. Down the corridor, into the office. And Bill Shankly closed the door. Bill Shankly sat down at his desk –

Sit down, Tommy. Have a seat, son.

Tommy Smith sat down.

I have decided to make Emlyn captain, Tommy. You'll still be the club captain, son. But Emlyn will be the captain of the team, Tommy. On the pitch, during the game. Is that OK with you, son?

Tommy Smith stared across the desk at Bill Shankly. And Tommy Smith nodded. And Bill Shankly leapt back up onto his feet –

OK then, Tommy. Thanks for coming in, son. I'll see you up at Melwood, Tommy. See you up at training, son . . .

Tommy Smith stood up. Tommy Smith walked out of the office. Down the corridor, out of the stadium. Into the car park and onto the bus. The bus waiting for Tommy Smith. But Tommy Smith was not laughing, Tommy Smith not joking –

Not any more.

. . .

In the summer of 1973, in the fourth week of July. All the players of Liverpool Football Club had to go and see Bill Shankly –

At the end of the last season, during the parade through the streets of Liverpool, John Smith, the new chairman of Liverpool Football Club, had climbed on board the open-top bus. John Smith had stood on the top deck of the bus. Between the two cups, between the two trophies. And John Smith had told the players of Liverpool Football Club they would all be getting new contracts for the following season. The new season. Now all the players of Liverpool Football Club had come to see Bill Shankly to discuss their new contracts for the following season. The new season. All the players of Liverpool Football Club standing in a line in the corridor outside the door to the office of Bill Shankly. Each player rehearsing the words he would say to Bill Shankly. Each player getting his words straight in his mind. And now Brian Hall was the player standing at the front of the line to the door to the office of Bill Shankly. Brian Hall rehearsing his words, Brian Hall getting those words straight in his mind. Brian Hall had decided he wanted a forty-pound-a-week rise as part of his new contract for the following season. The new season. But Brian Hall knew what Bill Shankly was like. Brian Hall knew Bill Shankly always got the better of him. Brian Hall knew if he asked Bill Shankly for a forty-pound-a-week rise, then Bill Shankly would blame the government and give him a twenty-pound-a-week rise. And that would be that. The end of that. And so Brian Hall had decided he would ask Bill Shankly for an eighty-pound-a-week rise. And then Brian Hall would let Bill Shankly beat him down to a forty-pound-a-week rise. Brian Hall smiled to himself. It was possible he might even get a fifty-pound-a-week rise. Brian Hall chuckled to himself . . .

The door to the office of Bill Shankly opened. And Chris Lawler stepped out of the office of Bill Shankly. Chris Lawler looked at Brian Hall, Chris Lawler smiled at Brian Hall. And Chris Lawler winked at Brian Hall. Chris Lawler held open the door to the office of Bill Shankly for Brian Hall. Brian Hall stepped into the office of Bill Shankly. And Brian Hall saw Bill Shankly –

Bill Shankly looked up from the pile of contracts on his desk. And Bill Shankly smiled –

Hello, Brian. How are you, son? Sit yourself down, son . . .

Brian Hall closed the door. And Brian Hall sat down.

Right, son. What do you think you're worth?

Brian Hall looked across the desk at Bill Shankly. Brian Hall took a deep breath. And Brian Hall said, I think an eighty-quid-a-week rise, Boss. I think that's what I'm worth . . .

Bill Shankly stared back across his desk at Brian Hall. Bill Shankly stuck out his chin. Bill Shankly stroked his chin. And then Bill Shankly stroked the sides of his face –

An eighty-pound-a-week rise, eh? That's a lot of money, son. That's a big rise. A very big rise, son.

Brian Hall shifted in his seat. And Brian Hall said, I know that, Boss. I know that. I know it is . . .

There won't be many folk who pay to see you play who have ever had an eighty-pound-a-week rise in their pay. In fact, I doubt there's one, son. Not one . . .

Brian Hall nodded. And Brian Hall said, I know that, Boss.

Well then, just as long as you do, son. As long as you remember that. Then OK, son. If that's what you think you're worth. Then that's what I'll give you, son. An eighty-pound-a-week rise. Now send in the next one, son . . .

Brian Hall stood up. And Brian Hall said, Thank you, Boss.

Bill Shankly looked back down at the pile of contracts on his desk. And Bill Shankly smiled –

After the parade, after John Smith had climbed down from the open-top bus, the new chairman of Liverpool Football Club had told Bill Shankly each player of Liverpool Football Club could have a one-hundred-pound-a-week rise as part of their new contract for the following season. The new season. Bill Shankly knew that was no way to run a football club. To run Liverpool Football Club. Bill Shankly knew no player of Liverpool Football Club would expect a one-hundred-pound-a-week pay rise. Bill Shankly knew no player of Liverpool Football Club would ever ask for a hundred-pound-a-week pay rise. And no player had asked him for a one-hundred-pound-a-week pay rise. Not one. Just as Bill Shankly knew no player would ever ask Matt Busby for a one-hundred-pound-a-week pay rise. Or ask Bill Nicholson, or ask Don Revie –

Not one player,

ever.

. . .

On Friday 24 August, 1973, the Friday before the first game of
the 1973–74 season. The first match of the new season. At home, at
Anfield. The players and the staff of Liverpool Football Club gathered
around the table in the centre of the dressing room. The home dressing
room. Around the green baize cloth on the table in the centre of the
dressing room. The Liverpool dressing room. The eleven plastic men
on the green baize cloth. The eleven red plastic men, each with a
number on their back. Bill Shankly picked up the players one by one –

We need our keeper to get the ball out quick to the full-backs.
To feed them fast. That's the way. OK, Clem?

And Ray Clemence nodded.

Bill Shankly picked up the two plastic men with the numbers
two and three on their backs –

And so we need numbers two and three to always be making
themselves available. Always ready to push up. OK, Chris? OK, Alec?

And Chris Lawler nodded. And Alec Lindsay nodded.

Bill Shankly picked up the two plastic men with the numbers
four and five on their backs –

Geoff Hurst will be up front for them tomorrow. You all know
what he's like. Big man, strong man. And good in the air. But he'll be
on his own. So numbers four and five, you should take it in turns to
mark him. That way one of you gets a wee rest, but he never does. So
talk to each other, work it out. OK, Larry?

And Larry Lloyd nodded. And Tommy Smith waited, waited
for Bill Shankly to say his name. But Bill Shankly picked up the two
plastic men with the numbers six and eight on their backs –

Six and eight. You need to be closing them down, cutting their
supply lines. Starving them. And then feeding the ball out wide, fast as
you can, out to the wings. To Cally and to Steve. OK, Emlyn? OK,
Peter? You got that? You know what you're doing?

And Emlyn Hughes nodded. Peter Cormack nodded. And
Tommy Smith waited. And waited. And Tommy Smith looked across
the room at Bob Paisley. Bob Paisley looking down at his feet. And
Tommy Smith looked across the room at Joe Fagan. Joe Fagan looking

down at his feet. And at the end of the meeting, Tommy Smith stood up. Tommy Smith walked over to Bill Shankly. And Tommy Smith said, Can I have a word please, Boss?

Sure, Tommy. Sure, son.

Bill Shankly and Tommy Smith stepped out of the dressing room. The home dressing room. Bill Shankly and Tommy Smith stood outside the dressing room in the corridor. The Anfield corridor. And Tommy Smith said, I never heard my name, Boss. I never heard you say my name. So I was just wondering if I'll be playing, Boss?

I have no made my mind up, Tommy. No yet, son.

Tommy Smith nodded. And Tommy Smith said, OK, Boss.

. . .

The next day, Stoke City came to Anfield, Liverpool. That afternoon, fifty-two thousand, nine hundred and thirty-five folk came, too. Fifty-two thousand, nine hundred and thirty-five folk to watch the first game of the new season. At home, at Anfield. Bill Shankly walked into the dressing room. The home dressing room. Bill Shankly took out a piece of paper from his pocket. And Bill Shankly read out the names on the piece of paper –

Our team today will be Clemence, Lawler, Lindsay, Thompson, Lloyd, Hughes, Keegan, Cormack, Heighway, Boersma and Callaghan.

And Tommy Smith stared at Bill Shankly. Bill Shankly looking around the room. From player to player. From Clemence to Lawler, Lawler to Lindsay, Lindsay to Thompson, Thompson to Lloyd, Lloyd to Hughes, Hughes to Keegan, Keegan to Cormack, Cormack to Heighway, Heighway to Boersma and from Boersma to Callaghan. Bill Shankly not looking at Brian Hall, Bill Shankly not looking at John Toshack. And Bill Shankly not looking at Tommy Smith –

Tommy Smith got up from the bench in the dressing room. The home dressing room. Tommy Smith walked out of the dressing room. The Liverpool dressing room. Tommy Smith walked down the corridor. The Anfield corridor. And Tommy Smith heard the dressing-room door open behind him. Tommy Smith heard the boots in the corridor behind him. Tommy Smith heard the studs on the stairs in the tunnel. The Anfield tunnel. And then Tommy Smith heard the roar of the crowd. The Anfield crowd . . .

That afternoon, there was a bomb scare at Villa Park,

Birmingham. There was a bomb scare at Belle Vue, Doncaster. That afternoon, there was fighting between some of the supporters of Derby County and Chelsea Football Club. Fighting between some of the supporters of Arsenal Football Club and Manchester United. That afternoon, there were stabbings at Euston Station, London. That afternoon, thirty-nine players were booked. And two sent off. That afternoon, there were forty thousand less people watching football matches than the year before. But not in Liverpool, not at Anfield –

In the sixth minute, Steve Heighway scored. And Liverpool Football Club beat Stoke City one–nil. At home, at Anfield.

Three days afterwards, Liverpool Football Club travelled to Highfield Road, Coventry. In the twentieth minute, Peter Cormack headed the ball down to Kevin Keegan. Keegan struck the ball. A perfect volley. And the ball struck the post. The Coventry post. One minute later, Stein headed the ball down to Hutchinson. Hutchinson struck the ball. A perfect volley. And the ball struck the back of the net and the back of the goal. And Liverpool Football Club lost one–nil to Coventry City. Away from home, away from Anfield.

On Saturday 1 September, 1973, Liverpool Football Club travelled to Filbert Street, Leicester. And in the fiftieth minute, John Toshack scored. But Birchenall scored, too. And Liverpool Football Club drew one-all with Leicester City. Away from home, away from Anfield. That evening, Leeds United had six points. And Leeds United were first in the First Division. Unbeaten. That evening, the Champions of England had three points. And the Champions of England were twelfth in the First Division.

On Tuesday 4 September, 1973, Derby County came to Anfield, Liverpool. That evening, forty-five thousand, two hundred and thirty-seven folk came, too. But not Alec Lindsay. Alec Lindsay was ill. At home, at Anfield. Bill Shankly walked into the dressing room. The home dressing room. Bill Shankly took out a piece of paper from his pocket. And Bill Shankly looked at Tommy Smith –

Our team today will be Clemence, Lawler, Thompson, Smith, Lloyd, Hughes, Keegan, Cormack, Heighway, Toshack and Callaghan. That's us tonight, boys. So come on . . .

In the thirty-fifth minute, from thirty yards out, Phil Thompson shot and Thompson scored. His first goal for Liverpool Football Club.

In the eighty-fifth minute, Kevin Keegan took a penalty. And Keegan scored the penalty. And Liverpool Football Club beat Derby County two–nil. At home, at Anfield.

Four days afterwards, Chelsea Football Club came to Anfield, Liverpool. That afternoon, forty-seven thousand and sixteen folk came, too. In the thirty-fifth minute, Kevin Keegan scored. In the second half, Keegan took a penalty. And Bonetti saved the penalty. But it didn't matter, it didn't count. Liverpool Football Club beat Chelsea Football Club one–nil. At home, at Anfield. That evening, Leeds United had ten points. Leeds United still first in the First Division. Still unbeaten. Burnley Football Club had nine points. And Burnley Football Club were second in the First Division. Liverpool Football Club, Coventry City, Leicester City, Manchester City and Derby County all had seven points. But the Champions of England were third in the First Division. On goal average.

On Wednesday 12 September, 1973, Liverpool Football Club travelled to the Baseball Ground, Derby. But John Toshack did not travel with Liverpool Football Club. John Toshack was injured again. Phil Boersma travelled to the Baseball Ground, Derby. And Phil Boersma played. In the tenth minute, Gemmill crossed for Hector. Hector shot. The shot was blocked, the shot rebounded. And Davies shot and Davies scored. In the twenty-sixth minute, Kevin Keegan passed to Boersma. Boersma shot. And Boersma scored. In the fortieth minute, Hector crossed the ball. McFarland met the cross. And McFarland scored. Five minutes later, Davies passed to Hector. Hector shot. And Hector scored. But the goal was disallowed. For offside. But in the fifty-fifth minute, again Davies passed to Hector. And again Hector shot. The shot hit Ian Callaghan. The shot flew off Callaghan. And the shot flew over Ray Clemence. Into the net and into the goal. And Liverpool Football Club lost three–one to Derby County. Away from home, away from Anfield. Bill Shankly walked down the touchline. The touchline at the Baseball Ground. And Bill Shankly shook the hand of Brian Clough –

Well played, Brian. Very well played indeed, son. I'd heard a whisper that all was not well here. But obviously not, son . . .

Brian Clough laughed. And Brian Clough said, Thank you, Mr Shankly. Thank you very much, sir. It's true we've had our ups and our downs. But it's nothing I can't handle, sir . . .

On Saturday 15 September, 1973, Liverpool Football Club travelled to St Andrew's, Birmingham. But Steve Heighway did not travel to St Andrew's, Birmingham. Steve Heighway was injured. Derek Brownbill travelled to St Andrew's, Birmingham. And Derek Brownbill played. His first game for Liverpool Football Club, his only game for Liverpool Football Club. In the seventy-first minute, Liverpool Football Club were losing one–nil to Birmingham City. And Bill Shankly took off Derek Brownbill. Bill Shankly sent on Brian Hall. And in the eighty-fifth minute, Hall scored. And Liverpool Football Club drew one-all with Birmingham City. Away from home, away from Anfield. That evening, Leeds United had fourteen points. Leeds United still first in the First Division. Still unbeaten. That evening, the Champions of England had eight points. And the Champions of England were eighth in the First Division. Eighth.

Four days afterwards, the Champions of England came to the Stade de la Frontière, in Esch-sur-Alzette, in Luxembourg, to play AS la Jeunesse d'Esch of Luxembourg in the first leg of the First Round of the European Cup. Some of the players of AS la Jeunesse d'Esch were part-time footballers. Some of the players of AS la Jeunesse d'Esch had other jobs. Some of them were steelworkers, some of them were postmen. In the forty-third minute, Brian Hall scored for Liverpool Football Club. But in the last minute, the very last minute, Gilbert Dussier scored for AS la Jeunesse d'Esch. And the Champions of England drew one-all with AS la Jeunesse d'Esch of Luxembourg in the first leg of the First Round of the European Cup. Away from home, away from Anfield.

On Saturday 22 September, 1973, Tottenham Hotspur came to Anfield, Liverpool. That afternoon, forty-two thousand, nine hundred and one folk came, too. Forty-two thousand, nine hundred and one folk and Alec Lindsay. Alec Lindsay no longer ill, Alec Lindsay fit to play. That afternoon, Phil Thompson did not play. Phil Thompson dropped. That afternoon, Peters scored first for Tottenham Hotspur. And in the twenty-eighth minute, Chris Lawler equalised for Liverpool Football Club. But Chivers scored again for Tottenham Hotspur. And in the seventy-sixth minute, Alec Lindsay equalised with a penalty. And in the last minute, the very last minute, Lawler scored again for Liverpool

Football Club. And Liverpool Football Club beat Tottenham Hotspur three–two. At home, at Anfield.

One week later, Liverpool Football Club travelled to Old Trafford, Manchester. There was wind and there was rain. High winds and heavy rains. And there was lightning and there was thunder. But there were no goals. And Liverpool Football Club drew nil–nil with Manchester United. Away from home, away from Anfield. That evening, Leeds United had seventeen points. Leeds United still first in the First Division. Still unbeaten. That evening, the Champions of England had eleven points. The Champions of England seventh in the First Division. Seventh.

On Wednesday 3 October, 1973, AS la Jeunesse d'Esch of Luxembourg came to Anfield, Liverpool. That evening, twenty-eight thousand, seven hundred and fourteen folk came, too. Twenty-eight thousand, seven hundred and fourteen folk to watch the Champions of England play AS la Jeunesse d'Esch of Luxembourg in the second leg of the First Round of the European Cup. In the forty-seventh minute, Emlyn Hughes shot. And the shot hit Mond. The shot deflected off Mond. And into the net and into a goal. In the fifty-sixth minute, Hughes shot again. Hoffman palmed away the shot. The ball fell to John Toshack. And Toshack shot. Into the open goal, into the yawning net. And the Champions of England beat AS la Jeunesse d'Esch of Luxembourg two–nil in the second leg of the First Round of the European Cup. At home, at Anfield.

Three days afterwards, Newcastle United came to Anfield, Liverpool. That afternoon, forty-five thousand, six hundred and twelve folk came, too. In the twentieth minute, Peter Cormack scored. In the eighty-sixth minute, Alec Lindsay scored another penalty. And Liverpool Football Club beat Newcastle United two–one. At home, at Anfield. That evening, Leeds United had eighteen points. Leeds United still first in the First Division. Leeds United still unbeaten. That evening, the Champions of England had thirteen points. The Champions of England fifth in the First Division. Fifth.

Two days later, Liverpool Football Club travelled to Upton Park, London, to play West Ham United in the Second Round of the Football League Cup. In the thirty-fourth minute, Peter Cormack scored. Five minutes later, MacDougall equalised for West Ham United.

In the fifty-fifth minute, Ian Callaghan passed to Steve Heighway. Heighway darted between Coleman and McDowell. Day came out towards Heighway. But Heighway stretched the ball round Day. Into the net and into the goal. But in the eighty-third minute, Brooking crossed the ball. MacDougall headed the ball back across the goal. The ball bounced across the goal. Robson raised his foot. His foot met the bounce. And the ball went into the net and into the goal. And Liverpool Football Club drew two-all with West Ham United in the Second Round of the Football League Cup. Away from home, away from Anfield. There would have to be a replay.

On Saturday 13 October, 1973, Liverpool Football Club travelled to the Dell, Southampton. In the seventh minute, Larry Lloyd hooked up Channon in the penalty area. Channon took the penalty. And Channon scored the penalty. And Liverpool Football Club lost one–nil to Southampton Football Club. Away from home, away from Anfield. That season, Liverpool Football Club had yet to win away from home, away from Anfield. That evening, Leeds United had nineteen points. Leeds United first in the First Division. Leeds United still unbeaten. That evening, the Champions of England had thirteen points. The Champions of England seventh in the First Division. Seventh again, only seventh.

One week afterwards, Liverpool Football Club travelled to Elland Road, Leeds. That afternoon, forty-four thousand, nine hundred and eleven folk came, too. Forty-four thousand, nine hundred and eleven folk to watch the current leaders of the First Division, the unbeaten leaders of the First Division, play the Champions of England. Forty-four thousand, nine hundred and eleven folk and Miljan Miljanić. Miljan Miljanić was the coach of Fudbalski Klub Crvena Zvezda Beograd. In four days, Liverpool Football Club would play Fudbalski Klub Crvena Zvezda Beograd in the first leg of the Second Round of the European Cup. Away from home, away from Anfield. On Saturday 20 October, 1973, in the thirtieth minute of the first half, Clarke passed to Bremner. Bremner passed to Lorimer. Lorimer crossed the ball. Jones met the cross. And Jones headed the ball. Into the net and into a goal. The winning goal. And Liverpool Football Club lost one–nil to Leeds United. Away from home, away from Anfield.

On Wednesday 24 October, 1973, Liverpool Football Club

came to the Crvena Zvezda Stadium, in Belgrade, in Yugoslavia, to play Fudbalski Klub Crvena Zvezda Beograd in the first leg of the Second Round of the European Cup. Miljan Miljanić had watched Liverpool Football Club play twice. Against Southampton Football Club and against Leeds United. And Miljan Miljanić had watched Liverpool Football Club lose twice. Miljan Miljanić told the gentlemen of the press, Liverpool Football Club are one of the teams of our time. An outstanding team. As outstanding as Real Madrid or Ajax of Amsterdam. They have a fine goalkeeper in Clemence. A pair of good full-backs, a tireless midfield worker in Hughes and a dangerous forward in Heighway. But I do detect a weakness in the middle of their defence. And we shall try to exploit it . . .

Bill Shankly had not watched Fudbalski Klub Crvena Zvezda Beograd play. In the two weeks since the draw for the Second Round of the European Cup had been announced, Fudbalski Klub Crvena Zvezda Beograd had not played –

But I like the Yugoslavs, Bill Shankly told the gentlemen of the press. They are like the people of the North. Mussolini tried to frighten them, Hitler tried to frighten them. And Stalin, in his turn, tried to do the same. They all failed. Now it's up to Liverpool Football Club . . .

In the fortieth minute of the first half of the first leg of the Second Round of the European Cup, Petrović passed to Lazarević. Lazarević passed to Janković. Janković passed back to Lazarević. Lazarević back-heeled the ball to Karasi. Karasi passed to Janković. And Janković shot and Janković scored. In the second minute of the second half of the first leg of the Second Round of the European Cup, Jovanović chipped the ball over the Liverpool defence. The Liverpool defence tried to spring the offside trap, the Liverpool defence too slow. Bogićević ran onto the chip. And Bogićević volleyed the chip. Into the net and into a goal. But in the seventy-second minute, Liverpool Football Club won a corner. Steve Heighway took the corner. Dojčinovski cleared the corner. But the clearance came out to Chris Lawler. Lawler on the edge of the penalty area. And Lawler shot and Lawler scored. An away goal, a dangerous goal. But Liverpool Football Club had still lost two–one to Fudbalski Klub Crvena Zvezda Beograd in the first leg of the Second Round of the European Cup. Away from home, away from Anfield.

Three days afterwards, Sheffield United came to Anfield, Liverpool. That afternoon, forty thousand, six hundred and forty-one folk came, too. In the twenty-sixth minute, Kevin Keegan scored. And Liverpool Football Club beat Sheffield United one–nil. At home, at Anfield. That evening, Leeds United had twenty-three points. Leeds United were still first in the First Division. Leeds United still unbeaten. Everton Football Club had eighteen points. And Everton Football Club were second in the First Division. That evening, the Champions of England had fifteen points. And the Champions of England were sixth in the First Division. Sixth.

On Monday 29 October, 1973, West Ham United came to Anfield, Liverpool, to play Liverpool Football Club in the Second Round replay of the Football League Cup. That evening, twenty-six thousand and two folk came, too. In the twenty-second minute, Peter Cormack passed to Steve Heighway. Heighway passed to Kevin Keegan. Keegan crossed low for John Toshack. Toshack dived low to meet the cross. And Toshack met the cross. And Toshack scored. And Liverpool Football Club beat West Ham United one–nil in the Second Round replay of the Football League Cup. At home, at Anfield.

. . .

The following Friday, after the training. Back at Anfield, after the meeting. In the dressing room, the home dressing room. Tommy Smith stood up. Tommy Smith walked over to Bill Shankly. And Tommy Smith said, Can I have a word please, Boss?

Sure, Tommy. Sure, son.

Bill Shankly and Tommy Smith stepped out of the dressing room. The home dressing room. Bill Shankly and Tommy Smith stood outside the dressing room in the corridor. The Anfield corridor. And Tommy Smith said, I never heard my name, Boss. I never heard you say my name. So I was just wondering if I'll be playing, Boss?

I have no made my mind up, Tommy. No yet, son.

Tommy Smith stared at Bill Shankly. And Tommy Smith said, If I'm not going to play, Boss. Then I'd rather stay here and play for the reserves. I'd rather do that than travel all the way down there, Boss. All the way down to London. Just to sit in the stands and watch everyone else play, Boss. I'd rather stay and play here . . .

Bill Shankly nodded. And nodded again –

464

I know how you feel, Tommy. I understand how you feel, son. But I've named you in the squad, Tommy. I've told the press, son. And I still haven't made up my mind, Tommy . . .

Tommy Smith nodded. And Tommy Smith said, OK then, Boss.

. . .

On Saturday 3 November, 1973, Liverpool Football Club travelled to Highbury, London. And Tommy Smith travelled to Highbury, too. But Tommy Smith did not leave his bag on the bus. The Liverpool bus. Tommy Smith brought his bag into the dressing room. The away dressing room. Tommy Smith put down his bag in the doorway of the dressing room. The Liverpool dressing room –

Bill Shankly walked into the dressing room. The away dressing room. Bill Shankly stepped over the bag in the doorway to the dressing room. Bill Shankly took out a piece of paper from his pocket. And Bill Shankly read out the names on the piece of paper –

Our team today will be Clemence, Lawler, Lindsay, Thompson Lloyd, Hughes, Keegan, McLaughlin, Heighway, Toshack and Callaghan. But Emlyn, you'll play at the back with Larry, son. And Phil, you'll play in midfield, OK, son? And Cormack will be the twelfth man today. So come on, boys. Come on . . .

Tommy Smith got up from the bench in the dressing room. The away dressing room. Tommy Smith picked up his bag in the doorway to the dressing room. The Liverpool dressing room. And Tommy Smith said, Good luck, lads. Good luck today. And I'll see you all in training, lads. Back in Liverpool . . .

And Tommy Smith walked out of the dressing room. The Liverpool dressing room. Tommy Smith walked down the corridor. The Highbury corridor. Out of the stadium and into the crowds. The crowds of supporters of Liverpool Football Club. And one of the supporters of Liverpool Football Club saw Tommy Smith –

What are you doing, asked the supporter of Liverpool Football Club. Where are you going, Tommy lad?

I'm going home, back to Liverpool. I'm not playing today. And I don't like watching. I'm not good at watching. So I'm going home . . .

The supporter of Liverpool Football Club shook his head –

If you're not playing, Tommy. Then I'm not watching, lad. I'm coming with you then, Tommy. I'll go back to Liverpool with you, lad.

I'll keep you company on the train, Tommy . . .

You're all right, son. I'm fine, ta. You must stay and support the team. They need you more than me, son. So you stay and support the team now. Please, son. Please . . .

And Tommy Smith walked away, away through the crowds. The crowds of supporters. To the tube station. And Tommy Smith took the tube to Euston Station. And Tommy Smith got on the train to Lime Street. The train back to Liverpool. And Tommy Smith sat on the train. In his seat, with his bag. And Tommy Smith thought about the game. The match. The game he was not playing in. The match he was missing. In his seat, with his bag. Tommy Smith fought back tears. Tommy Smith struggled to breathe. On the train, on his own. Thinking about the game, thinking about the match. The game he was missing, the match he was missing. And all he was missing –

In the seventy-seventh minute, Emlyn Hughes scored. In the eighty-fifth minute, John Toshack scored. And Liverpool Football Club beat Arsenal Football Club two–nil. Away from home, away from Anfield. Their first away win of the season. But in the corridor. The Highbury corridor. The gentlemen of the London sporting press were waiting for Bill Shankly, waiting to ask Bill Shankly about Tommy Smith. But Bill Shankly stuck out his chin –

It takes a good team to win at Highbury. It is one of the hardest grounds on which to succeed. So this victory came at just the right moment for us. Now I am confident we can score the goals necessary to beat Red Star Belgrade.

. . .

The next morning, the Sunday morning. Tommy Smith came into Anfield, Tommy Smith came in to train. To prove people wrong and to prove Bill Shankly wrong. Tommy Smith walked down the corridor. Past the door to the office of Bill Shankly. The door to the office of Bill Shankly open. Bill Shankly at his desk. At his typewriter. And Bill Shankly looked up. Out into the corridor –

Morning, Tommy. And how are you today, son? Come in, Tommy. And sit yourself down, son . . .

Tommy Smith walked into the office. But Tommy Smith did not sit down. Tommy Smith stayed on his feet.

Listen, said Bill Shankly. I know how disappointed you are,

466

Tommy. I know how hurt you feel not to be playing, son. I know how much you love playing, Tommy. How much you want to play, son. So I don't blame you for walking out, Tommy. For going home, son. I'd have done exactly the same myself, Tommy. If it had been me, son.

Tommy Smith looked at Bill Shankly. And Tommy Smith said, So will I be playing on Tuesday, Boss? Against Red Star Belgrade? Will I be playing, Boss? On Tuesday night?

Bill Shankly shook his head –

Now come on, Tommy. Come on, son. I have no made my mind up yet. It's still only Sunday . . .

Tommy Smith stared at Bill Shankly. And Tommy Smith said, If I'm not going to be playing, then I'd rather know. And if I know I'm not going to be playing, then I'd rather go somewhere else. Somewhere where I will be playing, where I'll be wanted.

I know that, Tommy. I know that, son.

. . .

On Tuesday 6 November, 1973, Fudbalski Klub Crvena Zvezda Beograd came to Anfield, Liverpool, to play Liverpool Football Club in the second leg of the Second Round of the European Cup. That night, forty-one thousand, seven hundred and seventy-four folk came, too. But not Tommy Smith. Tommy Smith was not in the Liverpool team. Tommy Smith was not even on the Liverpool bench. That night, Clemence, Lawler, Lindsay, Thompson, Lloyd, Hughes, Keegan, McLaughlin, Heighway, Toshack and Callaghan were in the Liverpool team. And Lane, Storton, Cormack, Hall and Boersma were on the Liverpool bench. And that night, under a silver moon, the supporters of Liverpool Football Club swayed and swayed. In a roaring sea of red banners and red scarves. And that night, under the silver moon, the players of Liverpool Football Club attacked and attacked. In a continuous wave of red shirts. Red shirts breaking against the white shirts of Fudbalski Klub Crvena Zvezda Beograd. Three times the white shirts of Fudbalski Klub Crvena Zvezda Beograd stood firm to clear the ball off their own goal line. But then the white shirts of Fudbalski Klub Crvena Zvezda Beograd turned defence into attack. And in the sixtieth minute, Pavlović beat Steve Heighway to the ball. Pavlović pushed the ball out to Janković. Janković flicked the ball on to Lazarević. Lazarević on the edge of the penalty area. And Lazarević struck the ball. And the ball struck the back of the net. The back of the goal. An away goal, a dangerous goal. Three minutes later, Bill Shankly took off John McLaughlin. And Bill Shankly sent on Brian Hall. And in the seventy-seventh minute, Bill Shankly took off Steve Heighway. And Bill Shankly sent on Phil Boersma. And in the eighty-fifth minute, Chris Lawler equalised. But in the last minute, the very last minute, Janković took a free kick. And Janković scored. And one minute later, the referee looked at his watch. The referee put his whistle to his lips. And the referee blew his whistle. And Liverpool Football Club had lost two–one on the night and four–two on aggregate to Fudbalski Klub Crvena Zvezda Beograd in the Second Round of the European Cup. And the Champions of England were out, out of the European Cup –

Out, out. Again.


## 44. SHEER POETRY, JUST LIKE ROBBIE BURNS

In the house, in their kitchen. In the darkness, among the fat. On his knees. Bill was cleaning and cleaning and cleaning. In the house, in their kitchen. On his knees. Bill heard Ness cough. In the house, in their kitchen. On his knees. Bill looked up. And Bill saw Ness –

How long is this going to go on, asked Ness.

I don't know, love. I cannot tell you.

. . .

In the dressing room, the home dressing room. On the Saturday, the next Saturday. Bill looked from player to player. From Ray to Chris, from Chris to Alec, from Alec to Phil, from Phil to Larry, from Larry to Emlyn, from Emlyn to Kevin, from Kevin to Peter, from Peter to Steve, from Steve to Tosh and from Tosh to Cally. And Bill said, Well, boys. I know you are all still hurting from Tuesday night. I know you are all still bitterly disappointed, boys. But I also know you all played your hearts out on Tuesday night. You all gave everything you had, boys. All played your hearts out for the supporters of Liverpool Football Club. All gave everything you had for Liverpool Football Club, boys. And so I know you can all hold your heads up high today. When you go out there today, boys. Because I know you'll all play your hearts out again. You'll all give everything you have again, boys. Because you'll have to play your hearts out, boys. You'll have to give everything you have, boys. If we are to catch Leeds United. If we are to be Champions again, boys. Because only if we catch Leeds United. Only if we are Champions again, boys. Only then will we play in the European Cup again. Only then will we have the chance to win the European Cup, boys. To give these supporters the one cup they have never had. The one thing that would make them happier than anything else, boys. The European Cup, boys. If we catch Leeds United and we are Champions again. That is the only ways, boys. The only way to get over the disappointment. To get over the hurt, boys. That is the only ways, boys. To be Champions again. And to play in the European Cup again. The only way, boys. The Liverpool way . . .

And on the bench, the Anfield bench. Bill and the thirty-eight thousand and eighty-eight folk inside Anfield watched the players of Liverpool Football Club give everything they had. They watched them play their hearts out. And in the twenty-second minute, they watched Steve Heighway score. And Liverpool Football Club beat Wolverhampton Wanderers one–nil. At home, at Anfield. That evening, Leeds United were still first in the First Division. Leeds United still unbeaten. But Liverpool Football Club were now fourth in the First Division. Liverpool Football Club now climbing . . .

On the bench, the Anfield bench. In the seventeenth minute, Bill and thirty-seven thousand, four hundred and twenty-two folk watched Kevin Keegan score. And five minutes later, they watched Keegan score again. And in the forty-fourth minute, they watched Peter Cormack score. And in the last minute, the very last minute, they watched Keegan score again. A penalty. And a hat-trick. And Liverpool Football Club beat Ipswich Town four–two. At home, at Anfield. That evening, Leeds United had twenty-eight points. Leeds United still first in the First Division. Still unbeaten. But Liverpool Football Club had twenty-one points. Liverpool Football Club now third in the First Division. Still climbing.

. . .

In the office, at his desk. Bill looked up from his typewriter. Bill saw Tommy Smith. And Bill said, Hello, Tommy . . .

Don't you hello Tommy me, said Tommy Smith. What the

hell is all this about Stoke City? About me going on loan to them?

Bill held out the palms of his hands. And Bill said, Are you not pleased, are you not happy, Tommy? Is it not what you wanted, son?

Not what I wanted, said Tommy Smith. I didn't know anything about it until Tony Waddington called me up at Melwood. Half an hour ago. That was the first I heard about it. Half an hour ago . . .

Bill nodded. And Bill said, Tony called me. He asked me if he could take you on loan. Just for a month. And I know you want to play. That's what you want. And so I thought you'd be pleased. Thought you'd be happy. And so I said yes. I said yes, Tommy.

But you never thought to ask me, said Tommy Smith. After all the years I've been here. After all the games I've played. As captain, as club captain. You never thought to talk to me? You never thought to ask me what I think about going to Stoke?

Bill shook his head. And Bill said, You told me you want to play. You told me that's all you want to do. To play. And they called me and told me they want you to play. So what is there to talk about, Tommy? What is there to think about, son? I thought you'd be happy. I thought you'd be pleased. Because you'd got what you wanted.

What I want is to play for Liverpool Football Club, said Tommy Smith. That's all I want, Boss. All I want . . .

And Tommy Smith turned his back on Bill. And Tommy Smith walked out of the office . Down the corridor,

out of Anfield.

. . .

In the cold, the bitter cold. The bus stopped at Skipton. In the cold, the bitter cold. Bill and the players and the staff of Liverpool Football Club got off the bus. In the cold, the bitter cold. Bill and the players and the staff had a meal at Skipton. In the cold, the bitter cold. Bill and the players and the staff ate their steak and chips. Their tinned fruit and cream. In the cold, the bitter cold. Bill and the players and the staff got back on the bus to Roker Park, Sunderland. But in the cold, the bitter cold. The heating on the bus had broken down. And in the cold, the bitter cold. The players and the staff of Liverpool Football Club were freezing to death, shivering to death. And in the cold, the bitter cold. Bill got up from his seat on the bus. In the cold, the bitter cold. Bill walked up the aisle of the bus to Jack Cross, one of the

470

directors of Liverpool Football Club. And in the cold, the bitter cold. Bill said, This is unacceptable. Unacceptable for the players of Liverpool Football Club. And so my lads will not be getting back on this bus, Mr Cross. My lads are not travelling back to Liverpool on this bus. So as soon as we get to Sunderland. I want this bus sent back. And I want a new bus sent. A bus with heating. Waiting for us after the match, waiting to take us back home. Back home to Liverpool.

In the cold, the bitter cold. Jack Cross nodded. And in the cold, the bitter cold. At Roker Park, Sunderland, Jack Cross arranged for a new bus. A bus with heating. And in the cold, the bitter cold. On the bench, the bench at Roker. In the twelfth minute, Bill watched Kevin Keegan score. In the forty-seventh minute, Bill watched John Toshack score. And Liverpool Football Club beat Sunderland Football Club two–nil in the Third Round of the Football League Cup. Away from home, away from Anfield. But in the cold, the bitter cold. In the dressing room, the away dressing room. Bill kept pacing up and down. Bill waiting for the new bus. The bus with heating. The bus to take them back home. Back home to Liverpool. And in the cold, the bitter cold. In the car park, the car park at Roker Park. At last Bill saw the new bus. The bus with heating. The bus to take them back home. Back home to Liverpool. And in the cold, the bitter cold. His coat stuck to his jacket. His jacket stuck to his shirt. His shirt stuck to his skin. Bill said, Come on, boys. Come on. The new bus is here. The bus to take us back home. Back home to Liverpool.

. . .

On the bench, the bench at Loftus Road. In the twenty-sixth minute, Bill watched Steve Heighway cross the ball. And Larry Lloyd headed the ball. Into the net, into a goal. But early in the second half, Bill watched Bowles equalise for Queens Park Rangers. In the seventy-fifth minute, Bill watched John Toshack score. But late in the second half, Bill watched McLintock equalise for Queens Park Rangers. And Liverpool Football Club drew two-all with Queens Park Rangers. Away from home, away from Anfield. That evening, Leeds United had twenty-nine points. Leeds United still first, Leeds United still unbeaten. That evening, Liverpool Football Club had twenty-two points. And Liverpool Football Club were fifth again. Falling again, not climbing. Falling and falling . . .

. . .

In the office, at his desk. Bill looked up from his typewriter. Bill saw Tommy Smith. And Bill said, Hello, Tommy. Hello, son . . .

What the bloody hell is going on, said Tommy Smith.

Bill smiled. And Bill said, Lovely to see you and all, Tommy. Good to have you back, son. Chris has done his cartilage in. Be out for a while. So I want you to play right-back for us, Tommy. You think you can do for that us, son? Play right-back for a while?

Aye, I'll do it, said Tommy Smith. I'll play anywhere. You know that. I'll do it for the team, I'll do it for the club. And for the supporters. But not for you. Not for you.

Bill smiled again. And Bill said, Great, Tommy. Thanks, son.

. . .

On the bench, the bench at Boothferry Park. In a time of energy rationing, in a time of power saving. At two fifteen on a Tuesday afternoon. To save power, to ration energy. Bill watched Liverpool Football Club play Hull City of the Second Division in the Fourth Round of the Football League Cup. And Bill watched Liverpool Football Club draw nil–nil with Hull City of the Second Division in the Fourth Round of the Football League Cup.

On the bench, the bench at Anfield. An hour earlier than usual, at two o'clock in the afternoon. Because of the power saving, because of the energy rationing. On a pitch that was too soft in some places, too hard in others. In a game that should never have been played. In the fourteenth minute, Bill and thirty-four thousand, eight hundred and fifty-seven folk watched Peter Cormack score. And Liverpool Football Club beat West Ham United one–nil. At home, at Anfield. And that evening, Leeds United had thirty points. Leeds United still first in the First Division, Leeds United still unbeaten. But the Champions of England had twenty-four points. And now the Champions of England were second in the First Division –

Climbing again.

On the bench, the Anfield bench. Bill and just seventeen thousand, one hundred and twenty folk were watching Liverpool Football Club play Hull City in the Fourth Round replay of the Football League Cup. At two o'clock, on a Tuesday afternoon. Because of the power saving, because of the energy rationing. And in the twelfth minute, they watched Ian Callaghan score. In the nineteenth minute, they watched Callaghan score again. And in the seventy-third minute, they watched Callaghan score his third. In his fourteenth season for Liverpool Football Club, in his six hundred and eighteenth game for Liverpool Football Club, Ian Callaghan had scored his first hat-trick for Liverpool Football Club. And Liverpool Football Club had beaten Hull City three–one in the Fourth Round replay of the Football League Cup. At home, at Anfield.

On the bench, the bench at Goodison Park. An hour early, at two o'clock. Because of the power saving, because of the energy rationing. Bill and fifty-six thousand and ninety-eight folk were watching Liverpool Football Club play Everton Football Club. But John Toshack was not playing for Liverpool Football Club. John Toshack still injured. And Steve Heighway was not playing for Liverpool Football Club. Steve Heighway had the flu. Alan Waddle was playing for Liverpool Football Club. And in the sixty-seventh minute, Alan Waddle scored. His first goal for Liverpool Football Club. The only goal of the match. And Liverpool Football Club beat Everton Football Club one–nil. Away from home, away from Anfield.

On the bench, the bench at Carrow Road. Blackouts had been expected and floodlights had been forbidden. But Liverpool Football Club had still travelled to Carrow Road. And Liverpool Football Club drew one–one with Norwich City. Away from home, away from Anfield. On the bench, the bench at Molineux. With overtime banned and with three-day working weeks about to start. Amid bomb scares and amid train crashes. At two o'clock, on a Wednesday afternoon. In the forty-sixth minute, Bill watched Tommy Smith try to head a long ball down to Emlyn Hughes. But the ball did not reach Hughes. Or Hughes did not reach the ball. Richards reached the ball. And Richards scored. And Liverpool Football Club lost one–nil to Wolverhampton Wanderers in the Fifth Round of the Football League Cup. And Liverpool Football Club were out of another cup. Liverpool Football Club off the pace. With overtime banned, with three-day working weeks about to start. Amid bomb scares and amid train crashes. The gentlemen of the press were talking about a time of crisis. A state of emergency. And the End of the World –

On the bench, the Anfield bench. An hour early, at two o'clock.

Bill and forty thousand, four hundred and twenty folk were watching Liverpool Football Club play Manchester United. Manchester United were fourth from the bottom of the First Division. Manchester United were in crisis, Manchester United were in trouble. In a state of emergency. And in the thirtieth minute, Bill and the forty thousand, four hundred and twenty folk watched Kevin Keegan score. A penalty. And in the sixty-fifth minute, they watched Heighway score. And Liverpool Football Club beat Manchester United two–nil. At home, at Anfield. In a time of crisis, in a state of emergency. Manchester United were still fourth from the bottom of the First Division. And Liverpool Football Club were still second from the top of the First Division. Leeds United still top of the First Division. After twenty-one games. Leeds United were still unbeaten.

On the bench, the bench at Turf Moor. In the mist, the Boxing Day mist. In the third minute, Bill watched James take a corner. And Dobson headed on the corner. Fletcher ran on to the header. And Fletcher scored. In the mist, the Boxing Day mist. In the sixtieth minute, Bill watched Kevin Keegan take a penalty. And Bill watched Keegan miss the penalty. But in the mist, the Boxing Day mist. In the eighty-fourth minute, Bill watched Peter Cormack equalise. But in the mist, the Boxing Day mist. One minute later, Bill watched Collins pass to Ingham. And Ingham passed to Hankin. Hankin shot. And Hankin scored. And in the mist, the Boxing Day mist. Liverpool Football Club lost two–one to Burnley Football Club. Away from home, away from Anfield. And in the mist, that Boxing Day mist. Liverpool Football Club had twenty-nine points. And Leeds United had thirty-eight points. In the mist, the Boxing Day mist. The Champions of England were nine points behind Leeds United. And in the mist, the Boxing Day mist. Bill knew the Champions of England had a mountain to climb.

On the bench, the bench at Stamford Bridge. On the last Saturday of 1973, in the twenty-first minute, Bill watched Peter Cormack score. And Liverpool Football Club beat Chelsea Football Club one–nil. Away from home, away from Anfield.

On the bench, the Anfield bench. An hour early, at two o'clock. With frost on the pitch and with ice in the air. On the first day of 1974, in the eighteenth minute of the match, Bill and thirty-nine thousand, one hundred and ten folk watched Weller shoot. And Weller scored.

But in the sixty-seventh minute, they watched Peter Cormack shoot. And Cormack scored. And with frost on the pitch and with ice in the air. Liverpool Football Club drew one-all with Leicester City. At home, at Anfield. The first points Liverpool Football Club had dropped. At home, at Anfield. Bill walked into the dressing room. The home dressing room. And Bill looked around the dressing room. The Liverpool dressing room. And Bill said, You tried your very hardest, boys. You gave your very best. And so do not let your heads drop, boys. Do not be downcast. It takes two teams to make a game of it, boys. It always takes two teams.

On the bench, the Anfield bench. An hour early again, at two o'clock again. Bill and thirty-one thousand, four hundred and eighty-three folk were watching Liverpool Football Club play Doncaster Rovers in the Third Round of the FA Cup. Doncaster Rovers were ninety-second in the Football League. Doncaster Rovers were bottom of the Football League. In the third minute, Bill and thirty-one thousand, four hundred and eighty-three folk watched Phil Thompson pass to Steve Heighway. And Heighway passed to Ian Callaghan. Callaghan crossed for Kevin Keegan. And Keegan headed the cross. Into the net and into a goal. But three minutes later, they watched Doncaster Rovers win a corner. And Liverpool Football Club failed to clear the corner. Woods crossed the ball back into the Liverpool penalty area. Ray Clemence failed to hold the cross. Clemence fumbled the cross, Clemence dropped the ball. And Kitchen pounced on the ball. Kitchen stabbed the ball. Into the net and into a goal. And ten minutes later, they watched Murray cross. And again Liverpool Football Club failed to clear the cross. O'Callaghan shot. And O'Callaghan scored. And the ninety-second team in the Football League, the bottom club in the Football League, were beating the second team in the Football League, the Champions of England. At home, at Anfield. At half-time, Bill walked into the dressing room. The home dressing room. And Bill walked around the dressing room. The Liverpool dressing room. Bill went from player to player. From Clemence to Storton. From Lindsay to Thompson. From Rylands to Hughes. From Keegan to Cormack. From Heighway to Boersma. And from Boersma to Callaghan. Bill patted each of their backs, Bill put an arm around each of their shoulders. And Bill said, Come on, boys.

Come on now. This is the FA Cup, boys. So let's get it going . . .

Back on the bench, the Anfield bench. In the fifty-seventh minute, Bill watched Callaghan cross the ball. Keegan met the cross. And Keegan scored. And then Bill watched Cormack shoot. But the shot was cleared off the line. And then Bill watched Wignall head the ball. But Lindsay cleared the header off the line. The Liverpool goal line. And in the last minute, Bill watched Kitchen meet a cross. And Kitchen headed the cross. But the header hit the bar. The Liverpool bar. And Liverpool Football Club drew two-all with Doncaster Rovers in the Third Round of the FA Cup. At home, at Anfield.

On the bench, the bench at Belle Vue, Doncaster. At half past one, on a Tuesday afternoon. In the fifteenth minute of the first half, Bill watched Phil Thompson send a long ball into the penalty area. And Alan Waddle headed down the long ball for Steve Heighway. Heighway chested down the ball. Heighway shot. And Heighway scored. And in the fifteenth minute of the second half, Bill watched Alec Lindsay send a free kick into the penalty area. And Peter Cormack headed the free kick. Into the net and into a goal. In the seventieth minute, Bill watched Doncaster Rovers score. But the goal was disallowed. Offside. The goal did not count, the goal did not matter. And Liverpool Football Club beat Doncaster Rovers two–nil in the Third Round replay of the FA Cup.

On the bench, the Anfield bench. An hour early again, at two o'clock again. In the fifteenth minute, Bill and thirty-nine thousand and ninety-four folk watched Kevin Keegan score. And in the thirty-first minute, they watched Keegan score again. And in the sixty-ninth minute, they watched Phil Thompson score. And Liverpool Football Club beat Birmingham City three–two. At home, at Anfield. That evening, Leeds United had forty-two points. Leeds United still unbeaten. And Liverpool Football Club had thirty-four points. Liverpool Football Club still eight points behind Leeds United.

On the bench, the bench at the Victoria Ground. Bill watched Hurst score for Stoke City. And Bill watched Kevin Keegan score for Liverpool Football Club. But the goal was disallowed. For handball. The goal did not count, the goal did not matter. And in the ninetieth minute, Liverpool Football Club were losing one–nil to Stoke City. But in that minute, that very last minute, Bill watched Tommy Smith score for Liverpool Football Club. And Liverpool Football Club drew one-all with Stoke City. Away from home, away from Anfield. And that afternoon, Leeds United drew, too. Leeds United still unbeaten. And Liverpool Football Club were still eight points behind Leeds United. Liverpool Football Club still with a mountain to climb.

On the bench, the Anfield bench. An hour early, at two o'clock. Bill and forty-seven thousand, two hundred and eleven folk were watching Liverpool Football Club play Carlisle United in the Fourth Round of the FA Cup. In the last round of the FA Cup, Carlisle United had beaten Sunderland Football Club. Last season, Sunderland Football Club had beaten Leeds United in the final of the FA Cup. Sunderland Football Club had been the holders of the FA Cup. And on the bench, the Anfield bench. Bill and forty-seven thousand, two hundred and eleven folk watched Liverpool Football Club attack and attack. Again and again. But Alan Ross, the goalkeeper for Carlisle United, saved and saved. Again and again. And Liverpool Football Club drew nil–nil with Carlisle United in the Fourth Round of the FA Cup. At home, at Anfield. There would have to be another replay –

On the bench, the bench at Brunton Park. At two o'clock, on a Tuesday afternoon. In the first half, Bill watched Liverpool Football Club have no chances. No shots on goal. But Bill watched Carlisle United have chances. Shots on goal. And Ray Clemence saved and saved. Again and again. But in the fiftieth minute, Bill watched John Toshack cross for Kevin Keegan. And Keegan turned the cross back for Phil Boersma. Boersma sidestepped a defender. Boersma shot. And Boersma scored. And thirty minutes later, Bill watched Brian Hall pass to Toshack. And Toshack scored. And Liverpool Football Club beat Carlisle United two–nil in the Fourth Round replay of the FA Cup. Away from home, away from Anfield. Liverpool Football Club were in the Fifth Round of the FA Cup.

On the bench, the Anfield bench. Still an hour early, still at two o'clock. In the sixty-third minute, thirty-one thousand, seven hundred and forty-two folk saw Bill take off Larry Lloyd. And Bill sent on Peter Cormack. And in the ninetieth minute, the very last minute, they watched Cormack score. And Liverpool Football Club beat Norwich City one–nil. At home, at Anfield. That evening, Liverpool Football Club had thirty-seven points. And Leeds United had forty-four points.

Leeds United still unbeaten. Liverpool Football Club still seven points behind Leeds United.

On the bench, the Anfield bench. At two o'clock, on a Tuesday afternoon. Because of the power saving, because of the energy rationing. Bill and twenty-one thousand, six hundred and fifty-six folk were watching Liverpool Football Club play Coventry City. Just twenty-one thousand, six hundred and fifty-six folk. The lowest attendance Liverpool Football Club had ever had for a First Division match. At home, at Anfield. Liverpool Football Club and Coventry City had asked the Football League to postpone the game. But the Football League had refused their request. Because Liverpool Football Club and Coventry City were both still in the FA Cup. And that afternoon, Bill and twenty-one thousand, six hundred and fifty-six folk watched Alan Waddle hit one post. And Waddle hit the crossbar. And Waddle hit the other post. And Waddle still could not score his second goal for Liverpool Football Club. But in the twenty-eighth minute, they watched Alec Lindsay score a penalty. And in the fifty-seventh minute, they watched Kevin Keegan score. And Liverpool Football Club beat Coventry City two–one. At home, at Anfield.

. . .

In the boardroom, the Anfield boardroom. On Friday 15 February, 1974. The Friday before Liverpool Football Club were to play Ipswich Town in the Fifth Round of the FA Cup. The chairman and the manager of Liverpool Football Club met the gentlemen of the sporting press. But the gentlemen of the press were not asking about the Cup. The gentlemen of the press were asking about Bill Shankly. About Bill Shankly's future, about Bill Shankly's new contract . . .

Mr Shankly's present contract expires at the end of May this year, said John Smith, the chairman of Liverpool Football Club. The very end of May. But I have already spoken to Mr Shankly about his future. And Mr Shankly assures me he will be delighted to stay with the club to which he has brought so much success. And so I have told Mr Shankly that he can decide the terms of the new contract. And he can decide whatever length of contract he wants. And I would be happy if it were for life. Because it is my sincere hope that Mr Shankly will stay with us for life. But that decision is not for us to make. However, we are completely at Mr Shankly's disposal.

Bill nodded. Bill nodded again. And then Bill said, It may be another year. Or two, or three. I don't know. But I know one day I will decide that enough is enough. That that is that. And then I'll leave straight away. Straight away. Because my career as a manager must have an abrupt end. I know that. I do know that . . .

But what would you do, asked Erlend Clouston of the *Liverpool Daily Post*, if you left, Bill? If you retired? What on earth would you do with yourself all day, Bill?

Bill laughed. And Bill said, I'll get out my tracksuit and my sweater. And I'll jog around. People will laugh at me, people will think I'm mad. But some of them will drop dead the next day. The very next day. And so I'll have the last laugh –

And die a healthy man.

. . .

On the bench, the Anfield bench. Half an hour early, at half past two. In the thirty-third minute, Bill and forty-five thousand, three hundred and forty folk watched Emlyn Hughes pass to Brian Hall. And Hall passed to Ian Callaghan. Callaghan passed back to Hall. Hall shot. And Hall scored. And in the fifty-fifth minute, they watched Alan Waddle pass to Kevin Keegan. And Keegan shot and Keegan scored. And Liverpool Football Club beat Ipswich Town two–nil in the Fifth Round of the FA Cup. At home, at Anfield. Liverpool Football Club were in the Sixth Round of the FA Cup.

On the bench, the bench at St James' Park. In the first half, Bill watched Alan Waddle mis-hit one shot. And then Waddle mis-hit another. And in the second half, Bill watched Phil Boersma pass to Waddle. Waddle with the goal at his mercy. An open goal, a yawning goal. And Waddle shot and Waddle missed. And then Bill watched Waddle have another chance. Another open goal, another yawning goal. And again Waddle missed. And Waddle still could not score his second goal for Liverpool Football Club. And Liverpool Football Club drew nil–nil with Newcastle United. Away from home, away from Anfield. But that afternoon, Stoke City beat Leeds United. And Leeds United were no longer unbeaten. But Leeds United were still first in the First Division. Leeds United still had forty-eight points. And Liverpool Football Club had forty points. Liverpool Football Club still eight points behind Leeds United. But in the corridor. The corridor at

St James' Park. Before the press, the sporting press. Bill stuck out his chin. And Bill said, Let no one dare suggest we have given away our title yet. Liverpool Football Club never give away anything. Not without a fight. A fight until the end. And there is still a long way to go. A very, very long, long way to go . . .

On the bench, the Anfield bench. At three o'clock, on a Tuesday afternoon. Because of the power saving, because of the energy rationing. Three minutes before the end, before the end of the game, Bill and twenty-seven thousand and fifteen folk watched Phil Boersma score. And Liverpool Football Club beat Southampton Football Club one–nil. At home, at Anfield. That afternoon, Leeds United did not win. Leeds United only drew. And in the corridor, the Anfield corridor. Bill stuck out his chin again. And Bill said, You can rest assured that the doubts will be niggling at Leeds United now. Because we are closing in on them now. We are breathing down their necks. And they can feel our breath. Hot upon their necks. I am not saying it *will* happen, gentlemen. But it's *possible*. It's always possible. Because anything is possible . . .

On the bench, the Anfield bench. In the last minute, the very last minute of the game, Bill and forty-two thousand, five hundred and sixty-two folk watched Peter Cormack cross for Kevin Keegan. And Keegan headed on the cross for John Toshack. Toshack spun, Toshack shot. And Toshack scored. And Liverpool Football Club beat Burnley Football Club one–nil. At home, at Anfield. That evening, Leeds United had fifty points. And Liverpool Football Club had forty-four points. Liverpool Football Club were now six points behind Leeds United. With a game in hand, with a game to come. And with a game against Leeds United to come, too. At home, at Anfield.

On the bench, the bench at Ashton Gate. In the forty-eighth minute, Bill watched Phil Thompson pass to Alec Lindsay. And Lindsay passed to Steve Heighway. Heighway passed to Peter Cormack. Cormack passed to Kevin Keegan. Keegan crossed for John Toshack. Toshack shot. And Toshack scored. And Liverpool Football Club beat Bristol City one–nil in the Sixth Round of the FA Cup. Away from home, away from Anfield. Liverpool Football Club were in the semi-finals of the FA Cup. That afternoon, Newcastle United played Nottingham Forest in the Sixth Round of the FA Cup at St

James' Park, Newcastle. Early in the second half, the referee sent off a Newcastle United player. The referee awarded a penalty to Nottingham Forest. Nottingham Forest scored the penalty. And Nottingham Forest were beating Newcastle United three–one in the Sixth Round of the FA Cup. And some of the supporters of Newcastle United in the Leazes End ran onto the pitch. Some of the supporters of Newcastle United attacked some of the players of Nottingham Forest. And two of the players of Nottingham Forest were injured. The referee took the players of Nottingham Forest and Newcastle United off the pitch. The referee waited until order had been restored. Until the players had recovered. Then the referee restarted the game. And Newcastle United won the game four–three. That afternoon, one hundred and three people needed medical treatment. That afternoon, thirty-nine people were arrested. That evening, the secretary of Nottingham Forest wrote to the Football Association. Nottingham Forest protested about the events at St James' Park, Newcastle. Nottingham Forest protested about the result at St James' Park, Newcastle. Ted Croker, the secretary of the Football Association, said the Football Association would investigate the events at St James' Park, Newcastle. Ted Croker said Newcastle United could be disqualified.

. . .

Outside the ground, outside Anfield. There had been queues since breakfast time. The gates closed one and a half hours before kick-off. And inside the ground, inside Anfield. For an hour and a half before kick-off, the supporters of Liverpool Football Club roared. And roared. And on the bench, the Anfield bench. From the first minute, the very first minute of the match, Bill and fifty-six thousand and three folk watched Liverpool Football Club thunder into attack. And Hunter cleared off the goal line. The Leeds goal line. From John Toshack. And Emlyn Hughes cleared off the goal line. The Liverpool goal line. From Lorimer. Liverpool Football Club attacking and then defending. Leeds United defending and then attacking. From front to back. From end to end. From back to front. From end to end. Attack and defence, defence and attack. And in the eighty-second minute, Bill and the fifty-six thousand and three folk watched Alec Lindsay lob the ball into the penalty area. The Leeds penalty area. And Kevin Keegan nodded the ball down to Toshack. Toshack touched the ball on to Steve Heighway. Heighway shot. And Heighway scored. And Liverpool Football Club beat Leeds United one–nil. At home, at Anfield. Liverpool Football Club had won thirteen games that season in the last ten minutes. Liverpool Football Club had conceded just one goal in their last nine games. And Liverpool Football Club were now unbeaten in their last sixteen games. Cup and League. Liverpool Football Club now had forty-six points. And Leeds United had fifty-two points. Liverpool Football Club still six points behind Leeds United. But Liverpool Football Club had two games in hand, two games to come. And in the corridor, the Anfield corridor. Bill stuck out his chin. And Bill said, Never mind the Championship. That was a great match. Just what the public needed. Just what the public wanted. After recent sad events . . .

And in the corridor, the Anfield corridor. Don Revie nodded –

Yes, said Don Revie. If nothing else, it was a first-class advertisement for football. If nothing else . . .

On the bench, the bench at Molineux. In the twenty-seventh minute, Bill watched Alec Lindsay pass to Steve Heighway. And Heighway passed to Brian Hall. Hall shot. And Hall scored. And Liverpool Football Club beat Wolverhampton Wanderers one–nil. Away from home, away from Anfield. That afternoon, Leeds United lost four–one to Burnley Football Club. At home, at Elland Road. Leeds United had fifty-two points. And Liverpool Football Club had forty-eight points. Liverpool Football Club now just four points behind Leeds United. Still with two games in hand,

still with two games to come.

. . .

On the bench, the bench at Old Trafford. Bill and sixty thousand folk were watching Liverpool Football Club play Leicester City in the semi-final of the FA Cup. And from the first minute, the very first minute, they watched the players of Liverpool Football Club attack. And in the thirty-fifth minute, Kevin Keegan headed the ball at the goal. And Rofe blocked the ball on the goal line. In the sixtieth minute, Keegan headed the ball at the goal again. And Cross blocked the ball on the goal line. And in the eighty-sixth minute, Keegan headed the ball at the goal again. And the ball hit the post. And in the ninetieth minute, the referee looked at his watch. The referee put his whistle to his lips. And the referee blew his whistle. In a match in which Liverpool Football Club had won thirteen corners. And Leicester City had won one. In a match Liverpool Football Club should have won. And won easily. Liverpool Football Club had drawn nil–nil with Leicester City. In the semi-final of the FA Cup. Away from home, away from Anfield. Bill walked into the dressing room. The Old Trafford dressing room. And Bill looked around the dressing room. The Liverpool dressing room. From player to player. Exhausted player to exhausted player. From Clemence to Smith. From Lindsay to Thompson. From Cormack to Hughes. From Keegan to Hall. From Heighway to Toshack. And from Toshack to Callaghan. From disappointed player to disappointed player. And Bill said, Now then, boys. Come on now. Chins up, boys. Heads up. I know we have got to go and play that lot again on Wednesday. Even though we have already beaten them once. I know we have to go and beat them again. Because the rules clearly state that unless either side puts the ball in the net, the score remains a draw. And so we have to go and play that lot again on Wednesday night at Villa Park. Play that lot again and beat that lot again. Even though we have already beaten them once. And so I know you are exhausted, boys. And I know you are disappointed, boys. But can you imagine how that lot are feeling? Can you imagine, boys? How would you feel if you were fighting George Foreman and you were getting clubbed to death for six rounds when – suddenly – the lights went out and you were forced to go back and fight him again four days later? Can you imagine how you would feel, boys? Can you imagine? You wouldn't look forward to that, would you, boys? Well, I can tell you, boys. I looked at the faces of those Leicester players as they walked off just now. And I looked into their eyes, boys. And I can tell you they looked as though they had been to hell and back. To hell and back, boys. And so I tell you. They are sat across that corridor, boys. In that dressing room. And they are not looking forward to Wednesday night, boys. Not one of them. Because they don't want to go through that again. And so on Wednesday night you go and finish the job, boys. You go and beat that lot again, boys. And you put them out of their misery . . .

On the bench, the bench at Villa Park. From the first minute, the very first minute, Bill and fifty-five thousand, six hundred and nineteen folk watched the players of Liverpool Football Club attack again. But this time the players of Leicester City attacked, too. End to end. Liverpool Football Club attacked and Leicester City attacked. End to end. Shilton saved and Ray Clemence saved. But thirty-five seconds into the second half, John Toshack headed down the ball. And in a scramble, a goalmouth scramble. Brian Hall knocked the ball over the line. Into the net and into a goal. But three minutes later, Earle shot. The shot cannoned off Emlyn Hughes. The ball fell to Glover. And Glover shot. Into the net and into a goal. But still the players of Liverpool Football Club attacked. And still the players of Leicester City attacked. End to end. Liverpool Football Club attacked and Leicester City attacked. End to end. Shilton saved and Ray Clemence saved. But in the sixty-second minute, Toshack lobbed the ball forward. And Kevin Keegan chased after the ball. Faster than the defenders of Leicester City, outstripping the defenders of Leicester City. The ball falling. Keegan chasing. The ball falling. Keegan chasing. Falling, chasing. Keegan caught the ball, Keegan struck the ball. Keegan volleyed the ball. From twenty yards out. Keegan volleyed the ball. Into the net and into a goal. A killer goal, a wonder goal. The goal of the season. Of any season. And then in the eighty-sixth minute, Peter Cormack passed to Toshack. Toshack shot. And Toshack scored. And Liverpool Football Club beat Leicester City three–one in the semi-final replay of the FA Cup. Away from home, away from Anfield. Bill stood in the corridor, the corridor at Villa Park. Bill cocked his head, Bill stuck out his chin. And Bill said, This was a magnificent match. Both teams were a credit. It was marvellous to watch. And the atmosphere was electric. But we played as well as we have ever played. We played class football from the back, moving the ball around with skill and flair. And I do not want to single out individual players. Because it was collective brilliance. Collective brilliance. But Smith was outstanding. And Callaghan. And Hall. And Cormack. All outstanding in a team of collective brilliance. And as for Keegan. Well, Keegan has scored many brilliant goals this season. But this was his most important. Because that was the killer goal for Leicester City. And it matched his all-round display. A fantastic display, an unbelievable display. But what is truly unbelievable to me is that the boy isn't even in the England side. It's nothing short of criminal. In fact, it's like hanging an innocent man.

And in the corridor, the corridor at Villa Park. The gentlemen of the press nodded. And the gentlemen of the press asked, But what about the Championship, Bill? You have to play nine games in the next twenty-four days. Can you still win the Championship? And the Cup? And do the Double? Because if you are to do that, if you are to win the Double. You'll have to win nine games in twenty-four days . . .

Bill smiled. And Bill said, I don't even know who we play on Saturday. Someone will tell me tomorrow. But I know we will try. Because we always try. Liverpool Football Club always try to win every game they play. Every game we play . . .

On the bench, the Anfield bench. Bill listened to fifty-two thousand and twenty-seven folk singing, *We're going to win the Cup! We're going to win the Cup! Ee-aye-addio, we're going to win the Cup!* And in the seventh minute, Bill and the fifty-two thousand and twenty-seven folk watched Alec Lindsay score a penalty. And in the twenty-ninth minute, they watched Queens Park Rangers score an own goal. And Liverpool Football Club beat Queens Park Rangers two–one. At home, at Anfield. Fifty-two thousand and twenty-seven folk still singing, now singing, *We're going to win the League! We're going to win the League! Ee-aye-addio, we're going to win the League!*

On the bench, the bench at Bramall Lane, Sheffield. In the fifteenth minute, Bill watched Woodward pass to Garbett. And the linesman put his flag up. For offside. But Garbett passed to Nicholl. And the linesman put his flag down. And Nicholl shot. And Nicholl scored. And the linesman kept his flag down. And the goal stood. And Liverpool Football Club lost one–nil to Sheffield United. Away from home, away from Anfield. Leeds United had fifty-four points. Liverpool Football Club had fifty points. But Liverpool Football Club still had two games in hand, still two games to come –

On the bench, the bench at Maine Road. In the eighteenth minute, Bill watched Peter Cormack score. But in the sixty-fifth minute, Bill watched Lee score. And Liverpool Football Club drew one-all with Manchester City. The next day, the very next day. On the bench, the bench at Portman Road. In the first half, Bill watched Whymark score for Ipswich Town. And in the second half, Bill watched Emlyn Hughes equalise for Liverpool Football Club. And

Liverpool Football Club drew one-all again. Away from home, away from Anfield. That afternoon, Leeds United drew, too. And Leeds United had fifty-five points. And Liverpool Football Club had fifty-two points. But Liverpool Football Club still had a game in hand,

still a game to come –

On the bench, the Anfield bench. In the third minute, Bill and fifty thousand, seven hundred and eighty-one folk watched Brian Hall score. In the twelfth minute, they watched Hall score again. In the sixteenth minute, they watched Phil Boersma score. And in the thirty-fifth minute, they watched Kevin Keegan score. And Liverpool Football Club beat Manchester City four–nil. At home, at Anfield. The supporters of Liverpool Football Club sang and sang, *We're going to win the Cup! We're going to win the League! Ee-aye-addio –*

*WE'RE GOING TO WIN THE DOUBLE!*

On the bench, the Anfield bench. Bill and fifty-five thousand, eight hundred and fifty-eight Merseyside folk watched Liverpool Football Club play Everton Football Club. But Liverpool Football Club did not score and Everton Football Club did not score. No one scored. And Liverpool Football Club drew nil–nil with Everton Football Club. At home, at Anfield. Liverpool Football Club had fifty-five points. And Leeds United had sixty points. But again Liverpool Football Club had two games in hand, again two games to come. And in the corridor, the Anfield corridor. Again. Bill stuck out his chin. And again. Bill said, It's not finished yet –

Not yet, not yet . . .

On the bench, the Anfield bench. Bill and forty-seven thousand, nine hundred and ninety-seven folk were watching Liverpool Football Club play Arsenal Football Club. Bill and forty-seven thousand, nine hundred and ninety-seven folk still believing. And they watched Kevin Keegan shoot. But Rimmer saved the shot. And they watched John Toshack shoot. And Rimmer saved the shot again. And they watched Tommy Smith shoot. But Smith hit the crossbar. And then they watched Ball pass to Kelly. And Kelly passed to Kennedy. And Kennedy shot and Kennedy scored. And Liverpool Football Club lost one–nil to Arsenal Football Club. At home, at Anfield. Their first defeat of the season. At home, at Anfield. That night, Liverpool Football Club had fifty-five points. And Leeds United had sixty points.

But Liverpool Football Club had only two more games to play, two more games to come. And Liverpool Football Club could not catch Leeds United. That night, in their homes. Leeds United were first in the First Division. In their homes, with their feet up –

Leeds United were the Champions.

On the bench, the bench at Upton Park. In the first half, Bill watched Alec Lindsay have a penalty saved. But in the second half, Bill watched John Toshack score. And in the last minute, the very last minute, Bill watched Kevin Keegan score. And Liverpool Football Club drew two-all with West Ham United. Away from home, away from Anfield. In the corridor, the corridor at Upton Park. Bill still had his chin stuck out. And Bill said, If the season had started at Christmas, we would have won the Championship by a street. And don't forget, we still have the most important game of the season yet to come. The FA Cup Final,

the Big One.

Up in Manchester, up at Old Trafford. That afternoon, in the eighty-fourth minute, Denis Law scored for Manchester City. And some of the supporters of Manchester United ran onto the pitch. And Matt Busby appealed to the supporters of Manchester United to get off the pitch. So the game could finish. For the sake of the club. For the sake of Manchester United. But some of the supporters of Manchester United would not get off the pitch. For the sake of the club. For the sake of Manchester United. And so the match could not finish. The match abandoned. But the result still stood. Manchester United had lost one–nil to Manchester City. At home, at Old Trafford. Manchester United were relegated from the First Division.

. . .

In the dressing room. The Wembley dressing room. Bill pinned a newspaper cutting to the wall. The Wembley wall. And Bill looked around the dressing room. The Liverpool dressing room. From player to player. The sixteen players of Liverpool Football Club. And Bill said, There you go, boys. That's what Supermac says he's going to do to us. How many goals he is going to score against us. How he is going to destroy us. And what he says about us. That we are overrated and that we have no pace. Well, he's done his talking. So now let's do our playing, boys. And so our team today will be Clemence, Smith,

Lindsay, Thompson, Cormack, Hughes, Keegan, Hall, Heighway, Toshack and Callaghan. And our twelfth man will be Lawler . . .

And in the dressing room. The Wembley dressing room. Phil Boersma stood up. And Phil Boersma shook his head –

My days of playing for this club are over . . .

And Phil Boersma walked out of the dressing room. The Liverpool dressing room. Down the corridor. The Wembley corridor. And out of the stadium. Wembley Stadium.

. . .

On the bench, the Wembley bench. Bill moved his arms, Bill moved his hands. For every ball, for every run. And every pass. And Callaghan passed to Lindsay. Lindsay crossed for Toshack. Toshack leapt for the cross. Toshack headed on the cross for Keegan. But Kennedy leapt. And Kennedy headed the ball over the bar. The Newcastle bar. And on the bench, the Wembley bench. Bill moved his arms again, Bill moved his hands again. For every ball, for every run. And every pass. And Heighway passed to Keegan. Keegan ran with the ball. Keegan beat Howard. Keegan crossed for Toshack. But McFaul got to the ball. McFaul saved. On the bench, the Wembley bench. Bill moved his arms, Bill moved his hands. For every ball, for every run. And every pass. And Smith passed to Keegan. Keegan chested down the ball. Keegan passed to Toshack. And Toshack shot. And Toshack missed. And on the bench, the Wembley bench. Again Bill moved his arms, again Bill moved his hands. For every ball, for every run. And every pass. And Callaghan passed to Heighway. Heighway ran. Heighway crossed the ball. But Howard cleared the ball off the goal line. The Newcastle goal line. And at half-time. On the bench, the Wembley bench. His vest stuck to his skin. Bill stood up, Bill got to his feet. And Bill walked down the touchline. The Wembley touchline. Bill walked down the tunnel. The Wembley tunnel. Bill walked into the dressing room. The Wembley dressing room. And Bill looked around the dressing room. The Liverpool dressing room. From player to player. From Clemence to Smith. From Lindsay to Thompson. From Cormack to Hughes. From Keegan to Hall. From Heighway to Toshack. And from Toshack to Callaghan. And Bill said, Well done, boys. Well played indeed. You'll win three or four–nil. I have no doubt, boys. No doubt at all. Three or four–nil. You mark my words, boys. Three–nil. You mark my words . . .

And back on the bench, the Wembley bench. Bill moved his arms again, Bill moved his hands again. For every ball, for every run. And every pass. And Hughes passed to Heighway. Heighway passed to Keegan. Keegan passed to Toshack. Toshack passed to Cormack. Cormack passed to Keegan. And Keegan shot. And Keegan missed. And on the bench, the Wembley bench. Bill moved his arms, Bill moved his hands. For every ball, for every run. And every tackle. And Lindsay won a tackle. Lindsay ran with the ball. Lindsay passed to Keegan. Keegan dummied the ball. The ball hit Howard. The ball bounced back to Lindsay. Lindsay struck the ball on the bounce. Lindsay volleyed the ball. Into the far corner of the net. The Newcastle net and the Newcastle goal. A goal of class, of different class. A disallowed goal. Offside. And so the goal did not count, the goal did not matter. But on the bench, the Wembley bench. Bill moved his arms again, Bill moved his hands again. For every ball, for every run. And every throw-in. And Heighway took a throw-in to Smith. Smith crossed the ball. Hall dived for the ball. The ball ran to Keegan. Keegan flicked up the ball. And Keegan volleyed the ball. Into the net and into a goal. A goal that counted, a goal that mattered. A goal that paid the rent. But on the bench, the Wembley bench. Bill was still moving his arms, Bill was still moving his hands. For every ball, for every run. And every free kick. And Cormack rolled a free kick to Hughes. And Hughes shot. And Hughes missed. By inches. And on the bench, the Wembley bench. Bill moved his arms, Bill moved his hands. For every ball, for every run. And every pass. And Toshack passed to Hall. Hall passed to Callaghan. Callaghan passed to Smith. Smith passed to Hall. Hall passed back to Smith. Smith passed to Keegan. Keegan passed to Heighway. And Heighway shot. And Heighway missed. And on the bench, the Wembley bench. Bill moved his arms again, Bill moved his hands again. For every ball, for every run. And every kick. And Clemence kicked the ball long up the pitch. Toshack flicked on the ball to Heighway. And Heighway shot. And Heighway scored. And on the bench, the Wembley bench. His shirt stuck to his vest. His vest stuck to his skin. Bill stood up, Bill got to his feet. And Bill turned to the supporters of Liverpool Football Club. And Bill raised his arm. His hand and his finger. In salute. And then Bill sat back down. On the bench, the Wembley bench. Bill moving his arms, Bill moving his hands. For every ball, for every run. And every header. And Thompson headed the ball down to Callaghan. Callaghan flicked on the ball to Keegan. Keegan crossed for Toshack. And Toshack shot. And Toshack missed. But on the bench, the Wembley bench. Bill still moved his arms, Bill still moved his hands. For every ball, for every run. And every pass. And Keegan passed long across the pitch to Smith. Smith flicked on the ball to Hall. Hall passed back to Smith. Smith passed to Heighway. Heighway passed back to Smith. Smith crossed the ball. And Keegan met the cross. Keegan hit the cross. Into the net and into the goal. The Newcastle net and the Newcastle goal. Newcastle United undressed now, Newcastle United stretched naked now. Naked and lost. In a nightmare, in broad daylight. And on the bench, the Wembley bench. His jacket stuck to his shirt. His shirt stuck to his vest. His vest stuck to his skin. Bill looked at his watch. And now Bill moved his arms one last time. Now Bill stretched out his arms. And now Bill moved his hands one last time. Now Bill waved his hands in front of him. And Bill said, That's it. It's all over . . .

And the referee put his whistle in his mouth. The referee raised his hands above his head. And the referee blew his whistle. And Liverpool Football Club had beaten Newcastle United three–nil. Liverpool Football Club had won the FA Cup. Again.

And on the bench, the Wembley bench. His coat stuck to his jacket. His jacket stuck to his shirt. His shirt stuck to his vest. His vest stuck to his skin. Bill stood up again, Bill got to his feet again. And Bill turned to the supporters of Liverpool Football Club again. And Bill Shankly raised his arm again. His hand again –

His finger again. In salute again –

And in thanks. Again –

Bill walked onto the pitch. The Wembley pitch. And two young supporters of Liverpool Football Club ran onto the pitch. The Wembley pitch. And the two young supporters fell to their knees on the pitch. The Wembley pitch. On their knees, at the feet of Bill Shankly, kissing the feet of Bill Shankly. And Bill laughed. And Bill said, Make a good job of them boots for me, will you, boys?

And Bill watched Emlyn Hughes lead the players of Liverpool Football Club up the steps. The thirty-nine steps. Bill watched Emlyn

Hughes receive the FA Cup from Princess Anne. Bill watched Emlyn Hughes hold the Cup aloft. And Bill heard the supporters of Liverpool Football Club roar, *Li-ver-pool, Li-ver-pool* –

*LI-VER-POOL . . .*

And on the pitch. The Wembley pitch. The gentlemen of the press and radio and television crowded around Bill Shankly. And Bill took off his coat. Bill handed his coat to a television producer. And Bill said, Look after that for me, please. But if you don't, you'll have to pay for it. And I got it in Rotterdam. And the fare to Rotterdam is very expensive. So make sure you look after it. But Christ, after today, you should be proud to be holding Bill Shankly's coat. Proud and humble. Because a lot of you people in the press were making predictions about the final. You were analysing our team when you hadn't even seen us play. When you had no idea how we play. And that annoyed me. It's like trying to analyse Jack Dempsey when you haven't even seen him fight. Well, now you know how we fight. How we fight for each other. And how we play. How we play for each other. And for the supporters of Liverpool Football Club. You have seen us and you have heard them. And I'm happiest not for myself, the players or the staff. But for the multitudes. Because I'm a people's man. A socialist. And I'm only sorry I couldn't go amongst them. And speak to them. But I'm happy that we worked religiously. That we didn't cheat them and that we have something to take back to them tomorrow. And so there's nothing more to say. So if you gentlemen will excuse me, now I'm going to get a cup of tea and a couple of pies . . .

*SHANK-LEE, SHANK-LEE, SHANK-LEE . . .*

And Bill walked off the pitch. The Wembley pitch. Bill walked down the tunnel. The Wembley tunnel. Bill walked into the dressing room. The Wembley dressing room. Bill looked around the dressing room. The Liverpool dressing room. And Bill sat down on the bench. The dressing-room bench. In the silence, on his own. His jacket still stuck to his shirt. His shirt still stuck to his vest. His vest still stuck to his skin. In the silence, on his own. Bill closed his eyes. And Bill whispered, That's it. All the arguments are won . . .

All but one. Just the one.

. . .

On William Brown Street. Before the Corinthian columns of

the Picton Library. With the players and with the staff of Liverpool Football Club and their families. And with the Cup. The FA Cup. Bill stepped forward again. Bill opened his arms again. And again the people, the hundreds of thousands of people, fell silent. *Just like that.* They all fell silent. And Bill said, Ladies and gentlemen, we have had many great memories at Liverpool Football Club during the last few seasons. But I think today I feel prouder than I have ever done before. Three years ago, I stood here and I said we would go back to Wembley. And yesterday we went back and not only did the team win the Cup, they gave an exhibition of football. But above all else, we are pleased for you. Because it is you who we play for. It's you who pay our wages. And not only did we win the Cup on the field, we won it on the terraces as well. But now we look to the future. Because that has always got to be done. And we have a great team. They can go on from here because we have been building to this for three years. During which time we have been the best team in the country. The best team in the land. And our consistency over the last three years proves it. We're good enough to win the League each season. If we did not have to play sixty or seventy games each season. But they are basically a young side. A side that is more than capable of winning the League next year. A young side playing great football, playing pure football. *Pure* football. And so there is no end to it –

There is no end to it . . .


## 45. AFTER THE WHISTLE, BEFORE THE WHISTLE

After the Cup, after the parade. The speeches and the parties. There was still another game, always another game. And on Wednesday 8 May, 1974, Liverpool Football Club travelled to White Hart Lane, London, to play Tottenham Hotspur in the last game of the season. And Bill Shankly walked into the dressing room. The away dressing room. Bill Shankly looked around the dressing room. The Liverpool dressing room. From player to player. From Ray Clemence to Tommy Smith. From Alec Lindsay to Phil Thompson. From Peter Cormack to Emlyn Hughes. From Kevin Keegan to Brian Hall. From Steve Heighway to Ian Callaghan. And from Ian Callaghan to Max

Thompson. And Bill Shankly walked over to Max Thompson. Bill Shankly sat down on the bench beside Max Thompson. And Bill Shankly put his arm around the shoulders of Max Thompson –

How old are you, lad? How old are you, son?

I'm seventeen, Boss, said Max Thompson.

Aye, said Bill Shankly. I know, son. I know that. You're seventeen years, one hundred and twenty-nine days old, son. Bob told me. And Bob told me you are the youngest player ever to play for Liverpool Football Club. Did you know that, son?

Yes, Boss. Bob told me and all . . .

And so are you nervous, son?

Yes, Boss. Very nervous.

That's natural, son. That's only natural. But you should be excited, too. Excited and proud. Proud to be pulling on that shirt, proud to be playing for Liverpool Football Club. For the supporters of Liverpool Football Club. And remember, son. There are fifty thousand men and boys on the Kop who dream of pulling on that shirt. Who dream of playing for Liverpool Football Club. Who dream of being in your shoes. In your boots, in that shirt. That red shirt. And believe me, son. Once you've pulled on that shirt. Once you've played for Liverpool Football Club. You'll never want to take off that shirt again. You'll never want it to stop, you'll never want it to end. So enjoy it, son. Enjoy every second and every minute of it. Every single second of every single minute. Because one day it will stop –

Believe me, son. One day it will end.

. . .

On Wednesday 8 May, 1974, early in the second half, Chris McGrath scored for Tottenham Hotspur. But in the sixty-seventh minute, Steve Heighway equalised. And Liverpool Football Club drew one-all with Tottenham Hotspur. Away from home,

away from Anfield.

# THE SECOND HALF

## EVERYDAY IS SUNDAY

*Shankly Agonistes*

## 46. THE BEST LAID SCHEMES

In the house, in their front room. After the whistle, before the whistle. In his chair, before the television. The World Cup on, the World Cup off. Bill turned to Ness. And Bill said, I've decided, love. I'll go now.

Are you sure that's what you want to do, asked Ness.

Bill shook his head. And Bill said, No, I'm not, love. I'm not sure at all. But I'm not enjoying life, love. I need to get it sorted out.

Well, if it's making you miserable, love. If it is making you unhappy. All this talking, all this thinking. Then you have to make a decision, love. One way or the other. It's like living with a time bomb.

Bill nodded. And Bill said, I know, love. And I'm sorry. Because it's hard on you, love. It's wearing you out, too. I know that, love. I can see that. But I thought you would bite off my hand, love. I thought you would jump for joy. And say, Yes, love. Now is the time.

I just don't want you to do anything you don't want to do, love. Football is your whole life. Liverpool Football Club is your whole life, love. I know that. And I know what a wrench it'll be for you, love.

Bill shook his head. And Bill said, I'd be leaving Liverpool Football Club. But I'd not be leaving the game, love.

I know that, said Ness. And nor would I ever ask you to, love. It would be too cruel. It would be too heartless.


## 47. O' MICE AN' MEN, GANG AFT AGLEY

After the season, before the season. In the boardroom, the Anfield boardroom. John Smith looked down the long table at Bill Shankly. John Smith shook his head. And John Smith said, But if it's a question of the new contract. If it's a question of the money. Then we are willing to double your salary. We're willing to triple your salary . . .

Thank you, said Bill Shankly. But it's not a question of money. It's never been a question of money. When I hear of the money that's bandied about, it makes my blood boil. There are men with tennis courts and swimming pools who haven't even got a Championship medal. But I have never asked for money. I came to Liverpool to make a success of this job for this club and for this city. Maybe I didn't get enough out of it for my family. I regret I didn't give Ness more. We're still living in the same house we moved into when we came to Liverpool. But at least it's a home, not a house. And I'm not looking for Buckingham Palace. And Matt is the same as me. They still live in the same semi-detached house in Chorlton-cum-Hardy they have always lived in. And perhaps my family are all right after all. They've all got a place to live and something to eat and I've got five bonny grandchildren. All girls. And every one with a Scouse accent. Now what more could a man want? So no, it's not a question of money. It is a question of time. And I have been around a long time. Twenty-five years as a manager, seventeen as a player. But during my time, I have always been so single-minded. And so my family has suffered. And I regret that. I regret that Ness has had to bear the brunt of my being away so much. And so I think I would like a rest, to spend more time with my family, and maybe get a bit of fun out of life. Because whilst you love football, it is a hard, relentless task which goes on and on like a river. There is no time for stopping and resting. That is not an option. So I'm retiring. Because that is my only option. And I think now is the right time. If we had lost the final, I would have carried on. But I thought, We've won the Cup now and maybe it's a good time to go. So I knew then, that day in May, I was going to finish.

John Smith shook his head again. And John Smith said, But what if we were to offer you a position as general manager? With an office here at the ground. Where you could come in when you want. And do what you want. At a different pace. At your own pace.

Thank you, said Bill Shankly. But that hasn't worked at United. It hasn't worked for Matt or for the club. They have been relegated. They are in the Second Division now. No, I've always said, when I go. When I leave. It will be a complete break. It must be a complete break. For you and for me. That is the only way.

John Smith said, But the thought of you leaving. Of you making a complete break. It is an horrendous thought for us. Would you not even consider becoming a director, Mr Shankly?

Thank you, said Bill Shankly again. But I'm not a committee man. So I could never be a director. That isn't me.

498

In the semi-detached house on Bellefield Avenue, West Derby, in their bedroom. Bill put on his shirt. His tangerine shirt. Bill went to the dressing table. Bill opened the top drawer. Bill took out his cufflinks. His gold cufflinks. Bill closed the drawer. Bill did up the cuffs of his shirt. His tangerine shirt. Bill went to the wardrobe. Bill opened the doors. Bill took out his suit. His freshly cleaned grey herringbone suit. Bill left the wardrobe doors open. Bill walked over to the bed. Bill laid out the suit on top of the bed covers. Bill took the trousers from the coat hanger. Bill put on the trousers of his suit. His freshly cleaned grey herringbone suit. Bill went back to the dressing table. Bill opened the second drawer of the dressing table. Bill took out a tie. The red tie his daughters had once given him for Christmas. The red tie he had worn ever since. Bill closed the drawer. Bill walked back to the wardrobe. The doors still open. Bill stood before the mirror on the back of one of the doors. Bill put on his tie. His red tie. Bill went back over to the bed. Bill picked up the jacket from the bed. Bill took the jacket from the coat hanger. Bill put on the jacket of his suit. His freshly cleaned grey herringbone suit. Bill walked back over to the dressing table. Bill opened the top drawer of the dressing table again. Bill took out one white handkerchief and one red pocket square. Bill closed the drawer. Bill put the white handkerchief in his left trouser pocket. Bill laid the red pocket square on the top of the dressing table. It looked like a red diamond. Bill brought the bottom point of the red pocket square up to the top point. It looked like a red triangle. Bill brought the left corner of the triangle to the right corner and then the right corner to the left corner. It looked like a long red rectangle with a point at the top. Bill folded the bottom almost to the top. Bill walked over to the mirror on the back of the wardrobe door. Bill stood before the mirror. Bill placed the red pocket square in the breast pocket of his grey jacket. Bill looked in the mirror. Bill adjusted the pocket square until just enough of the point was coming out of the pocket. The red point out of the grey pocket. Bill stepped back. In the semi-detached house on Bellefield Avenue, West Derby, in their bedroom. Bill looked at himself in the mirror. The suit too big, the tie too tight. And Bill saw a sixty-year-old man. The shadows around his eyes too dark, the lines in his face too deep. And Bill did not recognise him.


## 49. BUT GRIEF AN' PAIN (YOU'RE HAVING ME ON)

On the morning of Friday 12 July, 1974. In his office, at his desk. Peter Robinson rang around the press. And Peter Robinson said, There is a press conference at Anfield at twelve fifteen today. The board have a very special announcement to make. It is really important. It'll make front-page news. So make sure you are there. And don't be late.

Can you give us a hint what it might be about, asked the press.

Peter Robinson said, No. Just be there.

Is it to do with Ray Kennedy?

Peter Robinson said, No. It's nothing to do with any transfer deal. But at this stage, I can tell you no more.

At high noon, on Friday 12 July, 1974. In the lounge, the VIP lounge at Anfield. There were forty gentlemen of the press. Notebooks and microphones, television cameras and lights. The directors of Liverpool Football Club began to file in. In silent procession, in dark suits. They sat down behind the long table at the front of the lounge. Backs to the window, black against the light. They did not smile and they did not speak. In their dark suits, in a silent line. They waited. And then Bill Shankly marched in. Bill Shankly bounced in –

Hello, boys. Hello. How are you, boys? How are you all? Have you all had a good summer, boys? Good holidays? Have we got time for a quick cup of tea, May? A quick cuppa?

May nodded. And May poured Bill Shankly a cup of tea.

Thank you, May. Thank you very much, love.

Bill Shankly took a sip of his tea. And a bite from a brown-bread sandwich. And then Bill Shankly wandered over to the gentlemen of the press. Head cocked and jaw out –

The World Cup was very disappointing, wasn't it, boys? Very disappointing. If some of the stuff played in Germany had been played here at Anfield, the teams would have been hooted off the park. Hooted off the park. And I told you all before the World Cup that Yugoslavia wouldn't be any good, didn't I, boys? Didn't I now? They play for fun, not for keeps. They play cards for money and then give you back your money when they beat you. They are too sweet to be wholesome. Too sweet for this world, boys . . .

The gentlemen of the press all nodded. And the gentlemen of the press asked, So what do you think about Don Revie being appointed as England boss, Bill?

Jesus Christ, boys. The man is only forty-seven and he's gone into semi-retirement . . .

Bill Shankly stopped. Mid-sentence. Bill Shankly glanced at his watch. Ticking, ticking. Bill Shankly turned around. Bill Shankly saw the directors of Liverpool Football Club. Behind the long table, in their dark suits. Bill Shankly put down his cup of tea. His brown-bread sandwich. And Bill Shankly walked up to the long table at the front of the lounge. Bill Shankly made his way behind the backs of the chairs of the directors of Liverpool Football Club. Bill Shankly put down his hat on the window ledge. And Bill Shankly took his seat in the middle of the line of the directors of Liverpool Football Club.

One of the television crew switched on his portable sunlight. And Bill Shankly jumped back to his feet –

Hold it a minute, boys! John Wayne has not arrived yet!

The gentlemen of the press laughed. But the directors of Liverpool Football Club did not laugh. They did not even smile. In their dark suits and in their silence. They were waiting.

Bill Shankly sat back down behind the long table. Bill Shankly turned to John Smith. And Bill Shankly nodded –

And John Smith said, It is with great regret that I, as chairman of Liverpool Football Club, have to inform you that Mr Shankly has intimated that he wishes to retire from active participation in League football. And the board has, with extreme reluctance, accepted his decision. I would like at this stage to place on record the board's great appreciation of Mr Shankly's magnificent achievements over the period of his managership. Meanwhile, Mr Shankly has agreed to give every assistance to the club for as long as is necessary.

There were gasps from the press –

Gasps. And then silence.

Bill Shankly looked down at the table. At his hands, at his fingers. His fingers and his nails. And Bill Shankly nodded. And then Bill Shankly looked back up –

This is not a decision that was taken quickly, said Bill Shankly. It has been in my mind over the last twelve months. But I feel it is time I had a rest from the game I've served for forty-three years. My wife and I both felt that we wanted to have a rest and charge up my batteries again. It was the most difficult thing in the world to make a decision like this and, when I went to see the chairman to say I was retiring, it was like walking to the electric chair. I was going to be burned up, frizzled up. But when I've had a rest, there are plenty of things I feel I will still be able to do in football. I don't think it is the time to talk about them now. It will be part of my hobby. Whether I can live without it, I cannot answer now. I can only wait and see . . .

But there is no animosity between the chairman, the directors and me. None at all. These people kept me bartering, putting propositions in my way that possibly even Paul Getty would have taken. In the end I felt guilty, as if I was committing a crime . . .

But I said some time ago, I would go when I got the message to go. My wife felt it was time at the end of last season. In fact, she was quite hostile when I said no. Because my attitude was when I had finished one game, I began to prepare for the next. And when I think back now, I think I missed some of the fun out of life. Perhaps I was too dedicated. The laughs were there for the players but never away from the players. I was too serious. I lived the life of a monk. And I carried it to extremes. There is a happy medium which I should have tried to find. But my home has always been a haven. I'm only really comfortable there. It's what every man needs. There is nothing I like more than being with my grandchildren . . .

My wife thought at one time I wouldn't finish with the game until the coffin came in the house. But I think I will have years now before the coffin comes. I'm not saying the game would kill you, but being a manager is often like steering a ship through a minefield. But it's very sad for me to break away from football. And I shall continue to live on Merseyside. We won't move from here. The Liverpool crowd have been wonderful . . .

And I'll be here on Monday to meet the players when they report back for training. And if the new man wants any help from me while he is settling in, I'll be glad to give it. But if he doesn't, I'll go straight away. It will be a clean break. It will be a complete break with

Liverpool Football Club. When a new man comes in, I will be out.

But I'll still come to watch Liverpool and, when I do, I'll probably go into the Kop. Onto the Spion Kop . . .

In the lounge, the VIP lounge at Anfield. There was silence, still silence, still only silence. Until finally, finally, someone asked, Do you not fancy being a director, Bill? Are you moving upstairs?

No, said Bill Shankly. Not even if they paid me.

So how would you sum up your career, Bill?

Well, I think I was the best manager in the game and I should have won more. Yeah. But I didn't do anything in devious ways. I mean, I would fight with you. And I would break my wife's leg if I played against her. But I wouldn't cheat her. I wouldn't cheat anyone.

But what about regrets then, Bill. Any regrets?

Aye. Just one. Aye. Not winning the European Cup. But it's not about me. About the past. And about regrets. It's about the club. About Liverpool Football Club. And the future. The future of Liverpool Football Club. Not about the man who is going. But about the men who are coming in. And there's no doubt Ray Kennedy will do a good job for Liverpool Football Club. He is big, brave and strong. And his signing means that we now have the greatest strength in depth that we have ever had. We are so strong that you need to have a couple of international caps just to get into the reserve team. And I know Kennedy will cause plenty of trouble to defences. He fights all the way. And so he was at the very top of my list of wanted men –

So it's been a momentous day. Yes. But his signing shows that I'm not running away. And maybe it will be said that one of the last things I did at this club was to sign a great new player . . .

Bill Shankly stood up now. His suit too big, his tie too tight. The shadows around his eyes darkened, the lines on his face deepened. Bill Shankly looked at the gentlemen of the press. His eyes wet, his breath short. Bill Shankly nodded. And Bill Shankly smiled –

There'll not be many days like this, boys.

And then Bill Shankly was gone.

# 50. FOR PROMIS'D JOY!

In the house, in their bed. Bill opened his eyes. Bill closed his eyes. And then Bill opened his eyes again. In the dark and in the silence. Bill stared up at the ceiling. The bedroom ceiling. And Bill breathed out. Bill had been dreaming. Only dreaming. In the dark and in the silence. Bill turned to look at the clock on the table beside the bed. The alarm clock. Ticking, ticking. In the dark. Bill got out of bed. Bill shaved and Bill washed. Bill put on his shirt. Bill put on his suit. Bill put on his tie. His red tie. His Liverpool Football Club tie. Bill went down the stairs. Bill went into the kitchen. In the light and in the silence. Bill saw the cloth on the table. The cutlery and the crockery. The salt and pepper pots. The jars of honey and marmalade. The butter dish. The two glasses of fresh orange juice. And Bill smiled. In the kitchen, at the table. Bill and Ness ate breakfast. A slice of toast and honey, a glass of orange juice and a cup of tea. And then Bill helped Ness clear away the breakfast things. Bill dried up the breakfast things. Bill helped Ness put away the breakfast things. And then Bill kissed Ness on her cheek. Bill went into the hall. Bill put on his hat. Bill went out of the front door. Bill went down the drive. Bill got into the car –

And Bill went off to work.

Bill drove down the West Derby Road. And Bill saw people going into the newsagents. Buying their morning paper. Bill turned onto Belmont Road. And Bill saw people queuing at the bus stops. On their way to work. Bill turned into the car park at Anfield Road. And Bill saw the dustbin men and the postmen. Working. And Bill smiled. Bill got out of the car. Bill walked across the car park. Bill went into the ground. And into work.

Bill went down the corridor. Bill went up the stairs. Bill went into his office. Bill took off his hat. Bill hung up his hat. Bill walked around the bags of mail. The mountain of bags and bags of mail. Bill sat down behind his desk. Bill looked around his office. The filing cabinets and the shelves. The shelves of books. The books of names and the books of notes. The bags of mail. The mountain of bags and bags of mail. And Bill smiled. Bill reached into the first bag of mail on top of the mountain of bags and bags of mail. Bill took out a letter. Bill opened the letter. Bill read the letter. The letter of congratulations on winning the Cup. The letter of thanks for winning the Cup. And Bill smiled again. Bill put down the letter. Bill opened the top drawer of his desk. Bill took out a piece of paper. Bill closed the top drawer of his desk. Bill threaded the piece of paper into his typewriter. Bill turned the platen knob. And Bill began to type –

Bill began to work.

There were footsteps in the corridor now. There was a knock upon the door now. And Bill stopped typing. Bill looked up. And Bill saw Bob. Bob was standing in the doorway. Bill smiled at Bob. And Bill said, Morning, Bob. How are you today, Bob? You look a wee bit pale, Bob. Like you've seen a ghost, Bob. Are you all right, Bob?

Well, said Bob. I suppose I'm still in a state of shock.

Why, Bob? What's happened? What's wrong, Bob?

You, said Bob. Resigning. I had no idea. No idea at all.

Oh, that. Yes, well. I've made a decision, Bob. I've talked it over with Ness. And we both feel I need a rest. I mean, I'm still fit enough. I'm not ill. Don't worry. I'm fit, but I'm tired. And so I need a rest. I need to recharge my batteries. That's all, Bob.

But surely then there's no need for you to resign, said Bob. To call it a day. Have you not considered just having a bit of a break? Perhaps a cruise with Ness? Get your feet up for a bit. See the world. I could look after the shop for you. Keep things ticking over. You wouldn't have to worry. I'd keep things just the way they are. And then you could come back. Your batteries recharged, as you say. And things could go on. Just as they were. Just as they are.

No, Bob. No. I've made my decision. And I'm sticking to it. If you can't make decisions in this game. If you can't make decisions in life. Then you're a bloody menace, Bob. A bloody menace. You're better to go and be an MP or something.

Please, said Bob. Don't make me beg you, Bill. Please. Don't make me go down on my knees, Bill. But if that's what it'll take to make you change your mind. Then that's what I'll do, Bill.

No, Bob. No. I've said I'm retiring. And so that's what I'm going to do. I mean, I don't agree with the word. I hate the word! It's the stupidest word I've ever heard in all my life. It should be stricken from the record, retirement. Nobody can retire! You retire when you get the coffin. And they nail down the lid. And your name is on the top. That's retirement! No, Bob. No. But I've said I'm retiring from Liverpool Football Club. From Anfield. And so that is what I'm going to do. But not from football, Bob. Not from life. No.

But what about today, asked Bob. The training? The pre-season? What are we going to do, Bill?

Bill laughed. And Bill said, Same as we always do, Bob. I'm still here. Nothing's changed, Bob. I'll be down in a minute.

Bob stared at Bill. At his desk, at his typewriter. And Bob shook his head. And Bob smiled –

Well, if you say so, Bill. Then I'll see you downstairs. In a minute then, Bill. Downstairs . . .

Bill nodded. And Bill looked back down at his desk. At his typewriter, the unfinished letter. And Bill began to type again. To finish the letter, to finish his work. And then Bill looked at his watch. Bill got up from his desk. Bill picked up his bag from the floor. His kit bag. Bill walked around the bags of mail. The mountain of bags and bags of mail. And Bill went out of his office. Bill went down the corridor. Bill went down the stairs. Bill went into the changing rooms. Bill put down his bag on the bench. His kit bag. Bill took off his tie. His red tie. His Liverpool Football Club tie. And Bill took off his shoes. His suit. And his shirt. Bill put on his tracksuit bottoms. His sweater. And his boots. Bill went out of the dressing room. Bill went down the corridor. Bill went out of the ground. Into the sunlight. And Bill stood in the car park at Anfield, Liverpool. Ready for training,

ready for work.

Up at Melwood, in the pavilion. Before their training, before their work. Bill gathered together the players of Liverpool Football Club. But Bill did not look around the room. Bill did not look from player to player. From Liverpool player to Liverpool player. Bill stared into the distance. A slight shadow on the far wall. And Bill said, As you probably know, boys. As you've probably all heard. I had a big meeting up at Anfield on Friday. Because I have decided to retire. My time here is done, boys. And so a new man will come in. I don't know who. And I don't know when. But when he does, I will be gone. But I know you'll all try as hard for him and work as hard for him as you have for me, boys. Because I could not have asked for more. And so I thank you now, boys. For all your hard work. I thank you, boys. And I wish you all the very best of luck. And every future success, boys –

For all of you and for the club . . .

But you can't retire, cried Emlyn Hughes. Please, Boss. You just can't. Please don't, Boss . . .

Give it a rest, muttered someone. Pack it in, Thrush . . .

Bill breathed in, Bill breathed out. And Bill said, I've simply done enough and had enough, boys. I've been in this job a long time. And now I want to spend more time with my family. My grandchildren. And so I have to think about my health and my wife. But that's enough about me, boys. That's enough talking for one day. We've got a league to win, boys. A title to win –

So come on, boys. Come on –

Let's get it going . . .

And Bill led the players out of the pavilion. And round the training pitch. Bill joking, Bill laughing. Cajoling and inspiring. But running, still running, running harder, harder than ever. Then the players split into their groups. And the players lifted weights. The players skipped. The players jumped. The players did squats. The players did abdominal exercises. And the players sprinted. And Bill lifted weights. Bill skipped. Bill jumped. Bill did squats. Bill did abdominal exercises. And Bill sprinted. Bill laughing, Bill joking. Inspiring and cajoling. But sprinting, still sprinting, sprinting harder, harder than ever. And then the players passed the ball. The players dribbled with the ball. The players headed the ball. The players chipped the ball. The players controlled the ball. And the players tackled. And Bill passed the ball. Bill dribbled with the ball. Bill headed the ball. Bill chipped the ball. Bill controlled the ball. And Bill tackled. Bill joking, Bill laughing. Cajoling and inspiring. But tackling, still tackling, tackling harder, harder than ever. And the players went between the training boards. The players moving, the ball moving. Playing the ball against one board. Then taking the ball, controlling the ball. Turning with the ball, dribbling with the ball. Up to the other board. In just ten touches. Playing the ball against the other board. Then pulling the ball down, turning again and dribbling again. Back down to the first board. In just ten touches. And Bill went between the training boards. Bill moving, the ball moving. Bill playing the ball against one board. Then taking the ball, controlling the ball.

Bill turning with the ball, dribbling with the ball. Up to the other board. In just ten touches. Bill playing the ball against the other board. Then pulling the ball down, turning again and dribbling again. Back down to the first board. In just ten touches. Bill laughing, Bill joking. Inspiring and cajoling. But dribbling, still dribbling, dribbling harder, harder than ever. Then the players went inside the sweat box. Ball after ball. Into the box. Every second, another ball. For one minute. Then for two minutes. Then for three minutes. Ball after ball, into the box. And Bill went into the sweat box. Ball after ball. Into the box. Every second, another ball. For one minute. Then for two minutes. Then for three minutes. Bill joking, Bill laughing. Cajoling and inspiring. But sweating, still sweating, sweating harder, harder than ever. And then the players played three-a-sides. Three-a-sides then five-a-sides. Five-a-sides then seven-a-sides. Seven-a-sides then eleven-a-sides. And Bill played three-a-sides. Three-a-sides then five-a-sides. Five-a-sides then seven-a-sides. Seven-a-sides then eleven-a-sides. Bill laughing, Bill joking. Inspiring and cajoling. But playing, still playing, playing harder, harder than ever. And then, finally, the players ran one last time around the training pitch. And Bill ran one last time around the training pitch. Bill joking, Bill laughing. Cajoling and inspiring. But running, still running, running harder, harder than ever. Until the final whistle, until the job was done. The work complete. His work.

The players got back on the bus. Bob Paisley, Joe Fagan, Reuben Bennett, Ronnie Moran and Tom Saunders got back on the bus. And Bill got back on the bus. Bill still laughing, Bill still joking. All the way back to Anfield. Everybody now joking, everybody now laughing. All the way back to Anfield. Everything the same, the same as before. As though nothing had changed.

The players got off the bus at Anfield. And Bill got off the bus at Anfield. The players went into Anfield. And Bill went into Anfield. Bill laughing, Bill joking. In the dressing rooms. The Anfield dressing rooms. The players took off their boots, the players took off their tracksuits. In the dressing rooms. The Anfield dressing rooms. Bill took off his boots. Bill took off his sweater and his tracksuit bottoms. Bill joking, Bill laughing. The players went into the baths. The Anfield baths. And Bill went into the baths. The Anfield baths. Bill laughing, Bill joking. The players washed and changed. And Bill washed and changed. Bill joking, Bill laughing. And then the players said goodbye. And Bill said goodbye. Bill still laughing, Bill still joking. The players went out to their cars. The players went back to their houses. Everybody happy, everybody smiling. In the sunshine. The Anfield sunshine. Bill did not go out to his car. Bill did not go back to his house. But Bill was still happy, Bill was still smiling. The sun still shining. The Anfield sun. His day not done. His day not over yet.

Back in his suit, back in his tie. His red tie. His Liverpool Football Club tie. Bill went back down the corridor. Bill went back up the stairs. Bill went back into his office. Bill walked back around the bags of mail. The mountain of bags and bags of mail. Bill sat back down behind his desk. Bill reached back into the bag of mail on top of the mountain of bags and bags of mail. Bill took out another letter. Bill opened the letter. Bill read the letter. The letter on his retirement. The letter wishing him well in his retirement. And Bill shook his head. Bill put down the letter. Bill put the letter to one side. And Bill reached back into the bag of mail. Bill took out another letter. Bill opened the letter. Bill read the letter. The letter of congratulations on winning the Cup. The letter of thanks. And Bill smiled. Bill put down the letter. Bill opened the top drawer of his desk. Bill took out a piece of paper. Bill closed the top drawer of his desk. Bill threaded the piece of paper into his typewriter. Bill turned the platen knob. And Bill began to type again. Bill began to work again. To type and to type. To work and to work. To answer letter after letter. Letters of congratulations and letters of thanks. Bill typed and Bill typed. Bill worked and Bill worked. All afternoon. Until afternoon became evening. Bill worked.

Bill stopped typing. Bill looked at his watch. Bill got up from his desk. Bill picked up his bag from the floor. His kit bag. Bill walked around the bags of mail. The mountain of bags and bags of mail. Bill took his hat off the hook. Bill put on his hat. Bill went out of his office. Bill went down the stairs. Bill went down the corridor. Bill went out of the ground. Bill walked across the car park. Bill got into his car. Bill pulled out of the car park. Bill went down the Belmont Road. And Bill saw people getting off the buses. On their way home from work. Bill turned onto the West Derby Road. And Bill saw people going into the newsagents. Buying their evening paper. And Bill smiled. Bill pulled into the drive. Bill got out of the car. Bill opened the front door. And Bill saw Ness. In the hall. Waiting –

Where have you been all day, asked Ness.

Bill laughed. Bill took off his hat. Bill hung up his hat. Bill kissed Ness on her cheek. And Bill said, I've been at work. At Melwood and at Anfield. Where else would I have been, love?

I'm sorry, said Ness. I was worried, love. I thought you were just popping into the ground. I thought you'd be back sooner.

Bill shook his head. And Bill said, Oh no, love. There was too much to do. The training to take, the letters to answer.

Well, there are some more letters for you here, love, said Ness. Ness picked up a big bundle of envelopes from beside the telephone. And Ness handed the big bundle to Bill.

Bill looked down at the big bundle of envelopes. Of cards. And Bill said, What are all these, love? It's not my birthday yet, is it?

No, said Ness. They are probably retirement cards.

Bill put down the big bundle of envelopes back beside the telephone. And Bill said, That's nice, love. People are very kind. But I'll look at them later, love. After my tea. I'm starving, love . . .

You look exhausted, too, said Ness.

Bill shook his head again. And Bill said, Oh no, love. I'm fine. I've never felt better. I'm just hungry, love. I could eat a horse!

Well, it's your favourite, said Ness. Steak and chips.

Bill clapped his hands. And Bill said, Oh, that's grand. Thank you, love. There's no finer food to come home to. Just what I need.

In the kitchen, at the table. Bill and Ness ate their tea. A piece of steak, some chips and some peas. And then Bill helped Ness clear away the tea things. Bill dried up the tea things. Bill helped Ness put away the tea things. And then Bill and Ness went into the front room. Bill and Ness watched the television. They watched the news and they watched a documentary. Then Bill drew the curtains and Ness made another cup of tea. They read the papers and they talked about the girls. And their granddaughters. And then Ness stood up. Ness kissed Bill on his cheek. And Ness went up the stairs. Up to bed.

In the house, in their front room. In the evening and in the silence. Bill sat in his chair. His hands on the arms of his chair. His grip tight, his knuckles white. Bill felt his palms begin to sweat, his palms begin to itch. Bill began to drum his fingers. On the arms of the chair. Faster and faster, harder and harder. And then Bill stopped. In the house, in their front room. In the evening and in the silence. Bill got up from his chair. Bill walked out of the front room. Bill went into the hall. Bill opened his bag. His kit bag. And Bill took out a book. A book of names, a book of notes. Bill closed his bag. His kit bag. Bill walked back into the front room. Bill sat back down in his chair. And in the house, and in their front room. In the evening and in the silence. Bill opened the book. The book of names, the book of notes. A new book. Bill turned to the first page. A blank page. Bill stared down at the blank page. In the house, in their front room. In the evening and in the silence. Bill picked up a pen from the table beside his chair. And Bill began to write in the book. The book of names, the book of notes. Bill wrote out the names of the players of Liverpool Football Club. Bill made notes on the training they had done today. The first day of training. Of the pre-season. Before the new season. The 1974–75 season. Player after player, note after note, line after line, for page after page. Bill wrote and Bill wrote. Bill worked and Bill worked. All evening. Until evening became night.

In the front room, in his chair. In the night and in the silence. Bill stopped writing. Bill put down his pen. Bill closed his book. His book of names, his book of notes. Bill got up from his chair. Bill turned out the light in the front room. Bill went into the kitchen. Bill went to the drawer. Bill opened the drawer. Bill took out the table-cloth. Bill closed the drawer. Bill walked over to the table. Bill spread the cloth over the table. Bill walked over to another drawer. Bill opened the drawer. Bill took out the cutlery. The spoons. The forks. And the knives. Bill closed the drawer. Bill walked back over to the table. Bill laid two places at the table. Bill went to the cupboard. Bill opened the cupboard door. Bill took out the crockery. The bowls and the plates. Bill walked back over to the table. Bill put a bowl and a plate in each of the two places. Bill walked back to the cupboard. Bill took out two glasses. Bill closed the cupboard door. Bill walked back to the table. Bill put a glass in each of the places. Bill walked to another cupboard. Bill opened the door. Bill took out the salt and pepper pots. Bill closed the cupboard door. Bill walked back to the table. Bill put the salt and pepper pots on the table. Bill went to the pantry. Bill opened the pantry door. Bill took out a jar of honey and a jar of marmalade. Bill walked back to the table. Bill put the jar of honey and the jar of marmalade on the table. Bill walked over to the refrigerator. Bill opened the refrigerator door. Bill took out the butter dish. Bill walked back over to the table. Bill put the butter dish down in the centre of the table. Bill walked back over to the refrigerator. Bill took out a bottle of fresh orange juice. Bill closed the refrigerator door. Bill walked back over to the table. Bill poured orange juice into both of the glasses. Bill put the bottle of fresh orange juice down on the table. Bill walked over to the kitchen wall. Bill turned to look back at the table. At the cutlery and the crockery. The salt and pepper pots. The jar of honey and the jar of marmalade. The butter dish. The two glasses and the bottle of fresh orange juice. Waiting. For the dawn and for the light. And Bill smiled. Bill switched off the kitchen light. And Bill went up the stairs. Up to bed.

In the house, in their bedroom. In the dark and in the silence. Bill took off his tie. His red tie. His Liverpool Football Club tie. Bill took off his suit. Bill put on his pyjamas. Bill went into the bathroom. Bill switched on the bathroom light. Bill walked over to the sink. Bill brushed his teeth. Bill washed his face. Bill dried his face. Bill dried his hands. Bill turned off the bathroom light. Bill went back into the bedroom. Bill got into bed. And in the dark and in the silence. Bill stared up at the ceiling. In the dark and in the silence. Bill heard the clock on the table beside the bed. The alarm clock. Ticking, ticking. In the dark and in the silence. Bill knew Ness was still awake –

Did anyone mention the new man, asked Ness. Who they might be bringing in? And when he might be starting?

Oh no, love. Not yet. Give them a chance, love. Give them time. I mean, there's no rush. And there can be no rush. No haste, love. Not in a matter like this. A matter of this importance. And they know they've no need to rush. Because they know they've still got me, love. For as long as they need me. For as long as it takes, love. I'm still there. I'm still here, love. I mean, I'm not going anywhere, am I? I'm going nowhere, love.

## 51. THE KING IS DEAD, LONG LIVE THE KING

In the boardroom, the Anfield boardroom. John Smith looked down the long table at Bill Shankly. And John Smith said, You've not had a change of heart then, Mr Shankly? A change of mind, have you?

Oh no, said Bill Shankly. I've not had time. What with the training. And with all the letters and the telegrams. No. I've been busier than ever. I've not had a moment to myself.

John Smith nodded. And John Smith said, Well, we obviously have to think about the club, Mr Shankly. We have to think about the future. About who should come in. About who the new man will be.

Oh yes, said Bill Shankly. We must. Indeed we must.

John Smith said, And obviously the board very much value your opinion on the matter, Mr Shankly. We welcome your input.

Yes, said Bill Shankly. Of course. And I'm aware of all the speculation in the papers. The names being bandied about in the press.

John Smith nodded again. And John Smith said, Yes. And with Mr Revie also recently resigned as manager of Leeds United, it means that the top two managerial positions in English club football are both vacant at the same time. And that does complicate the situation.

Yes, said Bill Shankly again. I can see that it might.

John Smith said, And from what I have read, from what I have heard, Leeds have already interviewed Jimmy Armfield, Tony Waiters and Brian Clough for the job. Probably other men, too.

Ian St John, said Bill Shankly. I know for a fact they have spoken to Ian, too. And I believe he is in with a shout. A great chance. From what I have heard. So we might well have missed the boat with Ian. And that would be a shame. A great shame. But then of course there is Gordon. Gordon Milne. Joe Mercer speaks very highly of him. As a manager. He was even shortlisted for the England job. And of course Gordon knows the club. He knows it inside out. And then there is always Jack Charlton. I can't believe Leeds have not even considered Jack. From what I have heard. When you look what he has achieved at Middlesbrough. They were promoted with eight games left. With sixty-five points. I mean, the man is Manager of the Year. In fact, more than Ian, more than Gordon, I think Jack is our man.

John Smith shook his head. And John Smith said, Well, the

board are in agreement that we do not want to get into any kind of competition with Leeds United. Or any other club for that matter. No. It could make matters very protracted. And the clock is ticking. The new season getting closer by the hour. It could be most disruptive.

Yes, said Bill Shankly. Very unsettling for everyone.

John Smith nodded. And John Smith said, Yes. And so the board are thinking of offering the position to Bob.

Bob, said Bill Shankly. Bob who?

John Smith smiled. And John Smith said, Bob Paisley.

Oh yes, said Bill Shankly. Bob Paisley. I hadn't really thought about Bob. But yes. That is a good idea. A very good idea. If Bob will accept the job, that is. If Bob wants to be the manager.

John Smith said, Well, I have already spoken to Bob. Informally, of course. And he has told me he is willing to accept any job that Liverpool Football Club want him to do.

Yes, said Bill Shankly. Of course. That's Bob right there. In a nutshell. Thinking of Liverpool Football Club. Never himself.

John Smith nodded. And John Smith said, But of course I wanted to discuss the matter with you, too, Mr Shankly. Before we took matters any further. Before we made anything formal. Anything public. To see if you had any objections. Or any reservations.

No, said Bill Shankly. None at all. And why would I? After all, I'll still be here. I'll still be about the place. I can give Bob any help he needs. Anything at all. I'll always be here to help him.

John Smith coughed. And then John Smith said, Well, yes. Thank you, Mr Shankly. But Bob will be the manager of Liverpool Football Club. The team will be his responsibility. Now you have retired. The last thing we would want to do, and I am sure the last thing Bob would want to do, would be to burden you. Now you have retired. Now you have resigned from Liverpool Football Club. It would not be fair. Not on you. And not on Bob. It would not be right.

Of course, said Bill Shankly. Of course.

John Smith nodded. And John Smith said, And so the board will speak to Bob again tomorrow. And then we plan to announce Bob's formal appointment as manager of Liverpool Football Club at the annual shareholders' meeting on Friday.

Right, said Bill Shankly. I see.

John Smith stood up. And John Smith said, But finally let me say again, on behalf of the board, how very much we appreciate all the work you have done, all the help you have given us, during this period of transition. Thank you. But we all hope you can now, finally, enjoy your retirement, Mr Shankly.

## 52. ON WATERING THE GARDEN

In his suit, in his tie. His red tie. His Liverpool Football Club tie. Bill went back down the corridor. Bill went back into his office. Bill walked back around the bags of mail. The mountain of bags and bags of mail. And Bill sat back down behind his desk. Bill reached back into the bag of mail on top of the mountain of bags and bags of mail. Bill took out another letter. Bill opened the letter. Bill read the letter. The letter on his retirement. The letter wishing him well in his retirement. And Bill shook his head. Bill put down the letter. Bill put the letter to one side. And Bill stared down at his desk. At his typewriter, at its keys. Silent and waiting. Bill looked up from the keys. From the typewriter and from the desk. Bill looked around the office. At the filing cabinets, at the shelves. The shelves of books. The books of names and the books of notes. At the pictures on the wall. The history and the memories. The clock on the wall. Ticking and ticking. In the office, at the desk. Bill closed his eyes. Bill swallowed. And then Bill opened his eyes again. Bill looked at his watch. Bill got up from the desk. Bill picked up his bag from the floor. His kit bag. Bill walked around the bags of mail. The mountain of bags and bags of mail. Bill took his hat off the hook. Bill put on his hat. Bill went out of the office. Bill went down the stairs. Bill went down the corridor. Bill went out of the ground. Bill walked across the car park. Bill got into his car. Bill pulled out of the car park. Bill went down the Belmont Road. Bill turned onto the West Derby Road. Bill pulled into the drive. Bill got out of the car. Bill walked up the drive. Bill opened the front door. Bill stepped into the house. And Bill closed the front door.

Ness came out of the kitchen. In her apron –

You're back early. Are you OK, love?

Bill put down his bag in the hall. His kit bag. Bill took off his hat. Bill hung up his hat. Bill kissed Ness on her cheek. And Bill said, Yes, love. I'm fine. Thank you, love. But I thought I'd wash the car. And then I thought I'd make a start on the garden, love . . .

Bill picked up his bag. His kit bag. Bill went up the stairs. Bill went into the bedroom. Bill took off his tie. His red tie. His Liverpool Football Club tie. Bill folded it up. Bill opened the second drawer of the dressing table. Bill put the tie in the drawer. The red tie. The Liverpool Football Club tie. Bill closed the drawer. Bill sat down on the edge of the bed. Bill unlaced his shoes. Bill took off his shoes. Bill picked up his shoes. Bill stood up. Bill walked over to the wardrobe. Bill opened the wardrobe doors. Bill placed his shoes in the bottom of the wardrobe. Bill walked back over to the bed. Bill took off his jacket. Bill laid it on top of the bed. Bill took off his trousers. Bill walked back over to the wardrobe. Bill took out a hanger from the wardrobe. Bill hung his trousers on the hanger. Bill carried the trousers on the hanger over to the bed. Bill picked up his jacket from the top of the bed. Bill hung his jacket on the hanger over his trousers. Bill walked back over to the wardrobe. Bill hung his suit in the wardrobe. Bill closed the wardrobe doors. Bill opened his bag. His kit bag. Bill took out his tracksuit bottoms. Bill put on his tracksuit bottoms. Bill took out his sweater. Bill put on his sweater. Bill closed his bag. His kit bag. Bill walked out of the bedroom. Bill walked back down the stairs. Bill opened the cupboard in the hall. Bill took out an old pair of boots from the bottom of the cupboard. Bill closed the cupboard door. Bill sat down on the bottom stair. Bill laced up his old pair of boots. Bill stood up. Bill walked down the hall. And Bill walked into the kitchen.

Ness looked up from peeling the potatoes. And Ness smiled –

The kettle's just boiled, love. Would you like a cup of tea?

Oh no. No thank you, love. I've too much to do. Much too much to do, love. I best get a move on. Best make a start . . .

And Bill walked over to the sink. Bill bent down. Bill opened the cupboard under the sink. Bill took out the bucket from under the sink. The bucket and the cloths. Bill closed the cupboard doors. Bill put the bucket in the sink. Bill ran the cold tap. Bill filled the bucket. Bill carried the bucket and the cloths out of the kitchen. Down the hall, out of the house and into the drive. Bill put down the bucket on the concrete beside the car. Bill crouched down beside the bucket. Bill put the first cloth into the water in the bucket. Bill soaked the cloth in the water in the bucket. Bill took the cloth back out of the water. Bill held the cloth over the water in the bucket. Bill wrung out the cloth. Bill stood back up with the cloth in his hand. Bill turned to his car in the drive. Bill reached over the car. Bill began to wash the roof of the car. Back and forth across the roof of the car. Bill washed the dirt from the roof of the car. Back and forth, back and forth. From one side to the other. Back and forth, back and forth. From the front to the back. Bill washed the roof of the car. And then Bill crouched back down beside the bucket. Bill put the cloth back into the water in the bucket. Bill soaked the cloth in the water again. Bill wrung out the cloth again. Bill stood back up with the cloth in his hand. And Bill washed the windscreen of the car. Back and forth, back and forth. Bill washed the windscreen. And then Bill crouched back down beside the bucket. Bill put the cloth back into the water in the bucket. Bill soaked the cloth in the water again. Bill wrung out the cloth again. Bill stood back up with the cloth in his hand. And Bill washed the two windows on the near side of the car. Back and forth, back and forth. Bill washed the windows on the near side. And then Bill crouched back down beside the bucket. Bill put the cloth back into the water in the bucket. Bill soaked the cloth in the water again. Bill wrung out the cloth again. Bill stood back up with the cloth in his hand. Bill walked round to the back of the car. And Bill washed the back window of the car. Back and forth, back and forth. Bill washed the back window. And then Bill walked back round to the bucket. Bill crouched back down beside the bucket. Bill put the cloth back into the water in the bucket. Bill soaked the cloth in the water again. Bill wrung out the cloth again. Bill stood back up with the cloth in his hand. Bill walked round to the far side of the car. And Bill washed the two windows on the far side of the car. Back and forth, back and forth. Bill washed the windows on the far side. And then Bill walked back round to the bucket. Bill crouched back down beside the bucket again. Bill put the cloth back into the water in the bucket. Bill soaked the cloth in the water. Bill wrung out the cloth again. Bill put down the cloth. Bill picked up the bucket. Bill carried the bucket over to the drain. Bill tipped the dirty water down the drain. Bill carried the bucket back into the house, back down the hall and back into the kitchen. Bill put the bucket in the sink again.

Bill ran the cold tap again. Bill filled the bucket again. Bill carried the bucket back out of the kitchen. Down the hall, out of the house and into the drive again. Bill put down the bucket on the concrete beside the car. Bill crouched down beside the bucket again. Bill picked up the cloth. Bill soaked the cloth in the water again. Bill wrung out the cloth again. And Bill washed the bonnet of the car. Back and forth, back and forth. Bill washed the bonnet. And then Bill crouched back down beside the bucket. Bill put the cloth back into the water in the bucket. Bill soaked the cloth in the water again. Bill wrung out the cloth again. Bill stood back up with the cloth in his hand. And Bill washed the doors on the near side of the car. Back and forth, back and forth. Bill washed the doors on the near side. And then Bill crouched back down beside the bucket. Bill put the cloth back into the water in the bucket. Bill soaked the cloth in the water again. Bill wrung out the cloth again. Bill stood back up with the cloth in his hand. Bill walked round to the back of the car again. And Bill washed the back of the car. Back and forth, back and forth. Bill washed the back of the car. And then Bill walked back round to the bucket. Bill crouched back down beside the bucket. Bill put the cloth back into the water in the bucket. Bill soaked the cloth in the water again. Bill wrung out the cloth again. Bill stood back up with the cloth in his hand. And Bill walked round to the far side of the car again. Bill washed the doors on the far side of the car. Back and forth, back and forth. Bill washed the doors on the far side. And then Bill walked back to the bucket. Bill crouched back down beside the bucket. Bill put the cloth back into the water in the bucket. Bill soaked the cloth in the water again. Bill wrung out the cloth again. Bill stood back up with the cloth in his hand. Bill walked round to the front of the car. Bill crouched down again. And Bill began to wash the grille on the front of the car. Back and forth, back and forth. Bill washed the grille. And then Bill went back to the bucket. Bill crouched back down beside the bucket. Bill put the cloth back into the water in the bucket. Bill soaked the cloth in the water again. Bill wrung out the cloth again. Bill stood back up with the cloth in his hand. And Bill went from wheel to wheel on the car. Bill washed the four hubcaps of the car. Round and round, round and round. Bill washed and wiped the four hubcaps. And then Bill walked back to the bucket. Bill crouched back down beside the bucket. Bill put the cloth back into the water in the bucket. Bill soaked the cloth in the water again. Bill wrung out the cloth again. Bill put down the cloth. Bill picked up the bucket. Bill carried the bucket over to the drain again. Bill tipped the dirty water down the drain again. Bill carried the bucket back into the house, back down the hall and back into the kitchen. Bill put the bucket in the sink again. Bill ran the cold tap again. Bill filled the bucket again. Bill carried the bucket back out of the kitchen. Down the hall, out of the house and into the drive again. Bill put down the bucket on the concrete beside the car again. Bill couched down beside the bucket again. Bill put the second cloth into the water in the bucket. Bill soaked the cloth in the water in the bucket. Bill took the cloth back out of the water. Bill held the cloth over the water in the bucket. Bill wrung out the cloth. Bill stood back up with the cloth in his hand. Bill turned to his car in the drive. Bill walked over to the front of the car. Bill crouched down by the front of the car. And Bill began to wash the lights on the front of the car. Round and round, up and down. Bill washed the lights on the front. And then Bill stood back up. Bill walked back over to the bucket. Bill crouched back down beside the bucket. Bill put the cloth back into the water in the bucket. Bill soaked the cloth in the water again. Bill wrung out the cloth again. Bill stood back up with the cloth in his hand. Bill walked round to the back of the car. Bill crouched down by the back of the car. And Bill began to wash the lights on the back of the car. Round and round, up and down. Bill washed the lights on the back. And then Bill stood back up. Bill walked back round to the bucket. Bill crouched back down beside the bucket. Bill put the cloth back into the water in the bucket. Bill soaked the cloth in the water again. Bill wrung out the cloth again. Bill stood back up with the cloth in his hand. And Bill walked over to the wing mirror on the near side of the car. Bill washed the wing mirror on the near side. And then Bill walked round to the wing mirror on the far side of the car. Bill washed the wing mirror on the far side. And then Bill walked back round to the bucket. Bill crouched back down beside the bucket. Bill put the cloth back into the water in the bucket. Bill soaked the cloth in the water again. Bill wrung out the cloth again. Bill stood back up with the cloth in his hand. And Bill walked around the car. In the sunshine, in the drive. Bill looked for any dirt he had missed, Bill searched for any spot he had missed. But in the sunshine, in the drive. The car shone, the car sparkled. And in the sunshine, in the drive. Bill looked at his watch. And then Bill picked up the bucket and the cloths. Bill walked back over to the drain. Bill poured the dirty water down the drain again. Bill went back into the house. Down the hall, into the kitchen. Bill put the bucket in the sink again. Bill rinsed out the bucket. Bill rinsed out the cloths. Bill opened the cupboard under the sink. Bill put the bucket and the cloths back in the cupboard. Bill closed the cupboard again. Bill stood up. And Bill saw Ness –

How about a cup of tea now, asked Ness. A wee rest now? Before you go back out again, love?

Oh no. No thank you, love. Not now. I want to get straight into the garden. And get started, love . . .

And Bill walked over to the back door. Bill opened the back door. Bill stepped out into the garden. Their small back garden. Bill walked over to the shed. Their little garden shed. Bill opened the shed door. Bill picked up his gardening gloves from the shelf in the shed. Bill put on his gardening gloves. Bill picked up a big black bin bag. Bill walked over to one corner of the garden. With his gloves and with his bag. And Bill began to walk up and down the lawn. Their small back lawn. His head bent forward, staring down at the grass. Bill picked up every little stone he saw. Every little piece of grit and every little pebble. Bill pulled up every little weed he saw. Every little clover and every little dandelion. Bill put the little stones and the little weeds into his big black bin bag. Bill used the heel of his boot to tread down the ground. To fill in every little divot, to fill in every little hole. Up the garden and then down the garden. In a straight line. From one end of their small back garden to the other. Up and then down again. Four times, in four straight lines. Up and then down, up and then down again. Bill walked the length of their small back garden. Picking up stones, pulling up weeds. Filling in divots, filling in holes. And then Bill put down the big black bin bag on the flagstones beneath the kitchen window. Bill walked back over to the shed. Their little garden shed. Bill went back inside the shed. Bill picked up the lawn mower. The red Shanks manual lawn mower. Bill took out the lawn mower from the shed. Bill carried the lawn mower over to one corner of the garden. Bill put down the mower on the lawn. And Bill began to mow.

Up the garden and then down the garden. In a straight line. From one end of their small back garden to the other. Up and then down again. Four times, in four straight lines. Up and then down, up and then down again. Bill mowed their small back lawn. And then Bill set down the mower on the flagstones beneath the kitchen window. Bill walked back over to the shed. Their little garden shed. Bill went back inside the shed. Bill picked up a rake. Bill took the rake from the shed. Bill carried the rake over to the corner of the garden. And Bill began to rake. Up the garden and then down the garden. In a straight line. From one end of their small back garden to the other. Up and then down again. Four times, in four straight lines. Up and then down, up and then down again. Bill raked their small back lawn. Until there were four small piles of loose cut grass. And then Bill walked back over to the flagstones beneath the kitchen window. Bill picked up the big black bin bag again. Bill carried the big black bin bag over to the first small pile of loose cut grass. Bill gathered up the first small pile of loose cut grass. Bill dropped the loose cut grass into the big black bin bag. Bill carried the big black bin bag over to the second small pile of loose cut grass. And to the third. And then to the fourth. Until Bill had gathered up all four small piles of loose cut grass. And dropped them into the big black bin bag. And then Bill carried the big black bin bag over to the corner of the garden. The corner of the lawn. And again Bill began to walk up and down the lawn. Their small back lawn. His head bent forward, staring down at the grass. Bill picked up every little piece of loose cut grass he saw. Every little blade, every little scrap. Bill put the little pieces of loose cut grass into his big black bin bag. Up the garden and then down the garden. In a straight line. From one end of their small back garden to the other. Up and then down again. Four times, in four straight lines. Up and then down, up and then down again. Bill walked the length of their small back garden. Picking up blades, picking up scraps. And then Bill put down the big black bin bag on the flagstones beneath the kitchen window. Bill walked back over to the shed. Their little garden shed. Bill went back inside the shed. Bill picked up a pair of shears. Garden shears. Bill carried the shears over to the first border of the lawn. And Bill began to trim the first border. And the second border. And the third. And then Bill trimmed the border between the flagstones and the lawn.

And then Bill put down the shears on the flagstones beneath the kitchen window. Bill picked up the big black bin bag again. Bill carried the big black bin bag over to the first border. And Bill began to gather up the loose cut grass from the first border. Every blade and every scrap. And the fallen petals and the deadheads. Bill put them into the big black bin bag. And from the second border. The loose cut grass. The fallen petals and the deadheads. And then from the third. Until there was no more loose cut grass. No more petals and no more deadheads. And then Bill gathered up the loose cut grass from the last border. The border between the flagstones and the lawn. And then Bill put down the big black bin bag on the flagstones beneath the kitchen window. Bill walked back over to the shed. Their little garden shed. Bill went back inside the shed. Bill picked up a trowel. Bill picked up a bucket. Bill carried the trowel and the bucket over to the first border. And then Bill began to weed. On his lawn, on his knees. Bill weeded and Bill weeded. In the soil, on his knees. Between the flowers and between the plants. The first border. And the second border. And then the third. Bill pulled up weeds. Bill put the weeds into the bucket. Until there were no more weeds. And then Bill carried the bucket of weeds over to the flagstones beneath the kitchen window. Bill opened up the big black bin bag. Bill emptied the bucket of weeds into the big black bin bag. And then Bill cleaned the trowel. Bill cleaned the shears. Bill cleaned the rake. And the blades of the mower. Bill cleaned and Bill cleaned. On the flagstones, on his knees. And then Bill walked back over to the shed. Their little garden shed. Bill went back inside the shed. Bill picked up a broom. Bill carried the broom over to the flagstones beneath the kitchen window. And then Bill began to sweep the flagstones. To sweep up all the little blades of grass. All the little clumps of soil. Into a pile. And then Bill put down the broom. Bill gathered up the pile of grass. The pile of soil. Bill put the pile of grass, the pile of soil, into the big black bin bag. And then Bill picked up the broom again. Bill picked up the big black bin bag. Bill carried the broom and the bin bag back over to the shed. Their little garden shed. Bill put down the bin bag. Bill went back inside the shed. And then Bill began to sweep. To sweep up all the dirt and all the dust in the shed. Into a pile. And then Bill leant the broom against the wall of the shed. Bill gathered up the pile of dirt. The pile of dust.

Bill put the pile of dirt, the pile of dust, into the big black bin bag. And then Bill walked back over to the flagstones beneath the kitchen window. Bill picked up the lawn mower. Bill carried the mower back over to the shed. Bill put the mower back into the shed. Bill walked back over to the flagstones. Bill picked up the rake and the shears. Bill carried the rake and the shears back over to the shed. Bill put the rake and the shears back inside the shed. Bill walked back over to the flagstones. Bill picked up the trowel and the bucket. Bill carried the trowel and the bucket back over to the shed. Bill put the trowel and the bucket back inside the shed. And then Bill picked up the big black bin bag. Bill carried the big black bin bag back over to one corner of the garden. With his gloves and with his bag. Bill began to walk up and down the lawn again. Their small back lawn. His head bent forward, staring down at the grass. At the borders. Looking for any piece of loose cut grass he had missed. Any little stone or any little weed. A fallen petal or a deadhead. Up the garden and then down the garden. In a straight line. From one end of their small back garden to the other. Up and then down again. Four times, in four straight lines. Up and then down, up and then down again. Bill walked the length of their small back garden. And then Bill carried the big black bin bag back over to the shed. Bill tied up the top of the big black bin bag. Bill put the big black bin bag inside the shed. Bill took off his gloves. His gardening gloves. Bill put the gloves back on the shelf inside the shed. Their little garden shed. And Bill closed the shed door. In the sunshine, on the flagstones. Bill looked at the garden. Everything was neat, everything was tidy. And in the sunshine, on the flagstones. Bill looked at his watch again. It was half past four in the afternoon. Bill had washed the car. Bill had mowed the lawn. Bill had weeded the garden. And Bill had tidied up the shed. It was half past four in the afternoon. And there was nothing more to do. That was it,

that was all. No more work to be done. Here.


## 53. THE KEYS TO THE KINGDOM

Bob Paisley walked down the corridor. The Anfield corridor. Bob Paisley walked up the stairs. The Anfield stairs. Bob Paisley stood before the door to the office. The door to the office of Bill Shankly. And Bob Paisley listened. Listened for the sound of hammering, listened for the sound of talking. Bill Shankly talking on the telephone, Bill Shankly hammering on the typewriter. But Bob Paisley heard no hammering, Bob Paisley heard no talking. Bob Paisley knocked on the door. The door to the office of Bill Shankly. And Bob Paisley waited. Bob Paisley knocked on the door again. The door to the office of Bill Shankly. And Bob Paisley waited again. Bob Paisley put his hand on the handle. The handle of the door to the office of Bill Shankly. Bob Paisley turned the handle. Bob Paisley opened the door. And Bob Paisley stepped into the office. Bob Paisley looked around the office. The clock on the wall. Ticking, ticking. The pictures on the wall. The history, the memories. The shelves of books. The books of names, the books of notes. The filing cabinets and the bags of mail on the floor. The bags and bags of mail. The bags and bags of mail for Bill. The desk and the chair. Bill's chair. The typewriter and its keys. Bill's typewriter, Bill's keys. Silent and waiting. Bob Paisley stepped towards the desk. Towards the chair. Bill's chair, Bill's desk. And now Bob Paisley heard footsteps in the corridor. Footsteps Bob Paisley would recognise anywhere. Bill's footsteps. Bob Paisley turned around. And Bob Paisley saw Bill Shankly. In the doorway to his office. In his suit and in his tie. His red tie. His Liverpool Football Club tie. Bob Paisley smiled, Bob Paisley laughed. And Bob Paisley said, Morning, Bill. Morning. I was just wondering where you'd got to, Bill. I was just about to call the police. About to ask them to send out a search party for you, Bill . . .

No, said Bill Shankly. No, Bob. You can't be doing that now. You can't be worrying about me now. You've enough to worry about now, Bob. You've Liverpool Football Club to worry about now . . .

Bob Paisley shook his head. And Bob Paisley said, I didn't want the job, Bill. I wanted you to stay. For things to stay the way they were, Bill. That's all I wanted. You know that, Bill. But when they asked me, when they offered me the job, it was the proudest moment of my life, Bill. I would have accepted any job, any position they offered me. Anything they wanted me to do. But I took this job because I want to stabilise things for everyone. For Joe and Reuben, for Geoff and Tom. And for Ronnie. We have all had a big shock, Bill.

We were all very worried. About who was going to come in, about what would happen to us. But I thought if I accept the position, if I take the job, then your departure won't upset things too much. Because you know I believe in the same principles as you do, Bill. And you know I'll try and run the club on the same lines as you have done.

I know, said Bill Shankly. I know that, Bob. And that is exactly why I wanted you to be my successor. And why I was so relieved when the board and everyone agreed with me. That you should be my successor. And so I could not be more pleased for you, Bob.

Bob Paisley said nothing. Bob Paisley just smiled.

And you know I'm always here to help you, said Bill Shankly. Anything I can do to help you, Bob. To help you get run in . . .

Bob Paisley nodded now. And Bob Paisley said, Thank you, Bill. Thank you. I mean, I feel like an apprentice riding the favourite in the Derby. Or being given the *Queen Elizabeth* to steer in a force-ten gale. Because I'm finding there is a lot I don't know, Bill. A lot . . .

Yes, said Bill Shankly. There'll be a great deal, Bob. It's a big job managing Liverpool Football Club. A very big job, Bob.

Bob Paisley nodded again. And Bob Paisley said, Well, to be honest with you, Bill, I'm just trying to keep things the way they were. The way they are. For now. Just trying to take each day as it comes.

Yes, said Bill Shankly again. That's good, that's best . . .

And Bill Shankly put his hand into his jacket pocket. Bill Shankly took out his diary. His diary of dates, his diary of fixtures –

Yes, said Bill Shankly. But the days come thick and fast when you're the manager, Bob. I'll tell you that. There's no stopping, Bob. No respite. I mean, we've got the trip to Germany . . .

Bob Paisley said, Well, I know that's something you won't miss, Bill. All the travelling. All the trips abroad. At least that's one thing you won't be sorry to miss, eh?

And then there's the Charity Shield, said Bill Shankly. Bill Shankly still turning the pages of his diary. The pages of dates, the pages of fixtures. And it's at Wembley, too . . .

Bob Paisley said, But you'll be coming to that, won't you?

Oh yes, said Bill Shankly. Yes, of course, Bob. Thank you very much. That's very kind of you, Bob. I'd like that. I'd like that a lot, Bob. It would be a great honour. Thank you, Bob. Because there will be a great crowd there. With it being at Wembley, Bob. All the Kop will be there, I'm sure. All the boys from the Kop, Bob. Be a great chance for me to show my appreciation. Pay my thanks to them, Bob.

Bob Paisley nodded. And Bob Paisley said, Of course, Bill. Of course. I mean, from what Mr Smith said, from what the board told me, you don't officially retire until Monday 12 August. Is that right, Bill? Is that what you agreed with Mr Smith? And with the board?

Well, yes, said Bill Shankly. But then of course there's the testimonial that night. For Billy McNeill, up in Glasgow. I should be there, Bob. I want to be there. If that's OK with you, Bob?

Bob Paisley nodded again. And Bob Paisley said, Yes, of course you should be there. You don't have to ask me, Bill.

No, said Bill Shankly. No, Bob. I should ask. I must ask. Because the last thing I want is to be accused of sticking my nose in where it's not wanted. Where it's not needed, Bob . . .

Bob Paisley smiled. And Bob Paisley said, You could never do that, Bill. That'll never happen. I can promise you that now, Bill.

Well, said Bill Shankly. I don't want to be getting under your feet now, Bob. But I thought I'd just pop in and pick up some of these letters. If you don't mind, Bob? I'll just take a few home with me.

Bob Paisley laughed now. And Bob Paisley said, Of course I don't mind, Bill. I don't know how you deal with them all . . .

It does take time, said Bill Shankly. I won't lie to you, Bob. Reading all these letters, then answering them all. It's a big job, Bob. And a big part of the job. But it has to be done, Bob. When people have taken the time and trouble to write to you personally, then the very least you can do is take the time and the trouble to reply to them.

Bob Paisley looked at the bags and bags of mail on the floor. Bob Paisley looked at the typewriter on the desk. Bob Paisley shook his head. And Bob Paisley said, Well, I can't even type, Bill. I'd have no idea how to work that thing. Not a clue, Bill. Not a clue . . .

So you don't mind if I take it back home with me then, asked Bill Shankly. You wouldn't object, Bob? If I took the typewriter home? So I can answer all these letters at home, Bob? So I'm not in your way. I'm not under your feet . . .

Bob Paisley laughed. And Bob Paisley said, Be my guest, Bill.

Bill Shankly walked around the mountain of bags and bags of mail. And Bill Shankly picked up the typewriter from the desk. Bill Shankly put it under his arm. And then Bill Shankly picked up a bag of mail from the mountain of bags and bags of mail –

Well, I best get going, Bob. Get out of your hair. And get cracking on all these letters. I mean, they won't answer themselves . . .

Bob Paisley nodded. And Bob Paisley said, OK then, Bill. But don't you be overdoing it now. With all those letters . . .

Bill Shankly stopped in the doorway. The doorway to the office. Bill Shankly turned back to Bob Paisley –

So we are agreed then, Bob? That my last day will be Monday 12 August? My last official day. And that is OK with you, Bob?

Yes, Bill. Of course it is. Anything you want is fine with me, Bill. As I say, you don't have to ask . . .

How old are you, asked Bill Shankly. One foot in the office, one foot in the corridor. If you don't mind me asking, Bob . . .

Bob Paisley said, Fifty-five, Bill. Why do you ask?

I was just wondering, said Bill Shankly. I mean, we've worked together for a long time now . . .

Bob Paisley smiled. And Bob Paisley said, Yes. Fifteen years.

Yes, said Bill Shankly. Fifteen years. But all that time I never knew how old you were. I mean, I don't suppose it really mattered. I don't suppose it does. I mean, once you stop playing . . .

Bob Paisley nodded. And Bob Paisley said, But it can still catch up with you. With the best of folk.

Yes, said Bill Shankly again. But how old were you then when you stopped playing, Bob?

Bob Paisley smiled. And Bob Paisley said, I was thirty-five. March 13, 1954, was my last game. Here at Anfield. Against Charlton Athletic. We lost as well. Three–two. And you, Bill?

The same, said Bill Shankly. Thirty-five. But I felt I could have gone on, Bob. I felt I could have gone on forever.

Bob Paisley nodded. And Bob Paisley said, We all did, Bill.

Aye, Bob. But we were young then. And we were wrong, Bob. We were all wrong. No one goes on forever, Bob. No one is immortal, said Bill Shankly. And Bill Shankly glanced around the office. At the shelves, the shelves of books. The books of names, the books of notes.

At the pictures on the wall. The history, the memories. At the clock on the wall. Ticking and ticking. Bill Shankly smiled. Bill Shankly turned away. And Bill Shankly said, See you later, Bob. See you now . . .

And Bob Paisley watched Bill Shankly walk down the corridor. The bag of mail in one hand, the typewriter under his arm. In his suit and in his tie. His red tie. His Liverpool Football Club tie.

## 54. CHARITY IS A COLD, GREY, LOVELESS THING

In the hotel, in the room. Bill paced and Bill paced. Bill had travelled down to London with the team. Bill had checked into the hotel with the team. Bill had eaten dinner with the team. Steak and chips. Tinned fruit and cream. Just like always, just like before. And then Bill had said goodnight to the team. And Bill had come up to the room. His hotel room. And Bill had started to pace. Up and down the room. The hotel room. Two hours later, Bill was still pacing the room. The hotel room. But now Bill stopped pacing. And Bill picked up the telephone. The telephone beside the bed. His hotel bed. Bill dialled a number. And Bill listened to the telephone ring. And ring and ring –

Hello, hello? Who's speaking? Who is it now?

Hello, Don. Hello. It's only me, Don. It's only Bill. I just called to wish you good luck for tomorrow, Don. For the game tomorrow. And to say I'll see you tomorrow, Don. In the tunnel . . .

Oh no, you won't, said Don Revie. Because I'll not be in the tunnel, Bill. Brian will be in the tunnel. You won't see me tomorrow, Bill. Not unless you're planning to sit in the Royal Box. Because that's where I'll be sitting. In the Royal Box. Where you should be, Bill.

Bill laughed. And Bill said, I hope you're having me on, Don. I hope you're pulling my leg. What the hell would you be doing sitting in the Royal Box? You should be in the tunnel, Don. With your team, man. Where you belong, Don. In the tunnel . . .

They are not my team now, said Don Revie. They are Brian's team now. He's the manager of Leeds United now. Not me. It'll be his privilege to lead out that team tomorrow, Bill. Not mine.

No, Don. No. You won the Championship, Don. You won the League. Not Brian. It's you who should be leading out your team

528

tomorrow, Don. Not Brian. And I'm sure Brian feels the same . . .

To be frank with you, Bill, I couldn't care less what Brian feels. All I know is that it is his team now. And so it is his job to lead them out at Wembley tomorrow. It's Brian's job now. Not mine.

I can't agree, Don. I can't agree. And I'm sorry you feel this way, Don. I really am. I was hoping we would both be leading out our teams tomorrow, Don. Saying our goodbyes together . . .

I've said my goodbyes, said Don Revie. And now I have moved on. I am the manager of England now, Bill. Not Leeds United. But I'll be there. I'll still be there, Bill. And I'll be watching.

Bill laughed. And Bill said, Aye, Don. So you say. From the Royal Box. Well, I hope you have a nice time, Don. I hope you enjoy the view. And be sure to give my regards to the men with their brass and their wives with their jewellery. Goodnight, Don . . .

Bill put down the telephone. And Bill began to pace the room again. The hotel room. Up and down the room again. The hotel room. And then Bill stopped pacing. Bill took off his suit and tie. His red tie. His Liverpool Football Club tie. Bill put on his pyjamas. Bill went into the bathroom. The hotel bathroom. Bill switched on the light. The bathroom light. Bill walked over to the sink. Bill brushed his teeth. Bill washed his face. Bill dried his face. Bill dried his hands. Bill turned off the light. The bathroom light. Bill went back into the bedroom. The hotel bedroom. Bill switched off the light. The bedroom light. Bill got into bed. The hotel bed. And in the dark and in the silence. Bill stared up at the ceiling. The hotel ceiling. In the dark and in the silence. Bill could hear people in the street outside the hotel. Bill could hear people in the corridor outside the room. And in the dark and in the silence. Bill sat up. Bill got out of the bed. The hotel bed. In the dark and in the silence. Bill began to pace again. In the dark and in the silence. Up and down the room. The hotel room. In the dark and in the silence. Up and down. Bill paced and Bill paced –

Round and around, round and around –

Until night became day, until this room became another room. The dressing room. The Wembley dressing room. Bill pacing and Bill pacing. Round and around. The Liverpool dressing room. Buttoning his jacket, unbuttoning his jacket. His mouth dry and his palms wet. Bill paced and Bill paced. Round and around . . .

In the dressing room. The Wembley dressing room. Bob Paisley put a hand on Bill's arm –

Do you want to say something, Bill? Are you going to say a few words before the game?

Bill shook his head. And Bill said, No, Bob. No. In fact, I think I'll go and wait outside. Until you're done, Bob. In the tunnel. I'll be waiting outside, Bob. In the tunnel. Until you're done, Bob . . .

Bill walked over to the dressing-room door. The Wembley dressing-room door. Bill opening the door. Bill listening to Bob. Bob speaking to the team. The Liverpool team –

To be honest, Bob was saying to the team, I'm a bit worried about this game, boys. It's a bad time to have a game like this. Far too early in the season for a game like this. Of course, we want to win. And to put on a good show. But just go out there and knock the ball about a bit and try to enjoy yourselves . . .

Bill closed the dressing-room door behind him. The Wembley dressing-room door. And Bill stood in the tunnel. The Wembley tunnel. Between its high, bare walls. In its long, dark shadows. Bill waited for the team. The Liverpool team. In his grey herringbone suit. His red shirt, with the yellow stripes. And his dark tie. His loud, dark tie. Buttoning his jacket and unbuttoning his jacket. Bill waited and Bill waited. And then Bill heard the buzzer. The Wembley buzzer. And Bill turned. And Bill saw the Leeds team come out of their dressing room. And Billy Bremner shook his hand. And made a joke, a joke Bill didn't quite catch. But Bill smiled. And Bill laughed. And Billy smiled. And Billy laughed. And then Brian Clough shook Bill's hand. And Brian Clough said something to Bill, something like –

This must bring back some memories for you, sir?

Bill nodded. And Bill said, Oh yes. It does.

And then Bill saw the other dressing-room door open. The Liverpool dressing-room door. Out of the corner of his eye. Their boots in the tunnel, their studs on the concrete. Bill heard the team behind him now. The Liverpool team. Up and down his spine. In a line, in the tunnel. The Wembley tunnel. The two teams waiting, watching. In the shadows. The Wembley shadows. Bill felt Brian Clough watching him. But Bill tried to avoid his eyes. The thoughts in his eyes. But Bill could not avoid his words. The thoughts on his lips.

And Bill heard Brian Clough saying something else, something like –

So what are you going to do with yourself all season, Mr Shankly? What on earth are you going to do with yourself, sir?

And Bill said, Oh, I'll be busy enough. Don't you worry –

And then Bill nodded. Nodded to himself. And Bill started to walk towards the end of the tunnel. The Wembley tunnel. The light at the end of the tunnel. But someone put a hand on his arm. Someone stopped Bill. And asked Bill to wait. And so Bill waited. In the tunnel. The Wembley tunnel. In the shadows. The Wembley shadows. Another joke with Billy Bremner. Another joke he didn't quite catch. Didn't quite get. Another word from Brian Clough. Another word he didn't quite catch. Didn't quite hear. Buttoning his jacket, unbuttoning his jacket. Mouth dry and palms wet. Bill ran his tongue along his lips. Bill wiped his hands together. And then Bill saw the signal. At last, at last. And Bill nudged Brian Clough. Bill pointed to the end of the tunnel. The light at the end of the tunnel. And Bill began to walk towards the light. His shoulders stooping, his head bowing. Bill led out the team. The Liverpool team. Into the light, into the stadium. Still not sure if his jacket should be open, not sure if his jacket should be closed. Brian Clough still watching him, Brian Clough now applauding him. The stadium applauding him. The Wembley stadium. The supporters chanting his name. The supporters of Liverpool Football Club. And the supporters of Leeds United. All chanting –

*SHANK-LEE, SHANK-LEE, SHANK-LEE . . .*

In the light, the mid-afternoon light. In the stadium, the Wembley stadium. Across the pitch, across the turf. Bill walked. His shoulders stooped, his head bowed. Bill stared down at the grass. The Wembley grass. The weight of the wood. The wood on his shoulders. One foot in front of the other. Bill kept walking. Head bowed, staring down. Down at the grass, down at the ground. One foot in front of the other. At the bottom of the ocean, along the seabed. Bill kept walking. Head bowed, staring down. With feet of stone, in boots of lead. One in front of the other. Walking. And walking. Head bowed, eyes fixed on the ground. The Wembley ground. Bill walking on, Bill stamping down the memories, Bill treading down the fears. The voices in his head, the whispers in his heart. The wasteland and the wilderness. Under the ground, under the sea. Buttoning his jacket and unbuttoning his jacket. At last, at last. Bill reached the halfway line. The Wembley halfway line. And Bill stopped walking. And at last, at last. Bill looked up. Up from the ground and up from the grass. And his eyes met the stands. The supporters in the stands. And Bill raised one hand. His right hand. In salute and in thanks. To all four sides of the stadium. All sixty-seven thousand folk inside the stadium. And to the millions at home. The millions watching on television at home. And then Bill lowered his hand. His right hand. And Bill walked from the halfway line to the benches. The Wembley benches. One foot quickly in front of the other. And Bill sat down. On the bench. The Wembley bench. Between Brian Clough and Jimmy Gordon. His shoulders forward, his head forward. The wood across his back, the lead upon his feet. His raincoat across his knees. His left arm on his raincoat. His right elbow in his left hand on his right knee. His shoulders forward. His head forward. His chin in his right hand. His fingers stroking his chin. *Since I made my decision to retire, our front door has been besieged with people.* The whistle now. Thompson passes forward. Clarke keeps his foot in. The skin ripped from Thompson's ankle to his knee. First free kick to Liverpool. Now Jordan. Cherry. Giles. Clarke. Tommy Smith's tackle on Clarke. It's a booking. Number-ten Giles with the free kick. On the bench. The Wembley bench. Bill sat back. Bill crossed his legs. His right leg over his left. *I have received hundreds of letters and telegrams.* There's too much pace on it. Hall. Callaghan. Heighway. Thompson. Cormack saw that all the way and then took his eye off it when it arrived. But here's Hall again. Heighway. Hunter. Not a good tackle. Keegan. Good header by McQueen. Corner. Thompson coming up. Clarke almost deflecting that past Harvey as he came out. On the bench. The Wembley bench. Bill uncrossed his legs. Bill crossed his legs again. His left leg over his right. *Thousands of fans have written to me, pleading with me to stay.* Gray. Reaney outside Lorimer. Clarke and Jordan in the middle. Gray. Good blocking by Smith. Joe Jordan. Beautifully off the outside of his boots. Lorimer being forced wide. Reaney again on the overlap. Hughes in two minds. On the bench. The Wembley bench. Bill folded his arms across his chest. His right hand over his heart. *Everybody seems to be affected. I have had letters from Australia, New Zealand, Canada and Scotland, as well as from Liverpool.* Boersma. Keegan behind him. Heighway in the middle.

Here's Keegan. Trying to nick it in by the near post. Eddie Gray. Another good header by Cormack. Bremner. Hughes is a bit short. Thompson. Cormack. Keegan now out on the left. Only a crack on for him at the moment. Cormack coming up. He was unbalanced. But at least he saw that Keegan needed help. On the bench. The Wembley bench. Bill let go of his heart. Bill unfolded his arms. Both arms at his side. Bill uncrossed his legs. His left leg and his right. Both feet on the ground. *Two young men came to my house with a card signed by two hundred customers from the Derby Arms Hotel, wishing me well for the future. And almost all of the couple of hundred of signatures were signed in red ink. But there were three signed in blue. That is amazing to me. That even Everton boys said they were sorry to see me go.* Free kick to Liverpool for a push. Keegan. Good save. But it's going to go in. And it's gone. It's in. He was unlucky, David Harvey. He made a very good save from Keegan. It ricocheted around. It was Keegan's shot. But it may well have flicked off Phil Boersma. A goal out of nothing. On the bench. The Wembley bench. Bill sat forward again. His left arm on his raincoat again. His right elbow in his left hand on his right knee. His shoulders forward. His head forward. His chin in his right hand. His fingers stroking his chin again. *And I feel very touched. This makes me feel I have possibly achieved something at Liverpool.* Beautifully played, Keegan. There's another chance on here. And it's blocked. Boersma's shot. Corner. Reaney on the near post. Boersma with the back-header. Hunter. Leeds not quite themselves since that goal. Bad sort of goal to concede. On the bench. The Wembley bench. Bill sat back again. Bill crossed his legs again. His right leg over his left. *The tributes that were paid were wonderful, astonishing, emotional and touching.* Jordan on his own. Now he has Gray out to the left. Did well there, Joe Jordan. Bremner. Lorimer. Through the back, nicely. Clarke, unlucky. Appealing for a handball that never was. McQueen coming forward. Leeds' second corner of the match. McQueen stays up. Aimed for Reaney but too high for him. On the bench. The Wembley bench. Bill uncrossed his legs. Bill crossed his legs. His left leg over his right. *I know there is even an idea to change the name of Bold Street to Shankly Parade. It's all news to me. And anything that is in Liverpool that has my name to it I would be proud of. But I do not want anything to do with any controversy.* Leeds have got three back now. Reaney making it four. Keegan. Heighway in the middle. Marked by Cherry. Hughes. Jordan now back behind the ball for Leeds. Lindsay. Hughes. Brian Hall striding his way through. Well saved again, David Harvey. Superb stuff from Brian Hall and a good save by David Harvey. On the bench. The Wembley bench. Bill folded his arms across his chest again. His right hand over his heart again. *I came to Liverpool just to manage a football team. But the fact that these actions come from ordinary men and women in the street means more to me than money.* Giles. Bremner. Interesting. Jordan to his left. Clarke further over. Good leap by Clemence. On the bench. The Wembley bench. Bill let go of his heart again. Bill unfolded his arms again. Both arms back at his side. Bill uncrossed his legs. Both feet back on the ground. *They came from people my wife and I know. And from people we don't know. And they came from people in high places right down to the rank and file. The working men, just like me, who go to Anfield.* Now Boersma. Heighway. Good save again. Timed it superbly. But there are times when this Leeds defence is looking a bit short of pace. Cherry. Giles. Clemence gets there first. Keegan. Boersma to his right. Good early cross. Reaney's header. Cormack. Callaghan. Boersma. Hughes. Off the crossbar. Emlyn Hughes. A thunderous effort. On the bench. The Wembley bench. Bill sat forward again. His left arm on his raincoat again. His right elbow in his left hand on his right knee. His shoulders forward. His head forward. His chin in his right hand. His fingers stroking his chin again. *I class myself as one of them. I'm a working-class man. I used to work down the pit. I have no airs and graces. I might be better off now than some of them. But it has not altered my outlook on life or how I feel.* Giles. Lorimer finding Giles again. Reaney. Four to find. Here's Clarke. From Reaney's cross. Allan Clarke all alone. Bit wild by Giles. Another free kick. Lindsay to take. The whistle. And half-time –

On the bench. The Wembley bench. Bill stood up. Bill walked along the touchline. The Wembley touchline. Bill came to the mouth of the tunnel. The Wembley tunnel. And Bill stopped. Bill looked down the tunnel. The Wembley tunnel. Into the darkness, into the shadows. Bill started to walk again. Into the tunnel. The Wembley tunnel. The darkness and the shadows. In the tunnel. The Wembley tunnel. Bill stopped before the dressing-room door. The Wembley dressing-room door. In the darkness, in the shadows. Bill had his hand on the doorknob. The dressing-room doorknob. On the other side of the door. The dressing-room door. Bill could hear Bob Paisley talking. Talking to the team. The Liverpool team. In the dressing room. The Liverpool dressing room. Bill could hear Bob saying –

Just keep it up, lads. You're doing fine, you're doing well. So just keep it going, lads. Just keep it going . . .

In the tunnel. The Wembley tunnel. The darkness and the shadows. Before the door. The dressing-room door. Bill took his hand off the doorknob. The dressing room-doorknob. And in the darkness. And in the shadows. Bill paced. Up and down, up and down. In the tunnel. The Wembley tunnel. Bill paced and Bill paced. Up and down, up and down. And Bill waited and Bill waited. For the buzzer. The Wembley buzzer. And then at last, at last. In the tunnel. The Wembley tunnel. The darkness and the shadows. Bill heard the buzzer. The Wembley buzzer. And Bill saw the dressing-room door open. The Liverpool dressing-room door. Out of the corner of his eye again. Their boots in the tunnel, their studs on the concrete. Bill heard the team coming out. The Liverpool team. And Bill turned. And Bill saw the team coming out. The Liverpool team. And Bill greeted the players. The Liverpool players. Bill laughing, Bill smiling. Bill saying something, something like, Just keep it up, boys. You're doing fine, you're doing well. So just keep it going, boys. Just keep it going . . .

Buttoning his jacket, unbuttoning his jacket. His mouth still dry and his palms still wet. Bill ran his tongue along his lips again. Bill wiped his hands together again. Bill looked to the end of the tunnel. The light at the end of the tunnel. And Bill began to walk towards the light again. Bill walking back out with the team. The Liverpool team. Into the light, into the stadium. Still not sure if his jacket should be open, not sure if his jacket should be closed. Back around the touchline. The Wembley touchline. Buttoning his jacket and unbuttoning his jacket. Until at last, at last. Bill reached the benches again. The Wembley benches. And Bill sat back down. On the bench. The Wembley bench. Back between Brian Clough and Jimmy Gordon. His raincoat back across his knees. His left arm back on his raincoat. His right elbow back in his left hand on his right knee. His shoulders forward again, his head forward again. His chin back in his right hand.

His fingers stroking his chin again. *The only money I want is what I have earned. And all these tributes from the fans mean far more to me than anything like that. That was better than going around with the hat and collecting a hundred thousand pounds.* The whistle again. And Keegan. Being forced away by McQueen. Gray. Cherry. Lorimer. Giles. Gray. Reaney and Lorimer both out to the right. Reaney. Now Lorimer, number seven. Jordan in the challenge with Smith. On the bench. The Wembley bench. Bill sat back. Bill crossed his legs. His right leg over his left. *All these tributes, these letters, the press comment, have all meant more to me than money. But if you think I don't want money, you would be wrong! But all I want is enough to live on. That is all.* Clarke up forward. Looking for Jordan instead. It's a bit long. But it'll run for him. Bremner. Went one way, tried to come back the other. Jordan unable to bore in on that pass. Just forced him more to the corner. Clarke down hurt. On the bench. The Wembley bench. Bill uncrossed his legs. Bill crossed his legs again. His left leg over his right. *My mother was a very kind woman. And something she used to say still sticks in my mind. It was, If I have enough, I have plenty, and I don't want any more. That is a really great philosophy. And I've always tried to bear it in mind.* Boersma coming now. No one there. But that's where they ought to have been. Allan Clarke still down. Boersma. Nicely done. Good save. He'll try again. But if he had kept his head then, he wouldn't have gone for the second shot. He could have found Cormack. And then Harvey would have been committed in the wrong spot. The pressure still on. And that looked very much like a right hook by Johnny Giles. Keegan, the player down. Got up quickly. Giles going into the book. On the bench. The Wembley bench. Bill folded his arms across his chest. His right hand over his heart. *I'm not greedy. And I don't want anything to which I am not entitled. My father would always give rather than take.* Free kick never on. But more trouble off the ball. Keegan involved again. Billy Bremner being called over. McQueen being waved away. Keegan involved again. Kevin Keegan still having words with the referee. Keegan who was sent off in Germany when it was a case of mistaken identity. And he's off here. And he's absolutely livid about it. And Bremner is off as well. Bremner off as well. And they are both throwing their shirts down. On the bench. The Wembley bench. Bill let go of his heart again. Bill unfolded his arms again. Both arms back at his side. Bill uncrossed his legs. Both feet back on the ground. *They were one hundred per cent honest. My father and my mother. They didn't have much themselves. But they were always willing to help others as much as they could.* Gray now. Good play by Cherry. Giles just coming onto it. Jordan came a little bit too soon. Jordan went in on it. And it seemed to come loose. And in comes McQueen. On the bench. The Wembley bench. Bill sat forward again. His left arm on his raincoat again. His right elbow in his left hand on his right knee. His shoulders forward. His head forward. His chin in his right hand. His fingers stroking his chin again. *I would like to be judged not really on what I did but on the fact that I never cheated. I was not dishonest. I was never careless with money or with people. Basic honesty is the greatest thing any human being can possess. Some people cannot help being dishonest. But if everyone was honest, there would be none of the tangles there are in the world today.* Lindsay. Nicely played by Callaghan. Boersma. Heighway just around the penalty spot. Hall further over. Goal kick. On the bench. The Wembley bench. Bill sat back again. Bill crossed his legs again. His right leg over his left. *I have never begged for anything. And what I have received I have earned. And no matter what happens in the future, the memory of that will never be erased.* Lorimer. Cherry. And a goal. A good goal. One-all. On the bench. The Wembley bench. Bill uncrossed his legs. Bill crossed his legs again. His left leg over his right. *But all I have done has been for the club and for the people. For without the people, there would be no club.* Giles to Gray. Cherry. Reaney. Giles. Reaney going down the flank. Gray. Lorimer. And McKenzie was the player who very nearly forced it in. Goal kick. But pushing anyway. So a free kick. On the bench. The Wembley bench. Bill folded his arms across his chest again. His right hand over his heart again. *Because I appreciate everyone who comes to Anfield.* Heighway. And he's done well. Hall's going to take the free kick. Heighway up on one side. Boersma on the other. Callaghan arrives. Lovely stuff. Superb by Callaghan. And Cormack so, so near. Goal kick. On the bench. The Wembley bench. Bill let go of his heart again. Bill unfolded his arms again. Both arms back at his side. Bill uncrossed his legs. Both feet back on the ground. *Once I recall going onto the Kop about an hour before a match. Just to talk to the fans. And one of them thought I was going to watch the match from there. And so he said, Come and stand over here, Bill. You'll get a good view.* Cormack. Thompson. Smith. Heighway. He really hit that. And Harvey did very well. Tremendous piece of play by Heighway. On the bench. The Wembley bench. Bill sat forward again. His left arm on his raincoat again. His right elbow in his left hand on his right knee. His shoulders forward. His head forward. His chin in his right hand. His fingers stroking his chin again. *Now, perhaps, in future days, I will have more time to talk to these wonderful fans. These fans who have meant so much to me during my time here.* Hunter. Lorimer. Reaney. Hunter again. Corner. Four waiting. Giles. Looked as though he was going to trap, but instead flicked directly at it. Would have made a picture goal. Here's Hall. Reaney. The touch was enough. Lindsay. Boersma. Heighway. The tackle from Giles. And a penalty competition it is going to be. At the final whistle. One–one, the final score, over the ninety minutes. The penalties now. And then possibly the prospect of sudden death. After the first five penalties, then it will be sudden death. Sudden death, if nothing is decided. On the bench. The Wembley bench. Bob Paisley tapped Bill on the shoulder. Bill turned around. Bill leaned back. Bob Paisley whispered in Bill's ear, whispered something Bill did not quite hear, did not quite catch. But Bill nodded. And then Bill sat forward again. On the bench. The Wembley bench. His left arm on his raincoat again. His right elbow in his left hand on his right knee. His shoulders forward. His head forward. His chin in his right hand. His fingers stroking his chin again. *Since I made my decision to retire, our front door has been besieged with people. I have received hundreds of letters and telegrams. Thousands of fans have written to me, pleading with me to stay.* Ray Clemence and David Harvey. At the goal at the end by the players' tunnel. Bob Matthewson coming up. Alongside him, Peter Lorimer. So Peter Lorimer against Ray Clemence. One–nothing to Leeds United. Alec Lindsay now against David Harvey. One apiece. Johnny Giles. And a lot of whistles for him. But two–one to Leeds. Emlyn Hughes. That was the blaster. Two apiece. Eddie Gray the next to go. Three–two. Very calmly taken. A kick of a very different style to Emlyn Hughes. Brian Hall with the job of making it three-all. Which he does very comfortably. The penalty kicks so far of a very high standard. Norman Hunter. Four–three. Tommy Smith. Four apiece. So Trevor Cherry coming up for the last of Leeds' five penalties. Clemence not too far away from that. Five–four. Peter Cormack. Liverpool's number five in all possible senses. Five–five. To take us into sudden death. The goalkeepers looking to see who comes next. And Harvey is going to take against Clemence. And Harvey hits the bar. He's missed. But that's not it. Callaghan coming up to take now. So Clemence has not been given the responsibility. So Ian Callaghan, the Footballer of the Year, with the chance to give Liverpool the Charity Shield. Which he does. On the bench. The Wembley bench. Bill stood up. Bill turned. Bill looked for Bob Paisley. Bill reached for Bob Paisley. And Bill shook Bob's hand. Bill congratulated Bob. And then Bill walked onto the pitch. The Wembley pitch. His hand outstretched again. And Bill went from player to player. Liverpool player and Leeds player. And Bill shook their hands. The hands of the Liverpool players, the hands of the Leeds players. Congratulating them or commiserating with them. And Emlyn Hughes held Bill. Emlyn Hughes hugged Bill. Squeezed him as though he would never let him go. And Bill whispered, Go on, son. Go on and lead the team. And collect that shield. Go on now, son. Go on . . .

And Bill stood on the pitch. The Wembley pitch. And Bill watched Emlyn Hughes lead the players up the steps. The Wembley steps. Bill watched Emlyn Hughes collect the shield. The Charity Shield. The players ascending the steps, the players descending the steps. The Wembley steps. And then Bill joined the players. The Liverpool players. At the bottom of the steps. The Wembley steps. Bill posed for photographs with the team. The Liverpool team. And the shield. The Charity Shield. On the pitch. The Wembley pitch. Bill held the shield. The Charity Shield. And the photographers took their pictures. And the journalists asked their questions. And then Bill walked. Bill jogged. Around the touchline. The Wembley touchline. With the shield. The Charity Shield. With the team. The Liverpool team. On the track. The speedway track. Around the stadium. The Wembley stadium. Saluting the supporters of Liverpool Football Club, thanking the supporters of Liverpool Football Club. For the last time, the very last time. Saluting them and thanking them. For the last time, the very last time. The supporters of Liverpool Football Club chanting,

*SHANK-LEE, SHANK-LEE, SHANK-LEE . . .*

Some of those supporters of Liverpool Football Club on the pitch now. The Wembley pitch now. Embracing Bill, holding Bill. Tight, tight. Pulling him this way, pulling him that way. Harder and harder. And one supporter, one Liverpool supporter, reached out towards Bill. Across the pitch, the Wembley pitch. And this supporter, this Liverpool supporter, this supporter tied a scarf around Bill's neck. A tartan Liverpool scarf around Bill's neck. And another supporter, a supporter in a white boiler suit and a tall red hat, this supporter grabbed Bill. By the lapels, the lapels of Bill's jacket. And this supporter, this supporter in his white boiler suit and his tall red hat, with tears down his face and despair in his voice, this supporter held Bill. Tighter, tighter. This supporter hugged Bill. Harder and harder. Squeezed him as though he would never let him go. And this supporter begged and pleaded and cried, Please don't go, Mr Shankly. Please don't leave us. Please stay, Mr Shankly. Please stay with us, please . . .

Bill tried to pull back from this supporter, this supporter in his white boiler suit and his tall red hat, with the tears down his face and the despair in his voice. Bill tried to turn away. But Bill could not pull back, Bill could not turn away. And Bill reached out to this supporter, this man in his white boiler suit and his tall red hat, and Bill embraced the man. Bill held the man in his arms. And Bill said, It'll be all right, wee man. It'll be fine. Don't worry, wee man. Don't worry . . .

And Bill pulled back now. Bill turned away now. And Bill began to walk. To jog. And then to run. Across the pitch. The Wembley pitch. Towards the tunnel. The Wembley tunnel. The darkness and the shadows. And in the tunnel. The Wembley tunnel. In the darkness and in the shadows. Bill stopped running. Between its high, bare walls. In its long, dark shadows. His chest heaving, his heart racing. Bill caught his breath, Bill calmed his heart. In the tunnel. The Wembley tunnel. His breath caught and his heart calm. Bill knocked upon the dressing-room door. The Leeds United dressing-room door. Bill stepped inside the Leeds United dressing room. And Bill saw Billy Bremner. Billy Bremner sat on the bench. Still in his shorts, still without his shirt. Bill sat down next to Billy Bremner. And Bill said, What on earth did you do that for, son? Throwing your shirt off like that. Throwing it down on the ground like it was a piece of rag. What on earth were you bloody thinking? What got into you, son?

I don't know, said Billy Bremner. I am disgusted with myself.

Bill laughed. And Bill said, And so you bloody should be, son. But did you see you that picture of me and you and Jack Dempsey? In the paper? The one they took at the dinner the other night? Now that man could lick the world. That man knew how to really punch!

Aye, said Billy Bremner. It's a good photo. A good memory.

Bill nodded. And Bill slapped Billy Bremner on the top of his thigh. Bill got up from the bench. And Bill walked out of the Leeds United dressing room. Into the tunnel. The Wembley tunnel. And into the dressing room. The Liverpool dressing room. And Bill saw Kevin Keegan. Kevin Keegan sat on the bench. Already washed, already dressed. His father sat beside him. Bill sat down on the other side of Kevin Keegan. And Bill said, Forget it, son. Forget it. You were not the culprit. You were the victim. The victim of a heinous injustice!

I can't forget it, said Kevin Keegan. But I'm very sorry it happened, Boss. On today of all days. So I'm going to go home with my dad now, Boss. Because I need to think about things . . .

Bill nodded. And Bill said, All right, son. You go home with your dad. That's the best place, home. Keep your head down. And your nose clean. But your chin up. Your chin up, son . . .

Kevin Keegan nodded. And his father nodded. Kevin Keegan stood up. And his father stood up. And Bill watched Kevin Keegan and his father walk out of the dressing room. The Liverpool dressing room. And into the tunnel. The Wembley tunnel. Its darkness and its shadows. The door banging behind them. The dressing-room door. Bill heard the door banging. The dressing-room door. Banging and banging, echoing and echoing. And Bill looked around the dressing room. The Liverpool dressing room. Round and around. And Bill stood back up. Bill got back on his feet. And Bill began to pace again. Up and down the dressing room. The Liverpool dressing room –

Round and around. Round and around –

On the train. The train back to Liverpool. In the carriage, in his seat. Bill could feel the wheels of the train beneath him. Turning, turning. Round and around. Their movement and their rhythm. Round and around. On the train. The train back to Liverpool. In the carriage, in his seat. Bill had no book. No book of names, no book of notes. Bill had no diary. No diary of dates, no diary of fixtures. The dates to come, the fixtures to come. But on the train. The train back to Liverpool. In the carriage, in his seat. The wheels going round and around. Turning and turning. Bill did not look out of the window. Not at the sun setting, not at the night falling. The cattle dimming and the fields fading. The wheels going round and around. *So what are you going to do with yourself all season, Mr Shankly?* In the gloaming, in the twilight. Past the abandoned branch lines, past the mothballed stations. The wheels going round and around. *What on earth are you going to do with yourself, sir?* Bill thought about all the interviews he had done. All the broadcasters and all the journalists. The wheels going round and around. *So what are you going to do with yourself all season, Mr Shankly?* And Bill closed his eyes. Bill had had enough of dictating his own obituary. Bill had had enough of carving his own tombstone. Round and around. *What on earth are you going to do with yourself, sir?* Round and around. *So what are you going to do with yourself all season, Mr Shankly?* Round and around. *What on earth are you going to do with yourself, sir?* Round and around,

round and around. In the house, in their front room. In the night and in the silence. Bill paced and Bill paced. Round and around. In the house, in their front room. In the night and in the silence. Bill stopped pacing. Bill walked out into the hall. Bill picked up the telephone. Bill dialled a number. And Bill listened to the telephone ring. And ring –

Hello, said Maurice Setters, the manager of Doncaster Rovers.

Hello, Maurice. Hello. It's only me, Maurice. It's only Bill. And I'm sorry to bother you, Maurice. But I'm worried about Keegan. I am very worried about Kevin. After what happened today. I want him to come up to Glasgow with the team. We're playing in Billy McNeill's testimonial. It'll be my last game, Maurice. And I want him to be there. I don't want him brooding in Doncaster. I want to get things sorted. So will you go out and find him for me, Maurice. I called his house. I called his father. But the lad's gone to the pub. He'll be out drowning his sorrows somewhere. And that's no good for any man. So I want you to go and find him, Maurice. And tell him to call me. Because I'm back at my home now. And so I'll be waiting for him to call me. Whatever time. I'll be waiting. Will you find him and tell him, Maurice? Will you do that for me, Maurice?

Yes, said Maurice Setters. I'll do that for you, Bill. I will.

Bill sighed. And Bill said, Thank you, Maurice. Thank you. You are a pal, Maurice. You truly are. Thank you, Maurice.

Bill put down the telephone. And in the house and in the hall. In the night and in the silence. Bill paced and Bill paced. Up and down, up and down. In the house, in the hall. In the night and in the silence. Up and down, up and down. Bill paced and Bill paced. For hour after hour. Bill waited and Bill waited. Until at last, at last. Bill heard the telephone ring. And Bill grabbed the phone. On the second ring. And Bill said, Kevin? Kevin, is that you, son? Kevin?

Yes, Boss, said Kevin Keegan. It's me, Boss . . .

And Bill said, I've just spoken to Jock. And Jock wants you there. On Monday night, at Parkhead. For the testimonial, for Billy McNeill. Jock wants you to be there. To be up there. Because the people up there, they want to see you play, son. They don't care about what happened today. All that nonsense. They just want to see you play, son. So Jock wants you to be there. And I want you to be there.

If you'll be there, Boss, then I'll be there, said Kevin Keegan.

Oh, I'll be there, son. I'll be there. You just try and stop me, son. You just try and stop me . . .


## 55. IN THE HIGHLANDS, MY HEART IS NOT HERE

Before the testimonial, the testimonial for Billy McNeill. At the dinner, the dinner for Billy McNeill. Jock Stein got to his feet. Jock Stein picked up his knife. Jock Stein picked up his glass. Jock Stein tapped the knife against the glass once, twice, three times. And Jock Stein said, Ladies and gentlemen, we are here tonight to honour one of the greatest footballers in the history of the Celtic Football Club: the Big Man, the Caesar, King Billy himself – Mr Billy McNeill. Raised in Bellshill, a Motherwell supporter no less, he was spotted by Bobby Evans and, thankfully, signed for the Celtic Football Club in 1957. And so Billy was here when I came here. And by God, was I glad he was. Of course, it was Billy who scored the goal that won us the Cup in 1965. The first cup the club had won since 1957! And of course, he went on to score in two more cup finals. Not bad for a centre-half! But

I believe that goal back in 1965, that header that won that game, and that gave us that victory, I believe that was pivotal. Because that goal, that goal that won that game and that won us that cup, changed everything. Because that goal, that cup and that victory was the foundation of all the goals, all the cups and all the victories since. The five more Scottish Cups, the five League Cups, the nine consecutive League Championships and, of course, the European Cup. And I do not believe, in fact I know, we would never have won so much without Billy McNeill. Because it has been Billy's determination, Billy's strength and Billy's leadership as captain of the Celtic Football Club that have been the bedrock, the very foundation of all our success. And Billy has played every single minute of every single game he has ever played in. In all those games, he has never once been substituted. Because I would not have dared! Not that I ever wanted to, mind . . .

But for all his commitment, for all his dedication, his passion and his strength, you will never hear another player, another football man, speak ill of Billy McNeill. Because Billy McNeill has earned the admiration and respect not only of his teammates and the supporters of the Celtic Football Club, but the admiration and respect of all the players and the supporters he has played against. And so I think there can be no more fitting opponents, no more worthy opposition tomorrow night, than Liverpool Football Club. And so it gives me the greatest of pleasure to be able to welcome Liverpool Football Club. And to thank them for coming here to take part in this great occasion, this testimonial for Billy McNeill. However, in fairness, I'd just like to remind Liverpool Football Club that the Celtic Football Club do not play friendlies. We never have and we never will!

Bill Shankly jumped up. Up from his chair, up onto his feet –

Aye, John. Right you are, John. Well, that's lucky for you and for the Celtic. Because Liverpool Football Club don't play friendlies either! As you'll find out soon enough. . .

At the testimonial, the testimonial for Billy McNeill. In the centre circle of the pitch, the Parkhead pitch. Jock Stein embraced Bill Shankly. And Jock Stein said, Tonight is for Billy. But do you not hear that, Bill? Do you not hear the name they are singing now?

*SHANK-LEE, SHANK-LEE, SHANK-LEE . . .*

Aye, John, I do, said Bill Shankly. And I never dreamt, when I used to come to this ground as a schoolboy fifty years ago, that I would end my career here, with a finale as memorable and moving as this. I could never have dreamt of such a night, John.

And Jock Stein felt Bill Shankly grasp his hand. Bill Shankly grip his hand. Squeeze his hand as though he would never let it go. And Jock Stein looked at Bill Shankly. Bill Shankly in the centre circle of the pitch. The Parkhead pitch. And Jock Stein whispered, You know, I've never believed anything you've ever said to me, Bill. Not a word, a single word. The things you've said about your players. About Liverpool Football Club. If they were as good as you always said, they'd have not only won the European Cup, they'd have won the Ryder Cup, the Boat Race and even the bloody Grand National!

And they would have done, said Bill Shankly. But they never let me enter them. But they would have done. Believe me . . .

Jock Stein shook his head. And Jock Stein said, Well, I still refuse to believe that. And I also refuse to believe you are retiring, Bill. I cannot believe you. That you would walk away from this. From this game. From these players. These fans. I just cannot believe you, Bill. I refuse to believe you. Men like us don't retire, Bill. We go on and on until we die. Until we die at our posts, Bill. That is the kind of men we are. The kind of man you are, Bill . . .

But this is not about me, said Bill Shankly. And Bill Shankly let go of Jock Stein's hand. Bill Shankly walked over to Billy McNeill in the centre circle of the pitch, the Parkhead pitch. And Bill Shankly shook the hand of Billy McNeill –

Everything you have earned from the game. Everything you have gained from this game. You have done it honestly, son. So enjoy this night. Your night. Because you deserve it, son. Because you are honest. An honest man . . .

After the testimonial, the testimonial for Billy McNeill. In the dressing room, the Liverpool dressing room. Bob Paisley called for silence. And then Bob Paisley said, Have you got the time, Bill?

And Bob Paisley handed over a gold wristlet watch to Bill Shankly. And then Bob Paisley handed over a matching lady's gold wristlet watch to Bill Shankly. And Bob Paisley said, And will you give this one to Nessie, too, with all our good wishes, Bill . . .

In the dressing room, the Liverpool dressing room. Bill

Shankly looked down at the two gold watches in his hand. And Bill Shankly nodded. And Bill Shankly smiled –

It's funny how when you retire, they always give you a clock or watch, isn't it? The old gold clock, the old gold watch. The two things you don't need, the last two things you need. When you're sat at home all day. Watching those hands go round and around. Round and around all day. It's funny, isn't it?

But in the dressing room, the Liverpool dressing room. No one laughed. And no one spoke. Until Reuben Bennett said, Would you have preferred a pair of boots, Bill? A new pair of football boots?

Oh aye, Reuben. Of course, I would. If you had made them gold and all. Yes, a pair of golden football boots. Oh yes. And don't forget, boys. I'm always a size thirty in a golden boot!

And now in the dressing room, the Liverpool dressing room. Now everyone laughed. Almost everyone.


## 56. IN A DARK WOOD

In the house, in their bed. In the dark and in the silence. Bill could not sleep. His head on his pillow. His eyes open. Bill stared up into the darkness. Up into the silence. Everything dark, everything silent. Until at last, at last. The curtain edges grew light again. At last, at last. The wardrobe wood again, not shadow now. At last, at last. A ceiling on the room, a roof upon the house. At last, at last. The bottle on the doorstep, the paper through the letterbox. And at last, at last. Day was here again. A new morning come again. At last,

at last. Bill was out of their bed. Into the bathroom. Shaved and washed. Bill put on his tracksuit bottoms. Bill put on his sweater. Bill folded up his suit. His shirt and his tie. Bill put his suit, his shirt and his tie, into his bag. His kit bag. Bill took his boots from out of the bottom of the wardrobe. Bill put his boots into a plastic bag. Bill picked up his kit bag and the plastic bag. Bill walked down the stairs. Bill left his kit bag and the plastic bag in the hall. Bill went into the kitchen. Bill ate breakfast with Ness. A slice of toast and honey, a glass of orange juice and a cup of tea. Bill helped Ness clear away the breakfast things. Bill dried up the breakfast things. Bill helped Ness put away the breakfast things. And Bill kissed Ness on her cheek –

Are you going somewhere, love, asked Ness.

Oh yes, love. I thought I'd just pop in at Melwood. Just to see how everyone is doing, love. How they are all getting on.

But you saw them all yesterday, said Ness.

I know, I know. But I'm going to train as well. With the team, love. I might as well. To keep myself fit. I've got to keep myself fit, love. I don't want to be letting myself go now, do I, love?

I don't think there's any chance of that, love.

I don't know, love. I don't know. I've seen it happen to many a man. The minute he stops working. He starts to let himself go. To get idle and to get lazy. The minute he stops working. Because that's when the danger comes. The temptation to do nothing. To just sit around the house all day. Reading the paper and watching the telly. With his feet up and his guard down. Letting himself go, to rack and to ruin. No, love. No. I have to be on my guard. I have to keep myself fit . . .

But will you be back for your lunch, love?

I'm sorry, love. But I cannot say. I mean, if I'm needed at the ground, if I'm needed at Anfield. Then I'll have to go. And I want to go, love. I want to help. I don't want anyone to think I've abandoned them now. That I've turned my back on Liverpool Football Club. Because if I can help in any way, then I will, love. I must . . .

Of course, said Ness. Of course, you must. But you take care now, love. And I'll see you when I see you then . . .

Bill nodded. Bill smiled. Bill kissed Ness on her cheek again. Bill went into the hall. Bill picked up his kit bag and the plastic bag. Bill went out of the front door. Bill went down the drive. Bill got into the car. And Bill drove to Melwood. Just around the corner,

not three streets away –

His car in the car park at Melwood. Bill was leaning over the veranda of the pavilion. Already changed. Always, already changed. In his boots, his football boots. Bill was waiting. Always, already waiting. On the veranda of the pavilion. Bill watched the players get off the bus from Anfield. Bill waved at the players. Bill smiled at the players. And Bill shouted, Morning, boys. Morning . . .

Morning, Boss, said the players.

Bill laughed. And Bill said, A great day, isn't it, boys? A great day to be playing football. A great day to be alive!

Yes, Boss, said the players.

And Bill saw Bob Paisley, Joe Fagan, Reuben Bennett and Ronnie Moran. And Bill waved at Bob, Joe, Reuben and Ronnie. And Bob Paisley, Joe Fagan, Reuben Bennett and Ronnie Moran looked up at Bill. Bill leaning over the veranda of the pavilion. Already changed. And Bob, Joe, Reuben and Ronnie all smiled. And Bob, Joe, Reuben and Ronnie all waved back at Bill. And Bill shouted, Morning, boys. Good morning. And how are you all today, boys? All well, I hope?

Very well, shouted Reuben. Thank you, Bill. And you're looking well, too. Looks like you can't keep away, though . . .

Bill laughed. And Bill said, I'm just here to keep myself fit, Reuben. To keep on my toes. That is, if no one minds?

Course no one minds, said Bob. You're always welcome, Bill.

Thank you, Bob. Thank you very much . . .

And Bill jogged down the stairs. And out of the pavilion. And Bill joined the players running round the training pitch. Bill joking, Bill laughing. Cajoling and inspiring. But running, still running, running harder, harder than ever. Then the players split into their groups. And the players lifted weights. The players skipped. The players jumped. The players did squats. The players did abdominal exercises. And the players sprinted. And Bill lifted weights. Bill skipped. Bill jumped. Bill did squats. Bill did abdominal exercises. And Bill sprinted. Bill laughing, Bill joking. Inspiring and cajoling. But sprinting, still sprinting, sprinting harder, harder than ever. And then the players passed the ball. The players dribbled with the ball. The players headed the ball. The players chipped the ball. The players controlled the ball. And the players tackled. And Bill passed the ball. Bill dribbled with the ball. Bill headed the ball. Bill chipped the ball. Bill controlled the ball. And Bill tackled. Bill joking, Bill laughing. Cajoling and inspiring. But tackling, still tackling, tackling harder, harder than ever. And the players went between the training boards. The players moving, the ball moving. Playing the ball against one board. Then taking the ball, controlling the ball. Turning with the ball, dribbling with the ball. Up to the other board. In just ten touches. Playing the ball against the other board. Then pulling the ball down, turning again and dribbling again. Back down to the first board. In just ten touches. And Bill went between the training boards. Bill moving, the ball moving. Bill playing the ball against one board. Then taking the ball, controlling the ball. Bill turning with the ball, dribbling with the ball. Up to the other board. In just ten touches. Bill playing the ball against the other board. Then pulling the ball down, turning again and dribbling again. Back down to the first board. In just ten touches. Bill laughing, Bill joking. Inspiring and cajoling. But dribbling, still dribbling, dribbling harder, harder than ever. Then the players went inside the sweat box. Ball after ball. Into the box. Every second, another ball. For one minute. Then for two minutes. Then for three minutes. Ball after ball, into the box. And Bill went into the sweat box. Ball after ball. Into the box. Every second, another ball. For one minute. Then for two minutes. Then for three minutes. Bill joking, Bill laughing. Cajoling and inspiring. But sweating, still sweating, sweating harder, harder than ever. And then the players played three-a-sides. Three-a-sides then five-a-sides. Five-a-sides then seven-a-sides. Seven-a-sides then eleven-a-sides. And Bill played three-a-sides. Three-a-sides then five-a-sides. Five-a-sides then seven-a-sides. Seven-a-sides then eleven-a-sides. Bill laughing, Bill joking. Inspiring and cajoling. But playing, still playing, playing harder, harder than ever. And then the players ran one last time around the training pitch. And Bill ran one last time around the training pitch. Bill still joking, Bill still laughing. Still cajoling and still inspiring. And running, still running, running harder, harder than ever. Until Bill came back to where Bob, Joe, Reuben and Ronnie were standing. In the centre of the pitch. The training pitch. And Bill stopped running. Bill caught his breath. And Bill said, By, thank you, boys. Thank you. That was just what I needed, boys. Just what I needed. I tell you, boys. I tell you. I feel alive again, boys. Alive and kicking again! Thank you, boys . . .

You're welcome, said Bob. Very welcome, Bill.

The players started to walk back towards the bus. The bus back to Anfield. The players smiled at Bill, the players waved at Bill –

See you, Boss. See you tomorrow, Boss.

Bill waved back at the players. And Bill shouted, Oh aye. Rain or shine, boys. I'll be here. Rain or shine, boys.

Well, I suppose we'd best be getting on the bus, too, said Bob.

Oh yes, Bob. Of course you had. Don't let me keep you. You

can't be standing around here all day, gabbing with me. Oh no.

Bob, Joe, Reuben and Ronnie all nodded. Bob, Joe, Reuben and Ronnie all said goodbye to Bill. And then Bob, Joe, Reuben and Ronnie started to walk back towards the bus. The bus back to Anfield. Bill standing in the centre of the pitch. The training pitch. Bill watching them go. Back to Anfield, back to work. And Bill started to walk across the training pitch. To jog now, then to run. Bill caught up with Bob, Joe, Reuben and Ronnie. And Bill said, Actually, if no one minds. If I'm not in the way. Not under anyone's feet. Because that's the last thing I'd want to be. The very last thing. But I was wondering if I might just pop into the ground. To have a quick bath. If no one minds. I won't come on the bus. Don't worry. I've got the car. I'll drive. I don't mind. But I thought I might just pop into the ground. Just for a quick bath. After the players have gone, of course. Don't worry, don't worry. You'll never know I was there . . .

Of course, said Bob. You're welcome, Bill. And come on the bus, if you want. It doesn't bother me, Bill.

Bill nodded. And Bill said, Thank you, Bob. Thank you. But it's fine. I've got the car anyway. So I'll drive. But thank you again, Bob. Thank you very much indeed.

You're welcome, said Bob again. And you don't need to ask, Bill. You're always welcome.

Bill nodded. Bill smiled. And Bill watched Bob Paisley, Joe Fagan, Reuben Bennett and Ronnie Moran get back on the bus. The bus back to Anfield. Bill standing beside the bus. In the car park. Bill looked up at the windows of the bus. The bus back to Anfield. Bill smiled at the players in the windows of the bus. The bus back to Anfield. And the players smiled back at Bill through the windows of the bus. The bus back to Anfield. Bill waved at the players in the windows of the bus. The bus back to Anfield. And the players waved back at Bill through the windows of the bus. The bus back to Anfield. The bus pulling out, the bus going back. Pulling out of the car park, going back to Anfield. Leaving Melwood, leaving Bill. In the car park. Bill waving them off, Bill watching them go. In the car park. Bill walked towards his car. Across the car park, back to his car. And then Bill stopped. In the car park. Bill turned. Bill walked back to the training pitch. And Bill ran one more lap around the training pitch.

And then another. And another. And then Bill stopped running. Bill walked back to the centre of the pitch. The training pitch. Bill stood in the centre of the pitch. The training pitch. And Bill looked around the ground. The training ground. This ground that had been cold, this ground that had been dark. Where there were trees and where there were bushes. The grass long and the ground uneven. With hills and with hollows. An air-raid shelter and a cricket pitch. And Bill smiled. And then Bill saw a ball. Out of the corner of his eye. An old white ball, over by the fence. Bill jogged over to the fence. Bill put his foot on the ball. The old white ball. Bill pulled the ball back towards him. His foot on the ball. Bill rolled the ball back behind him. Onto the pitch. The training pitch. And Bill turned. Bill tapped the ball in front of him. Right foot, left foot. Across the pitch. The training pitch. Right foot, left foot. Back towards the pavilion. Right foot, left foot. Until Bill reached the pavilion. And then Bill flicked up the ball with his right foot. And Bill caught the ball in his hands. The old white ball. Bill held the ball in his hands. Between his fingers. Bill looked down at the ball. The ball in his hands. Between his fingers. And Bill smiled again. And then Bill put the ball down. Beside the steps. The pavilion steps. The ball ready for tomorrow, the ball waiting for tomorrow. The training tomorrow. And Bill walked across the car park. Bill opened the door of his car. Bill took out his shoes from the car. Bill took off his boots. His football boots. Bill put on his shoes. Bill put his boots back in the bag. The plastic bag. Bill got into his car. Bill pulled out of the car park at Melwood. And Bill drove to Anfield. Ready for his bath, ready for a soak. Bill pulled into the car park at Anfield. Bill parked the car. Bill got out of his car. Bill walked across the car park. The Anfield car park. And into the ground. The Anfield ground. Into the dressing rooms. The Anfield dressing rooms. The players long gone. But their smell still there. The smell of sweat, the smell of work. And Bill smiled again. And Bill took off his shoes. Bill took off his sweater and his tracksuit bottoms. Bill still smiling to himself. Bill went into the baths. The Anfield baths. And Bill stepped into the bath. The Anfield bath. The water still warm, the water still deep. Bill sank into the bath. The Anfield bath. The water deep, the water warm. Bill put back his head. In the warm water, in the deep water. And Bill closed his eyes. In the bath. The Anfield bath. Bill listened to the sounds of the bath. The Anfield bath. The water dripping, the water lapping. Dripping down the sides, lapping on the tiles. In the baths. The Anfield baths. Bill listened to the sounds of the ground. The Anfield ground. In the bath, in his ears. The footsteps in the corridors, the footsteps on the stairs. Coming and going. The telephones ringing, the voices talking. Laughing and joking. In the bath, in his head. The voices whispering, the voices wondering. Coming and going, coming and going. Bill could go up the stairs. Bill could knock on the door. Not with a demand, not with a threat. Just something he wanted to do, something they would want him to do. After this period of reflection, this period of rest. All things now considered, all things then restored. Just as before, just as they were. Yes, he would go up the stairs. And he would knock on the door. All things now considered, all things then restored. In the bath. The Anfield bath. Bill opened his eyes. And Bill sat forward. The water cold now, the water old now. In the bath. The Anfield bath. Bill stood up. And Bill stepped out of the bath. All things now considered, all things then restored. Bill reached for his towel. Bill missed the towel. And Bill missed his step. On the tiles,

on his back. His shoulder gone –

Bill fought back the screams, Bill fought back the tears. On the tiles, on his back. The blood draining from his veins. Bill tried to stand. Bill tried to get back on his feet. His palm flat against the floor, his other hand reaching for the side. The side of the bath. Bill slipped again, slipped back again. Cursing to himself, raging against himself. Fighting back the screams, fighting back the tears. On the tiles, on his back. The blood still running from his veins. The voices no longer whispering, the voices no longer wondering. Just cursing, just raging. And knowing, now knowing. On the tiles,

on his back. Bill could not go up the stairs. Bill could not knock upon the door. Not now,

not now.


## 57. A GREAT RECKONING IN A LITTLE ROOM

John Smith saw Bill Shankly walking towards him across the car park. The Anfield car park. And John Smith said, Hello, Mr Shankly. Good to see you. In fact, I was hoping I might run into you. I was hoping I would see you. To have a word, if I might? If you have the time?

Of course, said Bill Shankly. And it's good to see you, too, Mr Smith. In fact, I was hoping I might have a word with you, too.

John Smith nodded. And John Smith said, Well then, shall we go back inside? Up to my office? And have our chat there?

Great, said Bill Shankly. That would be great.

John Smith and Bill Shankly walked back across the car park. The Anfield car park. Back into the ground. The Anfield ground. Up the stairs. The Anfield stairs. Along the corridor. The Anfield corridor. And into the office. The chairman's office –

John Smith gestured at one of the chairs in front of his desk. And John Smith said, Please, Mr Shankly. Have a seat.

Thank you, said Bill Shankly.

John Smith sat down at his desk. John Smith looked across his desk at Bill Shankly. John Smith smiled. And John Smith said, So how are you keeping, Mr Shankly? How is retirement treating you?

Well, to be honest with you, said Bill Shankly. I've hurt my shoulder. I've been training. Keeping myself fit. And then I only went and slipped as I stepped out of the bath. Like a bloody fool.

John Smith said, Oh, I'm very sorry to hear that, Mr Shankly. I really am. And I hope it's nothing too serious?

No, no, said Bill Shankly. But I think I should lay off the training for a wee while. Just for a while, mind. Until it's right again.

John Smith coughed. John Smith cleared his throat. John Smith took a deep breath. And then John Smith said, Well, it was actually about the training I wanted a word, Mr Shankly . . .

Yes, said Bill Shankly. Of course. I mean, anything I can do to help. Then I will. Of course. Anything at all.

John Smith coughed again. And John Smith said, Well, to be very honest with you, Mr Shankly, I think what would be most helpful, the most helpful thing you could do, would be to come in and do your training on an afternoon. After the players have finished. In the afternoon. I understand you want to keep fit. I understand, Mr Shankly. Of course I do. And so you're always very welcome to come in every day. Every afternoon. And to use the facilities. The training ground. Of course. But after the players have left. I think that would be for the best. The best and most helpful thing. For everyone . . .

In the ground. The Anfield ground. In the office. The chairman's office. In the chair. The chair before the desk. In his suit and in his tie. His Liverpool Football Club tie. Bill Shankly fought back tears. Bill Shankly struggled to breathe.

And Bill Shankly nodded.

John Smith coughed again. And John Smith said, It's not that you are not welcome here any more, Mr Shankly. Please do not think that. It's not that you are being cast out. Please never think that. But we have to let Bob make his own mark. Let Bob be his own man. Not to live in your shadow. Bob has to be able to step out of your shadow. To stand or fall. On his own. As his own man. The man the players call Boss. Not Bob. Boss. The only man the players call Boss.

His heart breaking, his head nodding. His back already broken, his kneecaps shot and shattered. A cattle gun to his forehead. Bill Shankly tried to stand. And not to run. To get back on his feet. And to walk away. His head high, his chin up. But Bill Shankly could not stand. Bill Shankly could not get back on his feet.

And Bill Shankly nodded again.

John Smith said, I am sure you can see the difficulty, Mr Shankly. The difficulty of the situation for everyone. And so I'm sure you understand why I am saying what I'm saying, Mr Shankly. Not out of any disrespect towards you. Or any malice, Mr Shankly. Just in the hope of making the situation easier, making a difficult situation easier. Easier for everyone, Mr Shankly. For the players and for Bob. And for the club, for Liverpool Football Club, Mr Shankly. And, of course, for you as well, Mr Shankly. So I hope you understand . . .

Yes, said Bill Shankly. I understand.

John Smith smiled. John Smith nodded. And John Smith said, Good, good. Thank you, Mr Shankly. Thank you. Now you said there was something you wanted to talk to me about, Mr Shankly?

No, said Bill Shankly. It's not important now.

John Smith smiled again. John Smith nodded again. And John Smith said, Well then, Mr Shankly. If that is all . . .

Yes, said Bill Shankly. That is all.

And Bill Shankly gripped both arms of the chair. And Bill Shankly forced himself to stand. To get back on his feet. And to walk away, out of the office. The chairman's office. And along the corridor. The Anfield corridor. And down the stairs. The Anfield stairs. And through the door. The Anfield door. Bill walked. Out of the ground, the Anfield ground. Alone –

Bill walked alone.


## 58. OUTSIDE THE GATES, OUTSIDE THE PALACE

In the house, in their bed. In the dark and in the silence. His head on his pillow. His eyes open. Bill was exhausted, Bill was shattered. Exhausted and shattered by the hours ahead. The days to come. The long days to come. The long days without name. The long days marching on. Without flags, without songs. Exhausted and shattered. In the house, in their bed. In the dark and in the silence. Now Bill saw the curtain edges grow light again. Now Bill heard the paper through the letterbox. The paper on the floor. And Bill got out of bed. Bill put on his dressing gown. Bill walked down the stairs. Bill picked up the papers from the floor. The Sunday papers. And Bill smiled. Bill put down the papers on the table in the hall. Bill walked back up the stairs. Bill went into the bathroom. Bill washed and Bill shaved. Bill went into the bedroom. Bill took off his pyjamas. Bill put on his tracksuit. His red tracksuit bottoms and his red tracksuit top. Bill took his boots from out of the bottom of the wardrobe. Bill walked back down the stairs. Bill put his boots down on the floor by the front door. Bill walked into the kitchen. Bill ate breakfast with Ness. A slice of toast and honey, a glass of orange juice and a cup of tea. Bill helped Ness clear away the breakfast things. Bill dried up the breakfast things. Bill helped Ness put away the breakfast things. Bill kissed Ness on her cheek. And Bill said, I'm just going up to the rec for a bit, love. For a bit of a kick-about with the young lads up there.

That's a good idea, said Ness.

But I'll be back before lunch. Back in time to give you a hand. Don't you worry, love . . .

Don't be worrying about me, said Ness. You just go and enjoy yourself, love. Just don't overdo it. Not with your shoulder, love.

I won't, love. I won't. Don't worry, love . . .

And Bill kissed Ness on her cheek again. Bill went back out into the hall. Bill sat down on the bottom step of the stairs. Bill put on his boots. His football boots. Bill stood back up. Bill went out of the front door. Down the drive, down the street. And up to the rec –

And the young lads on the rec saw Bill coming. In his tracksuit. His red tracksuit bottoms and his red tracksuit top. The young lads ran towards Bill. The young lads gathered around Bill. Jumping up and down, smiling from ear to ear. Asking him about this and telling him about that. And some of the young lads ran to wake up their mates. To get their mates out of their beds and to fetch their mates up to the rec. And soon there were forty young lads on the rec. Forty young lads with their ball and with Bill. In his tracksuit. His red tracksuit bottoms and his red tracksuit top. In the middle of the rec, in the middle of the lads. At the heart of the game, the twenty-a-side game. In his tracksuit. His red tracksuit bottoms and his red tracksuit top. Bill laughing, Bill joking. Inspiring, cajoling. And playing. At the heart of the game, the twenty-a-side game. Playing harder than ever. In his tracksuit. His red tracksuit bottoms and his red tracksuit top. With no more minutes, with no more hours. No long minutes and no long hours. Just joking, just laughing. Cajoling, inspiring. And playing and playing. Until the game was done and Bill's side had won. And Bill said, Right then, boys. I best be getting back home for my dinner. And so should you, boys. Back to your homes, back to your families. But you all take care now, boys. And I'll see you all next week. Same time again, boys . . .

But what if it's raining next week, said one of the boys. What will we do? Will you still come, Bill? Will you still be here?

Bill laughed. And Bill said, Don't you worry, son. I'll be here. Even if it snows, son. I'll be here. Do you think Roger Hunt stayed in his bed when it rained? Or Ian St John or Kevin Keegan? Oh no, son. Oh no. I'll be here. And I'll be waiting for you . . .

And in his tracksuit. His red tracksuit bottoms, his red tracksuit top. Bill jogged away from the young lads. Across the rec. And Bill saw Mick Lyons. Mick Lyons stood beside the rec. Mick watching, Mick smiling. And Bill said, Hello, Mick. How are you, son?

I'm fine, said Mick Lyons. But how are you, Bill? How are you keeping? You're looking well, Bill. You're looking fit.

Bill laughed. And Bill said, Well, I am. I am, Mick. I've just had a great game. And we won. Nineteen–seventeen. A great game, it was. You should have joined in, Mick. You should have played.

Well, I'm taking the young Everton lads, said Mick Lyons. The under-twelves and the under-fourteens. I take them every Sunday afternoon. And we often come on here for a game.

That's great, Mick. That's fantastic. I'm very pleased to hear you're doing that, Mick. Very pleased.

Well, you should join us, said Mick Lyons. You should play.

Bill smiled. And then Bill rubbed his shoulder. And Bill said, Well, I will, Mick. I will. Thank you, Mick. Thank you very much. I'd like that. I'd like that a lot, Mick. And I'd play today. I would, Mick. But I promised Ness I'd be back. Because my shoulder's not too clever. I slipped and fell. Like a fool. And so I need to take it a wee bit easy until it's right. But I'll play next week, Mick. I promise. So thank you, Mick. Thank you. Because I'd like that. I'd like that very much.

Well, I'm very sorry to hear about your shoulder, said Mick Lyons. And I hope they're looking after you at Anfield, Bill?

Bill shook his head. And Bill said, Well, to be honest, Mick. To be very honest with you. I don't like to bother them, Mick. It's not my way. I mean, I don't want to be under their feet, Mick . . .

But you need to have that shoulder looked at, said Mick Lyons. You must, Bill. You must. So why don't you pop into Bellefield tomorrow, Bill? I know Jim McGregor would love to see you. He'd be happy to have a look at that shoulder for you, Bill . . .

Bill shook his head again. And Bill said, Oh, I don't know about that, Mick. I don't want to be a bother. Or a nuisance, Mick . . .

Don't be daft, said Mick Lyons. You could never be a bother, Bill. Never a nuisance. We'd all be glad to see you, Bill. Any time you want. You're always welcome, Bill. Always very welcome.


59. OH, WHISTLE, AND I'LL COME TO YOU, MY LAD

Jim McGregor, the physiotherapist at Everton Football Club, was waiting for Bill Shankly at the Bellefield training ground. The Everton training ground. Jim McGregor shook Bill Shankly's hand. And Jim McGregor said, Very good to see you, Bill. Great to see you. But Mick tells me your shoulder is giving you some gyp? I'm very sorry to hear that, Bill. I really am. But you're going to let me have a look at it for you then, aren't you? And let me get you fit and working again . . .

Thank you, Jim. Thank you, said Bill Shankly. But only if you've the time, Jim. If I'm not in the way. If it's no bother . . .

Jim McGregor laughed. Jim McGregor shook his head. And Jim McGregor said, Of course it's no bother, Bill . . .

And Jim McGregor led Bill Shankly down the corridors of Bellefield to the treatment room. Jim McGregor had a look at Bill Shankly's shoulder for him. Jim McGregor gave Bill Shankly a massage. And then Jim McGregor said, How about you and me have a quick jog round Little Wembley now, Bill? But only if you're feeling up to it. And only if you've got the time, Bill . . .

Oh, I've got the time, said Bill Shankly. That's the one thing I've got now, Jim. But I'd like that. I'd like that very much . . .

Jim McGregor laughed again. And Jim McGregor said, I thought you would, Bill. I knew you'd not say no . . .

And Jim McGregor led Bill Shankly out of the treatment room. Back down the corridors of Bellefield. Out onto the training pitches. And Jim McGregor and Bill Shankly jogged together around one of the training pitches at Bellefield. The one the players of Everton Football Club called Little Wembley. And when they had jogged around Little Wembley three times, Jim McGregor turned to Bill Shankly. And Jim McGregor said, So how do you feel now, Bill?

I feel great, said Bill Shankly. Really well. Thank you, Jim. In fact, I wouldn't mind dropping dead right now. On the spot.

Jim McGregor laughed. And Jim McGregor said, You what, Bill? You wouldn't mind dropping dead? You what?

Well, just imagine, said Bill Shankly. I'd be in my coffin. And folk would walk past. And they'd say, Look at Bill. Doesn't he look well today? In fact, he's the fittest dead man I've ever seen. There lies a fit, dead man. That's what they'd say, Jim.

Jim McGregor laughed again. And Jim McGregor said, Well, don't be dropping dead just yet, Bill. Not before Saturday . . .

Why, asked Bill Shankly. What's happening on Saturday, Jim?

Well, I told the Boss you might be coming in. And if you're not doing anything, Bill. If you've got no plans. The Boss has left a ticket for the match on Saturday for you, Bill. Because the club would love you to come to Goodison. And to sit in the directors' box, Bill. You'd be very welcome. Very welcome indeed, Bill . . .

At Goodison? I'm not sure about that, Jim. They'll be throwing eggs at me. Fruit, the lot, Jim. I'll be lynched!

Jim McGregor laughed. And Jim McGregor said, Don't be daft, Bill. You'll be very welcome. More than welcome, Bill. You mark my words. You'll see, Bill . . .

. . .

That Saturday, the first Saturday of the season. Billy Bingham, the manager of Everton Football Club, was waiting for Bill Shankly at Goodison Park, Liverpool. The Everton Football Club ground. Billy Bingham shook Bill Shankly's hand. And Billy Bingham said, It's great to see you, Bill. Very good of you to come . . .

No, said Bill Shankly. No. It's good of you to invite me, Billy. Very good of you. Thank you, Billy. Thank you. I just hope I'm not disturbing you, Billy. Not intruding . . .

Billy Bingham shook his head. And Billy Bingham said, No, Bill. No. Not at all, Bill. We are all delighted you are here. It's a great honour for us, Bill. And a great pleasure. I only hope you'll see us win, Bill. That you'll be a lucky sign . . .

Well, it's a tough one for you, Billy, said Bill Shankly. Derby County always are. And for your first match of the season, Billy. Very tough indeed. But then again, a big match at the start, it can help a lot, Billy. To get the players in the right frame of mind. Out of their deckchairs and off their sofas. To get them up on their toes, Billy . . .

Billy Bingham nodded. And Billy Bingham said, You're right, Bill. You're right. And we'll certainly need to be on our toes today, Bill. And no mistake. Up and running from the off . . .

And Billy Bingham led Bill Shankly up the stairs to the directors' box. And Billy Bingham said, Now you make yourself at home, Bill. And you enjoy the game. And I'll see you after, Bill . . .

Thank you, Billy, said Bill Shankly. Thank you. And good luck to you, Billy. The very best of luck to you all . . .

And Bill Shankly shook hands again with Billy Bingham. Bill Shankly walked into the directors' box at Goodison Park, Liverpool. And Bill Shankly shook hands with the directors of Everton Football

Club. And with their other guests. In the directors' box at Goodison Park, Liverpool. Bill Shankly took his seat. And Bill Shankly looked down onto the pitch at Goodison Park. And then up and around the stands of Goodison Park. At the folk in the stands at Goodison Park. And the folk in the stands at Goodison Park saw Bill Shankly. And the folk in the stands at Goodison Park began to applaud Bill Shankly. To salute Bill Shankly. And to sing his name –

*Shank-lee, Shank-lee, Shank-lee . . .*

And in his seat. Bill Shankly could not believe his ears. The reception from the enemy. In his seat. Bill Shankly smiled. Embarrassed. In his seat. Bill Shankly raised his right hand. His fingers. The arguments finished, the battles over. In his seat. Bill Shankly tried to smile again. In thanks,

in thanks . . .

Bill Shankly watched Everton Football Club draw nil–nil with Derby County at Goodison Park, Liverpool, in the first match of the season. And then Bill Shankly shook hands with the directors of Everton Football Club and thanked them for their hospitality. And Bill Shankly shook hands with Billy Bingham and thanked him for his hospitality and for his generosity. For the invitation and for the ticket. But Billy Bingham shook his head. And Billy Bingham said, You don't have to thank me, Bill. It's always great to see you. Always a pleasure, Bill. And you're always welcome. Very welcome, Bill. And so please remember. Please remember, Bill. There's always a ticket for you at Goodison. Because you're always welcome, Bill. Always . . .

Thank you, said Bill Shankly. Thank you, Billy . . .

And Bill Shankly drove home from the game. From the match. Every Saturday of the season. Bill Shankly drove home from the games. From the matches. The games at Goodison Park or the games at Old Trafford. The matches at Deepdale or the matches at Maine Road. Every Saturday. Every Tuesday. And every Wednesday. The games at Burnden Park or Brunton Park. The matches at the Victoria Ground or the Baseball Ground. Thursday. Friday. And Monday. Every night of the week, every game there was. Every match. Bill Shankly was there. And every night, Bill Shankly would drive home. From the game, from the match. Always thinking of another game, of a different match. The game he had not been to, the match he had not seen. And every night, Bill Shankly would open the paper. Looking for the result of that game. That game he had not been to. Every night, Bill Shankly would switch on the television. Waiting for the score of that match. That match he had not seen. And every night, Bill Shankly would close the paper. Every night, Bill Shankly would switch off the television. And Bill Shankly would wait for the telephone to ring. For the invitation to come. The invitation and the ticket. To the one game he wanted to go to. The only match he wanted to see. And every night, the telephone rang. Every morning and every afternoon. The telephone ringing and ringing. With invitations and with tickets. To games and to matches. The telephone ringing and ringing. But never with the invitation he wanted to come. The invitation or the ticket. The ticket for the game he wanted to go to. The match he wanted to see –

The only match Bill Shankly wanted to see –

The telephone ringing and ringing. Bill Shankly waiting and waiting. The telephone ringing and ringing –

Bill Shankly picked up the telephone. And Bill Shankly heard Ron Yeats say, Hello, Boss. How are you, Boss? Are you well, Boss?

Oh, I'm very well, said Bill Shankly. Never better, Ron. Thank you, Ron. Thank you. But how are you, Ron? How are you? I see you've a fight on your hands, Ron. A bit of a struggle . . .

Oh yes, Boss, said Ron Yeats. A fight and a half. And that's why I'm calling, Boss. To get your advice, to pick your brains. If you don't mind, Boss. If you've the time, Boss . . .

Of course I don't mind, said Bill Shankly. I was going to call you myself, Ron. But I don't like to intrude, to be putting my nose in. If it's not needed, if I'm not wanted . . .

Well, you're wanted at Tranmere, said Ron Yeats. You're very much needed at Tranmere, Boss . . .

Then there's not a moment to lose, said Bill Shankly. Because the clock is ticking, Ron. The clock is always ticking. And so I'll see you tomorrow morning, Ron . . .

And that next morning, that very next morning. Ron Yeats, the manager of Tranmere Rovers Football Club, was waiting for Bill Shankly at Prenton Park, Birkenhead. Ron Yeats shook Bill Shankly's hand. And Ron Yeats said, It's great to see you, Boss. And very good of you to come, too. Thank you, Boss. Thank you very much . . .

No, Ron. No, said Bill Shankly. I should have come sooner, Ron. You should have called sooner. Because there's not a moment to lose, Ron. Not a minute to spare. So let's get to work, Ron . . .

And Bill Shankly trained with the players of Tranmere Rovers. Every morning. Bill Shankly watched the players of Tranmere Rovers. Every training session. And every game. Home or away. Every match. In the stands or on the bench. Bill Shankly watched and Bill Shankly listened. But Bill Shankly did not speak. Bill Shankly just watching, Bill Shankly just listening. And after some weeks, and after more defeats, Ron Yeats said, What am I doing wrong, Boss? It's almost New Year and we're bottom of the division. We're going to go down. You've got to tell me what to do, Boss. Where I'm going wrong . . .

Well, you are making one basic, fundamental error, Ron, said Bill Shankly. Where do we change before training?

Up at Bromborough, said Ron Yeats.

Bill Shankly shook his head. And Bill Shankly said, No, Ron. No. Where do we change at Liverpool?

At Anfield, said Ron Yeats.

Exactly, said Bill Shankly. We change at Anfield, Ron. And then we travel out to Melwood. We train at Melwood. And then we travel back to Anfield. We always change at Anfield. Not at Melwood, Ron. Never at Melwood. Always at Anfield, Ron. Always at Anfield. And so you should be doing the same here, Ron. You should change here at Prenton Park. And then travel out to Bromborough. Train at Bromborough. And then travel back here to Prenton Park to change. It's the only way, Ron . . .

Ron Yeats nodded. And Ron Yeats changed the morning routine at Tranmere Rovers. Every morning. The players reported to Prenton Park. The players changed at Prenton Park. Then the players travelled to Bromborough. The players trained at Bromborough. And then the players travelled back to Prenton Park. Every morning. And Tranmere Rovers began to win. Home and away. Tranmere Rovers won some games. But then Tommy Docherty heard about a young lad at Tranmere Rovers. A lad Bill Shankly couldn't stop talking about. A lad Bill Shankly couldn't stop watching. A lad Bill Shankly thought was almost as good as Tom Finney. Almost. And Manchester United bought Steve Coppell from Tranmere Rovers. And Tranmere Rovers began to lose. Home and away. Tranmere Rovers lost too many games. And at the end of the season, Tranmere Rovers finished twenty-second in the Third Division. Tranmere Rovers were relegated. Ron Yeats was sacked. And John King was appointed as manager of Tranmere Rovers. John King telephoned Bill Shankly. And John King said, I know Ron's gone now, Bill. That it didn't end well. But I want you to know you're always still welcome at Tranmere, Bill. You're always very welcome. Whenever you've the time, Bill . . .

I'll help anyone, said Bill Shankly. That is my only aim in life. To help people. Anybody I can help, I will.


## 60. THE LONG GOODBYE

In the house, in their bed. Bill had not slept. Not slept a wink. His head on the pillow. His eyes open. Bill had stared up into the darkness. Up into the silence. All night. Bill waiting, Bill waiting. For the curtain edges to grow light. For the day to arrive. The day to come. The day Bill longed for. The day Bill dreaded. In the house, in their bed. Bill waiting and Bill thinking. Thinking of all the long meetings with the committee, thinking of all the hard work by the committee. The preparation and the planning. For this day. This day Bill dreaded, this day Bill longed for. Thinking and waiting. His head on the pillow. His eyes open. Until at last, at last. The curtain edges grew light again. And the day had arrived. The day had come. At last, at last. The day Bill had longed for. The day Bill had dreaded. Longed for and dreaded, dreaded and longed for. At last, at last –

Tuesday 29 April, 1975 –

At last, at last –

Bill got out of bed. Slowly. Bill went into the bathroom. Slowly. Bill shaved and Bill washed. Slowly. Bill went back into the bedroom. Slowly. Bill put on his shirt. His tangerine shirt. Slowly. Bill went to the dressing table. Bill opened the top drawer. Bill took out his cufflinks. His gold cufflinks. Bill closed the drawer. Bill did up the cuffs of his shirt. His tangerine shirt. Slowly. Bill went to the wardrobe. Bill opened the doors. Bill took out his suit. His freshly cleaned grey herringbone suit. Bill left the wardrobe doors open.

Slowly. Bill walked over to the bed. Bill laid out the suit on top of the bed covers. Bill took the trousers from the coat hanger. Bill put on the trousers of his suit. His freshly cleaned grey herringbone suit. Slowly. Bill went back to the dressing table. Bill opened the second drawer of the dressing table. Bill took out a tie. Bill closed the drawer. Slowly. Bill walked back to the wardrobe. The doors still open. Bill stood before the mirror on the back of one of the doors. Bill put on his tie. Slowly. Bill went back over to the bed. Bill picked up the jacket from the bed. Bill took the jacket from the coat hanger. Bill put on the jacket of his suit. His freshly cleaned grey herringbone suit. Slowly. Bill walked back over to the dressing table. Bill opened the top drawer of the dressing table again. Bill took out one white handkerchief and one red pocket square. Bill closed the drawer. Bill put the white handkerchief in his left trouser pocket. Bill laid the red pocket square on the top of the dressing table. Bill brought the bottom point of the red pocket square up to the top point. Bill brought the left corner of the triangle to the right corner and then the right corner to the left corner. Bill folded the bottom almost towards the top. Slowly. Bill walked over to the mirror on the back of the wardrobe door. Bill stood before the mirror. Bill placed the red pocket square in the breast pocket of his grey jacket. Bill looked in the mirror. Bill adjusted the pocket square until just enough of the point was coming out of the pocket. The red point out of the grey pocket. Slowly. Bill stepped back. Bill looked at the man in the mirror. And Bill said, I'm just glad the day has come. The worst thing in football is waiting for the match. It's always all right when it comes. But this has been even worse for me than waiting for the Cup Final. But I feel a lot easier now that the day has arrived.

And Bill walked down the stairs. Slowly. Bill went into the kitchen. Slowly. Bill ate breakfast with Ness. Slowly. A slice of toast and honey, a glass of fresh orange juice and a cup of tea. Slowly. Bill helped Ness clear away the breakfast things. Slowly. Bill dried up the breakfast things. Slowly. Bill helped Ness put away the breakfast things. And then Bill stood in the middle of the kitchen –

You're ready early, said Ness. Very early, love?

Well, I'm just glad the day has come, love. The worst thing in football is waiting for the match. It's always all right when it comes, love. But this has been even worse than waiting for the Cup Final.

But I feel a lot easier now the day has arrived, love . . .

I know, said Ness. I know, love.

I'm just looking forward to going to Anfield to see everybody again. All the people I worked with, all the people I worked for. I'm just looking forward to seeing them all again, love.

I know, said Ness again. I know, love.

Bill nodded. Slowly. Bill looked at his watch. Bill smiled. Bill laughed. And Bill said, But you're right, love. You're right. I'm ready too early. There's still a long while yet. So I think I'll go and read the paper for a bit. That'll kill some time . . .

And Bill walked out into the hall. Slowly. Bill picked up the paper from the table in the hall. Slowly. Bill stared down at the front page of the *Liverpool Echo*. Slowly. Bill read the headline on the front page of the *Liverpool Echo*: THANKS SHANKS, ALL THE VERY BEST! Bill read the subheading: HE'S UNIQUE, SAYS PAISLEY, AND THAT SUMS IT UP . . .

And Bill walked into the front room. Slowly. Bill sat down in his chair. Slowly. In the front room, in his chair. Bill read the paper. And the tributes. Slowly. Bill put down the paper. The tributes. And in the front room, in his chair. Bill looked at his watch again. And Bill closed his eyes. Waiting and thinking. Thinking of the night ahead, waiting for the match to come. The match ahead, the night to come. The night at Anfield, the match at Anfield. His testimonial match, his testimonial night. His last night, his last match –

At Anfield, at Anfield –

Slowly. Bill came out of the darkness. Out of the tunnel. The Anfield tunnel. Slowly. Bill walked along the touchline. The Anfield touchline. Slowly. Bill walked onto the pitch. The Anfield pitch. Slowly. Bill shook the hands of the players. The players of the Don Revie Select. Peter Shilton and Gordon Banks. Roger Kenyon and Alan Ball. Alan Hudson and Colin Bell. Liam Brady and Willie Donachie. Leighton James and Steve Whitworth. Colin Todd and Billy Bremner. Terry Cooper and Bobby Charlton. Malcolm Macdonald and Mick Channon. And then Bill shook the hands of the players of Liverpool Football Club. Ray Clemence and Tommy Smith. Phil Neal and Phil Thompson. Peter Cormack and Emlyn Hughes. Kevin Keegan and Brian Hall. John Toshack and Ray Kennedy. Ian Callaghan and

Steve Heighway. And then Bill walked back across the pitch. The Anfield pitch. Slowly. Bill walked back along the touchline. The Anfield touchline. And slowly. Bill sat down on the bench –

The Anfield bench. For the last time,

the very last time.

After the whistle. The final whistle. Bill stood up. Slowly. Bill got to his feet. Slowly. Bill walked down the touchline. The Anfield touchline. Slowly. Bill shook hands with Don Revie. And Bill embraced Don. Bill shook hands with Bob Paisley. And Bill embraced Bob. And then slowly. Bill walked out onto the pitch. The Anfield pitch. Slowly. Bill shook hands with the players again. The players of the Don Revie Select. And the players of Liverpool Football Club. And then Bill walked towards the centre of the pitch. The Anfield pitch. Slowly. Bill reached the centre circle. The centre circle of the Anfield pitch. And Bill stood in the centre circle. In the centre circle of the Anfield pitch. And someone handed Bill a microphone. So Bill could speak to the crowd. The Anfield crowd. And Bill said, The very word Anfield means more to me than I can describe. But there has always been pride at Anfield. And this is another night of pride. A night of great pride. The pride I have for Liverpool. The football club and the city. And the pride you the supporters have in the team. Your team. That is the way it is at Anfield. The way it is at Liverpool. And I hope it will always be so. And so to my successor and past colleague Bob Paisley, and all the players, I offer my very best wishes for the future.

But the greatest honour that could have been bestowed upon me has been the staging of this match tonight. And so I'd like to thank everybody connected with it. Bob and his board of directors. Don Revie and the players of both sides. All of whom I know personally. I'd like to also thank the testimonial committee, club secretary Peter Robinson and development manager Ken Addison for all their hard work and efficiency. But most of all I want to thank you all –

Thank you all for contributing so much to making this what is, quite simply, the greatest thing that has happened to me in all my life. It means the most that you all still came to support me after I had been away from you for months. And so I thank you all for your loyalty. And for your loyalty to me during all my years at Liverpool. The greatest part of my whole life. No man could ever have more friends than me. No man can ever feel more grateful –

And no man can ever feel more proud. I am a proud man from my head to my toes. This means more to me than anything else. God bless you, God bless you all . . .

And Bill handed back the microphone. Slowly. Bill walked back towards the edge of the pitch. The Anfield pitch. Slowly. Bill walked around the stadium. The Anfield stadium. Over forty thousand folk had come to watch the testimonial for Gerry Byrne. Fifty-five thousand to watch the testimonial for Roger Hunt. There were not fifty-five thousand folk here tonight. Not even forty thousand. There were empty seats in the stands. The Anfield stands. But Bill did not see the empty seats in the stands. The Anfield stands. Bill had eyes only for the Kop. The Spion Kop. There were no empty spaces on the Kop. The Spion Kop. The Kop full, the Spion Kop heaving. The Kop chanting, the Spion Kop singing, *Shank-lee, Shank-lee, Shank-lee . . .*

*Shank-lee, Shank-lee, Shank-lee . . .*

*Shankly is Our King . . .*

Before the Kop. The Spion Kop. His head bowed. His eyes closed. Bill fought back tears. Bill struggled to breathe.

*And you'll always be our king, you'll always be our king. You'll al-ways be our king . . .*

*OUR KING!*

Before the Kop. The Spion Kop. In a dream. His head bowed. His eyes closed. In a dream. Bill could not fight back the tears. Bill could not breathe. And slowly. Bill turned away. In a dream. From the applause and from the affection. Slowly. Bill began to walk back towards the tunnel. But in a dream, in this dream. The Kop would not let Bill go. The Spion Kop would not let Bill leave. In a dream. Some of the supporters climbed out of the Kop. The Spion Kop. To shake Bill's hand, to hold Bill tight. Draping Bill in scarves, garlanding Bill in scarves. Liverpool scarves, red scarves. In this dream. Three men dressed in white overalls, white overalls with red lettering, these three men gave Bill a plaque. A plaque entitled *The Road to Glory.* A complete record of Bill's years at Anfield. A plaque on behalf of the Kop. The Spion Kop. In a dream. Another supporter handed Bill a silver tankard. A silver tankard engraved *To Shanks, With thanks, A fan.* In this dream. A young supporter presented Bill with a card. Two feet square. With a thousand signatures. All in red, all in red. From the Kop. The Spion Kop. And in a dream, in this dream. Bill heard the applause, Bill felt the affection. Down from the stands, down from the terraces. In a dream, in this dream. Bill did not want to wake up. From this dream. Bill never wanted to wake up. From this dream,

from this life. Bill never wanted to leave.

Bill never wanted to say goodbye.


## 61. I AM A CHRISTIAN AND A SOCIALIST, DESPITE YOU

Ringing. The bottle on the doorstep. Ringing. The paper through the letterbox. Ringing. The letters on the mat. Ringing. The knocking on the door. Ringing. The telephone never stopped ringing. With invitations and with offers. With offers and with requests. The invitation to come here, the invitation to go there. The offer to do this, the offer to do that. That request and this request. Bill Shankly tried to answer them all. Bill Shankly wanted to answer them all. Bill Shankly tried to accommodate them all. Bill Shankly wanted to accommodate them all. Bill Shankly wanted to keep busy. Bill Shankly tried to keep busy. To visit this hospital, to speak at that dinner. And to host a weekly radio show on Radio City. Bill Shankly wanted to do it, Bill Shankly was happy to do it. If people wanted him to do it, if people were happy for him to do it. That was all Bill Shankly wanted. To give the people what they wanted, to make the people happy –

But the people were not happy,

the people were depressed,

depressed and angry –

The people were demonstrating outside the Radio City building. The people were protesting against Harold Wilson and his Labour government. But inside the building. Inside the studio. In the dark and in the silence. Harold Wilson looked across the table at Bill Shankly. Harold Wilson nodded, Harold Wilson smiled. And Harold Wilson said, I was very glad when I heard you were going to do this and you wrote to me, and I wrote, almost by return of post, I think.

Yes, said Bill Shankly. It was a tremendously quick reply. The leading statesman in the land. In fact, the prime minister of Great

Britain. I mean, for you to find time to come here is unbelievable. I mean, I thought that as a football manager I had a hard job . . .

Harold Wilson laughed.

But I can tell you one thing. Whereas I had to look after fifty-five thousand, you've to look after fifty-five million!

Yes, but it's a very similar job, you know? You know what they said about me? When I formed the Cabinet the first time? Hardly anyone had ever sat in a Cabinet before. We'd been out of office for thirteen years. And it was said, I used to say it myself, that I'd take the penalties, I acted as goalkeeper, I went and took the corner kicks, dashed down the wing. Now I've got a very experienced Cabinet and I said, I'm not going to do that. They didn't believe me. I said, I'm going to be what we used to call a deep-lying centre-half. I couldn't say sweeper because nobody would understand it outside football.

No, laughed Bill Shankly. No, no.

A lot of kind of people don't understand football, wouldn't know. And then, I think it was the *Liverpool Post* said, Funny, he's doing more than that. They said, In fact, he's being a manager. He's not even on the field. To which I said, I was very proud, from Liverpool, to refer to 'the Manager', which means Bill Shankly territory. I said this in a speech, I regard it as a compliment. But I went on to say this: where does the manager usually sit? On the substitutes' bench. I was reminding my team that I've got people on the substitutes' bench who think they are at least as good as anybody on the field. And I think that's the similarity of a prime minister's job and a football manager's job.

Yes, said Bill Shankly. In other words, you delegated the right men for the right job?

Right. But not only that. Like a manager's job, if your team gets relegated, as mine did in 1970, then some people start saying they want a change.

That's correct, said Bill Shankly. Yes. But you have proven, and I hope that you will keep proving, that you are the man.

I've been there nearly as long as you were in Liverpool.

In politics longer than that, said Bill Shankly. Than at Liverpool, anyway. Er, Mrs Wilson writes poetry?

Harold Wilson said, Yeah, yeah.

This is true?

Harold Wilson nodded. And Harold Wilson said, She does. She always has, since she was a girl. And then, a few years ago, she was asked to put some in a book, and I think, according to her publisher, it's the biggest sale of any book of poetry since the war.

Is that a fact, asked Bill Shankly.

Well, it's all genuine stuff that she still believes in. She writes about human things. She wrote about Aberfan. She was so moved by the Aberfan disaster, when all those schoolchildren were killed. I flew down that night. She came soon after. And she also writes about things like the Durham Miners' Gala . . .

Yes, oh yes.

And at Durham this year, she read them both out.

Authentic, said Bill Shankly.

Yes, that's right. That she feels.

I mean, actually, said Bill Shankly, I was born in the same county as Scotland's greatest poet, Robert Burns . . .

Harold Wilson said, Ah yes.

Who was not only a poet. A philosopher, a prophet. Everything. You name it. I think that if he had have lived until he was as old as Shakespeare and Wordsworth and them, I think that he would possibly have been in the First Division and they would have been in the Second Division.

Harold Wilson shook his head. And Harold Wilson said, I think, well, he is in the First Division, isn't he?

Yes, said Bill Shankly. Yes.

And I know his poetry less than my wife does. Though I've never known it, when I've been speaking in Scotland, that somebody on the platform hasn't quoted something. Either something familiar or something I didn't know. The Secretary of State for Scotland, who is a great Burns Night speaker, he can recite yards of it at a time. Most Scotsmen can, I think . . .

He, said Bill Shankly, in actual fact, was one of the early people on socialism . . .

Harold Wilson said, He was really, yes.

Possibly the first one was Jesus Christ, of course, said Bill Shankly. But after that, Burns was a real socialist. And one of the instigators of socialism, I think. Of course, he was a great character as well, Robert Burns.

Harold Wilson nodded again. And Harold Wilson said, Yes, he was. I haven't read as much about him as I should. But as a socialist, if one uses this phrase, and he was an early one as you say, it was because he felt it. It was because he loved his fellow men . . .

Yes, said Bill Shankly. Yes.

But he was not a theoretical socialist . . .

No, said Bill Shankly. No.

I don't think he'd understand anything about the theory of value or any of the scientific socialist writing that I don't bother much with myself, either . . .

No.

But he just felt a love of his fellow human beings and he wanted to see their lot improved.

That sums him up, said Bill Shankly. He was born in poverty. And he died in poverty.

Harold Wilson nodded. And Harold Wilson said, And he didn't believe that the Lord created people to be unequal. That he created one set of people designed to rule the earth and others, you know, to just be the hewers of wood and drawers of water.

His books have been translated for the whole of Russia, said Bill Shankly. Most countries in the world, in fact. But Russia more than anybody, I think.

I've found that. I've been in Russia many times and they really, I think, worship the ground he walks on. I think he's been translated into about one hundred and sixty Russian languages. And I remember, many years ago, they brought out a special postage stamp in his honour. Before it was thought of being done in Britain.

They did, said Bill Shankly. They did. For his anniversary.

That's right.

He was a well-known man for the women, of course?

Harold Wilson said, Yes. I think he got around a little bit . . .

Bill Shankly laughed.

And I think if he'd been in one of your football teams, you'd have been onto him about the hours he kept.

Yes, said Bill Shankly. I think I'd have had somebody, a

detective, watching where he went at night-time.

Harold Wilson said, I think, if he had lived today, he might be in the Scottish football team. Better not say that . . .

Well, it's a well-known fact, said Bill Shankly, that in his day, if a man committed fornication, he was reported to the local minister. And the minister sent for the man and he sat him in front of the congregation in a seat called the cutty stool. And he humiliated him in front of all the congregation. This was a well-known thing. Now it would appear that Burns was so often there that he had a season ticket.

Harold Wilson nodded again. And Harold Wilson said, Yes. It's what you call a sin bin in football.

That's correct, said Bill Shankly. Burns was in the sin bin. But, nevertheless, a fantastic man. Er, Huddersfield, Mr Wilson?

I was born there . . .

Yes, yes.

I was at school there until I was sixteen. And then I came to Merseyside . . .

Your background in Huddersfield, which I know well, of course. I was there five years.

Well, I know, yes. You were manager there.

And I used to play up at Oaks, said Bill Shankly. At the top of the hill there. And at the back of the field we started playing five-a-side football. On a Sunday afternoon. And it started off about five-a-side, then when it finished up there was about fifteen-a-side.

Harold Wilson nodded. And Harold Wilson said, My grandfather and grandmother were married at Oaks. Oaks Chapel. I was there until I was sixteen. Of course, I played football, but was never good enough. I used to go to watch Huddersfield Town every week. I played a bit of rugby league. But not professionally, of course. Then I came to Merseyside because my father lost his job, got another job on the Wirral, and I went to Wirral Grammar School, Wirral County School as it then was, and where I had to play rugby union. And I came to like that as well. But a lot of my formative career was spent on Merseyside as well as in Yorkshire.

Well, I think that, you mention rugby? I think it's a very good thing for character. I think that the rugby boys are good boys.

Harold Wilson laughed. And Harold Wilson said, Well, soccer

is, too. It's a good thing for character. And bad character sometimes.

I think that rugby union, said Bill Shankly, I mean, at school, I think it's a good thing for boys.

Yes. Well, I played it for two years. I was captain of the school team and a future England international was in the team when we played our first match and got beaten seventy-four–nil . . .

Bill Shankly laughed.

Well, it wasn't bad. We were thirty-seven–nil at half-time and we didn't deteriorate.

Who were you playing for, asked Bill Shankly. Everton?

No, we were playing for our school. You see, it was a young school. A new school. Only a year old. I was the only boy in the sixth form. And we asked one of the neighbouring schools to give us their fourth team. And they were suspicious. So they gave us their second team and they overwhelmed us.

Ah, yes. That was a form of cheating, wasn't it, said Bill Shankly. And Bill Shankly looked down at his clipboard –

Er, it's down here that you went to the Wirral Grammar School, and that was strictly rugby, was it?

Harold Wilson nodded. And Harold Wilson said, Strictly rugby. Well, at one point, the then headmaster, who was an excellent man, got worried that the boys had got nothing to do at lunchtime. So, as school captain, I said I would organise some healthy sports. And we played football every lunchtime. After lunch. Soccer. And I rather enjoyed playing soccer with ten-foot posts.

Aye, laughed Bill Shankly again. I bet you did. Because you had every chance of scoring a goal!

Harold Wilson laughed. And Harold Wilson said, Get the long shots in, yes. Well, I also did a lot of running. I ran for the Wirral Athletic Club. I got their youth championship. And then I ran in the Liverpool and District and we got the bronze, my team.

You were cross-country champion of Merseyside schools?

Harold Wilson shook his head. And Harold Wilson said, No, just the Wirral. I ran all sorts of other sports there. I once ran in the Northern Counties Athletic Championship, behind the man who set the record that year and was the English captain. And I got a good back view of him when we set off.

This cross-country, Mr Wilson? This is really a soul-destroying job, isn't it?

I'd never done much. I was short- and middle-distance. And then I went out to train at our cross-country headquarters and they asked me to run in the championship because they had a good runner who they, you know, wanted to give a chance. And somebody hadn't turned up. And I just stuck to him and beat him barefoot.

But this all leads up to the fact that you are prime minister of Great Britain. And you've played football, you've played rugby. You were cross-country champion. Now, I've run all distances . . .

Harold Wilson nodded. And Harold Wilson said, So have I, really. I could never decide what my distance was.

But the cross-country one is really soul-destroying?

Well, it is. And if you get a bit of a stitch. Or have the wrong thing to eat or drink beforehand . . .

You don't want to give in, said Bill Shankly. Do you?

No, no. You don't . . .

You want to go on until you die, said Bill Shankly.

Well, actually, that's good for politics. I remember when I was up and coming, really, one of the greatest journalists, now dead, said, Watch this man. He's a long-distance runner . . .

Yes, said Bill Shankly. Yes!

A long-distance runner who gets there in the end . . .

Yes, said Bill Shankly again. That's what I said at the beginning of the football season . . .

And keeps on running.

When they said, Who is going to win the League? I said, Listen. This is a marathon. This isn't a short sprint.

Harold Wilson said, It's very tight at the moment between the top ones. I heard you, actually, last season. Oh, I should think ten or a dozen matches before the end, saying Derby County were going to win. I heard you on the radio say that.

Well, I had seen all the teams then, Mr Wilson.

You were quite positive about it. And it was a near thing. But you were right. You were right.

Well, I think that they only used the bits they wanted to use.

Harold Wilson asked, Did they?

In actual fact, my first bet was Liverpool. And Derby County was my saving bet. And they edited it so that I was Derby County.

Harold Wilson smiled. And Harold Wilson said, Oh, I gave you credit for it then, you see.

Well, I did back Derby County. I had seen Derby at Liverpool. I'd seen all the teams. And I felt that Derby had enough class.

Harold Wilson nodded. And Harold Wilson said, Your Liverpool team was one of the greatest I've ever seen.

Oh yes . . .

It still is, of course.

Oh yes, said Bill Shankly again. Yes, yes. They've got character. And they are never beaten. They last the game. The game that we did play, it was geared to bring everybody into the game. And simplify it. Consequently, you didn't have more to do than me, if you were on the same team . . .

Harold Wilson nodded again. And Harold Wilson said, Yes, I know. Well, my theory about this is the same with politics. I often use the analogy. In fact, people say I get boring . . .

No, said Bill Shankly. No.

. . . the way I use analogies in the House of Commons. But it helps you understand it. So I always say, No team is going to win the Cup or the League unless it's got good reserves.

Yes, said Bill Shankly. Yes.

And I've paid as much attention to building up my reserves. As I say, after being out of office for thirteen years, I reckon that if my first team got under a bus, my second team could take over. And my third team shows in some ways more promise than any of them.

Yes, said Bill Shankly. This is true. This is true.

And you've got to give them responsibility young.

Exactly, said Bill Shankly. And if I had a well-known player, unable to play through injury, which would be a terrible blow. Some teams, if they lose a key player, that's them gone, you know? And the pessimistic will let that get them down. But when I had a key player injured, I used to say to the boy apprentice, Now listen, son. You're a better player than him. You see? And have a little bit of psychology.

Harold Wilson nodded. And Harold Wilson said, But I don't have the problem of temporary substitution. I have the problem of taking people off the substitutes' bench, like you do. I mean, for a very long time, you had five or six world-class forwards . . .

Oh, we did, said Bill Shankly.

And your problem was who to leave out.

We did.

Harold Wilson said, And they were always disappointed, whichever one was left out.

But our football was a form of socialism, said Bill Shankly.

Well, I think you know, you have the great advantage here – and it's true of certain other parts of the country – of tremendous schools' football. I mean, how often have my own constituents' boys gone on to the national championships, schoolboy championships, different parts of the constituency, different parts of Merseyside – and I've seen those kids playing and you'll find that kids of about ten or twelve are getting watched by the scouts.

Well, I've seen a few eleven-year-olds and twelve-year-olds recently. And there's a few of them can play, I can tell you.

Harold Wilson nodded. And Harold Wilson said, Yes, well they're born with it, they've got the gift, as long as they work at it.

They've got it, said Bill Shankly. And if they've got the ability, then a breakthrough is going to come out. And I've got my eyes on them, you know? So this is the thing. Er, back to the running. The grit that you showed in your cross-country. This is your character. And this is why you rose to be prime minister.

Harold Wilson nodded again. And Harold Wilson said, Well, you talk about Robbie Burns. But one of my favourite songs is from Harry Lauder. *Keep Right on to the End of the Road*.

Oh yes, said Bill Shankly. Yes.

If you've got a problem to solve, you've got to keep at it. You've just got to keep at it. And with us – again I'll take your football analogy – in politics timing is everything. People will nag you. Why haven't you done it? Why don't you get on with it?

Yes, said Bill Shankly again. Yes.

I was nagged all the summer about the anti-inflation policy. I knew what I wanted. And I was confident I'd get it. But it had to be the right time. So I had to get kicked in the teeth and everything else. Because I seemed to be complacent and lazy. But there's a time. And you know when that time is, you know when's the time to hit that ball. And it's the same thing . . .

And only you know that, said Bill Shankly. Only you.

Harold Wilson nodded. And Harold Wilson said, And only you know that. If you're a professional. And if you're not, you'd better make way for somebody else.

And only the manager knows of a football club, said Bill Shankly. What he's got to do. And when to do it. This is the thing.

Exactly. And how he's going to shape them . . .

And the man who's willing, said Bill Shankly, he takes the stick if it goes wrong.

And how you've got to bring this man on, and perhaps disappoint another, sometimes breaks his heart.

And he's not going to be told by somebody else when to bring him on, said Bill Shankly. He brings him in. The same as you bring your men in at the right time. And you make your statements at the right time. As you say, it's all timing.

And football managers. Politicians. Get it wrong sometimes . . .

Oh yes, said Bill Shankly. It's the simplest thing in the world.

And don't we hear about it?

Well, said Bill Shankly. It's a loud bang when a football manager does something wrong. But when you make a larger boob, with you then it's a bigger bang, of course.

Mind you, we have the right to answer back. In Parliament.

Sure, said Bill Shankly. Sure, sure.

Harold Wilson sat up in his seat. And Harold Wilson said, Our parliament, I think, is the greatest thing in the world. The Americans have got nothing like it. Nothing like it. And I don't know a lot about the Continentals. But it is democracy. The minister, whatever he's done, he's got to answer for it, to a pretty hungry crowd of experts. People who are out to either get him down or support him. And you can't touch it, you can't dodge the responsibility . . .

No, no.

If you've made a mistake, say so. And I've always had Question Time. And I was once told Macmillan, who was one of the greatest prime ministers – I didn't agree with him on a lot of things, nor he with me, but I respected him – and I was told that he used to be almost physically sick before questions, twice a week. I know how he felt. And when a prime minister isn't worried about questions, then democracy is in danger. But I've suddenly changed my psychology. I used to think of it like cricket, you know? If you are supposed to be a top-class batsman, they mustn't take your wicket. And it makes you a bit defensive, you know?

Yes, yes.

And I suddenly said, a fortnight ago, I've got it all wrong. I want to treat questions like football now. If they want to score a goal, let them score a goal, I'll go out and try and score two. And it's slightly changed my attitude. And it's also making the Question Time more exciting.

And you think this is advantageous?

Harold Wilson nodded. And Harold Wilson said, I think, if you think in sporting analogies, it helps you in other walks of life. You have a problem I don't have in the same way. But the jobs are similar in many ways. I went into the dressing room after a Huddersfield match. Huddersfield had won. They had played very well. So had the others, too. And I saw the manager talking to them. Although they'd won and he said they played marvellously, but he said, That marking was wrong. He said, Those little ones, you should mark the little ones. And let the big ones mark the big ones. I've often wondered what was said in dressing rooms. It was the first time I'd ever been in one. And I was in the Scottish one just after Frankfurt, you know?

Yes, said Bill Shankly. Ah yes.

In the World Cup. I went to see them when . . . well, I hoped they were going to pile up all the goals they needed, and they didn't. But it must be hard when your team has done badly and they know it, and you know it, to know exactly what to say to them.

Oh, it's a terrible feeling, said Bill Shankly. I mean, you know what it's like in politics if something goes wrong? I mean, it's a terrible feeling if you've had a bad day and you've got beaten.

Harold Wilson nodded again. And Harold Wilson said, And the first minute when you go in there, what do you say?

Oh, the first minute after it, said Bill Shankly. I mean, you may have something to say . . .

You can't chew them up too badly. Or you'll break their hearts.

No, no, said Bill Shankly. No. It's all psychology. I mean, what you have got to do is, you've got to know your Cabinet. You know all of these men in your Cabinet. You know their strengths and their weaknesses. I have got to know all these players. And I deal with them the way I think. One needs to be spoken to strongly, one needs a little handling. You know all your Cabinet and I know all my players.

You know what they'll take . . .

You know what is best for them, said Bill Shankly.

I think another thing with your job and mine. You've got certain people. Some are very, very good at this particular thing or that particular thing. And so I sometimes alter the system of government, the machinery of government, to make sure that a flyer of this particular kind can really develop on that side, so to speak, just as if you've got – well, let's not talk about any local footballers – but we were chatting the other night about Ray Wilson, who went from Huddersfield to Everton. Now if you've got a Ray Wilson there, you will develop, I guess, a particular style of play and tactics to make the greatest use of him . . .

Great, said Bill Shankly. Great.

If you've got somebody like Leighton James of Burnley – who, I think, he's a real, good old-fashioned winger of the kind I was brought up to respect and admire and cheer – then, in his case, I can imagine Burnley would build their tactics round a man like that, whereas, if they didn't get him, they'd be doing different tactics.

Mr Wilson, laughed Bill Shankly, you're going to be a manager of a football team soon . . .

Harold Wilson shook his head. And Harold Wilson said, I don't think I'd do it very well.

Because your tactics are right!

I'd rather be an amateur watcher of it.

But you played yourself at what level, Mr Wilson?

Oh, I was a goalkeeper in Huddersfield. I was a goalkeeper. I wasn't very good. I had a year off then because I had typhoid fever. And they didn't have the cures for it that they have these days. And then I went onto the wing. But shortly afterwards, as I say, I went to a rugby school. And the only thing I could do was run fast. And if I got the ball, I'd make for the goal line. Sometimes successfully . . .

Well, said Bill Shankly. I mean, there's another piece of your character coming out. Cross-country, the typhoid . . .

Harold Wilson nodded. And Harold Wilson said, I was camping at a Boy Scouts' camp. We had a local one, you know? We lived in the kind of textile valley. And it was up on the moors. We had an arrangement with the farmer who owned it. And I bought some milk from a local farmer, a milkman, who turned out to be a typhoid carrier. Twelve people got it. Six of them died. And I nearly did. And I lost nearly a year of my school.

You didn't die, said Bill Shankly. You didn't nearly die at all. Because you didn't. Because you weren't going to die . . .

Well, I didn't know how bad I was, actually.

No, said Bill Shankly. No, no.

They had to starve you out, you see, for many months. But I had a wonderful schoolmaster, a maths master. He never had a degree. And he was always in a bit of trouble. And he was a great socialist. I owe more to him than to almost anybody, in this way. And he was the maths master. I missed so much maths, over two terms. He said, If you are prepared to stay an hour a day after school, I am. And he said, I'll bring you up to date. And it was the happiest day, I think, he ever had in my time. And he was in tears when he told them that I'd finished third in the form in the maths exam . . .

That's fantastic, said Bill Shankly. Fantastic.

And I'll always owe that to him.

So the fact that the typhoid retarded you . . . I mean, you gained again. You were behind in the marathon and you made it up.

Harold Wilson nodded again. And Harold Wilson said, It was a challenge. And there were a lot of young masters at Wirral School. It was a new school. Apart from the head, there was nobody over thirty. And there was a wonderful chap taught classics. And he was a very good rugby player and cricketer. Played for Leicestershire seconds. And he was an example. He was killed at the age of twenty-seven, just only been appointed headmaster. Killed in the Lake District, climbing. Or walking, really. But he made an impression on everybody.

You see, said Bill Shankly, if you look at all the men, such as you, who have reached the peak of your careers . . . I mean, they all had setbacks, Mr Wilson . . .

Setbacks?

Without setbacks, you don't know what trouble is, do you? You don't know how to fight back!

Harold Wilson laughed. And Harold Wilson said, I had mine when I was relegated in 1970. You know, when we lost the election. And many people thought we were going to win. I wasn't so sure. And I had to set out and build it all up again. Keep the team together first, keep the team together. Don't let them get disheartened.

That's the thing, said Bill Shankly.

But that was a harder task, getting back, than actually running the government before. It's harder to be leader of a big national party in opposition than when you've got the responsibility of government.

So you say to me, How does it feel when you get beat in a big match? I mean, how does it feel when you lose the election?

Harold Wilson said, When you get relegated, yes.

But, in actual fact, vote-wise, I mean, there's more socialists than there are anybody else. But still you lose the election?

There's a lot of estimates . . .

I mean, how come, Mr Wilson, that a man can vote one way then change his mind?

Harold Wilson shrugged. Harold Wilson smiled. And Harold Wilson said, But they do. And sometimes they vote for personalities as well as policies. I read somewhere that, basically, people are committed Labour people, more than Conservatives. And of course, more young people are coming on that way. But they change from time to time. They get fed up with the government, like supporters get fed up with a team. And I think that's what's happened. I'll tell you, though, I was listening to the World Cup that Sunday night. The Sunday before. And we were winning two–nil, with about twenty minutes to go. And when I heard we lost three–two, I thought there'd be an effect. And I did hear there were a lot of voters saying, Oh, I can't stand anything after this. You know, it affected them. I think it had some effect on the election. Not decisive, of course.

In Mexico?

In Mexico, yes. And I think the mistake was to take Charlton off. That was the signal to the Germans. All they had to do was pile into the attack. As long as Bobby was there, they had got to cover their own goal and they weren't going to get the equaliser or the winning goal. But that's a matter of opinion.

Well, you see. That's, again, the same. Me, who was manager at one time. You, as prime minister. You've to make that decision. Now the manager made it and things went wrong. Now if he hadn't have taken Charlton off, they may have lost just the same.

May have lost the same, yes.

So he, in his wisdom, thought he was right. So you would have did the same thing, and so would I.

Maybe, maybe. Well, you've got to follow your judgement.

Sure you have, said Bill Shankly. If you can't make decisions, you're nothing. Nothing . . .

Well, you've got to take decisions that'll get attacked, misrepresented, sometimes praised. Sometimes you make a big mistake and you don't get attacked for it. They may not know it. May not see it. But you know you've made the mistake. And then you are lucky if other people don't find it out . . .

They don't know about it, said Bill Shankly. Because it's only you that knows it.

Harold Wilson smiled again. And Harold Wilson said, They are looking at a different part of the field.

Yes, yes, said Bill Shankly. Er, you've been thirty-five years on the Merseyside?

Harold Wilson sat back in his seat. Harold Wilson nodded again. And Harold Wilson said, I came here, yes, in 1932, to live here and go to school. Then I was elected for Ormskirk in 1940, which included a lot of Liverpool, thirty-seven thousand people within the Liverpool boundary, in West Derby, Dovecot and Croxteth. And then there was boundary changes. And I went to the new division of Huyton, still keeping Kirby. And now, of course, Huyton has lost Kirby. And all the time, it's been growing. Kirby's an entirely different place. It was a little farm village when I first represented it.

A big place now, said Bill Shankly. Been there many times.

Harold Wilson said, Yes. Big place now.

So that's a long time, said Bill Shankly. I mean, to be in the same place. Now, I mean, I know that everything is difficult in politics, Mr Wilson. Everything is difficult. I mean, you are the leader of the country. And not long ago, er, we went into the Common Market. I don't know anything really about the Common Market. Candidly, my whole life's been football. And I'm not exactly ignorant about other facts, of course. I mean, everyday life. But the Common Market? Er, you took us into the Common Market?

Harold Wilson shook his head. And Harold Wilson said, Well, it'd been going on since 1962. And we always said, It's good for us, if we're not going to be crippled by it, and if it doesn't break up the Commonwealth. And this is what the Labour Party said in opposition then. And when we were in government, we applied. And De Gaulle vetoed it, as he'd vetoed Harold Macmillan. Then the Conservatives took us in, Mr Heath, but I didn't think he had the country behind him. We said we would negotiate. And if we didn't get the right terms, we would recommend coming out. Then we had a referendum and the country decisively voted. Now nobody is in any doubt. We are a democratic country. People who fought hard against what I was saying in the referendum have loyally accepted it. I think that's the kind of country that we are. And we've got big problems to solve. We've got to strengthen our own economy to make us better partners as well as to survive and prosper there. And I have some criticisms of other European countries. But mainly their football style again. Back to football. Back to football again . . .

Yes, said Bill Shankly. Well, I mean, I think, whether we are in the Common Market or not, I think we've still got to work hard. So it wouldn't make any difference really.

Harold Wilson sat forward in his seat again. And Harold Wilson said, There is an argument for being in, an argument for being out. But on balance I came out strongly, in the end, for staying in. But it's a big league is this one. You can't go in as cripples. And you've got to build up your economic strength. I mean, people who say we're done for, they're totally wrong. There's more ingenuity and hard work, possibly, in this country than people realise. And we're showing it in our exports now, how well we're doing in a world of depression. But we've got to pull to our full strength or we can be a drag.

Mr Wilson, said Bill Shankly, ever since I can remember, there's been rumours that we were finished . . .

Yeah, yeah.

And pessimism. I mean, there's always a shortage of optimism and people willing to get their jackets off. But, I mean, I was born and brought up in the pits. I was in the pit when I was fourteen.

Which coalfield were you brought up in?

I was in the Ayrshire coalfield.

Yes, I used to know them very well. Very well. I used to know every miners' leader in Ayrshire, when I was younger.

Well, said Bill Shankly, we were in William Beard and Company, as they were then . . .

Harold Wilson said, Beard and Dolmillington.

It was. Beard and Dolmillington.

The managing director, I seem to remember, I'm going back thirty years, was called A. K. McKosh.

That's him, said Bill Shankly. Well, I was in that area. So that, even then, I mean, there was nothing but pessimism. Because it was a mining area. And if there was no pit. And you couldn't play football. You were out. You had no job.

Well, you know, we are developing new sources of coal mining in Scotland, areas that were nearly closed. We're putting in a lot of money now, to develop new seams, because there's new methods now, for mining . . .

Well, said Bill Shankly, this area where I am really was only scratched. And I think it's a full coalfield. Well, I didn't think that they should have shut down . . .

We're going out to sea. The North Sea has got coal as well as oil. And there are new ways of getting them.

Under the sea at Fife and all.

Harold Wilson nodded again. And Harold Wilson said, I know. I like going to coal-mining areas. I like getting out of London. I've got nothing against London, some wonderful people there. But if you're going to have any job to do with politics or running this country, you've got to get out and meet people where they are. Not just in London. I'm not worried about demonstrators. I don't worry about them. This afternoon I was surprised, even in Liverpool, where I've been, you know, a couple of times a month, there would be crowds outside. They weren't demonstrating either, when I was opening a community health centre. But I like to be out of London on a Friday and go around the country and meet people. Meet real people. Get away from the hot-house atmosphere of politics.

As you say, said Bill Shankly, I think the Houses of Commons is a hothouse. I mean, being in it all week. I mean, it must be a tremendous feeling to get out of it and get away?

Yes. It's a great job to do. But everybody who's there will do it better if they refresh themselves. As so many do, going to their constituencies, or going, as I've got to do, all over the country.

Yes, said Bill Shankly. You can be too close to it too long. You can't see the wood for the trees.

That's right. You need a breath of fresh air.

Especially if you come to Liverpool, said Bill Shankly.

Harold Wilson laughed. And Harold Wilson said, Fresh air in every way. I've been here three times in the last month. And I shall be coming up five times in the next couple of months . . .

Yeah, well, said Bill Shankly. And then, of course, there is two good teams here, too.

Yes, I once paid you that tribute at a football dinner. I said you were the fairest-minded man I've ever met when you said there were two good teams in football, in Merseyside.

Bill Shankly laughed.

No, I did say, if you remember, I criticised you a bit for that, for not mentioning Tranmere Rovers . . .

Yeah, laughed Bill Shankly again. Yeah.

You then agreed with me. And you did a lot to help Tranmere Rovers from Liverpool.

I did last season, said Bill Shankly. For a little while, yes.

Before that, though. When you were manager. I mean, there was the goalkeeper . . .

Oh yes, said Bill Shankly. Tommy Lawrence. We gave them some money and some players. We've done quite a bit. Mind you, we were trying to help ourselves as well.

That makes sense, doesn't it? Bread cast on the waters . . .

But we did try to help them, said Bill Shankly. There is no doubt about that. And we've helped many people. And if you can't help people, then it's a bad day.

Yes, you are helping yourself but finding honourable work for someone who was reaching the end of his First Division career. And, at the same time, helping to develop some young lads.

Yes, said Bill Shankly. Yes. Er, I've been playing, I have played football all my life. And I've been in the game forty-three years now. And I try to keep fit. I mean, I've got an easier task than you, of course. But you now tell me you've lost a lot of weight? And I think you have. You look well . . .

Harold Wilson nodded. And Harold Wilson said, I have lost about a stone in weight.

So how do you keep fit then, asked Bill Shankly.

Not in the ways I would like to. I would like a lot more exercise. When I was at Downing Street before, I used to play golf every weekend when I could, you know, and so I played a bit of golf. And then I got a gammy knee a couple of years ago. And now I've taken it up again this year. My problem is there's so much, things are moving at such a pace all the time, internationally and nationally, that I haven't had the exercise. I take the dog for a walk. He likes that. But I haven't had time to play golf since I came back from my holidays.

So, said Bill Shankly, in actual fact . . .

The answer is not enough!

Mr Wilson, said Bill Shankly, not enough. But I think that possibly dieting, if you're not getting too much exercise, would . . .

Harold Wilson leant forward. And Harold Wilson said, The real truth is, you know, it's not dieting. Although the doctor thought I was mad, I started drinking a lot of beer. I like it . . .

Yes, yes.

It makes me eat less. Now I think I am a bad guinea pig, because most people put weight on with beer . . .

They do, said Bill Shankly. They do.

But it works for me.

Well, said Bill Shankly, if you drink more beer and you eat less, then, I mean, and you are losing weight, then it must be working. Because you look fit now. And you must have shed a few pounds.

Harold Wilson nodded again. And Harold Wilson said, I'm much thinner. I'm lower now than I have been for fifteen years.

And is it possible that you could get a routine, said Bill Shankly. That you could go and have a walk? Two or three miles?

Harold Wilson shook his head. And Harold Wilson said, I can't get the time. But that dog is always waiting, if I get a chance of an hour. And he's now found the way to the local pub from Chequers.

That's your dog, Paddy?

My dog Paddy, yes. A great, big, soft, daft Labrador.

But is there any way you can get away from the people who are, you know, surrounding you all the time and have a walk?

Harold Wilson said, Oh yes. Yes.

You can do that, really? Do that daily or nightly?

I wouldn't have time. And I'd have to have security protection. Because there are a lot of strange people around these days . . .

I know that, said Bill Shankly. I know that.

Harold Wilson smiled. And Harold Wilson said, But they are good fun. We've played golf together, my detectives and I. We go boating together. Long holidays is my answer. I take a long holiday because I never know when I'll be brought back. Sometimes I've been brought back for a week, in the middle of the summer holidays. So I go for three weeks' holiday, as I get hardly any Saturdays or Sundays off. I go for three weeks' holiday. If I'm not brought back by a crisis – and I wasn't this summer – then it's a long holiday. And I enjoy it.

You go to the Scilly Isles, asked Bill Shankly.

Always. Yes. Walking, walking. Swimming, boating.

Wonderful, wonderful.

A bit of fishing.

But this is the whole thing, said Bill Shankly. If you keep fit, it's got to be regular.

Harold Wilson nodded. And Harold Wilson said, It should be, it should be. Yes.

It's got to be a little, often, said Bill Shankly. And the way to eat and keep fit and not put weight on is to eat a little, often.

Harold Wilson nodded. And Harold Wilson said, But there is a bigger thing than this. And that is sleep. I can always sleep. Last week, when I was tired, I slept for ten hours. And nine hours the next day.

Well, I tell you something, Mr Wilson: if you can sleep that well, you'll have a long life.

And the answer is: never worry. If you worry in the night, you say, If this question can be solved, I'll do it better at nine o'clock than three o'clock. I've taught a lot of people how to sleep.

This is good, said Bill Shankly. Er, and your dog, is it out of condition? I mean, because some dogs do, if they are lying about?

He gets a little bit of weight. On holiday, he walks. I walk him and he walks me. We both walk hard. And he's swimming for two or three hours a day. He's a beautiful swimmer.

Wonderful, wonderful.

And I swim a bit at Chequers. In Mr Heath's time, some generous people built a swimming bath there. That's a good way of doing exercise quickly.

Yes, said Bill Shankly. Yes. That's good for you, too. Not only that – the exercise you get – but the water refreshes you.

Yes, it does. I'm not a good swimmer. I'm a bad swimmer. But I learnt to swim on Merseyside at the Port Sunlight swimming baths, which is where we used to go from Wirral Grammar School.

But the water refreshes you?

Oh, it does. Nothing like seawater. Cold seawater. I like a swimming pool. But in Scilly the water is very cold, very pure and invigorating. And it's good for me.

Now, said Bill Shankly, we've come back to a question that is appertaining to football. What's England's chances in the World Cup? Now, first and foremost, of course, they have got to qualify. And I would say to you, really – change that – what chances have they got in the European Nations Cup?

Harold Wilson sat back in his seat. Harold Wilson laughed. And Harold Wilson said, Isn't it time for me to take over the interview and put that question to you? I'd rather hear your answer on that one. Well, I don't know. I'll simply say the only time we've ever won the World Cup was when we had a Labour government. So at least we've got that condition fulfilled. I think we were very unlucky in Mexico. It could have gone much better. We were unlucky. But I don't know. They are building up a new team. I think they had, in the end, to break up that very great team of 1966. Perhaps clung, tried to keep them together too long. But there's a lot of experiment going on. A lot of brand-new lads.

The next one is in the Argentine, said Bill Shankly. Which makes it more difficult. And possibly advantageous to the Latins.

Harold Wilson said, I don't think the high altitude in Mexico was good for countries coming from low altitude . . .

Mr Wilson, said Bill Shankly, the game never should have been played in Mexico.

No, no. Any more than the Olympics should. But I think we've a better chance now than I would have thought possible two or three years ago, when we saw that disaster of not getting into the finals, the disaster of not qualifying . . .

Not qualifying was a killer, said Bill Shankly. Scotland qualified. And they were a little unlucky.

Well, as I say, I saw them at Frankfurt.

Don Revie is in now, said Bill Shankly. And he's, he's, he's . . . Now he's searching out, er . . . What he can do for the best . . .

He's experimenting. Yes. Experimenting.

Well, said Bill Shankly, we were talking about getting the best players for the plan of campaign. And utilise them. And possibly it'll take him longer than people think.

Harold Wilson sat forward in his seat. And Harold Wilson asked, What were you naturally?

Right foot, said Bill Shankly. Oh yes. Right-footed.

But you could do both?

Er, I was a reasonable kicker of a ball with my left foot. But I was naturally right-footed.

What was your favourite position?

I played with four on my back, which then was called right-half. But I was a midfield player. Or I'd be a sweeper up. One of the two. We were talking about judgement, of course, which you and I had to have. What do you regard as your biggest mistake? If you did have a big mistake, that is?

Harold Wilson said, Oh, that's my secret!

Bill Shankly laughed.

I have had a number, including some that the commentators in the opposition have not got onto. I think one or two that I would say, particularly here: I think on Rhodesia, for example, in the 1960s, I thought they really were willing to negotiate and get a solution, and I went on. We had the meetings on HMS *Fearless*, HMS *Tiger*. I went there and I think I put a lot of energy into it that was wasted. Now the

589

situation has changed and I hope it is going to be all right. But, I think, other things: I underrated, for example, the economic situation in the 1960s. I didn't realise how virulent could be an attack on sterling. Sometimes, you know, from people just talking and gossiping without really knowing the facts. I was trying to build up the industrial strength and didn't allow enough, I think, for the fact that we could be knocked sideways by a run on sterling. We've learnt a lot from those days. But I think those are the kind of mistakes I would mention . . .

Well, I wouldn't call that a mistake, Mr Wilson.

And I think, like you, I sometimes put the odd person in the team that afterwards I thought had been a mistake . . .

Well, said Bill Shankly again, I wouldn't call them mistakes . . .

Not many . . .

I would call them happenings, said Bill Shankly.

Harold Wilson said, You say, in football, you don't have mistakes, you have happenings?

Happenings, said Bill Shankly. And I think it's the same in your case. Happenings.

Harold Wilson nodded. And Harold Wilson said, Well, I like the happenings to lead to a win, not a loss.

Right, said Bill Shankly. What made you become a socialist?

Really, very similar to the reason I think anyone you were brought up with would say. I was brought up in an area, the textile valleys of the West Riding, where unemployment, the Depression, was so great and where . . . well, my own father was out of work for a year or two. But we didn't have it hard, we didn't have it bad. But a lot of the kids – kids in my patrol in the Scouts, kids in my football team at school – their parents were out of work. Lads were in what we now call the eleven-plus and couldn't go on to the secondary school because of that. I think that's what really started it. But a lot of it was, as I say, also the influence of mostly the religious teachers.

Well, said Bill Shankly, I think to that question I would have said, I think you are what you are. You are born what you are. And I think that a man is a socialist at heart.

Harold Wilson nodded again. And Harold Wilson said, I think you are to a large extent born. My father voted Labour in 1906, though he also worked for Churchill, Winston Churchill, in the 1908 election, as his sub-agent. I was brought up on that legend. But perhaps in my mind the Tories never had a chance. Because I was a little indoctrinated the other way by my family.

Well, said Bill Shankly again, I think that you were a natural-born. And I think if I am born, the politics that is in me, is me.

That's right. Well, it is part of your whole make-up.

It is part of my make-up, said Bill Shankly. The same as my religion is part of my make-up . . .

Quite right. Absolutely right.

And football is my religion, said Bill Shankly.

Harold Wilson nodded. And Harold Wilson said, And I do not say that if a person is religious, he's got to be a socialist. All I say is, if he is a religious person, in my view, he should not feel that his politics and his religion are contradictory. Let him be, as so many are, a good Conservative, a good Liberal, a good Labour man. But he must feel that what he is doing in politics represents his conception of what religion tells him.

Oh yes, said Bill Shankly. Oh yes. Without doubt. Yes. Now who is the best player you ever did see?

It's difficult. Difficult. But Alec Jackson. Alec Jackson. Another Scotsman. Alec Jackson of Huddersfield.

The side that won the League . . .

And in those three years, they were in the Cup Final twice. And in the semi-final, with two replays in the middle year.

And the second team, said Bill Shankly, they won the Central League three successive seasons?

They did. And at the same time. That's right.

Now you mention Alec Jackson, said Bill Shankly, I'll tell you a story. Roy Goodall said to me that Alec Jackson used to go into the visiting dressing room, before the game at Huddersfield, and say to the left-back, I bet you a new hat I score three goals. And he used to go out and score three goals. This is the kind of cockiness the man had. He was so brilliant.

Harold Wilson nodded. And Harold Wilson said, He was. And it was tragedy when he was killed. I'm not saying there is nobody as good today. That sounds like a very old fogey. But I am saying, if I were to start picking out one or two today, I'd be unfair to a lot of others. I think there are people as good as he was today. And many would say better. We haven't seen them competing with one another.

Well, said Bill Shankly, I was lucky enough, and fortunate enough, to play in a team where a fellow called Tom Finney played. And of all the players I have seen, I would pick Tommy Finney.

You'd pick Tommy Finney?

Tommy had everything.

Well, what about that story, though, that when he replaced Matthews on the wing for a match, the centre-forward, Stan Mortensen, said, It's not the same? He said that Matthews always had the lace placed correctly.

Yes, said Bill Shankly. Correct. Great players both.

A wonderful combination.

Great, great.

Well, we've got some great players today. I've named one or two. And there are a lot more. And you've brought a lot of them on yourself, haven't you?

Well, said Bill Shankly, we have a team here. They complement each other. They play as a team.

You signed two players from Scunthorpe?

Clemence for eighteen thousand pounds and Keegan for thirty-five thousand pounds. Yes.

At a time when the ruling rate was a couple of hundred thousand for a first-class player?

Yes, said Bill Shankly. Clemence has been a brilliant player.

I've seen him play some good games.

Yes, said Bill Shankly again. Er, now, Mr Wilson, you and I are sitting here. Both from socialist backgrounds. That's not to say that we have no time for anybody else. Because, I mean, the whole world is with us. I've got friends in all walks of life. And I don't let politics or religion bother me. I'll tell you that now. That's a fact. But you were honoured with the OBE. And so was I. So it's one each.

Yes. We got one each.

Who's going to get the next goal?

Harold Wilson smiled. And Harold Wilson said, Well, actually, in some ways, I think I can pull a bit of rank here . . .

Bill Shankly laughed.

Mine was given me by Winston Churchill. In your case, it was a lesser prime minister who recommended you.

Very good, laughed Bill Shankly. A wonderful answer, Mr Wilson. And it's been wonderful talking to you. Thank you.

Harold Wilson nodded. Harold Wilson smiled. And Harold Wilson said, Well, thank you very much. I've enjoyed it. It's made a welcome break. A lovely change. Among friends . . .


## 62. BECAUSE YOU'RE MINE

In the house, in their bed. Bill could not sleep. Not a wink. His head on the pillow. His eyes open. Bill stared up into the darkness. Up into the silence. All night. Bill thinking, Bill wondering. Whether he should go or whether he should not go. In the dark and in the silence. Bill knowing and Bill not knowing. Whether he should go or whether he should not go. His head on the pillow. His eyes open. Until at last, at last. Bill saw the curtain edges grow light again. Bill heard the bottle on the step again. And the paper through the letter box. And Bill got out of bed. Bill put on his dressing gown. Bill walked down the stairs. Bill picked up the paper from the floor. Bill turned to the back pages of the paper. The sports pages. And Bill checked the fixture list again. Bill still thinking, Bill still wondering. Whether he should go or whether he should not go. In the dawn and in the silence. Bill still knowing and Bill still not knowing. Whether he should go or whether he should not go. Bill closed the paper. Bill put down the paper on the table in the hall. And Bill walked back up the stairs. Bill went into the bathroom. Bill shaved and Bill washed. Bill went back into the bedroom. Bill put on his shirt. His tangerine shirt. Bill went to the dressing table. Bill opened the top drawer. Bill took out his cufflinks. His gold cufflinks. Bill closed the drawer. Bill did up the cuffs of his shirt. His tangerine shirt. Bill went to the wardrobe. Bill opened the doors. Bill took out his suit. His freshly cleaned grey herringbone suit. Bill left the wardrobe doors open. Bill walked over to the bed. Bill laid out the suit on top of the bed covers. Bill took the trousers from the coat hanger. Bill put on the trousers of his suit. His freshly cleaned grey herringbone suit. Bill went back to the dressing table. Bill opened the second drawer of the dressing table. Bill took out a tie. Bill closed the drawer. Bill walked back to the wardrobe. The doors still open. Bill stood before the mirror on the back of one of the doors. Bill put on his tie. Bill went back over to the bed. Bill picked up the jacket from the bed. Bill took the jacket from the coat hanger. Bill put on the jacket of his suit. His freshly cleaned grey herringbone suit. Bill walked back over to the dressing table. Bill opened the top drawer of the dressing table again. Bill took out one white handkerchief and one red pocket square. Bill closed the drawer. Bill put the white handkerchief in his left trouser pocket. Bill laid the red pocket square on the top of the dressing table. Bill brought the bottom point of the red pocket square up to the top point. Bill brought the left corner of the triangle to the right corner and then the right corner to the left corner. Bill folded the bottom almost towards the top. Bill walked over to the mirror on the back of the wardrobe door. Bill stood before the mirror. Bill placed the red pocket square in the breast pocket of his grey jacket. Bill looked in the mirror. Bill adjusted the pocket square until just enough of the point was coming out of the pocket. The red point out of the grey pocket. And Bill stepped back. Bill looked at the man in the mirror. And Bill said, I promised I'd come on the Kop long ago. I promised I'd see the games from all parts of Anfield. From all sides of the ground. Because I am a citizen of Liverpool. A citizen of the Kop. The Spion Kop. But I wanted to come here. Onto the Kop. The Spion Kop. To be with all the people. To see all the people. To thank all the people. The people who have done so much for me . . .

And Bill walked down the stairs. Bill went into the kitchen. Bill ate breakfast with Ness. A slice of toast and honey, a glass of fresh orange juice and a cup of tea. Bill helped Ness clear away the breakfast things. Bill dried up the breakfast things. Bill helped Ness put away the breakfast things. And then Bill walked out into the hall. Bill picked up the paper again. And Bill walked into the front room. Bill sat down in his chair. Bill opened the paper again. Bill turned to the back pages again. The sports pages again. And Bill checked the fixture list again. Bill thinking again, Bill wondering again. Whether he should go or whether he should not go. In the front room, in his chair. Bill knowing again and Bill not knowing again. Whether he should go or whether he should not go. Bill closed the paper again.

Bill put down the paper on the arm of the chair. And then Bill stood up. Bill got to his feet. Bill walked back into the kitchen. And Bill said, I'm just popping out, love. But I might be a while . . .

OK, said Ness. Then you take care, love.

Bill smiled. Bill kissed Ness on her cheek. And Bill walked out into the hall. Bill opened the cupboard. Bill took out his coat. Bill put on his coat. Bill picked up his hat. Bill put on his hat. Bill closed the cupboard. Bill walked down the hall. Bill opened the front door. And Bill stared down the drive at the car. At the front door, on their doorstep. Bill still thinking, Bill still wondering. Whether he should go or whether he should not go. In the morning and in the silence. Bill then knowing and Bill then not knowing. Whether he should go or whether he should not go. And Bill stepped out into the drive. Bill turned back to the front door. Bill closed the door. Bill walked down the drive. Bill got into his car. Bill put the key into the ignition. Bill turned the key in the ignition. And Bill pulled out of the drive. Bill drove down the West Derby Road. And Bill saw the people walking in the street. In their scarves, their Liverpool scarves. Bill turned onto the Belmont Road. And Bill saw the people queuing for the buses. In their scarves, their Liverpool scarves. But Bill did not turn onto the Anfield Road. And Bill did not park in the Anfield Road car park. Bill turned into a side street. And Bill parked in the side street. Bill took the key out of the ignition. And Bill waited. Bill thinking again, Bill wondering again. Whether he should go or whether he should not go. In the car, behind the wheel. Bill knowing again and Bill not knowing again. Whether he should go or whether he should not go. But in the car, behind the wheel. Bill saw all the people walking down the side street. In their scarves, their Liverpool scarves. Bill saw all the people walking towards the ground, the Anfield ground. In their scarves, their Liverpool scarves. And Bill got out of the car. Bill turned up the collar of his coat, Bill pulled down the brim of his hat. And now Bill walked with the people. In their scarves, their Liverpool scarves. Bill walked with the people towards the ground, the Anfield ground. In their scarves, their Liverpool scarves. Bill walking, Bill walking. His collar up, his brim down. Bill walking, Bill walking. Nearer and nearer. Bill not daring to look, Bill not daring to see. Closer and closer. Until Bill was at the turnstile, until Bill had his hand in his pocket. The change across the counter, the ticket in his hand. And Bill was there, now Bill was here. Inside the ground, the Anfield ground. The collar of his coat still buttoned up, the brim of his hat still pulled down. Walking up the steps, walking onto the Kop. With the people, among the people. On the Kop, the Spion Kop. Now Bill looked and now Bill saw. All the people, all the people. In their scarves, their Liverpool scarves. Bill looked and Bill saw. And now the people looked and now the people saw. On Saturday 22 November, 1975. At ten to three. From every stand in Anfield. From every corner of the ground. People saw the Kop begin to part. Behind the goal. The Spion Kop forming a circle. A circle around one man. Around Bill. On the Kop. The Spion Kop. People patting his back, people shaking his hand. They gave him scarves, they offered him sweets. A stick of gum. A Murray mint –

Stand here, the people said. Stand here, Bill . . .

You'll get a better view from here, Bill . . .

And Bill thanked the people. One by one. Every one. Bill thanked them all. One by one. Every one. Bill patted their backs, Bill shook their hands. One by one. Each and every one. And then Bill raised his hands above his head. And Bill turned around. Bill looked up into the Kop. The Spion Kop. And Bill applauded the Kop. The Spion Kop. And Bill thanked the Kop. The Spion Kop. And now the Kop sang. Now the Spion Kop roared, *Shankly is a Kopite, Shankly is a Kopite, SHANKLY IS A KOPITE!*


## 63. ALL FLEAS ARE FIT

Bill Shankly could not believe his ears. Bill Shankly could not believe his eyes. Bill Shankly switched off the radio. Bill Shankly put down the newspaper. Bill Shankly refused to believe it. Bill Shankly would not believe it. Bill Shankly would not believe it until he had heard it from the man himself. And Bill Shankly switched on the television –

Prime Minister, asked the interviewer, what sort of prime minister do you think you will be remembered as?

Harold Wilson took the pipe from out of his mouth. He looked down, he looked up. And then Harold Wilson said, Not for me to say. But I hope I'll be remembered as one who, in the face of the biggest challenges – above all, economic problems – the country has faced in its history, kept the party together, kept the country together, kept the country united, secured a common effort from the people and an acceptance of the sacrifices that had to be made. I wish I could have been prime minister in happier times and easier times.

And looking back, can you pick out any one achievement which you are most proud of?

Harold Wilson looked down again. And Harold Wilson said, Well, there are some. Away from the kind of question I have been answering. For example, to have created the Open University, which was my own devising and which I saw through. And I think this will be remembered when many of the other arguments of today have been forgotten. But I think perhaps, in the last year, turning a divided country – and an eminent journalist, who has never been very friendly to me, last week said the governability of Britain was in doubt when we took over two years ago – turning a country facing that danger into a country that was united and determined, I think that is what I would like to be remembered for.

In your statement you made an interesting remark about the fact that you are determined not to succumb to the danger of being faced with a decision you have faced before, in case you mishandled it the second time round? I'm not quite sure what you meant . . .

Harold Wilson touched his neck. He touched his chin, he touched his cheek. Harold Wilson touched his tie. He smiled and he said, No, no. It was a problem I was aware of when I was a civil servant, very many years ago. You looked at a problem. You've looked at a solution people have put forward, you've turned it down. There is a danger that five years later, when circumstances may have changed, you say, Oh, we looked at that before. Or, I've been through this crisis before. And that you don't approach it with the freshness you should. I think that's a danger that can come after too many years. I hope I haven't done it. But I want to make sure that I don't. And that there will be a fresh approach to all the problems.

But that is one of the big things which has decided you to bow out at this moment?

Harold Wilson looked down again. And Harold Wilson said, No, I think the big things really are, first, that I have been here a long time. It's been a long run, a happy run. Almost the longest this century. I've got a wonderful team, I've got people almost of my own age group. Why should I sort of hog the thing? And cling on and prevent them from having the chance of succeeding and bringing their distinctive approach? That is one of the arguments; the other argument, I think we are now at a turning point. Things are beginning to pick up again. Very slowly, but beginning. Even unemployment is beginning to get more under control, I believe. But I would like new people to handle this. And of course, we are at a turning point on the biggest thing of all: the attack on inflation. When we've got acceptance, against all the odds as many people thought last year, by agreement, of what has to be done to fight inflation. The counter-inflation policy. The next stage, after the budget, will be to decide what we do for the next year. Now I think that is the moment to go. To leave others to do the negotiations. I would hate to wreck those negotiations, or even put them at risk, by an interruption for the need to have an election of a new leader. And when all the trade-union conferences are going on and so on. And there is a little lull before the budget, before any new negotiations can take place. So I think this is the time to do it. I've had a great deal of anxiety in working out what was the right time. But yes, I think that's right.

But that does mean your successor is going to have one of the most difficult jobs there could be, as almost his first task. And that is, obtaining agreement between differing opinions in the Labour movement and the trade-union movement about what that next stage of the counter-inflation policy should be . . .

Harold Wilson ran his finger along the top of his lip. He put the pipe in his mouth again. He lit the pipe. Then Harold Wilson took the pipe from his mouth again. And Harold Wilson said, I hope the way I handled it is going to help him. Because we start from a national consensus. As well as a consensus with the trade-union movement. Within Parliament, in the main. Certainly on our side. He starts from that. And he starts with the goodwill of the country.

Can I ask you, said the interviewer, if you feel you have a political weakness, what that is?

Harold Wilson looked down again. And Harold Wilson said, Well, I think it is always said I'm very forgiving. The man who kicks me in the teeth one week, I won't say I'm exactly promoting him – that usually takes a month – but I am forgiving. Because I know we are all human beings with our frailties. And sometimes I'm accused of another weakness: loyalty to my colleagues. That's not a weakness. I have always backed them. Even when, sometimes, they have put me in a spot. And I have tried to see them through. But loyalty by the prime minister to his colleagues is essential.

Can I ask one thing, about the burden on a prime minister, said the interviewer. Do you think our system puts too heavy a burden on each prime minister?

Well, it varies really. Depends on how the prime minister plays it. I like to know all that is going on. When I was prime minister in the sixties, hardly a single one of them had been in the Cabinet. I had to go in and do everything. It's like, you know, football? Taking the set piece occasionally. The goalkeeper. Taking the penalties and the corners. Now, of course, I have a very talented and experienced Cabinet. Even so, I like to know all that is going on. It's a heavy job. But a very enjoyable job. You don't get bored, you know? And if I don't get bored, I don't get tired. Others may do it differently. I've known prime ministers, not long ago, who were sitting in the garden at Number Ten here, reading novels in the afternoon. Well, I don't get a chance to read them even on a Saturday or a Sunday.

You've said today, said the interviewer, you are as fit as a flea. How fit is that?

Harold Wilson put the pipe in his mouth again. He lit the pipe again. He took the pipe from his mouth again. And he said, Well, all fleas are fit. And I feel fitter now than when I was forty. Certainly carrying less weight. But I think I was quoting the views of my doctor, who gives me regular check-ups. And he says I'm fairly sound.

Prime Minister, for the last time, thank you.

Thank you.

And Bill Shankly stood up. Bill Shankly got to his feet. And Bill Shankly walked over to the television. Bill Shankly switched off the television. And Bill Shankly walked over to the window. Bill Shankly looked out at the street. The empty street, the dark street. And Bill Shankly drew the curtains.

## 64. BRUGES

Bill waited and Bill waited. Bill still went to the games, Bill still watched the matches. But Bill waited and Bill waited. Bill had stood on the Kop, Bill had sat in the stands. Waiting and waiting. Not with the directors, the directors and their friends. Not in their box. Bill waited and Bill waited. On the Kop, in the stands. Bill waited and Bill waited. For the letter on the mat. The invitation and the ticket. Bill waited and Bill waited. For the knock on the door or the voice on the phone. Asking Bill, inviting Bill. To an away game, an away match. At Ayresome Park or White Hart Lane. But Bill waited and Bill waited. For just a letter or just a call. Until Bill gave up waiting. For the letter that never came. The invitation and the ticket. Bill stopped waiting. For the knock on the door and the voice on the phone. Until Bill said he gave up waiting. Still first to the post. Until Bill said he stopped waiting. Still first to the phone. Still waiting, still hoping. Hoping for a letter. An invitation and a ticket. First to the post. Not saying, just hoping. Hoping for a call. And first to the phone –

Hello, hello? This is Bill Shankly speaking . . .

Mr Shankly, said the voice on the line, this is Liverpool Football Club. We have a request for you to attend the second leg of the UEFA Cup Final. In Bruges next week. From –

Oh well. Yes. Thank you. Yes. Of course, I'd be delighted to be there. Thank you. But I think it's a bit late in the day. I mean, for the travel and for the hotel. A little bit late now . . .

No, no, said the voice on the line. Liverpool Football Club will make all the necessary travel arrangements.

Oh well, then. Then thank you. I would be delighted to come.

Great, said the voice on the line. Then we'll send you all the tickets you need. Everything you need. To your house.

Thank you. Thank you very much.

Bill put down the telephone. Bill walked back into the kitchen. And Ness looked at Bill. The look on his face. In his eyes –

Who was that, asked Ness. What was that about, love?

It was the club, love. Someone from the club. I don't know who, love. I didn't recognise the voice . . .

What did they want, love?

To invite me to Bruges, love. To the second leg of the final next week. As part of the club, love. The official party.

Really, asked Ness. I wonder why, love? It's taken them long enough, has it not? I wonder why now, love?

I don't know, love.

Well, what did you say, love? You're not going to go? After all this time, love. After waiting so long . . .

I know, love. I know. But I don't want anybody to think I'm being petty, love. I mean, I don't want anybody to say Bill Shankly is a petty man. A man who bears a grudge, love . . .

And so you said yes?

Yes, love.

But do you want to go, love? Is that what you want?

Well, I can't say it's something I've dwelt on, love. Something I've lost any sleep over. But now they've invited me, love. As part of the club. Then I'm happy to go, love.

Then if you're happy to go, you should go. I just wish they had done this before, love. They had thought of this before. But yes, then, you should go, love . . .

And Bill drove out to the airport. Speke airport. Bill parked in the car park at the airport. Speke airport. Bill looked for the bus. The Liverpool team bus. But Bill could not see the bus. The Liverpool team bus. Bill went inside the airport. Speke airport. Bill looked for the players of Liverpool Football Club. But Bill could not see the players of Liverpool Football Club. Bill checked in for the flight. The flight to Belgium. Bill stood in the line. The line for check-in. Next to people he did not know. Next to people he did not recognise. Bill boarded the flight. The flight to Belgium. Bill sat on the plane. The plane to Belgium. Next to people he did not know. Next to people he did not recognise. Bill got off the plane. The plane in Belgium. And Bill looked for the players of Liverpool Football Club. But Bill could not see the players of Liverpool Football Club. Bill looked for anybody. Anybody from Liverpool Football Club. Anybody he knew, anybody he recognised. But Bill could not see anybody he knew, anybody he recognised. And Bill took out the envelope from his pocket. The envelope filled with tickets. Tickets for flights, a reservation for a hotel. A hotel he did not know, a hotel he did not recognise. And Bill found a taxi. Bill showed the taxi driver the address of the hotel. The hotel he did not know, the hotel he did not recognise. And Bill sat in the back of the taxi to the hotel. The hotel he did not know, the hotel he did not recognise. And Bill got out of the taxi. Bill walked into the hotel. And Bill looked around the lobby of the hotel. Bill looking for the players of Liverpool Football Club. But Bill could not see the players of Liverpool Football Club. Bill looking for anybody. Anybody he knew, anybody he recognised. But Bill could not see anybody he knew, anybody he recognised. But Bill checked into the hotel. Bill signed the register. The hotel register. And Bill went up to the room. His hotel room. Bill sat down on the bed. His hotel bed. And Bill waited for dinnertime. Sitting on the bed. His hotel bed. Pacing the room. The hotel room. Up and down. The hotel room. Until it was time. Dinnertime. And Bill walked into the hotel dining room. Bill looked around the hotel dining room. Bill looking for the players of Liverpool Football Club. But Bill did not see the players of Liverpool Football Club. Bill looking for anybody he knew, anybody he recognised. And at last Bill did see people he knew, people he recognised. Bill saw the wives of the players of Liverpool Football Club. The wives and the journalists who wrote about Liverpool Football Club. And the wives and the journalists smiled at Bill. And they waved to Bill. And Bill smiled at them. And Bill waved back. And Bill sat down at a table. A table set for one. And Bill wished he had not come. He had not come. Bill wished he had stayed at home. He had stayed at home.


## 65. HOLIDAYS IN THE SUN

On the beach, on the sands. The Blackpool sands. The two little lads were building sandcastles. They filled their bucket with sand. They tipped up their bucket. They lifted up their bucket. But their castle collapsed. In grains, on the sands. The Blackpool sands. Every time. They filled their bucket. They tipped up their bucket. They lifted up their bucket. Every time. Their castles collapsed. In grains again, on the sands. The Blackpool sands. Bill Shankly knelt down beside the boys. And Bill Shankly said, That looks like Goodison Park, lads.

Looks like you need a hand from a master. A master builder, lads . . .

And Bill Shankly picked up the spade. The plastic yellow spade. Bill Shankly drew a square in the sands. The Blackpool sands. And Bill Shankly said, You'll need a castle on every corner, lads . . .

Bill Shankly filled the bucket with sand. Bill Shankly packed it tight. Bill Shankly patted it down with the back of the spade. Bill Shankly put the bucket on the first corner. Gently. Bill Shankly tipped up the bucket. Slowly. Bill Shankly lifted up the bucket. And Bill Shankly said, There you go, lads. As solid as a rock. That's how you build a castle, lads. How you build a fortress. Now you try, lads . . .

And the two little lads took turns to fill their bucket with sand. They packed it tight. They patted it down with the back of the spade. They put the bucket on the second corner. Then the third. And then the fourth. Gently. They tipped up their bucket. Slowly. They lifted up their bucket. And their castles stood. Solid. On every corner.

Bill Shankly stood up. And Bill Shankly said, There you go, lads. Just look at that! That looks like Anfield, lads. Like Anfield . . .

The two little lads stood up. The two little lads stared back down at their castle. Their fortress. On the beach, on the sands. The Blackpool sands. And the two little lads smiled. They beamed –

And Bill Shankly said, But you know what it needs now, lads? The only thing missing? We need a red flag, lads . . .

But then on the beach, then on the sands. The Blackpool sands. A football fell out of the sky. The Blackpool sky. And onto their castle. Their fortress. Destroyed and ruined. With one bad kick, with one wrong ball. On the beach, on the sands. The Blackpool sands. The two little lads turned to Bill Shankly. The two little lads looked up to Bill Shankly. With their lips trembling and with their eyes filling. On the beach and on the sands. The Blackpool sands. Bill Shankly picked up the ball. The football. Bill Shankly turned around. Bill Shankly saw an older boy coming towards them. The older boy saying, I'm sorry. I'm sorry, mister. It was just a bad kick . . .

On the beach, on the sands. The Blackpool sands. Bill Shankly looked at the older boy. The older boy in a blue football shirt. A blue Scotland shirt. Bill Shankly smiled. And Bill Shankly said, Aye, son. Aye. A bad kick, a terrible kick, son. Looks like you need help from a master. A master player, son . . .

And Bill Shankly turned to the two little lads. On the beach, on the sands. The Blackpool sands. And Bill Shankly said, Come on, boys. Come on! Let's get our revenge, boys! Let's teach them a lesson! And show them how we play, boys . . .

## 66. THERE'S NOTHING HERE BUT HIGHLAND PRIDE

John Roberts telephoned Bill. Bill knew John. John worked on the *Daily Express*. John had written about Liverpool Football Club for the *Daily Express*. John had talked with Bill about Liverpool Football Club. And Bill had shouted at John about Liverpool Football Club. But John had smiled at Bill. John had listened to Bill. And Bill liked John. John had also written a book. *The Team That Wouldn't Die: The Story of the Busby Babes.* Now John wanted to write another book. And so John asked Bill if he would like to tell his tale. His life story. John told Bill people wanted to hear his tale. His story. John told Bill people would be happy to hear his tale. His story. And so if Bill would like to tell his tale. His story. Then John would like to help Bill write his story. His autobiography. And John said Christopher Falkus of Weidenfeld & Nicolson would like to publish Bill's autobiography. His book. Christopher Falkus had published Matt's autobiography. His book. *Soccer at the Top: My Life in Football.* Bill had read Matt's autobiography. His book. And Bill had enjoyed Matt's book. And so Bill said, Yes. If people want to hear my tale. Then I will tell my tale. If it will make people happy. Then I will write my story.

Most afternoons. After Bill had finished his training at Bellefield. And Bill came home. Most afternoons. In the front room, in his chair. In his red tracksuit top. Most afternoons. Bill talked to John. About the morning training, about the morning game. The goal he had laid on, the knock he had picked up. Most afternoons. John listened. And John smiled. And then John asked Bill about the past. And most afternoons. In his chair, his red tracksuit top. For tape after tape. Bill talked and Bill walked. Most afternoons. Down Memory Lane. For chapter after chapter. Life in Glenbuck. The Road South. Change at Haltwhistle. Acting Corporal. Bitter End, New Beginnings. Law and Wilson. St John and Yeats. Body and Soul. Never Walk Alone. The

New Team. A Boy Called Keegan. Triumph Again. And Goodbye Anfield. Chapter after chapter, tape after tape. Bill talked and Bill walked. Most afternoons. Down Memory Lane. With the managers he had known, with the players he had known. Until Auld Lang Syne. And the tapes were full and the chapters written. The tale told and the book finished. *SHANKLY* by Bill Shankly. The book published. And the book banned from sale in the official club shop at Anfield.

In the house, in their bedroom. Bill walked over to the bed. Bill picked up the jacket from the bed. The freshly cleaned grey jacket. Bill took the jacket from the coat hanger. Bill put on the jacket. Bill walked over to the mirror on the back of the wardrobe door. Bill looked at the man in the mirror. In his grey jacket. The jacket too big. His red shirt. The collar too big. And Bill said, You couldn't even get from Carlisle to Preston on the train now for forty pound . . .

And now Bill heard footsteps on the stairs. Bill heard Ness tap on the bedroom door. And Ness opened the door –

They're ready, love. They're waiting . . .

Bill nodded. And Bill said, Thanks, love. I'm coming now.

And Bill closed the wardrobe door. Bill walked out of the bedroom. Bill walked down the stairs. Bill opened the front door. Bill went out of the house. Bill closed the front door. Bill walked down the drive. Bill walked over to the television crew. The television crew from Scottish Television. Bill shook hands with the television crew. The cameraman and the sound man. Bill shook hands again with the interviewer. The English interviewer from Scottish Television. And Bill said, So where do you want to do this? Where do you want me?

Just over here will be fine, said the interviewer.

In the sunshine. In the street. With cars passing and with dogs barking. Bill followed the interviewer to the spot they had marked. In the sunshine. In the street. In his grey jacket. His big grey jacket. And his red shirt. With its big red collar. Bill looked up at the camera. Into the television camera. And then Bill looked away. His hands in his pockets. Deep in his pockets. Bill looked down. Down at his shoes, down at the ground. Deep under the ground –

Bill, said the interviewer. Bill?

And Bill looked up.

Let's start at the beginning . . .

Yes.

Glenbuck? Some place, Glenbuck?

Well, at one time it was interesting. But you saw it. I mean, it's derelict now. But that's only one of a hundred villages that are derelict.

When we were down there, said the interviewer, somebody said, Oh, I remember Bill Shankly. He was never off the hills. Running up and down. Training. Playing in your pit boots . . .

Bill nodded. And Bill said, Ah well, yes. I mean, everybody, when you were boys, had big boots. They lasted longer, you know? With toe plates in them. Steel toe plates . . .

And Bill laughed. And Bill said, I mean, it's sure to break somebody's leg if you kicked them . . .

But how hard was it? Because I mean, to us, somebody of my generation, I mean, you say, Gosh, you can't live like that?

Bill nodded.

Big family, ten of you . . .

Yeah.

Small house . . .

Well, in the village there were some people had twelve of a family. And fourteen. Yes, it was hard. But I mean, not as hard as it would look, really. Because I mean, if there's a group of boys. Sisters and brothers. And you've got a good mother and father. You stick together. And you make things easier for each other. I mean, it's like playing football. You play collectively and then you're very difficult to beat. But if you've individuals in your team, then your team will fall down. Well, we were a team. And we helped each other.

And let's set the record straight about Glenbuck Cherrypickers. Famous team. But, in fact, you never really played for them, did you?

I played a trial when I were sixteen year old. And that season, they went defunct. They finished. That was their last season as a team. And so then, later on, I went to a little village called Cronberry. Near Cumnock. And played for Cronberry. Yeah.

How much money did you get for matches like that?

Oh well, I used to cycle to Cronberry. It was about twelve or fourteen mile. And I think it might have been two and six. Five bob. Maybe seven and six. Yeah . . .

And I mean, of course, it wasn't just you, was it? Every

brother, all your brothers played professional football, didn't they?

Bill nodded. And Bill said, They did. They did.

Who was the best? Yourself aside . . .

Er, it's difficult to say. I would think that possibly my brother Jimmy. Being he was a centre-forward and scored goals. He would have been, in modern football, possibly the best player.

How would you rate yourself, looking back? And comparing yourself to people you've managed?

Well, my record is that I reached international standard and I played in cup finals. And so, er, I got more credit than them. But maybe they didn't have the same chance as me.

How come you ended up in Preston, then? Because presumably a lot of Scottish sides would have liked to have signed you?

Well, I went to Carlisle on trial. And they signed me on. And then Preston saw me playing. After a season. They bought me for five hundred pounds. And out of that, I got forty pounds, I think. You couldn't get from Carlisle to Preston on the train now for forty pound.

The interviewer laughed. The interviewer nodded.

And Bill said, So Preston had been watching me the whole season. And after playing maybe about only six games in Carlisle's big team, they took me . . .

That's always been the thing with you, hasn't it? Driving onwards and onwards. And which, I think, is because of Glenbuck. And getting away from it. And getting on in life? And . . .

Bill said, Having seen the conditions that people had to live in. Having been in a pit, working in a pit. And it was either the pit or nothing. So that, I mean, that kind of environment really is good for people. And maybe that helped me. But being born, I think, with the determination is the thing. I mean, I think everything is inborn. I think that if anybody's got ability, I think that it's a natural thing for them . . .

Let's talk a little about some of the Scottish players you played with, back in those days. Who were the great ones amongst them?

Well, it's a difficult thing to say. But my first game for Scotland was at Wembley. And George Brown, who is now director of Rangers, he was playing. Captain of Scotland. Because I remember when the game was over. In the bath. George Brown said, Well, I think that will be my last game. He said, I'm thirty-three. And that was my first game. And it was possibly his last game for Scotland. George Brown was a class player. The great Tommy Walker was playing then, of course. He was brilliant. He was strong. He could batter them with both feet. He was fit. Jimmy Delaney played. I had these two in front of me. Jimmy Delaney was a powerful boy and all. And I remember playing over in Belfast. In the mud, one day. And at Tynecastle. In the mud, against Wales. And Walker and Delaney and I revelled in the mud. And I felt that the final game I played at Hampden, in thirty-nine, when England beat us. If Jimmy Delaney, who called off, had have been able to play. Then I think we would have beaten England.

Every kid in the country dreams of playing for Scotland. What's it really like, in the dressing room at Hampden Park, when you're pulling that dark blue jersey over your head? That must be the greatest thrill of them all, surely?

Oh well, it's unbelievable. Because I mean, as a Scottish boy, I mean your whole dream is to be, if you're football-minded, your whole dream is to play for Scotland. I mean, all Scottish people have got the fervour, you know? They want to fight. I mean, not fight like hooligans. I mean, they are all fighting people. They are warriors from the past. And small nations tend to be that way, you know? They think they are being sat on. And they fight back.

By the English?

Oh no, by everybody! Yeah, but then it was Scotland–England. Oh yes. Yes. I mean, as far as we were concerned, English people were poison, you know?

Yeah, said the interviewer. But tell me, are the Scots as good at football as they think they are?

Well, that's a difficult thing to say. I mean, I don't think that the best has been got out of the Scottish players that has been available to play at international level. And I think that they've got more natural ability than most of the other countries.

Yes, because you say in your book, don't you? That you wish Scotland had called on you in some capacity or another? To help out? So, I mean, you obviously think that you could have done something that hadn't been done, do it better? What . . .

Bill looked at the interviewer. And Bill said, Well, my record is one of success, as a manager. And I think that I have got the ways and means of motivating people. And if I had all the pick of the Scottish players at my disposal, then I think that I would have been successful. And that somebody was going to get an awful belting off us.

So who would you have picked, asked the interviewer. Say, for example, in the last two or three years? Do you think Scotland have left players out who should have been in?

Oh, I don't know about that. I don't know about that. In the midfield, at the moment, they've got tremendous strength. And the three boys that are playing – Rioch, that Archie Gemmill, Masson – and, of course, Lou Macari, who is playing brilliantly. And so they've got the greatest midfield strength of all, at the moment . . .

Macari can't even get in the side, laughed the interviewer. But you tried to sign him, didn't you?

Oh well, aye. Macari's not in the team, so the other boys must be brilliant to keep him out. I think, mind you, he may have been in. He was unfortunate. I think whoever got in now, would stay in. And if Macari had been in, he would have stayed in. But I think that Macari will play for Scotland soon.

I've always thought that one of the big reasons for Bill Shankly's success was he was a master psychologist?

Yes, well, conning is not really the word. I mean, I think that psychology is a form of exaggeration. And exaggeration is a form of psychology. And I was brought up in a village where all the men used to stand at the corner and tell terrible tales, you know? Long tales. Exaggerated tales. Now that's a form of psychology. Exaggeration.

How do you mean? What sort of tales?

Bill smiled. And Bill said, Tales about, er, I mean, an old man, he used to work in the pit. He says he pushed a hatch three hundred yards before he knew he was off the rails, you know? Things like that. We all used to wear little cloth caps. And we used to turn our caps upside down, you see? And this was a sign we didn't believe him. And then he used to go and say, Christ! I'll murder all of you! So I had psychology. I mean, I had a boy here. And he started off playing well. Then he tapered off. So I said, I need to work on him. Because he's got ability. So I used to give him the impression, when we were going to the away game, You're not doing too well, son, you know? That he wouldn't be playing. So he'd be sitting in the train or the bus thinking,

Well, I'm not playing. And when we got to the ground, I'd say, Do you want to play? And he'd say, Good God, aye. So he made his debut again. You see? That boosted him up.

I've been told a story about you and the table football . . .

Yeah. Yeah . . .

And getting that all organised . . .

Yeah . . .

Tell us that story.

You mean, the tactical talks?

Yes.

Oh well. I mean, we used to go and watch teams, and we only wanted to know what their basic formation was. And we had tactical talks. And there was anybody who would cause trouble, we would pay attention to them. But if we were playing against big teams, I used to take out big players, you know? The opposition. And put them in my pocket. And by the time half the big players were off, I said, We've cut them out already. We've beaten them. So I'd put the little Bobby Charlton and George Best in my pocket when I was talking. They weren't playing. And Denis Law. They didn't make any difference.

They weren't very good?

No, no. We had eliminated them. So I took them off . . .

And Bill nodded. And Bill smiled. And Bill waited –

So you became a manager, said the interviewer. And you started in some fairly far-flung places: Workington, Grimsby, Carlisle. What did you learn in those far-flung places that worked for you when you finally got to Anfield?

Yes, I started in the outposts. Carlisle. And Grimsby. And Workington. And Huddersfield. Hard places. But good places to be. I enjoyed myself. Yeah . . .

But what do you learn in a small club which then served you well, when you got to Liverpool?

Well, you learn you've got to work with very little money. This is detrimental, of course. But it's like being brought up in Glenbuck. A hard village, you know? That's a hard life. So being at Carlisle to manage. Being at Workington to manage, which is an outpost. I mean, that's hard work. So I think it's really a good thing to have been there.

You see, to my mind, all the really good managers I've met –

people like Jock Stein, for example, yourself . . .

Bill nodded. And Bill said, Yes.

The thing which separates them from all the other managers is not only this drive, but a kind of honesty. That you're looking after the club, that football counts . . .

Yes.

Well, I'm not putting this very well. But I suppose what I am trying to say is, there really is something which separates really good managers from the average managers. Now what is it? There's a marvellous story about Jock Stein. Celtic were playing away at Dundee United. And the match was called off at the last minute . . .

Bill nodded again. And Bill said, Yes.

And he drove out to Cumbernauld, on a Saturday, and stopped all the supporters' buses going to Dundee United. So that is what a good manager is about, isn't it?

Bill nodded. And Bill said, Now that is something. His first thoughts were for the people who pay. He's right. That was a wonderful thing to do.

Yes. Now going back, over all the years at Liverpool. They say the hardest thing in football is to have one good side, break it up, and create another one. You managed that pretty successfully?

Yeah . . .

But when you look back, were your affections for the first side really, more than the second?

Yeah, well, they were a great team. And I think that possibly there was very few teams in Britain would have beaten them. Over the last thirty years. To break it up – that was Ian St John, and Ron Yeats, and Peter Thompson, and Roger Hunt. Tommy Smith and Callaghan are still playing, of course – so to break it up was difficult. Because the one thing that surprised me was that I had vouched that I thought they would go on for another three years. Now they didn't. So they finished three years earlier than I thought they would do. So then my plans weren't working then. I was in the Third Divisions and Fourth Divisions, looking for players, like the Clemences. And Alec Lindsay and Larry Lloyd. And Keegan and them. But I went early to the Third and Fourth Divisions. I couldn't go and pay a hundred and fifty thousand pounds for a player and put him in the reserves. So I had to go to the lower leagues. And pick young boys. Eighteen, Clemence was, when I signed him.

What really comes across, when you were building that first Liverpool side, the great side, was that you were absolutely certain that you needed two players. And those two players were Ron Yeats and Ian St John. What was it made you so sure those were the two players that you needed to turn what was an ordinary side into a great one?

Some players are signed on with no doubt at all. No danger. Other ones, well, I hadn't seen enough of them to be sure of them. So there's always a risk and a gamble buying a player. Some of them I bought, there was no risk at all. In fact, it was stealing. Stealing!

What about Yeats, for example? Start with him . . .

Bill smiled again. And Bill said, Oh, Yeats was a colossus. Dear me. One of the biggest men in the game. Defended his box. He was one of the quickest men in the game. And possibly, over seventy, eighty yards, there were nobody in Britain could have lived with him. So he was a powerful man with a big heart. And a big frame. And St John and Yeats were the beginning . . .

And what has St John got? Because those were more sophisticated skills . . .

Oh, St John was strong. He was small but punchy and strong. And crafty and cunning. And a needle. He'd put his foot in, if he needed to put his foot in.

You mean, he'd kick his own grandmother?

Oh yes. Well, they're the kind I want. Yes. You don't want fellas that are yes, sir, no, sir, three bags full. They don't do me. I want men to be men. But to take it. If someone else is going to kick them, not to complain. So that it's a man's game.

Just go back to the psychology. Because that extended to referees with you, didn't it? You always had a fair old way of making your points to referees, didn't you?

Oh well, it's a difficult job, referees. It's a hard job. I mean, we tried to help them as much as we could. And in the end, of course, my idea of referees, for the players' point of view, was don't dissent. They give decisions against you. It's no good arguing. You'll only hurt yourself. You'll upset your system. You'll not be normal, if you're incensed. I said, So forget them. Take it. And if I drummed it into them long enough, then it would get to the point whereby they would take all the decisions and it wouldn't upset them. So I said, If he gives a free kick against you, you're all arguing the toss outside the box, and then you might even lose a goal because of this. I said, Now they may have given the decision against you. I said, But I'll tell you one thing. I've never seen a referee scoring a goal yet. They are all complaining about the referee giving a bad decision. I said, He didn't put the bloody ball in the net, did he? You see? So that was my psychology.

The interviewer laughed.

And Bill smiled.

And then tell us about the Kop, said the interviewer. Was it there before you came?

Oh yes.

The singing and everything else?

Yes, the noise was there. Yeah. Not the singing. The singing came later. The singing came along with the Beatles. And your Gerry Marsden's *You'll Never Walk Alone*. And *Ee-Aye-Addio*. That all came around the time we were beginning to move in sixty-four, sixty-five. And we win the Cup for the first time . . .

Is it worth a goal start? Or two-goal start? Because I mean, it must have been an intimidating place for other teams, Anfield?

No, they make a noise. But they are very fair. If you come here and play the game. Play football. They'll applaud you. If you come here with other intentions, it's a different story. They can be hard and all. But they are very fair. And they're very noisy, of course. There's a big band of them. And I would think that they are possibly the funniest crowd, you know? The humour of them. I mean, they can pick up things right away. I mean, I remember Leeds United coming here. And Sprake, in goal, was going to roll a ball out, you see? So he changed his mind, so he threw it into the net, you see? And inside of two minutes, they were singing *Careless Hands*. It's unbelievable. Bloody unbelievable. Yeah. That happened. That's absolutely true. Yeah . . .

Why did they make you almost into a god? Because I mean, you were their man, weren't you?

Well, we were successful. And we'd won the Cup for the first time. I think that was a big thing, you know? That made them proud. I mean, the fact that they hadn't won it. And they were speaking about hiding, you know? Kind of hiding with big coats on, so nobody would see them. That was one of the things, I think. Having won the Cup, and being successful, and going into Europe. And I was a people's man, you understand? I'm a socialist.

Still?

Bill nodded. Bill nodded again. And Bill said, Yes, yes. But that doesn't say that I've got very much time for politicians. Including socialist politicians. They've a difficult job. But I mean, they make a terrible mess of it. So that really and truly a man is his own politics. Your politics, you are born with. And so was I born with mine.

That's shades of Rabbie Burns in that . . .

Yes. Exactly. Yes. Burns was a clever man. When he wrote *To a Mouse*, he was in the field, with his brother Gilbert. Ploughing. And he said to Gilbert, I need to go home. And when he went home, and Gilbert come home at night, he had written *To a Mouse*. The whole lot.

Yeah, said the interviewer. Smashing . . .

And Bill said, Yep.

Why, asked the interviewer, just lastly, Bill, in the book, there's this bit, which has attracted all the attention, where you say you are not welcome at Liverpool . . .

Yeah.

I mean, surely that isn't true?

Bill swallowed. And Bill said, I've written a book about people. Praising people. Talking about people. Ninety-nine per cent talking and praising people. One per cent a little bit of criticism. And people pick out the one per cent. And if anybody is annoyed at me saying that, then that appals me. Because it's a fact. It's fair comment. And if anybody writes a book. About sport or anything. And it's ninety-nine per cent OK. Surely the one per cent is nothing, is it? You wouldn't win an election if you only got one per cent . . .

No, said the interviewer. But you see, what did strike me as odd in the book, you say that you went to Bruges with Liverpool . . .

Yeah.

After you stopped being manager . . .

Yeah.

And they wouldn't let you stay in the same hotel. Now that

seems awful to me. That the club would say, Go to another hotel. We don't want you . . .

Well, I went at the invitation of Radio City. And they must have got permission from the club for me to go on the plane. But I was in a different hotel, yeah. Oh yes.

Well, I would have thought Bill Shankly could walk into Anfield every day of the week, all the time, for what you have done?

Bill nodded. And Bill said, Oh, I could. For the home games, yeah. I could, yeah. But not the away games. I mean, I used to get tickets from Burnley. For the game at Burnley. I mean, maybe when I went to the home game, they might have said, Do you want a couple of tickets for the game next week? But no. No. It's mentioned a bit because it happened to me. You understand?

Yeah.

It happened to me.

Yes.

My life was spent there. Fighting to get them somewhere –

Bill stopped speaking. Bill stopped talking. And Bill looked away again. No cars passing, no dogs barking. Nothing. Nothing but silence. In the sunshine and in the street. Just the silence.

Would you like to go back?

No.

Into management?

Bill shook his head. And Bill said, No, no. I'd like to have some involvement. About games. And to help people.

Two last questions, I suppose: would you go through it all again? And is the football now as good as when you started kicking the ball around in Ayrshire?

Oh, I wouldn't like to go through the whole thing again. But having gone through it, I would like to be involved in some way. Because I think that I can do the game a lot of good. I mean, my psychology. My knowledge of the game. My knowledge of people. And I think it would be a terrible pity for that to be wasted . . .

And is the game today –

Because I'm still as lucid as I was. Yeah, yeah . . .

That's great, said the interviewer. Thank you, Bill. Thank you very much. That was great, Bill.

Bill nodded. Bill stuck out his hand. And Bill said, OK, then. If you're sure you've got everything you need . . .

More than enough, said the interviewer. More than enough. But thank you again, Bill. Thank you.

Bill smiled. And Bill said, Well, if you want a cup of tea. And a biscuit. Before you head back . . .

No, no, said the interviewer. We best get back. We best get off. But thank you, Bill. Thank you again. And to your wife, too.

Bill nodded again. And Bill shook hands with the interviewer. And with the cameraman and the sound man. And Bill said, Well, you boys have a safe journey back now . . .

Thank you, Bill.

In the sunshine. In the street. With cars passing and with dogs barking. Bill walked back to his gate. Bill walked back up the drive. Bill opened his front door. Bill went back into the house. Bill closed the front door. Bill went back up the stairs. Bill went back into the bedroom. Bill went back over to the bed. Bill took off his jacket. The freshly cleaned grey jacket. Bill picked up the coat hanger from the bed. Bill hung the jacket back on the hanger. Bill went back over to the wardrobe. Bill opened the wardrobe door. Bill hung the jacket back inside the wardrobe. Bill stepped back from the wardrobe. Bill looked at the mirror on the back of the wardrobe door. Bill stared at the mirror on the back of the wardrobe door. Into the mirror on the back of the wardrobe door. The man in the mirror on the back of the wardrobe door. In his red shirt. The collar too big. Bill looked at the man. Bill stared at the man. The man shaking his head. Fighting back tears, struggling to breathe. And Bill said, I have not written anything derogatory about anyone. I have just stated facts. My book is ninety-nine per cent about people and one per cent of criticism. And people have dived in to talk about that one per cent. But that one per cent is fair comment. About fact, about what has happened.


## 67. AND HIGHLAND SCAB AND HUNGER

People did want Bill Shankly to be involved in some way. People at big clubs, people at small clubs. People did think Bill Shankly could do the game a lot of good. At big clubs, at small clubs. His knowledge of the game. His knowledge of people. People called Bill Shankly. People invited Bill Shankly to their big club and to their small club. To share his knowledge of the game, to share his knowledge of people. Derby County called Bill Shankly. Derby County asked Bill Shankly if he would consider taking on an advisory role at the Baseball Ground. To share his knowledge of the game, to share his knowledge of people. I'm seriously thinking about this offer, Bill Shankly told the gentlemen of the local press. Because I would feel as if I were part of something again. I envisage going to the Baseball Ground once or twice a week. But that does not affect Colin Murphy's position at all. And I'm not being pushed for a decision. It's not like being asked to get a spade out and dig the road. But I would feel as if I were part of the game again without having the worries of a manager. When you are a manager, you have more worries than the prime minister. And he's got enough. But I would feel as if I were part of something. I would be helping with the training and the playing side of the club, working on little details like where to eat and what time to go to bed and so on. I could come and go as I please, maybe just going in one day a week, which suits me fine. But I would feel as if I were part of something again. I go to the games anyway, so I wouldn't be away from home any more than I am now. But I would feel as if I were part of something. I have been in football forty-three years and sometimes I get a bit moody and fidgety. Going to the games is fine but, having been involved, it's better if you go with the official party. And I would feel as though I were part of something again . . .

And Bill Shankly did seriously think about the offer. Bill Shankly seriously thinking, Bill Shankly seriously wondering. Whether he should go or whether he should not go. Bill Shankly knowing and Bill Shankly not knowing. Whether he should go or whether he should not go. Round and around. Bill Shankly thinking, Bill Shankly wondering. Whether he should go or whether he should not go. Until Bill Shankly did know. And Bill Shankly did not go. Bill Shankly stayed at home. In Liverpool. Bill Shankly waiting. Still waiting, always waiting. For the letter on the mat, the knock on the door. Or the call on the phone –

Tommy Docherty rang Bill Shankly. Tommy Docherty invited

Bill Shankly to Old Trafford. For the match against Liverpool Football Club. Tommy Docherty asked Bill Shankly if he would like to be the guest of Manchester United. For the match against Liverpool Football Club. And to share his knowledge of the game, his knowledge of people. And before the match at Old Trafford. The match against Liverpool Football Club. Tommy Docherty invited Bill Shankly into the dressing room at Old Trafford. The Manchester United dressing room. Bill Shankly walked around the dressing room at Old Trafford. The Manchester United dressing room. Bill Shankly shook hands with Alex Stepney, Jimmy Nicholl, Brian Greenhoff, Martin Buchan, Stewart Houston, Steve Coppell, Lou Macari, Sammy McIlroy, Gordon Hill, Jimmy Greenhoff, Stuart Pearson and David McCreery. Bill Shankly patted the backs of the players of Manchester United. Bill Shankly wished the players of Manchester United the best of luck. The best of luck for the match. The match against Liverpool Football Club.

After the match at Old Trafford. The match against Liverpool Football Club. The nil–nil draw with Liverpool Football Club. Tommy Docherty invited Bill Shankly to have a meal with him in the restaurant at Old Trafford. And Bill Shankly sat with Tommy Docherty in the restaurant at Old Trafford. Bill Shankly ate with Tommy Docherty. Bill Shankly talked with Tommy Docherty. Joked with Tommy Docherty, laughed with Tommy Docherty. Joked a lot and laughed a lot. Until Tommy Docherty needed a piss. And Tommy Docherty got up from their table in the restaurant at Old Trafford. Tommy Docherty walked across the restaurant at Old Trafford. Past the table of the directors. The directors of Manchester United and the directors of Liverpool Football Club. And Sidney Reakes stopped Tommy. And Sidney Reakes said, I see Bill Shankly is here . . .

Aye, said Tommy. Bill is welcome here.


## 68. O TELL NA ME O' WIND AN' RAIN

Bill drove to Manchester again. In the wind and in the rain. Bill parked in the car park at Maine Road. In the wind and in the rain. Bill got out of his car. In the wind and in the rain. Bill put on his hat, Bill turned up his collar. In the wind and in the rain. Bill went into the ground. In the wind and in the rain. Bill took his seat in the corner of the stand behind the goal. In the wind and in the rain. And Bill waited for the match to kick off. In the wind and in the rain. The FA Cup semi-final replay between Liverpool Football Club and Everton Football Club. In the wind and in the rain. Bill sat among the little boys and little girls who had travelled from Liverpool to Manchester. In the wind and in the rain. The little boys and little girls with no hats and with no collars. In the wind and in the rain. The little boys and little girls in their T-shirts and their singlets. In the wind and in the rain. The little boys and little girls soaked to their skins. In the wind and in the rain. Through to their bones. In the wind and in the rain. Bill watched the match with the little boys and little girls. In the wind and in the rain. Bill listened to them cheer. In the wind and in the rain. To cheer and to cheer. In the wind and in the rain. Liverpool Football Club. In the wind and in the rain. After the match. In the wind and in the rain. The match Liverpool Football Club had won. In the wind and in the rain. Bill got up from his seat. In the wind and in the rain. Bill soaked to his skin and through to his bones. In the wind and in the rain. Bill walked out of the ground. And in the wind and in the rain. Bill was recognised by a journalist. In the wind and in the rain. Bill was stopped by the journalist. In the wind and in the rain. The journalist asked Bill about the game. And in the wind and in the rain. Bill said, There was water dripping on me throughout the match. And there were little boys and little girls with only singlets on. They had spent all their money to get here. And they were soaked to their skins for their trouble. And then you people come out in the media and you say, These are the people we don't want. They are hooligans. Hooligans. And we don't want them here. And that really appals me. It appals me. The way you make them sit or stand in the rain in pens. The way you treat them like animals, worse than animals. Branding them as animals, branding them as hooligans. And hoping they will not come. Don't you realise that without these people, these boys and girls, there would be no game? Don't you realise that throughout the country these are the people who will spend all their money and do without a pair of shoes to support their team? Don't you bloody realise? Don't you fucking care?

## 69. IF PROVIDENCE HAS SENT ME HERE

Liverpool Football Club had won the League Championship again. For the first time, Liverpool Football Club had retained the League Championship. Then Liverpool Football Club had gone to Wembley Stadium. And Liverpool Football Club had lost the FA Cup Final to Manchester United. But Liverpool Football Club still had another cup final to come. The European Cup Final –

For the first time.

Liverpool Football Club travelled to Rome to play Borussia Mönchengladbach Football Club of West Germany at the Stadio Olimpico in Rome. And they were not alone. In their thousands. The supporters of Liverpool Football Club travelled to Rome. In their thousands. On planes or on trains. In their thousands. By car or by thumb. In their thousands. With tickets and without tickets. In their thousands. With their banners. *JOEY ATE THE FROGS LEGS, MADE THE SWISS ROLL, NOW HE'S MUNCHING GLADBACH.* In their thousands. With their flags. Their red and white chequered flags. In their thousands. With their songs: *Tell me ma, me ma, I'm not coming home for tea, I'm going to I-ta-lee, Tell me ma, me ma.* In their thousands. They were not alone –

Not alone.

Bill Shankly travelled to Rome, too. Along with the wives of the players of Liverpool Football Club. Along with the parents of the players of Liverpool Football Club. Bill Shankly was a guest of Liverpool Football Club. For the first time. An official guest in the official hotel. The Holiday Inn St Peter's Hotel in the centre of Rome. The Holiday Inn where the wives of the players of Liverpool Football Club were staying. Where the parents of the players of Liverpool Football Club were staying. And where the players of Liverpool Football Club were staying. But Bill Shankly did not hang around in the corridors and the dining room of the Holiday Inn St Peter's Hotel in the centre of Rome. Oh no. Bill Shankly did not want to be in anybody's way. Bill Shankly did not want to be under anybody's feet.

Bill Shankly woke up early. On the morning of the final. Bill Shankly went out to the Stadio Olimpico. On the morning of the final. Bill Shankly sat in his seat in the stands of the Stadio Olimpico. On the morning of the final. Bill Shankly was the first person in his seat. On the morning of the final. Bill Shankly was the only person in his seat. In his seat in the stands. Bill Shankly looked around the stadium. The empty seats, the waiting seats. In his seat in the stands. Bill Shankly looked down at the pitch. The grass and the lines. The posts and the nets. And Bill Shankly waited. And Bill Shankly worried. Bill Shankly worried that the players of Liverpool Football Club would be drained. The players of Liverpool Football Club would be tired. Drained and tired by the FA Cup Final defeat to Manchester United. Drained and tired by the heat of the Stadio Olimpico in Rome. On the morning of the final it was already eighty degrees. But in his seat in the stands of the stadium. Bill Shankly waited. And Bill Shankly hoped. Bill Shankly hoped Bob Paisley would make sure the players of Liverpool Football Club regained as much of their strength as possible. And Bill Shankly prayed. Bill Shankly prayed the players of Liverpool Football Club would find as much of their strength as possible. On the morning of the final. In his seat in the stands of the stadium. Bill Shankly smiled. Bill Shankly knew no one should underestimate Bob Paisley. Bill Shankly knew no one should underestimate the players of Liverpool Football Club. And Bill Shankly waited. And waited. Through the afternoon of the final. Bill Shankly waited. And Bill Shankly watched the supporters of Liverpool Football Club begin to arrive at the Stadio Olimpico. Through the afternoon of the final. Bill Shankly watched the supporters of Liverpool Football Club begin to fill the Stadio Olimpico. Through the afternoon of the final. Bill Shankly saw the banners and the flags of the supporters of Liverpool Football Club begin to take over the Stadio Olimpico. The red and white chequered flags. Through the afternoon of the final. Bill Shankly heard the chants and the songs of the supporters of Liverpool Football Club begin to overwhelm the Stadio Olimpico. *Ee-aye-addio, we're going to win the Cup. We're going to win the Cup, we're going to win the Cup. Ee-aye-addio, we're going to win the Cup!*

And through the afternoon of the final. In his seat in the stands of the stadium. The stadium now a sea of red and white chequered flags, the stadium now a storm of red and white songs. Bill Shankly smiled. And smiled. Bill Shankly knew no one should ever underestimate the supporters of Liverpool Football Club. On the evening of the final. In his seat in the stands. On the edge of his seat in the stands. Bill Shankly stared down at the players. The players of Liverpool Football Club. Ray Clemence. Peter McDonnell. Alec Lindsay. Tommy Smith. Emlyn Hughes. Ray Kennedy. Ian Callaghan. Alan Waddle. Kevin Keegan and Steve Heighway. The old and the new. Phil Neal. Joey Jones. Jimmy Case. Terry McDermott. David Fairclough and David Johnson. The players of Liverpool Football Club coming out of the tunnel. The players of Liverpool Football Club walking out into the stadium. To a deafening roar, to a glorious reception. On the night of the final. On the edge of his seat in the stands. Bill Shankly smiled again. Bill Shankly knew there was no way Liverpool Football Club could lose. No way on earth –

*Ee-aye-addio, we've won the Cup! We've won the Cup, we've won the Cup. Ee-aye-addio, we've won the Cup!*

Bill Shankly got up from his seat. His seat in the stands. Bill Shankly began to make his way out of the stadium. But a British journalist recognised Bill Shankly. And the journalist asked Bill Shankly about the game. About the team. Down there is the side you helped to build. What about that, Bill –

What a night for you?

This is the greatest night in the history of Liverpool Football Club, said Bill Shankly. Liverpool Football Club have been working towards this night for years. This night is the result of planning, of simplicity, and of how to play the game in a simple manner. And I think the whole world now realises that that's the way to play. The players were simply tremendous. And so were the crowd. They were unbelievable. This is what football is all about . . .

And the journalist thanked Bill Shankly. And Bill Shankly walked on. Among the supporters of Liverpool Football Club. In their thousands. Waving their banners, waving their flags. Their red and white chequered flags. In their thousands. Chanting and singing one song: *Ee-aye-addio, we've won the Cup.* Heading to the buses, heading back to town. Among the thousands. Bill Shankly headed back towards his bus. The bus back to the hotel. Among the thousands. Looking at all the flags waving. The red and white chequered flags. Listening to the one song being sung. *Ee-aye-addio, we've won the Cup.* Among the thousands. One supporter spotted Bill Shankly. And the supporter said, Is that really you, Bill? Is it really you, Bill?

Aye, said Bill Shankly. But keep it down, son. Keep it down. I don't want to start a riot with all the fans around . . .

But what are you doing out here, Bill? Why aren't you back in the stadium with the team, Bill? Your team . . .

Oh well now, said Bill Shankly. It's not my team now. It's Bob's team now, son. It's Bob's night tonight. Not mine, son.

The supporter shook his head. And the supporter said, No offence, Bill. But that's bloody rubbish, Bill. Everybody knows it's your team, Bill. It's your team, Bill. Everybody knows that, Bill. The team you built, Bill. The team you made, Bill. Everybody knows that, Bill. You should be celebrating with the players, Bill. With your players, Bill. With your team, Bill.

Well, thanks for saying that, said Bill Shankly. That's a nice thing to say, son. Thank you . . .

No, Bill. No. Don't thank me, Bill. Please don't thank me, Bill. Because I'm not just saying it, Bill. I'm not just saying it, Bill. It's true, Bill. It's true, Bill. It's us who should be thanking you, Bill. Us who should be thanking you, Bill. We wouldn't be here without you, Bill. This wouldn't have happened without you, Bill. Everybody knows that, Bill. It couldn't have happened without you, Bill. It could never have happened without you, Bill. Never, Bill. Never.

No, no, said Bill Shankly. It couldn't have happened without all of *you*, son. Without all of you supporters.

Well, come and join us then, Bill. Come and have a drink with us in town tonight, Bill . . .

Thank you, said Bill Shankly. Thank you, son. But I'm a wee bit tired now. I've been at the stadium all day, son. I'm going back to the hotel now . . .

But you haven't even got a scarf on you, Bill. Not even a Liverpool scarf on, Bill. Will you not take mine, Bill? I would be proud if you would wear mine tonight, Bill –

And the supporter untied the scarf from around his neck. And the supporter tied the scarf around Bill Shankly's neck.

And Bill Shankly looked down at the scarf around his neck. The Liverpool scarf. Bill Shankly touched the wool of the scarf. The red and white wool of the Liverpool scarf. And then Bill Shankly looked up at the supporter of Liverpool Football Club –

Thank you, said Bill Shankly. Thank you, son. And I will treasure this scarf. I will always treasure it. Because I know what this scarf must mean to you, son. On this great night for our great club . . .

The supporter of Liverpool Football Club nodded. And the supporter of Liverpool Football Club watched Bill Shankly walk on. Among the thousands of other supporters of Liverpool Football Club. Bill Shankly walked on towards the bus. The bus back to the hotel. Among the thousands. Other supporters now spotted Bill Shankly. In the coach park. And some of the supporters of Liverpool Football Club got down on their hands and on their knees. In the coach park. Thousands of supporters were now down on their hands and on their knees. In the coach park. On their hands and on their knees. Their heads bowed. The supporters quietly sang, *Shankly, Shankly, Shankly.* In the coach park. Bill Shankly walked among them. The thousands of supporters. On their hands and on their knees. Bill Shankly touched their bowed heads. Bill Shankly shook their outstretched hands. And then Bill Shankly climbed aboard the bus. The bus back to the hotel.

After the match, after the victory. There were the celebrations. And the party. In the dining room at the Holiday Inn. Bill Shankly looked around the room. In the centre of the room, tables had been arranged in a huge oblong. The tables covered with long white cloths. The tables piled high with food. But inside these tables. In the centre of these tables. There was another table. And on this table stood the European Cup. Bill Shankly walked over to the tables. Bill Shankly stood before the European Cup. Bill Shankly looked across the tables. The European Cup on the other side of the tables. Bill Shankly looked across the food. And Bill Shankly stared at the European Cup. Out of reach. Bill Shankly stared into the European Cup. Into the silver, the silver surface of the European Cup. And Bill Shankly saw his face reflected in the European Cup. Contorted and distorted. And Bill Shankly smiled. Some of the supporters of Liverpool Football Club had managed to get into the dining room of the Holiday Inn. The supporters were on their hands and on their knees. Under the cloths, under the tables. The supporters crawled into the centre of the tables. The supporters got to their feet. And the supporters touched the European Cup. The supporters had their photographs taken with the

European Cup. And one of the supporters came back up from under the tables, from under the cloths. On his hands and on his knees. The supporter saw Bill Shankly. Bill Shankly standing at the table. Bill Shankly staring at the European Cup. And the supporter said, This is all down to you, Mr Shankly. All down to you, Mr Shankly . . .

Thank you, said Bill Shankly. Thank you, son.


## 70. 'TWAS SURELY IN HIS ANGER

Bill was invited onto the bus. The open-top bus. And Bill went onto the bus. The open-top bus. For the parade through the streets of Liverpool. With the players of Liverpool Football Club and with the European Cup. On the open-top bus. With the players and their cup, with the players and their bottles. On the open-top bus. Many of the players were still drunk from the night before. The triumph of the night before. Kevin Keegan had a black eye from the night before. The celebrations of the night before. And on the open-top bus. Bill tried to get some of the players of Liverpool Football Club to calm down. On the open-top bus. Bill tried to get some of the players to put down their bottles. On the open-top bus. Bill wanted the players of Liverpool Football Club to see the supporters of Liverpool Football Club. The thousands of supporters of Liverpool Football Club. The hundreds of thousands of supporters of Liverpool Football Club. And not only the supporters of Liverpool Football Club. The supporters of Everton Football Club. All the people of the city of Liverpool were lining the streets of the city of Liverpool. Applauding the players of Liverpool Football Club, cheering the players of Liverpool Football Club. On the open-top bus. Bill wanted the players of Liverpool Football Club to drink in these scenes on the streets of the city of Liverpool. On the open-top bus. Bill wanted the players of Liverpool Football Club to never forget these scenes on the streets of the city of Liverpool. On the open-top bus. Bill wanted the players of Liverpool Football Club to always remember these scenes on the streets of the city of Liverpool. On the open-top bus. Bill wanted the players of Liverpool Football Club to always remember the supporters of Liverpool Football Club.

On William Brown Street. Bill got off the bus with the players and the staff of Liverpool Football Club. On William Brown Street. Bill walked up the steps to the platform in front of the Picton Library with the players and the staff of Liverpool Football Club. Before the Corinthian columns of the Picton Library. Bill stood with the players and the staff of Liverpool Football Club and their families. And before the Corinthian columns of the Picton Library. Bill remembered the first time he had stood here. Before the Corinthian columns of the Picton Library. The many times he had stood here. Before the Corinthian columns of the Picton Library. The last time he had stood here. But before the Corinthian columns of the Picton Library. Bill could not believe his eyes. Bill saw some of the players of Liverpool Football Club swaying from side to side. Some of the players of Liverpool Football Club struggling to stay on their feet. Some of the players of Liverpool Football Club too drunk to stand. And before the Corinthian columns of the Picton Library. Bill turned away, Bill looked away. Before the Corinthian columns of the Picton Library. Bill looked down, down at his shoes. Before the Corinthian columns of the Picton Library. Bill heard Bob Paisley say, In the thirty-eight years I have been here, this exceeds everything. It is the biggest day in the life of Liverpool Football Club. And before the Corinthian columns of the Picton Library. Bill could not believe his ears. Bill heard Emlyn Hughes grab the microphone from Bob Paisley. And Bill heard Emlyn Hughes singing, *Na na, na-na-na, Liverpool are magic, Everton are tragic. Na na, na-na-na, Everton are tragic . . .*

And before the Corinthian columns of the Picton Library. Bill could not breathe. Bill could not fight back the tears.


## 71. THIS WAS YOUR LIFE

Bob Paisley had won the European Cup. Jock Stein and Matt Busby had also won the European Cup. But Bob Paisley was the first Englishman to win the European Cup. Bob Paisley was the Manager of the Year. Bell's Whisky sponsored the Manager of the Year awards. Bell's Whisky asked Bill Shankly if he would like to present Bob Paisley with his Manager of the Year award –

Yes, said Bill Shankly. I will.

In the hotel dining room. In front of all the managers of all the football clubs in England. Bill Shankly stood up. Bill Shankly walked to the front of the room. And Bill Shankly stood before the room –

You probably all think I'm jealous at having to give this wonderful honour to Bob Paisley, the Manager of the Year, said Bill Shankly. Well, you'd all be damn right!

And in the hotel dining room. All the managers of all the football clubs in England laughed. And Bob Paisley stood up. Bob Paisley walked to the front of the room. Bob Paisley shook hands with Bill Shankly. Bob Paisley thanked Bill Shankly. And Bob Paisley said, When I took over from Bill, I said that I would settle for a drop of Bell's once a month, a big bottle at the end of the season and a ride around the city centre in an open-top bus! So thank you very much. Mind you, I've been here during the bad times, too. In my first year, we finished second . . .

And in the hotel dining room. All the managers of all the football clubs in England laughed again. And all the managers of all the football clubs applauded Bob Paisley. And Bill Shankly smiled.

The producers of *This Is Your Life* planned to surprise Bob Paisley in London after Liverpool Football Club had played Queens Park Rangers. The producers of *This Is Your Life* asked Bill Shankly if he would like to appear on this tribute to the life of Bob Paisley –

Yes, said Bill Shankly. I will.

In the television studio. In front of the audience. Bill Shankly stepped from behind the scenes. Bill Shankly walked towards Bob Paisley. Bill Shankly shook hands with Bob Paisley –

Bob and I never had any rows, said Bill Shankly. We didn't have any time for that. We had to plan where we were going to keep all the cups we won.

And in the television studio. Bob Paisley laughed. Eamonn Andrews laughed. And the audience laughed. And in their homes. The viewers laughed. Everybody laughed.

And Bill Shankly smiled.

## 72. DON'T LET ME KEEP YOU

In the house, in their kitchen. Bill helped Ness clear away the breakfast things. Bill dried up the breakfast things. In the house, in their hallway. Bill picked up the paper from the table in the hall. In the house, in their front room. In his chair. Bill read the paper. Bill finished the paper. Bill put down the paper. In the house, in their front room. Bill stared out of the window. Through the condensation on the inside of the glass, through the raindrops on the outside of the glass. Bill watched the people going to work. Bill watched the children going to school. In the house, in their front room. Bill heard Ness dusting in the hall. Bill heard Ness vacuuming in the hall. In the house, in their bedroom. Bill put on his suit. Bill put on his tie. In the house, in their hallway. Bill put on his coat. Bill picked up his umbrella. And Bill said, I'm just going to pop out for a bit, love. Have a walk to the shops for a paper.

It's raining cats and dogs out there, said Ness. You'll get soaked to your skin, love. You'll get soaked through.

Bill smiled. And Bill said, No, love. No. I've got my coat and I've got my brolly. And a bit of rain never hurt anyone, love. And the exercise will do me good. And get me out from under your feet, love.

Well, if you've made up your mind, said Ness, then you go, love. You go. But you take care, love. And I'll see you when you get back.

Bill kissed Ness on her cheek. And Bill said, Thanks, love.

In the cafe on the Eaton Road in West Derby, Liverpool. In his suit and in his tie. Bill sat in the window. The condensation on the inside of the glass, the raindrops on the outside of the glass. In his suit and in his tie. Bill stared out of the window of the cafe on the Eaton Road in West Derby, Liverpool. Through the condensation, through the raindrops. Bill watched the people in the street. In the rain. Bill watched the people going to work. In the rain. The people doing their shopping. In the rain. The people busy, the people occupied. In the rain. In the cafe on the Eaton Road in West Derby, Liverpool. In his suit and in his tie. Bill looked back down at his newspaper on the table. The newspaper he had already read. Twice. Bill picked up his cup of tea. Bill took another sip. The tea cold, the tea old. Bill heard the door of the cafe open. Bill looked up. And Bill saw a man he knew. A man who sometimes came into the cafe for his breakfast. A man who always had a good chat with Bill. And Bill said, Hello, son. How are you, son? You look soaked through, son. Sit yourself down, son. And get some hot food inside you, son. A nice cup of tea down you, son . . .

The man smiled. The man pulled up a chair. The man sat down at the table with Bill. And the man smiled again –

It's good to see you, Bill. Great to see you again. But how are you, Bill? Are you well?

Oh, I'm very well. Thank you, son. Thank you. Mind you, I picked up a wee knock in the five-a-side on Monday. But I'll be right for Friday. I'll be fit to play on Friday, no danger. But what about you? How are you, son? I've not seen you in here for ages. You must be busy, son. Are they keeping you busy at work?

Yeah, yeah. We're busy, Bill. We're busy. But I mean, I can't complain, Bill. I mustn't grumble. At least we're busy, Bill. At least I've got a job. I mean, I'm one of the lucky ones these days, Bill.

Oh yes. You're right, son. You're right. These are hard times for so many folk, son. I mean, these are desperate times for so many folk. It appals me, son. I mean, it appals me the way the country is going. It's going backwards, son. Backwards. So you do right to count your blessings, son. You do right. You have your job, you have your work. You have your family and you have your health. These are the things that matter, son. These are the important things.

And the football, said the man. Don't forget the football, Bill. At least we've always got the football . . .

Oh well, yes. Yes. You're right, son. You're right. We've always got the football, son. Always got the football. No matter what a mess the politicians make of things, son. No matter what a mess they make of the world. We've always got the football, son. We've always got that to be thankful for . . .

The waitress brought over a breakfast for the man. The man picked up the knife and the fork from the table. And Bill said, Go on, son. Go on. Get stuck in, son. Get stuck in. Get that inside you, son. A man needs to keep his strength up . . .

The man nodded –

And at least we're having a good season, Bill. Thank God we're having a good season, eh?

Oh well, yes. Yes. At Anfield, at home. We are. Yes. We are.

Not bad, not bad at all. But away from home, away from Anfield. It's a different story, son. A very different story. And to be honest with you, son. I'm worried. I'm very worried, son. I mean, I know they won away at Leicester on Saturday. But they've lost at City, they've lost at United. And they lost at Queens Park Rangers. Now you can't be losing at Queens Park Rangers, son. You can't be losing there, if you want to win the League. Not if you want to win the League, son. And they lost at home to Villa, too. At Anfield, son. And then there have been all the draws. I mean, five draws already, son . . .

The man nodded again –

But you think we can still win the League, don't you, Bill? You think we still can . . .

Well, it won't be easy. I can tell you that, son. It won't be easy. I mean, we've still to play Forest, son. Home and away.

But you don't think Forest can win the League, do you, Bill?

Bill smiled. And Bill said, Well, nothing would surprise me with Brian. Not with Brian Clough, son. I've always admired him. I've always respected him, son. And we often chat. He often calls me, son. To get my thoughts, to pick my brains. He's a very clever man, son. And a socialist, too. A man after my own heart, son . . .

But Dalglish is doing well for us, isn't he, Bill? I mean, I thought it might take him time to find his feet. Take him a while to settle, Bill. I mean, I'm very surprised how well he's doing for us . . .

Oh well, yes. But I am not surprised, son. Not surprised at all. I mean, I had my eye on Kenny since he was fifteen. I mean, when he was only fifteen, I had Kenny down here for a trial. And he was brilliant. He was brilliant, son. Even then, at fifteen. I remember it well. After the trial, me and Reuben. We drove him back to the YMCA. And I would have signed him then and there. No bother at all! But the boy was homesick. He was only fifteen. And he didn't want to leave home. And so I remember I called Jock Stein. And I said to Jock, I said, John, I cannot believe no one has signed this boy. This boy is brilliant. This boy is unbelievable. And Jock signed him. Then and there. Even though the boy was a Rangers fan! Jock signed him on. And that was good. That was great. I mean, if he wasn't going to come to Anfield. If he wasn't going to play for us. Then Celtic was the best place for him. With Jock to look after him, Jock to watch over him. So

I've had my eye on him for years, son. For years. So I'm not surprised how well he is going, son. Not surprised at all. And I tell you another thing, son. This is only the beginning. Only the beginning for Kenny at Anfield, son. And he'll not get carried away. No, Kenny's not that type, son. I mean, the night he signed for us. Big John Toshack brought him over to my house here in West Derby. Because John knows what it's like. No matter how old you are. No matter what you have done in the game. You are in a new city. You are stuck in a hotel. Away from your family, away from your home. So John brought him over to my house. For a cup of tea with me and Ness. And so we had a nice cup of tea and I had a wee chat with him. And I said to him, Kenny. I said, I've just got two pieces of advice for you, son. Don't go overeating in that bloody hotel. And don't lose your accent!

The man laughed. The man put down his knife and his fork –

So you think he'll score on Saturday then, Bill?

Aye. No danger, son. No danger at all.

And you'll be there, Bill, yeah?

Oh aye. Rain or shine . . .

The man glanced up through the window of the cafe. The man glanced down at his watch. The man shook his head –

Well, I suppose I best be getting back, Bill. Back to work . . .

Bill stood up. Bill picked up his umbrella. Bill handed the man his umbrella. And Bill said, Take this with you then, son.

Oh no, said the man. I can't do that, Bill. What about you? What will you do, Bill? You'll get soaked . . .

Bill shook his head. And Bill said, Take it, son. Take it. You've to go back to your work, son. Your need is greater than mine. I mean, I can stay here till it stops. Or I can dry off when I get home. But you've to go back to your work. You've your work to do . . .

Well then, thank you. And I'll drop it back here tomorrow for you, Bill. I'll bring it back then . . .

Bill shook his head. And Bill said, There's no rush, son. There's no rush at all. So don't be going out of your way, son. Don't you be making a special journey now. Not for me, son. Not for me.

Thanks, said the man. Thanks again, Bill. And I'll see you soon, I hope. So you take care now, Bill. You take care.

Bill nodded. Bill smiled. And Bill said, And don't you work

too hard now either, son. You look after yourself . . .

And Bill sat back down at the table in the window of the cafe on the Eaton Road in West Derby, Liverpool. In his suit and in his tie. Bill looked back down at his newspaper on the table. Bill picked up the paper again. Bill turned to the back pages of the paper. Bill heard the door of the cafe open. Bill looked up from his paper. And Bill saw a man he knew. A man who sometimes came into the cafe for his lunch. A man who always had a good chat with Bill. And Bill put down his paper. And Bill said, Hello, son. How are you, son? You look soaked through, son. Sit yourself down, son. And get some hot food inside you, son. A nice cup of tea down you, son . . .

## 73. AT THE TOP OF MY VOICE

Liverpool Football Club had beaten West Ham United two–nil. At home, at Anfield. Dalglish had scored in the thirty-seventh minute. And Fairclough had scored in the eighty-second minute. In the press box. The Anfield press box. With their pens and with their notebooks. The gentlemen of the press were scribbling away. The national press and the local press. The London press and the Liverpool press. The gentlemen of the press stopped their scribbling. The gentlemen of the press put away their pens. They put away their notebooks. And the gentlemen of the press walked out of the press box. They walked out into the corridor. The Anfield corridor –

Here they come, said Bill Shankly. Bill Shankly in the corridor outside the press box. Outside the Anfield press box. Bill Shankly standing there in the corridor, Bill Shankly waiting there in the corridor. In the Anfield corridor –

Here they are. Norman Fox of the London *Times*. Journalist extraordinaire. What a writer he is. Bob Greaves of Granada Television. Broadcaster supreme. What a presenter he is. Great professionals, true professionals. Always working, always digging. Looking for angles, looking for stories. Never off the clock. Here they all are. Looking for me, no doubt. To get my thoughts, to pick my brains. So come on then, boys. Here I am, here I am. You've found me, you've found me. So what do you want to know, boys?

Outside the press box. The Anfield press box. In the corridor. The Anfield corridor. The gentlemen of the press smiled. And the gentlemen of the press asked Bill Shankly who he thought should be the next manager of England. Did Bill think it should be Ron Greenwood? Did Bill think it should be Lawrie McMenemy? Did Bill think it should be Brian Clough? Did Bill think Brian Clough was even seriously interested in the job?

Oh well, said Bill Shankly. Brian and me, we often chat. We often talk. And so I know Brian well. And so I know Brian would not be going down to London if he did not fancy the job. If he was not interested in the job . . .

The gentlemen of the press nodded. And the gentlemen of the press asked, But do you think Brian Clough could do the job, Bill? Do you think he would do a good job as manager of England?

Oh, I have no doubt at all, said Bill Shankly. No doubt at all. Brian loves the game. Brian is passionate about the game. And his love for the game. His passion for the game. These are the things that have made him successful. And I believe he is the people's choice, too. Because he is a man of the people. A man like me . . .

Outside the press box. The Anfield press box. In the corridor. The Anfield corridor. The gentlemen of the press nodded. The gentlemen of the press smiled. The local press and the national press. The Liverpool press and the London press. But now the gentlemen of the London press looked at their watches. And now the gentlemen of the London press began to edge away. Away to pick up their phones, away to file their reports. But outside the press box. The Anfield press box. In the corridor. The Anfield corridor. The gentlemen of the Liverpool press did not look at their watches. The gentlemen of the Liverpool press did not begin to edge away. Outside the press box. The Anfield press box. In the corridor. The Anfield corridor. The gentlemen of the Liverpool press asked Bill Shankly about the game. Did Bill think it had been a good match? Did Bill think Liverpool had turned the corner now? After two wins in succession . . .

Oh well, said Bill Shankly again. It's difficult to say. Very difficult to say. I mean, it was good to see Thompson back. Very good to see him back. But he'll need to re-establish himself. Rebuild his rapport with Emlyn Hughes. Thompson will need to do that. Because

West Ham almost caught them out. They almost found them out. I mean, I think they were a little unlucky. West Ham United. I mean, to be a goal down at half-time, I thought they were unlucky. Very unlucky. I mean, Brooking and Curbishley were very quick. Those two were very sharp. And they passed the ball beautifully. Beautiful, neat passing. But their marksmen let them down. And I mean, losing Taylor didn't help their cause. That was a blow for West Ham. A big blow. And I don't think they ever really recovered. And I think if he had not gone off. If Taylor had not had to go off. Then I think it might have been a different game, a very different story, boys.

The gentlemen of the Liverpool press nodded. And the gentlemen of the Liverpool press asked, But what about the goals, Bill? The Liverpool goals?

Oh well, said Bill Shankly. They were good goals. Yes. They were great goals. I mean, I think Thompson's header would have gone in. I believe Dalglish got the last touch. I believe he'll get the credit. But Thompson deserves some of the credit, too. And then Heighway's corner for the second was a brilliant corner. And he had a brilliant game. Yes. In many ways, I think Heighway was the difference. He was brilliant. Brilliant. Some of his runs, some of his crosses. It was like watching Tom Finney at his best. Tommy Finney in his prime . . .

The gentlemen of the Liverpool press nodded. The gentlemen of the Liverpool press smiled. And the gentlemen of the Liverpool press said, You make it sound like a cup final, Bill . . .

Oh yes, said Bill Shankly. Yes. You see, every game and every day for me is still a cup final day. It always was. And it always will be. And nobody, no matter what they try to do or say. Nobody will ever take that away from me. Nobody. Because everything I do, every single thing I do. If I'm signing an autograph or if I'm cleaning the car. I do it with enthusiasm. I do it with pride. And that means there is a certain amount of pressure behind it. Like for a cup final. A cup final every day. Behind everything I do. Every single thing I do. Because I have always driven myself. All along the line. All along the way. And I'm not going to stop now. In fact, I don't think I could stop. Even if I wanted to. And I don't want to. I never want to stop. I want to keep driving myself. And to keep pushing myself. Because that is called ambition. And that's what keeps you going. Ambition keeps you going. And it's ambition that has kept me going. All these years. I mean, if you don't have ambition. If you have no ambition. Then you might as well get into your bloody coffin now!

The gentlemen of the Liverpool press nodded again. The gentlemen of the Liverpool press smiled again. And the gentlemen of the Liverpool press said, Well, it looks like it keeps you fit, Bill?

Oh yes, said Bill Shankly again. Yes. Keeping fit is the most important thing of all. If you are physically fit, then you are mentally fit. You are alert. And you are sharp. And so I am alert. And I am sharp. As alert as I ever was and as sharp as I ever was. I mean, I was always an athlete. And so fitness was always in my blood. Keeping me alert, keeping me sharp. In fact, I'm still only eleven stone thirteen pounds. That's only three pound heavier than when I was bloody playing! When I was playing thirty year ago!

The gentlemen of the Liverpool press laughed. And the gentlemen of the Liverpool press said, So you are not tempted by any of these offers then, Bill? These offers we keep hearing about. These offers we keep reading about. Because you're certainly fit enough, Bill. You are well enough. So you're not tempted then, Bill?

Oh well, said Bill Shankly. It's a difficult thing to say, boys. A very difficult thing to say. I mean, yes. I have had offers almost every single month since I packed in here. From chairmen and vice-chairmen of I-don't-know-how-many different football clubs. Almost every single football club in the land! And of course, I have been very flattered. And yes, I have been very tempted. But I mean, for one reason or another. The jobs were not right. The offers were just not suitable. I mean, many of them meant travelling too far away from home. Away from Liverpool. And while I don't mind travelling about. I don't mind travelling around with a club. I don't like to spend a night away from home. And so I don't want full-time involvement. That's not what I'd want. But I'd like to be involved with a football club. In an advisory capacity, you understand? Using my experience of the game, using my knowledge of the game. My experience of people, my knowledge of people. And to be one of the boys again. Yes. To be one of the boys again. I think it would take ten year off my age. Yes. It would take ten years off me.

## 74. THE MATCHES OF THE DAYS

In the house, in their front room. In the evening and in the silence. Bill got up from his chair. Bill walked over to the television. Bill switched off the television. Bill walked out of the front room. Bill walked into the hallway. Bill picked up the telephone. Bill dialled a number. In the house, in their hallway. Bill listened to the telephone ring. And ring. And then Bill heard Peter Robinson say, Hello?

And Bill said, Hello, Peter. Hello. It's only me. It's only Bill. Now did you just see the games? The games on *Match of the Day*?

Yes, said Peter Robinson. I saw them. I watched it.

And so what did you think, Peter? What did you think? I mean, I think that's a good result. A very good result for Everton, don't you think? I mean, I think many folk will have been surprised by that.

Yes, said Peter Robinson again. It's a good result.

But I can't say I'm surprised, Peter. I can't say I'm very surprised. I mean, the way Gordon has set them up.

Yes, said Peter Robinson. They looked very efficient. Very well organised. But I was surprised he kept McKenzie on the bench . . .

Oh well. I can't say that surprised me, Peter. Not really. Not the way Gordon is. Not the way he has got them playing as a team, Peter. You can see he believes in the importance of the team. In the importance of the individual knowing their place within the system. Within the team. Now McKenzie is skilful, I agree. Very skilful, I agree, Peter. But he has a tendency to show off. And to be that wee bit too greedy. And to not know his place, his place in the team. And so I can see why Gordon did not use him, why he kept him on the bench.

Yes, said Peter Robinson. He can be a little showy . . .

That's it, Peter. Exactly. That's it. He can be a little bit showy. And they were doing well enough without him. Without him and his bag of tricks. So Gordon had no call for him. He did not need him. Not when they were playing so well. I mean, I thought they took Chelsea for a walk in the park. To be honest with you, it was something of a stroll for Everton. I mean, they were happy enough to let Chelsea run. But only as far as the penalty area, mind you. Because they knew Chelsea would get no further. They could get no further. Not with Higgins, Jones and Pejic. Higgins, Jones and Pejic were very solid.

Very strong, Peter. I mean, they even allowed Cooke a yard start.

He did have two good chances, said Peter Robinson.

He did, Peter. Yes, he did. You are right, Peter. You are right. But his shooting is never up to his passing. And they know that. They knew that. Their eyes were more on Wilkins, I think. Now he was a danger. He's always a danger, is Wilkins. He does everything. He chases everything. He's a terrier. A terrier, Peter. But I mean, Buckley, Dawson and King always had control of the midfield. They never relinquished control of the midfield. But still, as you say. As you say, Peter, Chelsea still had their chances. Two good chances. And it might have been a different game. A very different story. If they had taken one of those chances. If Everton had had to chase the game. It might have been a different story. But to be honest with you, Peter, I could not see it. I could never see it happening. Because Chelsea need a man like Latchford. A player like Latchford. A player who will always take his chance. I mean, Chelsea lack that kind of player. That kind of man.

Did you think it was a penalty, asked Peter Robinson.

No, no. I did not, Peter. No. I mean, the lad Pejic said it was not his hand. It was the hand of the keeper. The hand of Wood. And the way the players protested. The way the Everton players reacted. I am sure it was never a penalty. And it would have been harsh if the lad had then scored. So I think justice was done. Justice was served.

What did you think of George Wood, asked Peter Robinson. I thought he made two very good saves, did he not?

Yes and no, Peter. Yes and no. Yes, they were good saves. Yes. But they were saves he should have made. That's his job, Peter. I mean, he was just doing his job. But you saw the other match, too? You watched the Birmingham–Forest match, Peter?

Yes, said Peter Robinson. I did, Bill.

Well now, then you saw a very good save there. An exceptional save by Shilton. I mean, Francis flicked it up beautifully. He volleyed it beautifully. He did everything right. But there was Shilton. With a glancing save, with a brilliant save. Not many keepers would have got to that, Peter. Not many men, I can tell you. That was going in, that was heading home. No danger. No danger at all. But there was Shilton. At full stretch. Incredible. I mean, for him to reach that. For Shilton to save that. Bloody unbelievable!

And Forest are still top, said Peter Robinson. And Peter Robinson laughed. And Peter Robinson said, I find that pretty unbelievable, too. If I'm honest with you, Bill . . .

Well, you know, Peter. You know what I think. I think they can go all the way. I think they can win the League. I really do, Peter. The way Brian has got them playing. The way he has set them up. As a team, Peter. As a team again. Not individuals, Peter. But as a team. A very balanced team. And Birmingham were no match for them. No match at all. And I mean, Alf will know that –

I do wonder why Sir Alf agreed to step in, said Peter Robinson. I mean, why now? Why would he, Bill?

Alf Ramsey is a football man. He loves being in football. After he was sacked, I know many clubs came knocking on his door. But they were either foreign clubs or Second Division clubs. But Alf always said he wanted to continue working. He said he still had a lot to give. And so when Birmingham offered him a directorship. He said yes. Because he wanted to be involved. And then when Willie Bell was sacked. And they asked him to be the caretaker manager. Again he said yes. Because he wanted to help. But they were never going to beat Forest. Alf knows that. Birmingham were lacking in the very basics. They have Francis. But just Francis. One man. An individual. And you can't win a game of football with just one man. Just one individual. No matter how good he is, how skilful he is. You can't win a game with just one man, Peter.

But it must have been galling for Sir Alf, said Peter Robinson, the way Burns played today. For Birmingham to have sold him to Forest before Sir Alf had even taken over. That must be very galling?

Oh well, I don't know about that, Peter. I don't know about that. Burns is a very difficult character. By all accounts. A difficult man to deal with. And so I'm not sure Alf would have got on with Burns. And then Burns is Scottish, of course. And Alf has never had any love of us. So I'm not sure he would have been able to get the best out of him. Not the way Brian has. I mean, Brian has reformed him.

And so you think he's the man to reform England?

I think he could, Peter. In fact, I'm certain he could. But I'm not sure he will be given the chance. I mean, I can't see the FA ever appointing a man like Brian. I mean, Brian would want to do things his way. Not their way. And he's never been one of them yes, sir, no, sir, three bags full merchants. And Brian never will be.

But they have invited him down for an interview, said Peter Robinson. They didn't do that the last time . . .

Aye, but I think it's just a sop. I think it's just for show. A show for the press, a show for the public. I mean, I think they've already made up their minds. I think in their minds they know who they want. And they want Ron. Ron Greenwood. And he may be fine. Ron may do very well. And I hope he does. But I think they are just wasting Brian's time. Inviting him down, interviewing him. They are just wasting his time. As I say, I think it's all for show. It's just a sop. And I think that's a shame, Peter. A very great shame. Because I think they could do with someone like Brian, with a breath of fresh air. I think they need a breath of fresh air.

It's a shame you're not an Englishman, said Peter Robinson.

Oh no. Never say that, Peter. Never say that. I've never thought that, Peter. And I never will. But you're right, Peter. You're right. I could teach them a thing or two. I certainly could.

I know you could, said Peter Robinson. I know you could, Bill. Well, I best be off. I best get to my bed, Bill . . .

Aye. Well, you sleep well, Peter. You sleep well. And I'll see you in the week, Peter. I'll see you on Tuesday. And thanks for calling, Peter. Thanks. And goodnight, Peter. Goodnight.

In the house, in their hallway. In the night and in the silence. Bill put down the telephone. Bill went back into the front room. Bill sat back down in his chair. And then Bill got back up from his chair. Bill walked over to the television. Bill switched on the television. Bill pressed the buttons on the television. Bill changed the channels on the television. And then Bill switched off the television again. Bill walked back over to his chair. Bill sat back down in his chair. In the night and in the silence. Bill picked up the paper. The evening paper. Bill turned the pages. Bill turned the pages. Bill turned the pages. And then Bill put down the paper. In the night and in the silence. Bill got back up from his chair. Bill walked out of the front room. Bill walked into the hallway. Bill picked up the telephone. Bill dialled a number. In the house, in their hallway. Bill listened to the telephone ring. And ring. And ring. And then Bill heard Jock Dodds say, Hello, Bill . . .

## 75. THE SPIRIT OF '78

Liverpool Football Club had not got their hat-trick. Liverpool Football Club had not retained the League Championship for a third season in a row. Liverpool Football Club had finished second in the First Division. Nottingham Forest had finished first in the First Division. Nottingham Forest were the Champions of England. Brian Clough was the Manager of the Year. Nottingham Forest had also won the League Cup. Nottingham Forest had beaten Liverpool Football Club in the final of the League Cup. Liverpool Football Club had not even reached the final of the FA Cup. Liverpool Football Club had been knocked out of the FA Cup by Chelsea in the Third Round. Ipswich Town had won the FA Cup. In the 1977–78 season, Liverpool Football Club had won nothing –

Yet.

Away from home, away from Anfield. In the first leg of the semi-final of the European Cup, Liverpool Football Club had lost two–one to Borussia Mönchengladbach. But back at home, back at Anfield. In the second leg of the semi-final of the European Cup, Liverpool Football Club had beaten Borussia Mönchengladbach three–nil. Now Liverpool Football Club were in the final of the European Cup. Liverpool Football Club had the chance to retain the European Cup. Real Madrid had retained the European Cup. Benfica had retained the European Cup. Internazionale had retained the European Cup. Ajax had retained the European Cup. And Bayern Munich had retained the European Cup. But no British football club had ever retained the European Cup. Now Liverpool Football Club had the chance to retain the European Cup. Now Liverpool Football Club had the chance to do something no other British football club had ever done before. If Liverpool Football Club could beat Football Club Bruges. At Wembley Stadium on Wednesday 10 May, 1978 –

Bill Shankly had been sent a ticket for the final. But Bill Shankly didn't really want to go to London. Bill Shankly didn't really want to stay in London. Bill Shankly didn't really like to spend a night away from home. Not these days, not any more. But Bill Shankly didn't want anyone to think he was a petty man. Bill Shankly didn't want anyone to think he'd turned his back on Liverpool Football Club.

Bill Shankly didn't want anyone to think he didn't care about Liverpool Football Club. Not anyone, not ever. And so Bill Shankly bought a train ticket to London. A day return –

And Bill Shankly sat on the first train to London. The first train to London full of the supporters of Liverpool Football Club. And some of the supporters of Liverpool Football Club spotted Bill Shankly. Bill Shankly in his seat on the train to London. And the supporters of Liverpool Football Club could not believe their eyes. They could not believe their luck. The supporters of Liverpool Football Club crowded around Bill Shankly. In his seat, on the train. And they said, Is that really you, Bill? Is it really you?

Aye, said Bill Shankly. It's me, lads. It's me. But sit yourselves down, lads. Sit yourselves down with me here. You don't want to be blocking the aisles now, lads. You don't want to be getting yourselves in trouble with the guard. And getting yourselves kicked off . . .

The supporters of Liverpool Football Club nodded. And some of the supporters of Liverpool Football Club took it in turns to sit with Bill Shankly at his table on the train to London. And they asked Bill Shankly for his autograph. And Bill Shankly smiled. And Bill Shankly signed his autograph for them. And the supporters of Liverpool Football Club asked Bill Shankly questions –

That same question –

Well, I *hope* we win, boys. Of course, I hope we win. But to be honest with you, boys. To be very honest with you. I do have my worries, boys. I mean, we've not had much luck at Wembley of late. It's not been a good ground for us, boys. Not since we won the Cup in seventy-four. That was the last time we won at Wembley, boys. And I mean, with no Tommy Smith. You know we've never won a cup without Tommy Smith, boys? And with Tommy being injured. With Tommy being out, boys. It'll be hard. It'll be tough, boys. Because Tommy is tremendous. A tremendous player, boys. And Tommy always makes a difference. Makes a very big difference, boys. And he's always been like that. Always been like that, boys. I tell you, from the start. From the very start, boys. Always ambitious. And with that arrogance, boys. That ambition and that arrogance. That arrogance you need, boys. If you're going to make something of yourself. If you're going to succeed in life, boys. I remember, Tommy was only sixteen.

Only sixteen, boys. The same age as some of you, no doubt. The same age as some of you boys. And I remember one game when he played for the reserves. Against City, boys. Manchester City. And Tommy was playing for us at right-half, boys. And Johnny Morrissey was at outside-left for us. And Johnny was a cunning player, boys. Very cunning, very crafty. And so I knew Johnny would be lying deep for us, boys. And so I said to Tommy. I said, When they are all down at your end, Tommy. They'll all be encroaching on this side. And they'll be leaving Johnny clear. You understand, boys? I knew what they would do. I knew they would leave Johnny Morrissey clear. And so I said to Tommy. I said, You make sure you hit the balls across for Johnny. And then Johnny will do the rest. And Tommy went out. And Tommy slashed the ball across the face of the pitch. Time and time again. Tommy was such a good kicker of the ball. Even then, boys. Even when he was only sixteen year old. Time and time again, Tommy slashed that ball across the face of the pitch. And Johnny cut City to pieces. He annihilated them, boys. And we won six–nil. Six–bloody–nil. And that was when Tommy was just sixteen year old. Unbelievable. Bloody unbelievable.

And the supporters of Liverpool Football Club sat on the edges of their seats. The supporters of Liverpool Football Club hanging on Bill Shankly's every word. And Bill Shankly smiled –

But come on then, boys. Come on. Who are your favourite players then, boys? Come on, who do you all like the best then?

And one of the supporters of Liverpool Football Club said, Emlyn Hughes, Bill. I just love Crazy Horse . . .

Oh yes, said Bill Shankly. Yes! What a player he is, what a great player he is. I remember, I saw Emlyn play his first game for Blackpool. His very first game for Blackpool. It was at Blackburn. It was at Ewood Park, I think. And I remember, Matt Busby was there and all. And I think Matt might have been there to see Mike England. To watch Mike England. But I remember within the first minute. The very first minute. I was watching Emlyn. Only watching Emlyn. And I mean, they were playing Emlyn at left-back. They'd played him all over. But by Christ, he didn't half play. He did everything. Bloody everything. And I remember, straight after the game, straight after the match. I went straight up to their chairman and their directors. And they were all puffing away on their fat cigars. Their big fat cigars. And I said, I'll give you twenty-five thousand now for Emlyn Hughes. You can have it now. No bother, no danger. But they were not in a generous mood. Not that night. They were getting offers for Alan Ball. Lots of offers, lots of big offers. And so they knew they'd be getting big money for Alan. And so they were in no hurry. They were not in a generous mood. Not that night. But I knew Emlyn Hughes was something special. And so I had my eye on him. And I kept my eye on him. And I followed him. And I watched him. And in the end I got him when he was still only nineteen. And I paid sixty-five thousand pound for him. But that was stealing. Sixty-five grand. For a player like that. It was still bloody stealing. One of the major signings of all time!

And the supporter of Liverpool Football Club nodded. The supporter of Liverpool Football Club smiled. And the supporter of Liverpool Football Club said, Thank you, Bill. Thank you . . .

But Bill Shankly shook his head. Bill Shankly took a piece of paper from out of the pocket of his jacket. Bill Shankly picked up his pen from the table. And Bill Shankly wrote on one side of the piece of paper, *This man is a true supporter of Liverpool Football Club. Please give this man a tour of Anfield on any day he wants. Signed, Bill Shankly.* And then Bill Shankly turned over the piece of paper. And Bill Shankly wrote his home address and telephone number on the other side of the piece of paper. And Bill Shankly handed the piece of paper to the supporter of Liverpool Football Club –

Don't thank me, son. Please don't thank me. It is me who should be thanking you, son. For supporting Liverpool Football Club. And so any day you want, son. You go to the players' entrance at Anfield. And you show them this piece of paper, son. And then you can go inside. And you can see the dressing room and the tunnel, son. And the trophy room. And make sure they let you see the pitch, son. Make sure they let you touch that grass. And then any time you want, son. Any time you are free. You just give me a call, son. And then you can pop in and have a cup of tea with me and Ness. And let us know how you are getting on, son. Because you'll always be welcome. You'll always be very welcome at our house, son . . .

And the supporter of Liverpool Football Club looked down at the piece of paper in his hand. And the supporter of Liverpool Football

Club struggled to breathe. He struggled to speak. And he whispered, Thank you, Bill. Thank you.

Now the train from Liverpool pulled into Euston Station. And Bill Shankly got up from his seat. Bill Shankly put on his raincoat. And Bill Shankly thanked all the supporters of Liverpool Football Club. Bill Shankly wished all the supporters of Liverpool Football Club a good day. He hoped they would be celebrating. He was sure they would be celebrating. But he asked them all to take care. And he hoped they would all have a safe journey home. A safe journey back to Liverpool. And he shook their hands. And he patted their backs. And then Bill Shankly said goodbye to the supporters of Liverpool Football Club. And Bill Shankly got off the train at Euston Station. Bill Shankly walked across the station concourse. Bill Shankly walked out of the station. Bill Shankly saw a taxicab. Bill Shankly flagged down the taxicab. And Bill Shankly took the cab out to Wembley Stadium.

In the corridor. The Wembley corridor. The gentlemen of the press saw Bill Shankly. Bill Shankly with his raincoat across one arm. Bill Shankly with his eye on his watch. And the gentlemen of the press asked Bill Shankly for his thoughts. They asked Bill Shankly if he thought Liverpool Football Club could win the European Cup again. If Liverpool Football Club could do what no other British team had done before. If Liverpool Football Club could retain the European Cup. If Bob Paisley could do what no other British manager had ever done before. And win the European Cup again, retain the European Cup.

Well, I hope so, said Bill Shankly. And I think so. But it won't be easy. Make no mistake. It won't be easy. Not without Tommy Smith. And possibly with no Steve Heighway. It'll be no easy matter. And I mean, this Bruges side beat Juventus in the semi-finals. Let's not forget that. We can't forget that. This Bruges team knocked out Juventus. Because to be honest with you. To be very honest with you. I think Juventus are the best side in Europe. Juventus are fit, very fit. And they are alive and they are urgent. Good minds, balanced and hard. By Christ, they are hard. Giving nothing away. Nothing. And the discipline of Italian clubs keeps them in phenomenal condition. And so I mean, the best team in Europe are not even in the bloody final. And so I can tell you one thing. If this Bruges side could beat Juventus. If this Bruges team could knock out Juventus. Then by Christ, Bruges must be a good team. They must be a very good team!

And the gentlemen of the press nodded. The gentlemen of the press thanked Bill Shankly for his thoughts. They thanked him for his time. And Bill Shankly looked down at his watch again. In the corridor. The Wembley corridor. Bill Shankly turned. And Bill Shankly walked down the corridor towards the dressing room. The Liverpool dressing room. In the corridor. The Wembley corridor. Bill Shankly stood before the door. The Liverpool dressing-room door. And Bill Shankly looked at the door. Bill Shankly stared at the door. The Liverpool dressing-room door. And Bill Shankly heard the voices on the other side of the door. Bill Shankly listened to the voices on the other side of the door. The Liverpool dressing-room door. And Bill Shankly did not recognise these voices. These different voices. And in the corridor. The Wembley corridor. Bill Shankly turned away from the door. The Liverpool dressing-room door. And Bill Shankly walked away. Down the corridor, the Wembley corridor.

In his seat in the stands at Wembley Stadium. The man sat next to Bill Shankly nodded. And the man said, You're right, Bill. You're right. But you still believe we can do it, Bill? We can still win?

And in his seat in the stands. On the edge of his seat in the stands at Wembley Stadium. Bill Shankly looked down at the pitch. The Wembley pitch. And Bill Shankly stared down at the players. The players of Liverpool Football Club. Ray Clemence. Phil Thompson. Emlyn Hughes. Ray Kennedy. Ian Callaghan and Steve Heighway. The old and the new. Phil Neal. Alan Hansen. Jimmy Case. Terry McDermott. Graeme Souness. Kenny Dalglish. David Fairclough. Joey Jones. Steve Ogrizovic and Colin Irwin. The players of Liverpool Football Club coming out of the tunnel. The players of Liverpool Football Club walking out into the stadium. To another deafening roar, to another glorious reception. And on the night of the final. The European Cup Final. On the edge of his seat in the stands at Wembley Stadium. Bill Shankly looked around the ground. At the sea of red, at the walls of red. And Bill Shankly smiled again –

Of course we can, said Bill Shankly. And of course we will. Because no one should ever underestimate the players of Liverpool Football Club. And no one should ever underestimate the supporters of Liverpool Football Club. So I'm certain we will win. I'm sure we will win. In fact, I think there is no way on earth we can lose . . .

No way on earth.

In his seat in the stands at Wembley Stadium. In the sixty-fourth minute, Bill Shankly watched Steve Heighway replace Jimmy Case. On the edge of his seat in the stands at Wembley Stadium. In the sixty-fifth minute, Bill Shankly watched Heighway pass to Terry McDermott. McDermott pass to Kenny Dalglish. Dalglish back over his head to Graeme Souness. Souness back to Kenny Dalglish on the right of the Bruges penalty area. On his feet in the stands at Wembley Stadium. Bill Shankly watched Birger Jensen come out of his goal towards Dalglish. Dalglish lifting the ball over Jensen. Into the net and into a goal. Dalglish jumping over the advertising boards. Dalglish running to the supporters of Liverpool Football Club. His arms aloft, his fingers outstretched. In celebration –

And in triumph.

On his feet in the stands. Bill Shankly looked at his watch. But Bill Shankly did not sit back down in his seat in the stands at Wembley Stadium. Bill Shankly turned. And Bill Shankly began to make his way out of the stadium. And one supporter spotted Bill Shankly. And the supporter said, Is that really you, Bill? Is it really you, Bill?

Aye, said Bill Shankly. It's me, son. It's me.

But where are you going then, Bill? Where are you off? The game is not finished, Bill. The match is not over. You're surely not going, Bill? You're surely not leaving us . . .

Aye, said Bill Shankly. I have my train to catch, son. My train back to Liverpool. My train back home. But I know we have won, son. I know we have won. And so I'll still be here in spirit, son. In spirit.

And Bill Shankly thanked the supporter of Liverpool Football Club. Bill Shankly wished him a good night. But he asked him to take care. And to have a safe journey home. A safe journey back to Liverpool. And Bill Shankly shook his hand. And Bill Shankly patted his back. And then Bill Shankly said goodbye to this supporter of Liverpool Football Club. And Bill Shankly walked out of Wembley Stadium. Bill Shankly searched for a taxicab. Bill Shankly spotted a taxicab. And Bill Shankly took the cab back to Euston Station.

In his seat on the train. The train back to Liverpool. The empty train back to Liverpool. Bill Shankly thought about the things he was missing. The victory and the celebrations. The party and the speeches. All the things he was missing. His home and his wife. His home he was missing, his wife he was missing. And Bill Shankly smiled.


## 76. COME LIKE SHADOWS, SO DEPART

In the house, in their hallway. Bill picked up the paper from the table in the hall. Bill looked at the photographs of the celebrations. Bill looked at the pictures of the parade. The faces of the players of Liverpool Football Club. Smiling, smiling. The faces of the supporters of Liverpool Football Club. And Bill smiled. In the front room, in his chair. Bill turned to the inside pages of the paper. Bill read the interview with the manager of Football Club Bruges. Ernst Happel had said, It was a weak final. It is no excuse but we were handicapped by lots of injuries. I would have liked to have been more offensive. But our injuries were against us. And I was disappointed with Liverpool Football Club. Because we played them two years ago. And tonight they were just a shadow of that team. They were just a shadow. And Bill shook his head. Bill closed the paper. Bill put down the paper. Bill got up from his chair. Bill walked over to the writing desk. Bill sat down at the writing desk. Bill opened the top drawer of the writing desk. Bill took out a card and an envelope from the top drawer of the desk. Bill opened the card. Bill picked up a pen. A red pen. And Bill wrote inside the card, *Well done, Bob. I'm very pleased for you. Liverpool have proved once and for all we are the real champions. The best team in Britain and the best team in Europe. Congratulations, Bill.* Bill put down the pen. The red pen. Bill picked up the card. Bill put the card inside the envelope. Bill held the envelope up to his mouth. Bill licked the two edges of the envelope. Bill sealed the envelope. Bill put down the envelope on the writing desk. Bill picked up the pen again. The red pen. And Bill wrote on the front of the envelope, *To Bob.* Bill picked up the envelope again. Bill got up from the chair at the writing desk. Bill walked out of the front room. Bill walked up the stairs. In the house, in their bedroom. Bill changed into his shirt. His tangerine shirt. Bill walked over to the dressing table. Bill opened the top drawer. Bill took out his cufflinks. His gold cufflinks. Bill closed the drawer. Bill did up the cuffs of his shirt. His tangerine shirt. Bill walked over to the wardrobe. Bill opened the doors. Bill took out his suit. His freshly cleaned grey herringbone suit. Bill left the wardrobe doors open. Bill walked over to the bed. Bill laid out the suit on top of the bed covers. Bill took the trousers from the coat hanger. Bill put on the trousers of his suit. His freshly cleaned grey herringbone suit. Bill went back to the dressing table. Bill opened the second drawer of the dressing table. Bill took out a tie. His red Liverpool Football Club tie. Bill closed the drawer. Bill walked back to the wardrobe. The doors still open. Bill stood before the mirror on the back of one of the doors. Bill put on the tie. His red Liverpool Football Club tie. Bill went back over to the bed. Bill picked up the jacket from the bed. Bill took the jacket from the coat hanger. Bill put on the jacket of his suit. His freshly cleaned grey herringbone suit. Bill walked back over to the dressing table. Bill opened the top drawer of the dressing table again. Bill took out one white handkerchief and one red pocket square. Bill closed the drawer. Bill put the white handkerchief in his left trouser pocket. Bill laid the red pocket square on the top of the dressing table. It looked like a red diamond. Bill brought the bottom point of the red pocket square up to the top point. It looked like a red triangle. Bill brought the left corner of the triangle to the right corner and then the right corner to the left corner. It looked like a long red rectangle with a point at the top. Bill folded the bottom almost towards the top. Bill walked over to the mirror on the back of the wardrobe door. Bill stood before the mirror. Bill placed the red pocket square in the breast pocket of his grey jacket. Bill looked in the mirror. Bill adjusted the pocket square until just enough of the point was coming out of the pocket. The red point out of the grey pocket. Bill stepped back. In the house, in their bedroom. Bill looked at himself in the mirror. And Bill smiled. Bill closed the wardrobe doors. Bill walked back over to the dressing table. Bill opened the top drawer of the dressing table again. Bill took out a badge. His Liverpool Football Club badge. Bill closed the drawer. Bill attached the Liverpool Football Club badge to the lapel of his suit. His freshly cleaned grey herringbone suit. Bill picked up the envelope from the top of the dressing table. And Bill walked out of the bedroom. Bill walked back down the stairs. Bill walked into the kitchen. And Bill saw Ness at the sink. The kitchen sink. Ness peeling the potatoes. The potatoes for their lunch. And Bill said, I'm just going to nip down to the ground for a bit, love. To drop this card in for Bob.

Ness looked up from the potatoes. Ness turned from the sink. Ness looked at Bill. In his suit and in his tie. His Liverpool Football Club tie. Ness nodded. And Ness smiled –

All right then, love.

Bill kissed Ness on her cheek. Bill walked out of the kitchen. Bill walked down the hall. Bill put the envelope in his pocket. Bill opened the front door. Bill stepped out of the house. Bill closed the door. Bill went down the drive. Bill got into the car.

In the sunshine. In his car. Bill drove down the West Derby Road. And Bill saw the people walking in the street. The people busy, the people occupied. In the sunshine. In his car. Bill turned onto the Belmont Road. And Bill saw the people getting off the buses, the people getting on the buses. The people busy, the people occupied. In the sunshine. In his car. Bill turned into the car park at Anfield Road. Bill parked in the car park at Anfield Road. In the sunshine. Bill got out of the car. The only car in the car park at Anfield Road. In the sunshine. The car park was empty, the place deserted. In the sunshine. Bill closed the car door. Bill took the envelope out of his pocket. In the sunshine. Bill walked across the car park. Bill walked up to reception. In the shadow of the Main Stand. Bill tried the door to reception. But the door was locked. In the shadow of the Main Stand. Bill knocked on the door. But no one answered. In the shadow of the Main Stand. Bill turned away from the door. And Bill walked round to the back of the Anfield Road Stand. And then round to the back of the Kemlyn Road Stand. The stands empty, the stands deserted. But in the sunshine and in the shadows. The stands were whispering, whispering to Bill. And Bill kept walking, walking round the ground. The empty ground, the deserted ground. Until Bill came to the back of the Kop. The Spion Kop. And in the sunshine and in the shadows. Bill stopped. Behind the Kop, the Spion Kop. Bill touched the bricks of the Kop. Bill touched the stones of the Spion Kop. Bill felt the bricks, Bill felt the stones. In the sunshine and in the shadows. The bricks were warm and the stones were hot. Red hot. The bricks alive, the stones living. Living and breathing. Bill listened to the bricks, Bill listened to the stones.

649

The bricks speaking now, the stones singing now. Revolutionary songs, revolutionary words. Words of anticipation, songs of transformation. Singing to Bill, speaking to Bill –

Bill? Bill? Is that really you, Bill?

Bill turned away from the bricks. Bill turned away from the stones. And Bill saw a little lad at his side. Maybe nine, maybe ten. The little lad in a pair of shoes that looked that bit too tight. The little lad in a pair of long trousers that had seen better days. The little lad wearing a red shirt. Not a football shirt, an official shirt. But a T-shirt, a red T-shirt. And on the left breast of the shirt someone had drawn a Liver Bird. And under the Liver Bird someone had written, *L.F.C.* And Bill smiled. And Bill said, Aye, son. It's me. How are you, son?

I can't believe it's you, said the little lad. I can't believe it, Bill. No one will believe me. My dad will never believe me . . .

Bill smiled again. And Bill said, Well, it is me, son. It is me. In the flesh. But how are you, son? How are you?

Great, said the little lad. I'm great. Ta, Bill. Ta. But I still can't believe we won again. I'm just made up. I'm still dead made up.

Bill nodded. And Bill said, Oh well, yes. That was great, son. That was great. A fantastic thing. It was brilliant . . .

Did you go, Bill? Were you there?

Bill nodded again. And Bill said, Oh yes. I was there, son. Yes. I was lucky enough to be there, son . . .

And you think we can do it again next year and all? You think we can win it again? My dad thinks we can. My dad thinks we will.

Well, I hope we can. I hope we will, son. But I think next season. In the European Cup next season, son. I think it might be Forest who will be our biggest challenge. Nottingham Forest . . .

Here, said the little lad. Where did you get your badge, Bill? I wanted to get one for my dad. For his birthday. Because he's mad, is my dad. He's mad on Liverpool Football Club. And he's always talking about you, Bill. Always telling me about you. About Liverpool Football Club, about all the things you did for Liverpool Football Club. He loves you, does my dad. Because he loves Liverpool Football Club. And so I wanted to get him a badge for his birthday. And so I went to the shop. But they never had one. They never did.

Bill smiled. Bill put the envelope back in his jacket pocket.

And then Bill reached up to the lapel of his jacket. Bill took off the badge. The Liverpool Football Club badge. Bill held it out towards the little lad. And Bill said, Then you give this to your dad from me, son. And from you. And you tell him I said thank you, son. Thank you to him. Will you do that for me now, son?

I can't, Bill. I can't. He'd kill me. My dad. He would. If he knew I took your badge, Bill. He'd kill me. He would. He'd kill me.

Bill took the hand of the little lad. Bill pressed the Liverpool Football Club badge into the palm of the little lad. Bill closed the palm of the little lad. And Bill said, He won't, son. No, he won't. Not if you tell him I gave it to you. I gave it to you to give to him. To thank him. To thank him for all the things that he has given me. And so you tell him that, son. You tell him that from me. From Bill . . .


## 77. WHAT CAN YOU SAY?

Liverpool Football Club had won their first five games of the 1978–79 season. Away from home, away from Anfield. Liverpool Football Club had beaten Ipswich Town, Manchester City and Birmingham City. At home, at Anfield. Liverpool Football Club had beaten Queens Park Rangers and Tottenham Hotspur. Liverpool Football Club had beaten Tottenham Hotspur seven–nil. This Tottenham side included Osvaldo Ardiles and Ricardo Villa. Ossie Ardiles and Ricky Villa had won the World Cup with Argentina that summer. But after this game, people said Liverpool Football Club would have won the World Cup. After this game, people said this Liverpool team was the greatest Liverpool team they had ever seen. This Liverpool team, one of the greatest teams they had ever seen. The greatest team they had ever seen. People said this game was one of the greatest games they had ever seen at Anfield. One of the greatest games they had ever seen. The greatest game they had ever seen. The last goal of the game, the seventh goal of the game, the greatest goal ever seen at Anfield. In the seventy-sixth minute, Ray Clemence passed the ball to Ray Kennedy. Kennedy passed the ball to Kenny Dalglish. Dalglish passed the ball to David Johnson. Johnson passed the ball to Steve Heighway. Heighway crossed the ball for Terry McDermott. And McDermott headed the ball into the goal. Five beautiful balls, five glorious passes. Into the net. One of the greatest goals ever seen. The greatest goal ever seen.

And after the game, Bob Paisley said, What can you say? That performance was frightening. That goal probably the finest ever seen on this ground. But we've got to keep our feet on the floor. Because this result won't help us next week. In fact, I'd rather have brickbats than praise. We seem to thrive on the brickbats, not the praise.

And then the gentlemen of the press had asked Bob Paisley about the European Cup. About the draw for the European Cup. The draw that had brought Liverpool Football Club and Nottingham Forest together in the First Round of the European Cup. The European Champions against the English Champions. Bob Paisley had shaken his head. And Bob Paisley had said, Even before we left Wembley. Even before our celebrations in London. I warned the players that the biggest stumbling block to our ambitions of retaining the trophy could be Brian Clough and his team. Now whether UEFA and the rest of Europe wanted two English teams in the European Cup, I wouldn't know. But the odds against us drawing Forest in the First Round were long, even though we were seeded and they were not. But that's how the draw went. And so that's who we must play . . .

In the First Round of the European Cup. At the City Ground, Nottingham. Bill Shankly had a pair of headphones on his ears. A microphone to his lips. Bill Shankly was commentating on the match for the radio. For Radio City, Liverpool. Analysing the game, dissecting the match. In the press box. On the edge of his seat. His body bent in his seat, his eyes fixed on the pitch. Bill Shankly watched the match, Bill Shankly transfixed by the game. The game Liverpool Football Club were losing. Away from home, away from Anfield. The match Liverpool Football Club lost. Two–nil.

His eyes strained, his voice hoarse. Bill Shankly put down his microphone. Bill Shankly took off his headphones. His ears sore, his body taut. Bill Shankly got up from his seat in the press box.

In the corridors of the City Ground. The gentlemen of the press saw Bill Shankly. Bill Shankly standing in the corridor, Bill Shankly standing in the shadows. And the gentlemen of the press asked Bill Shankly for his thoughts. They asked Bill Shankly if he could understand why Liverpool Football Club had lost two–nil to

Nottingham Forest in the first leg of the First Round of the European Cup. If Bill Shankly knew the reason why Liverpool Football Club had lost two–nil to Nottingham Forest in the first leg of the First Round of the European Cup. And Bill Shankly shook his head –

Well, it's difficult to say, said Bill Shankly. It's a very difficult thing to say. But I mean, to be honest with you. To be very honest with you, I was concerned before the game. Very worried before the game. I was concerned and worried that our players might be tempted to treat it as a League game. As just another League match. And I mean, I think that's what happened. I think that is what we saw. I don't mean to say the players were complacent. Oh no. Not that. Not that at all. What I mean to say is, when we were a goal down, we were still chasing the game. Still looking for an equaliser. An equaliser and then perhaps another. Instead of accepting a one–nil defeat as a reasonable result in the first leg of the European Cup. In the away leg. And so we were still chasing the game, when we were one–nil down. In the second half, we were still looking for that equaliser. And then possibly more. And then that allowed Forest to catch us. To nip in by the back door, you understand? Because we left ourselves exposed. And so Forest could then nip in and get that second goal. Because we allowed Forest to disturb us, we allowed Forest to harass us. Their midfield were set up simply to mark us tightly. When we were in possession. And then when they had possession, they simply bypassed their own midfield. They were just hitting long balls up the middle to their front men, over their own midfield. And their front men had the measure of us, their front men mastered us. And so then they got their second goal. And that second goal, you see? That now gives us a mountain to climb. When we get back home. Back home to Anfield.

And the gentlemen of the press nodded. The gentlemen of the press thanked Bill Shankly for his thoughts. They thanked Bill Shankly for his time. And Bill Shankly glanced down at his watch. And then Bill Shankly looked back up. The gentlemen of the press had gone. The gentlemen of the press had left. Gone to pick up their phones, left to file their reports. In the corridors of the City Ground, under the Main Stand of the City Ground. Bill Shankly now alone, alone in the shadows. Bill Shankly started pacing. In a circle, a small circle. Under the stands, in the shadows. Pacing and pacing, round and around. In a circle, a very small circle. Under the stands, in the shadows. Bill Shankly stopped pacing. Bill Shankly looked at his watch again. Bill Shankly walked towards another corridor. The corridor to the dressing rooms. The home dressing room and the away dressing room. The Liverpool dressing room. Bill Shankly walked down the corridor towards the dressing room. The Liverpool dressing room. And Bill Shankly stopped before the door. The Liverpool dressing-room door. In the corridor. The corridor of the City Ground. Bill Shankly stood before the door. The Liverpool dressing-room door. And Bill Shankly looked at the door. Again. Bill Shankly stared at the door. The Liverpool dressing-room door. And Bill Shankly heard the voices on the other side of the door. Again. Bill Shankly listened to the voices on the other side of the door. The Liverpool dressing-room door. Again. Bill Shankly did not recognise these voices, these different voices. Again. These different voices, these raised voices. And in the corridor. The corridor of the City Ground. Bill Shankly shook his head. Bill Shankly closed his eyes. What would he say? What could he say? And in the corridor. The corridor of the City Ground. Outside the door. The Liverpool dressing-room door. Bill Shankly opened his eyes. Bill Shankly sighed. And again. Bill Shankly turned away from the door. The Liverpool dressing-room door. Again. Bill Shankly walked away. Down the corridor, the corridor of the City Ground. Towards the door, towards the exit. Bill Shankly opened the door. The exit. And Bill Shankly saw the stairs. In the shadows. The stairs down to the car park. And Bill Shankly walked down the stairs. The steep, concrete stairs. Slowly, carefully. One hand on the rail. The cold, metal handrail. Slowly, carefully. One foot on the steps –

The steep, concrete steps. One foot, then the other. Careful of the steps, careful of his step, careful not to slip,

careful not to trip, not to trip,

and not to fall . . .

Bill? Bill? Is that you, called out a group of supporters at the bottom of the stairs. Supporters of Liverpool Football Club and supporters of Nottingham Forest. And the supporters came towards Bill Shankly. With their autograph books and with their football programmes. At the bottom of the stairs, in the car park. Bill Shankly touched his tie. Bill Shankly straightened his tie. And Bill Shankly smiled. He smiled at the supporters of Liverpool Football Club and he smiled at the supporters of Nottingham Forest. And Bill Shankly signed their autograph books, Bill Shankly signed their football programmes. And Bill Shankly answered their questions. The questions of the supporters of Liverpool Football Club, the questions of the supporters of Nottingham Forest –

That same question.

Of course, said Bill Shankly. Of course we can win. But it won't be easy. Make no mistake. Not with Peter Shilton and with Kenny Burns. And with Larry Lloyd, of course. Larry knows us well, of course. He knows Anfield very well. And Larry is very big, Larry is very strong. In fact, it was Freddie Ford who recommended Larry Lloyd to me. Freddie was one of my trainers when I was at Carlisle. And I remember, Freddie called me. Freddie was at Bristol City then. And Freddie said, You have to see this boy, Bill. This boy Larry Lloyd. And so I went down to see him play. Against Everton, in the League Cup, I think. And Bristol City lost five–nil. Five–bloody–nil! But even then, in that defeat. I could tell the boy had what it takes. Because I mean, his head never dropped. His head never went down. And that's the thing. Because I mean, you are always going to lose sometimes. You are never going to win every game. Every match. But it's how you lose. That's the thing. How you react when you are losing. Does your head drop? Does your head go down? Is that the kind of player, the kind of man you are? Or do you keep your head up? Do you keep competing? Keep fighting? Trying? That is what you are looking for. Fighters, triers. And without Larry Lloyd, they might have lost ten–bloody–nil! But his head never dropped, his head never went down. And so you see, I had my eye on him. And I kept my eye on him. And so when Big Ron was coming to the end of his time. When I knew Ron Yeats was not going to go on for very much longer. Then I bought Larry. And I paid fifty thousand for the boy. Just fifty thousand. And then, of course – after I left, after I packed in – Larry was sold to Coventry City. And I think they paid two hundred and forty thousand pounds for him. Two hundred and forty thousand pound! Unbelievable, bloody unbelievable! And I think that nearly bankrupted them. I mean, they overpaid. Because you always have to live within your means. You always have to cut your cloth. And then, of course,

Brian heard he could get him for sixty grand. Just sixty grand. And so Brian came in for him and Brian got him. For just sixty grand. And that is stealing. Bloody stealing! But a clever signing by Brian. A clever signing and a major signing. Because he's made a difference to this side. This Forest team. A big difference. And so we'll have to be on our guard when you come to Anfield. Because as I say, Larry knows us well. Very well. And Larry will have a point to make. A point to prove. But it'll be a different game, a very different game. More intense. Much more intense. And then, of course, there's the Kop. The Kop, you see. They'll make the difference –

They always make the difference.


## 78. ON YOUR BACK, LETTERS FROM AFAR

In the house, in their hall. The letters still came and the telephone still rang. The letters from clubs, the calls from chairmen. Clubs with problems, chairmen with vacancies. But Bill wasn't interested in jobs with other clubs. The problems of other clubs. Problems he had not made, problems he couldn't solve. Far from home, away from home. In places Bill didn't know, with people Bill didn't know. Not now, not these days. Now, these days. Bill wanted to stay close to home, in the place he knew, with the people he knew. The people of Liverpool. The people he knew and the people he loved. The people he cared about –

And in the house, in their hall. Other letters came, other calls. Letters from charities, calls from hospitals. Local charities and local hospitals. The Royal Society for the Blind on Merseyside and the Alder Hey Children's Hospital. Letters Bill wanted to answer, calls Bill wanted to take. If he could help, if he could make people happy. Then Bill was happy to help. Once or twice a week. Sometimes three, even four times a week. Bill would put on his suit, Bill would put on his tie. Bill would kiss Ness goodbye. And Bill would get in the car –

In the car park of the Alder Hey Children's Hospital. Bill got out of the car. In the car park of the Alder Hey Children's Hospital. Bill took out the letter from his coat pocket. And Bill read the letter again. The letter from Alf Thompson, the manager of the Lister Under-16s football team. The letter asking Bill if he would be kind enough to write a short note to a young lad called Ian Braithwaite. Ian played for the Lister Under-16s football team. But Ian had injured his spine playing for the Lister Under-16s football team. Now Ian was in the Alder Hey Children's Hospital. Alf Thompson thought a short note from Bill would cheer up the young lad. Because the lad was very down, very disappointed he was going to miss the rest of the season. And he was very worried, very frightened he might never play football again. If Bill didn't mind, if Bill had the time. In the car park of the Alder Hey Children's Hospital. Bill put the letter back in his coat pocket. And Bill walked across the car park. Bill walked into the hospital. Bill walked up to reception. Bill said hello to the nurses. The nurses who knew Bill Shankly. The nurses who smiled when they saw Bill Shankly. And Bill asked if he could pop in and see a young lad called Ian Braithwaite. A young lad who had injured his spine. To cheer him up, to give him a boost. If he wasn't in the way, not under their feet. And the nurses smiled again. The nurses nodded. And one of the nurses took Bill along to the ward to visit Ian –

In the hospital bed. On his back. The young lad could not believe his eyes. In the hospital bed. In traction. The young lad struggled to sit up. But Bill patted his hand. And Bill said, You lie still, son. You lie still. I don't want to disturb you now. I don't want to be getting you in trouble with the nurses now. So you just lie still now, son. You just lie still. Because I've just popped in to cheer you up. And to have a word. Because your manager, Mr Thompson. He wrote to me. And he says you are not feeling too good. Stuck in here, on your back. Missing your mates . . .

Yeah, said the young lad. I've got to be in here five week. And then they say I can't play again for the rest of the season. I've got to go easy when I get out. Or they say I won't be able to play again. And so then I've been thinking, what if I can never play again . . .

Bill shook his head. Bill smiled. And Bill whispered, Nonsense, son. That's bloody nonsense. Of course, you'll have to take it easy, son. But you'll be playing again. No danger . . .

Really, said the young lad. You think so?

Bill nodded. Bill smiled again. And Bill said, I know so, son. I know so. Because I've been in the same place you are, son. The very same place you are now. Long before you were born, mind. Probably before your dad was even born. I was playing for Preston at Halifax. During the war, in a war cup game. I took a kick to my knee, my left knee. And I'll never forget the night I done it. I was stationed in Manchester. Because of the war. So after the game, I came back to Manchester. On the bus, over the moors. And my leg was a terrible size. Enormous it was. Bloody enormous! And so I knew it wasn't right. I mean, you always get kicked. You'll always have bruises. And you'll always have cuts. But this was different. This was more serious. And so I went to the hospital. In Crumpsall, in Manchester. To let them take a look, to get the knee X-rayed. And when they took a look, when they saw the X-rays. They said I had a broken kneecap. A shattered kneecap. And so they put it in plaster. And when the fluid drained away. And the swelling went down. The plaster was wobbling all over the place. And so I got out of bed. And I remember, this nurse. This sister. She was from Ireland. And she said, What the hell do you think you are doing? You've got a broken leg, man. Get back in your bed and stop your messing around. But I said, How can my leg be broken? I'm standing on the thing. It can't be broken now, can it?

And so what did you do, said the young lad. Did you get back in your bed, Bill? What did you do? What did you do?

Bill smiled. And Bill said, I did, son. I did. Because she was fierce, this sister. Kind, but very fierce. But I gave her a dog's life. And so within a week, she sent me packing. Back to the camp. But when I got back to the camp, the medical officer there, he said to me, It might well not be broken, Bill. But it's your cartilage. And so I don't think you'll ever play again, Bill. Not with that knee. That's what he said. I don't think you will ever play again. And I thought, Oh aye? Is that right? Well, I'll show you. And after a few weeks, I was back training. And I was back playing. But it wasn't right. The knee was not right. But then three great things happened to me, son. All because of my knee. First, I got a posting back up in Scotland. In Bishopbriggs, in Glasgow. And when I was there, I played for Partick Thistle. This is still during the war, you understand? In the war league. And the people at Partick were good people. And they knew my knee was not right. Because in my very first game for them, I took another knock. And by Christ, it hurt. It bloody hurt. And so they paid for me to have the operation on my knee. They paid for me to have the piece of cartilage removed. And that was very good of them. Very good of them indeed. And so that was one good thing. The first good thing that happened . . .

And what was the second good thing, Bill?

Bill smiled again. And Bill said, Well, the second good thing. The very best thing, in fact. After the operation, after I had the piece of cartilage removed. Then I was training every day. Rain or shine. Whatever the weather. Me and my mate Jock Porter. Training and running. Getting back my fitness, building back my strength. Just like you'll have to do, son. Every day. Rain or shine. Training, running. Until you've got your fitness back, you've built your strength back. And so there I was, training. Running. Every day. In the rain and in the snow. And while I was doing my training. Doing my running. I used to see this young lass. And I liked her from the first time I set eyes on her. And I kept my eyes on her. And I started to chat to her, to pester her. And I remember, I used to take over toasted cheese to her section. Because she was in the Women's RAF. And she was stationed at the same camp. And do you know who she was, son?

No, Bill. Who was she? Who was she?

Bill laughed. And Bill said, She was my wife, son. That was Ness. Because I asked her to marry me. And she said yes. And so you see, son. If it hadn't have been for my knee. Injuring my knee. And then having that operation. And then doing that training. To get back on my feet, to get back playing again. Then I would have never met my wife. I would have never met Ness.

So that was really lucky, said the young lad. You broke your knee. But then you met your wife. That was really lucky, wasn't it?

Bill shook his head. Bill smiled. And Bill said, Yes and no, son. Yes and no. You see, I don't think it was luck. To be very honest with you, I don't believe in luck. I believe in hard work. And not listening to folk who are negative folk. The ones that will tell you you will never play again. And sometimes those folk are you. Your own voice. And so I believe you should never listen to those voices. Those voices that are always telling you what you can't do. Pessimistic voices. I believe you have to prove those voices wrong. And get back on your feet. Get training again, working again. Working hard to prove them wrong. And so you see, if I had just given up. If I had believed what that medical officer had said to me. When he said, You will never play again. Then I wouldn't have gone back to Scotland, to Partick Thistle. And I wouldn't have had that operation. And then after the operation. If I had just felt sorry for myself. If I hadn't wanted to get back on my feet, to get back playing again. Then I wouldn't have started training again. And then I wouldn't have seen Ness. And so you see, I don't believe it was a question of luck. I believe it was a question of determination. And a question of hard work.

You are right, said the young lad. You are dead right, Bill. And that's what I'm going to do. I'm going to do the same.

Bill nodded. Bill smiled again. And Bill said, Well, that's the best news I've heard all year, son. That's tremendous. Because you can. You can do it. I know you can. If you put your mind to a thing, you can do anything. If you work, work hard. And don't give up.

I won't, said the young lad. I promise you, Bill. But what was the third thing? You said there were three good things . . .

Bill laughed again. And Bill said, Oh yes. We won the Summer Cup. After the operation, after my cartilage. I thought, Well, I better thank Partick Thistle. For all they have done for me. It is the least I can do. After all they have done for me. And so I helped them win the Summer Cup. We beat the Hibs two–nil. At Hampden Park.

That's brilliant, said the young lad. That's just brilliant, Bill. Dead good. What position did you play, Bill? What were you?

Midfield, said Bill. What used to be called a right-half. But what about you, son? What position do you play?

I'm a defender, said the young lad.

In the centre, asked Bill.

Yes, said the young lad. In the middle of defence . . .

And is that how you did it, asked Bill.

Yeah, said the young lad. I jumped for this ball. I went up for it. And this other lad, their lad. He come in. And he clattered me. And I fell dead funny. I lost my feet. And landed on my spine . . .

Bill nodded. And Bill said, Now you see, that tells me everything I need to know about you, son. You saw the ball. You saw their man. And you saw him coming. But you still jumped. You still went up for that ball. You did not hide. You did not shirk your job. You jumped. For the team, for your mates. And so you'll do for me, son. You're the kind of player I'd have in my team . . .

Really, said the young lad. Really, Bill?

Oh yes. Without a doubt, son. You'd be the first name on the team sheet for me. Without a doubt . . .

In his hospital bed. On his back. The young lad blinked. Blinked back tears. The young lad struggled. Struggled to say –

Thank you, Bill. Thank you . . .

Bill shook his head. And Bill said, Don't thank me, son. At least, not with words. Don't thank me. You just promise me you'll keep your head up, son. And you'll not get down. And you'll just think about playing again, son. And not listening to them voices. Them voices that say you can't, that say you won't. When you hear them voices, you just stick your fingers in your ears, son. And you remember what we talked about. You remember our little chat, son.

I will, said the young lad. I will, Bill. I promise . . .

That's great, son. That's all I want to hear. Now I'm going to go and let you rest. But I'll be back to see you before too long . . .

Thank you, said the young lad. Thank you, Bill.

Bill smiled again. Bill patted the young lad on his arm. And Bill walked away, back down the ward. And out of the hospital.

In the car park. The car park of the Alder Hey Children's Hospital. In the car. Bill rubbed his eyes. Bill rubbed his face. In the car. Bill turned the key in the ignition. And Bill drove back home. Back home to Ness. Back home to his dinner. And in the house. In their kitchen. Bill ate his dinner with Ness. Their sausage and chips. Their tinned fruit and cream. And then Bill got up from the kitchen table. Bill picked up the plates. Bill walked over to the sink. Bill put the plates in the sink. Bill walked back over to the kitchen table. Bill picked up the salt and pepper pots. Bill put them in the cupboard. Bill walked back over to the table. Bill took the cloth off the table. Bill walked over to the back door. Bill opened the back door. Bill stepped outside. Bill stood on the step. Bill shook the cloth. Bill stepped back into the kitchen. Bill closed the door. Bill folded up the tablecloth. Bill put it in the drawer. Bill walked back over to the sink. Bill turned on the taps. Bill squeezed washing-up liquid into the sink. Bill turned off the taps. Bill picked up the scrubbing brush. Bill washed up the plates. Bill washed up the pans. Bill washed up the knives and forks. Bill put them on the draining board. Bill pulled out the plug. Bill dried his hands. Bill picked up the tea towel. Bill dried up the pans. Bill dried up the plates. Bill dried up the knives and forks. Bill put the pans in one cupboard. Bill put the plates in another. Bill put the knives and forks in the drawer. Bill walked back over to the sink. Bill picked up the dishcloth. Bill wiped down the draining board. Bill turned on the taps again. Bill rinsed the dishcloth under the taps. Bill turned off the taps. Bill squeezed the water out of the dishcloth. Bill put the dishcloth down next to the bottle of washing-up liquid. Bill turned around. Bill looked round the kitchen. Bill turned back to the sink. Bill bent down. Bill opened the cupboard under the sink. Bill took out the bucket from under the sink. Bill bent back down. Bill opened a box under the sink. Bill took out a Brillo pad from the box. Bill closed the cupboard door. Bill picked up the bucket. Bill put the bucket in the sink. Bill turned on the taps again. Bill filled the bucket half full. Bill turned off the taps. Bill took the bucket and the Brillo pad over to the cooker. Bill put down the bucket in front of the cooker. Bill opened the oven door. Bill looked inside. Bill could see the darkness. Bill could smell the fat. Bill knelt down on the kitchen floor. Bill unbuttoned the cuffs of his shirt. Bill rolled up the sleeves of his shirt. Bill picked up the Brillo pad. Bill sank the Brillo pad into the bucket of water. Bill pulled the Brillo pad back up, out of the water. Bill squeezed the water from the Brillo pad. The wet, steel wool. Bill squeezed it tighter. Bill put his hand inside the oven. Into the darkness, into the fat. In the kitchen, on his knees. Bill began to scrub. On his knees. Bill began to scour. Bill began to clean. To clean, and to clean, and to clean.

In the house, in their front room. Ness had finished the crossword. Ness put down her pen. Ness put the book to one side. And Ness got up from her chair. Ness said goodnight to Bill. And Bill said goodnight to Ness. Bill kissed Ness on her cheek. And then Bill sat back down in his chair. And Bill stared at the television. The dark, silent television. And Bill stared at the curtains. The closed, drawn curtains. And in the front room, in his chair. Bill listened to the rain. The rain falling on the house. The rain falling on all the houses. And Bill listened to the wind. The wind blowing around the house. The wind blowing around all the houses. And Bill thought about the young lad again. Bill could not stop thinking about the young lad. The young lad on his back in the hospital bed. The young lad Bill wanted to help.

The young lad who might never play football again. The young lad Bill wanted to help play football again. The young lad who might never play football again. The young lad Bill couldn't help play football again. And in the front room, in his chair. In the night and in the silence. His sweater stuck to his shirt. His shirt stuck to his vest. His vest stuck to his skin. In the rain and in the wind. Bill put his hands together. Bill closed his eyes. And Bill said a prayer.


## 79. ALL HOURS OF THE DAY, ALL DAYS OF THE WEEK

They came to the street. The street in West Derby, Liverpool. And they went up the drive. The drive to the house on Bellefield Avenue, West Derby. And they knocked on the door, they rang the doorbell. The doorbell to the house on Bellefield Avenue. And whatever Nessie Shankly was doing. Doing the housework, making the lunch. Nessie Shankly stopped what she was doing. And Nessie Shankly opened the door. The door to their home. And Nessie Shankly invited them into their home. Into their home to meet Bill Shankly. And whatever Bill Shankly was doing. Doing the gardening, answering letters. Bill Shankly stopped what he was doing. And Bill Shankly shook their hands. Bill Shankly thanked them for coming. And Bill Shankly welcomed them into their home. Bill Shankly invited them into their front room. Bill Shankly asked them to sit down. And Nessie Shankly made them a cup of tea. A nice cup of tea. And Nessie Shankly brought in some biscuits. On a plate, on a tray. With their tea. Their cups of tea. And Bill Shankly signed their autograph books. Bill Shankly signed their football programmes. Their memorabilia and their photographs. And if they did not have a photograph, Bill Shankly gave them a photograph from the pile of photographs. The pile of photographs Bill Shankly kept by the door. For the people who came to the street. The people who walked up their drive. And knocked on their door and rang their bell. All hours of the day, all days of the week. Bill Shankly smiled. And Bill Shankly answered their questions. Their questions about the season Liverpool Football Club were having, their questions about the seasons Liverpool Football Club had had –

Well, yes, said Bill Shankly. Yes. It was very disappointing to go out of the European Cup in the very first round. And I mean, we completely outplayed Forest. At Anfield, at home. In the second leg, the home leg. We completely outplayed them from start to finish. But you see, they had Peter Shilton and Kenny Burns. And Larry Lloyd, of course. And they were very strong. Very resolute. And so again, we were unable to score. And so yes, it was very disappointing, very depressing. But I am certain Forest will win it. I am sure Nottingham Forest will win the European Cup. And in fact, I am so certain. I am so sure. I've backed them myself. The day after the match. The goalless draw at Anfield. I put my money on Forest. That's how certain I am. How sure I am Forest can win the European Cup. And that would be a tremendous thing. Not only for Forest, not only for Brian. But for Britain, too. It would be a tremendous thing. A really tremendous thing for Britain. And of course, our season is not over. Oh no. Not over by a long chalk. I mean, I think we have every chance we can win the League. We can win the title. Because I think it'll come down to ourselves and Forest. And I feel Forest will be distracted. Distracted by the European Cup, you see? And so I think that gives us every chance. Every chance to win the League again . . .

And in the front room of Bill Shankly's home. On the edge of their chairs, with their tea in their hands. These people who had come to his home, these people who were sat in his home. They asked Bill Shankly about Everton Football Club, too. And Bill Shankly smiled. And Bill Shankly laughed –

Well, yes, said Bill Shankly again. Yes. It was very disappointing to lose at Goodison. And so I hope we can put that right on Saturday. Because it's always the worst thing in the world. If you lose a derby. It's a horrible feeling, a terrible thing. Because the city is split in half and you get so much banter. So many arguments and so many bets. And so this week before the derby, it always seems such a long time. Such a very, very long time. The longest week of the season. Because there are no games like derby games. No thrills like derby thrills. Because these games, they mean so much to so many. People have so many memories of so many derbies. And thankfully, I have a lot of happy memories. Because if you look at the results. The results since Liverpool Football Club returned to the First Division. Then you'll understand. Then you'll see why I have so many happy memories. So many very happy memories. Because we have beaten Everton more times than they have beaten us. That's a fact. A fact! And I can still see every goal that was scored in every game. In every derby game. And every time they got one. Every time they scored a goal. Well, that was like a knife in my back. But every one we got. Every one we scored. Then I was soaring, soaring with the astronauts. And so I have always wanted to win them all. Even when it was Liverpool reserves versus Everton reserves. I still wanted to win. To win every game, every derby. More than anything. And I remember the worst one. The worst one was when they came to Anfield and they beat us four–nil. At home, at Anfield. On the nineteenth of September, nineteen hundred and sixty-four. Oh yes, that's a day I'll never forget. A day I'll always remember. But I remember, too, the following season. The twenty-fifth of September, nineteen sixty-five. When we beat them five–nil. Because that was our revenge. Our revenge with interest. With bloody interest! But you ask me which was the best? Well, that's a difficult thing to say. Because I mean, there were so many great ones. So many great derbies, so many great victories. And I mean, I'll never forget the rubbing we gave them in the Charity Shield. That was after the World Cup, in nineteen sixty-six. And the records might show we won one–nil, only one–nil. But we gave them a pasting, a real pasting. And in fact, it turned out to be the best thing we ever did for Everton Football Club. Because after that match, after that rubbing. Off they went, breaking transfer records, signing Alan Ball. And that transformed them, Alan Ball transformed them. And that got them back on the rails. Alan put them back on the rails. But that was really down to us, thanks to us, and to the pasting we gave them in the Charity Shield. But I think the hardest and the most thrilling was the one in the November of nineteen seventy. When we were two–nil down. And they were in their blue heaven, in their seventh heaven. But we came back. And we beat them three–two. And that was like a bad dream for the Everton fans. A bloody nightmare. A red nightmare for them! Because they were two–nil up, you see. And they thought they were in Easy Street. But there is no Easy Street at Anfield Road. Oh no. No Easy Street at Anfield Road. Because you see, we never give up. And I knew with the players we had. The players we had that day. That was Ray Clemence and Chris Lawler. Young Alec Lindsay.

Tommy Smith, of course. And Larry Lloyd. Emlyn and Brian Hall. Phil Boersma, who I brought on for John McLaughlin. Steve Heighway, of course. Big John Toshack and Ian Ross. I knew we had the players who could come back. The players who could hit Everton like a whirlwind. And that is what they did. That is exactly what they did. They hit Everton like a whirlwind. A bloody whirlwind. A red whirlwind! And so we came back. And we beat them three–two. Three–bloody–two after being two–bloody–nil down. And so that was fantastic. A fantastic derby. The hardest but the most thrilling. And the best one for me, the best victory. And it tasted like champagne. Like red champagne. Because defeat is a bitter pill. A very bitter pill. But thankfully, we did not have too many of them. Not in my time.

And in the front room of Bill Shankly's home. On their feet now. These people who had come to his home, these people who had sat in his home. They thanked Bill Shankly for his time. They thanked Bill Shankly and Nessie Shankly for their hospitality. And Bill Shankly smiled. Bill Shankly shook his head. And Bill Shankly thanked them all for coming. Bill Shankly shook their hands, Bill Shankly patted their backs. Bill Shankly asked them all to take care, Bill Shankly wished them all a safe journey home. And then Bill Shankly said goodbye. At his door, on the doorstep. Bill Shankly waved goodbye to them all. And then Bill Shankly closed the door. The door to their home on Bellefield Avenue. And in their home, in their kitchen. Nessie Shankly washed up the cups and the saucers. And the plates. Bill Shankly dried up the cups and the saucers. And the plates. And then Nessie Shankly went back to what she had been doing. Doing the housework, making their lunch. And Bill Shankly went back to what he had been doing. Doing the gardening, answering letters. Until the next time there was a knock on the door. Another ring on the bell. Or the next time the telephone rang.


## 80. LOT 79: THE RELICS OF THE SAINTS

Joe Mercer was the president of the Eastham Lodge Golf Club on the Wirral. Joe Mercer asked Bill if he would like to come to speak after one of their dinners at the Eastham Lodge Golf Club. Joe Mercer said the members of the Eastham Lodge Golf Club would like to hear Bill speak. They would be happy to hear Bill speak. Bill didn't like golf and Bill didn't like golf clubs. But Bill liked Joe. And so Bill said, Yes then, Joe. I'll come to speak after one of your dinners. If that's what your people want, if that's what will make your people happy.

George Higham was the secretary of the Eastham Lodge Golf Club. George Higham was also a director of Tranmere Rovers Football Club. Bill knew George Higham and Bill liked George. George Higham wrote to Bill on behalf of the Eastham Lodge Golf Club to formally invite Bill to the club and to confirm the date that Bill would come to speak after one of their dinners. Bill checked his diary. Bill wrote the date in his diary. And Bill wrote back to George to accept the invitation to the Eastham Lodge Golf Club and to confirm the date he would come to speak after one of their dinners.

But Bill had never spoken at a golf club before, after one of their dinners. And so Bill did not know what he should say, what he should speak about. And every day. In the house, in their front room. Bill sat at his writing desk. Writing things down. Things he could say. Crossing things out. Things he couldn't say. Every day. Writing things down, crossing things out. Every night. Typing up his notes. His pages and pages of notes. Every day. Tearing up his notes. His pages and pages of notes. Every day. Starting again, stopping again. Writing things down, crossing things out. Every day until the morning of the day. The morning of the day Bill was due to speak at the Eastham Lodge Golf Club. His sweater stuck to his shirt. His shirt stuck to his vest. His vest stuck to his skin. Bill walked into the hall. Bill picked up the telephone. Bill called George Higham. And Bill said, George, George? I'm sorry, George, I'm very sorry, George. But I cannot come. I cannot speak. I'm not feeling too good. I'm not feeling myself.

Oh no, said George Higham. Oh no, Bill. Don't say that, please don't say that. Our members are very much looking forward to you coming, very excited about hearing you speak, Bill. They will be so disappointed, so very, very disappointed. Is there no way you can come, Bill? Are you feeling that bad, Bill?

Bill felt bad now. Very bad now. And Bill said, But I don't like golf, George. It's not my game. Football is my game. And so I wouldn't know what to say . . .

But no one is expecting you to talk about golf, said George Higham. People just want to hear your stories, Bill. Your stories about football, your stories about life. You are a great talker, Bill. A great speaker. And so they just want to hear you speak, Bill. About whatever you want. It's very relaxed. People have their dinner, they have a drink. And then they just want to hear you, Bill. Listen to you speak.

Bill felt worse now. Even worse now. And Bill said, But I just don't like golf clubs. They are not my kind of people, you see. And I'm not good at posh dos. They are not my kind of places, you understand? It's not me, George. It's just not for me . . .

But our club is not like that, said George Higham. Not like you imagine, Bill. Our members are from Liverpool, they are Liverpool people. They are looking forward to you coming, excited to be hearing you speak, Bill. They will be very disappointed if you do not come. They'll be very sad if you do not speak, Bill . . .

Bill felt terrible. Bloody terrible. And so Bill said, All right then, George. All right. I'll come, George. I'll come and I'll speak.

His sweater still stuck to his shirt. His shirt still stuck to his vest. His vest still stuck to his skin. Bill put down the telephone. Bill walked up the stairs. In the bathroom. Bill took off his sweater. Bill took off his shirt. Bill took off his vest. And Bill had a wash. A good wash. And then Bill went into the bedroom. Bill changed his trousers. Bill put on his shirt. His best white shirt. Bill put on his bow tie. His black bow tie. Bill put on his dinner jacket. His black dinner jacket. In the house, in their bedroom. Bill stood before the mirror on the back of the wardrobe door. Bill looked at the man in the mirror. In his dinner jacket. His black dinner jacket. His bow tie. His black bow tie. And Bill said, Good evening, ladies and gentlemen. And thank you, ladies and gentlemen. For inviting me to your club tonight. I, I, I . . .

In the bedroom. Before the mirror on the back of the wardrobe door. Bill stared at the man in the mirror. His shirt stuck to his vest. Again. His vest stuck to his skin. His bow tie. His black bow tie tight around his neck. Choking him, strangling him. And again Bill said, Good evening, ladies and gentlemen. And thank you, ladies and gentlemen. For inviting me to your club tonight. I, I . . .

Bill turned away from the mirror on the back of the wardrobe door. The man in the mirror. Bill closed the wardrobe door. Bill walked out of the bedroom. Bill walked back down the stairs. Bill went back into the front room. Bill went back to the writing desk. Bill bent down. Down under the writing desk. Bill pulled out the wastepaper basket from under the writing desk. And Bill took out all his screwed-up pages of notes. His pages and pages of notes. Bill straightened out all his screwed-up pages of notes. His pages and pages of notes. Bill picked out all his torn-up pages of notes. His pages and pages of notes. Bill stuck back together all his pages of notes. His pages and pages of notes. And then Bill took his pages and pages of straightened-out and stuck-back notes over to the chair. Bill sat down in his chair. And Bill began to read through all his pages of notes. His pages and pages of notes. And then Bill began to read out his speech from his pages of notes. His pages and pages of notes. And Bill swallowed. And Bill coughed. And then Bill said, Good evening, ladies and gentlemen. And thank you, ladies and gentlemen. For inviting me to your club tonight. I, I, I, I, I, I, I, I, I . . .

In the dining room of the Eastham Lodge Golf Club. On the little stage at the front of the dining room. Behind the lectern, on the little stage. Before the members of the Eastham Lodge Golf Club, behind the lectern. In his dinner jacket. His black dinner jacket. His bow tie. His black bow tie. Bill looked down at his notes. His pages and pages of notes. Bill swallowed again. Bill coughed again. And then Bill said, Good evening, ladies and gentlemen. And thank you, ladies and gentlemen. For inviting me to your club tonight. I, I, I . . .

But in his dinner jacket. His black dinner jacket. His bow tie. His black bow tie. Bill stared down at his notes. His pages and pages of notes. And Bill could not read his notes. His pages and pages of notes. Bill could not read his own writing. His pages and pages of writing. And Bill swallowed again. Bill coughed again. And Bill looked up. Up and out. Up at the dining room of the Eastham Lodge Golf Club, out at the members of the Eastham Lodge Golf Club. And Bill put down his notes. His pages and pages of notes –

And Bill said, I have to confess a few things. A few things about golf and a few things about me. Because you see, golf is not my game. Golf is not for me. In fact, this is the first time I've ever been anywhere near a golf club. But I've spoken to golf clubs. On the telephone. Many times. In fact, I think I must have called every golf club on Merseyside at one time or another. Because you see, I used to call them and tell them, You better not have any of my players. My Liverpool players. Up at your club, out on your course. Because you see, I never approved of my players playing anything but the game through which they earned their living. Because in my opinion, for a professional footballer, golf is a menace. Nothing but a bloody menace. Oh yes. You see, in my opinion, golf can put unnatural stress on the body of a footballer. Stress in places where they wouldn't normally have stress. If they didn't play golf. And when a player has these kinds of stresses. When they play golf. Then that is when a player gets injured. That's why they get injured. Oh yes. So that is why I never approved of them playing golf. And so I banned the players from playing golf. I banned them all. But they were a crafty lot. Very cunning, my players. Because that's the kind of men I like. Crafty and cunning men. But on the pitch, you understand? The football pitch. Not on the golf course. But I knew then, you see. I knew then they would be sneaking about, sneaking into golf clubs, sneaking in a quick game of golf when they thought I wouldn't be looking. When they thought I wouldn't know. But I was always looking. I always had my eyes on them. Oh yes. And so I always knew. And I remember one time, I had my suspicions about Tommy Lawrence and about Roger Hunt. Something about the way they were walking, the way they were whispering to each other. The kind of clothes they were wearing, the kind of shoes they were buying. These were not the clothes of a footballer, the shoes a footballer would wear. Oh no. I knew what they were about, what they were up to. They were sneaking about, sneaking off to golf clubs, sneaking off for a quick game. And so I remember, I called one golf club. The club I thought they were going to. And I called this club, and I said to their secretary, Have you got my boys there? And he said, No, no, Mr Shankly. But I could tell from the answer, the way the secretary answered. I could tell that Tommy Lawrence and Roger Hunt had warned the club, had warned the secretary that I might be calling, that I might be asking after them. Can you imagine? That is how crafty they were, how cunning they were. But you see, I could tell from the voice, the voice of the secretary. I could tell they were there. And I could tell they had warned him I would call. And so I knew they had told him to lie. Because I could tell by his voice that he was lying. He was lying to me. And so I told him, I said, I know you are lying to me. I know they are there. And so I'm coming over now. In my car. With my boys. With Bob, and with Joe, and with Reuben. In the car. And when we have finished with them. Then it'll be your turn. And now the man was shaking, his voice was shaking. And he said, Please don't, Mr Shankly. Please don't come, Mr Shankly. They are here, they are here. And so I told him, I said, Then you tell them from me to go home. To get themselves home. Or I'll be coming to your club with my club. My bloody club!

In the Eastham Lodge Golf Club. In the dining room. At their tables, after their dinner. With their cigars and with their drinks. The members of the Eastham Lodge Golf Club laughed. And the members of the Eastham Lodge Golf Club clapped. And in his dinner jacket. His black dinner jacket. His bow tie. His black bow tie. Bill smiled. And Bill said, But I have to confess. In one case. With one footballer. One footballer who took to the golf. I have only myself to blame. It was my own bloody fault. Because before one game, an away game. We were staying at this hotel. And we'd got there a wee bit too early. Even for me. Because I always like to be early. But we were too early. And the players were moping about, moaning. Moping about because they had nothing to do, moaning they were bored. And I tell you, there is nothing worse than a bunch of moping, moaning footballers. And this hotel, this hotel we were staying in. This hotel had a little course, a wee golf course. Nothing dramatic, you understand? Nothing spectacular. But to stop all their moping about, to stop all their moaning. I said they could go out for a game. A quick game, just this once. But I said, I'm coming, too. Not to play, just to watch. To make sure you don't do anything daft. Make sure you don't go and do anything silly and go and injure yourselves. Before the game, the match tomorrow. And so there I was, watching them, keeping my eye on them. And Tommy Smith, he was there. And he must have still been only a boy. Only just in the team. And Tommy had never played golf before, he'd never even seen a bloody golf course before. And so all the older lads. Your Ian St Johns and your Roger Hunts. They were teasing the boy, taking the mick out of Tommy. But Tommy being Tommy. Even then, even when he still just a young boy. He picked up a golf club. The very first time he'd ever picked up a club. And he

671

took his first swing, his first shot. His very first shot with a golf club. And he got a hole-in-one. A bloody hole-in-one! With his first-ever shot. Unbelievable. Bloody unbelievable! And that shut up all them older lads. Your Ian St Johns and your Roger Hunts. And I said, Jesus Christ, Tommy. You're a natural. A bloody natural! And Tommy was so made up. He was so pleased with himself that he decided this was the game for him. That golf was the game for him. And so you see, that was my fault. My own bloody fault. Because I encouraged him. I couldn't help myself. But in fairness, it didn't last long. I don't think golf is the game for Tommy, either. In fact, I think football is the only game for Tommy. I mean, I tried to get him interested in the boxing. Because as you all know, Tommy is a hard man. A very hard man. And so I used to try to get him interested in the boxing. In fact, I tried so hard, I even bought him a pair of gloves. A pair of boxing gloves. But actually, I bought a pair for every player. A pair of boxing gloves for every player. Because I used to tell my players. Every Friday night, the night before the match. I used to tell them all to wear their boxing gloves. To wear their boxing gloves in bed!

In the Eastham Lodge Golf Club. In the dining room. At their tables, after their dinner. With their cigars and with their drinks. The members of the Eastham Lodge Golf Club laughed. The members of the Eastham Lodge Golf Club clapped. And now they got to their feet for Bill. And they applauded Bill. And they thanked Bill. And in his dinner jacket. His black dinner jacket. His bow tie. His black bow tie. Bill nodded. And Bill smiled.

Now George Higham stepped forward. George Higham thanked Bill. And George Higham handed Bill a red leather binder –

Bill looked down at the red leather binder. And Bill said, What's this, George? It's not *This Is Your Life* again, is it?

Yes, said George Higham. It is, Bill.

And Bill opened the red leather binder. And Bill could not believe his eyes. Inside the red leather binder was the programme for the 1938 FA Cup Final. The programme for the 1938 FA Cup Final between Huddersfield Town and Preston North End. The 1938 FA Cup Final in which Bill had played for Preston North End. The 1938 FA Cup Final which Preston North End had won. And Bill stared down at the programme. And Bill could not speak –

Well, you know how I collect memorabilia, Bill. Football memorabilia, said George Higham. Well, we just wanted to get you something nice, Bill. And we knew you would never accept any money. So I hit upon this idea for you, Bill. And I managed to find one, through my contacts. My contacts with other collectors. Because I believe you do not have one, you do not still have yours, Bill?

Bill stared down at the programme. Bill shook his head. And Bill said, No, George. I don't. I don't have one any more . . .

Well, you do now, said George Higham. You do now, Bill.

And Bill stared down at the programme again. And Bill nodded. Bill fought back tears. Bill struggled to breathe. And then Bill whispered, Thank you, George. Thank you. I do all these events. All these events for people. And I'm happy to do them. I am happy to do them for people. But this is the first time anyone has ever thought what I would like. So thank you, George. Thank you very much.


## 81. AT SEA, ALL AT SEA; A SEA CHANGE

On Thursday 3 May, 1979, thirteen million, six hundred and ninety-seven thousand, nine hundred and twenty-three folk voted for the Conservative Party. That day, eleven million, five hundred and thirty-two thousand, two hundred and eighteen folk voted for the Labour Party. That evening, the Conservative Party won three hundred and thirty-three seats in the House of Commons. That evening, the Labour Party won two hundred and sixty-nine seats in the House of Commons. That night, the Conservative Party won the 1979 General Election. That night, Margaret Thatcher, the Member of Parliament for Finchley in London, who had been born in Grantham and who supported no one, became the Prime Minister of the United Kingdom. That night, James Callaghan, the Member of Parliament for Cardiff South East, who had been born in Portsmouth and who preferred rugby to soccer, was no longer the Prime Minister of the United Kingdom. In the house, in their front room, Bill Shankly got up from his armchair. Bill Shankly got to his feet. Bill Shankly walked over to the television. Bill Shankly switched off the television. Bill Shankly walked over to the window. Bill Shankly drew back the curtains. Bill Shankly stared out through the window. Bill Shankly stared down the street. The empty street, the silent houses. Their curtains drawn, their doors locked. Forever drawn and double locked.


## 82. WE MUST GET BACK TO SANITY

Despite the times, despite the world. The summer had still come again, another season come again. But Bill had not taken the train again. The train to Euston Station, London. Bill had not taken a cab again. The cab to Wembley Stadium. And so Bill had not gone down the corridors again. The Wembley corridors again. Bill had not stood before the dressing-room door again. The Liverpool dressing-room door again. And Bill had not taken his seat in the stands at Wembley Stadium. Bill had stayed at home, in his Liverpool home. In his front room, in his armchair. Bill listened to the 1979 FA Charity Shield match between Liverpool Football Club and Arsenal Football Club on the radio. In his armchair, in his front room. In his home, his Liverpool home. On his own, all on his own. Bill listened to Terry McDermott score for Liverpool Football Club. Bill listened to Kenny Dalglish score for Liverpool Football Club. And Bill listened to Terry McDermott score again for Liverpool Football Club. And then Bill heard Alan Sunderland score for Arsenal Football Club. And Bill got up from his armchair. In his front room. Bill got to his feet. Bill walked over to the radio. Bill switched off the radio. And Bill heard the telephone ringing. In the hall. Bill picked up the telephone. And Bill listened as a journalist introduced himself to Bill. And apologised for bothering him. Bothering and disturbing Bill. And then the journalist asked Bill for his thoughts. His thoughts on the match he had just listened to, his thoughts on the season to come. And in the hall, on the telephone. Bill breathed out. And Bill said, Well, we must get a wee bit of sanity back. That is the first thing, the most important thing of all. Because there is madness. Madness in the world, madness in the game. Madness in some of these fees that are being paid. It seems that suddenly everything has got out of hand, money-wise, transfer-wise. And the players themselves, they haven't helped. I mean, I was all in favour of freedom of contract. Don't misunderstand me, don't get me wrong. The clubs had things too much their own way. But now that freedom is being abused. They want freedom for themselves alone. I mean, everyone is out for themselves, every man out for himself. I mean, I bought players like Kevin Keegan, Ray Clemence and Larry Lloyd for the kind of money that today players are getting for their slice of the fee, their signing-on fee. Their own bloody fee! Now that to me is madness. That can't be right, it must be wrong. And some managers, they don't seem to mind what they pay. But the working man, he should be sick about it. He pays his money, too, more and more. And it is *his* money. His money they are throwing about. But in the end, I think the whole business will find its own level. It has to come to its senses. And maybe it will happen this season. That is what I would like to see. The first thing, the most important thing of all. A wee bit of sanity coming back into the game, into the world . . .

Talking of this season, Bill. This season to come, asked the journalist. Who do you think will win the League, Bill?

In the hallway, on the telephone. Bill smiled. And Bill said, Don't look further than Liverpool. Back the class horse. I mean, you'll only lose your money backing the triers. Your Aston Villa, your West Bromwich. I mean, it's a one-horse race. Not like in my day, not these days. I mean, in my day, in those days. You'd look at the Manchester teams. You'd look at Everton, you'd look at Derby. And you'd say, We've got something on our hands here. And above all, you'd look at Leeds. About this time of year, just before the season started. And you'd think about the likes of Hunter, Bremner, Giles and Lorimer. And you'd think about the manager, that fellow who's in the desert now. And you'd think, What's he up to? What is he planning for us? And you'd think about the confrontations, the confrontations to come. How they would go, what would happen. But not any more, not these days. There's no point. Not any more, not now. Now there's only Forest. They are a very talented side, a very well-managed side. And perhaps Ipswich, Ipswich Town. Again, they are a good side, a well-managed side. And I think they possibly should have won more things than they have. More than just the Cup. They should have won the League by now. The most important thing. But that's all there is now, these days. Just Forest and Ipswich. And I mean, that's the reason I did not go down for the match today. For the Charity Shield today.

Because I could have gone. Oh yes, I could have gone. But there's no point going all that way to find out something you already know now, is there? No bloody point. Not if you already know. No point at all . . .

But you still listened to the match on the radio, said the journalist. So who would you say was Liverpool's best player today, Bill?

Bill breathed in. Bill tightened his grip on the telephone. And Bill said, Liverpool! Liverpool was the best player. And Liverpool Football Club is always the best player. Because Liverpool does not have individual players like other teams. I mean, look at the Arsenal. Take the Arsenal today, for example. They are a good side, a capable side. But they depend on Liam Brady. They depend on one single man. One individual player. Liverpool Football Club depend on no single man. No individual player. Liverpool Football Club depend on every man! Liverpool Football Club depend on each other. And when you've people doing that properly, when they are the right men. Well trained, well prepared. Then they cannot be beaten. And so Arsenal couldn't beat them. Not if they played them for the next ten bloody years. Because Liverpool depend on each other. It's collective. Everyone working for each other. It is a kind of socialism. Pure socialism. Everyone doing what they can for the rest –

And Bill put down the telephone. In the hall. Bill heard a clock ticking. In the house. Ticking. And Bill felt old, two thousand years old. The clock ticking. So very old, so tired. Ticking. So very tired and so strained. The clock ticking. So very strained, his heart strained. Ticking and whispering. It was a different time, a different world. A world with no place for some men, some men left behind. In a different time, a different world. Men like him, men like Bill. His heart strained, his heart breaking. Left behind, with no place. In a different world, a different time. The clock always, already ticking. In the house, in the hall. Ticking and now a ball bouncing. On the ground, in the drive. Feet walking up the drive, hands knocking on the door. Little feet and little hands. And Bill opened the door. And Bill said, Hello, boys. How are you, lads? Did you listen to the match then?

Yeah, Bill. Yeah, said the boys. The boys with their red cheeks, their red shirts. Their red ball in their little hands. It was great, Bill. It was magic. And now we're going to play it, Bill. So will you come out to play? Will you come out and be the referee for us, Bill?

Bill looked at the boys. On his doorstep, in his driveway. With their red cheeks, their red shirts and their red ball. And Bill frowned. And Bill said, Aye, go on then. I'll come out to play. But I'll not be the referee. No way. If I'm coming out to play, then I want to play!

But then who will you be, said the boys. If you come out to play, then who will you be, Bill? Which player will you be?

Bill laughed. His heart beating. Beating and healed again. And Bill said, Liverpool, of course. I'll be Liverpool, boys . . .

What do you mean, asked the boys. With their red cheeks, with their red shirts. Their wide eyes and their open mouths. What do you mean? You can't be everyone, Bill. You got to pick one player. You got to be someone, Bill. You can't be every man now, can you?

Bill shook his head. And Bill smiled again. And Bill said, That's the thing, boys. That's just the thing. When you play for Liverpool, you play *as* every man, boys. Because when you play for Liverpool Football Club, you play *for* every man. You are not someone, you are everyone, boys. Every man. That's the thing that is different about Liverpool Football Club, boys. Different from every other football club in the land. In the world, boys. When you play for Liverpool, you play for everyone. You play for every man, boys. So you *are* every man. And then you are every player, boys. That's you, every man. And so I'm going to be Liverpool, boys. I'm going to be Liverpool. Now what about you, boys? Who are you all going to be?

Liverpool, shouted the boys. All the boys with their red cheeks, all the boys with their red shirts. And their red ball, their red ball up in the air now. We're going to be Liverpool, too, Bill! Liverpool!


## 83. I ALWAYS CARRY A PICTURE OF HIM

For the second successive year, Kevin Keegan had been named as the European Footballer of the Year. The Souvenir Press and the Wilkinson Sword company invited Kevin Keegan to London from Hamburg, West Germany. The Souvenir Press and the Wilkinson Sword company planned to present Kevin Keegan with a Sword of Honour in recognition of his achievement in becoming the European Footballer of the Year for the second successive year. And Ernest

Hecht of the Souvenir Press called Bill Shankly. Ernest Hecht asked Bill Shankly if he would like to surprise Kevin Keegan. If Bill Shankly would like to present Kevin Keegan with his Sword of Honour –

Yes, said Bill Shankly. I would, Ernest.

In London, at the presentation. Wide-eyed and thrilled to bits, Kevin Keegan watched Bill Shankly step out from behind the curtains. Kevin Keegan watched Bill Shankly walk across the stage. A sword in his hands. Bill Shankly held out the sword towards Kevin Keegan. And Kevin Keegan heard Bill Shankly say, This is for you, son. For all you have achieved in the game. For all you have done with your life, son. This Sword of Honour is yours. This sword is for you, son . . .

And Kevin Keegan took the Sword of Honour from Bill Shankly. Kevin Keegan stared down at the Sword of Honour in his hands. But now Kevin Keegan shook his head. And now Kevin Keegan handed back the Sword of Honour to Bill Shankly. And Kevin Keegan said, This is not mine, this is yours, Boss. Because anything I have achieved, anything I have done. It is because of you, Boss. It's all because of you. Because it was you who bought me from Scunthorpe, you who took a gamble on me when no one else would, Boss. And it was you who believed in me. You who always believed in me, Boss. You always encouraged me, you always supported and taught me. That was you, Boss. All you. So this sword is yours, not mine.

Bill Shankly shook his head. The sword in his hands, the tears in his eyes. Bill Shankly shook his head again –

No, no, said Bill Shankly. It's yours, son. Please take it. I cannot take it, son. I just cannot . . .

But Kevin Keegan looked at Bill Shankly. And Kevin Keegan whispered, Please. Please take it, Boss. You have given me so much. So very, very much, Boss. Please take this from me. Please, Boss . . .

At the presentation, on the stage. Bill Shankly stared down at the Sword of Honour in his hands. And Bill Shankly swallowed –

Then when I die, you can have it back . . .

On the train. The train from London back to Liverpool. Some of the passengers saw Bill Shankly sitting with a sword on the table before him. And some of the passengers stopped to ask Bill Shankly about the sword on the table before him. And Bill Shankly smiled –

Well, it was a great gesture by the boy. A very moving gesture

678

by Kevin. Perhaps even the greatest gesture since the world began! And it is certainly the greatest present I have ever had in my life. And when I get home, back to my house. I am going to display this sword in our home. So everyone can see this Sword of Honour . . .

Back in their house, in their front room. Nessie Shankly watched Bill Shankly prop the Sword of Honour up in the corner against the wall. Nessie watched Bill Shankly then step back. Bill Shankly standing before the sword, staring at the sword –

You must promise me this, love. That when I die, the day I die. You must pack up this sword, this Sword of Honour. And send it back to Kevin. Will you please promise me that, love?

Nessie Shankly nodded. Nessie smiled. And Nessie said, Well, yes, I promise you, love. But you know you'll be burying me. You'll bury us all, love. And so make sure you tell the girls and all.

Bill Shankly nodded. And then Bill Shankly turned away from the Sword of Honour. And Bill Shankly walked over to the bookcase. Bill Shankly took out one of his scrapbooks. His scrapbooks of cuttings, his scrapbooks of pictures. And Bill Shankly opened the scrapbook. Bill Shankly turned the pages of the scrapbook. Bill Shankly found the page he was looking for. And Bill Shankly walked back over to Nessie Shankly. Nessie still standing before the Sword of Honour, Nessie still staring at the Sword of Honour. Bill Shankly held out the scrapbook towards Nessie, the scrapbook for Nessie –

You see this, love? This sword here, in this picture here. That is the Sword of Stalingrad. King George commanded that sword be forged as a homage from the people of Britain to the people of the Soviet Union who had defended their city during the Battle of Stalingrad. King George commanded Churchill present Joseph Stalin with the sword at the Tehran Conference in 1943. But before Churchill took the sword to Tehran, the sword was exhibited all around Britain. And wherever it went, people came to see this sword, loads and loads of people. And finally, it was put on display in Westminster Abbey. And again people came from miles around, long queues of people. Not only to look at the sword, that magnificent sword. But to show their gratitude to our allies in the Soviet Union, to show their respect for the people of the Soviet Union. And it was like an icon to people, it was an inspiration to people. Not the sword, but the people of Stalingrad.

Their bravery and their courage. Their fortitude and their resolution. All their sufferings and all their sacrifices. This was an inspiration to the people of Britain, a lesson for the people of Great Britain. Their hearts, their hearts of steel. An inspiration and a lesson. And so on one side of the sword it says in English, *TO THE STEEL-HEARTED CITIZENS OF STALINGRAD. THE GIFT OF KING GEORGE VI. IN TOKEN OF THE HOMAGE OF THE BRITISH PEOPLE.* And on the other side, it says the same again in Russian. And you know what, love? That Sword of Stalingrad was forged by the same people who forged this Sword of Honour. The sword they gave to Kevin, that Kevin gave to me. The same people, the Wilkinson Sword people.

Nessie Shankly shook her head. Nessie smiled again. And Nessie said, I didn't know that, love. I didn't know any of that . . .

I don't think many people do, said Bill Shankly. And if they ever did, they probably don't remember now. People often forget.


## 84. IT WAS TWENTY YEARS AGO TODAY

Bill never forgot. Bill always remembered. Every hour of every day. Every day of every week. Every week of every month. Every month of every year. Every year and every season. Every season and every match. Every single match. From the first match to the last match. Bill always remembered, Bill never forgot. But Bill did not really care for anniversaries. Bill did not really celebrate anniversaries. The march of time, the passage of time. But people kept reminding Bill of this particular anniversary. People would not let Bill forget this particular anniversary. On his doorstep, on the telephone. In the house or in the street. In conversations and in interviews. Journalists and well-wishers. Asking Bill for his thoughts, asking Bill for his reminiscences. Asking him and reminding him. About the march of time, the passage of time. From that first match to that last match. And in the street or in the house. In interviews or in conversations. Bill smiled. And Bill said, Oh well, yes. It was very different then. A different time, a different world. And Anfield was very different then, when I first came. A different place, a different world. The Kop was open, yes. But the present-day stands had not been built, no. And gates had dropped to about twenty-one thousand. Unbelievable, really. Bloody unbelievable. When you think of what Anfield is now, the gates they get now. Every week, every Saturday. Bloody unbelievable. But then, back then. There was an air of depression about the place. Not like now, not like these days. And I remember when I came over to Liverpool with my wife to have a look around. And we went to the training ground. It was like a wilderness. A bloody wilderness. There was only the one pitch. And a tumbledown old shed for the lads to change in. And there was even an old air-raid shelter still there. A bloody air-raid shelter. Because nobody could be bothered to pull it down. Not until I came.

In the house or in the street. Bill smiled again. And Bill said, I mean, all you could really say was that it was there. But that was all. That was Liverpool Football Club then. A hell of a lot of potential. But not much bloody else. Not much else except the people, of course. And that was why I came. For the people, the Liverpool people. Even then, they were fantastic. Fantastic people. But I knew they were fantastic people. The Liverpool people. Before I came, I knew. Because I had seen some boxing contests at Anfield. Peter Kane against Jimmy Warnock. Ernie Roderick fighting the great Henry Armstrong. And I had a nose operation in Liverpool, too. Before the war. So I knew the people and I knew the city. I knew the city was like a Scottish city, the people like Scottish people. Full of a kind of Celtic pride, if you know what I mean? And so I mean, I've always identified with Liverpool people. And so I promised myself that we would build something here, something they could always be proud of . . .

In the street or in the house. Bill nodded. And Bill said, So that was why I came. Yes. Why I left Huddersfield Town. But I mean, if the board of Huddersfield Town had been ambitious, we would have won even more than Liverpool did! I mean, just look at the players we had there in those days, back in those days at Huddersfield. Denis Law, Ray Wilson, the Yorkshire cricketer Ken Taylor, Bill McGarry, Ray Wood and several more. What bloody players, what a bloody team. But Huddersfield was a seller's market. That was all it was. A bloody seller's market. I mean, I wanted to be buying, not bloody selling. I wanted the money to buy Yeats and St John. I wanted them for Huddersfield. And can you imagine, imagine if those two had joined the players we had at Huddersfield Town? Imagine what a team that would have been. What a bloody team. I mean, I think they would have won everything. But they wouldn't find the money to buy Yeats and St John or any of the players I wanted. And instead they sold the players we had. Bloody sold them. That's the difference. The bloody difference between Huddersfield and Liverpool. And so look at Huddersfield Town now, where Huddersfield Town are now. In the Fourth Division, the bloody Fourth Division. And it breaks my heart to see them there, it really does. I mean, when you think of the history of that football club. The things they did, the things they won. The managers they had and the players they had. And their supporters. It breaks my heart, it really does. But that is why Huddersfield Town are in the Fourth Division and Liverpool Football Club are the League Champions. And have been the League Champions six times since 1959, since I first came. And won the FA Cup twice and the European Cup twice. And the UEFA Cup. That's the difference.

In the house or in the street. Bill shook his head. And Bill said, But you know I was offered the job at Anfield eight years before? Eight years earlier. George Kay was still the manager then. And he had been the manager for fifteen years. It was George, of course, who was the manager when Liverpool won their fifth title in 1947. And he took them to the FA Cup Final in 1950, too. The final they lost to Arsenal. And did you know George also played in the very first Cup Final to be played at Wembley Stadium? Oh yes, he was the captain of West Ham in the White Horse final. Anyway, George was not a well man. He could not go on. And so Liverpool advertised for a new manager. And I applied for the job. I mean, I was at Carlisle. And I was still very new to the job. But I was ambitious. I have always been ambitious. Not for me, but for the supporters. I mean, right from the start I tried to show the supporters that they are the people who matter. The supporters, the team and the manager are the only people who really matter. Not the directors. But at Carlisle, it was the same story. The same story as at Huddersfield later. The directors lacked the ambition. The ambition and the belief. I mean, we had a good run in the Cup at Carlisle. Eighty thousand folk had watched the two games against Arsenal. And they had got good money for Ivor Broadis, too. But the directors would not use the money from the Cup or the money from Ivor. Again, Carlisle were a selling club. Not a buying club. And so I applied for the job at Liverpool. And I was invited over to Liverpool. I was very surprised to be invited. And I remember, when I got off the train at Lime Street, I saw Andy Beattie. Andy bloody Beattie! My good friend from my Preston days, my old friend from my Scotland days. And so I knew where he was going, why he was there. And he knew where I was going, why I was there. And I remember, we both looked at each other and we both laughed. And we both said, Well, that's two people who won't be getting the bloody job then! But you know, I was actually asked if I would be the manager? Oh yes, they offered me the job. But right away I said, Who picks the team?

In the street or in the house. Bill shook his head again. And Bill said, And of course, in those days. Back in those days. Nobody asked directors questions. Especially not a question like that. And so they told me they picked the team. They were in charge of selecting the team. They met in a little committee on a Friday and they made their choices. They made their selections. And then they would call in the manager. And they would tell him who they had picked. They would tell him who was playing. Whether he agreed or not, whether he liked it or not. And so I said to them, I said, Then you don't need a manager. You need a trainer. And I am not a trainer. I am a manager. And so I pick the team. I say who plays. And so you don't want me and I don't want you. So no thank you, gentlemen. And goodnight!

In the house or in the street. Bill laughed. And Bill said, But you see, they never forgot me. Oh no! Nobody else had asked them that question. Nobody else had spoken to them like that. Oh no. And so they always remembered me. Especially Mr Williams. He never forgot me, he always remembered me. My enthusiasm and my passion. But when they came calling, when they came calling in 1959. That was still the first question I asked, still the first thing I asked them, Who picks the team? But by then, you see. By 1959, they had changed their tune. They had learnt the hard way. Oh yes. And so they said, You do, Mr Shankly. Because you will be the manager. And so I said, Yes! Yes then, I will be the manager of Liverpool Football Club then. And so it's true to say, very true to say, I was the first genuine manager Liverpool Football Club ever had!

In the street or in the house. Bill smiled. And Bill said, Well, that's a good question, a very good question. What would have happened if Bill Shankly had come to Liverpool Football Club in 1951? Eight years earlier. Well, I have no doubt. No doubt at all. We would have conquered the world. The whole bloody world. I mean, I was thirty-six years old then. And I was at my best, I was in my prime. I had helped Carlisle to take sixty-two points in a season. And then later at Grimsby, we got sixty-six points from forty-two games. Because I was at my best, I was in my prime. The height of my ambition, my desire to succeed. For the people of the club, the supporters of the club. Whatever club I was at, whether it was Carlisle or Grimsby Town. Workington or Huddersfield. And so that was what I would have brought to Liverpool Football Club in 1951. And what I did bring to Liverpool in 1959. That ambition, that desire. And my passion. My passion for the game, my passion for the supporters . . .

In the house or in the street. Bill shook his head. And Bill said, But you know, it was a constant battle. A constant struggle. I mean, when we won the Second Division championship. When we were promoted to the First Division. The shareholders gave us all a silver cigarette box. You know, a wee little pat on the head. And I remember looking down at that silver cigarette box in my hands. And then I looked up at the shareholders. And up at the directors. And I said to them, I said, Do you think we have won something? We have won nothing! This is bloody nothing. This is only the start! Only the bloody start. Now we're going after the real prizes. The real bloody prizes.

In the street or in the house. Bill smiled again. And Bill said, And we won the First Division. And we won the FA Cup. And we won the League again. And we went into Europe. We went after Europe. And they were wonderful days. Oh yes! Truly wonderful days. Because it was all new, you see? All new. So people didn't expect you to win trophies all the time. And so the atmosphere was unbelievable. Bloody unbelievable. Because of the supporters. The supporters of Liverpool Football Club. They were unbelievable. They *are* unbelievable. Bloody unbelievable. And they inspire the team, you see? And so the team know who they are playing for, the players of Liverpool Football Club always know who they are playing for. Playing for the supporters, playing as part of a team. Because football is a team game. And so there is no room for prima donnas in a team. Because no man is more important than the team. And everyone is part of that team. Not just the players, the eleven players on the pitch. But the manager, the coach, the tea lady and the ball boys. Everybody is part of the team. They are all part of the team and so they have all got to be the best there is. The best they can be. Because they are all part of the same team. They are all the same. And I tell you this, our great team of the sixties. They were all paid the same money to a penny piece. There was no man who got more than another man. And that's the way it has to be. That's the way it must be. The only way . . .

In the house or in the street. In conversations and in interviews. The journalists nodded and the well-wishers smiled. And they said, Yes, it was twenty years ago today, Bill. Twenty years ago today.

And Bill said, I only wish I could start all over again . . .

But in the street or in the house. The journalists and the well-wishes thanked Bill for his thoughts and for his reminiscences. They thanked Bill for his time. And they said goodbye. Until the next time, the next anniversary. They left Bill alone. In the house or in the street. But Bill never forgot. Bill always remembered. Every hour of every day. Every day of every week. Every week of every month. Every month of every year. Every year and every season. Every season and every match. Every single match. From the first match to the last match. Bill always remembered, Bill never forgot. Bill bore these memories, Bill carried these memories. A great weight Bill bore, a piece of wood Bill carried. A piece of wood which left Bill with splinters, splinters in his back. In his shoulders and in his neck. But splinters which gave Bill faith, splinters which made Bill believe. Believe in the things that had been, once. Believe in the things that could be, again. After the resurrection, before the resurrection –

Bill said, I only wish I could start all over again . . .


## 85. BEFORE THE REVOLUTION

In the winter. Under dark and heavy skies. In the middle of the week, in the middle of the day. In his suit and in his tie. Bill Shankly stood before Anfield. Before the camera. The Italian television camera. The television crew and the interviewer. These men who had come from Rome to find out why English football was now the most successful football in Europe. These men who had come to ask Bill Shankly why. And in the winter. Under dark and heavy skies. They switched on their camera and they switched on their lights. And the interviewer looked up at the clouds and then back down at Anfield. At the houses around the ground, at the streets around the ground. The boarded-up shops and the paint-splattered walls. An abandoned old car and a smashed-up phone box. The newspapers and the crisp packets blowing across the pavements. Across the broken glass, across the dog shit. And the man from Rome said, This city is like a cemetery. This town is like a ghost town. Twenty per cent of this city's labour force is unemployed. In the town centre, in the job centre. There were just forty-nine jobs on offer. Everywhere we have been, we have seen derelict buildings. Empty factories. Huge tracts of wasteland. And wilderness. And everyone we have spoken to, everyone talks about closures and redundancies. About British Leyland and Fisher-Bendix, Dunlop and BICC, Plessey and GEC, Lucas and Girling, Courtaulds and Meccano. People don't seem to know what is happening here. People say there is nothing happening here in this town. Nothing here but the football.

The football is not nothing, said Bill Shankly. His eyes narrow now, his jaw set now. The football is everything! And now more than ever, in times like these. But I do not deny the things you have seen. I do not deny the things you have heard. No, no. But men hear what they want to hear, men see what they want to see. But there are some things some men cannot see, some things some men will never see. Some things some men do not want to see. Hidden things to some men, invisible things to some men. So where you only see empty factories and people on their knees. I still see a beautiful city and a great people. Proud people, passionate people . . .

And before Anfield. Before the camera. As Bill Shankly spoke. Men stopped to listen. Men and boys. In their coats. Their thin coats. With their scarves. Their red scarves.

And now more than ever, said Bill Shankly. His eyes wide now, his jaw forward now. Now in these times. It is the football that helps to keep them proud, it is the football that helps to keep them passionate. Because there is still an intense and powerful passion for football in this city. An intensity you will find nowhere else except in Glasgow. Because it comes from the heart here. And it flows in the blood here. In the blood of the people, in the hearts of the people. And what we do on Saturday provides a purpose and a focus for the people. For the working people, for the working man. Because football is the working man's sport. And so he is the club! The working man is the club. You cannot make a football club without him, without the ordinary working man. Oh no! And you cannot cheat him. Or he'll find you out. Oh yes! But if he trusts you, if the working man believes in you. Then he will follow you. And he will follow the team. Because he will recognise you are committed to him, the team is committed to him. And he will put all his pride and all his passion into the team. With fervour and with love. In his blood and in his heart.

Under the dark and heavy skies. In his broad-brimmed hat. The interviewer, this man from Rome. He smiled and he said, But perhaps it is only you who thinks like this now, Mr Shankly? Perhaps it is only you who is so passionate about this city. About Liverpool and about football. Perhaps it is only you now, Mr Shankly?

Well, you go back into the city again. With your fancy camera and with your fancy lights. And you talk to the men and women who live here again. But this time you ask them about the passion they feel for this city. The passion they feel for the football in this city. The things they want to be asked about, the things they want to talk about. And then you'll see. Oh yes. Then you'll see and then you'll hear. If you have the ears to listen, if you have the eyes to see. And then you'll go back to your city, back to Rome. And you'll always remember the day you came to this city, the day you were in Liverpool. And you will feel lucky, you will feel privileged. Lucky to have walked on these pavements, privileged to have spoken with these people! Real people.

And before Anfield. Before the ground. Bill Shankly stared into the camera. And now Bill Shankly nodded. And then Bill Shankly turned away. Away from the camera, away towards the people. The men and the boys. In their coats. Their thin coats. With their scarves. Their red scarves. And the men and the boys walked towards Bill Shankly. The men and the boys gathered around Bill Shankly. In a group, in a huddle. They patted his back and they shook his hand. And they thrust pieces of paper, scraps of newspaper. Into his hands. For an autograph, for a signature. And one of the men said, You know you are a genius, don't you? You know you are a genius, Bill?

Are you all going to the match tonight, asked Bill Shankly.

And one of the men said, Of course I am, Bill. I never miss a game. I've never missed a match yet, Bill. Never once.

But most of the men shook their heads. And one of the men said, I want to, Bill. Of course I want to go. But I can't afford to go, Bill. Not to every game, not these days.

I know, son. I know, said Bill Shankly. And I am sorry, son.

And again, one of the men said, But you know you are a genius, don't you? You know you are a genius, Bill?

Did any of you lads see the first leg, asked Bill Shankly.

And one of the men said, Yes, Bill. I saw it. I was there, Bill. For my sins. What a travesty, Bill! I could not believe it!

I know, son. I know, said Bill Shankly again. And you are right, son. You are absolutely right. I mean, we've now played Forest nine times and won only once. It's unbelievable. Bloody unbelievable! And that was a heavy pitch at the City Ground, a very heavy pitch. But to play like we did, on a pitch like that. And then to concede a penalty, in the last bloody minute, and lose the bloody match. It was a travesty! A bloody travesty! Because I really thought we had learnt our lessons, I really thought we had the measure of them. The way Bob had set them up, the way Bob had set Case up as a watchdog. A watchdog on Robertson. I mean, that was very effective. Very shrewd. It clipped their wings, it cut off their lines of communication, you see? And so Robertson never had a touch, not a bloody touch. Not until the last bloody minute and he steps up and scores a bloody penalty. Unbelievable. Bloody unbelievable! Very unfair, very unjust.

One of the men said, But you think we can still turn it around tonight, Bill? You think we can still beat them, don't you?

Oh yes, said Bill Shankly. Oh yes. I mean, we had some revenge in the Cup. In the FA Cup, of course. We already got the better of Forest then. And so I think that will have given the players a lot of belief. And of course, it's always a different game here. Always a very different game at Anfield. The belief of the supporters, the belief of the Kop. You see the players, they can all feel that belief. It's an incredible feeling. An incredible thing. The way the belief of the Kop, the way it flows from the stands onto the pitch into the players. The way it inspires the players, that belief. Their hope and their passion. It's unbelievable. Bloody unbelievable!

In their coats. Their thin coats. With their scarves. Their red scarves. The men and the boys nodded. And one of the men unbuttoned his coat. The man opened up his coat. The man untied the scarf around his neck. The man took off his scarf. And the man touched the tie he was wearing. The Liverpool Football Club tie. Under his coat, under his scarf. And the man said, I am sure you won't remember, Bill. Because it was ages ago now. Years ago now. So I am sure you don't remember, Bill. But I had gone to the club shop to buy a tie. But the club shop were sold out of ties. And then I saw you, you in the car park. And I stopped you. And I asked you for your autograph. And we started to chat. And you asked about me, about how I was doing. And I said about the tie in the shop, about there being no ties in the shop. And in the car park. You took off your tie. Your Liverpool Football Club tie. And you gave me your tie. Your Liverpool Football Club tie. And so this is your tie, Bill. The tie you gave me. And I have worn it every day, Bill. Every day since. I never take it off, Bill. Never. So thank you again, Bill. Thank you.

I do remember, said Bill Shankly. And I remember you, son. I remember you very well. But it was the least I could do, son. The very least I could do. To thank you, son. To thank you for supporting Liverpool Football Club. So thank you again, son . . .

And again, one of the men said, But you know you are a genius, don't you? You are a genius, Bill?

And now Bill Shankly shook his head. And Bill Shankly put his hand upon the shoulder of this man. And Bill Shankly said, Thank you, son. Thank you. But I am not a genius. I have only ever tried to be an honest man. And to make you proud. And make you happy.


86. WHATEVER THE SEASON

Not only in the summer. Not these days. But in the autumn. And in the winter and in the spring. These days. Bill and Ness would drive up to Blackpool. In all seasons, in all weathers. Or if Ness did not fancy the drive up to Blackpool. If Ness was busy. Bill would call a friend. And Bill and his friend would drive up to Blackpool. In all seasons, in all weathers. Or if his friends did not fancy the drive up to Blackpool. If his friends were busy. Bill would still go. Bill would still drive up to Blackpool. In all seasons, in all weathers. Bill parked the car by the Norbreck Castle Hotel. Bill crossed the tram tracks to the front. Bill walked along the Queen's Promenade. And Bill sat on the front, on the promenade. In a deckchair or in a shelter. Bill sucked a lozenge, a Fisherman's Friend. And Bill stared out at the sea, the Irish Sea. In all seasons, in all weathers. In a shelter or in a deckchair. Bill thought about the seasons that had been, Bill thought about the seasons to come. The things he had done and the things he would do. In all seasons, in all weathers. In his deckchair or in the shelter. Bill sucked a lozenge, a Fisherman's Friend. Bill stared out at the sea, the Irish Sea. And Bill said, I only wish I could start all over again. Oh yes . . .

I mean, I see some of these managers. I hear some of these modern managers. And they talk like gods. But they haven't won a thing. Not a bloody thing! And so I know, some of these top jobs. I could sit and do them with my eyes shut. With my bloody eyes shut!

Basic things, you know? Basic discipline, basic routines. The initial training period should take a long time. Oh yes. About five and a half weeks, I reckon. But you need to be cautious in these initial stages. You can't be going out and tearing people to bloody pieces in the first three or four days. Oh no. You don't put them in the sand or in the hills or on the road. You train them on the grass where they play. And you take it easy. I mean, if you saw Liverpool training in the early stages of my day, you might think they were being lazy. But the build-up was gradual, you see? Relying on experience, relying on knowledge. Our experience and our knowledge. Oh yes . . .

I mean, I would never ask players to stretch their legs until they were ready. Oh no. Injuries can be caused if the initial period is wrong. If a man breaks down two or three months into the season, it might well be because of his initial training. His initial training might well have been wrong, you see? It has to be a patient approach. Yes. It should be a very patient approach. I mean, Ray Clemence once pulled a muscle kicking balls too early into his training. It affected him for a long time. And he eventually missed a few games. And it cost us the League that season. I really believe that. I really do.

So I mean, you don't want to let them sprint too early. Or kick the ball too early. Oh no. Caution is the key. Patience is the thing. You train hard, yes. But only when you are ready. Cautiously, patiently. You build up the training, you build up the players. Always with an eye on the details, on the little things. Oh yes. The details and the little things. I mean, during serious training. When the season is in full swing, when the players are seriously training. Then the players will sweat. Oh yes, of course they will. And they must, they must. But they must still wear a sweater or a top to train in. Particularly if it is a cold day. Because they need that sweater or that top to cover their kidneys. And if you haven't worn one, you must put one on as soon as training is finished. To keep you warm, you must. Oh yes . . .

I mean, instead of stripping, training and showering at Melwood. And eating there and then going home. We stripped off at Anfield and then we went down to Melwood by bus. When it's still summer and pre-season and when you are still hot and perspiring, you don't want to be leaping into the bath five minutes after you have finished. Oh no. If you do, then you'll sweat all bloody day. So after training, I encouraged the boys to have a little walk around and then have a nice cup of tea. And then we'd all get on the bus back to Anfield. It takes about fifteen minutes or so to get from Melwood in West Derby back to Anfield. And so you see, about forty minutes would have passed from training until they actually got into the bath. And I am certain, bloody certain, this is one of the reasons why we were always fitter than the rest. Because most of the other clubs, they report directly to their training grounds. And they strip off there. And so then they come straight off the training pitch and into a hot bath. Now I always disagreed with that. Strongly disagreed.

I mean, our lads never felt uncomfortable. Oh no. They never had their lunch with sweat pouring off them. And in my opinion, this was very important and a key part of Liverpool's fitness. It actually prevented injuries from happening. Stripping off at Anfield and then getting the bus out to Melwood. And then having a cup of tea before getting the bus back to Anfield. It was very important. Oh yes . . .

So I mean, these are basic routines. Basic things, simple things. And the same things apply to the actual training sessions. The same basic things, very simple things. Footballers normally train for an hour and a half. But it doesn't mean they work for an hour and a half. Oh no. Some might be demonstrating a function while others are watching them, you see? And then it's your turn. And then the others are watching you, you see? So it's not how long you train. Oh no. It's what you put into it. Oh yes. I mean, if you train properly, thirty-five minutes a day might well do you. It might well be enough.

I mean, we built Liverpool's training on exhaustion and recovery with little areas of two-a-side, three-a-side and five-a-side. And in these little areas, you are working hard. Like a boxer, you see? Twisting and turning, turning and twisting. Training the basic skills, working on the simple things. Control. Passing. Vision. And awareness. Oh yes. Our training was based on these simple skills. These basic skills. That was what our training was based on. And on fitness. Because if you are fully fit, you have a huge advantage over everybody else. Oh yes. A tremendous advantage. Oh yes . . .

And I mean, then after all the training. After all the training was complete, on a Friday. We always had a talk about the impending game. All the players and the subs attended. And one of us, one of the staff. We would have watched the opposition. And they would bring in their report. You know, was it four–four–two, four–three–three or whatever. And did any of the opposing players have any little characteristics we might want to stifle? That kind of thing. But I never ever discussed the opposition at length. Oh no. The last thing you want to do is to talk about the opposition at length. It only builds up your opponents. And then it frightens your own players . . .

So I mean, we might have been playing Manchester United that weekend. But I wasn't going to be singing their praises. The praises of the bloody opposition. Oh no. I tell you, I remember once coming out of one of them meetings. And one of our lads, he said to one of his mates. He said, So are Best, Law and Charlton not playing then? And that made me smile, made me laugh. Because you see, we were only concerned about us. And our collective approach. And that was simple. Keep everything simple. And be patient. Even if it takes eighty-nine minutes to score. Keep it simple. And be patient. Because the number of times we won a match at the death was unbelievable. Bloody unbelievable. And when you sneak one like that, it's heart-breaking for the opposition. Bloody heartbreaking. Oh yes . . .

But I mean, before the game. Before the match itself. I always tried to have a joke up my sleeve, you know? To boost our lads and to knock down the opposition. I mean, don't misunderstand me. Don't get me wrong. We took our football seriously. But we always tried to get a laugh out of our team talks. And so I would always keep a few bombs for Saturday afternoon. Oh yes. I might say to the old boy on the Anfield door. I might say, Here's a box of toilet rolls. You hand them to the opposition when they come through that door. Because they're going to bloody need them. All the toilet rolls they can get. And often, I'd say it just as they were coming through the door. And I'd make sure my lads heard me, too. Oh yes! But I mean, don't misunderstand me. Don't get me wrong. It wasn't arrogance. Or over-confidence. Oh no. Because being overconfident, being cocky. That is a form of ignorance. It means you are talking too much. And if you are guilty of that, then an opponent will bring you down to earth. Oh yes. If you are cocky, then you'll get knocked down a peg or two. And I mean, we never lost a game. We never lost a match because we were arrogant. Or we were cocky. Oh no. And we didn't lose many. Not many at all. Not in my day, not in my time. But if we did lose, when we did lose. We were always ready to learn. Always.

I mean, we learnt a lot in Europe. Oh yes. We learnt a lot through playing the Latins in Europe. We realised a football match is like a relay race. Not a sprint. Oh no. And so we realised you can score a goal by playing from the back. I mean, it may be cat and mouse for a while. Waiting for the opening to appear. But as I say, if you are patient. If you keep things simple. Then you'll get your chance, your opening. If you are patient, if you keep things simple. And you can improvise. Oh yes! Improvisation. If your players can improvise, if your players can adjust to what is happening. You've got a chance. But as I say, it's not a sprint. It's a relay race. And the season itself, that is a marathon. A bloody marathon. And so in every game, all through the season. It's vital you conserve your energy. You make sure the opposition are doing all the chasing. They are doing all the running. I mean, when you are playing over sixty games a season, you can't afford to be running flat out all the time. Oh no. And so you have to make the opposition do the running. And you make sure the ball is doing all the work. So the system we devised, it was very economical. And so you want everyone to be doing their share . . .

I mean, the important thing is that everyone can control the ball and do the basic things. It's control and pass. Control and pass. Control and pass. So it's important to try and give everyone a touch of the ball as quickly as possible as soon as the match starts. If it comes to you, you chest it down simple and you roll it to your mate. And then he does the same, so everyone gets a touch. It doesn't look much, it might not look much. But it's important. It's something. Nothing fancy, nothing clever. If you try to do something clever, something fancy, and then it breaks down, then it can take the confidence out of you. That's not my way. Oh no. Because that's when the fear sets in. And then you are done for. You are lost. And you will lose . . .

And I mean, if you delay. Then the opposition are suddenly all behind the ball. Then you've all eleven of them to beat. And no space. And so you are looking for somebody who can control the ball instantly. And then give a forward pass. And then that gives you more space. And then you are all moving. All wanting the ball . . .

Because I mean, you see some teams playing and it seems as if nobody wants the ball. Nobody wants the bloody thing. They all turn their back on each other. But that's not my way. Oh no. At Liverpool, there is always somebody there to help you out. There is always somebody in space, somebody asking for the ball. Somebody there to help you. There's always somebody there to help you out. Oh yes . . .

So I mean, this is the secret. Get it. Give an early pass. Switch the ball around. You might not seem to be getting very far. But the opposition pattern is changing, the opposition are getting confused. And so then the space opens up for the next pass. And so all the players must understand that when they have delivered a pass, you've only just begun. You have only just started. You have to back up. And you have to look to help someone. You have to make yourself available. Available for the next pass. And then you get it again. And then you give it again. Early, always early. And then you move again. Into space again. Looking to help someone again, looking for the ball. That final ball, that final pass. And then the goal. Oh yes. The goal.

In all seasons, in all weathers. In the shelter or in his deckchair. Bill sucked a lozenge, a Fisherman's Friend. Bill stared out at the sea, the Irish Sea. And Bill thought about the seasons that had been, Bill thought about the seasons to come. The things he had done and the things he would do. If only he could start all over again.


## 87. IN THE NON-LEAGUE

Robinsons Barley Water had asked Bill Shankly if he would like to take on an ambassadorial role for them. Robinsons Barley Water had asked Bill Shankly if he would go and watch non-league games in the north-west for them. Robinsons Barley Water had asked Bill Shankly if he would then nominate his Man of the Match for them. And if he would then present his Man of the Match with a complimentary bottle of Robinsons Barley Water for them. Bill Shankly liked Robinsons Barley Water. Particularly their Lemon Barley Water. And Bill Shankly loved watching football. Any football –

Yes then, said Bill Shankly. I will take on this ambassadorial role for you. I will go and watch the non-league games in the north-west for you. And then I will nominate my Man of the Match for you.

Tony Sanders had spent most his working life in non-league football. Tony Sanders had been the manager of New Brighton. Tony Sanders had been the assistant manager of Skelmersdale United. Tony Sanders had been the assistant manager of Bangor City in Wales. Tony Sanders had even been the manager of Knattspyrnufélagið Víkingur in Iceland. Now Tony Sanders was the manager of Altrincham Football Club. Last season, Altrincham Football Club had won the Alliance Premier League championship. At the end of last season, Altrincham Football Club had applied for election to the Football League. The Big Leagues. But Altrincham Football Club had failed in their bid for election to the Football League. By two votes, just two votes. And so Altrincham Football Club were still in the Alliance Premier League. Still in the non-league, still in the little league.

But Tony Sanders was never far from the Big Leagues. Tony Sanders even lived close to Anfield Road. And Tony Sanders knew many men from the Big Leagues. The Giants of the Game. And Tony Sanders knew Bill Shankly. Tony Sanders had known Bill Shankly for a long time. Tony Sanders called Bill Shankly the Un-selfish Giant. Because Tony Sanders often met or telephoned Bill Shankly to ask for his advice or help. And Bill Shankly was always happy to advise or to help Tony Sanders. If he could, whenever he could. Bill Shankly would go to watch Altrincham Football Club play in the Alliance Premier League. And if he could, whenever he could. Bill Shankly would go with Tony Sanders to watch other non-league teams play. To help Tony Sanders assess the opposition, to help Tony Sanders assess potential new players for Altrincham Football Club. And before these games. And after these games. Tony Sanders and Bill Shankly would talk about football and talk about management. And Bill Shankly would stress the importance of training schedules and match preparation. Bill Shankly would always stress the importance of routine. Of a good routine. And Bill Shankly would always stress the importance of belief. Of self-belief –

The most important thing is to believe in yourself, Bill Shankly would always say. For the players to believe in themselves, for the players to believe in the team. In the club and in their supporters. And then nothing will stop you, Tony. Because you have all the ingredients needed for success here. You have a nice, clean and tidy ground. And you are a good manager. You have a good training schedule. You have the right approach to your matches. You have a plan that works. A plan you stick to. And so Altrincham are a fine football club.

And for the past three seasons, Altrincham Football Club had reached the Third Round of the FA Cup. In January, 1979, Altrincham had gone to White Hart Lane and drawn one-all with Tottenham Hotspur. And then Tottenham Hotspur had come to Moss Lane and beaten Altrincham three–nil. In January, 1980, Leyton Orient had come to Moss Lane and drawn one-all with Altrincham. And then Altrincham had gone to Brisbane Road and lost two–one to Leyton Orient. And now in January, 1981, Altrincham had drawn Liverpool Football Club in the Third Round of the FA Cup. Away from Moss Lane, away at Anfield Road, Liverpool.

On the bus, the Altrincham bus to Anfield. The Altrincham players saw Bill Shankly sat beside Tony Sanders at the front of the bus. On the Altrincham bus to Anfield. Bill Shankly not saying anything, Bill Shankly just looking out of the window of the bus. On the Altrincham bus to Anfield. Bill Shankly turned to Tony Sanders –

If you were to beat Liverpool today, Tony. If you were to win at Anfield today. It would be the giant-killing of the century, Tony. The biggest bloody giant-killing in history! David's victory over Goliath would have nothing on you and your boys, Tony.

Tony Sanders nodded. Tony Sanders smiled. And Tony Sanders said, And do you think there's any chance of that, Bill?

Do you want my honest opinion, asked Bill Shankly.

Tony Sanders nodded again. Tony Sanders smiled again. And Tony Sanders said, I've never known you give anything else, Bill.

Your problem is Liverpool, said Bill Shankly. Liverpool are different from any other football club. The players of Liverpool Football Club will treat your players as professionals. The players of Liverpool Football Club will treat your players with respect. There are no days off at Anfield, there are no slack days. And so Liverpool Football Club will treat this match like they treat every match. They will treat Altrincham like they would treat Manchester United. And so they will go out to beat you, Tony. They will go out to win.

Tony Sanders nodded. Tony Sanders smiled. And Tony Sanders said, Then we're going to need all the help we can get. And we could never thank you enough for all you have done for us already, Bill. You have strengthened us in so many ways. And you have saved us a great deal of money, too. Money we didn't have. And so as I say, I could never thank you enough, Bill. And I know you've said you don't want to talk about tactics. Not against Liverpool. And I understand your reasons, Bill. And I respect them, I do. But do you think you could just have a word with my lads in the dressing room? Before the match. Just a few words, Bill?

In the dressing room at Anfield. The away dressing room at Anfield. The Altrincham dressing room at Anfield. The players of Altrincham Football Club listened to the noise of the Kop. The chanting and the singing. The roar of the Spion Kop. And the players of Altrincham Football Club looked down at their boots. Their empty, hollow boots. And then the players of Altrincham Football Club heard the dressing-room door open. The away dressing-room door. And the players of Altrincham Football Club looked up. And the players of Altrincham Football Club saw Bill Shankly standing in the centre of the dressing room. The away dressing room at Anfield, the visitors' dressing room at Anfield. Bill Shankly looking from player to player.

697

From Connaughton to Allan. From Allan to Davison. From Davison to Bailey. From Bailey to Owens. From Owens to King. From King to Barrow. From Barrow to Heathcote. From Heathcote to Johnson. From Johnson to Rogers. And from Rogers to Howard. And the players of Altrincham Football Club waited for Bill Shankly to speak. To inspire them and to motivate them. In the away dressing room at Anfield, in the visitors' dressing room at Anfield. Bill Shankly opened his mouth. Bill Shankly closed his mouth. And then Bill Shankly looked around the dressing room again. The away dressing room at Anfield. The visitors' dressing room at Anfield. And Bill Shankly looked at John King. Bill Shankly pointed at John King. And Bill Shankly smiled –

You all see that man there? That man John King, lads? Well, I once tried to sign him. But he wouldn't listen to me. Oh no! And so he signed for Everton. Bloody Everton! But if he had listened to me. If he had signed for me. Then he would have been playing here every week. Every bloody week! And I would have curbed him. Oh yes! And I would have made him captain of England. But now he's got his chance to finally play here. And I tell you this, lads. He'll remember this day, he'll remember this game for the rest of his life. And so will all of you, lads. Because remember, there are many men who will play their entire careers, their entire football careers, without playing a game at Anfield, without kicking a ball here. In this ground, on this grass. And so this is a game, this is a day you will always remember, lads. And so make sure when you do look back, when you do remember. You can all say, I gave it my best. My very best shot. And I enjoyed it. Every minute of it. Every single bloody minute!

In the twenty-seventh minute, McDermott scored. In the thirty-ninth minute, Dalglish scored. In the fifty-fourth minute, Dalglish scored again. And in the seventy-first minute, Altrincham won a penalty. And Heathcote scored the penalty. In front of the Kop, the Spion Kop. And in the eighty-eighth minute, Ray Kennedy scored. And Liverpool Football Club beat Altrincham Football Club four–one in the Third Round of the FA Cup –

At Anfield, at home.

In the house, in their hall. The letters still came and the telephone still rang. But not the letters from clubs, not the calls from chairmen. Not these days. But in the house, in their hall. The letters from charities still came, the calls from hospitals still came. The Royal Society for the Blind on Merseyside and the Alder Hey Children's Hospital. Letters Bill always wanted to answer, calls Bill always wanted to take. And in the house, in their hall. Other letters came, other calls came. Letters from local businesses asking Bill to help them win contracts, calls from local radio and television asking Bill to appear on their shows. And if he could still help, if he could still make people happy. Then Bill was still happy to help. Once or twice a week. Sometimes three, even four times a week. Bill would put on his suit again. Bill would put on his tie again. And Bill would kiss Ness goodbye again.

In the car park of Granada Television Studios in Manchester. Bill got out of the car. Bill walked across the car park. Bill walked into Granada Television Studios. Bill walked up to reception. And Bill said, Hello. My name is Bill Shankly. I am here for the *Live from Two* show. I am to be a guest on the show today . . .

The man on the reception desk nodded. The man on the reception desk picked up the telephone. And then the man on the reception desk asked Bill to wait for someone to come down and take him along to the studio. And Bill waited in the reception. And then Bill followed a young woman along to the studio. Along to the dressing room. And Bill sat in the dressing room at the Granada Television Studios. On his own, in the dressing room. Before the mirror, in the dressing room. In his grey suit and his white shirt. And his red and white striped tie. In the dressing room, in the mirror. Bill waited for the other guest to arrive. And then the dressing-room door opened. And Sir Harold Wilson came into the dressing room. With his two bodyguards, his protection. His special protection. And Bill got up from his chair. And Bill shook hands with Sir Harold Wilson. And Bill said, It's good to see you, Sir Harold. It's great to see you. How are you, Sir Harold? How are you? I was very sorry to hear you were so ill last year. And so I was very pleased to hear you would be coming on this show today. In fact, it was one of the reasons I said yes . . .

Thank you, said Sir Harold Wilson. Thank you very much, Bill. It is very kind of you. Very kind of you indeed, Bill. And thank you for your card, your card when I was in hospital . . .

Bill shook his head. And Bill said, No, no. That was nothing, the very least I could do. I was very worried . . .

Yes, said Sir Harold Wilson. I wasn't sure myself if I was going to make it. If I was going to pull through. I had three operations, you know? And they were quite common ones. But they told me they had to take out half my guts to keep me alive. Half my guts, Bill.

But you are OK now? I mean, you look well enough. . .

Thank you, said Sir Harold Wilson again. And yes, now I am one hundred per cent. But as you know, I have decided to step down at Huyton, at the next election. I will not stand again, Bill.

Bill nodded. And Bill said, Yes, I was very sorry to hear that. And I did worry it was for health reasons. I was very concerned . . .

No, said Sir Harold Wilson. Not for health reasons, Bill. Not really. To be honest with you, Bill. I just feel there is no reason really to go on. I remember, within a week of meeting my wife, I told her, I told Mary, I said, I am going to marry you. I am going to become an MP. And become prime minister. And it is what I did. And I did it four times, Bill. And that is as good as any prime minister before me.

Bill nodded again. And Bill said, Yes. That is something.

Sir Harold Wilson sat down now. In the dressing room, before the mirror. His shoulders hunched now, his hair white now –

But I just feel I have done as much as I will ever do, said Sir Harold Wilson. As much as I can ever do now, Bill.

And then the dressing-room door opened again. And Shelley Rohde came into the dressing room. And Shelley Rohde shook hands with Sir Harold Wilson and with Bill. Bill liked Shelley Rohde. Bill liked her laugh. Bill liked her book on L. S. Lowry. And Bill liked the story Shelley told about L. S. Lowry. The first time Shelley went to interview Lowry. In his house. Lowry told her he had given up painting. Lowry told her he was too old. But then Shelley had looked again at the painting in the room. In his house –

The painting was still wet.

Now Shelley Rohde led Sir Harold Wilson and Bill along the corridor to the television studio. First Shelley would interview Sir

Harold. And Bill would wait in the wings. In the wings, behind the set. Bill listened to Shelley Rohde interview Sir Harold Wilson about his new book. His book on the State of Israel. His thoughts on Zionism. About his family, about his upbringing. Church and chapel. Unemployment and typhoid. Scouting and university. His career and his politics. The public image and the private man. With a slow pulse rate and with a quiet heartbeat. And then Shelley introduced James Conroy-Ward. And now James Conroy-Ward sang Admiral Porter's song from *H.M.S. Pinafore* –

Bill waiting in the wings, Bill listening in the wings. Waiting and listening, unbuttoning his jacket and buttoning his jacket until Bill heard Shelley say –

Welcome back. Now our next guest grew up in Ayrshire, one of five sons in a family of ten. Almost inevitably, at the age of fourteen, he went to work in the mines. And only when that pit closed, three years later, did he find his way from the dole into football. By the time he was twenty-five, he was not only an international but he also played for Preston North End in 1938, when they won the FA Cup Final. Now ironically, eighteen years later, he found himself manager of the club they had beaten in that final, Huddersfield Town. His subsequent triumphs with Liverpool are too numerous to mention. Suffice to say, when he retired as manager, he was offered a radio chat show which he accepted on the condition that his first guest was Sir Harold Wilson. So here now, for a return match –

Ladies and gentlemen, Bill Shankly!

Bill stepped out from the wings. Bill unbuttoned his jacket. Bill walked towards the sofa. And Bill shook hands with Shelley and with Sir Harold. Bill sat down between Shelley and Sir Harold. And Bill said, That was the reason I put the show on, because you were first . . .

But why did you particularly want him, asked Shelley.

Well, he's an MP for Huyton, in Liverpool. And I was Liverpool. And he was one of the people. A socialistic background. The socialistic background like me.

Is it true though, asked Shelley, that you wouldn't let him get a word in edgeways?

Well, I thought he was trying to steal the show. So I had to calm him down.

And Shelley laughed. And the audience laughed.

Bill smiled. And Bill said, No. It was a very interesting show.

Shelley sat forward. And Shelley looked over at Sir Harold –

I've often thought, Sir Harold, your support for Huddersfield Town is a little out of expediency? Or is that totally unfair?

Oh no, it's born loyalties. You're the same, Bill . . .

Bill nodded. And Bill said, Yes.

You are born that way, said Sir Harold. I still carry around with me – I won't bore you with it – but I've still got the little card from a newspaper called *Chums* – which I'm sure went out of existence a long time ago – with a picture of the Huddersfield Town team in 1926. My mother would give me a bob. I went on the tram right through. A penny each way. Three pence for a pork pie. Or fish and chips. Cheap in those days. Sixpence to get in. I had to be there at ten o'clock because of the crowds . . .

Bill nodded. Bill smiled. And Bill said, A fearless team, Huddersfield Town then.

I could tell you every team change, said Sir Harold.

Bill nodded again. And Bill said, They won the League three successive seasons.

They did, said Sir Harold. And they were in the Cup Final, the Cup semi-final two of those seasons.

Bill nodded again. Bill smiled again. And Bill said, Yeah. And I played against them in one Cup Final. But we won't talk about that . . .

But wasn't there a famous player who you brought down to Huddersfield, asked Shelley. When you were manager there?

Well, there was a famous player who was on Huddersfield's books, Shelley, when I went there as manager. He was fifteen year old. That was Denis Law. About eight and a half stone and very skinny.

And so what did you do with eight and a half stone's worth of potential, asked Shelley.

Well, he was fantastic. The boy was a genius of a player. So I had to then build him up, physically.

How did you do that?

Well, we got him steak and eggs to eat . . .

And Shelley laughed. And the audience laughed. And Bill smiled. And Bill said, Nearly made Huddersfield Town bankrupt. The steak was kind of expensive. And then we trained him properly. Because I had the experience of a brother of mine who overstrained his heart. Because he was training too hard when he was too young.

That was your brother, said Shelley.

Yes. My brother John. And he overstrained his heart.

All four of your brothers were footballers?

Bill nodded. And Bill said, That's correct. All five of us were professional players. Yes.

What do you think it is about hardship, asked Shelley, that seems to push people into games, really tough games?

Well, I think it's your upbringing. I mean, I was brought up in a mining district. And it was either the pits or football. And I think football was a little better than the pits.

But you didn't have much alternative, did you, said Shelley. Because the two pits closed?

They did.

Now did you find that unemployment had an effect on you?

Oh, it's the cruellest thing in the world, unemployment. You feel as if you are unwanted. I mean, this is a long time ago for me. But I can see them now. And it's coming back now, the word redundancy. And it's a terrible word.

It means unwanted, said Sir Harold.

Bill nodded again. And Bill said, It does. Exactly. And you could get into mischief and all kinds of things. It affects people's minds. And I think it is possibly the cruellest thing in the world, for boys to leave school and not have a job. A terrible thing. And so I worry about the youngsters these days. I mean, I love youngsters. I can always find the time to talk to them or sign an autograph. I never turned a kid away, if I could help it. Because basically I am sorry for them. I look at them. And I think, What are you going to be when you grow up? What is your destiny? I think it is a terrible thing if a grown-up doesn't help a youngster. Because kids can be hit terribly hard if an older person goes against them . . .

And many times each day, the front door rings at our home in West Derby. And standing on the doorstep will be a kid. Or a group of kids. Real Liverpool types. And they say to my wife, they say to Ness, Can I speak to Bill? It's never Mr Shankly. Oh no. But I don't mind that. Oh no. My wife has hundreds of photographs of me holding the FA Cup. And I sign one of them personally for the kid and give it to him. Best wishes to Jim or Joe or Jackie, or whatever his name is.

But there is one group of kids. Four or five of them who come up to the house every day while they are on holiday. They always ask me what I am doing. And whether I can come out to play football. They've had their autographed photographs by now, of course. But I usually end up giving them their bus fares back to Gillmoss. I don't know how they found out where I live. But so many of them do. And I don't mind, I don't mind at all. Because if I can help a kid along, then I will. They are broken-hearted if you snub them. And that I will never do. And I never have. I mean, there were always kids knocking around Anfield when I was there. They are the future Liverpool supporters, you see? They are real people to me, Shelley. Real people . . .

Shelley looked across at Sir Harold again –

What did you find it did to your father emotionally, Sir Harold? Because he was only forty-eight, wasn't he?

He felt unwanted, said Sir Harold. He didn't know if he would ever get a job again. I saw him one night, just in tears. He felt he had failed everybody.

And even mining was suffering, said Shelley. At that time . . .

Bill nodded. And Bill said, Oh yes. And it's come back again.

Do you feel, either of you, asked Shelley, that suffering of that kind helps build character. I know it's a corny old excuse for a lot of the evils that go on. But is it character building?

Bill said, Oh yes. You've got to fight back. If you can't fight back, there is nothing for you.

And those who collapse under it, said Sir Harold, they are never the same again.

Bill said, No.

But it's not my recipe or yours, Sir Harold said to Bill, for training people, is it?

Bill shook his head. And Bill said, No way. Not giving in is the thing. So you've got to try and fight it. I know that it is easy to talk and unemployment is a terrible thing. But you've got to try and fight it.

So you had no choice, said Shelley. It was either unemployment or football. But what have you got out of football all these years?

704

Well, everything I've got, everything I've got out of football, I owe to football. And the dedication I had and what I put into the game. You only get out of the game what you put into it, Shelley. And I put everything into it I could. And still do. For the people –

The people I was playing for and the people I was manager for. I didn't cheat them out of anything! So I put all my heart and soul, to the extent my family suffered.

Do you regret that?

Oh yeah. Yeah. I regret it very much. Yeah. Somebody said, Football is a matter of life and death to you. I said, Listen! It's more important than that. And that's true.

It's a religion, said Sir Harold.

Bill nodded. And Bill said, It is a religion. And my family suffered. They've been neglected.

How would you do it now, asked Shelley, if you had your time again. Would you do it the same way?

I don't know really. If I had the same thoughts, I'd possibly do the same thing again.

Both of you have wives who are very private people, said Shelley. But did they in any way share in your great moments?

Oh, Ness did to a certain degree. The Cup Finals, for instance. The sixty-five Cup Final . . .

A-ha, said Shelley. Strange you should mention that. We do also have a clip of that . . .

Have you?

Well, we thought it might just be your greatest moment . . .

Bill nodded. And Bill said, I think so, yeah.

It's coming up on that monitor there, said Shelley. Can you talk us through it . . .

Bill stared across at the monitor. And Bill nodded again. And Bill said, Well, that's the Cup Final. After extra time. And we beat Leeds United two–one. That was Ronnie Yeats picking up the Cup for the first time ever. After seventy-three years.

Seventy-three years?

Bill said, Yes. And that's the hardest cup in the world to win. It's a one-off job. Never mind the European Cup. That's virtually new. Winning the FA Cup is the hardest cup. It took seventy-three years.

And I thought that was a terrible disgrace that we had to suffer the taunts of people saying you hadn't won the Cup. Now that was the greatest moment of my life, winning the Cup. Not for me –

But for the people in Liverpool.

And you are still living in Liverpool, of course?

Yes. We're still living in the same house we moved into when we came to Liverpool. But it's not a house, it's a home. And I feel at home in Liverpool, with the people of Liverpool. I mean, the last holiday we had was a couple of years ago in Glasgow. Ness cannot really take long journeys and there's everything I need right here in Liverpool. And so I thank God for the wonderful people of Merseyside. I mean, the attitude of the people of Liverpool towards me and my family is stronger now than it ever was. You know, I never cheated them and they've never let me down. We are the same, you see? I mean, I'm just one of the people that stands on the Kop. They think the same as I do and I think the same as they do. So that it is a kind of marriage of people that like each other . . .

What is it about Liverpool that breeds this sort of fanaticism, asked Shelley. Whether it is politics or football or religion?

Or Everton, said Sir Harold.

Bill smiled. And Bill said, We're talking about the city of Liverpool now, Sir Harold. I think Shelley means Merseyside . . .

And Tranmere Rovers, said Sir Harold.

It is Anfield, though, said Shelley, that has something special for you, Bill . . .

Oh, Anfield has got everything for me. I mean, Anfield is the greatest shrine of all time. I mean, I would like to be buried at Anfield.

Not yet, I hope, said Sir Harold.

And the audience laughed –

Don't laugh, said Shelley. This is serious, isn't it?

Bill nodded. And Bill said, Oh yes.

There is a casket of somebody buried there, asked Shelley.

Yes, at the Kop end. In the net, behind the goals. There is a casket, a foot down. And all over the rest of the ground, around the Kop end. It is all spread with ashes . . .

But are you serious, asked Shelley, when you say you would like to be buried there?

Oh no. I'm not serious. No. I am serious. Oh yes. I mean, I'll be buried in spirit there. Even if my body does not go there. Because Anfield was the greatest thing that happened to me.

You also seem to have a particular affection for the players who have passed through your hands, said Shelley. So what are the qualities of a good footballer?

Oh, ability. And of course, dedication to the game. And living the life of an athlete. And giving people their money's worth. I mean, you go there and you pay your money and so you expect effort. And so all the players have got an obligation to do that.

You sound as if it is more of an entertainment, said Shelley.

Bill shook his head. And Bill said, Well, entertainment comes second for me. It's too serious for an entertainment. Entertainment is something you can laugh at. I don't laugh at football.

It's a religion, said Sir Harold again.

And Bill said, I think so, yes.

A way of life, said Sir Harold.

Bill nodded. And Bill said, Yes. It's a way of life. That's a good expression, Sir Harold. It is a way of life. And it's so serious, it is unbelievable. And I wonder what all the rest of the world does . . .

They become prime minister, laughed Shelley.

. . . I mean, they don't see the same things as me. And so I see the whole world differently, possibly.


## 89. WHO NOW WAVES THE BRIGHT RED FLAG?

Liverpool Football Club had had a very mixed season. They had been knocked out of the FA Cup in the Fourth Round by Everton Football Club. But Liverpool Football Club had beaten West Ham United in the final of the Football League Cup. In the replay of the final of the Football League Cup. Liverpool Football Club had won the Football League Cup for the first time in the history of Liverpool Football Club. But Liverpool Football Club had had their worst season in the Football League since the 1970–71 season. Liverpool Football Club had finished fifth in the First Division. But the 1980–81 season was not over yet. Liverpool Football Club were in the final of the European

Cup. Liverpool Football Club would play Real Madrid of Spain in the Parc des Princes, in Paris, in France, on Wednesday 27 May, 1981.

Liverpool Football Club had asked Bill Shankly if he would like to attend the final of the European Cup in Paris as an official guest of Liverpool Football Club. To travel on the plane to Paris with Liverpool Football Club and to stay in the hotel in Paris with Liverpool Football Club. And Bill Shankly had smiled –

Yes, said Bill Shankly. I would love to attend the final of the European Cup. To travel on the same plane and to stay in the same hotel. Thank you. Thank you very much indeed.

At Speke airport, some of the supporters of Liverpool Football Club saw Bill Shankly. Bill Shankly standing with the players of Liverpool Football Club, Bill Shankly talking with the staff of Liverpool Football Club. And some of the supporters of Liverpool Football Club patted his back and shook his hand. And they asked him about the European Cup. And Bill Shankly smiled –

Oh yes. It's been quite a journey. But a wonderful journey. I mean, the First Round was quite a cruise. In the end. But the Second Round, that was quite different. A very different tie, a much tougher tie. But that was a beautiful chip by McDermott up at Pittodrie. One of the goals of the season. And on his weaker foot, you know. But then we were very disciplined. And you need to be. In the Granite City. Very efficient. And then the return leg, the Anfield leg. Well, that was an excellent performance. Possibly the best performance of the season. I mean, Aberdeen held out fairly comfortably for the first twenty, twenty-five minutes. And I admit, I was beginning to worry. Because you see, we seemed a bit tensed up. Very tense. And we were perhaps a bit fortunate, possibly a wee bit lucky. I mean, the own goal from Willie Miller. But after that, after that own goal. We relaxed and we played some superb football. And as I say, for me, possibly the best football of the season. And Aberdeen had no answer. Simply no answer to the football we played. But having said that, I was still concerned about the Bulgars. Because I mean, in all our years in Europe. We had never played a Bulgarian team. And so it was a journey into the unknown. And I think, I do think, we were very fortunate to play the first leg at Anfield, at home. Now I would usually say, I would always say, it's better to play the first leg away. But not in

708

these circumstances, not when they were something of an unknown quantity. Though a team we did know had beaten Forest, had knocked out Forest. And I know Brian did call Bob. And Brian did tell Bob a few things about Sofia. But still, to beat them, to beat the Bulgars five–one. That set us up, set us up very well. For the away leg, the leg in Sofia. And by all accounts, that was a hard game. And we paid a price, a price in injuries. And then I did worry, worry when I saw we would be playing Bayern Munich in the semi-final. And when I saw we would be playing the first leg at home, I was very worried. And of course, it was not a great game. We were not at our best. Without Souness, without Johnson. And then with Ray Kennedy not fully fit and Terry McDermott going off at half-time. I mean, I think we were lucky to draw. And that they did not score. But you see, Bayern made a mistake. They just thought about closing us down. And yes, they closed us down. But they missed their chance. If they had gone for a goal at Anfield, if they had scored at Anfield. Then we would have had problems, big problems. But I know Bob was still depressed by the result, very disappointed with the result. And I was worried, too. Very worried. And I did not go, I did not go to Munich. But I saw the game, of course. On the television. And I mean, we were without Phil Thompson. Without Alan Kennedy. And having to use Colin Irwin and Richard Money. Good players, yes. Don't misunderstand me, don't get me wrong. But not our first choice, not our first team. And that has been the story of this season, the story of our season. And then to go and lose Dalglish so early in the game. I mean, that was a shocking tackle. Bloody shocking. And so I did think maybe we were out of luck, I did worry maybe this was not to be our season. But I have to say, the players responded. The team responded magnificently. And I don't like to single out individual players. That is never my way. Not my way. But I do think three players made the difference for us that night. I mean, for Gayle to come on so early in the game. In a game like that. Well, I think he did a magnificent job. And he gave their full-back a game and a half. He ran him bloody ragged. And then Ray Kennedy, of course. He kept his cool, he showed his class. I mean, with only minutes to go. And Johnson breaking on the right. And that was some break, too. And Johnson with a torn muscle, too. But Ray saw his chance, Ray went forward. And when that ball came, that

709

centre came. He kept his cool and he took his time. You saw the way he turned, the way he tucked the ball into the net. Now that was cool, now that was class. Because many a striker, many top-class strikers. They would have possibly whacked that ball first time and they would have probably wasted the opportunity. But not Ray, not Ray Kennedy. I mean, I was out of my chair. On my feet, in sheer delight. And so that goal, that goal was the away goal that took us through, that got us here. But I mean, another player stood out for me, too. Another player, in a different way. In a different way, Sammy Lee. The way he marked Breitner, the way he stuck to him like bloody glue. I mean, the man hardly had a kick, hardly had a touch. And it served Breitner right, it served the man bloody right. The things he had said after the first leg, the way he had gone on in the press about Liverpool being unimaginative. And unintelligent. Now you see, that was him being unintelligent. Breitner being stupid. Because that kind of thing, those kinds of words. They are like a red rag to a bull. They will always get a reaction, a reaction from Liverpool Football Club. And so that is what we got, that is what we saw. And I know Bob thinks that was possibly our best-ever European performance, the way we contained them, the way we were so considered and so thoughtful in everything we did. And with everything stacked up against us. The injuries and so forth. And so Bob is possibly right. I am sure he is right. And so as I say, it's been quite a journey. Oh yes. And a wonderful journey. But it's not over yet. Oh no. This journey is not finished. Not finished yet . . .

And at Speke airport. The supporters of Liverpool Football Club thanked Bill Shankly for his time. They thanked him for his kindness. They shook his hand and they wished him well. And Bill Shankly smiled. And Bill Shankly shook their hands. And Bill Shankly thanked them all. And Bill Shankly wished them all a safe journey. A safe trip to Paris. And the supporters of Liverpool Football Club watched Bill Shankly board the plane to Paris with the players of Liverpool Football Club and with the staff of Liverpool Football Club.

But on the plane to Paris. In the skies to Paris. There was thunder and there was lightning. Lightning which struck the plane, thunder which shook the plane. In the skies to Paris. On the plane to Paris. There was silence. And there were memories. Memories of other planes. Other weather. And there was perspective. And there were prayers. Answered prayers this time, thank God.

On the ground, at Orly airport. Some of the supporters of Liverpool Football Club saw Bill Shankly. Bill Shankly with the players of Liverpool Football Club, Bill Shankly with the staff of Liverpool Football Club. And some of the supporters of Liverpool Football Club patted his back and shook his hand. And said, We are so glad to see you, Bill. So pleased you are here. So very glad you could make it, Bill. So very happy you are . . .

And so am I, said Bill Shankly. So am I. But thank you, lads.

Outside Paris, at Versailles. Near the palace, the Grand Canal. The fountains and the gardens. The hotel was quiet, the hotel was tranquil. Away from the city, away from the pressure. Bill Shankly stayed with the players and the staff of Liverpool Football Club. But Bill Shankly did not bother the players of Liverpool Football Club, Bill Shankly did not trouble the staff of Liverpool Football Club. Bill Shankly walked around the hotel, Bill Shankly walked among its gardens. And a few of the supporters of Liverpool Football Club who had come out to Versailles saw Bill Shankly. In the hotel or in the garden. They stopped Bill Shankly. They patted his back and they shook his hand. And they asked him for his autograph. And they said, You know everyone is saying Real Madrid will win, Bill? Helenio Herrera and Paul Breitner. They are all saying Real Madrid will beat us, Bill. And the coach of Real Madrid, he sounds very confident . . .

Oh well, yes, said Bill Shankly. They have a clever coach. A very shrewd coach in Boskov. And I know he has said he thinks this Liverpool team are too old. He has called us veterans, yes. And so I know he thinks his team can outrun us. But I can tell you this, boys. When a coach starts making claims like that, starts saying things like that. Then it shows he is tense, it shows he is worried. And I know for a fact, the more they say things like that, the more they talk like that. Then the better Bob likes it, the happier Bob will be. Because I was always like that, I was always the same. Let them talk and then we'll play. Because that is where you win a game of football. On a pitch, not in a newspaper. And yes, they might have some good players. Some very good players in Camacho, of course. And Santillana and Stielike. And Cunningham, of course. If the boy plays, if the lad is fit. Because I know they have their worries, they have had their injuries. And I mean, this season Anfield has been more like a bloody hospital than a football ground! But I think from what Bob has said, I think Kenny and Sammy Lee will both be fit. And so I think we can name our strongest side. And so let them talk, but then we will play . . .

And some of the supporters of Liverpool Football Club said, And so it should be a classic match then, Bill. Liverpool versus Real Madrid. A real classic, don't you think, Bill?

Well now, said Bill Shankly. I don't know about that, boys. I mean, to be very honest with you. I cannot be sure of that. I mean, I doubt it will be a flowing game, a free-flowing match. But if we can win one–nil, then that will do for me. And I am sure that will do for Bob. Because then Liverpool Football Club will deserve to be ranked alongside the all-time greatest clubs in European football. I mean, Real Madrid are already there. Real Madrid have already won the Cup six times. But I mean, it's a very different competition now. A very different tournament. And for Liverpool Football Club to win this competition three times, this cup three times, then that would be one of the greatest achievements of all time, boys. Of all bloody time . . .

On the afternoon of the final, in the hours before the match. In the city, outside the stadium. Things had already started, things had already kicked off. Thousands of supporters of Liverpool Football Club had no tickets for the final. But thousands of supporters of Liverpool Football Club had still come to the Parc des Princes. To be near the final, to be near their team. But thousands of French policemen stood between them and the final, them and their team. Thousands of French policemen with batons and with guns. In their way, with tear gas. And some of the supporters of Liverpool Football Club threw empty beer bottles at the thousands of French policemen. Bottles in the air, bottles raining down. And some of the French policemen fired tear gas at the thousands of supporters of Liverpool Football Club. Tears in their eyes, gas in the air. Blowing into the Parc des Princes. Into the stadium, into the stands. The Kop of Boulogne. This stand named in honour of the Kop of Anfield. The Spion Kop.

In his seat, in the stands. Bill Shankly rubbed his eyes. Bill Shankly blinked. On the edge of his seat in the stands. Bill Shankly looked down at the pitch. Bill Shankly stared down at the players. The players of Liverpool Football Club. Ray Clemence. Phil Neal. Alan

Kennedy. Phil Thompson. Ray Kennedy. Alan Hansen. Kenny Dalglish. Sammy Lee. David Johnson. Terry McDermott. Graeme Souness. Jimmy Case. Steve Ogrizovic. Colin Irwin. Richard Money and Howard Gayle. The players of Liverpool Football Club coming out into the stadium, out onto the pitch. And on another night, at another final. Bill Shankly heard that reception again, Bill Shankly heard that roar again. And on the edge of his seat in the stands. Bill Shankly looked around the ground, around the stadium. All the grounds and all the stadiums. At all the banners, at all the flags. All the red banners and all the red flags. And Bill Shankly closed his eyes,

Bill Shankly closed his eyes. And Bill Shankly smiled.

Back at the hotel, back at the reception. Bob Paisley was standing at the bar, standing on his own at the bar. And Bob Paisley saw Bill Shankly. Bill Shankly on his own, Bill Shankly walking towards Bob Paisley. Bill Shankly shook Bob Paisley's hand –

Congratulations, Bob. Congratulations. I could not be happier for you, Bob. I just could not be more pleased for you . . .

And Bob Paisley said, Thank you, Bill.

I mean, after John won the European Cup with Celtic. I said to John, I said, You know you are immortal now, John. But I mean, you have won the European Cup three times now, Bob. Three bloody times. And so you are immortal, Bob. More than immortal!

Bob Paisley shook his head. And Bob Paisley said, No, Bill. No. There is only one immortal at Liverpool Football Club, Bill. And that immortal is you. That man is you, Bill. Because none of this, none of these cups. None of it could have happened without you, Bill. It's all because of you. All because of you, Bill . . .

That is very kind of you, Bob. Very kind of you to say that. But I know I'm not immortal, Bob. I know I'm mortal. Very mortal.


90. Y. N. W. A.

The game not finished, the match never finished. The pain in his heart and the smoke in his eyes. The city had been in flames, sirens in the air. Bill closed his eyes. On a stretcher, in an ambulance. Bill opened his eyes. And Bill saw Ness. His daughters and his granddaughters.

And Bill smiled. In the bed, in the hospital. Bill closed his eyes again. His eyes closed, for the last time. Bill was in the field. For all time. Bill had rolled the stone from the tomb. In the field. Bill saw the tree. Its blossoms gone, its leaves fallen and its branches bowed. In the field. Bill walked towards the tree. In the field. Bill stood before the tree. In the field. Bill looked up at the tree. Its branches that would rise up again, its leaves and blossoms that would come again. In the field. Bill touched the tree. This tree standing tall, this tree standing triumphant. Triumphant and resurrected now. Now and for all time. In the field. Bill knew this tree, Bill loved this tree. Her name was Liberty, her name was Liverpool.

## The Argument III (cont.)

On the train, at their table. Harold stared out of the window. Harold did not recognise the landscape, Harold did not recognise the place. Harold turned away from the window. And Harold took a postcard from out of his jacket pocket. Harold put down the postcard on the table. Harold slid the postcard across the table towards Bill. Harold smiled. And Harold said, You know who that is, Bill?

Aye, said Bill. Of course I do. It's the Huddersfield Town side that won the Championship three seasons running.

Harold shook his head. And Harold said, No, on the other side. Turn it over, Bill. Do you know who that is?

Bill picked up the postcard. Bill turned over the postcard. And Bill read the words on the back of the postcard:

*Up the Town, Nikita Khrushchev*

Bill looked up from the words on the back of the postcard. Bill looked across the table at Harold. And Bill nodded. Bill smiled. And Bill heard the whistle of the train. Bill heard the voice of the guard –

All change here! All change, please!

# SOURCES AND ACKNOWLEDGEMENTS

This book is a work of fiction. And so this book is a novel. The following books all helped to inspire this work of fiction, this novel. However, I would like to pay particular tribute to four books:

*SHANKLY: My Story* by Bill Shankly, with John Roberts (1976, 2011).
*Shanks: The Authorized Biography* by Dave Bowler (1996).
*It's Much More Important Than That* by Stephen F. Kelly (1997).
*The REAL Bill Shankly* by Karen Gill (2007).

And then . . .

*44 Years with the Same Bird* by Brian Reade (2009).
*A Strange Kind of Glory* by Eamon Dunphy (1991).
*Best and Edwards* by Gordon Burn (2006).
*Bob Paisley: An Autobiography* by Bob Paisley (1983).
*Bob Paisley: Manager of the Millennium* by John Keith (1999).
*Burns the Radical* by Liam McIlvanney (2002).
*Cally on the Ball* by Ian Callaghan and John Keith (2010).
*Crazy Horse* by Emlyn Hughes (1980).
*Dalglish* by Kenny Dalglish, with Henry Winter (1996).
*Dynasty* by Paul Tomkins (2008).
*Everton: The School of Science* by James Corbett (2003, 2010).
*Ghost on the Wall: The Authorised Biography of Roy Evans* by Derek
    Dohan (2004).
*Harold Wilson* by Austen Morgan (1992).
*Harold Wilson* by Ben Pimlott (1992).
*If You're Second You Are Nothing* by Oliver Holt (2006).
*In a League of Their Own* by Jeremy Novick (1995).
*Jock Stein* by Archie Macpherson (2004).
*Kevin Keegan* by Kevin Keegan, with John Roberts (1977).
*Kevin Keegan* by Kevin Keegan (1997).
*Life of Robert Burns* by John Stuart Blackie (1888).
*Liverpool 800* edited by John Belcham (2006).
*Matt Busby: Soccer at the Top* by Matt Busby (1973).
*Mr Shankly's Photograph* by Stephen F. Kelly (2002).
*RED MEN* by John Williams (2010).

*Secret Diary of a Liverpool Scout* by Simon Hughes (2009).

*SHANKLY* by Phil Thompson (1993).

*Shankly: From Glenbuck to Wembley* by Phil Thompson and Steve Hale (2004).

*Sir Alf* by Leo McKinstry (2006).

*Sir Roger* by Ivan Ponting and Steve Hale (1995).

*Soccer in the Fifties* by Geoffrey Green (1974).

*SOVPOEMS* by Edwin Morgan (1961).

*Talking Shankly* by Tom Darby (1998, 2007).

*The Amazing Bill Shankly* (CD) by John Roberts (2007).

*The Bard* by Robert Crawford (2009).

*The Best Laid Schemes: Selected Poetry and Prose of Robert Burns* edited by Robert Crawford and Christopher MacLachlan (2009).

*The Boot Room Boys* by Stephen F. Kelly (1999).

*The Essential Shankly* by John Keith (2001).

*The Football Man* by Arthur Hopcraft (1968).

*The Footballer Who Could Fly* by Duncan Hamilton (2012).

*The King* by Denis Law, with Bob Harris (2003).

*The Management* by Michael Grant and Rob Robertson (2010).

*The Saint* by Ian St John (2005).

*The SHANKLY Years* by Steve Hale and Phil Thompson (1998).

*The Unfortunates* by B. S. Johnson (1969).

*THOMMO: Stand Up Pinocchio* by Phil Thompson (2005).

*Three Sides of the Mersey* by Rogan Taylor and Andrew Ward (1993).

*Tom Finney* by Tom Finney (2003).

*Tommy Smith: Anfield Iron* by Tommy Smith (2008).

*Tosh* by John Toshack (1982).

*Winning Isn't Everything* by Dave Bowler (1998).

The crowd attendances, team sheets and goals for many of the games in the novel were taken from the website www.liverweb.org.uk. Chris Wood of the www.lfchistory.net website also kindly pointed out many factual (and grammatical) errors in the original proof. Thank you, Chris!

Many of the scenes involving Bill Shankly and the supporters of Liverpool Football Club were also inspired by the recollections of people on the many fan forums and websites dedicated to Liverpool Football Club.

There remains a great deal of debate about when *You'll Never Walk Alone* was first sung by the supporters of Liverpool Football Club. However, the closing scene of Chapter 12 was inspired by Wooltonian's post of 30 April, 2004, on the www.redandwhitekop.com forum. Thank you.

The original idea for this novel came out of a conversation with Mike Jefferies. I would like to thank Rob Kraitt for putting Mike in touch with me. And to thank Mike and Rob for all their encouragement, help and support during the writing of this book. I would also like to pay particular thanks to John Roberts: very generously, John lent me the tapes of his conversations with Bill Shankly and also a tape of the Radio City interview between Bill Shankly and Harold Wilson.

Astrid Azurdia, Sam Dwyer, Robert Fraser, Ann Scanlon and George Scott also very kindly provided me with documents and materials that helped in the writing of this novel. Thank you very much.

I would also like to thank the following people for their assistance and their support. In Liverpool: Ian Callaghan, Stephen Done, John Keith, Stephen F. Kelly and Paul McGrattan. In Huddersfield: Stephen Dorril and Michael Stewart. In Leeds: Stephen Barber, Emma Bolland, Anthony Clavane, Robert Endeacott, Rod Dixon, Chris Lloyd, Alice Nutter, Jane Verity and all the Red Writers at Red Ladder, Leeds. In Tokyo: as always, Hamish Macaskill, Junzo Sawa, Peter Thompson, Atsushi Hori and all the staff of the English Agency Japan; Motoyuki Shibata, Ariko Kato and all the staff and students of the Department of Contemporary Literature at the University of Tokyo; Mike and Mayu Handford, David Karashima, Justin McCurry, Akiko Miyake, Shunichiro Nagashima, Richard Lloyd Parry, Jeremy Sutton-Hibbert and David Turner. In London: Ruth Atkins, Ian Bahrami, Andrew Benbow, Lee Brackstone, Angus Cargill, Anne Owen, Anna Pallai and all the staff of Faber and Faber. Also Jake Arnott, Matteo Battarra, Andrew Eaton, Laura Oldfield Ford, Stephen Frears, Carol Gorner, Tony Grisoni, John Harvey, Michael Hayden, Richard Kelly, Eoin McNamee, Keith and Kate Pattison, Maxine Peake, Ted Riley, Katy Shaw, Steve Taylor, Paul Tickell, Cathi Unsworth, Paul Viragh and the staff of the Working Class Movement Library in Salford. Finally, I would like to thank all my family and friends, in Britain and in Japan, particularly Julian Cleator, Jon Riley and,

most of all, my father, Basil Peace,

and William Miller, always.